THE CHANGE TRILOGY

THE COMPLETE COLLECTION

AUDEEP CARIENS

Copyright © 2021 Audeep Cariens
Cover Design by Audeep Cariens
All rights reserved.
ISBN: 9798794361445

For Avi

"The people who are crazy enough to think they can change the world are the ones who do." - Steve Jobs

DESCRIPTION

The Change Trilogy Complete Collection combines all three novels in the trilogy; Maze: Form the Future, Cycle: Fight the System, and Dimension: Find the Change. Dive into this special edition book to experience the fifteen year journey of brothers, Ivo and Za, as well as the ups and downs of The Migrants. Follow our characters as they fight the Board, conflict with the ideologies of Migrant savior Nox, and stop the infiltration of dictators into the new virtual world of AltD and feel the full arc of our characters' emotions as they are torn apart and reunited countless times. Together, The Change Trilogy encapsulates the many intertwining narratives woven within each books, the world changing events, and the countless connections and clues that reach from the cover of Maze to the end of Dimension.

CONTENTS

DESCRIPTION
PAGE 5

MAZE: FORM THE FUTURE
PAGE 9

CYCLE: FIGHT THE SYSTEM
PAGE 267

DIMENSION: FIND THE CHANGE
PAGE 541

MAZE

FORM THE FUTURE

AUDEEP CARIENS

PROLOGUE

On October 11, 2029, the security forces of the largest national private corporations raided the capital of the United States and seized control of the government in the Takeover. For years, these corporations were aggravated by the government's constant close regulation of their power and, eventually, they took matters into their own hands and became too powerful to stop. The Presidency was replaced with the Board, a collection of the CEOs of the controlling corporations from the technology, medical, investment, merchandise, and manufacturing sectors. The Board didn't want to cause too much upheaval to the economy, after this shock to democracy, so they decided to maintain much of the country's infrastructure. That meant the public was largely unaffected, except for the change of hands in the governing powers.

But, with a drive for dominance, accelerated growth and, of course, profit, the Board needed increasing sources of labor to grow their various industries. They wanted the least expensive options; ultimately, they wanted labor for free. The expedient way to establish this was to return to what the country did best, in centuries past, enslavement based on racial identity. So, the Roundup began. The military was first 'cleansed' of its people of color who were sent to be labor workers like everyone else. Then, they were ordered to capture all people of color across the country. On each coast of the country, resistance groups started to form to provide refuge and safety for people of color who were trying to flee the machinations of the Board. The groups banded together to become the Migrants. As the Takeover wreaked havoc on the country, the Migrants were scrambling to survive; not too many were lucky.

In the aftermath of the Roundup, entire cities were left desolate and abandoned, the streets were barren, and the reins of power were firmly held by the Board. As news of the success of the Takeover was heard across the globe, similar insurgencies unfolded on almost every other continent: governments were replaced by corporations focused on accumulating profit by any means necessary, including discriminatory labor systems..

By 2031, the United States was a radically different place than it was even five years before, and so was the world.

IVO

MARCH 3, 2031

The concrete feels rough against my back and I grip it with my palms, for safety. I peer around the right corner, studying the area. I am looking for anyone who would throw me in jail—not ideal. It's one in the morning so, unsurprisingly, the coast is clear for now. All I see is an empty street, lined with garbage and skyscrapers. The ads are still running but the sound has been disabled. Thank god. I'm exhausted. Very exhausted. But Idrissa told me that rations were coming in late tonight, to be unloaded, and given out tomorrow. That means I have about a one hour window to make my move. If I can get this food, I won't just have my first meal in two days, but so will all of the Migrants.

I lean my head against the wall and take a deep breath. It's now or never. I spin off and sprint towards the Apple store. In a perfect world, I wouldn't try to enter the front door and instead shimmy my way down from the roof. But I don't have the parkour skills of my brother. As I near the never-ending glass, I take a moment to look around. It's been a while since I've been on Newbury street, I used to come all the time as a kid. As I reach the door, I glance to each side of the building. Since the Takeover, every store has had a security unit that the the owners can control. I find the small silver box drilled into the red brick of the next store over. I open the front flap and expose the red, blue, and yellow wires covering the dirty control panel. Reaching into my back pocket, I pull out my phone, navigate to the break-in code I wrote earlier and plug it into the control panel. After 30 seconds, I hear a click from the door handles. In five minutes, the security guards in the nearest police station will receive a warning and a direct camera feed to the store. The last thing I need right now is to get arrested. Again.

Quietly I push open the front door, heavier than I thought. All of the world's leading tech used to be housed and showcased in this ultra-modern space. Now, the Board turned it into their personal storage closet on the East coast. They didn't have to, but they did just to show that they own everybody and everything. So, instead of modern wooden tables with phones and computers displayed elegantly, there are boxes upon boxes of supplies, all identical, and all daunting. I need to read the inventory labels and find the food rations as fast as possible. Once I have located the correct packages, I will send a signal to my friend who will drive by. Every inventory label is about eleven inches long. Lucky for me, food labels are always stamped with a green circle, so they should be easier to find. I search for five minutes before I finally let myself believe it: the food's not here and Idrissa got it wrong.

Spinning around, I sprint out the door, grab my phone and run. My phone is buzzing like crazy and I glance at the screen which is illuminated from an incoming call. No time to see who it's from, I have to get out of here before the cops show up. Running down Newbury street, I can't help but be disappointed in what it has become. Instead of a bustling outdoor commercial center with trendy restaurants and stylish shoppers, it's an uncultured piece of government trash. I hear sirens in the distance.

Hopefully Idrissa got one thing right and he's waiting in the car by the Nike store. As I approach the curb, some people behind me yell.

"Hey stop! Police! We will shoot!" I ignore the warning, zigzagging my way across the street to avoid possible fire, I spot the busted old red Toyota Camry. Of course, in his predictable manner, Idrissa is absolutely tuned out. He has his earbuds in and is jamming out to a music library that hasn't changed in seven years. Damn. I slam on the roof of the car and jump in the passenger seat.

"Drive. Now." Idrissa steps on the gas he drifts around the corner, almost slamming a post with our rear end.

"What the hell Ivo, this was not the plan." Idrissa shouted in his thick Senegalese accent.

"I know I'll explain later."

"Forget later, I am currently speeding away from the cops and you're here empty-handed. You are going to tell me right now what the hell happened." I'm fuming. Who is he to demand answers? He's the one that got the intel all wrong and now I'm the one in trouble. I almost died because of his mistake. Or worse, I could have been captured. We take a sharp right nearing the outskirts of the city. Our speed is ninety miles per hour and I'm starting to worry that the car might break down.

"You got it wrong, that's what happened."

"No, I swear, this time the intel was good. There is no way that the rations weren't there."

"Well they weren't."

"Did you check the back room storage?" Dang, the back room. I always forget that the front of the Apple stores are only half of them. They always have tons of stuff stashed away in the back.

"Dammit. No I didn't."

"See...not my fault."

"Fine. Not this time. What's your plan for getting us out of this? I count three cops behind us, two motorcycles flanking a Dodge." This happens every time the mission doesn't go smoothly. We need to find a way to shake these guys so that they don't find where all of us are hiding.

"You know that alley with a dead end?"

"Yeah"

"Well I'm gonna go there."

"But how does that help us, Idri? We'll get stuck right with them."

"Six days ago the building adjacent to the end of the alley was abandoned. It hasn't been renovated in forever so neither the previous business nor the Board wanted to use it."

"I really don't see where you're going with this. Can you please stay on task?"

"You'll see" A normal person would freak out in this situation. But I know Idri and if he says he has a plan, he has a plan.

We take a quick left onto a main road. There are a few people waking up and getting their shops ready but very few cars. I look up and scan the building windows to see everyone staring out their windows at us, and then at the cops, and then back at us. Ever since the Takeover, there haven't been many situations like the one we're in now. I recognize the crumbling brick building as the corner point of the alley Idri was talking about. This could either go really well or we could die. Going at full speed we drift right into the alley. I check the passenger seat window and see that one of the motorcycles hit the curb while the other one was forced behind the cop car. One down, two to go. Idri hits the accelerator and we are nearing the end of the alley.

"Idri, slow down. We're gonna hit the dead end. You need to slow down!" He doesn't listen to me, he's focused. Right before we hit the end, he slams on the brakes, swings the steering wheel as far left as possible, and drives straight through the massive side-window of the abandoned building, catching a ramp on the way up.

I look behind us and see both the bike and the car crash into the wall and each other, catching fire before I hear an explosion.

"Haha. I knew that would work. Wow, am I good or what?" Idrissa is ecstatic as he weaves past pillars and leftover furniture within the building. Good thing the entrance to this building is just a ratty garage door. Idri rams right through it and speeds away.

"Not gonna lie, that was pretty clean, Idri. You did good. What am I gonna tell everyone though? We're coming back empty handed."

"It's fine. Hopefully someone else had more luck on their assignment," Idrissa reassures me. "Worst comes to worst, we don't eat." Now we really are on the outskirts of Boston, near the harbor. Nearing the coast with tumbling water and rough sand, Idri takes out his phone. Unlocking it and typing in a command the road in front of us drops down like a ramp. Driving in, we turn into a parking space and get out of the car.

This is our base, the home of the Migrants. That's what we call ourselves anyway. The Board calls us rebels but the Takeover wasn't our fault or even our plan, so we don't see how we could be called that. Don't ask me how leaders of the biggest corporations in the world all happened to be white supremacists, but they were. That means, when they decided to raid the government and take over, that was one of the first things added to their mission statement. Basically, the big companies wanted free rein. Those that were able to flee fled here, to the Migrants.

Our base is pretty nice seeing how we should all be homeless at this point. There's a control center with all of the technology we could scramble to find, small concrete rooms that resemble jail cells but are actually for sleeping, and storage for food. There are two locations like this, the other one being on the other side of Boston. As we walk down the hall, Aiko approaches us.

"Did you already drop the food off in storage because I was just around there and I didn't see you guys." Immediately, my heart sank. When you have nothing, every little thing matters. Not getting this food leaves people hungry. Idrissa and I had a larger responsibility to more people than just us. And we failed.

"There is no food. We didn't get it." Idri replied before I could. Both of us are disappointed in ourselves, we can only hope that someone else had more success.

"Why? What happened?" Aiko sounded worried more than disappointed. "Are you guys ok?"

"We're fine. Idri managed to finesse our way out of a cop chase. At the expense of a perfectly useable building of course. Collateral damage I guess." Aiko chuckled at my comment. If I'm good at anything, it's getting someone that is on edge to calm down, with my humor. Meanwhile, Idri is just shaking his head, disappointed.

"It's fine guys. Let me go check if the others brought anything back. You guys get some rest, you're gonna need it if the news is true."

"What news?" Idri and I both question at the same time. We both had been in undercover mode for the past two days preparing for the mission. When we monitor public feeds we don't want our phone to have a traceable location.

"You didn't hear? The Board has decided to do another Round Up, which targets all of the people of color that had found some peace in public. That means innocent people are going to be moved to labor camps."

"That can't happen." Idri sounds worried. He has a family history with labor camps. His family are immigrants who came to the United States years ago before the Takeover. The reason they decided to escape Senegal was because they were being held by the corrupt government there for no reason. Of course, every government is corrupt now, but the US was a better and safer place compared to most nations back then.

"You're right, it can't happen. And it won't if we have anything to do with it. Which means I need both of you ready when we make our move." Aiko always sounds confident and calm. She's one of our leaders for a reason.

"You got it." I reply. Of course I'm gonna fight. Right now, these people are my family, and I'll protect them at all costs.

"Great. See you soon." Aiko walks in the opposite direction, preparing for possible shipments that others brought in. Everyone here is sensitive to resources. We all come from different backgrounds and countries, and none of us ever grew up privileged. Then again, how could we. We don't exactly blend in with the ocean of white privilege.

I say bye to Idri and head to my room. It's nothing fancy but after three years of living here, I made the space my own as much as I could. My small bed sits to the left side of the room, a thin mattress that lays on a fifty year-old iron base. To the right is my desk. It's pretty clean at first glance, just my laptop and a few books but looking closer you see I shoved everything else in the drawer below. On the wall above my desk is a few of my drawings which used to be a hobby of mine and a lot of flyers collected from the ground that the Board gave out. All warnings to people to follow orders or be punished. Coercion is the Board's middle name. Next to my desk is my bookshelf. These are all my parents' books that I could salvage. On the ground there are three soccer balls. Soccer was my thing until the Takeover happened. Now there's no time to play, I grew up faster than I ever imagined I'd have to. Above the head of my bed is the picture of my intact family, a long lost memory now. My parents stand behind me with my brother by my side. We're all smiling. Taped to the other wall adjacent to my bed is a three by four foot map of the city. A red line follows a convoluted route through the city. I made that line in an attempt to track down my brother. I don't know if I'll ever find him.

I climb into bed, the sun is just beginning to come up and shine into my room. I'm exhausted. I have been up all night trying to get rations that I couldn't even get. I pull the covers over me, rest my head against my pillow, the only soft thing in my entire room, and shut my eyes.

***

We are running as fast as we can, trying to get the buzz of the helicopters behind us. Jumping roof after roof, I follow my brother's lead, trying to copy his same movements. One wrong footing, hold, or one moment of bad timing could lead to a twisted ankle, and an end to our freedom. I feel the pressure and burn in my knees as my feet slam onto the hard rock.

"Come on, hurry up." Za yells behind his shoulder. It annoys me that I'm the one behind. Everyone knows there's no one faster than me in the entire Migrant community. If I am running on the ground that is. When it comes to absurd scaling of buildings and jumping across unimaginable chasms, leave that to my brother. Not to mention, I am frightened of heights.

"I'm trying, you know this isn't my forte. Plus you're the one that got us into this stupid mess anyways." I barely get the sentence out between breaths and I don't even know if he heard me, and he definitely won't admit to it being his fault.

"Stop your panting, old man." He shouts back, midway through a jump. "Plus, nothing's your forte anyways." God, do I want to punch him right now. He always does this, getting under my skin, seeing if I'll break. But I'm better now, since I was forced to level up to be the parental guardian of Za as well.

"In the name of the Board, we are ordering you to stop. We will use lethal force." A speaker from one of the helicopters blares. I'm not intimidated, they will probably use lethal force anyway, they have before. I glance over the edge of the building. I immediately get sick to my stomach but fight through it. I'm surveying the area, seeing if there is a graceful way to dismount from the high ground. Unfortunately the police has about ten cars and bikes following us on either block. We are definitely screwed.

"Intersection up ahead!" That's not good. Intersection means we have to jump over an entire two-lane street, which for me is nearly impossible, or we get to the ground and either fight our way out or run for our lives. Za is lost now. I'm usually the one with directions so the fact that he's out in front is not only confusing for him, but absolutely terrifying. I disabled communication back to the base because I don't want anybody tracing calls. This would be a perfect example of when I don't anticipate correctly. Either way, there would be no way a migrant could get a car through all these cops without being shot or captured. Let's put it this way, there are no good options.

"What's the plan Ivo! We are getting close." I quickly turn around looking for a way out. Behind me the helicopters are about a block behind us but gaining quickly. Beside us are the cars. In front of us in an impassable gap. Some would say we are stuck, but I never say the "s" word.

"Zashil! Shift to the right!" He takes two steps to the right and I toss a sticker bomb to his left, twenty feet in front of me. We stole a weapons load that was headed for a nearby military fort. At first we were disappointed because the load only had a few guns, but I argued that these discrete bombs would come in handy. Two seconds later the bomb quietly explodes opening a gap in the roof.

"Jump in!" I yell, hoping he hears me and doesn't go on to do something stupid. Luckily, he does, and he jumps in. I follow suit. I'm not sure what building this is, we were going too fast for me to keep track and label it on my mental map of Boston, but luckily it's an abandoned office space. Falling in I look around for Za.

"Za?!"

"Yeah, over here." He peeks his head out from underneath the desk. Good. He listened to me. I made him memorize steps of action in case a situation like this ever happened. The first step was to run, and the second step was to deceive and find cover. I go over and duck beneath the desk next to him. I look at him and put a finger over my mouth, listening. I hear the sirens getting farther away, but the helicopters are hovering above us, they probably have low visibility because they have to stay high up. Most of the tall buildings around Boston were recently outfitted with extra satellite connectivity so their antennas could get caught in the helicopter.

"Ivo!" Za whispers, not realizing that there's no one around that could hear us anyways.

"What? It'll be ok Za don't worry."

"It's not that. I know we'll be fine." He takes a deep breath and sighs.

"Then what?!" I'm kinda getting impatient now because we still have a lot of work to do.

"Well....Ya see..."

"Zashil, I'm not mad at you but you really just need to spit it out."

"I forgot step three." Phew. I let out a sigh of relief. Thank God it wasn't serious. I don't think I even remember step three.

"That's ok, don't worry. It's time for improvisation anyways." I say calmly in the best reassuring voice, which is not very good. I listen again for any noise. I hear thuds against the roof which means the soldiers are dismounting, they will be ready to jump down, guns firing, in a couple minutes. Ok Ivo, think. Think. I peek over the desk. There's a small computer with paperwork and pencil to one side. On the other side there's a small container. I get up, knees on the ground, and open it. That's what I'm talking about. Business cards. I grab one and retreat back under the desk.

"Ivo, what are you doing? This is not a time for shopping."

"Shh." I locate the name on the top of the card. It read "Boston Real Estate" just what I was hoping for. Real Estate companies used to have massive office spaces, but the Board needed all of the parking space they could get as they upped security within the city, after the Takeover. That means that there's a parking lot beneath us, that's our way out.

"Everyone armed? When we get down there, disperse and find them. Our orders are shoot on sight." I hear the commander above us.

"Za, we need to go down. There's a parking lot and we can escape."

"You're not a very good driver, Ivo." He sounds worried.

"We aren't carjacking, but the cars are the perfect cover, tons of places to hide."

"Oh yeah, that makes sense."

"Whatever happens, stay close alright?" If he didn't hear anything else, I hope he at least heard this. I run out towards the exit door, ducking down as I go. Za follows behind me. I open the door to find an emergency exit staircase. Time for the thing we practiced. Instead of descending the stairs like we do normally, Za and I position our hands onto the railing and flip over, so we are hanging off the railing. I nod at Za and he goes first. He pushes off the side of the staircase with his feet and turns around in time to grab the opposite railing. After he had jumped down a few stories, I follow him. We meet at the bottom. We both duck beneath the nearest wall, the rough concrete scraping our knees. I peer over and see that the cop cars have circled back, there are two cops about to come in through the front door, which is twenty feet to our right. Game time.

I nod at Zashil again and we run along the edge until we are right next to the door. Taking one last deep breath we wait for the door to be pushed open. The cops don't even have time to think before Za and I both take a man. I jab mine in the stomach before ramming him into the wall. Pinning his hand down with my feet I grab his gun and elbow his neck, knocking him out. I turn around to Za who has done the same. He hands me the other gun as he pulls the knife out of the cop's back pocket. He's not a big fan of guns and I am the only one who actually knows how to use them. We run through the door. The cop cars are to our left and the cops themselves have their backs turned. We round the corner and sprint for our lives.

"Stop!" One of the cops turns around to see us and he starts running after us; two others follow and one gets on the motorcycle.

"Za, keep running!" I yell as I quickly turn around and take aim, a gun in each hand. First, I take out the first cop with my left hand and then fire at the tires of the motorcycle right as it's about to take off. I turn around and keep running. We run for two blocks and then I spot a familiar building: this was where we used to practice our roof jumps.

"Zashil, up there!" He doesn't look back before he pushes through the glass door and starts running up the stairs. I follow him, looking back over my shoulder to see two cops still trailing us. We get to the top and start to jump roofs, making our way slowly towards the outskirts where the cops lose surveillance and confidence. We jump our third roof when I look to my left across the road. I spot a man peering out of a window in the building parallel to ours. He's on the top floor and has a sniper out. Tracking the position of the sniper with my eyes I see that he's aiming for Za. Makes sense seeing how the cops still want to recruit me for special ops, they don't care much if Za is alive or not.

"Za watch out!" He doesn't hear me. We are about halfway across this roof. Damnit. I put everything into my sprint trying to catch up to him. Just as I'm about to touch his shoulder I hear a pop and dive in front of Zashil's head. I slam against the ground and Za looks down in horror. The bullet grazed my shoulder. It burns so bad. Za kneels down.

"Ivo! Ivo! Are you ok?"

"Za, you have to keep going, they can't get both of us!" I yell, the pain in my shoulder overwhelming.

"But you said never to leave your side."

"For once, don't listen to me." I am desperate. I don't want anyone laying a finger on Za. At least if he's with the Migrants, he's with people I trust.

"Fine." He turns around and runs, scaling down the next building and cutting across the street. I crawl my way over to the ledge so I can see him. I grab my phone out of my front pocket, enable communications and type "Track Za's phone and pick him up. Mission failed." I look back towards Za, my vision getting blurry. I see him hesitate in the middle of the road and then a helicopter drops down a net around him. He tries to run but can't escape. Men close in around him and attach one of those god-awful ankle bracelets. My head feels woozy. No. Zashil. Everything goes black.

ZA

MARCH 3, 2031

I wake up to a blaring fog horn. Dazed and exhausted I look around the room as everyone gets out of their cots and starts to get dressed. Two armed soldiers stand guard by the only exit out of this large jail cell. One of the new captives lays in the bed next to me, still sleeping. He only got here yesterday, but by not waking up, already he has made a mistake that will haunt him for at least a year. The general holding the fog horn walks through the door and straight towards me. I look to the floor and focus on getting dressed as fast as possible. Instead of scowling at me, like he does everyday, he walks past me and stares at the sleeping boy next to me. Putting the fog horn right next to his left ear he lets it fly, almost definitely leaving permanent hearing damage. The kid wakes up confused and damaged, but he has no time to recollect his thoughts before the general grabs him by his neck and drags him out of the cell. Everybody just stares as the boy's flailing feet barely scrape the floor and his wailing soon diminishes down the hallway.

"Hurry the hell up. We don't got all day," yells one of the soldiers. We all finish getting dressed and stand up saluting the air, showing our obedience. We file into a single line. I'm one of the shortest ones there and the man in front of me, about fifty years old, towers above my head. We all start marching out of the door, as each man passes through, the guard hands us each a personalized piece of paper. These sheets are given out everyday and explain our instructions for the day. If not fulfilled, we are either punished or killed, depending on the constantly shifting mood of the supervising officer. I am hoping to get the same assignment as yesterday. The guard hands me my piece of paper, and, before I have a chance to look at it, I'm shoved forwards and I continue marching towards the cafeteria.

I fold the piece of paper twice into a small square that can fit in my pocket. I'm wearing the usual prison clothes, bright orange baggy pants with a matching top. The only modification made was that they sewed in pockets as some of the jobs require them, even though they claim that the pockets made our clothing more humane. The sneakers are the only thing they don't provide. Basically, whatever shoes you were wearing when they arrested you are the shoes you have for the entirety of your stay. Luckily, my trusty black Adidas sneakers were on my feet on that terrifying day. In hindsight it was the only luck I've had in ten months.

As we get close to the familiar cafeteria, the large open space looms above me. The high rafters and unique dome shape of the building reminds me that we are in a repurposed aircraft hanger. Instead of planes, there are twenty feet long wooden tables with matching benches lined up in rows across the entire space. People are filing in from all six entrances to the cafeteria, each in the same attire and every person with a weary look on their face. I'm coming out of exit five. All of the lines converge in the middle of the cafeteria where the food is being served. Old guards scoop the meals out of ten large metal barrels, almost certainly contaminated, with a large metal ladle. We only get to drink something at dinner, which is usually stale water from a previous shipment of rations. Slowly, I make my way towards the food. The guard takes one look at me, his cruel and wrinkled face hands me a bowl with the most minuscule scoop of oatmeal. He's nice enough to top it with a ball of spit.

Now's the hard part. I maneuver my way through the crowd to find either an empty table, or one with a familiar face. Of course, by now, I know almost seventy percent of the labor workers here, but I classify the ones that aren't going to bully, fight, or kill me as the familiar ones. After wandering and scanning the massive space, I find an empty table near the edge of the cafeteria. Relieved that this morning won't be the worst I've ever had, I sit down and start eating. The oatmeal is dry today, like so dry I'm almost positive that they didn't even cook it. Either way, it's food and I need all of the nutrients I can get to make it through the day as alive as I can be.

As I eat, I reach into my pocket and grasp the instruction sheet. Slowly unfolding it, I read my first task. I let out a sigh of relief as I see that my task today is in fact the same as yesterday, data-inputting. This job is less labor intensive because all I have to do is sit at a computer and input all the criminals located, tracked, or captured today and put it into the system where facial recognition, courtesy of the big tech companies, helps the Board ID the person. Then all of the thousands of cameras around the country can send an alert if they get a match on any person they see. However, the real reason I like this job is because I can look for my brother discreetly. The entire system is there, so if they get a hit, I can be the first to know. Knowing Ivo, he will definitely find a way to add some code to the system, some kind of message for me.

My relief turns into terror as I see that further down the page I have been assigned a second task. This almost never happens, it either means that you're moving up in the ranks, or they so badly want to get rid of you that they want to work you so hard that they have an excuse to punish you. Even worse, the job was mining. I have only had this once before, and it was horrible. I will get put into a high speed train that brings me underground to a mine. The worst part is, there's a quota for how much I have to mine in a certain amount of time. For most, the quota is reasonable. But for me, a frail fourteen year-old, it's almost impossible. Last time I did this job, I unsurprisingly didn't fulfill the requirements. They were considering killing me but because I'm so young, they still wanted to keep me for further development. The Board likes capturing kids like us because they have plenty of time to convert us into soldiers. So, on this particular occasion, I was put into The Fridge as punishment. I had to sleep there, barely escaping full body hypothermia. I am not looking forward to a similar experience tonight.

Finishing my meal, if you can call it that, I stand up and head towards exit five. At this point, I have pretty much the whole place memorized. Architecturally, it's much nicer than I would have imagined for an airplane hangar, too bad it's become a prison. I reach exit five, its entrance is a thirty foot arch made of strong metal. The chain-link fence is up now, you can see the end of it sticking out from the top of the entrance, but during the nights it comes down like a garage door to keep people from stealing food. I start my walk down the tunnel, it's very dimly lit but illuminated signs help you know where you're going. Navigating these tunnels was hard at first, but I noticed a pattern the more time I spent here. The airplane hangar cafeteria is in the middle, at least from what I can tell. Then the six tunnels stem out in different directions and lead to smaller rooms. Each time a room shows up, two more tunnels connect to it. It keeps going like that, doubling the number of rooms and tunnels each time. I have only gone past room three of any given exit, I have no idea how long it keeps going. All of the tunnels are lined with tracks, this is where carts with resources or soldiers speed along, they make us walk of course. Some of the tracks gradually lead lower underground while others lead higher up, I'm not sure if there are multiple floors because no labor worker ever goes up. The word going around is that the Board has a bunch of labs and soldier-training facilities up above. If that were the case, I would be in a very tall building, which seems wrong seeing as I would have seen it on the Boston skyline with my brother.

After about ten minutes of walking, I come to my first fork on the path. To the left, there's a half shattered sign that reads "To Cells" and below it in small red lettering there's a warning but a part is missing. To the right there's a neon sign that has illuminated letters, it looks pretty cool because it was welded together with pieces of neon signage from restaurants and that sort of thing. This one reads "To Labor." That's the one, so I turn right and keep walking. I am virtually alone in these tunnels but that's just because I left early. Technically, I could have been in the cafeteria for another ten minutes, but I always get pushed the wrong way or into the wrong tunnel in the crowd. I learned that the hard way when I checked-in for a much harder job than I had been assigned to.

After another five minutes I reach a small brick room. There's nothing in here except for a battered wooden desk with an accompanying war veteran. They always stick the war veterans of color here. It's the Board's way of keeping up their promise to take care of war veterans from before the Takeover, while still maintaining their white supremacy. Since I got assigned this computer job a lot, I have gotten to know some of the guys stationed down here. They're the only people I talk to because I don't want to rile up the older and larger prisoners and I certainly am not going to talk to the white soldiers. So these are the people I'm comfortable with. This time, however, I don't think I've ever seen this guy before. He was dark-skinned, probably African from one of our previous allies. He looks miserable. I stride towards him.

"You new here?" I ask inquiringly but to my surprise he's not as relieved to see a harmless teenager as the other guys usually are.

"Not in the mood today, kid. Nothing against ya, I'm just in a general state." He seemed down, down in the way where all his negative feelings have converged; frustration, anger, disappointment, and sadness.

"Yeah, I get it. Most guys are in that state when they realize the Board couldn't care less about them or the promises they made." I try to be reassuring, that's my one good quality in terms of social interaction. "I'm sorry they did this to you. They did the same to all of us. If you have anything left in you, try to keep fighting for equality, it might be the only way out of this reality." I could see I was starting to make him feel better but I didn't want to pressure him into a therapy session with a fourteen-year-old so I just unfold my instruction sheet and hand it to him. He takes the sheet, his burly hand covered in bruises. Silently looking it over, he stamps it with the green 'approved' stamp and looks up. He is visibly tired.

Handing me the instructional sheet back he said "My name's John."

"Nice to meet you, John." I stick out my hand, hoping this will start a possible friendship. "My name's Zashil, but everyone just calls me Za."

"Alright then Za, you best be going before the rampage comes." I nod and walk past the table, he presses a button beneath his desk and part of the brick wall slides open. I walk in and the wall shuts behind me. This room is narrow but long, tables on tables put together with hundreds of computers set up, their bright displays providing extra lighting for the entire room. The only other source of light is the fluorescent lights above, their white glare is harsh and nauseating. Of course, there are no windows, not here and not in the entire compound, it's so easy to lose track of time. You will think you're doing pretty well when, in reality, only fifteen minutes have passed.

I find a computer near the corner of the room at the end, and sit down in the cobwebbed office chair. I login with the username and password on the instruction sheet, they change them every time so no one has unauthorized access to the internet or any computer database. Doesn't really matter if we could do something wrong, we would be knocked unconscious before we could even touch the keyboard again. The computer keeps track of what we are doing. If it senses any suspicious behavior it sends a signal to the cameras hung from the ceiling. From there, the camera on the ceiling locates the position in the room I am in, accessing the webcam of the computer I am using, runs facial recognition, activates the brass bracelet locked around my ankle, and electrocutes me. And it does all of that in less than a second. Some people have tried to trick the system and wrap something around their eyes so that facial recognition can't work. But then, instead of accessing our ankle bracelets, two sets of cuffs come out from the ground and the table, lock the hands and legs in place while a warning goes out to the nearest guard. However, that takes a few extra seconds, so whoever is trying to get in attempts to use that time to finish what they're doing, only the best hackers in the world can finish a command that fast—only one hacker in the world actually. My brother.

After logging in, I start to get to work. Notifications appear in the top right corner of the screen; there I can see my dashboard. Basically, I have to go through all of the new criminals or vigilantes that the authorities have either located, captured, or arrested. Each criminal has a current profile, just a bunch of messy information that was quickly entered by whomever was responsible for the find. My job is to open the criminal database and input all of that information. It's the boring work that the Board has someone else do. I start working as more people file in. They all glance at me from the corner of their eye when they come in, but most of them are used to me being early to labor work so none of them think twice.

After I go through a few people I find a face that I recognize. The girl has blue eyes and blonde hair, I don't personally know her but I have seen her around. It must have been when Ivo and I visited the other migrant base. It's too bad she was caught, she's only thirteen. The fact that the Board is starting to collect migrants is not a good sign. It means they are either getting close to our locations, or they are starting to catch on to our looting patterns. We had split up the city into different sub-areas and assigned people to each. When there was any kind of resource drop in your area, then you're responsible for attempting to steal that stuff. Along with that, everyone had to memorize alternate road routes and shortcuts so there was never a distinct traceable route back to the base. Ivo and I were special. We were the only two people not assigned to a sub-area. Instead, they told us we were floaters. That meant that we did our own thing, going on higher profile missions and providing reinforcements to whoever needed it. I loved our job. We were never split up and everyday was something different, not to mention the migrant community saw us as some kind of heroes. I miss not being able to do that. Assuming Ivo is still alive, I wonder if he's still a floater and if he works alone. I'm not sure he's even looking for me. His attitude towards attachment is pretty unique. When our parents died he didn't even shed a tear. Instead, he told me that we must live the way they wanted us to in order to properly honor their lives. I tried to listen to him but I couldn't stop crying for a couple of months. Being the way he is, he could've just accepted that there was no way he could save me. I mean, I've done this database job countless times in the last ten months and there's not even a side note that mentions anybody like him.

After three hours of working, a soldier walks through the door and tells us it's time for the shift change. This will be my first time experiencing this. Usually, I get assigned the same thing for both shifts so I never have to move for the entire day. I know they do this on purpose because they assume that us kids are inefficient and slow so they don't want to give us an excuse to elongate our trip across the compound. Not really knowing what to do, I follow everyone out of the room and through the tunnels, heading back towards the cafeteria. I reach into my pocket and, for a second, I think that I forgot my instruction sheet back in the database room. Luckily, I remember that I had tucked it into my shoe so no one could pickpocket me. That's been a recent issue as people realize the sheets themselves don't have a personalized code or picture or anything. So, prisoners have been stealing other people's sheets in order to get easier work. It's never happened to me, but I always play it safe and not wait for the bad to come to me.

Once we get into the familiar cafeteria, the rush of sound hits me, almost immediately giving me a headache. There are so many people moving so fast to get to their next shift. I get pushed and turned around so many times that I almost miss which exit is which, and where to go. I run over to the same corner that I ate at this morning and get a moment of peace. Sitting down, I reach into my shoe and find the folded piece of paper. Reading the bottom again, I understand that I have to go through exit two and then catch a train headed down towards the mine. I jump up onto the cafeteria table so that I can look around and reorient myself. I turn around until I see the number two above a large arch. I get down and start walking in that direction, dodging people, weaving in and out amongst the tables. Finally, I make my way across the cafeteria and into exit two. Looking down at my sheet, which is carelessly still in my hand, I realize that the departure time of the train is in two minutes. Crap. I was never good with time and I scold myself as I run as fast as I can down the tunnel. The problem is I haven't been down this way in a while and I don't remember how long this exit is. Finally, I found a fork in the path. Squinting at the signs and trying not to let my sweat drip into my eyes, I turn right towards the mine. Starting my run up again, I near a group of people going in the same direction. I slow down to a walk, satisfied and slightly impressed with myself that I made it on time. I catch up to the group and decide to linger behind them. All of these guys are huge, each and every one of them looking like an Olympic bodybuilder. I knew that the Board likes to assign strong men to the mines but these guys are on another level. They literally look like they could punch me through three walls. I stare at my feet, making sure not to make eye contact. Out of everyone I have seen here, I definitely don't want to get on these guys' bad side.

Soon we get to a raised platform on the left with a stolen sticker from the subway that says "Step Away from Ledge. Train Approaching." As if right on cue, a bright light further down the tunnel starts to get bigger and the sound of rusty train wheels on tracks whining slowly gets louder. The train comes to a screeching halt in front of us. It's less of a train and more of a cart that was poorly outfitted to slide down tracks. It's an incredibly dilapidated brown rectangular box, with the entire top non-existent. Instead, there are just railings off the side. Everyone gets in, holding on to the railing and preparing themselves for departure. The screeching starts again and the train begins to build up momentum as it slides downhill through the tunnel.

"First time on the transport, bud?" I'm almost surprised by the softness of the voice. I turn around and a large golden-brown man towers over me. On closer inspection he looks Hawaiian and has long dark hair with piercing brown eyes.

"Yeah, actually." I try to sound confident and strong, like someone who has been surviving in the labor camps successfully, which I have. Instead, I sound like a timid kid who was unfortunate enough to be separated from his guardians and is now in mortal danger. Which also has some truth to it.

"Well, it's not as scary as it sounds." He replies earnestly, calming me down. "And we aren't as scary as we look." He remarks. Two of the guys around him chuckle. All I manage is a smile but I appreciate this guy's demeanor, it makes me feel that extra bit more comfortable and secure.

"My name is Ano."

"Nice to meet you Ano. My name is Za." I try to sound comfortable and make him feel as good as he made me feel.

"Za. What an interesting name. Where are you from Za?" His voice is smooth and tender, not what I believed a man of his stature would have.

"I was born here in Boston but my parents were immigrants. My father was German. On his way out of Germany, he decided to stop in India first. That's where he met my mom. Then, they came to the United States." For some people, talking about their dead parents might make them sad. And while a part of me is still scarred, I love talking to other people about them. Not only does it make me feel better, but talking about my mixed background is always fun.

"Sounds like your family are interesting people. I'm purposefully not going to ask how you got here. Nobody around here will ask you. We keep that to ourselves, as it brings too much pain to think about the past. But if you hang with us, you'll learn the best ways to navigate this place. Don't tell anyone, but we will find a way out and if you're with us when that time comes, you'll be right by my side." Soothing and confident. I like Ano and he might be my first real friend around here. Hopefully. The only thing I don't trust about him is his attitude towards getting out. It's much harder than it seems and I was smart enough to examine the ways to get out right from the start. There is none, not counting the coding thing that only one person in the world can do. Ano's confidence in his ability to escape might lead him astray, and I don't want to be by his side when he's executed for a failed attempt.

My thoughts are cut short as the cart, or transport, comes to a halt. Jumping out, I follow Ano down steps into the mine. The only other time I was assigned mining, it was in a different location and as the cave opens up I quickly realize that I am in a drastically different place. We walk down into a massive black cave, it's incredibly dark and our footsteps echo and bounce back at us. A handful of barrels and tools lie on the ground but the darkness overwhelms me as only a few candles and handheld lights barely illuminate the space. A guard approaches the group and has everyone take out their instructional sheet, stamping them. There's something off about this though. The guard isn't only stamping the sheets without even glancing at their contents, but he's also greeting the men and smiling at them like they're long lost friends.

Finally it's our turn in line and the guard vigorously shakes Ano's hand. "It's good to see you Ano, how have you been?" The guard has a thick Caribbean accent.

"I'm good Usain, how are you holding up?" They both speak to each other with so much comfort. It's almost as if the vast power imbalance doesn't exist with them, like they aren't on completely opposite sides.

"Ya know, the same. I'm hanging in there. Being assigned to this crap hole is a massive downgrade, but seeing you guys makes me feel a lot better about the whole thing. Maybe I won't mutter profanities at my supervising officer today." Everyone laughs, even me. "And who's this little fellow? Don't tell me you're into kidnapping. Or even worse, did you voluntarily adopt him and become a father." Usain punches Ano in the shoulder jokingly.

"This little guy's name is Za, a fellow labor worker. It's his first time down here and I thought I might take care of him, at least through this shift." There's that kindness again, it's getting to be almost unnerving.

"Well nice to meet you Za. I would shake your hand and get to know you but I'm a guard and not supposed to do that. So, instead I'll let you guys get to work." He winked at Ano as we both stride away from him and further into the cave. Struggling to keep up with Ano I inquire about that odd encounter.

"Ano, what was that?"

"That was an old friend. Just because they're soldiers doesn't mean that they aren't still people. Not everyone working for the Board is with them. They just chose the side that worked for them at the moment. Usain over there was given a lifeline by the Board. If he had refused, which he wanted to, he would've been killed. Instead he listened to me and accepted the offer. From then on he has been safe and unharmed." This was kind of mind-boggling. Not in a million years did I think I would see an interaction like that. Nor did I think I would ever see a prisoner of the Board talk about the Board like that. It was a lot to take in but my mind was being changed about the Board. They are still my enemy, but I'm starting to think it's not the Board as a whole with all their people, but instead the people that are responsible for making the Board how it is. Either way, I'm excited about the new things I could learn from Ano and reassured that I can make it through this day safely with him by my side. All of a sudden, life wasn't seeming as bad as it could be.

I V O

MARCH 4, 2031

"Wake up. Ivo, wake up." My eyes slowly open to see Aiko's face leaning over. For some reason she is still vigorously shaking me, her hands on my shoulders. "Oh, good you're up." Almost embarrassed, she withdraws her arms and slowly backs away from the bed. I push myself up into a sitting position.

"What's going on? What time is it?" I'm not really one to sleep in. I used to be a pretty deep sleeper, I still am, but my sleep cycle is always off now that my missions are getting earlier and earlier in the morning.

"It's 6 am."

"Oh. Jesus Aiko, you made it seem like I was in a coma. Why are you waking me up if it's only 6 am?"

"Well, I was kinda worried because while it's only six, you have been sleeping since you got back from your mission yesterday with Idri, which actually means you have been sleeping for sixteen hours." Weirdly enough, she did sound worried. But she's almost always worried about me for some reason and that's the kind of person she is. Born to be a mother basically.

"Oh ok, that makes sense. Jeez, I don't think I've ever slept that long." While I am worried that I slept that long, there's a part of me that is kinda impressed. It's the kind of thing that I would run to my brother and brag at him about. After all, he is the king of sleeping in.

"Well, I'm glad you slept. I'm going to need all of your energy today."

"Why? What's happening today?"

"You don't remember? I guess you really did pass out. Today's the Board roundup. We need to be out there to protect the public. At least, protect them the best we can." Of course, the roundup. How could I forget? All of a sudden, Aiko's tone is sounding a bit unsure. I need to make sure she can count on me today.

"Of course, now I remember. Don't worry Aiko," I look her straight in the eye, "I'll be ready. I always am."

"I should've never doubted you." She says with a smile on her face. "Well, I'll leave you to get ready." She turns around and walks out the door, pausing and looking back at me before she disappears down the hallway.

I slowly and reluctantly get out of bed. My legs feel numb after being inactive for so long and a tingling feeling starts to shoot down my legs as they wake up. I look down and realize I had fallen asleep in my mission clothes. Damn, I must've looked like an absolute doofus when Aiko saw me this morning. Oh well. I changed out of my sleek athletic pants and into new ones. These are the favorite pieces of clothing that I still have from before the Takeover, the pants are matte black and made with special woven fibers that make them waterproof and crazy durable. I can always rely on these to add some stylish stealth to my missions, or at least that's what I think they do in my head. Taking off my dirty and sweaty grey t-shirt, I decide to change into a black one made of lighter material. No matter how peacefully we are going to try to defend these people, we are still going to end up getting into a fight so I need to be prepared with the proper attire. In the end, what I'm wearing underneath is just for me because we, specifically me, have a trick up our sleeves that the Board definitely won't expect.

A couple months ago I was out on a mission with Aiko and Idrissa. Initially, the intel was for a new shipment of fresh food. The Board ships fresh food to on site soldiers very rarely so we were very excited to get our hands on this. Turns out that the Board had called the shipment of fresh food in a ploy to keep people from wanting to take it, they mostly expect us rebels to go for the processed food rations because they last longer. Instead the shipment was actually for some super high-tech weapons, straight off the assembly line and never used in battle. It was the Board's response to the soldiers in Boston that complained they weren't armed well enough to fend off the increasing number of rebels. Too bad, cuz they never got to see their shiny new weapons. Instead, we did.

Ever since the Takeover, the Board told all major tech companies to focus their efforts on military innovation. Basically, the United States was intent on defending themselves against other countries and their insane dictators and leaders. The military tech got so innovative and futuristic that most soldiers complained and just wanted their old stuff back. Instead of wasting all of the work that went into the high tech stuff, they limited production to a very few amounts of those weapons. Dividing it out, every major military shipment had mostly old but enhanced weapons as well as one or two items of the new stuff. The weapons include pistols, rifles, machine guns, and other kinds of artillery, as well as bombs, grenades, and blades of all kinds. If you were lucky then the people ordering the shipment were low on bullet proof vests and helmets and you could swing some of those too.

That was the case for the shipment that we hijacked. Everything went very smoothly. Idiotically, the guards and drivers surrounding the shipment weren't even well armed and since all three of us are highly trained in combat, it was not a problem. Specifically, the shipment included about thirty vests, fifty pistols, twenty five machine guns, twenty rifles, ten big bombs, fifteen sticker bombs, and twenty grenades. At first we thought that the shipment didn't have a special tech thing but, then again, we didn't know what we were looking for. The special tech thing ended up being a suit of some kind hidden beneath the vests. That's where my speciality comes in. All three of us, Aiko, Idrissa, and I, are so admired by the Migrants because we each possess a highly specialized skill that almost no one else has, including anybody within the Board.

Aiko is extremely well-versed in every kind of martial art as well as a master sword fighter. Idrissa is an expert of espionage and the sharpest shooter you will ever find. His father was an international spy for the FBI, back when that was a thing, and he trained Idri to follow in his footsteps. Idri can hit any target from half a mile away without a good scope. Then there's me. While I can do a bit of martial arts well, I can shoot fine, and can go undercover without much trouble, I'm certainly not a master at any of those things. My speciality is tech and science. No one, and I mean no one, can code or tinker better than I can. And that makes me very special. It means that I'm the only non-governmental person that can understand and mess with all of the tech and software that the best in the world make for the Board. My brother was a specialist too. He was the best at parkour and no one else could maneuver a space like he could.

That meant that when we found this suit everyone was disappointed except me. Millions of dollars were pumped into this one object and I was curious as to why and what its potential was.

After a few days of examining it and unlocking the software I realized that this could be the most advanced weapon I had ever seen because of its customization. The gist of it is that the suit conforms to the body of the user, creating an extremely lightweight and durable robotic layer. It's as if the suits of Iron Man and Spider-Man had a baby, if that's even an accurate analogy. The robotics are extremely complex and configurable, similar to Iron Man's suit. But the elasticity and thinness of it makes it much more usable in close combat missions. While I was able to unlock most of its software potential, I couldn't get into the settings that define the suit's size. Lucky for me, the suit was set to a size that was almost a perfect fit for me. All of the Migrants agreed that it would be best served in my hands, with someone who knew how to manage it and use it.

At first, the suit was colored in army green camouflage with an accompanied helmet. To get the suit on you would have to slide on the shirt and it would spread and cover your entire body with nanotechnology. Then you would put on the helmet which had built in AI and access to government information and catalogs. The suit allowed you to generate certain weapons from your hands, like simple knives or certain guns. There was stored material throughout the interior of the suit that fed through the hands. It was an advanced version of 3D printing that was super fast.

I didn't like any of it except for the concept. If I were on a mission, taking the whole thing out of my bag, helmet and all, and then installing it on myself would just take too much work and time. That's where my engineering skills came in and, in my opinion (which is shared by most other migrants), I made it ten times better. Diving into the software, I located the design specifications which outlined the limits of the suit and why it was made the way it was, this was in case any soldier got the suit damaged in action and needed to fix it. The helmet was included because there was no way to fit the amount of technology, screens, processing power, and batteries into a device that was compressible, so they made the helmet separately. The suit was made with a larger starting point because it had to house all of the material, for instant weapon generation. After taking a step back and realizing what I could really use the suit for, I began my modifications.

It took weeks, three months actually, to get it just right without malfunction. And even then, the suit was liable to glitches. But, finally, many more months later, I was done, and it was perfect. Instead of the shirt being the starting point of the suit, it became a gold necklace. The necklace is just a gold rope chain with a cube as the center piece. I was able to configure the material that generated the weapons into a much more condensed form. The drawbacks of these changes meant that I had to have a checkpoint for the suit to know how to form. Before, the shirt already knew the basic shape of the body because it was a tight fitting shirt. So, I placed those checkpoints on my wrists and ankles. I started off having to wear four bracelets all of the time, which got uncomfortable so I changed them to line against the inner openings of my jacket and pants, which was much easier. The other drawback was the change in material meant I could only generate two weapons, a high quality pistol and a knife. But I realized those are the only two weapons I use anyway and in the off-chance that I need a bigger weapon, I'll just physically take one. The necklace was configured to also form the suit around my head, eliminating the need for the helmet. It made the whole process more discreet but it meant I lost some software functionality. I got rid of all of the screens except a large one right underneath my eye-line. And I kept the AI.

So after getting the rest of my outfit sorted, I grabbed the necklace on my desk, slipped on my matching black sneakers and walked out the door. I turned the corner and almost bumped right into Idri who appeared to be waiting for me.

"C'mon, Aiko asked us to go scout out the area."

"Alright, you ready?" I asked, kind of skeptical of his minimal outfit and artillery, he needs guns after all.

"Of course, I'm ready. And I thought today might be a nice opportunity to try out the news toys you've been working so hard on for me." He winked and we started walking down the hall. Idri is wearing black clothing like me but his pants are baggy cargo pants and he has military boots on that he has painted black as well. Further up, he has a tight-fitting long-sleeve black shirt on and a bullet proof vest on, which I don't have because my suit is kinda bullet proof. It only fails if the same place is hit multiple times. Idri also has a black beanie on, which he insists is to complete the stealth of his outfit but he wears it every time, probably because it's the last thing his dad gave him before he left. Virtually every single pocket on Idri's body, six on the vest and six on the pants, is full. He has grenades and knives. Not to mention he is also carrying a duffel bag with guns and ammo. Hanging off his belt loop are the so-called toys he was talking about. They are two miniature guns that I configured to turn into large machine guns and rifles. Not that much effort went into them but ever since I gave them to him, he can't stop smiling at me and gesturing towards them before a mission.

Walking down the hallway from my room, the labs and engineering rooms are to our left. All of the smart people are hanging out in there, talking about concepts or just gossiping. No one has hardline jobs around here, you kinda do what you wanna do and need to do, but we all work towards the common cause of restoring some kind of equilibrium back to society. Anything is better than this. More bedrooms are on our right and, soon enough, the space opens up into the garage. There's only a few old cars, we are working on stealing high-end lightweight transportation, namely motorcycles, but this is what we got for now. While the entire space is floor-to-ceiling concrete, the garage is made of bricks. Our entire base is a repurposed ancient subway station that the city eventually filled in, built around, and forgot. When we moved here, we went into the Board database and erased all the history of this location. Idri steps up to the Camry and turns the key to unlock, I hop in the passenger seat and he drives. Emerging out of the ground we head towards the city's center, what used to be Chinatown and now is home to most of the city's residents.

It takes us about fifteen minutes to get there because we have to avoid all of the cops and the traffic. We park in an alley adjacent to a massive parking building. Idri slides his bag over his shoulder and we pick the lock to the building's side door. Crouching down as we move through the lot I get flashbacks of ten months ago, I've been dreaming about losing Za a lot lately. This time though, I push the thoughts away. I need to stay focused. We weave through all of the cars and make our way to the emergency stairwell next to the elevator. Climbing them as fast as we can, we reach the final platform which has a ladder leading up to the roof. After climbing the ladder, we lay down on the roof facing the block perpendicular from where we parked the car. Idri takes out his binoculars and starts to inspect the area.

"Aight, what are we sayin? Is it bad or doable?" I ask, hoping he'll see there are no feds and we can just stroll down there and round up the people of color, giving them a code to get into our base.

"It's not great." He replies, still scanning the area from right to left. Actually, I change my mind. It's bad. The feds are everywhere and have already shoved a bunch of people in trucks. This is bad Ivo, we might be too late." He seems worried but I stay confident. Idri has a habit of exaggerating.

"Calm down. It can't be that bad. Here, hand me those." Idri hands me the binoculars and I point them in the same direction. Let's just say, Idri wasn't exaggerating this time. There are about fifty cops, maybe more.

Some are stationed around the trucks and outside the houses while others are knocking down doors, slowly making their way down the block. Zooming in on the truck it seems that they hit the jackpot. There are probably around 40 families, about 100 people, in each of the three trucks, one being empty.

Handing the binoculars back to Idri, I slouch down. "Damn, you're right. There's no way we can take them. I guess we should get back before they notice us and tell the others before they walk into something horrible." I'm disappointed and angry. This keeps on happening. We think that we can get there before the Board and save some people, but they always win and always take away innocent lives from their homes and jobs.

"Maybe we don't have to Ivo."

"What do you mean, there's no way we can take them." I say, slightly confused as to where Idrissa is going with this.

"We don't have to save them now if we can save them later." He says excitedly that he finally beat me to an idea. "We don't need to fight for them now, if we can get where they are going without the Board knowing." Genius. He's onto something with this, but I don't know how we are supposed to find that out. We've been looking everywhere for government compounds ever since they took Za and we haven't found anything, not even a clue.

"How are we supposed to get that information?"

"When you were looking, did you see the phones by their side?"

"Yeah I think I saw that. Still, how does that help us?"

"Only soldiers on lower level tiers in the ranks are given phones. They are programmed to have their supervisors number in case of trouble and more importantly, they have all of the routes to bases and such because the Board doesn't want lower-level soldiers knowing the locations before their missions so there is no way the intel can be leaked." This is where the whole intel and spy thing really comes in. "So, all we need is one of those phones and then we can track down their location later." He was really happy with himself now.

"That's genius Idri. Now we have to figure out how to take the phones."

"Should I call Aiko? She could bring some help."

"No, don't do that. We need to be discreet and not attract the attention of all of the soldiers." I know that Aiko and her team would be helpful but this new mission could go very wrong and I don't want anybody else getting hurt. "Idri, you position yourself up here with a sniper, taking out anybody I don't see that will interfere. I'll go down, take out a few guys, grab their phones, and leave a smoke bomb so we don't start a full on war."

"Sounds good." He turns away and starts assembling his weapons. I grab a smoke bomb from his open bag and then turn back towards the ladder, heading down to where we entered. Crouching down by the front door, I open it just enough so that I can survey the area and make my plan. I need to see which soldier I would go for. Everyone except for one guy in front of an alley has their phones securely strapped into their belt. This guy seemed to be checking something because he is holding his phone close to his face. I look above him and see that there is a catwalk on the side of the building that is adjacent to the alley that the guard is standing in front of. That's my play, I get him by surprise, drag him into the alley, and no one should even notice he's gone. Now I just need to figure out how to cross the street.

I quietly open the door and stand right in front of it. The building casts a shadow right over me and, with the black clothes I have on, someone would have to look twice to spot me. Leaning against the wall as flat as I can, I peer up and see Idri's sniper mounted on the ledge. I wait to see if he'll look down but he doesn't so I make my move. Checking to make sure no one is looking, I sprint straight across the street towards the opposite building. Turning into an alley, I'm about one block away from where I need to be. Roof-jumping skills, don't fail me now. Climbing up the emergency fire staircase which is inconveniently very fragile, I make it to the roof, about six stories up. I look one more time across the street to catch sight of Idri and luckily he sees me. We each give each other a thumbs-up and I start running and jumping over gaps. The jumps are only six or seven feet, completely doable for me when I'm running at full speed. The only problem is that landing makes a lot of noise, so quieting that down and completing the jump is difficult. Za always told me to roll into the landing so I try to do that as softly as possible. Thirty seconds later, I'm standing above the alley with the guard and one jumps away from the building with the catwalk. I take one deep breath and run into the jump, immediately rolling and staying flat down on the concrete surface of the roof. As I army crawl towards the ledge of the building with the catwalk I hear a crack beneath me. Crap. Lifting my leg, I realize I had crawled right over a stick.

"Hey, what was that?" I hear a soldier exclaim in the distance.

"Nah, it's nothing. Probably just a stupid bird. Leave it be and start looking out for real threats, the boss said there might be some rebels crawling about, thinking they're all heroes or whatever." Phew. Thank god for that idiot. It seems as though the guard I'm targeting is completely oblivious to their entire conversation so I slowly climb onto the catwalk, my back to the alley. I rotate myself so the hands are grabbing the catwalk behind me and my feet are against the wall. Doing a quick check for cameras, I notice there is one on the opposite building turned away from me, but it looks like it's about to pan. I need to make sure they don't notice my suit when I activate it, they already have my face or at least I think they do, so that doesn't really matter. When I'm sure the camera isn't panning for a few seconds, I touch the cube around my neck and feel the suit start to morph around me. The helmet is the last to come and I have to lift up my feet and hands one at a time so that the suit can go over them.

Once it's done, I'm finally ready. Turning my body to the left so it's facing the guard I leap off of the catwalk and directly behind me. Quickly putting my hand over his mouth I drag him backwards into the alley. He struggles, lashing his elbows behind himself, but I easily move side to side, dodging his blows. I'm trying to think how I can quietly knock him out, ultimately deciding to punch the guard in the back to stop him squirming. I lean him up against the wall so that his face is almost touching and then I remember that I added a new electricity blast to the suit. I lift my left hand to the side of his neck and press my thumb into my point finger, triggering an electric shock, and subsequently knocking him out. Wow, I'm glad I added that because everyone told me it wasn't ever going to be useful. Slowly letting the guard crumple to the ground, I position his body so he's leaning against a dumpster, hidden from the other guards. I take the phone, which is surprisingly still in his hands. Making sure it's not damaged, I realize I won't need the smoke bomb at all and am about to grin when I hear gunshots in the streets.

"He's up there! The two of you go up the stairs, we'll secure the prisoner back here." I hear the same soldier as before yell. Crap, they definitely saw Idri. I climb back up to the roof and look across the street. Idri is nowhere to be seen on the roof. I check the sides of the building and sure enough, Idri is crouching down on the left side of the building, not too far from the car. I see two or three guards enter the parking garage with the same door we used. I take out the smoke grenade, pull out the pin, and toss it into the middle of the street. Covering my ears I hear a quick boom followed by some swears and the footsteps of the soldiers' boots coming away from the garage and back into the street. Nice. I climb back down into the alley, exit on the other street, take a right, and run to where I think the car is. Hopefully, Idri has done the same thing and isn't waiting for me. I get to the Camry and see the headlights are already on. Fantastic. Hopping into the passenger seat I see that Idri is completely calm, satisfied with how the plan was executed.

"That worked out well." He says as we pull out of the alley and speed towards the base.

"Yeah. To be honest, I didn't really expect it to go that well." I'm speaking the truth, the odds were definitely against us on that one. "Did you even have to take a shot?"

"Nope, thanks to you I kept all of my precious ammo." We both smile at a job well done and I examine the phone in my hands. While everyone is going to be happy that we found a way to possibly save those captives we saw, I'm looking at a phone that could finally lead me to Za.

ZA

MARCH 4, 2031

Database input. Mining. I'm reading my instructional sheet as I eat my breakfast. I've done the same two tasks for the past three days, probably because Ano has some connections. Not that anyone ever bothered me before, but, ever since meeting Ano, no one has even glared at me. It's gotten to a point where people I have never seen or met have nodded at me. Even today, I'm sitting across from two full grown black guys that I have literally never seen but they just came over and sat with me, not a word out of their mouths. I definitely could get used to prison life like this, it's not too bad when you're not completely alone. I was really starting to soak in the morning when all of a sudden a crazy loud siren started blaring. Everyone gets up but doesn't really move or go anywhere. From the looks of things, this hasn't happened before so we are all new to this.

"Stay with us bud." Says one of the guys that is sitting with me. I guess they do know how to talk. I just look their way and nod in approval. Trust me, if two men with that amount of muscle say they'll protect me, I am not leaving their side.

"Everybody stay calm!" A general says as he walks in through exit five with a whole squadron of soldiers and guards behind him. The guards and soldiers file out and all take up position, covering the entire perimeter of the cafeteria. When the commotion continues, the general pulls out a loudspeaker.

"I said. Everyone stay calm and sit down." His voice rings and echoes throughout the airplane hangar as all of the prisoners start to sit down and be quiet.

"What's going on here! Can't we just eat in peace?" A random unseen prisoner yells.

"Will you SHUT UP!" The general yells in response, his bright blue eyes flaring as his blonde hair flops around.

"Are we in trouble?" Another prisoner asks.

"Jesus. What is it with you people? Someone detain that idiot." He says gesturing towards the guards. We all watch as a guard handcuffs the prisoner who ends up being a middle aged brown man and drags him out of the cafeteria, his heels audibly scraping the floor.

"Ahh. Ok. Finally some peace and quiet. Here is what's happening. Some crazy guy, who shall remain unnamed, just tried to escape. I don't know why he did this as everyone knows this prison is the most secure prison ever made. Heck, I don't even know where we are. Anyways, obviously this man is now dead." He waited for us all to nod in approval, it is what we all expected so the nod wasn't that out of place.

"But, the fact that he tried to escape means you guys are getting a bit too comfortable with the current setting. So, congratulations. All of you will be getting transferred. It's actually good timing because the Board just captured a bunch of people and they're going to need a nice place to stay, which of course is going to be this lovely place." A few people gasped at the news and there were murmurs around the place which were not stopped by the general this time.

"I, unfortunately, was not blessed with knowing where you are being sent. But rest assured, it's either worse than this place or much much worse than this place. Both, two solid options." Some more murmurs follow, some people frightened by this, others really didn't care. I mean how much worse can this possibly get. Personally, I was unmoved. I couldn't care less about a change in scenery. If anything was a problem, this would make it significantly harder for Ivo to find me, assuming he's still looking that is.

"Well, that's all I got. So pack up your things after work today, and you'll be off tomorrow." The general turns and walks out the way he came, the squadron following him.

I go back to my food, fairly unfazed and refocus myself on getting through this day. After I'm finished, I set off to the database center, leaving early as usual. I nod to the two guys that said they were going to protect me. They nod back and I head off on my usual lonely walk through the tunnel. Making my way to the database center, the guard stationed there is John again. It was nice to see a familiar face. He acknowledges me, stamps my instructional sheet and opens the door for me.

"After tomorrow, it doesn't look like we are going to see each other again, bud." He says, as I'm walking through the door.

"Guess you're right, John. Can't say I'll miss you but I hope your next job is a bit better. You deserve it." I always try to be nice to John. I've only seen him a few times throughout the last couple days, but he always looks depressed. I would be too if I was mistreated the way he was, but I can't help him because I'm not in any better of a position.

"Thanks, kid." He muttered deeply, and then turns around, staring at his desk as some more prisoners approached. I walk through the door and get settled at my usual station. I login and get to work, remembering to tuck the instructional sheet back into my shoe.

After a couple of hours I find something very interesting, something I've never seen before. There is a new criminal that they wanted entered into the database. However, the only thing they have on them is a grainy video from an outdoors surveillance camera. That's weird because you can't determine if he's a person of color or not, so he must have done something pretty disruptive to be pushed so early onto the criminal list. That's not even the most interesting part. After I got the notification of the criminal, I tried to move the data into the database, which is my job. But every time I tried to do it the database said "ERROR, Criminal Duplicate." It thinks that whoever this is has already been filed into the database. But the computers around here are smart enough not to send me a notification for a new criminal if the criminal already existed. The whole point of this database is for that not to happen because if the database knows the criminal. Any new material can be assigned to someone's profile based on facial recognition. After a few tries I decide I might as well look at the video. All of a sudden I have a bunch of time on my hands because the computer won't send me new notifications until I finish with this one, which isn't going to happen anytime soon.

The video is grainy and I can only view it in a small window, but there is something eerily familiar about the figure. From what I can tell, the figure is wearing all black, but because of the darkness of the alley, there is nothing definitive about any of his features. The body type suggests it's a male. He seems to be looking at something that's in the camera's blind spot, he almost looks hesitant, like he's waiting for something. And then the camera pans in the opposite direction and that's it. There is nothing here to suggest any criminal action. Of course, I don't have access to any news or government watchlists to determine if this guy was included in some kind of attack. I watch the video a couple more times and notice that the clip stops playing a couple of seconds before it's finished. Interesting. I feel a quick sharp pain in my ankle. It's a warning sign from the system telling me to get back to work. Eventually I'm going to have to signal for a guard to come fix this glitch but I really want to recover those last seconds of the video before I have to do that.

After a couple minutes of brainstorming I have an idea. I go into the user settings which allow me to change how things show up on my screen. For instance, I can change how big or small the notification panel and the different grid views I can get that display the criminal information. They give us access to this stuff because they think it will make us more efficient workers. I decide to minimize the notification panel as small as it will go in the hopes that the dashboard section will get slightly bigger. I exit out of the settings and try to play the video again. Great, it worked. The video is slightly bigger and now it displays a video playback bar so, not only can I rewind, but I can slow down the content. Finally I might be able to catch the last couple seconds of this twelve second video. I watch it once more on normal speed. After the camera pans, it pans back to where the guy was except that he's not there anymore. Nothing out of the ordinary, it seems as though he just left. I decide to slow it down by fifty percent. Once I get to the part where it starts to pan back, I pause. Zooming in to even worse resolution, I notice a couple blurry black things off to the right of the frame. I keep playing the video but it's the same as before. I lean back in disappointment ready to call a guard to come fix my computer. I can't believe I went through all of this trouble to get a couple of blurry black sticks.

I exit out of the video and get a prompt on the top of the criminal profile saying "Data Updated" and prompting me to reload the page. I do so and another copy of the video shows up labeled "Enhanced Video." I cannot believe my luck. In the time between opening up this notification and viewing the video, some secret service professional ran a video enhancer and immediately uploaded the file to the profile. Whoever it was must've though that since the notification was pressed a while ago, the profile had already been entered into the secure database. Otherwise, the person wouldn't have done this because they don't want us prisoners seeing any confidential information. Lucky for me.

I press the video which looks ten times better now. I can see the figure more closely now, he has a black shirt on with black pants and black shoes. All regular clothing, nothing special. The guy has black hair and seems to be of brown complexion. That would solidify the reason why he was considered a criminal, regardless of what he did. Unless you work directly within the Board (which is rare) or own a shop that supplies the Board (more common) then all people of color are deemed criminals. I skip forward a few seconds, not seeing anything that I didn't get before. I really wanted to see the enhanced black sticks. The video takes a while to load but once it does it reveals two legs, almost mid-jump. I assume that whoever this criminal jumps off of the wall and onto the ground, that seems to be his general trajectory and I'm quite an expert on jumps if I do say so myself. Zooming further in there is something off about the legs. They aren't the black pants and shoes like before. So either this is a different person or he changed which seems impossible seeing how the camera only panned away for a few seconds.

Just as I finish the video I feel a much harsher electric shock in my ankle. That's it for my playtime. I quit out of the profile labeled "Anonymous" which is misspelled with an "i" instead of the first "o" and a "v" instead of the "y". Whoever writes the code for these machines must really be an idiot. I navigate up to the "I Need Help Button" and the computer says that a guard is on the way from somewhere else in the base.

Soon enough the guard gets here, kinda spooking out the other prisoners since they haven't ever seen a guard in here before.

"What seems to be the problem, masala?" He asks condescendingly. This guy does not look like he knows tech. I ignore his racism and tell him the problem.

"When I try to transfer this profile into the database it says it's a duplicate."

"Alright, idiot. Did you try just trashing the profile." Of course I had thought about it but we were informed to never do that without approval.

"I was told never to do that." I replied timidly, afraid of his threatening look.

"Well you obviously weren't listening. You're not supposed to do that if it just says error. But any of this duplicate crap is just nonsense and you can toss it." He presses a button on the remote in his hand and gives me a quick shock. "Next time only ask for help if you actually need it. Better yet, just don't ask for help and get electrocuted all day. It'll serve all of us better." He walks away, a couple of the braver prisoners snarling and frowning at him. Of course, us prisoners are never taught those exceptions just so that the guards can do stuff like that.

I keep working through the next hour, nothing really out of the ordinary happening. Then the doors open and I head to my second shift in the mines. Once we get to the cafeteria, I find a table to climb up onto and I start to look around for Ano. I like it more if I walk into the mines with Ano because then the guards know my affiliation and pretty much don't bother me at all. Not able to find him in the sea of moving heads, I walk towards the appropriate exit holding on to a chance that I'll run into him there. Weaving my way through people and trying to avoid running into anybody that will pick a fight, I make my way to the entrance with no Ano in sight. I decide that he must have just gone down to the transport early so I make my way there. As I approach the platform, I recognize absolutely no one. Nobody at all looks at me or even gives me the slightest positive nod. On the contrary actually, some of them even give me dirty looks. This is strange because usually Ano's friends are at least hanging around because the mines are their favorite labor job. As the transport approaches, I guardedly make my way into the cart, avoiding eye-contact or physical contact with anybody else. I position myself in the corner and look away from the interior of the cart and its passengers. This day just keeps getting weirder.

Once the transport stops, we all get out. I look up to see Usain standing out front as usual. Happy that at least one friendly face is around, I make my way to the front of the line. Grinning, I approach Usain holding my instructional sheet in my hand and am about to greet him before he leans over next to my ear and whispers.

"Don't get all soft on me now kid. Your protection ended this morning and now you really have to do your work. If not, I will personally see to it that your last night in this place is hell." He lifts back up into a standing position, snatches my instructional sheet, stamps it, and pushes me along.

Shaking and afraid I pick up some tools and get to work. What did he mean by my protection ended this morning. I never asked for the protection, Ano just conversed with me once and then all of his prison friends and guards looked out for me, not letting anyone bother me. But before, I was doing just fine for myself. I hadn't gotten beaten up and I was getting my work done. I was in nobody's business and that was how I wanted it. I knew there was something fishy about Ano and his whole gang. I should've stayed away like Ivo always taught me. I guess I was too caught up in the excitement of having some kind of friend that it clouded my judgement.

The morning thing still didn't make sense though because Ano's buddies were still guarding me this morning when that general had his whole speech. Unless. Oh god. The guy that the general was talking about was Ano. I knew it. He always said he had a way to escape, I just thought that he was trying to act tough and was bluffing. Everyone knows that this place is legitimately inescapable otherwise I would've been the one to find a way out. The guys that were with me probably didn't know that Ano was planning to do it, and the guys that were going with him probably backed out when they realized he was crazy. Oh well, looks like I'm back to square one. And, finding my place in the next prison the Board is taking us just became ten times harder.

Letting out a stressful and anxious shy, I start hammering down at the rock. The only thing that would make this day worse was if I didn't meet my quota. The problem is, there is no chance that I can actually mine the amount that I have to. I am physically not capable. Accepting my fate, I mess around for the next three hours, banging at the rock and hoping for a diamond to just pop out like a gift from god. At the end of the shift, before anyone can leave for dinner, Usain comes around and checks everyone's progress saying pass as he approves of their load. He checks everyone else off last and waits to dismiss them until he gets to me. Glancing down at my pile of rubble he smirks. Looking back into my eyes he has a piercing glare. At this moment, I genuinely think he is going to kill me. At the very least, I thought he is going to drag me into The Fridge. And then he turns, says "Pass," and starts walking away. He has a heart after all. I can imagine that Ano's approval of me meant something to him.

Letting out a sigh of relief, I walk out of the mine, take the transport back to the cafeteria, and get in line for some food. Every night it's the same exact thing, mashed potatoes made from rotten potatoes and unidentified meat. I get served after waiting for fifteen minutes in line, of course my wonderful meal was topped with a ball of spit, and I make my way to my corner table. Alone once again I eat as fast as I can, dump my plate, and make my way to the bunks. They told us to pack up but I have nothing to pack. Once they realized that all of my things were stolen from the Board anyways, they left me with nothing.

I curl up into bed, the hardness of the bunk piercing into my stomach, and rest my head on the pillow. I immediately start drifting asleep, tired from the unusual action of the day. Maybe, just maybe, I can get some sleep before tomorrow's transfer. Ivo always told me to get to sleep before an important day.

***

I don't want to leave. I don't want to leave. My hand is soaked with blood as I hold my brother's shoulder.

"Go, Za." He mutters. But I can't, I won't. At least if we are captured together, we are together. I can't imagine life without him. But there is something telling me that once, just this one time, I should actually listen to him. Getting away might give me a chance to save him. I nod back at him, and run, tears flowing down my cheeks. I almost miss the first roof jump, pulling myself up with my fingertips. I jump down into an alley and cross the streets, finding cover behind a dumpster. I look up to see the helicopters moving toward Ivo. Target acquired I guess. I shouldn't have been so stupid. This failed mission is my fault. I'm not sure how, but I could've avoided this. I need to take responsibility for my actions. Glancing up towards the roof with Ivo, I don't see him. He must've passed out. He will be so mad at what I'm about to do. But hopefully, one day, he can find me so that I can explain everything. I need to take responsibility, for once. I step out into the middle of the street, waving my hands over my head.

"Hey!" I yell. "Over here!" The helicopters turn towards me and I hear sirens coming closer. Soldiers start to drop down and dart towards me in all directions. I pull out my phone from my back pocket, shattered. Tapping the SOS button twice, I toss the phone as close to the building with Ivo as possible. The soldiers get closer, guns pointing towards me. My ears ringing from all of the chaos, I get down on my knees and put my hands over my head. The soldiers circle around me as a helicopter drops a net over me from above. I crumple to the floor from the weight of it. Barely conscious, I get picked up and shoved into a truck. Someone attaches a silver bracelet to my ankle. Everything is blurry.

"We have a rebel. Repeat. We have a rebel." I hear a soldier talking into his coms. My knees are stinging and battered with bruises. My legs are so tired they feel almost numb.

"Hey, he's still awake." Someone says. "We can't let him remember our location." I see a foot get lifted above my head, I turn as the foot comes down, in an attempt to knock me out. I manage to dodge it. "Stupid kid." He says. I notice a silver remote in his pocket. He takes it out and hovers his finger over a button. "This will make him take a nap." I feel a quick shock in my leg and then through my entire body. And, finally, my head.

IVO

MARCH 5, 2031

Holding the phone in my hand, it's almost daunting. All of the information that I thought was impossible to get accessible on this little device. Idri's and my mission ended yesterday, but Aiko made us wait until today to unlock it, just because she wanted everyone available in case anything urgent happened. The goal for the Migrants is to locate where all of the innocent captives are being kept, the people the Board caught yesterday. So, I have to attend to that first. Afterwards, I'm going to look for where the 'criminals' are being kept, because that's where Za will be.

"Earth to Ivo. Hello?" Idri is sitting next to me as I play with the phone in my hands, passively observing it. He catches me drifting off into my other plans.

"Yeah. Yeah. Sorry. I was just...thinking." I reply, stumbling over my words. "About how to find the recent captives." I awkwardly add.

"I know you, Ivo. And I know you have something else going on up there." He says, pointing a finger towards the top of my head. "And whatever it is, I know you won't tell me. But I'm here if you need help. I'm always ready for any kind of secret mission." He winks and I let myself smile, trying not to seem too grateful but it means a lot that Idri is here for backup. Aiko walks into the research lab, at least that's what we call it. In truth, it's just a bunch of dated scientific equipment accompanied by all of the computers that we could salvage.

"Alright guys. You are good to go." After she gives us the all clear to start our software break-in, I immediately place the phone on the desk in front of me and plug my own phone into it. I start running unlock commands. "And…I'll just be sitting over here, in case you need anything." Aiko backs away, already intimidated by my haste and intensity.

A ping comes from the guard's phone, indicating it's been unlocked. I navigate to the GPS section and find the route history. From what I can tell, there are only two routes programmed. The first one is to the Board military headquarters, which everyone already knows about. No one ever attempts to break in there, it's basically suicide. At all times there are four military tanks patrolling, let's just hope the prisons aren't that heavily guarded. The second one must be what we are looking for so I copy down the route directions onto a piece of paper and take out a map of the city. Starting from where the trucks were when we took the phone, I use a red pen to follow the route direction and trace the path. It stops at an abandoned airbase on the far outskirts of the city, not too far from where we are, actually.

"Found it." I say excitedly. Idri turns his head, he was kinda zoned out, and Aiko gets up and walks towards me, she hadn't taken her eyes off me this entire time. Creepy, if you ask me.

"Great." She says. "Where is it?" No one acts like I just hacked into the entire government cyber-system because that's just their expectation nowadays. It's kind of disappointing to not have this hero moment like Idri got yesterday, not that I'm jealous or anything.

"It looks like it's about two miles away from here, even further in the outskirts." I reply, pointing to the red dot I made on the map.

"Alright, let's go." Idri said, getting way ahead of himself. He dismounts from his perch and starts walking out of the lab.

"No, Idrissa. Not gonna happen. We need to be super prepared with a full team. I'm not going to be caught out like you guys were yesterday. That was too risky." Aiko seems firm and confident in her authority. Technically, no one has power over anyone but for some reason Aiko kind of became the one in charge. She's more responsible than Idri, that's for sure.

"Fine. Tell me when you're ready." Idri says, sulking. He walks out of the lab and heads towards his room which is further down the hallway.

"What do you need?" I ask.

"I just need you to be on your A-game," she says, walking out and touching my arm. "No one is being captured on this mission, especially not you." She smiles and walks away. Looking back, she adds "Make sure Idri isn't going to try anything stupid, and get some rest."

Sitting alone in the lab, I take a deep breath. This is it; the chance I've been waiting for. I turn back to the phone, disappointed that it didn't have any more routes. I can only hope that there is one prison, for criminals and everyone else. Sitting at the desk, I close my eyes and try to find a moment of silence when my brain can recharge.

***

"What's the plan for today? Do you have any tests or anything?" Baba has his hands on my shoulder as I eat my breakfast which is the same as always, cereal.

"I think I have a math test." I reply in between spoonfuls.

"Well did you study last night?" Mama shouts from the kitchen.

"Yes, of course I studied." I lie. I actually barely studied. But, in my defense, I never have to. I smash every math test with ease and studying would just be a waste of time. If I told all of this to Mama she would freak. Baba doesn't really care though.

"And how many times have Za and I told you that you're not eternally speaking through fifteen walls. At this point, I have permanent hearing damage." I add and Baba chuckles from behind me. He loves when I make sarcastic comments. Mama steps out from the kitchen so she can see us at the dining table, returning Baba's chuckle with a scowl.

"I don't shout. I just want to make sure you can hear me." She says, in haughty defense .

"The only one you need to scream at is Baba. He has the hearing capabilities of a ninety-year-old." Za says, coming downstairs and striding into the dining room, his head wet from a shower. This time, there is no chuckle from behind me.

"Alright. Both of us have some flaws. But, since everything is genetic, you guys have one, if not both, of these problems. So, who's the impaired one now?" Baba comments, moving into the living room so he can watch the news before work. "How about you Zashil, do you have assessments today?" He asks, before sitting down and almost spilling his coffee.

"No, I don't think so. Math was yesterday so I get a break today." Za replies as he places a bowl on the table, holding the cereal in his hand and the milk underneath his arm.

"How did that go?" Mama shouts again, she is going to pry every detail about this math test out of Za. He's not the greatest at math, so there is always more pressure for him to do well. Our parents act like math and science are the only things that matter while I try to stay more positive about the other things that Za is good at.

"Let's just say that the report card this semester won't accurately represent my math ability." He replies, smiling at me.

"That's not acceptable, Zashil." Mama continues shouting, stepping out of the kitchen with her I'm-an-Asian-Tiger-Mom face.

"Take it easy, a couple math tests aren't going to tear apart his entire future." Baba supports Za. He's always, almost exclusively, thinking about the future for us. He's always saying the world is going to be a different place with different job opportunities. So, he is constantly telling us to go with the flow, expand our passions and skills, so that we can be more flexible. When he starts having conversations about this stuff he sounds pretty apocalyptic.

After all, the country is thriving right now with tons of money and support from other nations. Yeah, we have a pretty mediocre president but the government is not too bad. There hasn't been as much racism and generally Za and I have had a pretty great childhood. Mama is doing great with her science work and Baba is once again coming up with new life changing ideas in engineering. Everybody's lives seem put-together and there is almost no poverty. It seems pretty unrealistic to think that everything is going to drastically and negatively change in the next few years.

All of a sudden, we hear the screeches of the school bus, and we are late again. Za and I get up and grab our bags. It used to be that high schoolers start school earlier than younger kids but that changed a while ago, in order to be more efficient. We are heading right out the door when we both go to zip up our bags and the lunch box is missing.

"Mama, where's our lunch." We both yell into the kitchen.

"Oh, damn. Sorry, excuse my language. I totally forgot about making your lunches". We both run out the door. Great, another day of not eating a real lunch in the most prosperous time in this country's history. This happens more often then it should. Now, it means that Za and I have to grab school lunch, which doesn't really work because our cards don't have any money because Mama always says that we are better off eating her food. Which is actually true. But, only when she makes the food. Za looks at me and just laughs, realizing that I had predicted this would happen this morning after Mama had told us she would be finishing up some last minute work this morning. Oh well. We both get on the bus, finding our friends in our respective grade sections. One last glance at each other before we see each other at the end of the day. I give him a thumbs-up and he mouths "good luck" for the math test. He does it every time because I hate it when he gives me good luck wishes.

***

"Ivo! Time to go." Idri's voice wakes me out of my trance and I spin around to see him standing in the entrance. "Are you even ready?"

"Yeah. Of course I'm ready." I'm not. I haven't even gone back to my room since finding the location this morning. But I need to portray myself as a responsible leader, which I am. That is, most of the time. Idri goes back down the hallway towards the car and I sprint out of the lab and into my room. Grabbing my necklace off of the desk and looking down to check that what I have on is adequate. Taking one last look at the picture of my brother and quickly memorizing all the routes out of the prison, I make my way towards the garage. Idri is already in the Camry but Aiko is standing and briefing seven other team members. I recognize most of them but I don't remember any of them really being the warrior, infiltrator type. I suppose it's all we got and I trust Aiko to choose the right people.

"Alright team, let's move out." She ends her motivational speech and then walks towards me. "I've always wanted to say that." She whispers with a huge grin on her face.

"Can I ride with you guys?" She asks Idri. I laugh as Idri gives me a look of pure rage. He hates when anybody else gets in the car, he likes to think of it as our private vehicle. He looks back at Aiko and gives a fake smile.

"Of course. The more the merrier."

"Ok, thanks!" Aiko replies, Idri and Aiko always act like they have never been the best of friends, it's as if they have something against each other, despite the fact that I know they are close. It's pretty impressive that I haven't found out what the tension is for yet.

"I call shotgun!" She exclaims as she opens the passenger side door and starts to get in. But, once she takes one look at Idri's angry expression, she gets out. "But, the back is even better."

I just laugh at the whole encounter. I get into the passenger seat and we drive out of the base and into the open air. It's a pretty cloudy day and cool. I glance into the rear view mirror, checking to see if the van with the other team members is behind us. They don't know the location, only the three of us do. So, if we get lost, they will get really lost. We drive on for a few more minutes, speeding, of course, through the outskirts. It's amazing to see all of these abandoned buildings, some flooded if they are close to water. Climate change really started to hit Boston hard in terms of the rising water-levels. Most of these places haven't been touched for a year. I notice crumbling parking garages and former high-end office buildings.

We tried to take one of these buildings for an additional base, but we couldn't get the electrical wirings to work without the Board noticing. It's too bad, because the buildings are very modern looking and would have been a nice place to get some sunlight, unlike our current underground hideout.

"I have a question." Idri asks, directing it towards Aiko as he continues to drive.

"Ok. Shoot." She replies, confident that she knows the plan inside and out. Leave it to Idri to find a loophole.

"What are we going to do with all of the people we find?" He asks, a little bit concerned. "In case you haven't noticed, we don't exactly have enough space in the Camry. And, we don't have enough space or food for all of the people at the base."

"Great question, Idri. Luckily, I have a solution." Idri just rolls his eyes as Aiko continues to explain her master-plan. "First, let's stop referring to the Camry like it's our collective prized possession. And, to your point, that's why we are going to have to steal some transport vehicles and find a place to securely and secretly park all of them on our way back." Idri lets out a sigh of disappointment.

"So, basically, our entire plan is just to wing it." He looks at me, almost begging me to punch him and drag him out of this nightmare. "We are so…so…so…screwed. And, for the record, the Camry has single-handedly saved countless lives." He bangs his head against the steering wheel to get his message across. I glance back and see that Aiko's positive grin has shifted to a glum resting face.

"We'll figure it out and I can personally attest to the Camry's prowess." I add, not to anyone in particular. I'm trying to support both Aiko and Idri. However, in truth, we are very screwed. The only reason I have to support Aiko is because she is the one who came up with the plan, so it's not like we have an amazing alternative that we can just switch to. If we have to use her plan, might as well have her in a good mood to lead us through it. When we start to get near the prison, we slow down.

"Ivo, go check it out." Idri says, quietly. I hop out of the car and look back, giving a stop signal to the van behind us. We are about half a block from where the prison is supposed to be and our cars are parked on the parallel street. I go down an alley towards the street with the prison. Stopping at the intersection, I peek my head out and around the corner. I let out a sigh of relief. I see the airplane hangar with what seems like a bunch of tunnels coming off of it. Some are short and others are long. Strange. But, the good thing is there are no tanks or anything on guard out front. They were really banking on no one being able to find this place. That means we will only have to defend against some heavily armed guards. With Aiko, Idri, and I, that shouldn't be a problem.

I run back to the cars, give them a thumbs-up and gesture to come park in the alley. They do so and Idri hops out of the car first while everyone gets their gear sorted.

"What does it look like?" he asks.

"Well, we should be fine. No military vehicles out front so I'm just suspecting there are guards with a bunch of guns."

"Great. Looks like I don't have to die today after all." He says sarcastically.

"The only problem is that the place is huge. It's going to take forever for us to search the place if we don't split up and you know how I feel about splitting up." Honestly, I was initially never against the whole 'split up and we'll find each other' plan. It's always more efficient. But, Za and I never split up, we were like one unit. And then the first time we did, something bad happened.

"Ok. I'll go with you and Aiko can divide up the team. Hopefully, we can all find each other again with some success." I nod in approval. I feel better with Idri by my side. We both walk over to Aiko who is addressing the team again. I guess she was way ahead of us because she is already dividing up the team into groups.

"Remember. Find the recent captives and get out. That's it. No picking fights; only engage guards that are in your way." They all nod. It's kind of strange seeing Aiko, an eighteen year old, talk to a bunch of adults. As soon as we are ready, Idri takes his big gun off of his shoulder and we head out towards the building. At first, I am worried because the front of the hangar doesn't appear to have any kind of door or way in. Luckily, there's one single door off to the side.

Opening it slowly, we all fan out with our guns at the ready. It's a huge open space, scattered with, what seem to be, very large picnic tables. This must have been some kind of cafeteria. But, a cafeteria usually has people and it's scarily silent with nobody in sight. There are six big arches around the place, each with entrances into one of the tunnels that I saw from outside. I look behind me and already see Aiko pointing to where groups should go. No one is talking because we are afraid it will echo. Idri and I head towards the arch labeled five. Entering the tunnel, it gets creepy fast. There are only dim lights and the tunnel seems as if it goes on forever.

Finally, we reach a fork in the path. The sign to the left says 'prisoner bunks' and the one to the right says 'mines.' As much as I want to see what 'mines' means, we both decide that the prisoner bunks are the best bet. After a couple more minutes of the daunting tunnel, we reach a hallway with big rooms crammed with the most uncomfortable beds. All of the beds are empty, not a single belonging to be found. It's like no one has ever been here. We walk between the beds, grimacing at the awful living conditions. I feel a vibration in my back pocket and take out my phone. It's a text from Aiko that says "we got them." I show Idri the phone.

"Thank the lord. This was starting to feel like a horror film. These tunnels are never ending." He exclaims, already walking out of the bunk room and back into the tunnel. I start following him but something catches my eye. "Ivo, let's go. The guards are probably already looking for us." He nags.

"You go, I'll catch up." I say. He shrugs and walks down the hallway.

"Don't do anything stupid" are his parting words. I look down at the cot that caught my attention. All of the beds are made the same way except for this one. Most of them have the sheets made with a threadbare blanket on top. On all of them, the blanket is folded once back so you can see a bit of the sheet underneath. But on this cot, the sheet is also folded back, revealing the bare mattress. I keep examining the cot, knowing that my chances of escaping are dropping by the second. This entire prison has an impersonal uniformity. So, even the slightest irregularity feel strange. And then, I find something. In-between the cot and the mattress there is a corner of a piece of paper sticking out. I pull out the paper and my heart drops. It's the same picture that I have in my room. My parents and Za stand next to me. He was here, he was just here. That explains why I was attracted to the bed, that strange way of making a bed is exactly how Za does it.

I fold the piece of paper and shove it into one of my pockets. Sprinting back through the tunnel and towards the cafeteria, I almost tripped three times. I need to find him. When I get there, the seven team members are consoling the recent captives, some I recognize from the day before. Idri and Aiko are sitting, nervously waiting for me.

"What the hell, Ivo. We have to go. We had to take out the guards that were holding the prisoners so they sent out a distress signal. Tons of soldiers will be here any minute. What was so important?" Aiko is losing it. And, she has every right. I just put everyone in harm's way. But, I can't explain it all right now. I'm panting from my sprint.

"Where are the others?" I ask, trying to stay calm.

"What others, Ivo? This is everyone. We counted twice." Idri answers.

"Where are the others?!" This time I'm screaming and everyone looks in my direction.

"We don't know who you are talking about. Can we talk about this when we get back to the base." Aiko tries to calm me. I'm angry. But then I hear the sound of engines starting up behind the hangar. I sprint through the back door of the hangar just in time to see twelve transport trucks driving away. One of those had Za and I missed him.

I slowly walk back inside. Everyone must have thought I had gone crazy because I see them all exiting through the front. Only Idri is waiting for me. He doesn't inquire about anything, we just walk out together. Everyone is loading into more transport trucks that some of the team members found as Idri and I head towards the Camry. We hop in and head back to the base.

"Aiko said that we'll wait for tomorrow to look for a place for the people to stay. For now, we'll all just cram into the base. There are too many cops around to risk anything." I don't answer. I'm speechless. I had almost given up hope that I would ever find him. And then, I get one chance and I'm too late.

Z A

MARCH 5, 2031

The fog horn wakes us up extra early. I expected we would head to the trucks to be transported to who knows where. By everyone else's reactions, I suspect that they thought the same thing. For a couple of minutes we just stand there, staring at the guard to give us different directions than usual. But he just stares back. So, we all file out like usual and we are handed instruction sheets again. I fold it up and shove it into my pocket. If everything is going to be the same then I'll just look at the instructions during breakfast like usual. I follow the bodies into the cafeteria and get in line for my oatmeal. Because Ano is gone, people give me weird and threatening looks again since I'm a vulnerable kid. Sitting in the corner alone, I take the instruction sheet out and notice a few differences.

We have a first-shift as normal. I've been assigned the database stuff again which is ideal. Then, it seems like we have five minutes of free time before being put on the transport. Sounds like a much more relaxing day compared to the usual. I finish breakfast early again and head to work. I hope that today is as exciting as yesterday. I keep thinking about that mysterious man. In ten months of doing database work, I had never seen anything like that. It's at times like this that I wish I had some friends that I could talk with. Right now, it's just me speculating and making things up in my head.

I'm early as always and I hope to see John so I can at least talk to one person today but the guard there is someone I have never seen before. He gives me a slight nod. Stamping my instruction sheet and opening the door, I walk into the room and find my usual place by the corner taped off and labeled 'out of order.' I guess that incident made the guard suspicious and he just didn't admit it. I sit at the station right next to it, hoping I can get a similar sensation of being secluded. Looking at my instruction sheet, the password for the login information is exactly the same as yesterday. That's never supposed to happen. Having the same login means that I will have access to what profiles I uploaded in the last session, kind of like a history. I will be able to view those profiles with any sort of updates made recently. Usually I would just get a guard to give me a different login because I don't want to get in trouble, but I am very interested in this mystery man and really want to see if there is anything new on him.

I login and immediately try to find the history section. Obviously this has never happened before, so I have no idea where to look. I would imagine they would hide it deep in the settings just in case a mistake like this happened. That is, assuming this is a mistake and someone isn't anonymously helping me out or laying a trap. After not being able to find any button, I dive into the settings and find a button that just says "recents" under the advanced tools section. This section has always been there but nothing ever showed up when you pressed on it. I scroll through the profiles, all of which I remember going through, until I find the unnamed one. I press on it and see that a bunch of new stuff has been added. They didn't add any new personal information like height, race, or age but there are new videos meaning that the computer thinks the "criminal" in these videos are the same unnamed person. I look up from the screen to see people filing in so I exit out of the recents page and go back to the dashboard. I don't need anybody peeking over and seeing what I'm doing.

So, for about an hour, I just do the normal thing, going through new notifications and easily entering information into the database. I'm quickly realizing that this work is very repetitive, almost every profile is the same process which means the work could easily be done by a computer and some well-written code. I guess the Board just really wanted to give us busy work. Once I'm confident that everyone is in the groove and won't get distracted easily, I go back to the recents page.

Once I open back up the unnamed profile again, I start going through the new photos and videos. Most of them are either too blurry or the computer got it absolutely wrong. A large number of them are just of someone walking and minding their own business. This profile is meant to be a criminal profile and, since none of the videos or photos are connected with any criminal activity, I don't really see why they are here. I keep going through them because at least I get to see how Boston is looking after ten months. It looks largely the same, if not worse, with more abandoned buildings and government takeovers. When we were younger, Ivo and I would love to just walk around because of how much diversity and culture existed within the city. Now, it's not a place that I would want to be. Unfortunately, since the Takeover most places are starting to look more and more like Boston and turning into dirty cities with nothing but pollution. Seeing the new billboards on the sides of buildings in these photos is interesting. I guess certain companies for clothing and other consumer goods are having a comeback thanks to Board funding.

I go through thirty files before I find something mildly interesting. It's a picture of the Apple store that was repurposed for government storage. The door is open which is weird because the time of the photo is really early in the morning. Nothing happens this early, especially not shipments of any kind. I zoom in to look closely around the store. The picture is of good quality but, because it's from a camera across the street, you can't see much without zooming in. At first everything seems normal, but then I find the security console which is open for some reason. Zooming in further reveals a smartphone, the same kind most people have, plugged into the console. This is not normal. No one messes with government security like that and getting into the building just requires a key or a card swipe. Everyone knows that plugging in something like this would just alert the cops who would be there in a few minutes. Obviously, this is criminal activity, but still. There is no evidence of the unnamed guy. No one even makes an appearance in the photo. So, how did the computer identify this one? Scrolling into the details part of the photo where it outlines the date and quality of the file, I see there are some attached links. Lucky for me, I have access to them because the computer still thinks I'm uploading data. There are more pictures, almost identical to the one I just looked at except taken from a slightly different angle. I'm about to exit and give up before I see that the last file is a video.

The video is very short but it shows a guy in all black, similar to the original video of this unnamed character, running across the street. I rewind to the last half second and slow it down, pausing right before the end. I want to see if I can catch a glimpse of where he is headed. Zooming in, all I see is the backend of a Toyota Camry, nothing special and not enough to see the color of the car. The license plate is not detailed enough to read. I can't remember any of the Migrants having a car this old when I was around. So unless they decided to go steal an old car, which is very unlikely, then this is not them.

I close out of the videos, realizing that chasing this unknown person is not leading me anywhere. Not even the computers are smart enough. I move on for the next two hours, going through notifications and entering data into the database. It's amazing that I have gotten to the point where I look forward to getting a job like this, it kinda speaks volumes about the conditions of my life lately. I can only hope that the labor is a bit more fulfilling at the next place, no matter how unlikely that is. After the shift is over, everyone gets up instead of just the ones with a different second shift, and we all head towards the cafeteria.

When we get there, I don't think I have ever seen so many people and heard so little noise. It's unbelievable. Everyone is just mulling about, no conversations, quarrels, or fights. It's almost as if everyone has just entered a phase of deep depression. Remembering the schedule for the day, I realize that this is the ten minute break. I decide to walk back towards my bunk, take one last look and make sure I didn't forget anything, not that I own anything that I could forget. Once I get to my bunk, I sit on the bed just staring into space. I really hope that Ivo is looking for me. Then I realize that, if they ever find this place after I leave, I should leave something behind that would tell him that I was here. Ivo works off of motivation and he can become unmotivated pretty quickly. So, if he saw that he was getting closer to finding me, then it would keep him going, which is what I want. I take a quick look at all the bunks, thinking about what I can change to mine that would make it unique enough to catch Ivo's sharp eye.

Ever since I got here, I was told exactly how to do things. How to make a bed, how to fold clothes, most of which I already did anyways. The ways they made us do things were pretty conventional. But, there was one habit that I had to break when making my bed. Ever since I was a kid, I hated getting into bed, and having to find the bedsheet to get under. To me it was annoying and I always just ended up falling asleep under the comforter but on top of the sheet. Mama would always get so upset with me, complaining that I was making the blanket too dirty. I looked once more at all the beds, realizing that they are all made the same way, as they should be.

Basically, the bed is made with the sheet underneath the pillow and the blanket on top folded slightly back, revealing a bit of the sheet and bed underneath. In order to solve my unique problem, I would not tuck the sheet underneath the pillow but instead fold it over in unison with the blanket. That way, it was no trouble to get in the bed. Assuming no guards came in to fix it once we leave, Ivo's eye would definitely catch this change. I turn back to my bed, feel for the end of the sheet beneath my pillow and fold it over the already folded blanket. Ok, great. But this is not enough to show Ivo that it was me, specifically, that was here. This will only catch his eye. I doubt he would immediately jump to the conclusion that this was my doing. I sit back down on my bed and keep thinking. I don't have any belongings to leave behind, no clothes or shoes or anything. Everything I own, I'm wearing.

Feeling in my pocket I find something. It's a picture of our intact family, our parents in the back with Ivo and I in the front. This is the only thing that the soldiers didn't take, it was a rare moment when they were being human. All of the prisoners have some kind of thing to remind them of their life before this. I look at this every night before going to bed, my worst fear is forgetting how my parents look or, even worse, Ivo. But, this is the only way that Ivo will ever know that I was here. Glancing at the clock, I realize I only have two more minutes until our break. I fold the piece of paper two times in half and then tuck it between the mattress and the iron frame of the bed. I fidget with it until just one corner is poking out enough to be noticed. I take one last look at my work. I don't expect anyone to come by and fixe it. Hopefully, Ivo will be here before that happens.

I leave the bunks and walk back towards the cafeteria at a brisk pace. I think I will be a minute late, but, luckily, when I enter the hangar, everyone is busy and occupied with the transport stuff. It looks like there is one giant snaking line throughout the entire place and exiting out the back. Everyone is kinda jumbled together but then a guard gets up and yells to get in alphabetical order by first name. All of sudden, it gets very chaotic. People that don't like each other or have never talked to each other are suddenly asking what each other's name are in order to find their place. Thank god I know exactly where I'm headed so I don't have to mess with all of that. I make my way to the far back of the line. Some people come back to ask me what my name is and all I say is "Z" so they step in front of me. I wait for almost two hours in line before I get even remotely close to the front. I peer around the line to see what's taking so long. Every single prisoner is being catalogued and given a printed out version of their entire criminal profile. We have never gotten to see our own profile so this is kinda exciting. They are probably doing it this way so there is no messing around when we get to the new place. It's about to be my turn when a guard runs through the front door.

"Hey! We spotted rebels! We've got to get these prisoners out of here and guard the new captives." He yells from across the hangar.

"Ah, damn. I knew this would happen." The guard handing out profiles mumbles. "Alright let's go people," he starts shoving prisoners through the exit, "you'll get your profile before we get to the other place." He's about to push me through before he hands me my profile, "Your the only 'Z' kid, so that's easy."

I get shoved through the door into a transport van. Looking around, there are at least thirty people in here, which means it's really cramped seeing how these vans are only meant to have fifteen at most. Let's hope this is a short drive. I'm sitting on the right side, squished between a beefy dude and the metal side of the truck. I won't be surprised if my entire body loses circulation by the end of this. As we start to pull away, I peek through the crack of the door, hoping to see my first glimpse of the outside world in ten months. Just as the crack in the door is closing, I spot the front of a red Toyota Camry sneaking out of an alley. I squint to see the license plate, it's the exact same as the one I saw in the picture earlier. Then the door shuts and the most uncomfortable drive of my life begins.

IVO

MARCH 19, 2031

"Ivo, you have to eat something. You can't just starve yourself." Aiko begs through the door. I don't answer. Eventually she just sighs and walks away. I've basically locked myself in my room. It's been two weeks since we saved all of those captives. While I tried to stay positive at first, thinking about how close I got or how many innocent people I saved, it didn't work. Eventually, I just recoiled. I haven't gone on a mission. I've only eaten from the rations I have in my room. I have barely talked, not even to Idri and Aiko. I can barely function. Somehow, getting so close to Za and then failing feels worse than losing him. I blame myself for both times, but so much more effort, hope, and heart went into finding him. Now, he's being shipped off to who knows where. As soon as he leaves the city, there is no chance I'll find him. I don't really have a way out. Traveling between cities requires going through too many security stops. And, I can forget about leaving the state. Unless I'm going to drive cross-country without being spotted, I don't really have a way to get from point A to point B.

I lay in bed, a book open, trying to get my head out of this lull. I love helping people. Which I have been doing ever since the Takeover. I wasn't going to let some stupid set of dictators ruin people's lives, especially not mine. But losing Za was a whole different thing. Not that I would trade lives or anything, but not knowing what the Board is doing to him makes me angry. And, by my statistics, there has got to be almost no other kid in high security prison. The Board mostly spares them because they see an opportunity to turn them into soldiers.

I spend all day just passively reading and feeling bad for myself. I have never been less productive in my entire life. I'm about to turn off the lights and go to bed when I hear a sound on the other side of my wall behind my desk. Technically, this wall is exposed on the other side, in some random part of the outskirts. But no one has ever messed with it because it looks harmless from the other side. And, we haven't ever heard anybody outside because it's in the middle of nowhere. The noise sounds like crunching footsteps. I get out of bed and walk towards my desk. Leaning over, I put my head to the wall trying to listen.

I hear the footsteps getting closer until I assume, whoever it is, is standing right in front of the wall. The person pauses for a second, I hear a zipper unzip, and then he or she starts walking away, the crunching getting fainter and fainter until I can't hear it anymore. That was weird I think to myself as I walk back towards my bed. I sit on the edge of my bed, going through possible reasons why someone would be there.

I'll go check that area out tomorrow. Staring at the ground I see a small white piece of paper. How did that get in here? Picking up the paper without looking at its contents, I scan the wall for possible points of entry. Low and behold, in the top hand corner where the wall meets the ceiling, there is a small gap, just big enough for a small piece of paper to slip through. I sit back down on the edge of my bed and turn the slip over. It's about the size of a fortune from a fortune cookie. It reads "I Know Where

He Is" with the first letter of each word capitalized and bolded. The other side is literally just the side of the fortune cookie with lucky numbers.

Tons of questions immediately jump into my mind. Who is this person? How did they know where we are? Who is the he? Is he talking about Za? How the heck would he know where Za is? Nevertheless, this gets me excited. I have to go check out the other side of the wall tomorrow. If there is a one percent chance that this person knows where Za is, I'll take it. I decide I'll take Idri with me. He's the only one that won't think I'm insane and making up stories. This incident would just seem staged to them, especially considering the state I have been in these past couple of week. I place the piece of paper gently into the drawer of my bedside table. Getting into bed and pulling the blankets over me, I shut my eyes. Already, I know I won't be getting any sleep tonight.

2 A

MARCH 6, 2031

The drive seems to go on forever. For a little bit, I'm almost positive we are just going in circles. My understanding of the time is so warped, we could have been on the road for eight hours or two days. Banging around in the metal interior of the truck was sickening and I couldn't find a moment of peace, or even sleep for that matter. Finally, the truck stops but, before we can all get out and stretch, two guards come in and cover our heads with bags. Unsurprisingly, this whole situation feels similar to when I was first captured. I feel a rope being tied around my wrist and then to the person next to me. They're just tying us together so that we can't run, not that anybody would try anyways. We get tugged out of the truck and into the outdoors, the fresh air would feel much nicer if I had a chance to breath it in. As suddenly as we were outside, we are being shoved back into another vehicle. I try my best to feel around and it just feels like the same truck we were in before. This ordeal might have been another way to disorient us, seems like a lot of trouble for that though. Just as I'm convinced that we are in the same truck, I hear the familiar sound of a plane starting up and then before I know it, we are in the air. Guards walk around and take the bags off of our heads. I immediately look around and see that we are in a military air transport. That's just great.

We fly for a few hours, everyone's face solemn. Getting in a plane really sucked the hope out of all of us. Whoever was coming to save us definitely can't get to us now. We land smoothly, but I can't shake this feeling that we probably should've been descending for longer. It almost felt as if we kept rising and then we got to our destination. I guess everything really has been messing with my head because there is no chance that we are not just at another stupid military prison. We all get out of the plane, no hands tied this time. The platform we are on is slowly lowering like an elevator and we stop when we are in the middle of what seems to be a concrete, metal, and glass cube.

"Welcome to The Maze." A general says as he approaches us. There it is again, a stupidly dramatic name for absolutely no reason. First it was The Fridge in the last place and now it's The Maze, they really must've done their research into teen novels to get names like this. Unlike the other generals, this guy looks legit. He is at least six two with massive arms and legs, and he looks to be no older than thirty. All of the other generals have been old white fat dudes that have no right to boss anybody around. Already, I'm more intimidated by this place.

"This is the most fortified and inescapable prison ever built." Yeah, right. That's what they said about the last place. "And I know what you're thinking, you've heard that before. The only reason they said that is because this place is so fortified that whoever told you that didn't even know it existed." Damnit, I really hope this guy is joking. He grins at all of our faces, everyone starting to get a little bit intimidated.

"Now's the time that I would give you a tour, but that would be pointless. This place is too confusing for it to do any good. But, I'll at least show you your bunks." We all smirk. If he won't show us this whole place, we'll show ourselves. I toured almost every tunnel I could get to at the last place at least ten times, it didn't result in anything except knowing my way around like the back of my hand, which was fine. I've never been good at direction so that was quite a feat.

We start to exit the plain gray concrete cube. We walk through a large doorway that leads us onto a suspended path over a long fall. Looking around, it looks like another concrete cube. We keep walking on the path, through the layer of the second cube which seems to have rooms for labor workers and then, into another larger cube. This time, there are multiple floors and much more depth to the interior. As soon as we pass over the second overpass, basically a bridge with no sides, we take a sharp left and start walking down a hallway. Bunks flank either side, some independent cells are also there, probably taken by higher profile criminals. Finally, after turning left two times, we get to a room full of bunks, almost identical to the room at the last place.

"Make yourself comfortable and see you at dinner ." The general is sinister as he motions before him and his guards walk away. He forgets to mention where the hell the cafeteria is in this place but I realize there is some kind of map on each of our beds. There are many more of us than before because there are people from all six exits. I find a bed and sit down, surprised to find it significantly more comfortable than the last place. It might end up being that this place is more of a permanent situation while the last place was just a pit stop. The room is situated horizontally, so that the long part of the room is faced out into the interior of the prison. This entire back wall is glass, really thick glass at that. Having no stuff to put away, I walk towards the back. The room is massive, but bare. I reach the glass wall and look out into the interior. There are four of those overpasses coming out of the inner cube which is somehow suspended. I wonder how many cubes there are and I doubt that

I'll ever find out. I can tell that this place must've taken forever to build though. The inner cube has a strip of glass around it, probably the back walls of rooms like this.

I make my way back to my bunk, forgetting three times where it is, and sit down, grabbing the map from my pillow. Before looking at it, I glance up to see everyone sitting on their bunk doing a similar thing. I look back at the map. It seems to be a top down view of the prison. At the center is the landing pad where we came in. It looks like the first cube we passed through is for security and databases. Then the cube that we are in is all for bunks. That's crazy because that means there must be at least two thousand prisoners here, assuming the entire cube is lined with cells and rooms just like ours. Then the next outer cube is shown as three floors. The middle one, which the bridge passes through, seems to be the cafeteria, the upper one is where the guards live, and the bottom one is just labeled 'Work.' And then there are arrows at the four corners of the page, suggesting the cubes keep going. But that space is just labeled, 'More.' I'm guessing we are not allowed to enter the 'More' section. I put the map down, checking it to make sure there is nothing on the back. It's just a small QR code in the middle, and in fine print below it, the words 'keep this at all times.' I fold the map and shove it into my pocket.

I look around to see what everyone else is doing and see that they are looking at something beneath their beds. I crawl down onto my knees and push the blanket and sheet out of the way. I see two big metal bins, no lock or anything so I assume it's for us. I pull both of them out, trying to avoid getting too close to the person next to me. I lift them onto my bed and sit next to them. They weren't very heavy so I can't imagine anything super substantial is in them. I open the first one and can't help but smile. There are more clothes, in many different sizes. Two different outfits, one all black and one all white with accompanying Adidas sneakers. I'm starting to get a little skeptical of this place. Why are they giving us stuff? I open the second one and it's empty except for a small piece of paper. The piece of paper just says 'Name Tag' on the front with a line below it. There is a pen in the box that I didn't notice before. I write just my first name because no one ever has the same name as me. I'm about to find a way to attach it to myself when I see the back. It says "put at foot of bed." Sure enough, I look at the foot of my bed and there is a laminated slot for the name tag which I slide in. This place is giving off different vibes then the last place, that's for sure. I close the boxes and stick them back beneath the bed.

A few minutes later, after just sitting on my bed and staring into space, a guard stands at the doorway, calls us for dinner, and then walks away. We all get up and I follow the crowd to the nearest overpass so that we can cross over into the next cube. I glance across the gap and see other prisoners crossing over their bridge. I guess that's how they keep all of them streamlined into different spaces, we never leave our own linear path. My group enters into a brightly lit space with cafeteria seating. Except this time, the seats are padded, and the place where you get your food is like a restaurant complex. The back wall is lined with buffet stations, each labeled with a different cuisine. I get closer to the food and see that it's not gourmet but it's definitely not your average prison food. Excited about making a food choice for the first time in ten months, I choose to go with Chinese. Different barriers and railings are keeping people in order and when I get to the station, I grab a plate and utensils and scoop some white rice and orange chicken onto my plate, taking as much as I think I can physically eat. I head back towards a table that seems relatively empty, each table fits about fifty people, and start eating. I'm halfway through my meal when I hear the general's voice and turn around to see him in the middle of the cafeteria.

"Hi everyone, I'm going to need your attention here for a few minutes. You may keep eating but I hope that you listen to me." Everyone is already dead silent, in awe of how great this place seems to be compared to the last one.

"I hope you are all getting a chance to see how this is not a normal prison. You are still prisoners but hopefully this environment allows your labor work to be better and more efficient. My name is General Lee and I am head of The Maze. I wanted a chance to properly introduce The Maze to you and how it works. You must have noticed the cubes that make up this prison, we call them Layers and the first four Layers contain everything you will need or use. The codes on the back of your maps will be scanned shortly and that code will be matched to your profile. When you go to work, you scan it. When you eat, you scan it. When you sleep, you scan it. Everything you do will be recorded and documented. There are no secrets here. Ever. Your work here will be assigned tomorrow morning. Anything you will need for any job you ever receive will be placed in the empty container underneath your bed. The work you are assigned will be based on any expertise you might possess or lack thereof. You will be able to serve the Board in the most productive and useful way possible. That is it, now enjoy your meal." General Lee exits the cafeteria and we all resume eating.

After I finish, I head back to the bunks and realize that scanners have been attached to everyone's bed. There is a small screen that says "please scan your code." I take out, unfold, and turn over the map, holding the code beneath the screen to be scanned. "Code Accepted" this time the device speaks in a robotic female voice. "Please look at the camera." The voice says as a camera pops out of the top of the screen. "Facial recognition successful. Welcome Zashil Wolf." It says again and then a card pops out of the side. It looks like a driver's license with my age, height, and other general information. "Please scan to go to sleep." The voice says. I scan my card and it says "Goodnight, Zashil." I haven't been around this amount of technology in a while. I stick my card into my pocket and get into bed, tossing my shoes beneath my bed. Tomorrow, I will finally put on different clothes. Closing my eyes I can't help but feel nervous. I'm fifteen, what skills do I have that can aid the Board? Suddenly, I start feeling very nervous about tomorrow morning. Hopefully it's not as bad as I think it's going to be.

I V O

MARCH 20, 2031

Inevitably, I wake up early, barely any light peeking through my rustic brick wall. Rolling out of bed, I start to get dressed. I reach towards the drawer in my bedside table, checking to make sure the piece of paper wasn't just in my imagination. I open the drawer and see the piece of paper, message and all. I grab it and shove it into my pants pocket as I pull them on. After my completely blacked-out outfit is complete, I grab my phone and start to walk out of the door. Before I leave, I hesitate, and head back towards my desk, grabbing the necklace, putting it on, and tucking it underneath my shirt. You never know what you're going to run into, especially in the outskirts. Recently it's been reported that government officials are going undercover as civilians in an attempt to reveal rebels and other anti-government behavior. I'm going to have to get Aiko to come up with some sort of protocol, we don't want a dangerous spy waltzing into our secret base.

I walk into the hallway and head a couple rooms down to Idri's. I quietly knock on his closed door.

"Idri." I whisper. After no response I gently turn the door knob and peek my head into his room. He is fast asleep, covers over his head, and a mild snore coming from beneath the bed sheet. I close the door and stand against the wall. I was going to do this with Idri. Not only does he make me feel safer but his skills also come in handy in situations just like this. I decide that I'm going to go alone.

I exit the base through the garage door. I don't need a car unless some kind of clue on the outer wall of the base gives me a place to go. I head down the road after the base door closes behind me, roughly in the direction of my room. I walk for a few minutes, turning around until I'm fairly confident I'm standing above my bedroom. I'm kind of on the edge of the road where there is a railing, a fence, and multiple warning signs for a drop. The wall that I'm looking for should be the one facing outwards on this edge.

Now, I just need to figure out how to get down there. I walk back and forth, checking to make sure there isn't any easy way down. In the distance to my right there are a bunch of abandoned buildings, most of which are occupied by white people that are against the Board. The Board doesn't really care about them, they kind of just treat them like homeless people. Except, there is no homeless shelter. At least they aren't criminals. We've tried talking to them, and while they are on our side, they aren't going to pick a fight with the Board any time soon. It's a shame because so many of them live right by our base.

I stare one more time at the fence, I'm just going to have to jump it. I grab the chain link and step up onto the railing. Propping my right foot up and squeezing it into the fence, I give one big push and launch myself to the other side. Using my feet and hands, I slowly dismount from the other side. It wasn't as big of a jump as I imagined, maybe fifteen feet from the top of the fence to the ground. I look around. Right where the bottom of the fence stops, brick starts for eight feet until touching the bottom. Realizing that that's about the height of my ceilings, I'm reassured that I'm in the right place. I turn around to see a small stream and more buildings in the distance. There is a lot of fog this morning so there isn't much visibility from where I'm standing. Looking back at the wall, I survey it for anything out of the ordinary. All I see are cracks in the wall and old red bricks. There has got to be something here that I'm missing. This is not just a place where someone goes for a nice stroll. Whoever sent this note knows exactly who he was giving it to and, somehow, knew where we were. I start to look at the ground, there's just a bunch of rubble and trash. Some soda cans, trash from takeout meals, glass, and a bunch of rocks and remnants of older bricks. I can't believe I'm doing this, but I start rummaging through the trash, checking to make sure there isn't anything written on the trash or hidden in the bags or cans. Nothing.

I sit down, my back against the wall. Pulling out the note from my pocket I stare at it. Something about the way it is written seems off, like there is more to the text than just what is says. The beginning of each word is capitalized and bolded. Maybe it's an acronym. "I Know Where He Is" as an acronym would be "IKWHI" which is nowhere close to any word. Damnit. What could I possibly be missing?

I turn over the piece of paper and look at the numbers. They are just a bunch of random numbers, with no pattern at all. Which is not a surprise seeing how I'm literally looking at the back of a fortune cookie ticket. I pick up a rock and throw it into the water out of frustration. Right where the rock I threw used to be is a fast food bag. The logo is a samurai sword with the name of the restaurant in red text: "KHIWI." I've heard of this place before. They have always been a huge Chinese fast food chain but they became a big deal after the Takeover. The white Americans loved the food so much that the restaurant owners were pretty much the only rich people of color that weren't captured. In fact, the Board actually gave them a bunch of money to fund more locations. The founders of the chain are billionaires. What a life.

I get up, scolding myself for thinking that this could actually lead somewhere. I guess I was getting way ahead of myself. For all I know this could be a trap. I forgot to check for cameras when I got down here. I look back down at the bag. "KHIWI." Why is my brain interested so much by that. I'm still holding the note in my hand and holding it away from my face so it's right above where the logo is. Oh wow. "IKWHI." What are the chances. Those letters can easily be rearranged into "KHIWI." Well, it looks like I got myself a lead, no matter how weak. I take out my phone, it's five in the morning. I open the internet and look up the Khiwi location downtown. It says they open at seven which means there are definitely people arriving soon to set up.

I go back into the garage, trying to find a vehicle to use. I'm about to head towards Idri's room to steal his keys for the Camry when I spot a brand new military motorcycle in the back of one of the new transports. I guess I've been so cooped up that I never noticed that other stuff was in those transports. I climb into the truck and start up the bike. On the seat there is a note that says "For Ivo. From Idri and Aiko." I take a step back and notice that the bike has already been painted matte black, my favorite, and has a bunch of custom features. Usually, I'm the one that does the tinkering so this is a nice surprise. I guess Idri will have to give me the rundown of my new ride when I get back. I roll the bike out of the truck, hop on, and slide on my helmet which is also already painted matte black.

A screen turns on right underneath my sight line from within the helmet. I guess this is standard in military helmets now, because I know for a fact Idri doesn't have the expertise to add this. I see that he did disable the stupid AI voice that is in all military electronics. Thank God. I start up the motorcycle, I'm relieved that it's electric because otherwise the engine would have woken up everybody in the whole base.

Exiting the base, I head towards downtown. The helmet screen says it is 5:15 AM so I'm right on schedule. I'm hoping that the staff arrives around 5:30. The screen asks me to enter my destination but I just ignore it. I know where I'm going and I'm still slightly skeptical that Idri knew how to disable all of the Board data tracking.

It takes me ten minutes to get into Chinatown, I saw almost no cars along the way and the city was still quiet. I decide to park my bike in an alley a few blocks away from the restaurant. Getting out, I take my helmet off, realizing that I have nowhere to put it. If I leave it here, then someone will definitely steal it and, if I take it, then people will know that I have a motorcycle. I place it on the seat of the bike and, to my surprise and relief, the seat has a mechanism that locks the helmet into place. I make sure that the remote keys are in my pocket and I start walking at a brisk pace towards Khiwi with my hood up.

The problem with venturing into Chinatown is that I am always weary of the number of cameras that this part of the city has. Mostly because it has a history of being the most crime-ridden, even if those statistics were from before the Takeover. Unfortunately, the Board took control of all the existing surveillance systems. When I finally get to Khiwi, I put my face up to the window to see if anybody is there. There is just one Chinese guy at the cashier. I bang on the window and when he looks up, I wave. He walks towards the door, unlocks it, and cracks it open.

"We don't open until seven." He says, you can tell that he just woke up. The guy is skinny and uninterested but has a stern expression that makes me not want to mess with him. Despite the fact that they are protected by the Board, employees like this will never call the cops on any migrants.

"Oh, I know." I reply. "I am actually looking for someone, he or she, I actually don't know, told me to meet them here." Saying it out loud makes me realize how crazy I sound.

"Well you can come back when we open. I'm sure whoever you're meeting just got the time wrong." He's about to close the door so I panic.

"Wait, sir. Please. I have a code for you." I pull out the piece of paper, hoping it means something to this guy and hand it to him. He takes it and looks at the numbers on the back, completely ignoring the message on the front. Opening the door, he ushers me in.

"Welcome, he has been waiting for you." He says as I walk in. This is getting weirder and weirder. I walk into the restaurant. There are small tables in the middle with larger booths on the side. I wait for a minute so that the guy can get in front of me and show me where I'm going. He leads me behind the cashier counter and then just stops and stares at me.

"Do you need anything else from me? Am I in the right place?" I ask. I'm nervous about this whole situation. He doesn't answer and just looks down at the floor. I look down to where he is looking and see a square drawn out with red tape. He is standing within the square but my feet are on the tape. I step into the square and he nods at me. Then, he presses a red button hidden beneath the counter and suddenly the platform starts lowering like an elevator. It stops after a couple seconds, lowering into some kind of secret basement. I step off of the square platform and look behind my shoulder to see the guy headed right back up.

"Hey! What am I supposed to do down here?" I'm freaking out now. This is definitely a trap. I can't believe I was this stupid. I look around. It's dark and musty. It doesn't feel like a secret military base.

"I hoped you would make your way here." A man's voice comes out of the corner. Startled, I immediately put my right hand up in a fist and reach towards my necklace with my left, turning my body towards where his voice came from. The man steps out from the darkness. He's wearing the classic military guard uniform. Crap. I knew this was a setup. The only thing is this guy is black, which doesn't really make any sense. It doesn't matter though, he's with the Board. I clench my fist and start bouncing on my toes, ready for some combat action.

"Woah. There is no need for that. I'm on your side." I start to relax after hearing his smooth tone of voice.

"But, you're with the Board. Who are you?" He takes one step closer.

"I'm the one who sent you that message. You're a smart boy for picking up on those clues, I wasn't sure if I had made it too hard." I put my fists down, convinced that this guy isn't a threat, even if he is with the Board. As he stands in the light, I notice that he is older. His face is worn and his hair is grey, there is something calming about his demeanor, like he has already seen the worst that he possibly could. He walks closer towards me and, just as I'm about to punch him, he puts his hand out for a handshake.

"My name is John. And I've met your brother." I shake his hand softly, at least I know that Za is definitely alive.

"How?" I ask.

"Please. Sit." John replies, gesturing towards two wooden cartons near the wall. I walk over and take a seat.

"Let me explain" he starts. I just nod, still in shock. "I was a guard at The Fridge." He sees my confused face. "It's a prison inside of the first prison where your brother was held for the last ten months. The same one that you broke into. That was impressive by the way." He smiles.

"But you're...you're..."

"Black. Yes. I'm not exactly a high ranking official. I'm a war veteran." That explains his weary look and his role within the prison. I'm familiar with the Board agreement that pre-dated the Takeover and pledged to take care of war veterans. Of course, they modified the agreement for veterans of color after the Takeover was complete.

"Then how do you know my brother?" I'm getting a little impatient.

"Yes. I'll get to that. I was assigned to be a guard for the database labor workers. I didn't really do anything because, well, no one wanted me to. Basically, I just stamped people's instruction sheets." I really don't know what many of these terms mean but I let him continue because I want to know how he knows Za.

"I only arrived a couple of weeks before Za left but I saw him a couple of times when he was assigned database work. He was the only one that greeted me and treated me like a person. He's a very nice kid. One day, Za was obsessing over a criminal profile. Of course, I'm supposed to stop them but I had a soft spot for your brother. When a guard finally came downstairs to fix it, he told me to modify the criminal profile that Za was looking at. That's when I found your hidden message. The letters that were changed in the word 'anonymous' spelled out your name." I had completely forgotten about that. I had programmed a hack so that if a camera ever caught sight of me and uploaded it to the criminal database, it would alter the spelling of anonymous. Too bad Za didn't notice it himself.

"But how did you know I was his brother?"

"Well, you boys are quite famous within the Board. Everybody knows about the two brothers that wreaked havoc on the Board systems. Each, very specialized. One maneuvers space and the other is a tech genius. We never got to see your faces, but us guards of color, always rooted for you boys." That's interesting. I didn't know we were that well-known.

"So, I connected the dots."

"But, why sacrifice everything for us? And, how did you know where I was?"

"I have always been against the Board. Reuniting you two would be a way to take them down. As for finding you, that wasn't actually hard. You see, I have a nephew that's a migrant. He would always tell me to come find him when I got back from the war. That I would be safer there. He told me how to find the two migrant bases. For the one he's in; go to the outskirts and find the crack in the road."

"That makes sense. So why didn't you join us when you came home?"

"I couldn't. They captured me at the border and immediately took me to government training. " He seems sad, disappointed.

"I'm sorry." I reply, John really got the short end of the stick. "So, do you know where my brother is?"

"He is in a very secretive new prison that no one knows about. It took me a while to find the location, I had to ask a favor from an old friend. He gave me the location." He handed me a piece of paper with longitude and latitude coordinates on it. On the other side is a phone number.

"Thank you so much, John. Why don't you come with me?"

"I can't right now, I have to return to work, but please, call me, whenever. I'm here to help." I nod and stand on the tape square. I would stay and talk more with John but my friends must be getting worried and I have a lot to process. I have suddenly been given hope again. Just as the platform is moving I look back at John.

"John. What's your nephew's name?" He looks up and smiles as if he knows I know him. And just as I'm back at the top he says it.

"Idrissa."

ZA

MARCH 7, 2031

I wake up to a high pitch beep coming from every console at the foot of our beds. While we are still forced to wake up, at least it's not an ear-splitting fog horn. This is the morning. I don't exactly know what they are going to assign a fifteen year-old that never finished high school but if it's anything different from what I did last time, I'm sure that I'll appreciate it. I get up and sit on my bed, looking around, wondering where the guards are. And then, I remember that I have new clothes. Excited, I drag the bin out from under my bed and pull out the all-black outfit. It is extremely comfortable and fits me perfectly. Sliding the shoes on, I'm pretty sure that my feet are already thanking me. For the first time in a while, I take a look at my old shoes. They are in bad shape, with tears, rips, and stains after everything they have been through. I've had them for so long that my toes have already busted holes through the top. Basically, for the last ten months, I have been wearing glorified sandals. They may actually be more useless than sandals at this point, now that I think about it.

I look up and suddenly see everyone getting up and leaving. We don't have to wait for someone to lead us to breakfast? That seems wrong. I look at the people nearest to me, they all have notes that they are reading. Probably work instructions. But where did they get them? I frantically check every part of my bed, making sure I didn't miss anything. This is bad. I see the guy in front of me pull out his second bin. Within it, there are tools for engineering of some sort. He must have been assigned to repair something. I pull out the second bin and take off the cover. Inside, there isn't any note, just a thin black jacket. Nothing about the jacket seems to represent any kind of occupation or work but I put it on anyway. It reminds me of the wind breakers that Ivo and I would always wear, they were our favorites because they could be worn all year round, which, in turn, meant that we didn't have to buy a different jacket for each season.

I wait around for a couple of minutes, sitting on my bed, as I watch everyone find their new tools and clothes and follow the map on their work instructions. They are definitely going to get to eat before me. My stomach starts to rumble and soon that's all I hear as the entire place empties out, all of the bunks perfectly made. It's pretty weird to see the place in its entirety like this.

After another ten minutes I decide I'll just walk to the cafeteria and get something to eat. Maybe, I'm lucky and they just forgot I existed. I'm about to get up when General Lee walks in, flanked by two heavily armed guards. Oh, great. They probably realized they have no use for a kid and they might as well just execute me now to avoid wasting resources. One of the guards keeps walking until he is right in front of me.

"Is your name Zashil Wolf?" He asks. I'm almost taken aback by his politeness.

"Yes...sir." I stumble as I respond. How did I just mess up saying yes.

"Come with me, please." He turns around and walks away, checking his shoulder to make sure I'm following him. I get up and make sure I grab my ID card, putting it in the lined pocket of my new pants. I follow

General Lee out of the room and we start walking towards the nearest bridge.

"Come." He says. "Walk next to me." I hurriedly catch-up to him. We are walking at a very brisk pace. It would always annoy the hell out of me when Ivo would do this.

"I've been waiting a long time to see you, Zashil. I actually tried to have you transferred almost five months ago but the Board insisted on keeping you at the last place for reasons I never quite understood."

"How do you know who I am?" I ask timidly. Even though General Lee seems calmer than any other government official that I've met, I'm still afraid of the power he has. He just chuckles.

"Everyone knows who you are. Ivo and Zashil Wolf, the most highly specialized, trained kids in the world and the biggest thorn in the Board's ass for the last eighteen months." I did not realize we were that famous. I wonder if Ivo knows we are that well-known. I knew we were always fighting against the Board but I felt as though we were doing it at a pretty low level, not necessarily catching the attention of high-ranking officials like General Lee.

"You are in demand. After we captured you, we thought it was a gift from god. We never thought you kids were going to be caught. We are still looking for your brother. It would really be something to have both of you, but, for now, you'll do just fine." He talks about us with a sense of admiration that makes me uncomfortable. What do they want with me? We get to the bridge and start walking across. When we get to the cafeteria we walk straight through it and then one of the guards scans his card near the door, and we continue onto the next bridge. We are now in the "More" part of the map which makes me nervous because that means they aren't given me any regular job.

"What do you want with me? I'm just a kid." I ask, really trying to understand the point of all this.

"Oh no. You're not just a kid. You are the kid. Master of parkour, expert in combat, extreme athleticism. Not every fifteen-year-old can hold a gun and a knife in both hands and use both of them masterfully at the same time." Well this just gets weirder and weirder. This guy has done his research— how does he know my signature move? The knife and gun combo I invented myself, just to prove to Ivo that they could both be used together. We cross the bridge and enter the next cube. This time, it's all glass. If I didn't know I was in the most top-secret and secure prison in the world, then this would all seem pretty cool. We stop in the hallway before entering any rooms.

"In terms of what we want with you. Well, you're just going to have to find out." He opens the closest door and reveals a massive training facility. There is a section with shooting practice, an entire modular obstacle course, a track, weights, and a massive board for designing tactics. And it's all completely empty, not a single soul in sight. General Lee's voice breaks me from my awe.

"You, Zashil, are going to be the Board's secret weapon. With you, we have the youngest, most combat-ready individual we will ever find—you don't require further training at all. Did you know that in the time span of three months, you took out over two-hundred of our most highly trained soldiers. You did it with such ease you made it look like a video game. I know this because I have been watching you. Every time a soldier has reported you infiltrating our missions, I have tuned into their bodycams and seen everything you do. It was more tiring switching from cam to cam just to keep up with you than it was for you to single-handedly dismantle our entire objective. That is why you're here." This is making me very nervous. I don't want to be used as a weapon. I don't want to help the Board. But if my other option is death, then I don't think I have a choice.

"Bring them in." The general orders the guards next to him. They rush to the corner of the facility and open the door. A line of twenty men come in, most of them in their mid twenties. "Meet your squad. These are the twenty most highly trained fighters we could find. Every single one of them is a complete soldier having one unique skill. To them, you are Agent Wolf and their commander."

"What if I don't want to do this? What if I don't want to help the Board?"

"You know that jacket you have on?" I look down at the windbreaker. Seems completely harmless. "That jacket was formed directly to your body specs, it is now locked onto you and can only be removed using my personal ID. The jacket is lined with micro bombs. One in itself is not lethally harmful, as you know. But your jacket has three hundred of them woven within the fabric. If at any time, you refuse to help us, are off-task, or attempt to escape, I will press one button on my phone and you will be blown to smithereens. Now, obviously the choice is yours. But maybe, if you help us, then we'll help you."

"And how would you help me exactly?"

"Does freedom appeal to you?" That catches my attention. "With conditions, of course. You won't be able to fight against the Board anymore but we'll let you be a normal kid with a normal kid's life." I just nod. Those terms are agreeable. Basically, to not die, I have to train this team to be mission-ready. And then once those missions are completed, I could be set free and get to see Ivo again. While the job is not exactly what I was expecting, the rewards are certainly better than nothing. I look up at General Lee and nod.

"Excellent," he says, obviously pleased with himself. "Here is your new ID." He hands me one that looks exactly like the ones he and the other government officials carry around. "You have complete freedom in this place. If you do anything wrong, we'll just kill you. So, you train on your own schedule, you eat when you want, you sleep when you want. Anything you need or want you can have, just ask. As long as your team is mission-ready when we need them there is no need for you to be our prisoner." This seems cool at first until I realize that instead of being their prisoner, I'm a prisoner of death. General Lee just turns around and leaves with his guards. For a minute I forget that I'm not alone. I try my best to address my team, if I'm even going to call them that.

"Ok...." Not really knowing how to start. "I know this is weird. You have been trained by elite generals and commanders for your entire life and now your fate rests in the hands of a fifteen-year-old." I'm really trying to sound confident but I'm pretty sure I just sound stupid. I glance at the twenty faces staring at me, all eyes focused and faces blank. Knowing that they are listening, I continue.

"I have never received formal training like you have. So in that aspect, you win. But, I fought against the Board for long enough to know the weaknesses in those soldiers. You will not have weakness. I am going to form this squad into one that I'm proud of, even though I don't really want to." I'm happy with my little speech, hopefully I gained a small amount of respect in their eyes. I can only hope that they will listen to me. First, I wonder how I'm going to teach them to be rebels. My stomach rumbles, reminding me not to be more emaciated than I already am. I quickly realized that I am the boss, and therefore I can do whatever I want.

"Has anyone eaten breakfast?" I ask the group. They all shake their heads in unison. "Alright, then that's what we do first." I start walking out the door and then realize that they are all waiting to follow me.

"Oh right. I'm the boss." I chuckle to myself. "Well, I don't know where the food is for you guys so you're going to have to show me where we eat." They all start walking in the opposite direction towards the end of the training facility. I guess I wasn't even close.

As we walk, I think about what my life is going to look like for the next few weeks. It's going to be different. Very different than it has been. Then it hits me. I am officially working for the Board. I am on their side. Kinda. And I've certainly envisioned worse ways to collaborate with the Board. I'm starting to question if I'm still loyal to the Migrants. Do I even want to leave?

18 MONTHS EARLIER

IDRI

OCTOBER 10, 2029

I'm sitting on my bed, flipping through my journal. I haven't really written in it since moving to the United States but I still enjoy looking back at old memories. Right now, I'm trying to find an entry that I look back on often, to remind myself of an intact family. Finally, I find it. I move myself towards the top of the bed so that I can lean myself against the wall. I take a deep breath and then glance towards my journal, almost unsure if I should read it. I always get emotional after reading this, even though my father taught me never to show emotion. I can't help at least feeling it.

Uncle left today. He said he will be back soon, but I know he won't. He's going to fight in the war, they didn't tell me what war, or for whom he will be fighting for. I wanted to know. But they told me that eight-year-olds are not meant to know these things. It makes me mad to not be able to understand the struggles of my family. Father and I are leaving soon. His work is taking him to the United States. It's supposed to be special there. Lively, and with many different kinds of people. There is no fighting. At least that's what Mother told me. She is not coming. I'm going to miss her. Father said she'll come when we have a home, and know that it's safe. But here, it's not safe. So I'm confused. I don't want to leave her alone. Father said to be strong, don't let my emotions get in the way of doing the right thing. But I will lose my friends, and my mother. I don't want to go. Here, it is small. There, it is big. Here, it is familiar. There, it is strange and new. Father said the schools are good there and I can learn more than I would have ever learned here. I've never gone to school before. Uncle taught me everything I knew. Father always left for work and Mother took care of the house. So Uncle would help me learn, how to speak, how to live. Today is a sad day.

It's a short passage. But my eight-year-old self had no idea how great the United States would be. I have a good life here. Mother still hasn't joined us, but Father said she'll be coming very soon. It's been almost nine years since I last saw her. I haven't talked to Uncle since he left, but he sends letters to my father. He seems to be doing well, he hasn't been injured yet and he hopes that he can come back soon. Both my father and my uncle have United States passports because they were born here. Right after they were born, they went back to Senegal where they stayed. But my father had friends here and I now know that his work was with the secret service. He is constantly training me to follow in his footsteps. He always says "if you work with the people in power, they don't have a reason to hurt you."

I live by that. I always work with the people that are more powerful than myself. So far, it has worked for my father. We have a nice house here outside of Boston and we are comfortable in terms of money. He gets called into work but because there is so much to be done in Boston, he doesn't end up needing to go too far.

IDRI

"Idri! Breakfast!" Father yells from downstairs. I drop my journal on my bed and run downstairs, grabbing my backpack on my way out. School has been hard for me because Father keeps taking me out to learn how to do secret service work. He says that the specific things they are teaching me at school will not help me be the self-sufficient adult following in Father's footsteps. I make my way to the kitchen table, a large round piece of wood. My father is making waffles this morning, my favorite. He only ever makes this meal when he wants to talk to me, otherwise he just makes toast or something.

"Idri," he says, walking to the table with a plate of waffles in one hand and syrup in the other. "I have a job for you."

"Really! Just for me!" I reply, excited to be independent.

"Well, no. Technically it's our mission. The agency now accepts you as an agent-in training, so they can give us missions together. The reason I say it is your mission is because I'm going to stay more in the background on this one." This is weird because Father never lets me go on a mission alone if he has a say. He likes to train me as we are going.

"Why aren't you coming? Do you have another mission? Are you too busy?" I ask, curious.

"No. It's just about what the mission is. Here is the report." He slides over a folder that was sitting on the table. I open it up and start reading over the introduction. Something about a criminal who is taking out government officials. Seems like a pretty low-stakes mission. So low-stakes that I'm wondering why they would give it to secret service agents and not just the police. My father works for the United Nations secret service. It's a fairly new group designed to keep down terrorists and criminals on a global scale. Once governments across the globe became stable and peaceful, the United Nations shifted to being a global point for any secret service countries needed. The idea being, the most qualified agents would be available to all nations. For so long, the United States government and the United Nations would send my father missions to Senegal. Now, we get missions that are relevant to our area, specifically Boston. Usually petty crime like this mission is easily taken care of by the police.

"Basically, it's a young girl," Father continues. "She is Asian and has been attacking government guards all over the city. No one has been able to find or capture her because she happens to be a better fighter than everyone. She carries a sword with her wherever she goes, and apparently she knows how to use it expertly. Not only is carrying a sword around as a weapon is illegal, but a minor attacking government officials successfully is unheard of." He seems surprised by this case, as am I. It seems like something straight out of a comic book.

"So that's why you only want me going in. You think that, because I'm a kid, I will be able to get to her?" It makes sense, teenagers can connect easier than adults.

"Exactly."

"Ok. When are we making our move?"

"Now."

"You can't be serious. I have school and it's an important day because I have a math test." I have never been good at math. And it's not helpful that I keep missing my tests. The test today is one that I had kept rescheduling to take for at least a month. Honestly, at this point I forget what the test is even about.

"Can't we do it another day. It doesn't seem like she's stopping anytime soon which means she's not going anywhere. Plus, we don't even have a lead." Boston is a massive city. Without a hint of some kind, there is no way we can find her. She could be in plain sight, or be hiding in any number of places. I'm not missing my math test for a stupid wild goose chase. I'd like to think that Father is a practical person, but things like this really make me doubt that.

"No, it has to be today. We have a lead. It's in the folder. I'll email your teachers, tell them you're sick and that the doctor says to stay home for a few days. I need you on this one." He says as he starts to get up. This is when he activates his boss voice, like he is demanding I do this.

"Eat your breakfast and read through the report. We leave in thirty minutes."

I drag my waffles closer to me. They are cold now, my excitement for breakfast has dwindled now that I know what the next few days are going to look like. It's only been a couple of minutes before I hear the bus screech to a halt across the street, wait for thirty seconds, and then leave. It's not that I don't like these missions. But sometimes, it seems like I haven't had a very normal childhood. When I'm not in school, I'm being trained. That means no time for hanging out with friends, no time for a girlfriend, no time for a sport, even though I'm very good at track and field. Sometimes, like on this occasion, it means no time for school.

I eat and continue skimming the report. It's amazing how much information they can get on somebody without even contacting them. Obviously, this girl, who is unnamed in the report, didn't think her plan through because she still has an active social media profile. That unlocked facial recognition which is still in its developmental stages but the government is trying to reach out to tech companies to secure that capability. This girl seems to have no known relatives, which means she she doesn't have close contact with her parents, although the report states that she does have parents according to her social media bio. She is trained in swordsmanship and close combat, which is evident in the many times she successfully took out guards and soldiers. The report mentions that the guards she attacks are mostly ones that defend large tech corporations and predominantly white-owned businesses which is strange. In fact, all of the guards she has attacked are also white. You don't see racial patterns in attacks very often nowadays, the United States is the most racially equitable place in the world and the last racially charged attack was involved in police brutality and that took place over five years ago. The report also mentions that she keeps being spotted near the outer edge of Chinatown and that she is seen there specifically during meal times. I guess that's what Father was talking about when he said that we have a lead.

I finish my breakfast, which ended up being quite satisfying after all, and then head upstairs to get ready. Right now I'm wearing blue jeans, a white t-shirt, and a pair of Converse, which doesn't cut it in terms of mission attire. I get undressed and pull on sleek black cargo pants with a matching black long sleeve shirt. In terms of shoes, I grab the trusty unbranded black sneakers that Father snatched from the Board center. I head out of my room and down the hallway. At the end of the hallway, there is a large window. I grab the bottom window sill and slide it to the right, revealing a red button. I press the button and a part of the wall, to my left, slides open. There are some cool parts to this house because the government tricked it out for Father when we moved.

I step into the room and the wall shuts behind me as the lights go on. This room is like a large walk-in closet. Except, instead of clothes, there is an obscene number of guns, knives, grenades, and spy equipment. This mission isn't one where we are trying to intimidate the enemy. Actually, it's the opposite. So the less armed, the better. I'm going to try to get close to this girl and at least talk to her long enough to understand her motive. So instead of guns and knives, I grab a pen that turns into a knife and some small paper-thin grenades. I stuff all of that into the pockets of my cargo pants and exit the room. I almost bump into my father as I leave the room, which I like to call the weapons closet.

"Are you ready to go?" he asks.

"Yep, all ready. We are headed into Chinatown, right?" I need to make sure I didn't miss anything important in the report. I just skimmed it, whereas my father carefully read each word. Usually we get about the same out of it, or at least the information that's needed. But, sometimes I miss something.

"Yes. Meet me downstairs." He slides the windowsill, presses the button, and walks into the weapons closet as I grab my phone from my room and head downstairs. I'm really hoping that this mission can be completed today so that I don't have to miss a few days of school like my father said. That would be a real pain in the neck. I sit on the couch in the living room, waiting for Father. It's taking him an unusually long time to grab weapons. When he finally comes downstairs, he is carrying an entire duffel bag of weapons.

"I thought this mission was low key. I'm making contact with her, not shooting her." I say skeptically.

"You never know what could happen. She doesn't just take out the guards. She kills them." I guess that's the part I missed. I should've grabbed more weapons. Oh, well. We head into the garage and jump in the car. It's an old red Toyota Camry. It's the first car that my father ever got in the United States. As soon as he got here the Board told him he needed a better car and they keep urging him to get one. At one point they just said they will pay for any car he wanted. The point was, the car is red which is not exactly discrete. But Father said that he loves this car, he never told me why he wanted to keep it so much, he's not a very sentimental character. We both hop in and get driving. Neither of us talk. Father isn't really a fan of talking in the car before a mission. He wants to focus. Except this time, it's just me going in. He's just here in case I really need him.

It takes twenty minutes to get into Chinatown. There are tons of people everywhere, just like there always is in the middle of Boston. I can't really imagine a time when downtown isn't crawling with people. It's going to be very difficult to pinpoint faces. When we finally get into the area of Chinatown where the girl is frequently spotted, we slow down and start to circle the area. We both scan the streets, making sure we don't miss her. After an hour of circling I spotted someone. It's a young girl, about my age, with a sword around her back. She is wearing normal teenage girl clothes. I notice that everyone is looking at her. Probably because she is carrying a sword but also because a girl her age should be in school right now.

"I see her. I see her!" I grab Father's arm and start shaking. "Pullover." He pulls off and puts his hazards on. I jump out before the car even stops. I scan the road until I spot her again. She is walking briskly down the crowded block, weaving through people. It seems as though she is walking with purpose so she must have a destination. I start following her, at first going faster than she is going but then slowing down as I get closer to her, keeping a safe distance. A few times she looks over her shoulder and when she does I duck into an alley or hide behind a stranger in front of me. It's important that she doesn't notice me because I'm also a kid who should be in school. After a few blocks, the girl goes into a sushi restaurant. I lean against the wall of the building adjacent to it. I pull out my phone and call Father.

"Where are you?" He immediately asks.

"I'm right next to the sushi restaurant a few blocks down from where you dropped me off."

"Ok. I'll park in the garage across the street. Call me if anything changes. For now, wait outside until I say otherwise." He hangs up.

I wait for what seems like a long time but I look at the time on my phone and realize it's only been forty five minutes. At least we found her. I thought that was going to take the whole day. She is definitely just eating a meal which means she'll probably be done within the next fifteen minutes. It's around noon and I wait a few more minutes before calling father. Then I grab my phone and dial his number.

"Hey, she's been in there for around an hour. Should I check it out?" I ask, hoping he'll say yes so I can do something a little more exciting than just waiting around for something to happen.

"Yes. Proceed. But don't hang up, talk me through what you see." I walk towards the restaurant and open the door. The place is pretty busy, most of the tables are full, that might be the reason why she chooses to eat at this place.

"How many?" I'm almost startled by the server in front of me. She could see my confused face so she asked again as though I didn't hear her the first time. "How many will be in your party today?"

"Oh, no thanks. I'm actually just looking for someone who's already here." The server walks away.

"What was that?" Father asks over the phone.

"Nothing. Nothing. Just a waitress." I scan the restaurant tables and only see old couples or families, no sign of the girl. "She's not here."

"Are you sure? Check again. You were looking at the doorway the whole time. How could she have left?" He's right. There is no way she could've exited through the front door without me seeing her. I check again to make sure.

"Nope. She is definitely not here."

"Damnit!" Father sounds frustrated. I'm about to hang up and exit the restaurant when I hear a crash. A table has been turned over, all of the food and dishes sliding onto the ground. The girl is sprinting into the back of the restaurant near the kitchen.

"I see her! She's running through the back kitchen. Swing around and try to catch her on the other end. I'm in pursuit!." I yell through the phone as I push people aside and run in the direction of the kitchen. I push through the metal swinging doors and catch sight of her sword on her back.

"Everyone move." I say as all of the cooks get out of the way. I keep sprinting, trying to catch up to her. I have to hand it to her, she's pretty fast. But not fast enough to outrun Father when he pulls the car around. I run through the kitchen and out the back door into an alley. No girl in sight. I look to the right and see the red Camry pulling up at full speed. Father jumps out of the car.

"Where did she go?"

"I have no idea. She just disappeared." We are both frantically looking everywhere in the alley to find something, anything.

"She can't just disappear Idrissa." He sounds mad and frustrated.

"I swear, I was right behind her." And then something jumps onto my shoulders, tying a piece of cloth over my eyes. I stumble backwards and trip on something, banging into the wall. I rip the blindfold and see the girl slide across the hood of the Camry, hitting my father with the handle of her sword. He stumbles back, not able to pull out his gun in time. She sprints out of the alley and turns right into the crowd of people. We both get up and sprint after her but as soon as we exit the alley we look in the direction we saw her go and realize there is a massive crowd of people on this street getting ready for an event. All of them with masks and costumes on, meaning there is no way we can find her now.

"God damnit!" Father yells. He storms off towards the car, and I follow. We both get into the car, I grab the blindfold she used in case it gives us any clues. "We wake up early tomorrow morning." Father says as we reverse out of the alley. It doesn't matter. She will be looking out for us now, which means this mission just got ten times harder.

AIKO

OCTOBER 10, 2029

I peer over the catwalk as silently as possible. The kid that was chasing me has his back turned and I can't see much of his facial features, so I won't be able to recognize him again. I can't believe I was almost caught. How could I have been so careless? I look down and see a red car approaching and an older man gets out of the car. They keep quarreling about where I went and how I can't disappear. It's what they all say when I escape. This isn't my first time being found and chased, but I'm always faster and smarter. Those traits help me to get away, especially because I'm never stronger. I wish that these people knew that what I'm doing isn't wrong, or at least it's not completely wrong, even if it might be slightly extreme.

I peer down again and shuffle my feet, waiting until I'm confident that they are too busy complaining to notice me moving. I slowly inch my way towards the edge of the platform and then in one motion I swing my legs over the edge and jump onto the back of the kid, knocking him over. I start sprinting towards the car, which is blocking the alley. I lift off of my left foot and slide across the hood. At the same time, the other guy starts to come towards me and I grab my sword, pull it over my shoulder, and hit him with the handle. I dismount the car hood and run into the street, taking a sharp right and sprinting into a crowd of people. There must be some kind of celebration because everyone has costumes and masks on. I steal one of the closest masks when the vendor isn't looking and tie it around my head. I slow down to the pace of everyone else and take a quick glance over my shoulder in time to see the two guys turn around. I'm sure they'll be back again, but now I know what their car looks like. I take a deep breath and let out a sigh of relief. Usually I would lose whoever was chasing me just by running, but whoever that kid was, was ready. No one has ever gotten that close. And I must admit, cutting off the alley with the car was one of the smarter moves I've seen, even if it took too long. I continue walking down the street, moving in and out of the crowd.

After a few minutes, I turn right into an alley. On my left, there is an old brick wall and on my right there is the side of a worn down gray cement building. I walk halfway down the alley until I reach a trash bin. I push the trash bin to the side and look both ways, making sure no one is watching. When I'm sure that no one is looking, I stand up and, as discreetly as possible, push in one of the bricks near the bottom. A part of the wall, about the size of a small doorway opens up and I quickly walk through. The door closes behind me. I'm in pitch darkness, so I grab my phone and turn on the flashlight. Walking through a dark tunnel I make it into a back room. This is the backside of a Japanese restaurant, I'm friends with the owner who happens to also own the sushi place I just trashed in my rather inelegant departure. There are a few guys playing cards to the right and I walk over to them.

"Hey. Anyone know where Shinji is?" They all look at me wondering why a teenage girl is looking for one of the richest restaurant owners in Chinatown. Finally one young guy speaks up.

"He's in the kitchen." He quickly mumbles before going back to the card game.

"Thanks." I climb the ladder in the center of the room and make my way into the kitchen. I see the back of Shinji's head, who is currently screaming at one of the cooks.

"This is not good enough." He yells into the poor guy's face. He's a tough boss.

"I don't understand what I did wrong." The guy retaliates. Bad mistake.

"Fired." Shinji demands. The cook takes off his apron and turns around, dragging his feet as he leaves the kitchen.

"Sir. Mr.Shinji." Another cook approaches him, with a little more bravery in his demeanor.

"What is it?" He snaps.

"That was the wrong cook. He wasn't the one that messed up the sushi order."

"What!" Shinji replies. "Well I didn't like him anyways. Couldn't stand up for himself." Shinji turns around and smiles as he sees me standing in the middle of the kitchen.

"Aiko, how good to see you." He says calmly as he walks towards me. "How much of that did you see?" He adds, almost embarrassed.

"Enough, Shinji. You can't be so mean." I say, looking into his eyes. He's a short man, about sixty although I never actually asked how old he is. His grey hair sticks up from his head, stopping abruptly at his high hairline. Wrinkles cover his face, making him seem like a wise old soul. He wears a white long-sleeve collared shirt, rolled up to his elbows, with sleek tailored suit pants that are a deep black. His shoes are very expensive black leather sneakers. This is the outfit he is wearing almost every time I see him. He just smiles at me but his smile slowly turns into a frown as he sees the solemn look on my face.

"What's wrong, Aiko?" He asks.

"I'm sorry Shinji. I was trying to get away from these guys that were chasing me. But I messed up your restaurant and scared some of your guests. I'm sorry. I shouldn't have let them track me to your restaurant but it was the only place I felt safe." I start crying, tears streaming down my face as all of the other cooks just stare at me, confused. I look up at Shinji's face, ready to get yelled at. But instead his face looks calm and unmoved. He pulls me into a hug and pats my back.

"Why aren't you mad?" I ask, surprised as I pull away from the embrace.

"I already knew, Aiko. Of course my people phoned as soon as it happened. It's ok. I don't like those government guys anyways." Shinji doesn't know what I've been doing. He just thinks I'm a poor Japanese orphan girl who is being chased down by the government to be put into a foster home. Most of that is true so I'm not really lying, I'm just withholding some information. He wipes away my tears and I smile at him. Shinji found me hungry on the strects one night as he was walking home. He brought me to his house where he gave me food and a bed. He doesn't have any family, no wife or kids, so I think he felt like I could be something like a daughter to him. He showed me his restaurants and the secret rooms he has to take care of fellow Japanese people. He told me I can stay anywhere, in any of his properties. I still go to school and stuff because technically everyone still thinks I live with my adopted parents in the middle of the city. I ran away because I couldn't stand how they worked for the government. Ever since, I lie to everyone and avoid seeing them and instead hang out here with Shinji. Despite his usual aggressive demeanor, he's more relaxed with me.

"Can I stay here tonight Shinji?" I mutter.

"Of course." He answers. "But I need to go take care of something now. Will you be ok?" I nod and he turns around, walking out of the kitchen and into the seating area. I turn around and climb down the ladder, sitting down in the corner of the room opposite from the guys playing cards. I pull out my phone and start reading the news, mentally making my plan for the next attack. I only take out people that are doing bad, or are becoming corrupt. I have gathered enough information to confidently say that the government is headed towards a big change in power. My foster parents were high up in the corporate world and I overheard some conversations about the corporations taking over or something. As soon as I knew, I ran away and have been trying to find out more ever since.

With nothing to do, I scroll through the news for god knows how long. At least a few hours. I grab the pillow and blanket that Shinji always leaves for me and I head to bead early in the hopes I will wake up early and have time to complete a mission before those guys come back looking for me.

I look down onto the government building. I'm crouched on the roof of an office building across the street from where most corporations go to suck-up to government officials. Scrolling through the news last night, I saw something that mentioned a high-ranking guy from some major corporation has an important meeting today. I'm actually not sure if this is where it's happening, but if it's not here, at least I'll be able to take a picture of the people that come here.

After waiting for a couple of hours, I finally see him. He has two security guards next to him, which is actually not a lot compared to other people I've watched. I recognize the bright blonde hair and height of the guy from the pictures I saw online. Funny enough, I never actually got his name, but it doesn't really matter. Anybody that is conspiring to basically destroy democracy deserves what I'm about to give them. I don't take out the high officials, because that would mean the entire government would come after me. Instead, I take out one or two of the guards, kind of like a warning and a statement, just to let the guys know that not everybody is a fan of them.

I turn around, ready to run down the stairs of the building just in time to attack one of the guards before they go inside but when I do, I see an African kid, about my age standing right behind me. Damnit. I didn't even hear him come up. How? Also, where is his bigger friend?

"Hi." He says and just smiles. I swing my sword from around my back and lower my hips and knees. He doesn't even flinch. Instead he just takes a step forward.

"I'm not here to hurt you. I mean technically I am supposed to capture you." He lets out a chuckle. I have never met someone that is so confident that I won't kill him. And I won't. He's not a white government bureaucrat. I stay dead silent, although my shoulders start to relax. He notices and takes another step forward, now only a few feet away from me.

"If my father were here, he would shoot your foot and then handcuff you. So, you're lucky I convinced him to stay in the car. You do know you've killed a lot of people, right? Technically, you've killed enough people to warrant me, a person in the government, permission to kill you in turn. But in case you haven't noticed, I'm not the executioner type. What's your name?" In any other situation I would've slashed part of his body and been on my way, unfazed. And I definitely wouldn't give anybody my actual name. But this kid seems nice and for some reason, I think he would understand my perspective and reasoning. It almost seems like he's fishing for it.

"Aiko." I mumble under my breath, almost making sure he doesn't hear me.

"Well, Aiko…" He says as he takes all of his weapons out of his pockets and drops them onto the concrete roof of the building. He's in black cargo pants and is wearing a bulletproof vest. What is someone of his age doing working for the government?

"I want to talk to you before I let my father get a hold of you. If that's alright with you?" He sits down cross legged and just stares at me, waiting for an answer. I don't really have a choice so I sit down with my arms holding my knees toward my chest. I feel the rough concrete scratching my clothes and skin. I drop my sword next to me, just in reach. I nod in approval.

"Great." He says, obviously satisfied. "Who are you legal guardians?" I look at the ground. I might as well tell him the truth. Either I do now, or they interrogate it out of me later.

"Danny and Samantha Anderson," I answer, not adding the fact that they are my adopted parents. I look up and he raises his eyebrows as though he either knows them or something just clicked in his mind.

"Ok. And how old are you?"

"Seventeen."

"Same here. What is your ethnicity?"

"Japanese." These just seem like normal questions you would fill out on any government form.

"How long have you lived in the United States?" I'm starting to notice his accent more and more.

"Six years."

"And have you always lived in Boston?"

"Yes."

"Where did you learn how to use that sword?"

"Japan." I don't mention specifics. I started learning when I was very young. My neighbor was an extremely experienced sword master and he found me and taught me how to fight with the sword. He said that if I'm going to go through life alone, I need to be able to defend myself. I'd say I've been doing more than just defending myself with the sword.

"Aiko," he starts, as he shuffles a little bit closer to me. "Why are all your victims white?" I perk up in surprise. No one has ever noticed that about my victims. He didn't ask why I kill. He knows that I have a motive.

"I only kill the racist ones." I say back.

"But they haven't harmed anyone."

"They harm many people by working for evil companies."

"Those companies are serving our country in many ways." I can tell he's trying to understand but having a hard time. I can't blame him. The last hate crime was forever ago and monopolies have been developing but not hurting the public due to government regulations. From face value, everything is completely fine. Maybe if I tell him what I've found, he'll be able to tell someone that has the power to make change. I lower my knees and tuck my feet under myself, now I'm sitting how he is. I look up at him.

"They won't be soon."

"What do you mean by that?"

"You won't understand." I want to see if he really wants to know.

"Please. Help me understand. I know that someone like you won't just go around killing people because you feel like it. So tell me why?" I take a deep breath. I have never tried to articulate this to anyone before. I need to make sure I don't sound totally crazy.

"Why do you think the bosses of major companies have suddenly started to meet with government officials way more?"

"Because they want to help the public." He can't help it. The government controls the schools, so the schools teach what the government wants them to teach. It's not his fault that he is blind to the corruption that is beginning.

"No. The companies are meeting with the the government because they want less regulation. Every large company will soon band together to seize power of the government. The most powerful political figure won't be the President of the United States, it will be the people that control these companies." I can't tell if he's following because his furrowed brow suggests that he's confused but I keep going anyway.

"The people that control those companies are often white men. White men that have a history of racism within their family and have no conception of their own white supremacy. Once this transition happens. The government will not exist. Democracy won't exist. Instead a few white, rich, and powerful men will have whatever they want and control the public however they want. And when that happens, they are going to need people to work for them, which will probably be people of color."

"That's not possible. How could all of this be happening without anyone realizing it? And why would they do this? The United States is one of the strongest democracies in the world. The country worked extremely hard to get to this point. Why would they throw that all away?"

"Because, these people have complete control and this is how they will get it. These companies have always controlled parts of our lives that we didn't know they did. They control money, houses, and technology. The big corporations want to control everything and the only way to do that is to control the government that already have been influencing people's lives. It's all part of a single big master plan."

"How do you know all of this? Or, is this just all a conspiracy theory?"

"My parents were…are…important people in these corporations. I overhead some conversations." I try to share as little as possible about my parents.

"Even the race thing?"

"That's a theory. But, a good one."

"I can't say that I believe everything you're saying, or any of it, for that matter." He starts to get up, leaving his weapons on the ground. "But I can't shake this feeling that you're telling the truth, at least what you think is the truth. And there is only one way to find out. You need to come with me." No way I'm going straight into the belly of the beast. I will never comply with the government, not even nice kids like this one.

"No. No way." I reply as I start to grab my sword handle, waiting for the chance to make another inelegant escape.

"You don't understand," he says, still very calm. "I do not work for the United States government. I work where my father works. We work for the United Nations secret service. If you can explain what you just explained to me to my father and show us some kind of proof, he can warn the United Nations and hopefully get an explanation for all of this." Not the government? Huh. Some part of me really wants to trust this guy.

"I'm not going to make you come with us. I'll tell my father that I looked everywhere and couldn't find you. You can go out through the back door of the office building. But if you want to help save people from whatever domination you're describing, then this is the only way that you can get help. Because, trust me, no one else is going to believe you."

"Fine." I say, getting up. As long as I'm not being forced to go with them, I'll go. I want the chance to help people, because killing some guards isn't sending the message that I thought it would anyway. I stand up, grabbing my sword and swinging it over my shoulder. He picks up his weapons, there weren't many, to be honest, and then he gestures to follow him. We walk down the emergency staircase and out the front door where that same red car is parked. He opens the door in the back seat for me and before I get in, he looks at me.

"My name is Idrissa by the way. And no matter what people are telling you, my father and I are here to help."

IDRI

OCTOBER 11, 2029

We sit in silence for most of the drive.

"Why isn't she handcuffed?" Father asks, adding to the awkwardness.

"Why would we handcuff her if she came by her own free will?" I reply with a question of my own. In my mind, I'm really hoping Father agrees with me because I promised Aiko that we aren't really capturing her, but talking with her.

"You handcuff her because she's a criminal. She's actually a murderer." I look over my shoulder and see Aiko staring out the window. She is definitely listening to us. I feel bad, my father won't talk to her with the same calmness and understanding as I do.

"Father. We aren't capturing her as a criminal. She gave me some very intriguing and important information. There is a pattern to her actions, and a reason." He doesn't respond for a while. His philosophy is that criminals have nothing to contribute. I strongly disagree. If Aiko was a pickpocketer I might have a bit more leniency from him. Her being an outright murderer under the age of eighteen operating under her own free will does not pose a case where Father would push aside his beliefs.

"Tell me when we get home." He finally replies. We drive the remaining ten minutes home through traffic in complete silence. Our lack of conversation leads to me eavesdropping on people walking by. Father taught me to always absorb and remember as much information as possible, so you can analyze it later. I take in everything I hear, all of which is pretty useless information. We pull into the garage and get out of the car. Father starts to walk towards the passenger door with handcuffs in hand.

"I got her. You go inside. She can sit in my room."

"Fine." He replies as he walks towards the door. I reach towards the passenger door and open it.

"This is our home." I tell Aiko as she gets out. "Follow me. I'll show you where you can stay." She takes a minute to look around before looking back at me and nodding. I walk into the house and up the stairs, leading her to my room. As I get to the top of the steps I notice that the weapons closet isn't completely closed. I have to remember to close it. Aiko has killed dozens with just a sword—what she could do with those weapons defies the imagination. I take a sharp left into my room as quickly as possible so she doesn't have time to look around.

"This is my room. You can stay here. I'll come back with food in a minute. Make yourself at home." I purposefully made my room a place without any weapons or anything like that, unlike Father who has a gun that is hidden within the backboard of his bed frame. I wanted to make sure my room was somewhat of an innocent haven for situations like this. Since the United Nations secret service is a global diplomatic organization, we don't have prisons and that sort of thing like the government. So on the rare occasions where we have to capture people and keep them secure and comfortable, we need a place to put them. I head out of the room and close the door. Immediately, I rush to the end of the hallway and close the hidden door before heading downstairs.

Father is sitting at the dining table, head in his hands, and obviously very tired. We barely slept last night because we needed to figure out how we were going to find Aiko, now that she knew what our car looked like. Based on who she was going after, we realized that they all somewhat connected to the government. We didn't realize how but we were lucky because the only governmental meeting happening today was a meeting with a high ranking official from a major company. We decided that that's where we needed to go. I make my way to the dining table and sit down on the opposite side of the table. Father looks up, eyes weary.

"So, tell me again why she shouldn't be handcuffed."

"We had a conversation on the roof. I wanted to know what her motive was. She told me, and I told her that you could help, so she came on her own free will. I didn't feel like she was a threat to us, because all of her targets were white, so I thought it best not to give her the wrong impression."

"If you think I'll help her kill high-ranking officials then you're mistaken. That's not my job." He sounds frustrated. First, he is given a frustrating moving target and, now, he has to host a murderer. I could see how this is not the most appealing situation. A part of me just wants to give in. But I can't not tell him what Aiko said. I know she was telling the truth.

"Please, just let me explain," I beg.

"Fine. You have five minutes to convince me why our friend isn't in restraints." I tell him everything. Almost everything she said word for word. I tell him about who she kills, why she kills, and the information she has about the end of democracy.

"Please. Just call your connections at the UN and make sure that there isn't some intelligence that might confirm what she says? That's all I ask. If it isn't true then you can do whatever you feel is necessary. But if it is true, you have to treat her like an ally."

"Ok. When, not if, they confirm that it's not true then we have to have a talk about how to handle persuasion in the field. You are too soft." He walks away and takes his phone out of his pocket. I walk into the kitchen, grab an apple and some chips, and make my way back to my room. I knock on the door and, before Aiko can reply, I open the door. She is sitting on the ground, her back against my bed, looking at something on her phone.

"Here, I brought you some food." I drop the food next to her and sit to her left in the same way, four feet away to make sure she doesn't catch me by surprise.

"Thanks." She mumbles, taking a quick glance at me out of the corner of her eye.

"I just talked to my father. He is calling his contacts at the United Nations to confirm your findings."

"Really!" She turns towards me and smiles. All of a sudden she is a lot more animated. "I didn't think he would believe me. Thank you."

"Well, not so fast. He doesn't completely believe you. But I promised you that we would try to warn people if what you are saying is true and that's what we are doing. I want you to know that if what you're saying isn't true then my father wants to take you in as a criminal."

"Yeah, I know." That's a surprise, I thought she was about to bolt. "I'm confident that you will see I'm not lying. Plus, I'm too good to be held as a prisoner. You would have to kill me before that happens." The intensity and confidence in her voice is a shock—she had only whispered and mumbled to me since I talked to her. I'm about to ask her where she goes to school before Father comes running into my room.

"She's right," he exclaims as he exits the room and makes his way down the hallway to the weapons closet. Aiko and I both get up and follow him.

"What do you mean she's right?" I ask, struggling to keep up with him as he starts grabbing virtually every weapon in the closet. He takes down two rifles and hands one to each of us. He did not just hand a fully loaded gun to a murderer.

"Father. What are you doing?"

"She was right. About everything," he pants. "I called my underground contacts at the United Nations, they said it's starting to happen in every powerful country in the world, but the United States is the farthest along. They have been infiltrated. All of my colleagues have been killed and they are going to come for us. The monopolies are working together on a takeover of some kind. They are going to force all people of color into submission, using as much violence as necessary." Oh, this is bad. I wanted to trust Aiko but I didn't want to believe that what she was saying could be true.

"We need to stop this. We can't just defend ourselves." Aiko says as she confidently steps out from behind me.

"No. It's too late. They are already starting the process. The best we can do is find a place to hide and we can save people if we bring them to that place." He is noticeably scared, an emotion that I haven't seen in a long time. Maybe ever, actually.

"Ok. Where are we going?" I ask. Aiko has wandered off into the weapons cabinet, filling her pockets with grenades and basically anything she can carry.

"There is this bunker, an abandoned underground train station, that the UN has for any of us in the secret service that need it. We can go there but I have to first erase it from the government database so they can't track us there."

"How do we do that?" Aiko asks, circling back towards us.

"That's the hard part," Father continues. "The only way to do that is from within. So we have to go into the government center."

"But that's where all of the soldiers and military are going to be." I say in retaliation. This is very quickly becoming a suicide mission.

"I didn't say it was going to be easy." He replied. "But that's all we got." I nod and start grabbing more weapons, grenades, bombs, and literally whatever else I can fit. Running back to my room, I grab a black duffel bag which I start to stuff large guns into. It's at these times that I wish large guns would be more compact. Maybe one day someone will make that happen. I run back to the weapons closet.

"Ready?" Father asks.

"Ready," Aiko and I say in unison. We all jump into the red Camry and Father starts driving fast towards the government center. As we get closer, we all look on in horror as hundreds of soldiers line up in front of military vehicles and tanks. Looking up, dozens of helicopters circle around the city. It's almost as if all of this happened within the last fifteen minutes. I have no idea how we haven't noticed anything in the last two days. Maybe that meeting was more important than any of us thought. Father takes a sharp left into a side road.

"What now?" Aiko asks from the back.

"I don't know," Father replies as he glances at the government center to get a feel for things. I lean around the wall and take a look. There are significantly fewer guards flanking the sides of the building compared to the front. But the front remains the only way into the building. The dome shape of the building makes it difficult to be stealthy and the glass that covers it means the reflection can reveal our movement to our opponents as we try to get closer. The only way in would be to sneak in somehow and we can't do that with the way we are dressed.

"I got it." I say, turning back towards Aiko and Father who have their backs leaned up against the wall, rather deflated. They both turn their heads towards me as if to say to continue. "We can't fight our way in, but we don't have to. If we can go around the back of the building and sneak around to one side. We can take out a few guards and steal their uniforms. Then we can enter the building without being easily noticed. As long as we keep our heads down and get in and out quickly, I don't think we should run into any problems."

"That's a great idea, Idrissa. Good evaluation of the situation." I love when he uses spy talk to express encouragement. We all hop back into the car and Father drives us a few blocks away so that we can cross into the next street over. We pull up from around the back and park right behind the building. Jumping out of the car, we run towards the side until we see guards. I look at Father who signals to us to go to one side, while he'll take the other. There are four guards who have their backs turned. We all rush to them and take them by surprise. I wrap my arm around the neck of one guy and slowly drag him back, using my heel to kick down his flailing leg. I let the guy slowly crumple to the ground. Looking to my left it looks like Father did the same with the two other soldiers. Meanwhile, Aiko leaves behind a pool of blood underneath her target. I grimace.

"Well, good thing there are four guards because we can't use that uniform anymore." Father smirks, as I scold Aiko. It's starting to become evident that Aiko doesn't exactly care about whether she is drawing attention or being restrained with her combat. Hopefully that doesn't become a problem later on because we are about to willingly walk into a building with hundreds of people who are trying to kill us. We change and scurry around the dome, our backs to the glass and slide along as far as we can before being seen by the guards standing out front.

"Hey what are you soldiers doing here? We have a mandatory meeting inside." I almost forgot we were in military clothing and I turn around to make sure that Aiko and Father both have their helmets on. I look to my side to see a guard with no helmet on, gun in hand, and expressionless. He doesn't look like he has any intention to hurt us or suspect anything out of the ordinary.

"Sorry, sir. We were just checking out the other side, the guards here left their posts and we thought we heard some people over here." Father chimes in. He's always first to think of a solution.

"Very well then. Finish your check and then head inside. The Boston general has some information for us, before we head out." The guard walks away towards the entrance.

"Phew. That was really close." Aiko exclaims. She looks the youngest out of everyone from her stature so she doesn't exactly fit in. I turn back towards Aiko and Father.

"Ok. We all act normal as we walk in. Let's mix into the crowd and see if we can find anything out about what's going on. And then we can peel off. Father, do you know where the database center is in this place?" I lay out the plan for them, feeling the most confident I ever have. Father trained me well--I'm coming into my own and Father is listening.

"I'm pretty sure I came here when we first got to Boston. But that was before the renovations. If they didn't move the database center then it should be down the right side of the corridor, at the end of the hallway."

"Great. Father, you peel away from the crowd early so you have time to erase the catalogue of the base before we start to march out. Aiko and I will try to get as much intel as possible and get into some government vehicles so we blend in. I'm guessing civilians aren't going to be on the road for all this." I'm guessing that this stuffs is getting televised as we speak. Everyone nods so I turn around, stand up from my crouching position, and walk out towards the entrance, standing tall like the guards always do. I check over my shoulder to make sure Aiko and Father are doing the same thing. At first, I walk at a normal pace, but then I realize we don't have weapons in our hands like everyone else. I'm surprised that the last guard didn't catch that. I speed up, walk up the wide steps, and into the large entrance to the dome, where the ten foot steel doors have been propped open.

We immediately hit a crowd of people who were all grouped in the lobby. They are looking up towards an overhanging balcony constructed of more glass but held up by metal rails. I'm assuming that's where the general will be delivering his speech. I look up and around. The dome's interior glass is not completely translucent, the blue sky clearly displayed at the top of the building. The balcony goes almost the entire circumference of the dome and hallways exit out from the sides of this lobby space, which is a smaller circle within the building. If I wasn't on a life or death mission, I would take more time to admire the architecture.

I'm snapped out of my observations by a flurry of clapping. I look up to see the general approaching the podium, which stands near the edge of the balcony. I clench my teeth as I think about how easy it would be to shoot the glass from under him and end this whole thing. Of course, there would probably be someone else that would take over. But still, that would bring me a lot of satisfaction.

"Soldiers! Many of you already know me and others of you are just now joining my army." The general starts speaking. He is wearing the same uniform as everyone else but it's covered in various badges. He has a commander's hat on but from this distance I can't see any of his facial features.

"My name is General Fox. I'm here to lead you through the most glorious moment of the century. Together we will subdue Boston and serve our government in the most honorable way. You will all have a chance to work with me as long as you want. Each squadron has been assigned addresses where they must capture the people who live there. But keep them alive. The Elite Group has been given the names of people that are the greatest threat to our mission. Those people must be eliminated and the Elite Group has been formed with the best of the best from around the country to make that happen." I look to my side to see Aiko's frightened expression, but I see no signs of Father. That's good because it means he already peeled off to find the database center, hopefully all of the soldiers and guards are here and, at most, he only has to take out some unarmed people. Meanwhile, the general keeps adding to his maniacal plan.

"The reward for everyone's compliance is complete freedom. You can live where you want, eat what you want, and offer the Board the highest form of service. Once this mission is complete, the Board pledges to have all of the greatest minds innovate on new military technology and you bet that you soldiers, will be first in line. Now, let's head out and make this happen!" I guess the companies are calling themselves the Board. This guy really is crazy and the even crazier thing is, there are hundreds just like him all over the world right now. Basically, these people are fighting just so they can earn basic human rights. Food and a home.

Everyone starts marching out of the entrance. I check my phone and there is a message from Father saying that he found what he needed and he'll meet us at the back end of the building. I turn to Aiko who's trembling in rage.

"Aiko. Focus. We need to get out of here alive. It's the only way that we will be able to help people before these guys get to them." She nods.

"What do we need?" She asks as we start moving with the crowd. Everyone's so busy getting ready that no one even turns to us to ask us who we are.

"We need a military vehicle. We can't keep driving around in my father's car, it's way too obvious." Once we get outside, we stand on the steps and look around. There are a bunch of military vans and stuff, packed with soldiers. I look towards the far right where a driver just gets out of one, no keys in his hand.

"Aiko, look. That's the van we need to take." From what I can tell, there's no one in the back so now's the time. We jog over, trying not to draw any attention to ourselves. I get into the front seat and Aiko climbs into the passenger side after she closes the back doors. I make sure the keys are still in the ignition and I take a hard right, squeezing into the alley on the left side of the building. I take another right and park against the curb on the backside of the building. We are only waiting fifteen seconds before Father runs up to the car, opens the back doors, and climbs into the back.

"Drive, Idrissa!" I step on the accelerator.

"Did you do it?" I ask over my shoulder.

"Yes. But, I was almost caught. Good thinking on the military vehicle but they will find my car soon and be able to iD it, so we don't have much time. We need to go straight to the base."

"But all of our stuff is at home. Everything is at home. We can't just leave it there. And Aiko needs to get her stuff as well." I look towards Aiko.

"Actually, I don't. I don't have anything worth going back for."

"See! She's being more rational than you, Idrissa. Sometimes you have to make hard decisions so you can complete the mission." There's the secret service talk again.

"Fine." I reluctantly agree. "Once we get to the base, I'm heading back out." There are things there that remind me of life in Senegal.

"Here." Father leans over my shoulder and hands me his phone which has an address and coordinates on it. I take one look at it and memorize the location. Stepping on the accelerator, I speed towards our temporary reprieve.

AIKO

OCTOBER 11, 2029

I said I didn't need anything. But, now I'm worried about Shinji. What's going to happen to him? I'm about to ask Idrissa to turn around but that would be selfish. Especially after everything that Idrissa and his father have done for me this past day. They trusted me when no one would. Of course I was right. I knew that all along. But I never thought it mattered because I wouldn't ever be able to find people that would actually believe me. I look out the window, seeing innocent families having fun outside or watching TV in their houses. They have no idea what's about to happen. No one does. We turn onto a highway that runs along the edge of Boston. This is where tons of companies have their storage buildings I know because I used to sneak in and sleep in them when I had no where else to go.

"I'm confused." Idri says, looking back at his dad.

"Why?" His dad replies, leaning over Idrissa's shoulder.

"Because this is it. These are the coordinates you gave me. But it's just in the middle of the road."

"No. That can't be. This base was protected by the government. What was the government, I suppose. But anyways, they wouldn't just destroy it." Idrissa's dad says, obviously worried.

"Well, is it possible that you gave me the wrong location?" Idri asks. I'm just observing the conversation while I also unbuckle my seat belt and look around through the windows. From what I can tell, it really is just the middle of the road.

"No. I definitely gave you the right location, Idrissa. I don't understand. It should be right here. My partners have come here before and reported back. How can it just disappear?" I'm about to sit back in my seat, deflated, but I decide that it's my turn to remain positive.

"How about we get out of the car and look around." I chime in. I don't even wait for their answer. I just hop out and start scanning the area. The water is only a few yards away and the office buildings are in the distance. Not many people drive this way so I don't think we have to worry about any cars coming up behind us. I crouch down and look at the ground. Then something catches my eye. At first glance it just seems like there is a crack on the road beneath the front tires of our military van. But the crack is oddly very straight. Like perfectly straight.

"Guys, check this out." I say, peeking over the hood of the van. They are both looking across the water trying to see if the base is over there. Idrissa turns around and walks towards me.

"What is it?"

"Look at this crack. Doesn't it seem abnormal how straight it is?" He drags his finger along the crack next to the tire.

"Yeah, that is weird." Idrissa starts to get up. "Wait a second," he adds. "Father said that the base was a recycled train station right?" I just nod. "So the likelihood of the base being underground is high since most old train stations were essentially all subways." He's right. We are in the right place, we are standing over the hidden base. Idrissa stands up.

"Father, we found it." His dad turns around.

"What? Where? How?" He rushes towards us.

"Aiko found this crack and then I remembered that you told me the base was an old train station. We are in the right place. We are standing over the base."

"You're right." His father replies. "There's only one problem. We don't know how to open the entrance." Crap. I hadn't thought of that. I look behind me where the road meets a rocky ledge, on the opposite. Walking over, I feel the rock. It's rough and sharp but there is one patch that looks a bit smoother. I push with my hand and the piece of rock pushes back and slides to the side, revealing a blue lever.

"I found it." I say, looking back at them. "Idrissa, back up the car so it's behind the crack." Idrissa's father walks towards me while Idrissa hops in the car and starts to back it up. Once he's done he leans out of the car.

"Ok. Hit it!" He yells. I push down the lever and the road in front of the van starts to dip down, becoming a ramp that goes underground.

"I underestimated you, Aiko." Idrissa's father says from behind me. I turn around. "I'm sorry I doubted you and treated you like a criminal, even if you are still technically a criminal. I never truly introduced myself. My name is Kalidou and it is very nice to have you around." I shake his hand and then we both run down the ramp which Idrissa has already driven the car down. As we walk down into it we see large brick walls surrounding an open concrete area. The concrete floor has distinct lines showing where it covered up the old tracks. A couple corridors lead off but the space is pretty much empty. Idrissa runs towards us as he emerges from one of them. It's like a tiny train station was completely gutted and cement was put down for floors. Extra concrete walls were also added to create rooms on the sides of the tunnels with some glass elements for aesthetics. Generally, it's quite barren.

"I thought you said this was a secret service base." Idrissa directs his comment towards his father.

"It is." He responds.

"Well there is absolutely nothing here. It's less of a base and more of a bunker really. I just ran through the corridors and every single room is empty apart from beds, although there are a lot of rooms. Should be good for housing people even if we don't have any food or resources for them."

"What are we going to do about that by the way?" I ask. My focus is on helping the most people. We did our part by finding this base but my job isn't over. I need to help the civilians that are being captured as we speak. But there is no point in bringing those people here if they are just going to starve to death.

"We are going to have to go back out and find rations. Father has the intel of where the people are that the soldiers are taking. If we go out to gather people, you can head out and find us some food. Get as much as you can because we don't know how long we have to survive in this place or how many people will seek refuge here." I nod in approval. I like this plan. I know how to scavenge and there is no point in me wandering around trying to save people when Idrissa knows exactly where to go.

"I don't know if I want us splitting up." Kalidou says as he walks back towards the car and pulls the duffel bag full of weapons out of the trunk. "We are better off staying together. Without the three of us, there is no way anybody is getting saved today."

"But it's our only option. I state. I respect Kalidou's experience but now is the time to be a little reckless. "There is no way we can do everything before the military finds everyone. Idrissa's plan is the only way we can get what we want."

"Fine. But I'm sending Idrissa with you. I'm the parent and I can more than handle myself out there. You two need each other." I'm willing to make that compromise even if I do work better alone.

"Ok then. It's a plan," Idrissa says heading towards the van. "Aiko and I will go get some resources while Father rounds up as many people as possible. We are going to need another vehicle."

"I'll drop you two off in the city and you can find another vehicle. Then I'll meet you back where I dropped you off." Idri and I both nod and we all jump into the military van.

"Wait, I saw something by the entrance." Idri says. He jumps out of the car and hops back in thirty seconds holding a remote. "I'm guessing this controls the door which is going to be helpful in speedier operations." We drive up the ramp, the road sealing closed behind us after Idrissa presses the remote. We head into the city, using as many back roads as possible. I spot at least five trucks full of soldiers out of the back seat window, maybe more. Some of them are just monitoring a situation but others are dragging, cuffing, forcing people out of their homes. All of them people of color. When we get a couple of miles from Chinatown, Kalidou pulls up the curb and lets us out, each of us pulling our military helmets over our heads.

"Good luck. And one last thing before you go." Idrissa and I lean our heads through the van windows. "If I'm not back in three hours, then leave without me. It's not worth risking everyone you guys get. You guys are the lifeline for people around here. They need you." Idrissa is troubled by this but he nods with me anyways, he's been trained to put many lives over one. Nevertheless, I am confident that Kalidou will be back here with plenty of time to spare and a van full of people. Kalidou pulls away and I look towards Idrissa.

"What's the plan boss?" I ask, trying to refocus him. I can see that my words get his mind going.

"I think our best bet is to find a vehicle and then load it up with stuff from a local grocery store. Most of them are owned by people of color who are going to be captured anyways, so we might as well get them to help."

"Ok. Where are we going to find a truck?"

"How about that one." Idrissa points across the street. Parked clumsily is a rickety white pickup truck with more than a few dents and scratches.

"Really, Idrissa. Can't we find something that looks a little bit more....usable." He just grins as he crosses the street. I shake my head and run behind him. We get to the driver's seat window and Idrissa punches clear through. The car alarm starts blaring.

"Not exactly a stealthy approach, spy guy." I say as I stand behind him, checking to make sure no one is around.

"Just hold on." He mutters as he reaches into the car, playing with wires. All of a sudden the alarm stops and the car door opens.

"How did you do that?" I ask as I climb into the passenger seat and slouch down into the very uncomfortable chair.

"That thing that I put over the ignition is a device that can trick the car into thinking it has the right key in it." I look towards the ignition and see a black disk, maybe the size of a quarter with a blue light circling around the edge. I guess I've really been missing out on some cool gadgets. My sword is slowly starting to look much more archaic. I'm surprised no one questioned it when I carried it around earlier. We speed off down the road.

"Keep your eyes out for any grocery or convenience store. Anything that would have water and essential rations." Idrissa says. I love how he says rations. Both him and his dad are so governmental.

"There. I see a place." We pull off to the right side of the road and jump out. Homemade ads cover the storefront and the entire place looks like it hasn't been renovated in two decades. The sign says open so we walk straight in. But the place is deserted, not a soul in sight. Why would the owner not lock the place?

"Hello!" I yell. "I don't know Idrissa. I don't want to steal."

"Says the person that has killed people. The owner is obviously gone and this entire block is mostly occupied by people of color so I'm guessing whoever owned this place just fled to safety. I'm sure they won't mind— we are trying to save this city." When he puts it that way it does make sense.

I follow him as we grab cartons of water and canned foods, loading them into the back of the truck. Once we gather all of the supplies that can fit in the bed of the pickup truck we drive back towards where Kalidou dropped us off after a worrisome rumble from the engine. We get there and check the time, it's been almost three hours.

"Don't worry, he'll be here." I reassure Idrissa. We sit in the truck for another half an hour. Once a military truck drove by and we thought it was Kalidou but it ended up being the military and we crouched down near the floor until they passed.

"Idrissa. We have to go. Your father gave us very clear orders. I'm sure he'll just meet us later."

"I'm not leaving until he gets here." I can't imagine the situation he is in so I wait for another few minutes. But then I look behind the truck and an entire squadron of trucks is coming up our street with a massive tank behind us.

"Idrissa! We have to go! They are going to kill us." I yell. Pulling my seat belt over my chest.

"We can fight them. I'm not leaving without him!"

"He probably just saw them and went back to the base." I know that today could be the last time he sees his father but we can't help anybody else unless we get the stuff in this truck back to the base. With tears streaming down his face, Idrissa puts on his seat belt and drives away right before the military notices us. I don't talk to him. I don't mention anything else. I don't try to make him feel better. I know how he feels. I also lost my parents. But not in this way. This way feels a lot more violent.

We drives towards the outside of the city and Idrissa stops the car before the crack. I pull out the remote from his pocket and open up the entrance. We drive through and get out of the truck. Idrissa frantically looks around for anyone else. When he doesn't see another car he kneels on the ground, still crying. I go to close the entrance before three shadows emerge from the entrance of the base.

"Wait! Please." I don't press the button and go up to meet the people as Idri looks up, wiping his tears. The figures end up being two brown kids with black hair, one my age and one younger, carrying an old man beaten up. As I get closer, I realize it's Shinji. His shirt is drenched with blood and his head is scraped. The boys drop him into my arms.

"This is for him." The older one says, holding a piece of paper and weakly pointing towards Idrissa. Idrissa comes up and takes the note. The boys help me carry Shinji into a bedroom.

"His wounds are stable. He just needs water and some rest." The older one says. I go back out into the garage and see Idri depressed. His hands on his face and the piece of paper laying on the ground next to him. I pick it up. It only says "I Love You Idri" followed by a series of numbers, I think it's a flight number. But it has an attached picture. The picture has a younger Idrissa with Kalidou and what looks like his mother standing over him, each with a hand on his shoulder. I fold the note and put it into my pocket. I'm not going to let Idrissa lose this. I turn around and see the boys carrying things off of the truck.

"I'm sorry about his father." The younger one says. "He saved many people. He gave them the location of this base and we hid them until we could go back and get them. He died trying to save that man."

"Who are you?" I ask both of them.

"I'm Ivo and this is Zashil. We are here to help stop the Takeover."

PRESENT DAY

IVO

MARCH 21, 2031

Making my way towards the garage, I put on my necklace. I have my helmet underneath my arm with a duffel bag around my shoulder. The bag has various guns and grenades, hopefully I won't need them. Suddenly Aiko rushes past me, bumping my shoulder along the way.

"Where are you going so fast?" I ask, turning around to face her.

"The team's almost ready, I just forgot food rations. I'm going to grab them and then we'll be good to go." Aiko never listens to me.

"Aiko. I told you this is a solo mission. We have no idea what we're up against and I'm not going to have an entire team's lives on the line. It's not fair to them and it's way too dangerous. They aren't even fully trained." I'm almost pleading at this point. When I got back yesterday I decided I'd come up with a plan and then go the next day—today. Originally I was going to bring Aiko and Idrissa. But I realized that the base needs Aiko for protection and she also never leaves without a team now. For Idri, the news hit him pretty hard. It was less of a motivation to go find his uncle but more depressing because it reminded him of all the tragic things that happened. I didn't know his father well but I know Idri well himself to realize how much he meant to him.

"It's too late." Aiko replies with a smile. "We are already geared up and our truck is blocking the entrance, so it's not like you can leave without us even if you wanted to." This is so frustrating. No matter how many times I make a request or say I'm going alone, Aiko never listens. It's crazy to me that she ever used to work alone. But I'm almost sure that Idri is making that up. Just like he made up the fact that she was an assassin hated by the government. That has got to be the least believable story I've ever heard. But then again, nothing is impossible. I mean we just found Idri's uncle after all.

"Fine. You can come on one condition." I say in my best spiteful voice, although it never intimidates anybody.

"I'm listening." She says with a huge grin on her face. She is getting everything she wants.

"You and your team have to stay behind as backup so I can at least check out what we are dealing with before anybody gets hurt." She nods. I guess we finally found a compromise she agrees with. Shocking.

"Ok. Then let me grab the food and I'll be right back." She spins around and sprints towards the pantry. I find my bike and lean against it, waiting for Aiko to get here so she can move the damn truck.

"You look good on that bike." I spin around to see Idri standing there with an expressionless face. I don't think he will ever be in a state of being that prevents him from making fun of me.

"Your touch-ups were questionable. Remind me to teach you how to tinker with things." I smile and he smiles back. I haven't seen Idri in probably twenty hours. He basically hasn't left his room.

"Where are you headed?"

IVO

"To the coordinates your uncle handed me." I grimace as I realized I brought up a sore subject. "Hopefully we can find Za. I was just going to go by myself but Aiko parked this stupid truck in front of the entrance so I'm stuck with her and her beloved team." Hopefully I saved it. Idri seems unfazed by the mention of his uncle but if I had made peace with the destruction of my family and then all of a sudden one just popped up, I really don't know how that would make me feel.

"Can I come?" Oh my god. Why is everyone begging to come with me? Of all people, I had ruled out Idri first. But we work so well together and I would feel much better with him around. I mean, Aiko is great. But she's always interfering with my plans.

"Of course you can. But we are about to leave and you look like crap. No offense of course." He really does though. He has his stained pajamas on, his hair is a far cry from his usual groomed mini-afro, and it's evident that he hasn't taken a shower from where I'm standing and I'm standing at least ten feet away from him.

"Just wait like five minutes. Please, Ivo. I really want to help you. I think reuniting you and your brother would really help me deal with things." I give him a nod.

"Hurry up!" He turns around and rushes towards his bedroom, passing Aiko down the hall who is carrying way too many food rations.

"Aiko. We aren't leaving for the rest of our lives. If it goes according to plans then we will literally be there only for the day. In other words, we will only miss lunch." Everything she does is a little much. Her tendency to kill any enemy on sight without hesitation, her planning, and she certainly has a problem with managing and gauging quantities.

"I just don't want anybody to get hungry," she retorts.

"The food is going to go bad if it has to live in the truck all day." She chuckles.

"Fine, I'll put some back. And what was Idrissa doing up so early?"

"He's coming."

"He's what?!" She exclaims.

"Why are you so surprised? He was always going to come. He just waited until the last minute."

"Oh, so he just gets to ask you and then all of a sudden he's part of the mission. I have to beg on my hands and knees to just bring some damn food." She's got a little bit of a point.

"Because you come with baggage. Baggage that includes enough rations for a small nation and a team of twenty people. Plus you leave blood everywhere that sword goes." That really shuts her up. She sulks as she offloads twenty percent of the food into the truck and drops the rest of the packages on the ground. She gives me a grumpy face before climbing in the driver's seat of the truck. Idri comes running down the hall, now showered with his classic black cargo pants and bullet proof vest.

"Ok. Now I'm ready." He says as he hops into the Camry. "Except I think someone took all of my guns." I try to hold back a laugh as he realized I have a duffel bag over my shoulder. He's about to complain but the entrance opens and the truck drives out.

"You are so annoying. I can't believe you took all of my guns." He says over the rumble of the truck going up the ramp.

"Sorry, I can't hear you!" I yell as I put on my helmet and pull out, grinning. I did some tinkering of my own last night with this helmet and my suit. I first programmed the coordinates into the helmet's built-in GPS system. But I also made some modifications to the helmet and bike so that it works well with my suit. If I need to, my suit can morph with the bike and kind of tuck me into a more aerodynamic shell. Plus the suit knows when I have a helmet on so it attaches to the helmet and then stops. My dream is to somehow have a bike like this one be generated by something like my necklace. I'm almost positive that's something the Board is already working on. Too bad I know that I could make it better. The coordinates lead us just outside the state so our drive should only take at most an hour. Once we get outside of the city, I swerve in front of the truck so they can follow me. I purposely didn't give anyone else the location because I didn't want anyone going without me.

We mostly drive in silence for a while. Everything is that of a city landscape but all of the buildings are pretty much owned by the same people. It's kind of freaky, like we are driving in a loop. Eventually we get closer to the coordinates, fewer buildings around now. Suddenly grass and trees open up, a rare sight to see. We almost never see a forest, and even though this isn't the forest it used to be, it's still nice to see. We turn off the highway and onto a small dirt road. We drive, trees flanking us on either side, and sun-dappled shadows of overarching branches on the road. Then we are there. But there is nothing except a strange, open meadow. I pull off the road which stops ten feet ahead, so there is nowhere else to go. I hop off of the bike and get out, Aiko and Idri do the same.

"This is it?" Idri says as he walks towards me. Aiko is just standing in the middle of the road, head turning around.

"These are the exact coordinates." I reply, wondering the same thing as everyone else.

"Where is it then?" Idri says, as he starts to wander around the meadow. "Maybe my uncle was wrong."

"I don't think he was," Aiko replies as she walks up from behind us. "See the middle of the meadow. It has indents from helicopters and planes landing here. Someone is interested in this location."

"So you think it's underground?" I ask.

"Possible, but it would have been a massive project to make an underground base here from scratch."

"I'm getting mixed signals here." Idri walks back over to us. "Are we in the right place or not? And if we are in the right place, then shouldn't we be hiding."

"Hiding from who? There isn't anyone for miles in sight. No one lives in nature anymore. You can't survive," I reply. "Ok, let's think about this. If the location is correct, then it must be underground. And if it's underground, then we have to find something that can trigger an entrance, or at least find proof of electricity or human life." Idri and Aiko both nod.

"Aiko, go tell the team, so they can help us look." Idrissa and I head out into the middle of the meadow, the long grass coming up to our knees, while Aiko goes back to the truck. We both crouch down and start scouring the ground, looking for anything unnatural. I touch the grass, which is pretty wet.

"Idri, has it rained recently?"

"No, hasn't rained in the area in a while. There's been somewhat of a drought. Why do you ask?"

"Because the grass is wet."

"Oh yeah, that is weird. Probably just morning dew or something, moisture doesn't always have to come from rain." Then I feel a drop on my back, and then more.

"Is it raining?" Idri asks. He puts his hand out in the air and we see drops fall on his palm. I look up through the rain, my hair starting to get wet and stick to my head. I see Aiko just getting people out of the truck.

"Aiko," I yell. "Go back inside the truck, it's starting to rain!" She has a very confused expression on her face.

"No it's not!" she replies. Holding up her completely dry hair to prove her point. Idri and I look at each other in complete astonishment. It's raining in the meadow. But thirty feet away, on the road, it's not raining.

We both get up and run towards the cars. As soon as we start getting to the edge of the meadow and onto the road, we both stop feeling the rain drops against our backs. Our feet hit the completely dry dirt of the road and my eyes dart to the blank windshield of the Camry, not a drop on it.

"Jeez. You guys are soaked. Ivo, what the hell is going on?" Aiko asks as the team of twenty just stares at us in utter confusion.

"Now I'm really lost." Idri says as he grabs two white towels out of his car and hands one to me. I wrap it around my shoulders after drying my hair.

"This can't be the weather, because the weather just doesn't do this."

"Sometimes if there is moisture on the exterior of a helicopter or plane, it will drip down." Aiko remarks.

"Yeah, but we would have heard a plane or helicopter, the Board hasn't made them completely silent yet." Idri says. Both of them look towards me as if I have the answers to everything.

"What?"

"Well you're the science and technology guy. So if anybody can figure this one out, then you can." I just smirk. I know I can figure this out, but it might take some time to do so. Suddenly I hear the chopping of air coming from a helicopter.

"Now that is the sound of a helicopter," Idri says. He peeks his head out and looks up. "Specifically a military helicopter. Ivo, we've got to go."

"Everyone back in the truck, we are going back!" Aiko tells her team. I grab my helmet and jump onto my bike, driving ahead of the Camry and truck as both of them follow me. I guess I'm going to have to figure this one out at home. I'm hoping that if I hack the Board database, it might have information I could use. We rush home, all of us speeding. Getting that close to the Board freaks everyone out. Thankfully, we don't run into anyone else on our way home. It helps that I use as many side roads as possible.

When we get back, I head immediately to the lab and computers. I hack into the Board database but there is no record of a building there. Not even any construction. I made sure that no other parties were hired to work on something there and all I could find was that a cargo plane had been used in that area a while ago. They make a lot of noise so there was a noise complaint from a citizen. But other than that, there is nothing. I lean back in my chair, thinking. The drops we felt could not have been rain. So the only way that could happen was from condensation. But it was way too much water for it to be condensation from a plane or a helicopter, plus we would have heard if either of those had flown above us. It would have to be something large. Oh no. I rush into Idri's room. Aiko is also there, talking to him.

"I figured it out."

"Well that was quick." Aiko says looking up.

"Well I guess I won the bet then." Idri says towards Aiko. He turns towards me. "We bet on how long it would take you to figure it out. I just won myself some money. Thanks for being so smart, Ivo." He grins at me, obviously way too happy with himself.

"Shut up Idrissa and let Ivo explain himself." They both look up at me.

"Ok. So the rain thing was weird. We knew it couldn't be rain so it must've been condensation. But it couldn't have been condensation from a helicopter or plane because we would have heard those and there was way too much water." I know I'm going way too fast and they aren't keeping up but I needed to get it out. "And I looked it up and the only construction-like thing that was brought to that area in the last five years was a cargo plane. The building that we are looking for is in the air, floating above the clouds. The cargo plane was bringing stuff up for constructions and supplies. And the marks that Aiko saw on the meadow were from the building's base taking off with thrusters. The water we felt was the condensation from the entire building being released." I'm almost out of breath by the end of that.

"Woah." Aiko and Idri say in unison.

"How the hell are we supposed to stealthily infiltrate a floating building?" Idri asks, discouraged.

"We'll figure that out later. For now, we need some rest." Aiko says. "I have a feeling tomorrow is going to be a long day."

We all head out to our rooms. I take off my necklace and sit on my bed. If what I'm saying is actually true, then we have our work cut out for ourselves. I really hope Za is in there.

ZA

MARCH 21, 2031

It's my first mission today and I'm stressed. I've been poking at my waffles for ten minutes. On one hand, I think my team is ready. Actually, I know my team is ready. But I don't know if I'm ready. It's one thing teaching them how to fight like me. But I'm not my brother. I'm not good at organizing or leading a group of people. If we don't succeed, I die. So those are my options. Death or success.

We leave in fifteen minutes so everyone else already left to get ready. They are like robots. Eat, train, sleep. I'm in the private cafeteria which is open and modern with professional chefs that make whatever we want. Usually, I can't get enough of these waffles, perfectly golden brown with just the right amount of fruit, syrup, and whipped cream, food I haven't had in years. But now, the waffle is soggy, the white of the whipped cream slowly dissipated into the waffle, and the syrup became dark brown streaks across the waffle. I decide that it's pointless just sitting here so I get up and go to my room. It's painful for me to waste food.

Walking into my room, I still can't believe that it's all for me. When I was first asked to bring my things from the bunks and come live here, I thought that we were making a pit stop to talk to the general. Low and behold they basically gave me an entire suite. There is a mini-kitchen with a large king size bed, with teal sheets, my favorite. There is a large television on top of a mantel with a fireplace, all sitting in front of a large couch. Glass looking out to the interior levels, tinting with just the press of a button, is the icing on the cake. Our house in Boston was never as nice as this. It got me curious to see what mission I would be going on. Seeing how they are treating me, it must be some important stuff.

I walk towards the right side of my bed, opening up my walk-in closet, barely full. I grab my ops outfit which is the classic black cargo pants with a long sleeve black shirt and military vest. I still prefer wearing a good pair of sneakers over military boots, so that's what I slide on over my black socks. I actually never got used to wearing black. I preferred how I looked in white. Plus, blue is my favorite color. But Ivo told me that wearing black would conceal me better in the shadows and drew less attention. Now, it's just become a habit to walk out the door wearing as much black as possible.

I walk towards the mantel and slide its right corner. The mantel splits in the middle, each side circling behind the shelf and pushing out all of my new toys. This is the hidden weapons closet, and probably the best thing to happen to me since I've been at The Maze. I got all of the bells and whistles. All of the new spy tech and all of the new guns. My brother would be jealous of the amount of technology in this stuff. I have to admit, some of this stuff is better than the weapons my brother used to tinker and make, and that's saying a lot. All of the high-tech weaponry that my brother and I used to chase and find is here. Turns out, this is where all of the shipments were going for soldiers that were going to be in a team like the one I'm leading. I grab a couple guns, including a pistol and rifle, and then reach towards the more interesting things.

First, is the spark grenade, at least that's what I call it. It's a small grenade that, when activated, releases ten more bombs in all different directions. You never know when you really just need to blow stuff up. After putting that in my right pants' pocket near my knee, I grab two knives that can transform into swords and attach them to my belt. Finally, the holy grail. Custom-made for my team, they call it the Rod. Wicked stupid name if you ask me, but what it does is ridiculous. It's a small matte black cylinder with a diameter of about an inch and a half, really dense for its size. The Rod is pulled apart to generate a staff kind of thing that can be customized by the user. I like mine blunt, but some of my soldiers have their's sharp. The best part is, the Rod can also generate a vehicle. They call it a Hover Bike. Basically it's an electric cycle but the wheels have each been split vertically in half, each facing the ground, and now located at the side of the vehicle. They are like thrusters that are very flexible, so can go in many different directions. It's a real fun to ride in the gym, and should be even better on the mission. I grab my customized one, which has the ability to control everyone else's, and attach it to my back. The only thing that would make this better is if we had one of those fancy suits that forms around your body. But apparently that was stolen. Kind of a bummer, I would have liked to play with one of those. I close up the mantel, and just as I'm walking towards the door with my rifle around my shoulder, someone knocks on the door.

"Come in!" I shout across the suite. In walks General Lee.

"Are you ready for your first mission?" He asks. He has increasingly become softer and gentler with me. Less like a general and more like an advisor. The change is probably because I've been putting all of my effort into the team, not fighting back against his order. After all, I could die at any moment with the mechanism they have on me. A couple days after wearing that suicide vest, it was replaced by a thin attachment over my chest. Same use, smaller package.

"My team and I are very ready. We've been training hard for this first mission." I reply confidently. Even with my doubts about my mentality, I can lean on my soldiers who are the best of the best. Usually when generals say that, they are just using rhetoric. But General Lee wasn't kidding this time, these guys are the real deal.

"That's fantastic to hear." He smiles in satisfaction and continues. "Here's how it's going to work. I'm going to give you a very thorough briefing of the mission. And then you communicate to your team however you see fit. Sounds good?" I nod. I actually don't agree with this approach as I'd rather have everyone know what's going on at the highest level possible, but complaining wouldn't change anything.

"Ok, let's get started then." He hands me a folder which I open and start to flip through as General Lee starts explaining the mission. "Some international fugitives have stolen a very important item from the Board. You don't need to know what it is but the operation will be difficult. These criminals took a boat from Europe and are now trying to steal weapons from the Board to take back to their home countries. We think that these countries are preparing to declare war on the United States." This is interesting news. No one messes with the United States. But other countries do have the means to do so, especially if they get their hands on our weapons technology, and if they disagree with US policy. I refocus my mind back on the mission and my face stays expressionless.

"Currently they have a base further up the east coast near Canada, right by the water. Your mission is to take out their vessels so they can't leave our borders and retain the property of the United States government. Take out as many of the criminals as possible but we don't know how many there are. From our intel, there is anywhere from thirty to one hundred men. You will see in the folder that we have gotten a picture of the organizer of the group. He should be taken out at all costs. Is the mission clear?"

"Yes, General." I say as I examine the picture of the man, trying to memorize the face. He has long gray hair and is pictured with a maniacal smirk on his face. His grey stubble facial hair completes the criminal look.

"Ok, then. Your team is waiting for you at the landing pad and best of luck to you all." He walks out the door and down the hallway. My room is in the fifth cube so making my way towards the inner cube takes some time. I pass through the cube with the gym and then walk through the cafeteria for labor workers. As I walk through the second cube, a couple of prisoner heads turn as they growl at me. They are probably wondering why I'm so special. Why I get to hang out with the general and have my own room while they work all day, everyday. The ironic thing is, I would rather be in their position. At least I would then have my life in my own hands. I might have all of the food and space that I want, but I don't have the control or choices that I want.

I finally make it to the launch pad, where each of my twenty super soldiers are already in the plane with their seatbelt on. It's bizarre to me that we are taking a plane to this mission. After all, we could just drive there. Now that I think about it, everybody takes a plane off of this thing. There are no windows when I get strapped in and, after giving the pilot the thumbs up, we take off.

For probably twenty minutes, I am positive that we are going in circles. I'm not a prisoner this time, so the fact that they are still paranoid about the location is strange. We are flying for an hour before we start moving. We all get out and immediately feel an ocean breeze. I haven't seen the ocean in what feels like ages. I used to love hanging out there with my parents, although Ivo always stayed inside. It's too bad that sightseeing isn't in the itinerary for the mission. I turn towards my team, who are all geared up and waiting for directions. It's like they're robots. I tried to have normal conversations with these guys, asking them where they are from, how old they are, and that kind of stuff but I got stonewalled every single time. So I gave up.

"Ok. Here is the deal. Based on the coordinates that I have been given, we are about three miles out from the target. The enemy is a group of criminals from Europe who have stolen government property. Not only do we need that property back, but we need to destroy their vessels and kill this man." I hold up the picture. "We do not know how many men are there, but use lethal force on as many as possible. Five of you will come with me while the others split up. We don't know where the Board property is being held, so radio that in as soon as you can see it." They all nod towards me. It's interesting talking in the general kind of voice. I'm surprised they didn't laugh at my lack of military terminology.

I start running at a jog and slowly build up pace. Pulling the Rod from behind my back, I separate it and a hover bike forms beneath me. Landing on it safely, buttons on the Rod appear on each side, becoming handles and controls. I look behind my shoulder to see my team following my lead and speed towards the criminal base. It only takes a few minutes to get there and when we are a third of a mile out, I disengage the cycle and we start walking towards them. Each of the soldiers has a unique skill set, which I helped to utilize. The criminals might be prepared to fight military forces but we aren't trained like them nor do we fight like them. We fight like vigilantes except that we are highly skilled. They all know their groups. The soldiers that will always come with me are the scientist, the shooter, the health specialist, the massive guy, and the combat guy. I like having people that can do what I can't do. Everyone else can handle themselves without me.

When we approach the base, we hide behind bushes. The base is a series of metal buildings surrounded by thick foliage. The edge of the base has a dock where I count ten ships. I give the signal and we head out. As we get closer we see where the guards are. About five guard each of the seven buildings and some more scattered about. By the look of it, they don't have very good weapons and don't seem highly trained. I send the other two teams towards the middle of the base and the others guys and I head towards the dock. I start to hear gunfire behind me as we approach the dock, weaving between buildings, and crouching behind structures as we get closer.

The dock has two soldiers on each side. I pull out my two knives as I approach the right two who notice us and start to aim their guns. I throw the knives at them before they can fire their weapons. Meanwhile two more soldiers each pull out their pistols and hit both of the other guards—headshots. We go towards the dock before I have an idea. I put up a fist to tell the soldiers behind me to stop. I reach down into my right leg pocket and grab the spark grenade. If this works, I'm a legend. I activate it and slowly roll it out into the middle of the dock. It tosses ten more grenades, one going onto each of the ten boats, and I cover my ears as the dock and all of the ships explode at the same time. God, I love technology.

We are making our way back towards the middle of the base when a radio comes into our ear coms.

"We found the Board property, it's in a small silver crate in building number six but is heavily guarded. Requesting backup."

"We are headed your way." I reply. All of us start to run faster towards building number six which is on the opposite end of the camp. Guards start trying to stop us but we all have our weapons up and ready to fire. We finally make our way to the building but when we get there I see someone getting in a car behind the building and starting to drive away. I was going to leave it alone before I saw the long silver hair. Damnit.

"You guys go ahead. I'm going to get this guy." They all start to file into the building while I take a sharp right down the side. The guy looks behind his shoulder and starts the car, then accelerates. Too bad he's not getting away. I pull out the Rod again and rush after him. He's following a faint dirt road that seems to be going straight inland so I veer off and weave through trees, making a large arc before turning right in front of the car. The car brakes suddenly and the guy clumsily tries to get out of the car and escape.

"Please. You don't understand. You're on the wrong side." He says as he starts to crawl away desperately. "You don't want to kill me. I am trying to save people."

"I'm sorry, but I'm not acting on my own free will." I'm doing what will keep me alive. I look away as I pull out my pistol and shoot him. I hate killing people, despise it. But it's either I complete this mission, or the only hope of the Migrants gaining any kind of internal power within the Board is killed with the press of a button. I hover back to the base where my men are all waiting, one of them holding the silver crate. He goes to open it.

"Don't open that. That's not part of the mission." We head back to the plane which takes us back towards the base, landing after another hour of circling around. When we get out, General Lee is there to greet us. I hand him the silver crate.

"Well done Zashil. I am very pleased with your results. Please rest and congratulate your team on a well-executed mission." I barely manage a nod. I have no energy left. Passing through the levels, I stop to eat at the cafeteria. I'm suddenly starving and I choose to eat some Indian food that somewhat reminds me of home. After finishing up, I make my way to my room in the fifth cube. I'm about to unlock the door with my iD but I just hesitate. Looking at the iD, I realize I have clearance everywhere in this place and I've been so hard at work that I haven't had a chance to explore yet.

    I decide that I deserve a bit of exploration before heading to bed so I keep walking through the cubes. The next one over is where the general sleeps and where other government officials stay while they are visiting. The one beside is a massive lab. I peek through the windows to see scientists hard at work on various things from weapons to biology. I should talk to some of those people sometime. I keep walking. The next one is just storage. And finally I get to what seems like the last layer, cube nine. I walk through it and see that there are exits to what seems like a balcony. Excited to breath fresh air and possibly see where we are, I jog towards the glass door, pushing it open.

    Immediately my face is hit with a gust of wind and I walk towards the railing, excited to look down. But to my horror, I see nothing. Looking forward, I see the sun in the distance and a layer of clouds passing through The Maze. The exterior is covered in condensation. I look left and right while walking the entire perimeter of The Maze before I let it sink in. I still have no idea where we are. Because we could be anywhere. I really am stuck here. And until I learn to fly, it's going to take a miracle to get me out. Never in a million years would I have thought that I'd be stuck on a floating prison.

IVO

MARCH 24, 2031

"Found one!" Aiko shouts from the lab. I run out of my room and Idri joins up with me halfway down the hallway. We've spent three days just researching nearby hangars and air fields where we can find a helicopter or a plane. And that research doesn't include us finding a pilot. Idri claims that he was taught how to fly but Aiko and I both agreed that we aren't putting twenty people's lives in the hands of Idri, that would just be poor judgment.

"Where?" I ask as I run into the lab and towards the computer station to the right of the room. Recently, Aiko has been even more committed than I have been to find a way into the floating prison. She's been crouched over the computer for hours, without food or water.

"Well it's on the East Coast." She replies.

"That's great!" Idri remarks. "I'll go get the cars ready."

"The only thing is, I don't recognize the coordinates." Aiko looks towards me with that same look. The you-have-the-answer-to-everything look.

"Let me see." I lean over Aiko's shoulder and glance at the coordinates, 42.3245° N, 70.9859° W. Then I pull my phone out of my back pocket and punch those in. It takes forever to load even though the coordinates aren't far from Boston. Slowly the map zooms in from the view of the country and when I'm about to let out a sigh of relief as it goes towards the coast of Massachusetts, it veers right into the Atlantic Ocean, to a small island. On my map it's colored in blue, showing that it's completely government property and requires permission for access. I turn my phone around and show Idri and Aiko.

"Well, that doesn't bode well. Are you sure you didn't find any other aircraft locations, Aiko?"

"I'm sure. This is the only one I found where aircrafts are easily accessible."

"Well, not easy enough. I know you guys think I'm capable of it but I'm telling you now that I can't single handedly take out an entire military base with just a few guns." Idri chimes in.

"We never ever thought you were anywhere close to being that good." Aiko jokes. I chuckle at their argument before thinking to myself: what's the best way to infiltrate an island? This is a tough one to say the least. The fact is we have to infiltrate a floating base on water in order to then attack another floating base. How do I get myself in these situations?

"Guys, let's focus." I urge. "We are going to need a boat so does anybody have any idea how to make that happen?" Boats aren't really a thing anymore. There are no recreational activities on boats that survived the Takeover. And all ocean territory has been claimed by nation states, meaning that the only boats in the country are ones that are owned by the United States government.

"We could just make a raft and float there." Idri comments.

"C'mon Idrissa. We need real ideas. Stop messing around." Aiko scolds him.

"What if we just go check out the dock where the boats are coming to and from the island? Then we can get a better sense of what we need." I say. They both nod towards me.

"Just us this time." I add as I eye down Aiko. I don't need to march up to the dock with twenty bodyguards.

"Fine. But I still get to come, right?"

"Yeah, as long as you don't slow us down." Idri jokes as he lightly punches Aiko in the shoulder and walks out of the lab. Sometimes they glare at each other, sometimes they joke around. I just don't get it. I look at Aiko and we both smile before following Idri to the garage. We all climb in the red Camry, Idri driving and Aiko in the backseat.

"Hold on a sec." I run back to my room, grabbing Idri's duffel bag which is still full of weapons from our last outing and I quickly put the necklace on around my neck. I run back and jump into the passenger seat, throwing the duffel bag backwards into Aiko's lap.

"We never know what we might come up against and I'd rather not be unarmed."

"Good call," Idri says as we drive out of the base and start making our way towards the coast.

When we get closer, we park the car off to the side behind some small houses. Slowly, we survey the area and find a place to take cover. The dock is a semi-circle extending from the coast. It curves around with smaller rectangular docks stemming out at perfect intervals. We crouch behind large wooden crates, away from the water.

"Now what?" Aiko whispers into my ear. She's sitting to my right, both of us having our backs against the crates. Meanwhile, Idri is on the other side of the stack, craning his neck with his binoculars held up, facing the ocean.

"I guess we'll wait." I replied. "Idri." I lean over Aiko and tap Idri on the shoulder, getting his attention. He turns back and puts his binoculars down. "What do you see?"

"It looks like there is a sizable ship coming towards the coast. Based on the direction it's coming from, I'm guessing it's the transport vessel between the island and the mainland." I nod as I lean back against the crates. If it's a big enough ship, I'm thinking that our way in is by sneaking onto the transport and hoping to god we find a plane on the island without being caught. The only downside is that we could hypothetically be trapped on the island without any food or water.

"The ship's getting closer." Idri whispers over to Aiko and me. "We need a plan because I'm pretty sure these are the only crates on this dock so we know where they are headed as soon as they get here."

"Yeah, I think I got it." I start to explain. "We need to let whoever is guarding the ship get out so we know who and how many we are dealing with. I think that if we are stealthy enough we can probably make our way onto the ship and find a place to hide. It shouldn't be too long of a trip. But the emphasis is on stealthy." I look up to get their reactions and Idri is just staring down Aiko. "Am I missing something?" I ask.

"Well Aiko is not the most stealthy to say the least." Idri says, still staring Aiko down who is making direct eye contact with Idri. I have never known Aiko to be not stealthy, apart from her having to always bring a team everywhere she goes. I'm still a little annoyed by that. She almost never uses the sword around her back. It's almost if that's just for decoration at this point. I guess I'm going to have to ask them about that later because I hear the docking of the boat followed by the shuffling of feet.

"Alright. Everyone ready?" They both nod and I point towards a ladder that lowers down from the dock. I can't confirm that there is anything below the dock—most times there is another lower platform for smaller boats. But I'm completely basing that assumption off of my very limited research of government docks.

I start scurrying off to the ladder which is to the right of the dock. I take a quick glance over my shoulder to make sure everyone is following me, confirming that Aiko is still carrying the duffel bag full of weapons around her shoulder, and then I quickly look over to see where the ship is. It's docked pretty much at the center stem.

Once we get to the ladder I start to hear voices in the distance and immediately hop down. To my delight, there is a lower platform beneath the dock. We have to crouch down but it's better than having to swim. We start making our way towards the center of the dock. The splashing of the water against the shore and the smell of sea water is all I can sense but I try my best to listen for anybody walking above us. We are almost there when I see four shoes through cracks right above us. I put my hand up to tell Aiko and Idri to stop. I quietly listen to what they are saying.

"Did you hear that? It sounds like something is underneath us." I wince at the prospect of us not even making it to the ship. The voice is a deep male voice with a thick southern accent. The other guy has a similar accent but his voice is slightly higher.

"Nah, it's probably like some animal or something. No one ever wants to sneak into our butthole of an island. Don't worry about it. I just wanna get this shipment of supplies and get back to my house, all of this movement is making me exhausted. I swear, they don't pay us enough for this crap." I let out a sigh of relief.

I try my best to look through the cracks and discern if the soles of their shoes are military boot soles but they just look like normal sneakers. If it wasn't for the mention of someone paying them, I would think that these two guys don't even work for the Board. After all, the Board has become so orderly since the Takeover that almost everyone that works for them, no matter how far down the food chain, are always in some kind of uniform and definitely don't complain about their quality of life. I look back at Aiko who is directly behind me, her mouth being covered by Idri's hand. I really gotta ask why Idri is so paranoid about Aiko on missions like this. They both shrug as though to say don't worry about it and just keep going. I see the footsteps moving away and, as soon as I hear the sound of their feet hitting the wooden planks of the dock start to fade, we travel the final twenty feet to the middle of the dock.

There is another ladder leading back up to the top; this time it's silver metal. I put up my finger towards Idri and Aiko as I move towards the ladder. I climb it ninety percent of the way, just far enough so that my head peeks over the floor of the dock. The two guys both have military weapons, so now we know they are definitely working for the Board, but they are pretty low-grade it seems. Both of them are occupied loading the crates we were hiding behind onto a pallet jack so I wave my hand down and usher Idri and Aiko to come up. I waited for them both to be on the dock, then we quickly run onto the ship. It is big with a large cubicle in the center. We crouch behind there while all of us look around for a better place to hide. I see a hatch near the end of the ship, facing the water and I crawl over to it. Opening it, I see that there is just a bunch of junk and stuff. It looks like the space is just used for storage. Holding the hatch open, I signal to Idri and Aiko to head down the steep steps. I follow them, closing the hatch above me.

"I can't believe that actually worked." Idri whispers over to Aiko and I, who are leaning against a bunch of soup cans that are taped together. He starts to sit across from us, himself resting against a few crates similar to the ones we were hiding behind on the dock.

"What, you didn't believe in my plan?" I remark.

"Let's just say I was prepared to take the ship by force. But your plan ended up being way better. Plus, these guys don't seem very dangerous or threatening." Idri replies.

"Well thanks for the vote of confidence Idri."

"Yeah no problem. Anytime." He grins at me, knowing that he's getting under my skin. I just look away. Looks like his mood has improved sufficiently. Soon enough, we hear footsteps above us again, the sound of the engines going and eventually we are moving, leaning back and forth as the water passes beneath us. It only takes thirty minutes for us to get to the base and we wait for a few minutes until I am sure that the two guys are off and gone.

"Ok, let's make this as quick as possible. It would be best if we didn't have to use these." I gesture towards Aiko who's holding Idri's duffel bag. We climb back up the ladder and make our way off the ship. The island is very much developed. Three massive metal buildings are centered on the island with ramps coming out in all directions. We start walking closer as we use cars, crates, and trees as cover.

"There!" Idri says. He has his binoculars out again. He's pointing off to the left, where a large hangar is open at the building to the far left. He hands me the binoculars and I take a look before handing them to Aiko. That hangar has at least ten small military planes.

"Let's head over there. Hopefully they don't have any guards for the planes. But I doubt it, seeing how we haven't seen a single other soul. For all we know, we have already met the only people at this base." I suggest.

"I wouldn't be too sure about that, Ivo. If this is in fact a government base, then we should expect a lot more people." Idri comments as we start heading towards the hangar. We are about halfway there, walking along the side of an empty driveway, when I spot a sign across the road. It directs pilots in the opposite direction for "Pilot Check-in and Training."

"We might have a problem." I say as I turn towards Idri and Aiko who had kept walking and are now ten feet in front of me. They start to stroll back.

"What is it?" Aiko asks.

"See that sign." They both look as I keep talking. "It says that the pilots are going to be on the opposite side of the base. And unless we are suddenly putting our lives in the hands of Idri, we need one of them. What I'm saying is that I think we need to split up."

"Yeah, that's not a good idea." Idri replies, worried. "How are we supposed to know if you've been hurt or captured? We have no means of communication."

"Yeah, for once I agree with Idrissa." Aiko adds.

"This is the only way. Plus, we don't need communication if we have a good plan. How about this: Aiko and I will go find a pilot, because that is probably going to be more difficult. And then Idri can go and take hold of a plane. Once Aiko and I have found someone that is compliant, then we'll bring them to the hangar." While I'm talking, Idri has taken out his binoculars and is looking back at the hangar.

"Yeah, I think we might have to revise your plan, Ivo. A bunch of soldiers just showed up near the plane. They aren't doing anything but I have a feeling it's going to have to get violent. I think Aiko should come with me and you can go find a pilot, which shouldn't be as difficult or involve any shooting." That's surprising. Aiko and Idri never want to be paired up. But his plan does make more sense.

"Ok, let's do that. I'll meet you guys back at the hangar. And please try not to kill anybody. Just knock them out." They both nod and keep walking towards the hangar. I sprint across the street, crossing a lawn, and then put my back against the middle building. I crane my neck up and see a security camera panning to each side. It seems like standing against the building is in its blind spot so I slowly shuffle against the wall, towards the building to the right of the base. The entire side of this main building is completely flat with no windows, so I think it's the back of the building which makes me more reassured that I shouldn't run into anybody.

Finally, after several minutes of shuffling with my back uncomfortably flat against the wall, I make it to the corner of the main building. Inching towards the edge, I look for the pilot building and see it across from me, but separated by a dirt road that's about fifteen feet wide. I check both ways before crossing the road and immediately putting my back against the wall again. I'm on the back right corner of the pilot building and this time there are windows that start right above my head when I'm standing. This building is significantly smaller than the other buildings in terms of surface area as well as the fact that it is only one floor. I grab the windowsill with my fingertips and slowly lift my body slightly up, just enough so I can see through the window which is thankfully not one way glass. It's a large open space, with airplane simulators to the far right side and a desk to the left. At first I see the backs of current pilots, with badges on the upper arms of their uniform. But when one of the three steps away, I'm shocked to see who they are training.

The pilots in training are all kids of color, some brown and others black, all wearing the same grey Air Force academy t-shirt with black sweatpants. I can't quite tell if they are here in captivity or if they really are training of their own free will. I hop back onto the ground. The fact that they are people of color worries me about the Board's plans for the future, but it also means that I should have an easier time convincing one of them to come help us. I tap my necklace and crouch down as I wait for my suit to morph around me. I don't need anybody seeing my face and I don't know how many more armed soldiers were in my blind spots when I was looking through the window. I wait as the black synthetic material forms over me, followed by nano tech, before turning the opposite corner and walking along the left side of the building.

Peering around the corner, I don't see anybody guarding the door. There is no way that the guards will ever leave without the trainees with them, so waiting around is not an option. I take one more deep breath as I stand in front of the large metal door. Pushing the door open I generate two pistols in each of my hands and take aim at the three guards I saw through the window. They don't see me coming so I shoot them in the leg. While they collapse, I notice two armed guards, one in each corner. I roll through the middle of the room as they take aim and then reverse my position so that I'm crouching with my back to the back wall. I stretch out each arm and aim for the legs of both the guards, two shots from each gun is all it takes for them to crumple to the ground, each holding their legs in agony. Meanwhile, the trainees, each between fourteen and my age are scurrying back towards the door, every one of them still on their butt.

"I'm not here to hurt you. I am one of the leaders of the Migrants." I state as I deactivate my suit. A few jaws drop in awe as they see the guns drop to the floor and the suit slowly minimizes back into my necklace. "My friends and I infiltrated this island in order to acquire a plan for an important mission we have. However, we need a pilot. Are any of you comfortable flying and would like to help us. We are the only hope of kids like you ever living normal lives." All of them hesitate and some of them even get up and walk through the door. I'm not going to hurt any of them. And, while I do want to ask why they are here, that's going to have to be a question for whoever wants to join us. As more people file out of the building, I start getting nervous that I won't be able to find a pilot until a young boy, about Za's age, stands up and steps towards me.

"I'll help." He volunteers and I smile. He's a small skinny boy but looks mentally strong. His face is a similar brown tone to mine and his long dark hair swings around as he moves. "My name is Riz. My parents were captured from the Board and I want to help anybody that can get them out."

"Nice to meet you Riz. How well can you fly?" I ask, overjoyed that someone stepped forward but also slightly worried that this young boy is going to be flying the plane.

"I'm the best here by a long shot." He brags. As he finishes the sentence an alarm starts blaring.

"Good, cuz it looks like we have to get going." We run through the door and sprint as fast as we can back behind the buildings towards the hangar. They already know we are here so there is no point trying to find the blind spots of the cameras. It only takes us a couple of minutes to make it to the hangar where Aiko and Idri are waiting as they lean against a small military transport plane.

"What the hell is going on?" Aiko asks. "And who's the kid?"

"This is Riz, he's our pilot. And the whole stealth approach didn't go completely to plan." We all jump in the plane and Riz quickly fires it off. We are speeding down the runway well before the guards start shooting from behind us. Once we take off I let out a sigh of relief. The only problem is, we don't have a place to land.

LA

MARCH 24, 2031

The last three days have gone by in a daze. I haven't gone back to the balcony. And no one knows that I've been there, even though I have access so it's not like I was going against the law or anything. If my brother were here, he would be amazed at the technology. He would examine this entire place, coming up with a mental blueprint and an astute scientific explanation. But I just find it creepy how I'm in a floating building. And it's even worse that no other prisoner knows. This all explains the half an hour of circling every time we leave or come back on an aircraft. A part of me was still hopeful that I could somehow figure out a way to escape this place. Now that I know the only way out is by plane or helicopter, it's starting to hit me that I actually have to do this whole fight for your freedom thing that General Lee proposed forever. It sucks not to have anyone to talk to. I am quickly getting very lonely.

I'm laying horizontally across my couch, mulling everything over in my head while I stare unconsciously into the warm blazing fire in front of me. I'm twirling a knife around in my hand. It's crazy that only a couple years ago I hadn't ever seriously handled a weapon. Now it feels like I'm missing a body part whenever I don't have a weapon on me. I'm about to get up and head to dinner when, as if on cue, I get a knock on my door.

"Come in." I say, expecting the calm figure of General Lee to come in with a new mission brief or one of his daily check ins.

"I'd really rather not." A teenager's voice answers. Sounds about my age. Surprised, I get up and open the door. Three feet away from me stands a brown boy, maybe a year of two younger than me, with dark black wavy hair and piercing green eyes. He's wearing normal street clothes which immediately confuses me. I don't even wear normal street clothes and I can wear whatever I want. I'm about to welcome him but when I look up he looks almost frightened. His eyes staring at my right hand, horrified. I look down and realize that I'm still twirling the knife around in my hand.

"Oh my god. I'm so sorry." I say, scrambling to somehow put the knife away. I settle for awkwardly leaning down and setting the knife down on the floor. So much for a good first impression. "I'm obviously not going to hurt you. I just…I just had this in my hand before. It kind of helps me calm down and think." I shake my head as I realize I just made it so much worse. Now I sound like I'm an actual crazy person. He laughs as he notices my reaction to what I just said.

"No offense taken. Trust me." He holds up his hand, which is worn and scraped. Not what I expect from an innocent looking kid. "My name is Aziz. General Lee told me to come see you." This has never happened before but I open my door wider and gesture for him to come in.

"Please, sit anywhere you'd like." I tell him as I close the door behind me. He sits down on the couch while I drag a chair in from the kitchen. "So why are you here? Does General Lee need something?"

"Not exactly. He said you were the leader. I'm part of the team now, at least that's what they told me." He pulls up his yellow cotton t-shirt, revealing the same black bomb thing that they put on me.

"How did you get captured?" I ask.

"It was in the early days of the Takeover. We avoided the military for a while and we were in a migrant camp in Boston. But eventually, they found us. My entire family, mother, father, brother, and me, were out getting supplies when they spotted us. We didn't have any weapons, so we surrendered. My parents and I were brought to a prison while my brother was taken somewhere else. They said he had really good awareness and vision or something, whatever that means. We were at that prison for a few months before I was taken here." He's obviously nervous. His hands have a slight shake and his right hand keeps gripping and tugging at his left pointer finger. His right foot keeps tapping the ground and his back is completely straight. If there was any body position that screamed nervous more than this, I would be surprised.

"Not to be rude, but what's so special about you?" I'm about to elaborate on what I mean but he answers right away.

"I have a photographic memory. Which means, in terms of what's useful for the Board, I am literally the sharpest shooter you can find. Mostly because I memorized all of the science and math books I could find, meaning I can calculate every shot I take mathematically. Basically, I never miss." Well, I guess Aziz is joining the club of obscenely talented teenagers, along with me and my brother. You can count on General Lee to find these kids. It seems like he has quite the urge to utilize their abilities for the Board.

"I guess you're going to fit right in here." I reply, smiling. "I was just about to go to dinner, why don't you come with me. I'll show you how things work around here." We start to walk out of the room. "Oh, and just one more thing. Did you circle around in the plane for about thirty minutes before landing?"

"Yeah, thirty two actually. I looked at the clock. How did you know?"

"I'll tell you later." We head down the hallway to the private cafeteria for my team. We sit down at the nearest wooden table, and soon the chef comes over.

"Nice to see you Mr. Wolf. Who's your new friend." Chef Silva has been nice to me ever since I got here. I think he's nice to everyone, but something about his actions towards me makes me think it's been a while since he's seen kids. He looks like a Spanish guy, so I don't think he's here by force. But at this point, you never know. The Board put a damn suicide module on Aziz and I.

"It's nice to see you too, Chef Silva. This is Aziz and I think he'll be staying here for a while." Chef Silva smiles. He's not supposed to know about the team or anything like that. It's funny because, technically, I rank higher than him.

"It's nice to meet you Aziz. What would you like to eat today?" Aziz turns to me in shock. He leans over, across the table towards me, and whispers like Chef Silva can't hear him.

"Is this a test?" He asks.

"What? Why would this be a test?" He quickly glances at Chef Silva who is innocently smiling and waiting.

"I haven't gotten to choose food in like a year."

"Well now you can. I'll explain to you how things work around here. For now, just pick something to eat." He sits back in his chair like he's thinking before immediately leaning back over the table.

"Where's the menu?"

"There isn't one. He can make anything you want."

"Oh, ok." He leans back again. "Can I have Cheerios?" I slap my forehead.

"Yes...sir." Chef Silva replies, obviously confused and rightfully so. He turns towards me.

"I'll have my usual pizza. And excuse Aziz over here, he's just getting used to how things work."

"That's no problem Mr. Wolf. I'll be back soon with your meal." He spins around and heads back into the kitchen.

"Cheerios. Really. What are you five?"

"It's my favorite. And I haven't had them in forever."

"Hey, I'm not judging. Well I kind of am. But I'm not going to complain about your choices. I think it's time I tell you how things work. But first, tell me what you already know." I laugh a little to make him feel more comfortable. But I am questioning the maturity of this guy.

"I pretty much know nothing. I got here, and this weird guy, I think his name was Lee or something, started praising me and stuff. It was really weird. And then they slapped this thing on me." He points to his chest. "And then he told me to see you. What is this thing anyway?" That's not a lot at all. I guess I'm still more important to General Lee, as he told Aziz nothing.

"Ok. For one, that thing attached to your chest is a bomb. So yeah. You are now part of my team which means you've joined twenty other of the highest trained soldiers in the country. Your job is to help me to complete the mission. We fail, you die. You try to escape, which is not even possible, you die. Otherwise, you can pretty much do whatever you want. You can ask for whatever, and they will bring it. You have your own room now. But we train everyday for seven hours and you're still pretty much a prisoner. Did they give you an ID?"

"Yeah, it's in my pocket."

"That can get you into whatever level of this place that you want to. This is The Maze, so every level looks the same."

"Wow. That is a lot of information. So, basically I have been put in the highest security prison possible so that I can train to be on your team and complete missions for the Board or I die. But I can pretty much get whatever I want because they want me to think that I'm cool or whatever." Maybe I was wrong about this kid, he's kinda funny despite his young age. But, who am I to talk? I guess that's why he's not the leader.

"Yeah pretty much." The food is placed on our table—my pizza, a three cheese pizza with sausage and pineapple, and Aziz's bowl of cheerios with a cup of milk on the side. He pours the milk in, picks up his spoon, and is about to take his first bite when I add something. "Oh yeah. By the way, this place is floating." His metal spoon falls with a splash into his bowl.

"What? How is that even possible?"

"Long story. I just want to make sure you're not the idiot that actually tries to escape. Because unless you can fall hundreds of feet without dying, then you are most definitely stuck here." I pick up my pizza, pleased with myself that I caught him off guard. There is something very satisfying about that. I take my first bite, and Aziz follows after. We pretty much sit in silence which is fine by me. I really hope Aziz isn't the kind of kid I have to babysit.

16 MONTHS AGO

RIZ

DECEMBER 17, 2029

"Do we have to go Mama?" I complain, as I follow behind her. I'm getting pushed left and right as we swerve through the dense traffic of people. Aziz is in front because he is so sure that he remembers the signs that point to the airport. Mama doesn't answer of course. I don't want to go because America doesn't seem like the most appealing place to be right now.

"Yes, sweetheart, we have to go. Any place is better than India right now." She keeps saying that. Literally every time that Aziz and I complain she replies with that sentence. Not to mention the fact that Aziz and I both agree that America is not necessarily better than this. I look around as we head through the center of Kolkata, billboards everywhere are now covered with national messages and alerts. All of them have the British flag plastered across them with the words, "Welcome Back". As every other country goes through changes because of corporations taking over, everyone says we have it worse than most. I mean, we are one of the few actually being re-colonized, which I didn't think was a thing. Our government wasn't exactly going in the best direction. But at least it was still our government. That's why we are leaving. Our father left two years ago to find a job and make sure we would be safe there. We haven't heard from him in months, but then we saw the news. Baba is a very smart person, he taught at a university here in India as a professor. Once we saw what was happening in America, we were sure that he found refuge. It was then that Mama became so adamant about leaving. Aziz keeps saying he thinks it's a trap. That the British colonizers will just be waiting for us there. I believe him but there is absolutely nothing we can do to change Mama's mind. It is what it is now.

We keep walking the busy streets, once crowded with food stands and crazy rickshaw drivers. Everyone stares at us. No one is headed to the airport now. No country can be any kind of a new beginning right now. We are going to be prisoners here in India, and we will be prisoners anywhere else. The life of a brown person is definitely changing. I don't think we'll ever come back. I take a deep breath in to get the last smell of India and immediately regret it. I breathe in ninety percent dust, dirt, and car exhaust, which doesn't complement the turmeric and masala that hits me at the end from the few remaining street vendors.

After what seemed like hours of shoulder bumping work, but was realistically just ten minutes of walking down a street, we finally come up to Dum Dum airport at the edge of the city. It's a stark contrast from what it used to be. For once, I can actually see ten feet in front of me, and taxi drivers aren't fighting each other just to take a tourist through the streets without killing people. Aziz walks behind Mama and comes up towards me as she rummages through her purse for passports and tickets.

"I told you I could do it." Aziz always has to brag about his skill. It's not even a skill. It's not like he trained himself to have photographic memory.

"Yeah, whatever. Congratulations, you finally did one thing right." He punches me lightly in the shoulder and we both laugh. It's not like I don't have my skills. My awareness of my surroundings is second to none. If Aziz and I were one person, we would be a heck of a person.

"Let's go boys. I found the passports." It still amazes me that it takes Mama so long to find things in her own small purse. We keep walking, Mama dropping a few crumpled candy wrappers on the ground, collateral damage from her intense rummaging through her bag. We push through the revolving doors and step onto the slippery white marble floors. We weave through the empty line dividers. I have a backpack on and Aziz is rolling our one carry-on suitcase. I really hope not burning anything won't come around to bite us later. We make our way to the check-in desk, but no one is there. A small silver bell sits on the counter and Mama taps on it, sending an echoing ring through the entire terminal. After five minutes an Indian woman makes her way to the desk.

"Hi. How are you doing today?"

"Good. We have a flight departing in two hours." Mama hands her the passports and tickets.

"Oh. That won't be necessary." The lady replies, pushing the passports back across the counter. She then takes the tickets, crumples them up, and tosses them into the chain-link recycling can next to her.

"Excuse me?" Mama asks, starting to panic.

"All transportation by air is about to be completely under the jurisdiction of the Board. So any existing flights will just be boarded and then depart. There is no need for any tickets or anything like that. If you want to leave the country then we won't stop you." Wow. I guess people really don't believe in going anywhere.

Confused, Mama turns around and starts to walk towards security. We follow her and continue to walk through the empty security checkpoint. I guess not even criminals want to leave the country. We make our way towards the correct terminal, passing empty stalls and restaurants. Only half the lights are turned on and the sound of our feet stepping on the glossy floor is all we can hear. It is eerie. When we get to the right place, no one is there to greet us for boarding. Instead, the door is open and we walk the boarding ramp onto the plane, the air pressure hissing through the cracks. Mama guides us to the back where our seats are. No one else is here so I don't see why we have to sit in the cheap seats next to the bathroom but Aziz and I don't complain. We sit down and, before we can even get buckled, the plane starts moving.

"Welcome aboard. We are so glad you chose us to fly. You will notice that there are not many people on the plane. That is due to most tickets being refunded. Please enjoy your direct flight to Boston." The artificial voice repeats the same message again in five more languages. I tap the plastic screens of the in-flight consoles. They are unresponsive and all I get is static. I push my backpack further beneath my seat, hanging one of my legs over the edge. I'm sitting on the aisle with Mama in the middle and Aziz on the window side. Leaning back, I start to close my eyes. Slowly I start rolling around different possibilities in my head of how our landing is going to go. How are we going to find Baba? How are we going to find anyone when the Board of every country hates us?

AZIZ

DECEMBER 18, 2029

I wake up right before we land. Looking to my left, Riz is still fast asleep. He looks stupid with his left leg hanging over his armrest into the aisle. Who the hell can sleep like that? Mama is already gathering her overstuffed purse from under the seat in front of her.

"Mama, wake up Riz." She nods and taps Riz on his right leg. Slowly Riz's eyes start to open. He reorients himself. I can't stop laughing as he grabs his left leg with both hands and pulls it over the armrest. It must have fallen asleep. He sees me laughing and scowls as he pulls his backpack out from under the seat. Sometimes, Riz is just hilarious.

When the plane lands, we walk back through the entire empty airplane. I look on in envy at the first class seats that could've been ours if Mama hadn't been so damn stubborn about sitting in the seats we were assigned. She doesn't quite understand that nothing matters anymore. The overpacked carry-on suitcase drags behind me, crippled by its two broken wheels. It ping pongs off the aisle seats as it clumsily makes its way through the plane. When we make it out, we are greeted by more emptiness. We've never been to Logan airport before, but I'm pretty sure that it's never this empty. We walk past a ridiculous number of

McDonalds and fake bookstores. Who is actually buying those books? When we finally make it to customs, nobody is there. That was expected but Mama still insists on standing there to wait for someone.

"Mama, no one is going to come." Riz complains. "No one had been anywhere in any of these airports."

"But if we don't check in with customs. It won't be legal." She retaliates.

"Oh my god, Mama. Nothing is legal or illegal anymore. The laws don't exist, there are all new laws. Can we please just walk through the airport and try to find Baba." She finally listens to me. Without Baba, there is absolutely no reason or logic to Mama's thinking. She is obviously confused by this whole thing, even though it's pretty straight forward: everything is changing and falling apart. When we make it to the exit of the airport, no one is in sight. Mama starts freaking out as she stares at the empty currency exchange station. But without stubbornly waiting this time, Mama lets us direct her out through the revolving glass doors. Riz and I breathe in fresh air as we step outside. It smells so much cleaner than India. It's a slightly overcast day. The clouds, some grey some white, litter the blue sky as the sun attempts to seep through. It's cold. Very cold. And all we have on are our basic hoodies. I look up and see the worst sight possible. Two massive tanks are headed our way, with ten soldiers in front. So far, not so good. A general steps forward once they get closer.

"Welcome to the United States of America. You are unwanted visitors and are therefore prisoners of the Board. Please step forward to be transported to the nearest prison camp." Well at least we aren't being slaughtered. Mama starts crying and Riz starts anxiously shaking his legs. I drop the suitcase and step forward.

"What are you doing Aziz?" Mama scolds me.

"Doing what they told me. We won't need our stuff in prison. Might as well listen to these people, they all have guns." I look straight ahead as the soldiers come and handcuff me.

"This one is very smart to listen to us." The general continues, as he looks at me. "It's a shame that he is brown, otherwise he would've made a very obedient and promising soldier." Mama and Riz are about to step forward with their fists out to be handcuffed as a man in military uniform interjects.

"Stop!" He yells from afar. The general glares towards the on rushing man. As he gets closer I notice he's a black man but is decorated with badges and is obviously was or is a member of the American military.

"And who must you be?" The General asks.

"My name is John Mane. I'm a United States commander from the army. Thank god you found these people. They are my war prisoners, requested by the Board. They are in my custody. Thanks for your help, but I can take it from here." He speaks with such authority that I don't think anybody will question him. And it turns out I was right.

"Ok, Commander. Try not to lose your war prisoners next time." He winks and signals for his forces to turn around. Immediately Commander Mane turns to us with haste in his eyes.

"We can talk later. For now, you have to follow me." We pick up our stuff and speed walk behind Commander Mane. He rushes towards the opposite side of the parking lot which is completely empty. His car sits lonely in the middle of the parking lot. He crumples the pile of parking tickets left on his dashboard, fumbles the keys in his hands, and then unlocks the driver side door. He quickly runs around the car and opens the passenger door for Mama. When we are all in the car, he takes a deep breath and then starts to exit the airport.

"Thank you, sir." Mama says, as she also lets out a sigh of relief.

"It's the least I can do. The order hasn't yet been sent out to also capture war vets of color. I'm just trying to help as many people as I can before that happens." He looks over his shoulder and smiles at Riz and me. "So, where are you guys from?" Commander Mane's accent is very interesting. It sounds American but it has a Senegalese undertone. His background story must be very interesting. Riz is the first one to answer, as always. He always thinks the fastest which means he always knows what to say first.

"We are from Kolkata, India. Our father came here to America a couple of years ago and we haven't heard from him in months. We are here to reunite with him." Riz sounds nervous. Our first experience in America hasn't gone exactly to plan.

"I see. And what are your names?"

"I'm Aziz and my brother here is Riz. Yes, we are twins so you don't have to ask. And the way you can tell us apart is our eyes. I have green eyes and Riz has brown eyes." Commander Mane chuckles from the driver's seat.

"I wasn't going to ask, but that is certainly good to know. I'm sorry about your father but if he is a smart man then he would've found refuge at the same place where we are going." He sounds hopeful which makes me feel a bit more confident.

"Where exactly are we going?" I ask.

"I don't know much about the current situation so don't quote me on this but I know just enough to get you guys somewhere safe. Ever since the Takeover, a group of people worked to establish hidden places for all people of color that were going to be captured. I think they call themselves the Migrants. My nephew told me about one of these places. I am going to try to find the closest one now and drop you folks off." So that's what they are calling all of this stuff. the Takeover. Sounds intense but I guess it is intense.

"And why won't you be joining us?" Mama asks.

"It's a bit complicated for me. You see, I am just now coming back from the war where I fought for the United States. That makes me a war veteran. When I signed up for the draft, I was promised all of these benefits if I returned from war. But then the Takeover happened. The Board will want to see me and renegotiate the terms of our agreement. So, that's where I'm heading. As much as I would like to stay with you guys. It's just too risky. I wouldn't want to draw too much attention to innocent people and put them in danger." We sit in silence for the rest of the drive. All of us are now satisfied with the information we have. Commander Mane has seen so much, I wish I could ask him about where he comes from and how the war was. Or even what war he fought in. But, I feel bad for his situation. Once respected by his government and nation, now he has been pushed aside. It takes us fifteen minutes of speeding to get close to our destination.

"What I'm about to do might seriously freak you guys out. Do you trust me?" We all nod, convinced that Commander Mane knows what he is doing. But then he starts doing what he was warning about. We are just about to enter the city but there is a hill next to the road. Once John sees a break in the highway railing he veers right through the gap and drives towards the hill.

"Commander Mane, what did we do wrong?!" Mama starts screaming.

"Please don't kill us!" yells Riz. We drive at full speed right into the hill and at the last minute a part of the rock pulls away and we drive right into a cavern, the door closing behind us. Mama stops her screaming and starts to calm down, breathing loudly. Meanwhile, Riz and I get out of the car, our mouths wide open in awe. This is ridiculous. The interior of the hill is hollowed out and is lined with reinforced metal. John starts feeling around the metal on the outside. There is very little light and none of us move. We just turn around in a single spot.

"I'm pretty sure something should be around here." John says as he runs his hands over the side of metal. "Oh here it is." He pushes a piece of metal in. It recesses and soon the platform that the car and we are on starts to lower down. Mama clings onto the car even though we aren't lowering at any kind of a dangerous speed. Eventually the platform presses into the floor of what looks like a massive base. There are rooms and people everywhere, cars are all parked next to the platform. We walk over the crack of the platform and Mama holds our hands as we take everything in. People from all different places of all different ages are running around, eating, reading, bustling about, anything. They all look safe and healthy.

"I can't believe you made it." A man steps out from the crowd and I immediately recognize him as Baba. His black hair wavy just like ours, and his brown skin healthy and smooth. We run towards him and give him a huge hug. Mama soon followed, tears running down her face.

"It's so good to see you Baba." Riz says. He steps backwards and looks us up and down.

"You boys are now men, all grown. We can catch up later, but you must be hungry. Come along." Riz and I start walking down a hallway while Baba kisses Mama on the forehead and embraces her again. Now that we are altogether, any place can be our home.

RIZ

DECEMBER 25, 2029

It's been two weeks. Baba told us everything. How he was almost captured. How a super sketchy guy told him about this place. How he has tried to help all of these people by teaching the children basic subjects. But no matter how many positive things he has told us, it doesn't do anything to fend off the general sadness of Aziz, Mama, and I. Baba has been living like this for months, not being able to communicate because of fear he will be tracked. But we just got here and, while the base is very nice, there is so much uncertainty. I get off of my bed, looking across the room to the sleeping Aziz. I walk into the hallway and towards my parent's room. As I approach, I notice that the door has been left open and as I peer into the room, the bed is made and there is no sign of Baba or Mama. I decide to head into the cafeteria, or that's what the Migrants call it.

As I get into the cafeteria, I walk straight past the long worn wooden picnic tables and into the pantry. I look for something to eat and as I finger through the different preservatives and canned foods, Aziz comes up from behind me.

"How long have you been up?" He asks as he shoves me to the side and grabs the remainder of Cheerios that he hid behind the cans of soup.

"Maybe ten minutes." I reply as I decide to go for the fruit cup. We walk back to a table and sit down together. "I think we are pretty low on rations. Maybe this time, Baba will let us come with him to gather resources."

"Yeah, hopefully. The only reason that he doesn't let us come is because he refuses to have us see him commit crimes and do illegal things." That is pretty much true. Baba always wants us to see him as the nice guy that follows the rules. It's his fairly useless way of setting an example for us.

"By the way, do you know where he is? I couldn't find Mama or him anywhere."

"Yeah. He took her to an underground restaurant place that actually serves migrants. Some place called Khiwi I think." Aziz knows everything and it's incredibly annoying. It might have been helpful if they had told me too before I went wandering around the entire base trying to find them.

"How do you even know that? Did they tell you or something?" I ask, already frustrated by this morning.

"No, they didn't tell me. When I said goodnight last night I saw a reservation time written on one of their business cards." Somehow, it's even worse that he knows more than me without them even telling him. I don't answer and peel the plastic off of my fruit cup.

"Hey, I want to show you something. It's crazy cool." Aziz says as we start to get up. I follow him as we walk out of the cafeteria and towards the parking lot where everyone exits and enters. Then we head straight down a hallway in the opposite direction. I've never been this way but according to the confidence of Aziz, he has.

"Where are we going?" I ask as we pass more bedrooms and some more storage.

"I was exploring this place yesterday and went down to the end of the hallway. And then, I was just going to take a break so I leaned against the back wall. And then this happened." We make it to the end of the hallway where there is a red brick wall. Aziz sits down with his back against the wall and leans back, pressing the wall with his spine. I'm about to tell him that he dreamed this all up, but then something gets triggered in the wall and the whole thing slides to the side.

"It's sick right? C'mon." I follow him into the room, the brick wall closing behind us. There are lab materials scattered everywhere as well as an unsafe amount of exposed wires. At the center of it all, sits a black kid, a few years older than us, sitting at a small metal desk. He looks up and smiles as he sees Aziz walking towards him. Aziz always makes friends way faster than me. I like to think that my judgment of people is better because I'm more cautious but he insists that I'm just weird.

"Aziz, it's great to see you." The kid gets up and initiates a customized handshake with Aziz. Ridiculous.

"Marques, this is my brother, Riz. I wanted you to meet him and show him this place." Marques walks towards me and grabs my hand, shaking it vigorously. I can already tell that this guy is one of those geniuses that is just enough crazy that you can tell.

"It's great to meet you, Riz. And welcome to my workshop." He sweeps his arms around the room before centering back on me. "This is where all of the technology that the Migrants need are made. At least everything that Ivo doesn't make because I'm still not as good as him."

"Who's Ivo?" He opens his mouth like he's about to answer my question and then changes his mind at the last second.

"It doesn't matter. For now, you get to see the stuff that I have been making. And you kids are the best people to use them." He hurriedly guides us to the back of the room, where weapons, toys, and anything in-between are haphazardly organized on glass shelves. Marques picks up a small silver metal disc and hands it to me, the coolness of the metal hitting my hand. "Now this is my latest invention. It's a disc that you can slap on to an enemy and it will sense its activation and electrocute them. The really impressive part is that it's so small and thin!" He's way too excited. This is not exactly mind-blowing technology.

"What's this?" Aziz asks as he picks up a small black rectangle. He presses a red button at the bottom and it starts to flip out and transform into a full-on rifle. Now that is cool. I start to gain some respect for Marques until he squashes it.

"That's a prototype for one of Ivo's new weapons. We don't have to focus on that. Guns are old news. Electrocution is the new mainstream weapon." He goes on blabbering about his new zap toy while I go rummaging in one of the bins labeled Ivo. Some of the stuff he has in here is actually really cool.

"I was wondering where you kids were." Baba's voice comes from near the doorway. Aziz and I walk over. "I was waiting until the day one of you would find this place. I didn't tell you about it because I thought it would be cool if you found it yourself. Hey Marques, how are you doing?" Baba waves at Marques who is still holding his electrocuting thing. He timidly waves back.

"I'm good, how are you?"

"Better now that these boys are here." He taps both of us on our heads. "What have you kids been doing anyways?"

"We ate breakfast and Aziz showed me this place," I explain.

"And we are almost out of food rations." Aziz chimes in.

"Ok. Well I think I'll head out now so that I can gather some stuff before the sun goes down."

"Can we go please?" Aziz begs. We have barely been out of the base since we got here and it would be nice to gain some experience in surviving out here. At least that's how we see it.

"No. We have gone over this. It's too dangerous for the three of us to leave and we shouldn't leave Mama here on the base by herself." Baba retaliates. This is pretty much the same argument that he has used every time.

"But what if we bring Mama with us? Like we all go out together." I add, hoping that the idea that our family would stick together would appeal to Baba.

"Please, Baba. You always tell us that we need to be prepared for life without you and Mama. How are we supposed to be prepared if we don't know how to survive? We need to learn how to get food and resources because we probably will be living in this base for a while." Aziz keeps on begging, he is apparently a little more desperate for this family mission to happen than I am. Baba puts his head down like he has lost the battle.

"Fine." He sighs. "Go get your mother and then we'll leave. And before you go, grab some weapons from Marques. Aziz, remember what I've been teaching you." I go and get Mama, trusting that Aziz will get enough weapons for the both of us. I don't know the details of what Baba has been teaching Aziz but it has something to do with snipers and stuff. Aziz can memorize entire books so I think that Baba has found a way to incorporate that into shooting.

I head straight back to our parent's bedroom where the door is still open. This time, Mama is reading something on her bed.

"Mama, we are leaving. Baba says that if you come with us, then he'll show Aziz and I how to find food and stuff." She looks up, obviously surprised that Baba agreed to anything like that. I don't think she really cares. She has much more faith in Aziz's and my abilities.

"I'll meet you at the parking lot. Just let me get dressed real quick." I nod back and head towards the parking lot. Baba is already in the driver's seat of his car, an old black Nissan. Aziz comes up to me and hands me a knife and pistol.

"Thanks." I say.

"My gun is still bigger." He brags as he shows me his long sniper. I'm just surprised that Marques didn't somehow convince Aziz to bring the new toy.

"Whatever." I reply as I open the right back seat door and hop in. Soon, Aziz follows and, after a couple of minutes, Mama gets in the passenger seat. We drive out and turn right onto the highway.

"The number one rule is not to be seen. As soon as you're spotted, then the Board will not stop for anything until they successfully capture you." Baba talks over his shoulder towards us. You can sense that he is a bit nervous. "Usually, we would make sure not to be seen by cameras. But the Board already knows that we aren't accounted for within their prisons, they just don't care if we don't bother them." We take a sharp left turn off of the highway and onto a smaller road. "Right now we are just going to get food. Most of the food that is in the city is brought in from the Board as a supply to the personnel that work here, at prisons and other things like that. The way that the food comes in is through transports. Our job is to find one of those transports that is the least guarded and then take the food that we need. We want to avoid as much violence as we can but there are almost always a couple of guards on these transports."

"Is that why we have these?" Aziz asks, holding up his gun.

"Yes. But again, only use those if you have to. They are acting as more of a warning to others." We drive through the city and then we pull into a random alley and park the car. We all get out and start sneaking around the city in a three block radius around where we parked. About two blocks away from the car, we see a transport parked at a gas station. We hide behind a building that's across the street. From what I can tell, there is no one in the truck, they are probably in the convenience store. Aziz starts to walk around the building towards the gas station but then Baba grabs his wrist and pulls him back.

"Be patient." He urges. Soon enough, two guards exit the store and walk towards the transport vehicle. "Aziz, now is the time. Do what we have been practicing." Aziz steps in front of me before kneeling down on one knee. He takes his sniper off of his shoulder and starts to take aim, keeping a steady hand. He starts to draw lines in the air with his movement, I have no idea what he's doing. Just as I'm about to warn Baba that the transport is getting away. I watch as the two guys crumple to the ground. I glance back at Aziz who is very pleased with himself.

"Was that one shot?" I ask, still in shock. I guess that's what he's been learning from Baba. It's actually more likely that's just what he's been learning from the books that Baba has given him. Aziz just looks at me and smiles before swinging the sniper around his back and walking towards the gas station. Baba follows him and I pull Mama with me as she is still in complete shock. We make it to the gas station and Baba opens the back of the transport.

"It's empty." I observe. "Why is it empty?"

"Oh no." Baba says. In the middle of transport there is an alarm that starts to blare. "Run. Everybody run!" Baba demands. We start running but it's too late. A group of soldiers drive up on us in cars from behind. Ten soldiers get out of the car and circle around us.

"I knew we'd get you guys eventually." A man with a tablet wearing all black gets out of one of the cars. We all put our hands up as multiple guns are pointed at us. He walks up to each of us, scanning them with his tablet. He smiles once he scans Aziz and I. "Take that one." He says, pointing at me. "He has good vision and awareness. The rest can go to the nearest prison." He doesn't even look me in the eye before he gets back in his car and speeds away. Mama cries as they handcuff me and shove me in a different car than them. I try to scream but they cover my mouth. We start driving away to who knows where. I try to look out the window but I can't see anything.

After thirty minutes, my eyes are covered by a rag. They force me out of the car, walk me across some wooden planks, and shove me onto a platform where I sit down. I start to rock back and forth as I realize that I'm on a boat. They take the blindfold off once we dock. I look around and see a few trees surrounding three massive metal buildings. I feel the my feet sink into the sand of shoreline and look around to notice we are on an island.

"Let's keep it moving kid." A soldier says behind me as he shoves me forward. I walk towards the base and am directed to the middle building. Pushing through the front door, I look above me as I see a hanging air force plane within a large empty space. They force me up the stairs to the right and I walk down a hallway with plain metal rooms flanking each side. When we get near the end of the hallway, they take off my handcuffs and push me into an empty room. It has a bare mattress in the middle with a silver metal toilet and small wooden desk on opposite sides of the bed. They shut the heavy door behind me and I sit down on the bed.

"Welcome to the Air Force training camp." The same soldier's voice says from behind the door. "This will be your home for a long time so get comfortable. You have been chosen to be trained obediently and to serve the United States government because of the natural skills that you have. See you in the morning." He knocks on the door and I hear his footsteps walking back down the hallway. I lay down on my bed, clutching my stomach as it rumbles. I stare at the bare grey ceiling as I try to think about what skills I have that make me a good pilot.

AZIZ

DECEMBER 25, 2029

Mama can't stop crying as we keep driving to who knows where. I look out the windows, trying to memorize signs as much as possible, but the vision from the windows is so low that it's not even worth it. I lean my head against the window and put my left hand on Mama's leg, trying anything to soothe her. Baba is completely tuned out on the opposite side of the car. All of us have the same question rolling around in our head. Why Riz? If anything, I'm the one with the rare talents.

It takes only ten minutes before we reach our destination. After they handcuff us, we are pushed out of the car and into a very tall brick building. The bricks are all painted matte black and the building is probably at least twenty stories. We walk through the front door which is made of reinforced metal but decorated with horizontal wooden planks.

"What is this place?" I whisper to Baba.

"Shut up!" The soldier in front of us says. We walk into the center of the building, which is square at its base. Starting on the left hand side there is a spiraling staircase that, when looking up, I notice keeps on going through the entire building. Oddly, there is no elevator. It's almost like this is a prison made two hundred years ago. The guards that were directing us step away and go back through the front door. A man wearing a general's uniform, similar to one we saw when we first got to America, steps in front of us.

"Hello. My name is General Lee. Welcome to The Maze." He ushers us to follow him and we start climbing the steps. "Actually, I'm not sure if this is still called The Maze because there is a new one they are building. Is this still called The Maze?" The general asks a guard standing post on the second level. He just shrugs. "Anyways, it doesn't matter. I am currently in charge of this prison until the next The Maze is built, whenever that's going to happen. It's a very complicated construction process. This prison is very old and is very confusing. The steps go on for the entire length of the building as you will soon find out. However, because each floor is made completely identical and certain obstacles prevent you from knowing which floor you are on, you will almost always be scratching your head. Trust me, it doesn't only confuse the prisoners." We hit the fourth level and I glance down. Instead of seeing the floor where we came from, I just see a reflection of where we are going, making it seem like we are going down forever. Looking up, there is no obvious end to the staircase. By the time we finally stop, I have completely lost count of which level we are on. But I guess that's the point.

"Is this where we are staying?" Baba asks. From what I can tell, General Lee isn't necessarily a legitimate general, he seems a little bit too nice and light humored.

"Yes. This floor and this prison is where you will be staying. I'm not sure why they put you here, maybe because it was the nearest place. Usually this place is reserved for higher profile criminals. Anyways, this is your room." He ushers us into a room on our right. The doorway is just an opening in the brick wall. We walk in and see three separate cots with a bookshelf, toilet, and desk nearby. "Food will be given to you occasionally. And tomorrow you will be directed to your labor work which must be completed to ensure your survival."

"Where is Riz?" Mama asks the general.

"I have no idea who that is and therefore have no clue where he is. But you better get used to life without him because this is your situation for the time being." General Lee awkwardly nods to us and leaves the room, disappearing up the maze of stairs. I go and sit down on my cot, immediately feeling how hard and uncomfortable it is. Baba sits at the desk, rubbing the wooden surface with the palm of his hand. Mama stares at the empty bookshelf. We all need to get used to this because, for once, nothing's going to help us.

MAZE

PRESENT DAY

IVO

MARCH 25, 2031

"So what's the plan boss?" Riz asks.

"Ummmm..." I hesitate. There is nowhere for us to land that wouldn't be swarming with soldiers as soon as we get there. I'm quickly realizing that I didn't think this plan all the way through.

"Are you kidding me, Ivo. You're telling me that you devised this whole plan for us to get a plane and a pilot but you didn't think about how to land the damn plane. You really are something else." Idri complains from the back seat. This small plane only has four seats, which is fine for now but once we attempt to save some people from that crazy prison, it might become more of a problem.

"Calm down, Idrissa. I'm sure Ivo can think of something." Aiko attempts to reassure Idri who is having a full-on panic attack.

"I'm starting to regret coming with you guys. I mean you seemed pretty legit when this guy walked in with that suit." Riz points to me without looking. "But now it seems like you people have nothing figured out. I didn't enjoy where I was but at least I was alive."

"Everyone, shut up. I think I have a plan." I say, only somewhat convincingly.

"See Idrissa, Ivo always comes up with a plan." Aiko says, glaring at Idri.

"For the record, I don't always want to be the one responsible for making the plans. It's not like you two are incapable." I comment.

"If I have to listen to you three bicker any longer, I'm going to crash this plane. Can you just tell me what's next?" Riz shouts from behind his back, clearly perturbed.

"Ok. The plan is to head straight to the prison. Basically, we have nowhere to land so might as well do what we got the plane to do." Saying it loud makes it sound a lot more stupid than it did in my head.

"That's your plan. Are you freakin kidding me? Your plan is suicide. We barely have weapons. We have no backup. Maybe we are better off with this kid coming up with a plan. At least whatever stupid thing he comes up with, will be better than that." Idri continues his complaining.

"Hey man. I'm right here. And, for the record, I'm not that dumb. I am the one flying this thing ya know." Poor Riz, he's the last one that deserves to be grilled.

"Well, if no one else can come up with a different plan, then we better be prepared to fight. Who knows how many people they are going to have or how good they are." Aiko says. Idri puts his finger in the air like he's going to argue again but then realizes that there is really no point in wasting time when he could be getting his weapons ready. Instead, he dives into his bag and starts loading his weapons.

"People! No one has given me a place to go." Riz complains. I lean over and punch in some coordinates into the GPS system. "Thank you. You know, usually, the pilot should know the destination first."

"Yeah, sorry kid." I pat him on the shoulder as he shakes his head. I sit back down in the passenger seat and grab a rifle from the duffel bag. It takes only fifteen minutes for us to be in sight of the prison.

"Oh. My. God. Are you guys sure you want to go to this place? Excuse my language but that thing is god damn massive." Riz comments.

"Is it just me or does that thing look significantly bigger when we are this close?" Idri says as he looks up from his weapons. "Yeah, I agree with the kid. Forget the plan, I'm not stepping foot in that place." The exterior of the cube is completely metal with just a balcony and railing surrounding the perimeter. The only way in, it seems, is through the hole in the top that would land us in the middle of the prison—not ideal. All of sudden, an alarm starts blaring. Great, second security alarm of the day.

"Well, we can't turn back now," Aiko says. "Riz, fly us down that hole."

"What?! No, it's not too late. Please Ivo, can we please turn around?" Idri starts shaking my shoulders.

"C'mon, Idri. Get a hold of yourself. We have a mission and we are going to complete it. If we turn around now with nowhere to land, then we might as well sign our own death certificates." I push Idri's hands off me. He has never freaked out like this before. I think it's because this new plan kind of took him by surprise and he doesn't like surprises. I look towards the prison as Riz is trying to maneuver the plane into a position for landing. I scan the top surface of the cube just in time to see turrets popping out of the top.

"Riz, how are we doing over there?" I ask as I hop into the back and start gathering more weapons.

"I'm working on it man!" He shouts.

"Well you might want to work a little faster because we got some serious guns pointed at us!"

"This day just keeps getting better, doesn't it?" He yells back. We start swerving from side to side, I'm assuming it's to keep the guns from taking aim. Gradually, we make our way closer to the opening and once we are there, Riz slowly lowers us down.

"Everyone get your weapons ready. They know that we are coming, so be prepared for god knows how many soldiers." I tell the crew.

"Here, kid. Take this thing. If you don't know how to use it, just point it at somebody and make them scared until we can take them out." Idri hands Riz a gun. I'm not sure if he is joking or being completely serious because the technique he just described is one hundred percent not practical. Riz grabs the gun and looks at me with a very confused expression. I just shrug my shoulders.

"We are landing in ten seconds, people!" Riz yells. When we hit the ground I reach over Aiko and swing open the double door on the side of the plane. Aiko jumps out and I follow, with Idri behind me, as he stands in front of Riz. For a moment I think we are alone on the landing pad. There are two bridges on each side of the platform leading to other levels of the prison. Then a group of about thirty massive guards march from each of the bridges and circle around us on the platform. I activate my necklace and get a rush of adrenaline as I feel the suit's nanotech morphing around me. I swing the rifle from around my back into my arms.

"What, no fancy general to come and greet us?" I joke, trying to distract the soldiers. Aiko and Idri know that, when I make a joke, it's time to fight. Immediately, I generate a grenade from my suit, which I upgraded recently, and roll it out in front of me. It erupts, tossing seven men over the edge. Meanwhile, out of the corner of my eye, I see Aiko slide underneath the front of the plane and to the other side, followed by the sound of a smoke grenade. Aiko likes to blur the enemy's vision so that she can get closer and use her sword. The soldiers from the side start to move towards me. As one approaches me, I slide underneath his legs, attached a splinter bomb to his back as I get up on the other side. Two more try to take aim before I generate knives and throw them into their stomachs. Three more come but I shoot them with my rifle before they can even move. Then it's silent.

I look around and see all of the soldiers either crumpled or hanging off the edge of the platform. Aiko comes up from behind me, two cuts on her legs.

"You ok?" I ask.

"Yeah, just some minor injuries. You don't look so good though." She points to my upper right arm. I hold it up and see blood dripping, staining my suit. I trigger my necklace and my suit starts to disappear, revealing a glancing gun wound. I didn't even notice it. I was too busy fighting.

"We can patch it up later. Right now, we have to find the prisoners." I start to walk to one of the bridges but then turn back around to face Aiko. "Where's Idri?"

"Over here!" I hear Riz's voice from inside of the plane. Aiko and I rush over to see Riz holding Idri's head. "He got shot in the leg trying to save me. It's not a fatal injury but he's losing a lot of blood. I dragged him into the plane because I didn't know what else to do."

"You did the right thing," I reassure Riz as I kneel down inside the plane and look at Idri. He has already passed out and his left leg is bleeding through his black cargo pants right above the knee.

"The plane has a med kit." I turn to see Aiko grabbing something from the back of the plane. "I can help him but I'm going to need Riz's help here." I nod back.

"It's fine. I can handle this. You guys helped with the hardest part." I step out of the plane and steadily walk across the first bridge, my rifle ready to fire. The second level has a bunch of empty bunks so I keep walking. When I cross the next bridge, I see someone in a prisoner uniform. He hears me coming and runs right into the hallway. I guess I found the prisoners. I turn right and then left, into a large room. The back wall is just a big piece of glass and tons of bunks litter the room. Some of them are made and there are only a few people in here.

"Hey! I'm here from the Migrants. If you want to get out of this place, head to the landing pad. We have a plane." I'm ignoring the fact that the plane can barely even fit one more person.

"You're too late." The young man that ran away from me says, getting off of his bed and walking towards me. "They already gathered them up."

"Where?" I frantically ask.

"In the next level. Please save them."

"I'll try." I run out of the room and turn back down the hallway. Turning left, I run down the next bridge. I make it to the next level and walk into to what looks like a cafeteria. I slow down to a walk as I look left and right. Then I see a group of prisoners gathered at the far right corner. I walk towards them but then two soldiers, each wearing black and a plain grey mask over their faces, step in front of me.

"Hand over the prisoners and I won't hurt you." I threaten. The smaller guard to the right lifts up his gun but then the other lowers the gun down. He takes two steps towards me and I reach towards my necklace. And then he pulls his mask back over his head and I drop my gun, clattering to the floor.

"Ivo?"

ZA

MARCH 25, 2031

I wake up to my ringing alarm. Without looking I hit the top of my alarm four times until it stops. Tired, I sit up in my bed and grab my phone. It's six in the morning and time for training. I hobble out of my bed, still a bit sore from our first mission. My feet drag against the wooden floor as I make my way to my closet. I open the door and scan the closet for today's attire. Scattered among black shirts, I find one grey athletic trainer and pull it over my head. Taking off my pajama pants, I pull on generic black track pants. Briefly, I walk to the mantel and trigger the weapons closet. I take a quick look over my weapons, trying to remember if it's weapons training today or not. Not being able to make up my mind, I grab the Rod. Putting my phone in my pocket, I slip on my black sneakers, and walk out the door towards breakfast. I walk into an empty cafeteria.

Over the last couple of weeks, I've learned that my team eats breakfast, or brunch I should say, after our first session of the day. Apparently, Aziz does too. They say that there is some scientific reason why they do it but I don't think I can break my habit of just waking up and eating. As soon as I sit down, I notice Chef Silva walking towards me.

"What's it going to be this morning?" He asks. Chef Silva is always so enthusiastic in the morning. Sometimes, it helps me feel that much less exhausted.

"Just some yogurt and fruit today, thanks." He nods, and returns two minutes later with a completely overkill breakfast. The white ceramic bowl is filled with vanilla yogurt and topped with different berries. Mixed in on top, there is some granola. I smile at Chef Silva and he nods as though he knows that I think it's way too fancy for me. I've complained about that to him before, but he never seems to care. He turns around and goes back to the kitchen, waiting for his next lucky customer. I quickly eat my breakfast as I scroll through the news on my phone. Apparently some migrants broke into an Air Force training facility. "Good for them" I think to myself. I keep convincing myself that I'm still on their side. It does make me wonder what on earth they need from a place like that. Getting a plane would be difficult and not worth it, as they would just be shot out of the air as soon as they are spotted. I finish my breakfast and walk to the gym. Swinging open the metal doors, I'm greeted by a busy room. All the guys are either working out or talking amongst themselves, waiting for me to show up. They quickly huddle around me and I mentally take attendance. Everyone is accounted for, I think, but then I remember that Aziz is supposed to be here.

"Anyone seen Aziz?" I ask the group. Now that I think about it, I don't think they have even met Aziz. Their confused faces confirm that. "Never mind. Just give me a minute while I grab him." I walk out of the gym and down the opposite hallway where the soldiers' bunks are. I make it to the end, where Aziz is supposed to be sleeping. I knock on the door.

"Aziz. You in there?" After no answer I use my card to open the door and let myself in. I see a sleepy Aziz just starting to wake up. His covers kicked to the ground and one of his pillows was still over his head.

"Dude, it's like six in the morning." He whines.

"It's six thirty and time to get up. We have training." I command. He doesn't budge.

"Just let me sleep a little longer." He begs. "I'm so tired and this bed is so comfortable."

"Well the bed isn't going anywhere and that's also not how things work around here." I walk over to his exposed weapons closet. I open it up, pick up an automatic rifle, make sure it's not loaded, and shoot it at Aziz. The sound of the gunshot rippled throughout the room and Aziz scrambled out of bed.

"Great, now you're up. Now get dressed. We are all waiting for you." I sit on his couch as I watch him slowly get dressed. I'm definitely going to need to work on his commitment. I still don't understand how we are almost the same age. It's shocking, really. He turns towards me barely dressed. He has some baggy sweatpants on with a white t-shirt. He pulls on socks and shoes.

"I'm ready." He says confidently. He is obviously shaken up. But he deserves it for being so late.

"I don't think you are, but let's get going anyway," I reply, ushering him out of his room. He has no idea how intense our training is. I guide him towards the gym and open the doors to see my twenty beautiful soldiers standing exactly how I left them.

"Boys, this is Aziz. He's new around here so please don't be nice to him. He's the next member of our team and apparently remembers a lot, so yeah." I shove Aziz to the end of the line. "We are going to do some tactics today and then run through some simulations. Shouldn't be too bad if everyone is alert and ready to roll." I glare at Aziz who timidly backs away.

We run through training pretty easily. Aziz does an ok job of keeping up, although his close combat technique is questionable. When we make it to the end, he wearily walks towards me.

"So this is like a real thing. You're pretty harsh, man." He starts complaining again.

"Just doing my job. Let's head to lunch and I'll give you a little bit more of analysis of how I think you did today." He follows me back towards the cafeteria but, as soon as we sit down, General Lee sits down next to us.

"How was this guy's first training session?" He asks, patting Aziz on the back.

"He has a lot of work to do. But not bad for a first go. And you weren't wrong to bring him in, he is quite the sharp shooter. Not to mention, he really helps out with my poor memory." General Lee laughs.

"Well, I'm glad everything is going well. And I promise, you will get another mission very soon. But for now, I have some very interesting news for you Zashil. Aziz, would you mind giving us a second in private." Aziz, still intimidated by General Lee, rushes to get up, hitting his knee on the top of the table. I hold back a laugh as I see him limp away.

"What's the news?" I ask, turning back to face the general.

"All of the top officials are having a meeting in two days. They have already been very impressed with the team I have put together and they have requested the attendance of their leader, which is you."

"Wow." I start. "I don't know what to say." I actually don't. I would really rather not be recognized as this amazing warrior fighting for the Board. How can these people forget that I'm still a prisoner?

"You don't have to say anything. I already arranged your flight and I'll be accompanying you there, all of the details were sent to your phone." He gets up, joyous, and scampers away. That's not exactly how I thought my time here was going to go. If only there was a way that I could tell the Migrants when and where that was happening.

Aziz doesn't rejoin me until after lunch at our second training session. We are about to begin when the security alarm goes off. Unsurprisingly, no one in the gym panics and instead starts to gather weapons.

"What's going on?" Aziz asks as he starts to load his sniper.

"I have no idea but I'm sure that General Lee will be here soon to tell us." As if on cue, General Lee storms through the gym doors.

"Listen up, people. We have some intruders. I sent some soldiers already but if they were able to find this place and make it this far, then I have a feeling it will only take a few minutes for them to get dispatched." General Lee looks at me. "Zashil, I need your men to gather as many prisoners as possible and hold them hostage in the cafeteria. You and Aziz will stand guard there. You're two of our best so I expect you to handle this threat." I'm about to complain but then I remember that he can just kill me so I decide against it, and instead nod my head in agreement.

"On it, sir." General Lee exits the gym and I turn to my men. "You heard the man, get to work!" Aziz follows me to my room where I grab my fighting clothes and start pulling them on. I grab a couple of masks and hand one to Aziz. "Here, put this on." He does while I grab a bunch of weapons from the closet, tossing a couple knives and grenades back to Aziz. When we make it the cafeteria, I turn to my left to see the prisoners already tied up. It looks like they were only able to gather about seventy percent. We are standing on the bridge when I catch a glimpse of a figure moving towards the prisoners. I can only see his black hair, rifle, and black shoes from where we are. I motion for Aziz to follow me and then we step off the bridge and into the cafeteria, we intercept the guy and stand in between him and the prisoners. But as soon I take a look at his face, I recognize the eyes, nose, and hair. It's Ivo. I push down Aziz's gun which is pointed at Ivo and take two shaky steps towards him. Pulling my mask off, my eyes start to water.

"Ivo?" I say, rushing towards him. He hugs me as soon as I get close enough.

"I never thought I'd find you." His familiar deep voice says through my ear. "But we have to get out of here now. We have no time." I step away and look at him.

"I can't." I say.

"What do you mean you can't?" I pull up my shirt, revealing the bomb over chest.

"It's rigged to explode on command. The General has the remote. He has one too." I point back to Aziz who takes his mask off.

"Riz?" Ivo asks.

"Who's Riz? That's Aziz." I reply. I'm so confused.

"Wait, you know my brother?" Aziz asks rushing towards Ivo.

"Yeah, I think I do. He's actually with us." Ivo replies as he starts checking out the bomb module. "I think I can temporarily disable it. Just enough time for you to get out of range of the remote." He reaches into his back pocket and pulls out two very thin disks.

"Oh, Jesus. Not those things. Those things are so damn stupid." Aziz says from behind. I'm really starting to question if I know anything about Aziz.

"How do you know what these are?" Ivo asks.

"Because I was at the migrant base with Marques when he invented them. They are ridiculous. Wait, that must mean you're the genius, Ivo."

"Yeah, I am. Not a genius though. And they usually are pretty useless but they will send a very strong electric shock through that thing on your chest and temporarily short circuit them." Ivo slaps one on each of us and then pressed a button. I feel a slight electric shock before I see a red light pop up on the top of the bomb.

"I cannot believe that Marques just saved my life." Aziz says. I really don't know anything about him or his supposed brother.

"Ok, time to get out of here. We have a plane." Ivo says as he starts to walk towards the landing platform.

"We?" I ask. He must've brought Idrissa and Aiko. I don't know them very well because they both left shortly after we got to the base. They went to establish the second place for the Migrants.

"I'll tell you once we are there."

"What about these prisoners," I say. Ivo never leaves anybody behind.

"I know, but with you two guys we won't have any space in the plane. We are going to have to come back for them." I nod back and follow behind Ivo as we run towards the landing platform. Once we get there, I notice all of the bodies. Ivo must've gotten a lot better because even he didn't used to be this good. We hop in the plane.

"Riz, let's get going buddy." Ivo says, tapping a kid on the shoulder who is sitting in the pilot seat. He turns around and I swear to god I thought Aziz teleported for a minute before he jumps from behind me and gives him a hug.

"I can't believe I found you Riz!" Aziz says. I have a lot to catch up on. I look behind me and see Idrissa and Aiko strapping in. They both nod at me. At this point, they probably know more about me than I do about them.

"The reunion is going to have to wait until we are safely in the air, guys." Ivo suggests from the passenger seat. Aziz clobbers back towards me and sits on the ground, holding a handle on the plane. We slowly lift off and fly away. Looking down through the window, I see General Lee rushing onto the landing platform just as we take off. I see him take out the remote and try to kill Aziz and I, but it does nothing. For now, I'm safe. For now, we are all safe.

IVO

MARCH 25, 2031

We decide to find a nearby field to land in, and hopefully make a quick exit. Za and I try to catch up on as much as we can on the way there.

"Are you serious? John is the one that helped you. That is absolutely insane, I always knew that he was more than he let on. And he's your uncle?" Za points at Idri who is quietly listening in the back of the plane. He just responds with a slow nod.

"And then the rest is history. We found a place that had a plane, that's where we found Riz over here, and then we went straight to the prison. What's it called again?" I ask.

"The Maze." We both laugh, knowing that the stupid government nomenclature never stops.

"Tell me, what happened with you? Where did they take you?" I want to know as much details as possible.

"When you told me to run, I tried to cross the street. That's when they picked me." Za starts. "They took me to that prison that has an airplane hangar."

"So, I was close. I was there saving some prisoners. I found this picture." I pull out the picture of our family. "I just missed you, you must've been in one of those transports." I shake my head. I always thought that I was close but now to know that I almost had Za then.

"Yeah. I mostly did some database stuff in prison, that's how I met John. After they transported me, they flew me to that place. That's when they attached this thing to me." He points to the bomb on his chest. I need to figure out a way of taking that off without it blowing up. For now, I'm pretty sure I stopped its functionality but that doesn't mean I shouldn't try to take it off. I don't want Za living with a bomb on his chest. The same goes for Aziz as well.

"They told me my skills were highly valued and they wanted me to lead a team of super soldiers. They wanted us to do the dirty work of the Board for them. I was dispensable in their eyes. But that General Lee guy liked me way too much. It was kinda weird." It's amazing how much Za has matured in the last eighteen months. I wish I was there with him but it's good to know that he handled himself well.

"I am so happy to see you Za. I really thought you were gone. I can't lose you too."

"I know." We do our secret handshake. It's really not that complicated but only we know it.

"What's the plan, boss" Idri asks from the back.

"The plan is to get everybody back to the base, get you patched up, and then head out and save the rest of those people in The Maze." I reply. Seeing all those people strapped up for no reason made me very frustrated. But, at the time, there was no way we could've actually saved them.

"No." Za says. "We can't."

"Why?" Aiko asks.

"Because, as much as I want to save those people too, there is something more important." He takes a deep breath. Za never used to be this calm. He always rushed into things without thought. If he wasn't so good at what he did, he would definitely be dead by now. "General Lee told me about something before the alarms went off back at The Maze. He told me that the top Board officials were all going to have a meeting."

"About what?" I ask.

"I don't know." Za responds.

"Why would he tell you that?" Idri finally tunes in. "I mean you were still a prisoner after all."

"He told me because I was invited to the meeting. Something about the Board being impressed with my team or whatever. We only went on one mission so I don't really get it."

"Ok. You're telling us this, but what are we going to do about it?" Aiko asks. I know that it's just a matter of time before they look at me for a plan.

"If we can pull it off, I think we should take them all out. It won't fix things permanently, but it will put the Board in enough disarray for us to have some more time." Za says. His plan is risky but it could be done and we won't get another chance like this again.

"But what if they have already been warned?" Idri asks.

"Then I wouldn't still have access to all my files on my phone." Za holds up his phone, displaying an email with coordinates and attendance. "I think that General Lee didn't inform them because I saw him press the button. I'm pretty sure he thinks that Aziz and I were blown to pieces when we tried to escape. But that would've made an explosion, so maybe he just forgot I still had access." I save the coordination and then, as if on cue, they disappear. "Nevermind, he didn't forget."

"I think we give it a shot." Aziz says. Looking up from his phone. He hasn't spoken in a while and I don't blame him. Everything that is going on is all a little much.

"It's impossible. There will be tons of security. There is no way we can get anywhere close to the meeting," Idri says, always the realistic one.

"Just hear me out." Aziz continues. "Za goes in like he belongs there, because they still think he does. We make sure that General Lee doesn't ever make it inside to dispute Za's story who is going to say that General Lee couldn't make it. Za keeps them distracted while also finding us a way to get in without having to knock down the front door. Meanwhile, the rest of us start to set up bombs around the building. We get out, Za leaves early. At that point it doesn't matter if he blows his cover. And then boom." Aziz makes an explosion with his hands. I really like this kid. I couldn't have come up with a better plan myself.

"I'm the sharp shooter." Idri sits up at that comment, obviously offended. I'm also a little suspect.

"Actually, I think Idri is the sharp shooter." I defend Idri who nods back in thanks,

"No offense to you, you seem like a nice guy, but I'm sharper. I have a photographic memory that leads to a one hundred percent success rate." Well, you can't argue with that. "So, I'll be across the street to cover you guys for any threats that blind side you. Now, do we have enough bombs?"

"We do at the base." Aiko replies.

"That's good because we have to go back to the base anyways. The meeting isn't for another two days." Za mentions.

"Well, let's hope nothing drastic changes between then and now," I say.

"Landing now!" Riz shouts from the pilot seat. I almost forget that he was even here, he was being so silent. We land in the middle of a field and all jump out. Idri immediately starts looking for a car.

"Check this out bro." Za says to me. He then pulls out a black rod and starts running. Jumping up, he pulls the rod apart and a floating motorcycle thing generates beneath him.

"Holy crap!" I say, walking up to the bike to admire the technology.

"I thought you might like this." Za says.

"Well, I guess it's a good thing I brought these." Aziz says from behind us. He reaches behind his back and pulls out four more rods along with the one he already has in his hand. "I grabbed a few extra from the collapsed guards before I got in the plane." He tosses one to each of us. "Now, can we please get going because I'm freakin' starving. I never actually got a chance to eat a full meal thanks to this guy's strict time constraints." Aziz glares at Za. I start cracking up.

"You're telling me Za was the one to keep you on a strict time constraint. That Za?" I point at Za, struggling to keep my breath.

"Hey man. I've gotten better, you'd be proud of me," Za retaliates. I can't stop laughing but I copy what Za did and the hover bike generates beneath me. I have got to incorporate this thing into my necklace.

"Let's get moving." I command, looking back to make sure everyone had the hang of their new toy. Everyone's got it except for Riz who is seriously struggling. He keeps just diving into the dirt. Eventually he gets it, after five dirty attempts, and we make our way around the city and towards the base. When we make it, Aiko shows Aziz and Riz around the base while Za walks into his room, completely the same as how he left it.

"Man, it's good to be back." He says, smiling at me. I give him time to get readjusted and head to my room. I take off my sweaty clothes and put my necklace down on my desk. We have two days before the fight of our lives and for the Migrants' sake, I really hope we are ready. I sit on my bed and then hear a knock on my door.

"Come in." I say loudly, not moving. Idri walks in first and then a larger man walks in behind him. I look at his face and immediately grin, recognizing him as John.

"Any chance you guys need some more help?"

ZA

MARCH 27, 2031

For two days we have been preparing like it's the end of the world. We trained everybody that is staying in the base on how to defend themselves during physical threats, and we stored away tons of extra food which we smuggled from the Board's cache. There are way more people here than when I left. That last time I was here, there were still some empty rooms. Now, the place is swamped and, not only is every room full, but every room is at least doubled-up. Ivo says that after they took all those prisoners back home, they thought that they were going to find a place for them to stay. Turns out, there was nowhere for them to go.

"Bro, you ready? We leave in a few." Ivo says as he gives a light knock on my door. Everything in my room was exactly how I remembered. I can tell that Ivo never lost hope that I was going to eventually find my way back.

"Yeah, just gathering the last of my things."

"Ok. Sounds good. Meet us in the garage when you're ready." He gives me a quick smile and then walks away. We decided to go with Aziz's plan. I'm kind of happy for him in a way, like I'm a proud dad or something.

Going with his plan means that we are running a pretty tight ship. Ivo and I are going, along with Idrissa, Aiko, Riz, Aziz, and John. We decided that the officials are less likely to ask questions of me if John comes with. Meanwhile, Riz is lookout and Aziz is backup. Aiko, Idrissa, and Ivo will handle everything else.

While everyone was gathering things, Ivo was hard at work trying to get this bomb off of me. He was able to disable it, but he said there was something connecting it to me and Aziz that was out of his area of expertise. He was going to go out and find a scientist or something, but then I told him that it wasn't worth and we had more important things to do. I tap on the black bomb. Now it's dirty and the matte black paint is starting to wear off. It makes a hollow noise when I tap it, reminding me that it's made of premium materials. I don't want the bomb on me but, if it has to stay on, then I'm glad it's not plastic.

I stand up from my bed and reach into my duffel bag. It has my mask, and a few of the weapons I was able to take from The Maze. Meanwhile, the Rod is hanging on the back of my pants and the pockets of my cargo pants are filled with various bombs and grenades. I don't want to pack so much that anyone gets suspicious, just enough that I look the part. After all, I'm supposed to be the ruthless teenage fighter that leads a team of government super soldiers. It's kind of daunting when I stop to think about it.

I grab the duffel bag and walk out of my room. Giving one look back to memorize how it looks. I was always confident that I would find my way back here some way or another. I guess I already did that so, this time, I really don't know. I walk down the hallway and into the garage. Everyone is standing by their vehicles. Aziz and I are used to our hover bikes so we are just holding our Rods. But it seems like Idrissa is in a relationship with his red car and Riz has had a problem with the hover bikes since the beginning so they are both sticking with the Camry. I shake my head as I make the connection between the Camry and the car I saw earlier.

Aiko insists on bringing a van just in case we have to make a quick getaway all together. I've been talking to her more in the last couple of days and the more that I talk to her, the more she sounds like an overprotective mom. It's kind of amusing. John says he's the most experienced driver so he is going to be driving the van. Meanwhile, Ivo's fancy new bike is nowhere to be seen and he's just standing in the middle of the garage. I look at him knowing that he must've come up with some new crazy invention.

"What are you driving for this one?" I ask him. He gives me a wide grin.

"Let's just say, I made your rod thing a little better." He pinches his fingers together for added rhetoric. Then he whips the Rod that Aziz gave him out of nowhere. He jumps up while he pulls the rod apart and his bike generates underneath him.

"No way," I say. The bike was way cooler than anything I had from the beginning. Now he made the whole damn thing fit in the Rod.

"That's not all." He brags. He presses a button on the bike and the two wheels each vertically split in half and raise up so they face the ground. Suddenly the sick bike is also now a hover-bike.

"I hate you." I joke, taking out my Rod. He just laughs and then gives the signal to Aiko to open the door. She opens it, pressing a remote in her hand, and then jumps in the passenger seat. We all head out, the coordinates locked in on everyone's GPS. It takes us twenty minutes of silent driving to get there. When we finally do, we all park behind the building that's across the street from the meeting. The meeting is on the top floor of a very tall glass skyscraper. We are parked behind an old concrete office building. Aziz waves goodbye as he heads up to the roof with his sniper, he'll be in pole position to take out anybody that tries to take Ivo, Idrissa, or Aiko by surprise from behind. John gets out of the van and approaches me.

"You ready kid?" He asks,

"Yeah, just one sec." I walk past him and over to Ivo, who is getting his bombs ready. "I never asked you about that necklace you're always wearing." Ivo looks up.

"Oh, this." He says, holding the small silver cube in his hand. "This is nothing." He smiles as he presses it. Immediately, a black suit starts to develop around him like nano-tech that I see on some of the military magazines. My jaw drops as I see this suit quickly cover his entire body.

"Oh my god. So that's where that transfer went." I think to myself how I didn't assume that it was Ivo. Of course, it was. I look down at the ground to see the final bits of the suit morph over Ivo's foot and then it hits me. The anonymous unnamed criminal in the database back at the prison was him. It was his suit that I saw. That's why the foot was different. I slap my forehead in frustration.

"What?" Ivo asks.

"It's nothing. I just figured out something that I should've a long time ago. But that thing," I do a sweeping gesture towards his whole suit. "Is pretty amazing, Ivo."

"Well, I'm glad you like it." He minimizes his suit and pulls out another necklace from his pocket. He tosses it to me and I catch in my hand. "Because I made one for you. It's a little different. Lighter because of your movement. Instead of guns, I added technology that stores energy you're hit with and you can use later. It still has knives though." He winks. I look back down at the necklace. It's gold instead of silver and the cube has thin etchings on it. "Maybe you'll give it a try when you go all Bruce Lee on those nut jobs."

"Thanks," I say, grinning.

"Hey man, it's what I'm here for. Now go get your job done so that we can hang out in some peace and quiet before the entire Board comes after us." I nod, put on the necklace which fits perfectly around my head, and walk back towards John.

"Now I'm ready." I tell him.

"Alrighty. Let's do this thing. We walk around the concrete building and straight through the front doors of the skyscraper. Two guards are standing at the front.

"And who are you?" One of them asks. John steps in front of me and starts to harangue the guards.

"He's goddamn Zashil Wolf. Leader of the super soldiers and probably the most bad-ass fighter in the world. Now if you want to ask him another stupid question then he might consider killing you just for the inconvenience." The soldier, scared, leans over to the other guard.

"He's on the list." The other guard whispers.

"I apologize, sir." They each move to the side and we walk right through. When we get in the elevator, John starts cracking up.

"Did you see the looks on their faces." He says, leaning over because he's laughing so hard. I start laughing too.

"That was pretty smooth John, I'm not going to lie."

"Smooth! Smooth does not begin to describe the grace that I did that with. Oh my god. I'm probably the best bodyguard ever." I let out a last chuckle before the elevator beeps. The doors slowly open to reveal a long dark marble hallway leading straight to a conference room surrounded by glass. When we get closer, I notice that's it's full of people. Each seat occupied by a tall, blonde, white man. It would be an understatement to say that I stand out. Technically, I'm still a criminal to them. John holds the translucent glass door open for me. Looking out the opposite side, you can clearly see the stunning Boston skyline. I move around the table towards the two empty seats, John follows behind me. All of the conversation that was happening has stopped and each and every man in the room is now staring at me.

"And who are you?" The man at the head of the table asks. I recognize his face from the newspaper as the current director of the Board. It's unknown how much actual power he has by himself but, seeing how he's at the head of the table now, it seems the he has enough.

"I'm Zashil Wolf." I answer as I sit down.

"Ah yes. It's great to see you Zashil. I am a big fan of your work." He smiles after giving me the first judgmental look over. "And I was under the impression that General Lee was going to be joining you today."

"Oh, I'm sorry I thought you had heard from him yourself. He has recently fallen very ill. Instead, my close advisor here will be joining us." I say confidently. Still trying to figure out the best way to fit my character and hide my satisfaction that General Lee didn't say anything to them.

"No, we haven't heard anything from General Lee over the last couple of days and I'm sorry to hear that. We usually don't check our messages leading up to an important meeting. Does your advisor have a name?"

"John Mane." John replies and it's good that he did because I didn't know his last name.

"It's good to meet you Mr. Mane. Now, shall we get started?" John gives him a nod and then the director opens up a folder that I'm assuming has talking points. "We are going to war, folks. And I, more than anybody else, wants us to win." I sit so still I think I'm paralyzed from shock. Meanwhile, there's no reaction from everyone else, as if they all have known for ages. Which they probably have. John bumps me on the shoulder as if to say 'snap out of it.' I relax my shoulders and regain my confident posture.

"Our war on Europe is going to be taken very seriously. We barely won the first time. And it disgusts me that we needed the help of colored people to do it." I cringe. "This time, I want to bury them to the ground. Take their land." He looks towards me. "And that's why I invited you. Your work leading the super soldiers has been incredible and I would like your help with tactics, strategy, and method." I'm still in shock so it takes me a minute to gather my thoughts.

"I'm humbled to be of service in this very important time." I try to suck up to him and it works as the director cracks a quick smile and a nod. "As you have seen, a small elite team led by incredibly skilled individuals will only ever result in success. I did not attain my skills through military training but I found a way to twist the strategy of the opponent to work in my favor." I'm speaking mostly nonsense but I'm pleased to see everyone nodding along like they think what I'm saying is actually important. In reality, I'm basically telling them how to street-fight.

"If you ignore the military basics of fighting, you are able to become more ruthless. You may become more violent, but you will almost certainly win. I suggest that you create many teams just like mine. Put them in a top-of-the-line facility to train and then dispatch them as needed on Europe with specific missions. They can be espionage, assassinations, or whatever you like. You will have very targeted threats and be able to neutralize Europe's government within days. I believe that's how you win." I finish and lean back in my chair.

"That is very inspiring." The director replies. "And very correct. I think that this should be what we do and I would like all the men in this room to consult Zashil after the meeting to plan the best way to contribute to this. The plan of attack is…" He doesn't get to finish his sentence before an explosion starts to ring through the buildings. As smoke enters the room, I

MAZE

press my necklace and feel the suit come over me. It looks like the plan worked. As I had all of the attention on me, John was secretly providing intel on the building through his glasses while he sat right next to me. No more messing around, it's game time now.

IVO

MARCH 27, 2031

Once Za leaves with John I walk over to the group and hand them coms. John also has a com to use on the inside. The only one that doesn't is Za because we don't want him to be distracted plus, let's face it, way more people are going to be focused on Za then on John.

"Everything we do has to be completely in sync. If we place the bombs at the wrong time, we will blow one of us up. Does everyone get that?" Idri nods and so does Aiko as they put in their earpiece. I look to Riz who is already sprinting away. "Where is he going?"

"I think Aziz forgot his earpiece." Idri says.

"Oh ok, I thought that I stressed him out or something. He has had a stressful, few days and I'm just glad that he didn't kill us on that plane." I reply, relieved.

"I thought he was pretty good honestly." Aiko, once again, defends the youngest. It only takes about a minute for Riz to run up to the top floor and come back.

"Ok, I'm also ready if that wasn't already clear." He states as he rushes back to join the group.

"Ok, great. Does everybody have their bombs?" They all hold up the bombs I designed. I basically took the most powerful grenade and put it into something discrete that can stick to places. It wasn't that hard to do but the integrated timer means that we'll have time to get out without blowing ourselves to smithereens. I nod back and we head around the building. I activate my necklace as I'm walking and we run across the street and around to the other side of the glass skyscraper. I looked up the blueprints of this place before, it's just another industrial glass building which means it has side doors like everywhere else. I find the one on the side which is locked of course. I attach a miniature bomb and place it inside of the door handle which then blows up and the metal door swings open.

"Wait, isn't that General Lee?" Idri says, he's peering around the building's corner to the front on lookout.

"Crap, I forgot that we had to wait and take him out." I whisper. All of us are slowly creeping our way around the corner when General Lee just collapses, blood slowly coming out of the back of his head.

"You're welcome." Aziz's voice says over the coms. Riz is already shaking his head.

"You always have to show off don't you." Riz complains as we head back around the corner while General Lee's guards look around until Aziz takes them out too.

"Everyone shut up and make this quick." Idri hisses over the coms. Thank god, he said that because I wasn't going to be as nice. Once we step inside the door we start getting intel from John over our phones. I pull mine out, it looks like he is texting everything to us which is not the most discrete.

"Uncle John always had the ability to do tactile things with his eyes closed." Idri explains. I'm just glad he has hasn't been caught yet. We continue to walk through the basement as I read the texts I'm getting.

"John says that they're on the top floor in a glass conference room." I put my phone back in my pocket, that's realistically all of the information that we need. "I think our best bet is to line the ceiling of the floor underneath with bombs and then see if we can toss some on that floor or nearby. Hopefully, Za can get some off too."

"We should also put one where it won't affect the top floor so that Za knows when to move." Idri says.

"Good idea." I reply. We find the elevator and press the button. It slowly comes down to our floor and I cross my fingers that there aren't any guards inside. The doors slowly open and Idri and Riz both raise their guns, but the elevator ends up being empty. As long as no one calls the elevator while we are going up, we should have a straight shot to the top. Aiko presses fifty-four and the button lights up. We are almost there when the elevator starts to slow down. "Everyone be ready." I generate two pistols from my suit. The elevator gradually comes to a stop on the forty-ninth floor. The door starts to open and a very old woman who is hunched over is revealed. I put my guns down.

"I'll take the next one then. Looks like your busy." She slowly says as she hobbles backwards. She pushes up her old glasses as the elevator doors close again. I can tell that her vision was so bad that she probably only saw general figures without any detail. Idri and AIko can't help but start laughing.

"Everyone shut up." I command. We make it to level fifty-four with no problem. Hopping out, I immediately look up at the ceilings. They are the basic punch-in square ceiling boards, the beige ones. "Take some of those off and put the bombs in there." I whisper. "Idri, go find a place to put that side one in, that you were talking about before." Idri nods and runs towards the emergency stairwell. Riz, Aiko, and I start to fan out, grabbing chairs to stand on from the mess of cubicles as we place the bombs all around the massive office space. I put mine near the middle, the place that I think is directly underneath the conference room. I grab a black office chair, which is very hard to balance on, and push in the panel, sliding it to the side. I see a metal beam and take out the bomb, which is about the diameter of a soccer ball. I turn it upside down and the grips grab on to the metal beam. I repeat the process down the middle of the space. When we are all done, we meet back in front of the elevator. We wait a couple of minutes and then Idri finds his way back to us.

"Where did you put it?" I ask.

"It's off the side of the building, two floors below us. It should go off in…" He glances at his watch. "Three, two, one." And then we hear a sharp explosion form the left side of the building.

"Ok, I'm starting the timer." I press a button on my phone and that triggers a five minutes timer for the bombs. We have to get out of this building and back to our cars. There will be every police car, ambulance, and military anywhere near the city here in minutes after the explosion, and we have to be gone by then. Aiko starts to walk into the elevator.

"No! No elevator. It might stop working, we have to take the stairs." She glares at me as she swings open the door leading to the emergency stairwell. We start running down the stairs, each of going as fast as we can and checking our watches for time. About half way down, we run into some guards that are running up the stairs. I flip off of the platform before they reach us and over them while Idri slides down the railing. I generate my suit and then create two pistols and hit two guys in the back while Idri dismounts the railing from right behind him and puts his left arm over the right chest of the guy while his right leg kicks into the right leg of the soldier. In one fluid motion Idri flips him over and he falls down the middle of the stairs. We both do that in seconds. I look up and see Aiko stunned, her sword trembling in her hand and Riz just drops his gun to the floor.

"What?" I ask. "You know what, never mind. Let's go!" Idri goes first and we all start running down the stairs again. I look at my watch, we have two minutes left.

"Hustle people!" I scream. We pick up the pace. Once we get to the bottom, we take a sharp right and sprint down the basement hallway, pushing through the side door again. We turn right and run into the middle of the street where about ten guards are standing. "Everyone, get near me!" I shout. Riz, Aiko, and Idri crouch near me. I toss three smoke bombs over their head followed by a few splinter bombs. We make a sharp sprint towards the opposite building and run our way around, holding our sleeves up to our faces to block the smoke. We make our way to the back where the van is waiting. Aziz is already leaning up against the building. I frantically look around, up and down the street. I look at my watch, we made it with a minute to spare.

"Where's Zashil?" Aiko and Idri ask at the same time.

2 A

MARCH 27, 2031

I flip over the table as I generate guns in my hands, firing at as many people as possible, while also guarding John who is exiting the room. One guy tackles me to the ground but I see that the suit is charged with energy. I thrust up and he flies across the conference table. Nice. John goes through the door and I follow, taking one last glance back at the director who is staring at me as everyone else crouches underneath the table. He knows it's the end. Twenty guards start to close in on us from every angle, blocking our way to the elevator. Out of the corner of my eye, I spot a grey door that says "Emergency Exit" written on it.

"John! Go there! I'll be right behind you!" I point to the door and John makes a b-line for the stairwell. I back pedal after him, throwing bombs and shooting at everyone I can see. They are about to load their guns when I toss a smoke bomb and back into the door. John is already making his way down the stairs. By my calculation, we have three and a half minutes to make it out of this building before it blows. I see a doorstop next to my foot and I pick it up, shoving into the door handle of the door to block it. That will give us at least a minute.

"Go, John! Go!" I yell at him as we rush down the stairs. Good thing John isn't a non-athletic old dude. We frantically run down, each of us skipping steps and sometimes sliding down the railing. I hear the voices and sounds of the guards breaking through the door barricade and running down after us. The sounds of their footsteps echo throughout the stairwell. Meanwhile, I see hands of soldiers grabbing the railing on the lower parts of the staircase and making their way towards us. I look at my watch, a minute and a half left and we are only a third of the way down. We aren't going to make it.

"John, follow my lead!" John stops and looks back at me confused.

"What?! Kid we have got to go!" He starts stumbling down the next flight of stairs.

"No. We won't make it. You have to trust me on this one." I really hope he trusts me. I swing out my rod and jump into the chasm in the middle of the stairwell. As I fall, I pull apart the Rod and wait as the hover bike generates beneath me. I fall flat on the seat before thrusting the handles upwards. I make it to where John is, who is still running down the he stairs. I guess he didn't trust me.

"Jump on!" I say as I move my butt as far forward as it can go. John jumps clumsily, making his way over the railing and grabs my shoulders when he sits down on the bike, which immediately loses four feet of altitude from the weight. I turn the hover bike off and we free fall all of the way down. John takes my rifle and starts firing from side to side at anybody he sees. I stare at the quickly approaching concrete floor. Not now. John keeps firing. Not now. John runs out of ammo and tosses the rifle at somebody's head. Not now.

"Kid, I don't feel good about this. I mean, I lived a good life I guess." Now. I pull up on the handle and turn the bike back on. The thrusters kick in and we hover right above the ground. John is amazed. We hop off and I grab the rod as when the bike deactivates. I step over a body who is very much dead, looks like he took a fall. John rushes down the basement hallway, trying to find the side door. I look the opposite way and see a silver door on the right side of the building.

"John!" I shout down the hallway. He looks back at me and starts to run towards me. We sprint as fast as we can through the hallway and to the door. Our boots cracking against the concrete surface. I push through the door and a wave of smoke hits me. I hold my watch up to my face so I can see it through the smoke. Thirty seconds. I run through the smoke, John hot on my tail. We use our sleeves to cover our faces. We almost trip over multiple bodies and I hear the sharp sound of many sirens becoming louder and louder. We make our way across the street and stumble to the side of the building. I feel two hands grabbing me and try to fight back.

"It's us. It's us." I recognize Aziz's voice and glance to see Riz helping John. They drag us towards the van and pick us up, tossing us in. I rub my eyes which are stinging like hell. We drive quickly away. I look up and see Ivo's face.

"We did it man." I hear a massive explosion and the sound of glass crashing against the pavement. The echo of the explosion gets fainter and fainter as we head back towards the base. We actually did it.

IVO

MARCH 28, 2031

"Jeez. We really did a hefty number on that place." Aziz exclaims from the couch. We are all in the tech room, huddled around the TV. Just as we had hoped, there were no suspects. Every single news feed plays the clip over and over and over again. Silence, followed by a small explosion. Then more silence. Then the entire top of the building collapses in on itself and glass sprays around the block. Then the authorities show up. Then repeat. No one can quite believe that was us. Of course, it was in the news yesterday but everyone was so tired that we all just rolled into bed. Some of them cut to scenes of people escaping prisons amidst the chaos, although there aren't as many escapees as we would've liked, probably since we didn't take down the military or anything.

None of us even spoke. Even now, Aziz and Riz are the only ones jumping out of their seats with excitement. To the rest of us, it just feels like our duty was done. By leading the Migrants, Za, Idri, Aiko, and I made a promise to make things right. Now it feels that we are getting closer. Of course, you cut off the head, multiple heads in this instance, more grow back. We just killed the heads of the Board. But there is an assistant-director who will become director and there are vice-leaders that will take over, too. All we actually accomplished was a few days of peace, the people in power have to clean up the mess that, if we are being honest, they created in the first place. I have no sadness about what we did. We just killed the cruelest people on the planet. Maybe that's ruthless of me.

"Now what?" Za asks. He walks over to the office chair I'm sitting in. He grabs another one and rolls it over.

"I don't know, man. I'm tired of always running. We aren't enacting real change." I'm exhausted, depressed, and am the least driven I've ever been. Za leans over and pats my shoulder.

"Dad would be proud of you," he says. I look into his eyes, just like our father's. It kills me that we haven't even confirmed our parents' deaths yet. "You know, I forgot to tell you something from the meeting because I didn't want to stress you out." He says it like he is disappointed in himself.

"What?" I ask.

"The Board may or may not be planning a war on Europe." I stand up in my chair.

"What!" Everyone looks my way.

"What is it Ivo?" Aiko asks from the couch.

"You know what Za, why don't you tell them." I'm flailing my arms around and I start pacing.

"The Board is going to attack Europe." Za says quickly before retreating to the back of the room. Everyone starts shaking their heads.

"Great, that's just great." Idri gets up and walks out of the room and I don't blame him. He just found his uncle and now it feels like we all have to go back to war.

"What if we can stop it?" I ask.

"Not another grand plan again, Ivo." Aiko says. John gets up to go after Idri. "We are all too tired."

"But that's not what we do. We don't get tired and then stop. Aiko, you didn't let me give up when I couldn't find Za. If we had given up, Za would still be in prison now. We can't just give up."

"I'm sorry, Ivo. Not this time." Aiko gets up and gives me a hug before leaving the room. Aziz and Riz say nothing, they just get up and leave as well. I look at Za, who is still by my side.

"Let's do it," he says. I smile, he's just trying to be nice.

"Thanks, man. But you don't have to make me feel better this time." Now it's my turn to pat him on the shoulder.

"I'm not making you feel better, I'm serious. At the meeting, they asked me be the head of tactics. I explained to them what I think they should do. I know how they are going to do this, which means I know how we can stop them. If we get to Europe before them…"

"Then we can warn them of what's coming. We don't have to stop the Board from here. We stop them by having allies on the other end." I finish his thought. This could work.

"You ready for another adventure?" Za asks.

"It's already a better adventure because you're going to be here this time."

ZA

MARCH 31, 2031

It took us a while to figure out how we were going to get to Europe in the first place. But, we decided that we should take our own boat. Ivo spent the last two nights memorizing water territory and finding loop holes. If we go in the right direction, we won't run into any other boats at all. I gather the last of my things, all of which are fitting into one duffel bag, Ivo believes in traveling light. In terms of when we get there, we have absolutely no idea what we are to do. To be honest we could try to find our grandparents in Germany who we haven't seen in ages. There is a high possibility that they are dead. If they are dead, then we may even try to find our uncle who is, god knows where. I think he's rich though. Either way, we can only hope the racist policies haven't taken hold there yet. I get up and go to the garage where Ivo's bag is already sitting. It's been there for almost a day, credit to Ivo's concept of preparation for travel. Very unnecessary if you ask me. I lean against the Camry, waiting for Ivo until Idrissa looks down the hallway and glares at me for doing so. I stand for a couple of minutes and then sit on Ivo's bag and then stand again. What is taking Ivo so long? Then he emerges out of the lab, his hair so out of order that I'm pretty sure he just slept in there.

"What took you so long?" I ask him as he wanders down the hallway. He is already in the right clothes which I cringe at because it means that he's been in those clothes for more than twenty-four hours. It doesn't matter, I guess.

"Just whipping up a little surprise." He winks at me. I roll my eyes. If it's another one of those stupid trinkets that add nothing valuable to how I do things, then I'm going to kill him. In his defense, the last thing he made me was this necklace which came in handy when I was trying to find my way down fifty-five stories. Aiko follows Ivo close behind and eventually Idrissa walks out of his room and joins us. I swear to god he was still glaring at me. How is that even possible?

"Well, at least the base is in semi-good hands." Ivo says, turning around to face Aiko and Idrissa. Idrissa stands up all confident, as if he's taking all of the responsibility.

"Aiko is, of course, in charge." Ivo adds, looking at Idrissa who deflates into a slouch. "And take care of those twins. Trust me, you're going to need them." Ivo gets an awkwardly long hug from Aiko.

"Please don't die," she begs. Then she gives me a little pat on the back. Idrissa comes over and ruffles my hair before performing his handshake with Ivo. It won't be the last time we see them.

"I left devices for encrypted communication in each of your rooms." Ivo says as we start to walk out the door. "Oh, and I made quite a few upgrades to the base last night." He doesn't tell them what they are and we walk up the ramp. The base entrance closes behind us and we stand in the middle of the winding empty road. I take out my Rod to generate my hover bike.

"Not so fast, there." Ivo says.

"What? Is this the surprise?" He smiles and I follow him as we jump the fence and step onto the beach. For a minute, Ivo just stares back at a crack in the brick wall. I was going to make fun of him for it, but it was clear that something significant happened there, so I let it be and remember to ask him later. He then turns around and takes out what looks like the Rod but is much longer and thicker in diameter. Instead of matte black, it's a matte chrome. He pulls apart the handles and then starts to run towards the water. He jumps right before his foot touches the ocean and in seconds, an entire electric motor boat is generated.

"Hop on, why don't you." He says over his shoulder. I jump on the rear end, setting my bag down at the back of the boat. We speed away for a few miles and then Ivo presses a button. A matching chrome cover starts to cover the black boat and once it attaches on all ends, the boat sinks into the ocean, becoming a submarine.

"Didn't see that coming did you?" I laugh at the brilliance of it all.

"Good thing neither of us knows what's coming next. This time you can't make me look dumb." I stare into the dark ocean, severely lacking in fish, empty and deserted, crushed by the effects of global warming.

"What upgrades did you make to the base anyways?"

"You're going to have to wait to find that out from Aiko and Idri."

I shake my head in frustration.

"What's the plan, bro?" I ask.

"No one gets shot."

CYCLE

CYCLE

FIGHT THE SYSTEM

AUDEEP CARIENS

PROLOGUE

Five years after the Migrants blew up the Board conference in Boston, a lot changed and a lot didn't. The United States were never able to harness the momentum of the Migrants, the Board returned in full force, and the United States remained controlled by private corporations. The effects of the Roundup remained, people of color continued to be bound by labor work, and the Migrants never stopped their fight.

However, the rest of the world that had been decimated by Boards of their own were inspired by the work of the Migrants and, after the Wolf brothers warned the European government of the impending war with the United States, the rest of the world converted back to how they were before the Takeover. It took time for society to adjust once again but, eventually, the world seemed settled again. The United Nations became the government of government that oversaw global protection and continents acted together instead of smaller countries. The world seem to be united, safe, and inclusive. Except for the United States, who were stuck in the ages.

The Wolf brothers settled in Europe. After warning the European government of the war, Ivo was hired as an elite fighter. With the world reaching a point of stability, Za was able to have an ounce of a childhood for the first time in years and Ivo immediately enrolled him in school. But, it's hard for Za to enjoy his new life when he is constantly thinking about one question: what's happening with the Migrants?

ZA

March 1, 2035

It's been a hard day—more than usual. I had watched the clock all day in class, the time moving so slowly it was torture. Finally, I step into my home, swing my bag off my shoulder, and onto a hanger in the hallway in one swoop, as I kick back my ankle to close the bright orange front door. Slipping off my shoes and using my toes to toss them by the others, I flop, stomach first, onto my rigid leather couch, bounce up straight and turn on the TV.

The bright screen illuminates the dark room, my eyes still not used to the new TV. I flip to the local news channel, and another reminder of my brother's fame greets me. His annoyingly symmetrical face cropped into a square frame on the screen. The headline reads "Ivo does it again!" referring to Ivo's crime-fighting prowess. I flip through the channels, seeing the same picture of Ivo on repeat, until I finally settle on a Premier League Football replay. I stare in a haze until my stomach rumbles, reminding me to eat, and do my nightly check-in with the government.

Ever since Ivo and I successfully warned European leaders of the incoming invasion, they have welcomed us into their inner-workings. I begged Ivo to bring us back home, but he insisted we start a new life, moving forward from our painful past. Part of me agreed with him, but a

CYCLE

part of me wanted to return to my vigilante past. Even when a bomb was strapped to my chest, at least I felt the rush of adrenaline, knocking down soldiers twice my size. Of course, the European government spoke to the United Nations Secret Service. The UN appointed us as global protectors, whatever that means, and enlisted us in Europe. Ivo works on the frontlines every day while he makes me go to school. Something about how I have the potential to be smarter than him or something. I still help him and the government when I can, but I'm in my final year of high school and can't really imagine myself going to college, so I guess I'll be a regular with them soon.

After the leaders of Europe saw how wack the United States had become, they did a total 180 on the Board and corporate takeover. Instead, Europe became one entity and is back to being a functional democracy, what America had always hoped to create. We kept up contact with the Migrants for a bit, but eventually, it became too risky. Ivo keeps saying that once the government respects him, he will convince them to save the Migrants back home. We'll see if that ever happens because he has already become somewhat of a celebrity.

I finally stand up and stumble towards the kitchen. Clumsily, I swing open the right fridge door, peering into the emptiness. I finally set my eyes on the one-week-old remainder of a pizza. I hit my head against the top of the fridge before I reach into the back of the fridge to grab the plastic container and then hit it again as I pull back, closing the door. I grumble to myself in annoyance as I rub the top of my head. I take out the pizza and place it on a plate before shoving it into the microwave and pressing the one-minute button twice. As the familiar sound of the misaligned microwave plate hitting the interior microwave walls runs in the background, I go over to my desk in the corner and open my laptop. As I put in my password, my phone from the living room buzzes, the vibrations muted by the couch.

I walk back over the living room and glance at my phone screen, contemplating whether I answer. As soon as I see Ivo's name on the screen, I pick it up and answer.

"Yo," I say, sounding intentionally monotone, so he knows that deserting me at school for weeks does not maintain my happiness.

"What's wrong?" He inevitably asks. I smile to myself, glad that my ploy worked.

"What? Nothing. I'm just getting ready for my meeting." I know that he's shaking his head behind the call as he realizes that he played right into my hand.

"Okay, good. Well, that's what I was calling about. There is no meeting tonight. We need you to get over here as soon as possible."

"Why? What's going on?" I frantically ask as I shove my laptop into my bag. The microwave starts beeping at me, and I run over and start shoving the pizza into my mouth.

"No time now. I'll catch you up when you get here."

"Wait. Ivo. How am I supposed to get there? I don't know if you forgot, but I live on the other side of town, so I can be closer to my school." I take the opportunity to take a little jab at him and hopefully get him cursing his decision to have me live so far.

"There's already a car waiting for you outside." He hangs up, and I run over the window, looking down at the road where a black Mercedes is waiting for me. God damn it, I think to myself, mad that Ivo is still always one step ahead of me. I sling my backpack over one shoulder and open the door. Before I leave, I push in one of the wall panels and reach behind it to find my Rod.

Shutting the door behind me, I push through the emergency exit door further down the hallway and slide down the staircase railings. After I finish making my way down the ten flights of stairs, I find myself at the back of the building. I'm about to run to the front, but the same black car pulls onto the curb and stops right in front of me. The passenger side window rolls down and reveals a familiar face.

"I thought you might skip the elevator again. It's never easy with you, is it?" Virgil says with a smile. Virgil is basically our parental guardian, even though Ivo is an adult.

"C'mon, get in." I smile back and open the passenger door, throwing my backpack into the back seat.

"Jeez. You still use that old thing," Virgil comments, nodding towards my Rod, which is still in my right hand as he speeds towards the secret service center.

"What are you calling old?!" I retort. "This is a pristine, modern, cutting edge piece of technology. And mine is even better since the one and only Ivo Wolf made some custom tweaks." Virgil just smiles.

"No. This is modern, cutting edge technology which the one and only Ivo Wolf also designed." Virgil reaches over and opens the glove compartment, pulling out a small metal square. "This is his latest invention. He told me to give it to you as an apology for not spending more time with you." I stare at the square. It's as thin as paper, and I wonder to myself what it could be.

"Yeah, right. No gift is gonna replace hanging out with him." I say.

"I don't know, man. If any gadget can do it, it's that one. It's the first one in the world that Ivo has given to someone else," Virgil replies.

"What's so special about this little thing?" I ask.

"It goes behind your ear. You can test it out on your next mission." I shrug and put it delicately into my pants pocket. I look out the window, surveying the London city streets as I imagine my next mission.

IVO

March 1, 2035

"What's up, Ivo. The boss man told me that you needed something." Will asks as he peeks through the cracked open door.

"Yeah. I needed someone else's opinion on this case to make sure I'm not completely insane." I respond. For the last few weeks, I've been picking up criminals here and there. On the surface, they were largely unrelated, but I might've found a way that strings them all together. If I'm correct, we could be able to stop the criminals at their roots. As I'm looking back over the papers, Will hesitantly enters my office. His timidness goes well with his lean figure. His white shirt is buttoned up all the way to the neck, but his jeans take away somewhat from the professional look. After a few seconds of contemplation, he pulls out a chair opposite my desk and takes a seat, his thumbs starting to whirl around each other nervously.

It's rare for me to ask for help from anyone else, especially just another office guy. I'm not sure why, but Will seemed like an interesting person to me. I was walking down the office hall this morning and saw him. He stuck out like a sore thumb among the football-size secret agents that populate most of this place. I lean back in my black leather chair as I take my feet off my desk. I track Will's eyes to my retro Jordans. They soon observe my tracksuit. My blackout pants grip my legs, and pulled over my head is my matching black hoodie. When I came here, they gave me a list of strict office rules—dress code and manners. I really couldn't be bothered to care in the end. They aren't going to fire me because they need me, and, realistically, they need me so much that they really can't tell me to do anything. I know I sound arrogant in my head, but I sometimes have to let myself realize how far I've come. I stop staring at the wall and suddenly realize that Will has silently been waiting this whole time. Looking at the clock, it seems like he's been sitting with his back upright and his legs shaking for about three minutes.

"So, Will," I start, seeing his head perk up, and his brain visibly starts to tell itself to listen extremely hard. "I'm sure you know about the criminals that have been popping up all over Europe recently." It takes a few seconds for Will to realize that I'm waiting for a response.

"Oh, yes, of course. The bank robbery and hijacked cars being the latest accounts, if I remember correctly." I nod in approval, relieved that I didn't pick a person that has no idea about the inner workings of the service.

"I might have found a way to connect all these crimes. So, I need your help to make sure my theory isn't too much of a stretch." I see the color fall from his face as he realizes that he suddenly has to express his opinion about something I did. "I need your honest opinion, Will. Don't worry. I won't be mad at you if you call me crazy. We are already a bit too close for that." I wink at him, and he smiles. I can't tell if he's nervous or happy.

"Here's the deal. All of these crimes have been next to epicenters in the city. The first ones were minor but right next to the statehouse. And, the others took place next to the houses and buildings of the richest and most elite. Now, that could just be a coincidence. But, I scrubbed through the security footage and noticed that every criminal came with something in their pockets. However, they left with nothing except for what they stole." I swivel around my monitor and point to one of the bank robbers who has what looks like a cube in his jacket pocket.

"You see that?"

"Yeah. Ok..." Will responds. He is evidently not catching on yet. I continue.

"This is where it gets interesting. About a week before these crimes started, there was a continental tech conference. The headliner was military tech genius Tirique. He unveiled his newest mini-bomb, capable of exploding a city block and can be remotely triggered from wherever in a 1000 mile radius." Will starts to nod as he sees where I'm going. "That bomb looks like this." I turn the monitor around again and show Will a picture of a blue cube with a "T" embossed in silver on the top. The only visible indent is one at the bottom that, when pulled out, reveals the control panel, and there is a very faint pattern. Otherwise, it's simple and anonymous.

"So you think Tirique is the man behind all of this?" Will asks, suddenly excited.

"No. Tirique is too nice to do something like this and has way too much to lose. But, whoever it is, has been in contact with Tirique and is planning to assassinate every elite person on the continent. I have a slight feeling in my gut that this someone is American." Will nods and thinks to himself.

"I believe you," he says defiantly. "And I'm being honest." He adds before I can question him.

"Ok. Thanks, Will." He starts to leave, and before he shuts the door, I add one more thing. "And Will..."

"Yes?"

"You're now my guy." I don't think he knows what that means, but he looks pretty excited about it. However, instead of doing the usual thing and saying thank you, he just nods slowly, acting like he is so cool that he was expecting this all along. I chuckle after he closes the door.

A few hours later, I gather all of my materials and bring them to the boss. No one knows his name, and everyone thinks it's cheesy and stupid that we just call him the boss, but that's another story. I walk into his massive office, covered in oak and outfitted by the newest computers.

"Sir?" He looks up, his hulking shoulders leaning back and resting as he sees my face.

"Ivo! Please come in." He smiles.

"I might have a theory. Actually, I do have a theory, and I think I'm right."

"Well, you're rarely wrong," he responds in his deep and husky voice. I respect the boss a lot because he used to be in the military. He knows what it feels like to be in the field, so I think he appreciates our effort more. I explain the theory the same way I did to Will.

"It does seem as if you might be onto something, Ivo. But you know I'm stretched thin. I don't have enough bodies to explore speculation with an organized mission right now." I slump in my chair but immediately stand up with an idea.

"With your permission, sir. I want to call in Zashil." All it takes is a nod, and I'm out of his office and dialing Za on my phone.

ZA

March 2, 2035

I stare through the floor-to-ceiling window at the Eiffel Tower, now the central cell tower for what used to be Paris. What once was a tourist attraction for culture and food has quickly been turned into a hub for tech companies. Skyscrapers are plastered across the horizon, their height extended by an abundance of antennas and satellites.

"So tell me again why we are here?" I ask Ivo who is on the couch doing whatever 'research' he's doing. As soon as I got to the government center, Ivo was already outside. I didn't even get out of the car before Ivo hopped in and had Virgil drive us here. Ivo filled me in, as much as he could, but it was so much to take in that none of it really resonated with me. Ivo lets out a sigh of either disappointment or annoyance (they are essentially the same thing for him) as he hears my question.

"The tech guy that is head of the company that released the bomb is somewhere here in the HUB. We need to find him and ask him some questions."

"So why don't we just go to the company headquarters and arrange a meeting?" I ask, not knowing yet if it's a dumb question or not.

"If it were literally anyone else, we would. But this guy operates under a veil of secrecy. He's not a very public character in general, and it definitely doesn't help that his company is the biggest producer of military and spy technology. So finding him is going to be the hardest part. After that, we can leave this dump of a place and get to the real fun." He looks up and grins at me as he references the Wolf brothers back in action.

"Ok…So where to, first?" I ask as I plop myself down on the couch and lean over to Ivo's laptop.

"Food," he replies and closes the laptop right after I get a glance at an internet search: 'Where to eat in the HUB.' I swear under my breath, considering for a moment that Ivo's 'research' might be no more than trying to find good food to make up for his abysmal and nonexistent cooking skills.

He gets up and grabs his glasses, throwing mine behind him. Nowadays, you never leave the house without your glasses, especially for secret service officials. They give you information at a glance, and they are crucial to navigating the HUB. We run down the stairs and out the front door of the hotel we are staying at. The HUB is basically a series of identical skyscrapers. They are all entirely glass on the exterior and are similar in size and shape. The layout of the city, if you can call it that, is just a grid. That's why you have the glasses. They can give you directions and overlay visuals over the buildings that tell you what they are and if you're allowed inside or not. The entire system is highly sterile and confusing but very secure, precisely what these massive tech companies want for their headquarters.

I look up to see the deteriorating floating tracks of the Hover Train. When the revolution happened, these tracks were put up all over Europe to ease transportation around the entire continent, which had become one entity. Everywhere else had completely torn them down except for the

CYCLE

HUB because they 'sucked the humanity out of the cities' or whatever. But, as you can see, the HUB doesn't care about that. The truth is, the Hover Train is very efficient but, with the lack of funding, no one wants to risk their life on one if they can just walk. I keep my glasses in my pocket as I follow Ivo's lead. He had sent Virgil home already, to my disappointment.

We weave through the bland skyscrapers for about fifteen minutes before Ivo finally takes a turn into a building. He looks back at me for the first time as if he completely forgot that I was even with him.

"Put your damn glasses on. This restaurant is supposed to be pretty good, but the people here know this place's under-workings well. They won't even attempt to talk to me if my little brother doesn't have his glasses on." He starts to open the door as I reach for the thin and modern frames in my pocket and perch them on the arch of my nose.

"Plus, you can't see the menu if you don't have those on," Ivo adds, swinging open the thick and heavy steel door. We walk through, and I double-tap the right edge of my glasses to turn them on. I'm almost taken aback by how different everything looks; I haven't put these on in a while. They are banned in school, and most of the lower class can't afford luxuries like these. I'm not supposed to be advertising that I have access, (we aren't really rich), or that I work for the government in any way.

As I continue to stride behind Ivo, I look around at all of the holograms popping up on the walls. Pictures of the chefs and the restaurant's achievements appear on the dark walls of the hallway, now covered in an ocean blue wallpaper. As we step into the seating area, the bios of everyone seated at the table can be accessed through a red button above their heads. Meanwhile, the description of what they're eating comes up below their food. I immediately start getting glares for staring, but quickly realize it's not as much that, as it is the fact that they have no idea who I am. Secret service glasses like these improve the functionality, but they also don't let people see your bio.

"Psst!" Ivo catches my attention and hurries me towards him. He's already being led to the table, and we start making our way to the back of the restaurant.

"Thank you." He says to the waiter as we sit down. Once the waiter leaves, I lean over the black wooden table.

"Where are the menus?" I ask him. He just grins at me, and I immediately know that he's about to show me some technology that excites him. He signals for me to watch him. I see his thumb and pointer finger of each hand form a rectangle on the table. Slowly, he drags his hand in opposite directions. I lean back in my chair, take a deep breath and repeat the action on my side of the table. As soon as I put my fingers on the table, a white rectangle shows up between my hands reading 'menu.' I pull my hands apart as Ivo did, and suddenly a full menu starts to visualize on the table. Pleased with myself, I look up at Ivo, who curiously swings his fingers all over the place. I look back down on the menu and see the option for some ravioli. I press on it, and, to my surprise, a three-dimensional hologram of the dish starts floating over the menu. I spin it around with my finger and, after a while, some instructions appear below it: 'pinch and remove any unwanted items.' I see the basil on the top, which I know I don't like, and pinch at it before making a tossing motion. Suddenly, the basil disappears, and the text reads 'basil removed.' I keep playing around with the menu until the waiter comes before I press on the pizza and make a pushing motion towards the waiter. I'm assuming he sees it through his glasses because he nods and minimizes it.

I look up to Ivo, who smiles, and I see some bright neon text in the top left of my eye. "What did you get?" It reads. I shake my head and place my glasses on the table.

"These things are starting to give me a headache," I complain as Ivo takes off his glasses and pushes them into his jacket pocket. I admire the exactness and minimalism of his outfits. They are always so plain but end up looking very sharp. Today, he's wearing a pair of sleek black sneakers with grey tight-fitted suit pants. His jacket is a zip-up black bomber coat that perfectly wraps his shoulders. I reminisce about when our only home was in a secret basement and we had two sets of clothes. We were poor, we smelled horrible, and we always looked as homeless as we actually were. It amazes me how far we have come, especially Ivo. Sometimes I wonder if he ever misses those times. He always despised those wealthy governmental officials, and now he is one. I think he sometimes gets annoyed when he catches himself stooping down to their level but I guess the UN government is different than the Board.

"There she is." Ivo leans over and whispers to me. He nods behind my shoulder, and I quickly turn around and glance at a very tall blonde woman wearing a short, but expensive, black dress.

"Who's that?" I ask as I turn back around before she can notice me staring.

"She's the owner of this restaurant. Everyone uses this restaurant as a meeting place for top-secret work. Therefore, she knows everything there is to know about what goes on around here. She's our best bet at finding Tirique." I look down at the table and see it shake in a clean rhythm as Ivo starts to bump his knees into the bottom nervously. Ivo is an extremely calm person, always in complete control of his emotions. So, even when it's just a tiny tick like this, you know that something is up.

"What's the plan then?" I ask. I'm about to look back behind my shoulder when Ivo jumps out of his chair and starts striding towards her. Surprised, I hurriedly gather myself and go after him. By the time I am next to him, almost out of breath, he's already in conversation. Based on her furrowed brows and fake smile, I can tell she feels ambushed. It gets worse when Ivo all of a sudden flashes his badge. In one fluid movement, she backs away and starts to rush towards the back door. Her two bodyguards immediately step in front of us, both moving the corner of their coats to the side and revealing their awe-inspiring collection of weapons, including knives and guns. And, just like that she's gone.

"C'mon. Let's get out of here." Ivo grabs my sleeve and tugs me away. We slowly walk out of the restaurant.

"What the actual hell was that, Ivo? I thought I was the one that was clumsy in undercover situations, but that was godawful. Why would you flash your badge?" I anxiously pace back and forth as Ivo leans against a cellphone pole, grabs his glasses out of his pocket, and slowly slides them up to his nose. His shoulders are relaxed, his legs comfortably crossed, and his face is back to being completely expressionless. The only thing off about his appearance is a wave of his jet black hair is slightly frizzy and out of place. "Hello! Earth to Ivo. You're freakin' me out, man."

"That's the plan," he abruptly responds. "You still have the device that Virgil gave you?"

"Yeah, but…"

"Might wanna take that out now." I stumble around in my pockets until I find the thin black device and attach it behind my right ear, as Virgil taught me.

"I still don't understand anything that's happening. You know I hate when you keep me out of the loop Ivo, even if it makes you look cooler when you finally tell me your master plan." Ivo always does this when we are on missions together. He has a strategy in mind and just leaves me hanging. He says he does it to see the expression on my face when he explains that he knew what he was doing all along. The sad thing is, I definitely fell for it this time.

"All I needed to do was get near her. When I walked up to her, I immediately shook her hand. My hand had oil that has nanodes in it that are trackable. I flashed my badge so it would make her uncomfortable. Inevitably, she's now going to go home to feel safe. As long as she doesn't wash her hands between now and then, she's going to lead us right to her house, exactly where I want to be. I have a hunch she's hiding something useful to us there." I slap my forehead in disbelief. Since when is goddamn oil trackable.

"So what's this thing for? Is it a transmitter?" I ask as I tap the gadget behind my ear. Ivo smirks.

"You really think the next generation invention I've been working on is just a smaller transmitter? I feel underestimated, bro. Tap twice on it and then hold," he says as he grabs his, which is chrome, and puts it behind his ear.

I do as he says and feels a slight vibration on my neck. A deep robotic voice says, 'calibrated.' Suddenly, a suit starts to form around my body as the nanotech creates a solid but flexible metal suit around my entire body. Last, it goes around my face. I can see like usual, but there are also screen overlays across my sight-lines. The robotic voice comes back, 'Welcome, Zashil Wolf.' I hold up my arms and look at myself. A matte black surface is all over me with no visible seams and some gold accents. I look across to see Ivo in a matching suit, except it has chrome accents. Suddenly I hear his voice in my ear.

"How's this for an upgrade?" I can tell he's smiling behind his suit.

"It's sick. But why?" I ask. The suit is impressive but other than for protection, I can't think of a purpose for it.

"Well, Virgil told you it replaces the Rod, right?" I nod before realizing he can't see it. "Put your fists together like you're holding a Rod and then pull away." I see him do it, but nothing appears. I copy his movements, and, sure enough, a virtual rod appears. I'm assuming the helmet uses the same technology as the glasses, and I'm looking at a virtual hologram. "That's your Rod. I'll show you some more of the perks later. But the tracker is getting away from us, so we have to go." Ivo starts running on the road and then jumps as a high-tech motorcycle appears right below him. I smile. It's just like old times now. I do the same and follow him, literally racing into our next adventure.

IVO

March 2, 2035

I listen to the soothing sound of rubber gliding over asphalt. I take a glance behind my shoulder to see Za staying right behind me even though he has a bit of wobble. I laugh to myself as he starts to veer off to the right before catching himself. I get a notification telling me the tracker has stopped moving in the top right of my vision. It comes as no surprise that it stops at one of the enormous mansions in the HUB. I activate my transmitters to give Za a quick update.

"Yo. We are about five minutes away. Be ready. We aren't just walking in through their front door." I can tell he's shaking his head.

"Seriously, Ivo. Can't we ever do things the civilized way? I mean, we are in the secret service, for crying out loud, we don't have to act like criminals anymore."

"I know. But, it's just more fun this way." I grin as I continue to annoy him. He hates when I do this. I just keep doing whatever and expect him to follow. I probably should keep him in the loop more often, but I don't like the fact that he's growing up, it feels like I can't protect him.

I take a sharp right turn off of the main road. We spiral around in a descending loop before turning left and passing beneath the road we were just on. This is where the HUB gets very confusing. Not only does everything look the same, but the added layers, bridges, and overpasses mean it's virtually impossible not to get lost. This is where all of the rich people live, inevitably. They like the bonus of knowing every person that wants to visit them has to try. Luckily, I have experience navigating convoluted spaces. We continue weaving above and underneath roads until we get to the property sector. Most skyscrapers are still the same, except they now have little virtual markers that show up above the doors to indicate who is living there. Most people use aliases, so this isn't very helpful in terms of our intel-gathering.

You know you have reached the wealthy part of the HUB residency area when the secret tunnels begin to show up. It's not uncommon for people to die lost in the tunnels. I had done my research on the drive over to the HUB, so I know what I am doing. At first glance, everything seems the same. The buildings are still dull and tall. However, to get to certain parts of the city, you must actually drive through buildings.

"Za, stay as close to me as you possibly can. However stupid you think I'm being, don't back out. It will only make it worse." I don't wait for him to answer. I veer quickly to the left so that the next building is straight in front of me. I see my map in the top left corner, ensuring that I have this right with red markers that I had set up before. I take a quick look over my right shoulder to make sure Za is doing what I ask. I nod at him as I see his front tire as close to my back tire as possible. I look back ahead right before we hit the building. My body tenses as it braces for impact on instinct, but the glass quickly folds in on itself as we pass through. The ground immediately slopes downwards, and we are now safely driving in a secret underground tunnel.

"Holy crap. My stomach did not like that one at all." Za complains behind me. I smirk and accelerate, invigorated that the plan has gone well so far. After a few minutes, we slowly drive on an incline, making our way back to ground level. Once we get above, the harsh wind immediately hits me, and rain slides down my suit.

This part of the HUB is a haven. Lush wildlife suddenly fills all of the space in between the buildings. Looking behind, I can see the HUB center where we just came from, the skyscrapers still covering the horizon. As we keep driving, more and more normal houses pop up. They are still sterile and modern, but at least they resemble a place where someone could live. I check that the tracker still hasn't moved in my peripheral vision. The blinking dot hasn't moved for the last fifteen minutes, and I slow down to enjoy the brisk weather.

After five minutes of calm cruising, we reach our destination. Skylar, the owner of the restaurant, lives in a boxy mansion. One-way glass covers the entire front, and the roof, made of black stained wood, is at a sharp downwards angle, giving the house an unwelcoming vibe. The exposed support beams are steel, with some areas complimented with black marble. The entire feel of the place is industrial–certainly not homey. I jump up, squeezing the two handles together, and the cycle disappears beneath me before my feet hit the ground. Za walks up from behind me, the rod, which I can't see, apparently still in his hands. He shoves his arms in front of me, demanding assistance.

"Push them together harder," I whisper as I usher him to follow me around the back of the house. He does as I say and gets the rod to disappear after a few tries.

"So, what's the plan," Za says as he hurries to catch-up before matching my crouch.

"The plan is to ambush." I abruptly answer. I keep scurrying around the house, but Za puts his arm in front of me to stop me.

"Wait, wait, wait. Let me get this straight," he whispers. "You plan to break into her house, fend off her one bajillion bodyguards, and then take her hostage." I nod, agreeing with everything he's saying. Based on how fast he talks, I think he thinks this plan is much more unreasonable than I do. "First off. Where the hell are you going to take her? Second, how in god's name are we fighting those big-ass guards? And third, did you ever consider calling for backup?"

"Umm…no. Why would I do that? I know that we can handle this." I swipe his arm out of the way, and I continue my venture to the back of the house. He stands up, shaking his head but eventually follows. Before turning the corner, I check to make sure no one is standing guard behind my back. Unfortunately, there are two giant dudes on either side of the massive two-doored entrance. I turn back around and give hand signals to Za. I point up and swoop down with my arms, finishing with a punching motion. He is nodding, and I'm ninety percent sure he gets what I'm saying.

We move back along the right side of the house, looking for any footholds. Za points to a slight two-inch-deep blemish in the wall, obviously convinced he could use that. I signal him to go first. I'm not trying to look like an idiot. From where I'm standing, it seems damn near impossible to use that slight indent for any support, but my brother is a master at pulling off the impossible in these situations. He lifts his right leg about three feet to the foothold and uses his momentum to lunge his body upwards. He grabs a support beam high up with his right hand before settling into a hanging position with both arms. He then does a quick pull-up to get some force and lifts off, snagging the roof and eventually rolling onto the roof gracefully.

Nope, I tell myself. There is no chance in hell I can do that without making any sound or falling. And then I remember some of the last-minute modifications I made to the suit. I lift my right leg and double-tap my ankle bone. Suddenly, hundreds of little nubs come out of my soles. Grip. Yes. I take a few steps back until I feel the fence against my back. I take a quick lookup to see Za lying down on his stomach. He throws his arms up in the air. I shake my head and wave my left hand to shut him up. I take a deep breath and then sprint towards the wall. I lift off my right foot, my left toes hitting the wall first. I don't pause to think. I keep thrusting my knees forward, and when my right foot hits the wall, I push my body forward, rolling onto the roof. My brother cringes at the thud the impact makes against the wood, and we both don't move for a few seconds to make sure the guards below didn't hear anything.

Army crawling towards the edge of the roof, we are careful not to slide down the harsh angle. Za taps my shoulder as we near the edge.

"What the hell was that?" He whispers.

"Grip. I added it a few days ago."

"Do I get that?" He inquires.

"No. I'm testing it first. Plus, it's not like you need it anyways. You're a monkey when it comes to these things. Now, can we focus back on the task at hand?" I can tell Za is pouting behind his helmet.

"Yeah yeah, whatever. What's the gameplay here anyway?" He asks as I signal him to stop. I peer over the edge of the roof. Both guards are standing as they were before. I scoot back a few inches and turn back towards Za, retracting my helmet.

"Here's the deal. We are both going to take out a guard as quietly as possible. Then I will go first and scout it out, while you go back around front and keep a lookout. Remember, communicate through your transmitters and try not to initiate. We don't have to advertise to the whole HUB that the secret service is snooping around. You got it?" I wait for him to nod before I crawl to the right, so I'm above the other guard.

We both swing our legs over the edge. I countdown with my fingers. Three. Two. One. I jump, each of my legs landing on either of the guard's shoulders. I immediately put my left hand over his mouth and activate the taser in my right hand. I put it up to his neck, spin around in front of him, and flip his body, so he lands on his back, his feet closer to the house. I look over to Za and just shake my head. His arms are struggling to keep a grip around the guard's neck as he tries to suffocate him, and Za's feet are flailing around, wildly jabbing at the guard's torso. I keep shaking my head as I calmly walk over and tase the guy near his hip.

"Really, man. How can you be so smooth when you scale buildings and still not be able to take a dude out."

"He was big, ok. Plus, I didn't know this suit was capable of everything known to mankind. Why didn't you just tell me? You're so annoying." He kicks his feet at the grass as he walks away and back around the house. I chuckle to myself before slowly creaking the door open.

I walk into an open plan home. A giant TV and a row of ceiling-high bookshelves dominate the massive room. The kitchen contains three granite islands to the right, and I see the inside of the front door straight ahead. After a few seconds, Za's figure comes into view through the massive windows. The house is empty and eerily silent. Skylar must live by herself. I activate my helmet again and turn on the heat signature sensor. I pick up some heat on the stovetop. The tea kettle seems to be hot. She's home, but who abandons a tea kettle without making tea? I look down below, but there are no heat signatures in the basement.

I'm about to walk out of the house disappointed before a spot of color starts getting larger and larger, coming right towards me. I quickly turn off my heat signature and am welcomed by Skylar, samurai machete in hand, running straight towards me. The red ribbon on the bottom is flapping around. It's definitely a showpiece and not a weapon. I allow myself to relax, knowing that the sword will not be sharp enough to do any real damage to my suit. When she gets closer, she throws a couple of jabs that I dodge with ease. I grab her right wrist and slap the machete away, making a loud clatter as it impacts the concrete floors. I spin her arm around as I reach down and tear the ribbon from the sword. She struggles to no end before I grab her opposite arm, which is trying to slap me and force it back around her back like the other. I quickly tie the ribbon around both wrists and sit her down on the massive brown leather couch in front of the TV. Based on the smoothness and glossiness of the leather, I can tell the sofa has never been used. I quickly tie the shoelaces of her white designer sneakers together and take a seat on the back armchair to her right.

"Who are you, and what do you want?" She nervously spits, a hint of anger and violence still polluting her voice. I minimize my helmet and wait for her to recognize me. It doesn't take her long. "You again. God, I hate you secret service people, always so unprofessional and playing around with other people's affairs. What happened to my guards?"

"Do you know who I am, Ms.Garcia?" She shakes her head. "Look really hard," I add. And then it hits her.

"You're that Ivo character aren't you?" She answers, suddenly a bit of tremble in her voice.

"So you know why your guards weren't a problem in the slightest. Maybe you should consider getting their hearing checked or something."

"What do you want with me?" She stumbles on her words, now annoyed that I'm so calm.

"I don't really want anything from you. I simply want to talk." I wait for her to answer, but she avoids making eye contact and turns her head away. "I know that you are quite familiar with all of the people and business that goes on in the HUB. So, I simply need your help finding someone." I wait again, but she's now staring at the ground, defeated.

"His name is Tirique. I'm sure you've crossed paths before. He's around quite a bit these days. I have a few questions I'd like to ask him."

"I'm sure you know he's an allusive man then. No one knows where he is at any given time." She answers, her face twisted with scorn.

"How about this, you tell me anything about his recent whereabouts, and I'll get out of your hair." I stare at her for a few seconds until she finally talks.

"Ok. Fine. All I know is that Tirique loves staying underneath the center of the HUB when he wants to get away." That's bizarre. I had no clue that the center of the HUB had an underground scene, but I suppose it's plausible. I'm about to ask her more questions, but I hear some scratching over the transmitters. Finally, Za's voice comes in.

"Ivo! We got company!" He says. I take a quick look out the window to see some black vans pulling up. I look back at Skylar, who is just smiling.

"I do a little more than just gathering information, Mr. Wolf." I scramble myself up from the chair and start rushing towards the back door.

"Welcome to the HUB, Ivo. Nothing is normal here."

ZA

March 2, 2035

God, is he aggravating or what? I kick at the ground a few times and curse at myself as I walk back around to the front of the house. No wonder it took him less time to take the guy out. He had a goddamn taser built into his hand. Sometimes, I want to challenge him to a fight. Just to prove to him and everyone else that he has far less natural ability than me without his little inventions and tricks. Whatever.

I go to the front of the house. Green hedges create diagonal barriers in front, creating a triangle with the road as it funnels to the front door. The path intersects the hedges and leads to the front door. I decide to crouch low in the hedge to the right of the house. I retract my helmet to get some air and decide to start pressing random places on the suit to see what it does. After pressing some random areas on my arms and nothing happening, I'm about to give up. But, then I tap the inside of my left wrist. Suddenly a light starts to shine from my palm. I activate my helmet again so I can see the hologram. It appears to be a menu. This is good. Now I can find out about all the features myself.

I press the vehicle's button on the top right. The first one shown is the cycle we were just using. The hologram is animated, with a person using the rod and the cycle appearing underneath them, then it rotates around the 3D model of the cycle before repeating. I start swiping right, and more vehicles show up.

"Holy crap," I say to myself as I furiously swipe through all of them. There have got to be at least ten different options. One of them is a clean-looking sports car. Another looks like a fancy glider. All of them say 'beta testing' right above the name. I guess these are a bunch of vehicles that Ivo is working on currently. I exit the vehicle menu and start looking for things out of the ordinary. Suddenly, I hear a crash coming from the house, which sounds like metal against granite or something. I just shrug it off. If Ivo needs my help, he'll say something. Plus, I'm still a bit salty that I don't get to interrogate anybody. I focus my attention back on the menus. At the very end, there is a folder called Za. This could be a bunch of cool stuff for me or a bunch of useless things he put in to make fun of me. I open the folder, but it comes up with an error message: 'You do not yet have access to these items.' I remember that there is a voice inside this suit and decide to ask it some questions.

"Hey, dude?" I ask, just to see if the voice responds.

"Yes, Zashil?" Woah. The deep voice is working, which is a bit creepy, if I'm honest.

"Why can't I see what's in this folder? I mean, it's named after me."

"Ivo put a lock on this folder. Its contents will become available when the suit recognizes a certain level of achievement and your progress meets the requirements." The deep male voice is more natural than it sounded at first, but its rigidity still makes me cringe a little.

"So, what are the requirements?" I ask. Of course, Ivo won't let me see the stuff he made just for me. It was stupid for me to even get my hopes up. I'll probably never meet the dumb requirements anyways. I don't know why I'm wasting my time.

"I'm not at liberty to say." The voice responds, inevitably.

"Alright. Thanks, creepy voice."

"Anything you need, Zashil."

"Wait. Do you have a name by any chance?"

"You are to give me any name you like." The voice responds. I think for a while what I want to call him, but I can't think of anything, and eventually, the little icon that indicates that the voice is listening disappears. I take a lookup and see three black vans roll up in front of the house. Damn. I activate my transmitter.

"Ivo! We got company!" I yell as I crouch down lower, so they don't see me. For a minute, I don't think Ivo heard me, and I back up to check on him. But then he runs into me from behind.

"Aight. We gotta go," he says, rushed. His voice is slightly more unstable than usual but still more calm than you would expect.

"Did you get what you needed?" I ask.

"No time. I'll tell you later." We both look up to see a bunch of guys in black suits get out of the van. They are all carrying some serious weaponry. "Let's go out the back and cut through the neighbor's yard. Then we can loop back towards the center of the HUB." I follow him as we start running back behind the house.

"Aw, man. Do we have to go back to the HUB? That place sucks." I complain. I'm not too fond of the vibe of the place. Everything about it makes me feel like I'm being watched, which makes sense seeing how it's where all of the wack tech companies reside.

"Yes, we do. It turns out we aren't too far away from our guy," he says over his shoulder. We jump the stone wall that surrounds the massive backyard.

"There they are!" I hear the restaurant owner's voice from before shout from behind us. On the other side of the fence is an even more enormous mansion, this time in all white. Ivo ushers me to huddle underneath a tree next to a fountain.

"Take your right hand and swipe down from your elbow to your wrist on your left forearm," he says. I copy as he does it. Nothing seems to change, but then I look down. My entire body looks extremely reflective. "Now be quiet and still. They can't see us unless we move suddenly." We both crouch as still as possible next to the tree. The men in black suits hop the fence extremely clumsily as they try to keep hold of their guns. They look around, scanning the environment to see where we went. One guy looks straight at me. I swear we make eye contact, but then he turns around.

"All clear." A few of them swear to themselves before hopping the fence again and circling back. Ivo slides upon his forearm, and his suit reverts to its normal state. I do the same.

"That was amazing. When did you whip that up?" Ivo minimizes his helmet, revealing a slight smile.

"I added it with the last batch of updates. I'm pretty proud of it, but it only can last for three minutes." We walk to the front of the massive white house and use our rods to activate our cycles. We head back towards the center of the HUB. I follow Ivo, sometimes swerving from left to right, enjoying the ride.

We retrace our steps, weaving back underneath roads and above the terrain. Finally, we drive out of a building and turn back onto the road. We deactivate our cycles before it gets too crowded and minimize our suits. We smoothly walk back towards the hotel where we are staying and make our way up to our room. I collapse against the couch, the sun starting to glimmer on the horizon as a new day begins. The light washes over me as my legs stretch out on the couch. After taking a few breaths, I gather myself and sit up. Ivo is already looking things up on his computer.

"So, what's next?" I ask. He shuts his laptop and looks up at me. His eyes are tired, but he seems awake enough to go another day without sleep.

"So, I talked to Skylar. I didn't get to squeeze all of the information out of her that I wanted, but I was able to get a rough estimate of where we can find Tirique." I nod as I follow. I'm almost enthralled to have another classic and convoluted mission with Ivo. And the fact that I get to miss school helps the cause. Ivo continues. "Basically, Tirique likes to go to the HUB when he wants to hide or get away."

"But weren't we just in that area? Why did we come back to the center."

"Because. Apparently, there is a whole underground scene below the HUB that no one knows about."

"Jesus. Ok. How do we get down there?"

"I'm not sure. I still have to do some research. We might need to do some wandering and see if we pick up any clues." I let out a big sigh of exhaustion and then get up, ready to go.

"Aight. Let's go." Ivo laughs.

"Slow down their little bro. We both need some sleep first. Otherwise, we aren't going to find anything when we go hunting."

"Oh, thank god. I thought you would never say that." I turn around and stumble towards my bedroom. The white sheets of the hotel bed are still perfectly in place, unused. I don't even bother getting undressed. I flick off my shoes using my opposite toes and then deflate onto my bed. In a matter of seconds, I'm out, recharging for the next endeavor.

IVO

March 3, 2035

I peek into Za's bedroom to make sure he's asleep. He's sprawled across his bed, his shoes randomly thrown on the floor, and his face rested directly down on the clean white pillows. When I'm positive he's asleep, I head towards the kitchen and make myself some coffee. According to my research, most of the ways down to the underground are through various establishments. I'm going to need as much energy as I can get. Hopefully, Za doesn't wake up any time soon. I whip up some instant coffee and chug it before heading out the door. I make sure I look presentable and check my pockets to confirm that I have my glasses.

Once I'm outside, I amble down the roads. Most of the businesses and such are already opening even though it's still dawn. I put my glasses on to check the names and hours of the places. The first place I saw on my search was a casino called Trapped. If the name isn't a clue enough, that place is dangerous. In general, it's usually a good rule of thumb to never go into a casino or a bar in the HUB. Because everyone wears their glasses, these places find it very easy to trap them through enticing visuals and rewards. Since Trapped is open all day and through the night, I thought I would start there.

I take a right and then a left, weaving through some skinnier and less public alleys. I always make a mental note of where the security cameras are, not because I can't be spotted but because I can usually trick them into thinking I'm going somewhere where I'm not. I notice that one camera has a visual cut off right before the door into a hotel. I move towards the door as if I'm going into the hotel, and, once I'm sure I've tricked the camera, I quickly inch away with my back against the building. I do that a few times until I reach the casino.

As soon as I approach the door, a massive hologram alert pops up in front of me. It reads, "no entry without glasses. Glasses must be worn at all times." After that, it lists a bunch of offenses and fines for not abiding by the rules. I have my glasses on but now turn them off. Most glasses can't do that, but I modded these for situations like this one. I take a deep breath and then push through the heavy metal door. Immediately, neon lights and empty tables greet me. Of course, if I had my glasses on, I would see all of the games, scores, and prizes within the casino and holograms would be scattered everywhere.

"Would you like a drink, sir?" A waiter comes towards me, holding a metal plate with various alcoholic beverages in smaller than typical sizes.

"I'm fine, thanks," I respond, pushing past him and searching for anything out of the ordinary. Other than in the main area, not many places could act as an access point to the underground. It can't be with all of the games because that would be too out in the open. I wander towards the bar in the back. A long oak counter separates me and high chairs from the bartender and his arsenal of drinks. I nod at the bartender, dressed in all black, his sleeves slightly rolled up to before the elbow, revealing tattoos. I know I'm missing out on the full effect from the faded look of the line by not having my glasses on. A lot of people embed a description or an animation that compliments their tattoo. If you're in the HUB, what you see without your glasses is never the whole story.

I mill about, spinning around in my chair for a few moments until the bartender goes to attend to someone else and make a drink. I quickly heave myself up so I can look at the floor behind the counter. Nothing seems astray, and the continuous cement flooring means there are no secret doors or anything. I push myself back and leave the bar before the bartender can say anything. Wandering for a while longer, I make eye contact with a few other customers whose faces are either littered with disappointment or lit up from adrenaline.

After exploring the whole expanse of the first-floor casino, I'm about to head upstairs to the hotel and lounge area before I see a man in a very luxurious velvet purple suit walk into the women's bathroom. Curious, I lean against a wall next to the bathroom door. I grab the least alcoholic-looking drink I can find from a waiter and sip it as I try to look like I belong. After ten minutes, the guy doesn't come out, which is suspicious. I scan the ceiling for cameras, and indeed, there is a security camera on rotation. That means that every two minutes or so, it should rotate far enough for the entrance to the bathroom to be out of sight for at least ten seconds, plenty of time for someone to sneak in unseen. After tapping my feet for a minute, the camera rotates, and I spin-off and into the women's bathroom. I check below the stalls to ensure no one is here and then lock the swinging blue door behind me—the same glossy white tile line both the floor and wall. I rub my hand over the crevices, checking to make sure there isn't anything special about them. I check the three stalls and, other than them being all immaculate, there is nothing out of the ordinary.

I go to wash my hands in the far-right sink, taking a look in the mirror before turning on the faucet. Then I see it. There is a single, tiny, hairline crack down the mirror that continues through the middle of the sink and all the way down to the floor. I roll up my sleeves and push each side of the sink as hard as possible, but nothing moves. I step back to see if the crack continues down to the floor. It doesn't, but I notice that the tiles are slightly lighter below the sink and continue to the stall across from it. This is either a coincidence, or they removed some tiles after completing the bathroom at a later date and installed something extra beneath the floor, covering it up with newer tiles. I walk back into the stall where the pristine tiles lead into the toilet. I scan the toilet, but nothing seems out of the ordinary. I pull off the old industrial top and take a look at the pipes. A red switch hides in the back, hidden underneath some old piping and a waterproof covering. I switch it on and head back out of the stall and to the sink. I give it one more push, and the entire right side of the sink falls to the side, the hydraulics in the hinge stopping it right before it hits the ground. In the space where the sink's base should be, a single pipe interrupts a narrow granite staircase leading down. I go back and unlock the bathroom door to avoid suspicion and then jump down into the stairs, grabbing the inside edge of the sink and pulling it back into place. I listen and hear the switch go back and then head down into the darkness.

    I have to squint to get down the narrow staircase, which continues to wind as it progresses. A faint light at the bottom helps illuminate my path, but it's clear that these steps weren't a recent installation. The staircase seems to go down forever, continuously winding, the faint light getting slightly brighter every step. By the time I get to the bottom, I have completely lost track of how deep I am. I step down into a library. Tall wooden bookshelves are on both sides of me, creating a corridor. I walk into the open space where thousands of books are against the circular wall, rising into the ceiling. The entire area is very un-HUB-like, everything is warm in color, and the space almost feels cozy. However, that feeling ends as I keep walking. I take a right into the main area and follow the descending number of books out into a hallway. Now it quickly becomes sterile. The floor is a slippery black marble, and the walls are black. The space is lit by harsh white lights, embedded in the ceiling, arranged in a row down the hallway. Rooms stem off left and right. I step into a few of the rooms and am greeted by more old-fashioned spaces—some cafes with nobody home, others old museums with barely any art. The entire space feels eery.

Finally, the hallway ends, and a spinning door leads me out onto a city street. The road is cement, obviously laid down on dirt with the grainy brown particles messing up the sidewalk. There aren't many people around, but I realize it's still only eight in the morning after checking my phone, which has full service. Tall buildings line the main road, appearing to go on forever. I'm assuming the buildings also have other secret entrances down to this place. This place looks more like a typical city than the HUB itself. A generally comfortable but musty warmth circulates, and the buildings don't all look the same. Brick is a sight for sore eyes, and the lack of glass is a breath of fresh air. I spot a few people milling about; they ignore me. I notice that no one is wearing glasses here, and when I turn mine on, nothing changes in the environment.

I see a cafe is already open for business, and I step in. Small wooden tables are scattered around, complimented by wood chairs with red leather seats. There's one guy, in work uniform who is sweeping up the floor. I walk over, and he scrambles to get behind the cash register at the sight of seeing me.

"Oh no, that's alright. I just stepped in to talk to someone from around here." The waiter's tense face relaxes, and his shoulder droops. His dusty blonde hair looks odd against his browner skin, and his unbuttoned shirt hints at how casual he actually is.

"Ok good, because I haven't put out the baked goods yet. What can I do for you?" I fold my arms and rest my elbows against the counter in front of the register, taking my glasses off and putting them in my pocket.

"So, what's the deal with this place....Richard?" I take a glance at his name tag.

"Sorry, sir. I'm not sure I know what you mean."

"Who's the big dog? Who runs the underground? I'm a businessman passing through the HUB and couldn't resist coming down here when I heard about it. It's quite the establishment. Amazingly, no one knows about it." Richard seems to find comfort in talking about something he knows about. He smiles.

"It's secretive for a reason—only the best of the best know about this place. In terms of the big dog, I usually wouldn't spoil the excitement of finding out, but since you are just passing through, maybe I'll give you a jump start. His name is Tirique. I mean, I'm sure you know him. Everybody does at this point. Man, he is a genius. He spends a lot of his time down here and saves all his most secret work for the specialists living here. Rumor says that he's working on something huge and that whoever works down here will be the first to try it. That's why my mom made me take this job, says it's a once-in-a-lifetime opportunity."

"That's cool, man. I'll get out of your hair so you can do your job. But, by any chance, do you happen to know where Tirique lives around here? He's an old friend of mine. He is actually the one that invited me down."

"No one ever actually sees Tirique here, but his compound is at the end. It's maximum security, but I'm sure they will open it up for you." Richard pauses like he's going to say something else but then shakes his head and starts unloading drinks into the fridge. I wave goodbye and leave the shop. A few more people are now walking around, all of them speedy and with purpose. I'm about to turn right and check out Tirique's secret compound, but I remember that I have to be back before Za wakes up.

I start retracing my steps, and it takes me thirty minutes to run up the steps and back out into the casino. Harsh light greets me as I leave the casino. I squint as my eyes readjust to the searing sunlight, and I make my way back to the hotel. Once I get into the room, I notice the lights are on. I don't remember leaving them on when I left. Although the small table is slightly askew, the living room looks intact, and a couch cushion is a little out of place. We were both so tired that we could've done that before, and I hadn't noticed.

"Za! You up, bro? I found the underground. It looks pretty exciting." I hear no answer and start making my way to his room. "Za, are you serious? You're still sleeping. I thought you're used to pulling all-nighters for school." I push through his door, which is left a crack open like how I left it. I step on the covers, which are now on the floor. Footprints stain the white sheets. Everywhere pillows have been thrown, one resting against the cracked television screen. I frantically check every corner of the room and the rest of the apartment before punching the couch cushion and sitting down, head in hands. Za's gone.

ZA

March 3, 2035

"Rise and shine, Zashil." I wake up to cold water pouring on my head. I brush my hair out of my eyes and frantically look around my room. Two guards stand on either side of the bed, wearing green camouflage military uniforms. The one on my right is holding the bucket, still letting it drip on the bed.

"That's enough, Kyle. Jesus. The boy is up. We aren't trying to freak him out, remember." The sound of a new voice draws my attention forwards. At the foot of my bed, a young man, maybe mid-twenties, in a clean-cut striped black suit, sits in one of our kitchen chairs that he dragged into my room. His American accent reminds me of home, and it's nice to hear after years of European conversations. We make eye contact, and he smiles, revealing one of those perfect sets of American teeth.

"Hi, Zashil. Sorry about the antics, but you are a hella deep sleeper. All of this must be giving you a bad impression. Damnit. I told myself I wouldn't do this." I interrupt him, already annoyed by his personality.

"Where's my brother? Who the hell are you? And, what do you want?" I ask, quickly sitting up in my bed, causing the two guards to tense up momentarily. I keep my sightline pointed towards the young man, but I think about how to get out of this. I could either combat my way out, but, based on how these guys are standing, I don't like my chances without weapons. I could engage in conversation and then find a way to dip out later. Or, I could just make a run for it, jump out the window, and hope to use my skills to cushion my landing. Before I can make a decision, the man starts talking again.

"Wow. So many questions. Uhhhh…ok. In all honesty, I have no idea where your brother is because he wasn't here when we got here." That's bizarre. I thought that Ivo was going to sleep when I did. Where would he have gone, and why would he have left?

"Which is a real shame because I was quite proud of the plan I had come up with to detain him. It was quite elaborate in my opinion. It would've been nice to execute it." He pauses and meets my killer glare. "Oh right, the other questions. My name is Serge Adams. I would tell you what I do, but it would ruin the surprise for later." God, I want to punch this guy so bad right now. I realize that I will have to deal with him for even longer if I choose the second option, which seems the most realistic anyways.

"As for the third, I'm just here to have a quick chat. A few of my friends and I are whipping up a little project. Well, I say little, it's actually quite large. But we wanted you to be part of it. We are big fans of your work in general…." Nope, I can't do it.

I whip the covers onto the guy to my right in one fluid motion, temporarily blinding him. Then I kick up into the other guard's head, putting him off balance, and jump to the floor. As the one on the right starts to regain his balance, I grab two pillows and toss them into his face as I stride towards him. I shove him into the back wall and knock him out. Serge is now on his feet as he quickly realizes that two soldiers may not have been enough. I dive over the bed and throw both legs in unison at the man's chest. He spirals away and crashes into the TV. I flip over the helplessly diving Serge and into the kitchen. I look for anything, my shoes, phone, literally anything I could use. But I have no time. The guard is back on his feet and rushing towards me. I grab a pot of coffee that's at arm's length and splash it into his eyes, hoping it's hot. Then, I make a B-line towards the door. I push it open and sprint down the hallway. What to do. What to do. Then I remember. I feel behind my ear and activate my suit. Thank god. I find the emergency staircase and jump down the middle, grabbing onto the outside of the railing to help swing down. As I jump, the suit finishes wrapping around my body, my helmet finally materializing over my head.

Once I get to the bottom, I shove through the 'no exit' door, an alarm going off as I run into the side alley. I turn right but am greeted with a massive black van decked out with artillery weapons. I turn around and start sprinting, but another van turns into the alley. I look to jump and scale the opposite building wall, but electric rope swings around my ankle, and I fall in a heap as I jump. Four men get out of the vans and push me against the exterior wall of the hotel. They use a metal strip along my neck that magnetically connects to the wall, almost choking me.

"Well, that was quite the skeptical Mr. Wolf." I suck in my neck to turn to see Serge casually walking down the alley towards me. "See, people. That's the kind of skill and ambition we need. Very well done. I thought that you were going to jump out the window. That would've been something, definitely movie material. As he stands in front of me, he leans down and squats to my level. He grabs my chin and forces me to look up into his emerald eyes. He slaps my cheek.

"I appreciate your passion Zashil. But you would've been better off just listening to what I had to say. Now poor Karl is taking a nap in the back of a van and we give him enough time off as it is."

"I swear to god, Serge. If you don't let me go." I shout as they drag me towards a van. Before I can say anymore, I feel a needle go into my neck, and everything starts to fade to black.

IVO

March 3, 2035

Shoot. I pace back and forth through the middle of the hotel room. I should've never left him. Was that wrong? I don't think so. How was I supposed to know he would be abducted? And why on earth would someone want him instead of me? I pick up my phone and dial the office, but I hang up right after it starts ringing. No. I can't tell them because then they will send a search party, and then I'll lose my cover, if I had any in the first place, and everything will just come to nothing.

Okay. Think. I can hack his phone. Good idea, Ivo. I go into the living room and grab my laptop. I sit down, open the computer, and activate the tracker on his phone in a matter of seconds. Then I hear a beeping from the kitchen. I walk over and, there, sitting perfectly on the kitchen counter, is Za's phone. Great. Just great. I start pacing again, my legs strained and tired, and my head all over the place. I keep putting on my glasses, turning them on, looking around, turning them off, taking them off, and putting them back in my pocket.

I must do that five times before thinking of another idea. His suit chip. There is no way that, in his tired haze, he remembered to take off his chip.

I guess he's going to learn the hard way that it won't come off at all if you keep it on for more than 24 hours. I stride back to my laptop and start trying to track his suit. Even though I invented it, I had purposefully made it extremely difficult for anyone to get in, even if they had the code themselves. However, I had left a loophole for myself and, in a few minutes, I'm in and looking at the map. The suit seems to be moving, so Za must be in a vehicle of some sort. I can also track his health analytics, and he seems to be okay, just knocked out.

I let out a sigh of relief. I legitimately thought he was dead for a second. My computer says that they are very far away, so even if I went as fast as possible, they would easily have too much time with him in whatever base they are going to. I have to, at the very least, cut them off. I guess we are going to have to try it, I tell myself. Within the suit, I put in more vehicles than just the classic cycle. There is also a glider. If I don't die trying to use it, that will get me there in plenty of time.

I close my laptop and head out the door, making sure to put the 'I'm busy' tag on the door handle. The last thing I need is the hotel getting suspicious of anything. I don't even want to think about the broken TV right now. I head down the hallway to the emergency staircase but go up instead of down. I have no idea how well this is going to work. In theory, I should get myself in the air, and the motors and everything will make sure I essentially become a miniature airplane. On the other hand, I could easily just fall fifteen stories to my death because I'm jumping off a building without ever testing it. I climb a few stories and exit through a silver door.

The roof is entirely flat, with almost no protrusions. Even during the day, the darkness of the buildings glooms the mood. There is a small one-foot lip around the roof's perimeter, but I should be able to jump off of that with no problem. I activate my suit and stretch out my legs as it

CYCLE

forms around me. I turn on the map in my top right to keep an eye on the tracker. Once my suit is complete, I back up to the edge. Starting with a jog and then increasing to a sprint, I run the length of the building. Forming the rod in my hand, I push in twice with both hands and then pull out. The plane starts to form around me as I jump. First, it's not unlike the cycle; my body positions are the same but there are long wings that jut out from around my torso and an extra top enclosure that keeps me inside appears, almost like a windshield. Just as I'm about to tip forward and start falling, the engine kicks in, and I'm off to the races. I designed this so it would also be like driving the cycle. The handles have now turned on a ninety-degree angle and moving them left or right in unison is what makes it turn.

Okay. The first step is complete. I veer off to the right to get in line with the tracker and accelerate as much as possible. After a few minutes, I leave the HUB behind me, the precise city landscape now replaced with miles of lush green forest, only interrupted by small bodies of water. I would do anything to feel the fresh air against my skin, but I start to sweat when I think about Za. Maybe I should've just asked for backup when he told me. I thought, I guess I still think, that I can do this mission by myself. But I must admit, it's getting a bit more complicated than what I intended. It only takes a few minutes to gain speed and start shortening the distance between myself and Za.

Suddenly I get a call from the boss. I think about not taking it but realize it would be more alarming if I didn't answer, and I want him to believe that everything is going to plan. I answer the call after attempting to get my mind in the right headspace.

"How are you doing, boss." I almost yell, unsure of how much noise pollution is coming from the air currents. He answers normally, so I assume the yelling will be necessary for the duration of the conversation.

"Well, it's busy over here. But I called to see how my favorite agent is doing. Any progress with your little excursion?" His hoarse voice is weirdly comforting to hear. It might be because it's something familiar for once.

"Everything is going to plan, sir. I have gathered enough intel to track down Tirique, and we should be getting to the bottom of this very shortly." I stay as definitive as possible, not letting any doubt creep into my voice. I don't mention my discovery of the underground HUB because, for one, I haven't had time to process and think about it myself, and, for two, I know that the moment I mention it, the boss will immediately send a whole crew out here to crawl around.

"Well, that's great to hear, Ivo. I'm sure having your brother is a massive help. I don't want to keep you too long, but I tried to contact Zashil and got no answer." I shake my head.

"Za is with me. I told him to leave his phone and stuff at home, so he didn't get any distractions. You know how high schoolers are these days." I cringe at my unconvincing cover-up.

"Very well then. I wish you the best of luck, and I expect victory calls from both of you very soon. Be well." He hangs and up, and I let out a sigh. That was a close one. I get an alert from my map telling me I'm two miles away from the tracker. It only takes me a couple minutes to reduce that to one mile.

As I'm closing in, the worst possible thing happens. Out of absolutely nowhere, the tracker just stops. It disappears. No one could have taken the tracker off because, by now, the suit can't be removed from Za's neck. The only way that they could've stopped the tracker was if they went underground. But they would have had to go very, very underground. This is not good. I land in the area where the tracker was seen last. It's a broad dirt road. Tracks from at least two vans mark the road but abruptly stop where I'm standing. I kneel and scan the ground. There's a crack that

CYCLE

goes around in a fairly large circle in the middle of the road, but I don't see any control panels anywhere. I walk around and examine every tree within ten feet of the circle. Every single tree has a rectangular indent facing the circle. I push the panel in, but nothing happens until I get to the last one. This one moves in and slides behind into the tree. Inside is a bunch of wires and a small LED screen. By looking at the way it's set up, it looks like the hatch or whatever only opens with remote access. I'm about to tug at some wires to hotwire the door open before I see the screen blinking: 'all weapons available.' Damnit. I quickly realize that all of the indents in the trees must house automated security weapons triggered when someone tries to do what I'm about to do.

    I turn around, sliding down the tree and sitting down. I sit with my back to the tree, facing the road, my head buried in my arms. What am I supposed to do now? I could wait here for anybody leaving or coming. But if I were going to do that, I would either need more people or more firepower. I could go back to Paris and plead for backup. With an agent in danger, I don't think the boss would deny me any assistance. Either way, I need to head back to the hotel and figure stuff out.

    I get a running start, activate the rod, and use my cycle to ride smoothly back. I need to think. What else could I possibly do? If Za used the suit, which I'm sure he would, and he tried to escape, then there should be a way I can see what he saw. There are miniature cameras that record everything. It was a feature requested by the UN secret service for when I hand these suits out to more agents. They were adamant that they needed a body cam so the general or whoever can direct them remotely. That's what I'll do. I'll check if he used the suit and then see what information that gives me and go from there. Just keep it together, Ivo, and you can figure this one out. These are the moments where my dad would be so calm. He died before he could ever teach me that skill.

It takes me forever to get back, but I eventually make it to the edge of the HUB and walk the rest of the way to the hotel. Now there are people everywhere. Everyone is moving with purpose and looking around through their glasses. When I make it upstairs, I go straight to my laptop. Please, please, please, for once in your life, Za, accept some assistance from technology. I see a video file from early this morning. This has to be it. I open it, and a lot of blurriness greets me. When it focuses, it looks like Za is jumping down the middle of the emergency staircase, swinging from the railing. That's his classic move. It's good to know that they didn't entirely catch him by surprise and he put up a little fight. I regret not telling him about all the other stuff in the suit. That would've been helpful. Oh well. I play the footage and see Za run out the door and get ambushed by two vans and multiple big guys in suits. And then one guy, who looks like the choreographer of this situation, gets real up close. I pause the footage. He seems weirdly familiar, but I have no idea why. There is no audio to the clip, which is unfortunate because someone could've said his name.

I keep the clip paused and attempt to run facial recognition software on the man's face. It doesn't come up with much except a name, Serge Adams, and a list of possible aliases. I head into the secret service database and go to the video section. This is where all security footage is collected, analyzed, and marked with any people in the video. I search Serge Adams, and a bunch of videos pops up. This guy has been pretty busy lately because most of the videos are tagged with dates within the last year. I keep flicking through the videos, most of them just useless footage of him heading into a coffee shop or something like that. I notice a strange pattern. Every week, on a Monday, he is in London and goes to coffee at the same place. Since he's not in London in any of the other clips, I can assume he goes there for a specific recurring meeting.

CYCLE

I replay the clips over and over. Every time, all it shows is Serge walking into a cafe. There is nothing else that the camera picks up. I start studying if there are any other clues in the clips. I notice that the cafe has a massive window. I zoom in to see if I notice anything. And then I see her. Skylar is sitting in a seat by the window, wearing many layers and a big hat to conceal her identity. That is probably why she isn't marked in the clips. However, I can recognize her hair and height from anywhere. I quickly scroll through the other clips and, now that I'm looking for her, I find her in every one of the cafe meetings. What could these two people have in common? I'm still thinking about them when I get to the very last clip from the year, and then I see something that's even more shocking.

It's a clip of a street corner. It looks like it's in Paris, but I could be wrong. There is no location tag on the clip, which is odd. There, standing on the corner, is Serge, leaning up against the building. Out of nowhere, Tirique walk by, hands Serge a folder, and then keeps walking, getting in a black car around the corner. I close my laptop and lean back in my chair. So all of these people are connected. Tirique, who is either responsible for or supplying the criminals who are robbing a bunch of buildings, Serge, who has kidnapped Za, and Skylar, the know-it-all of the HUB. Yes, it's three powerful people. But what could they possibly share as an objective?

ZA

March 3, 2035

I open my eyes to a dark room. It almost looks like an apartment living room. I'm lying down on a leather couch. I check my hands and wrists for tags or handcuffs, but they have nothing. I sit up and look around. In front of me is a large fireplace, a couple of abstract sculptures on the mantle. There are bookshelves on both sides of the room, and behind me, there is a fridge and table. Some snacks, fruit, and yogurt are already on the table. I get up and hesitantly grab a banana, doing one more scan of the room. Other than the lack of a door or windows, this room is comforting. I peel and finish the banana swiftly, my stomach growling for more as I toss the remains in a small trash bin next to the table. Instead of grabbing food, I sit back down on the couch and try to remember what happened. The last thing I remember is getting knocked out as I was dragged towards the van. That's it. I wonder where Ivo is. He's probably going crazy trying to find me. I'm sure he'll find a way eventually. I just need to make sure that I'm not gone or dead by the time he gets here.

The bookshelves on my right suddenly swing open, and a very refined-looking brown man walks in, around Ivo's age, wearing a very sharp-looking tracksuit underneath a trench coat. He slowly walks towards me after gently pushing the bookshelf back into place. He starts to talk as he makes his way towards me and sits in the armchair to my left. His voice is extremely measured and smooth.

"Zashil Wolf. It's an absolute pleasure to finally meet you." He sits down and reaches out his hand for a handshake. I hesitate, but his calm nature and reassuring glance prompt me to return the gesture. "Before we start talking about why I'm so intrigued by you, I want to apologize for the shambolic handling of your invitation from Serge and his crew. He's a bit messy sometimes and has no clue how to take orders. He was supposed to, at the very most, pick you up and put you in the van." I can tell by his disgusted expression that he's very unhappy with Serge, which makes me think that I'm sitting across from the head guy of whatever operation I'm being brought into. I look into his eyes and see no signs of scorn or negative energy. He's honest and, for whatever reason I'm here, he wants me to feel at ease. I settle myself, squirming around on the couch until I'm comfortable, and then speak, trying to match his tone of voice.

"Yeah, that wasn't very well handled, if I'm being honest." He chuckles as he stares at the floor. "I need to know why I'm here. Who are you, what is going on, and why, instead of my brother, do you want me?" He takes a deep breath, almost like he is centering his chi or something, and then proceeds to answer my questions. His wavy black hair, which has hints of silver, falls over his forehead as he leans in, complimenting his clean-shaven face. To say the least, he looks professional.

"My name is Nox, and I want what you want, but I think I'm a bit more radical. I come from where you come from. I was an orphan growing up in the United States on the West Coast. When the revolution happened, I escaped my white adopted parents and found the Migrants. I rebelled against the Board but was never convinced I was ever going to get a better life. So, I left. I hid in a cargo ship headed to China. I was nomadic, moving from place to place around Asia. I stuck out less there, and I was less bothered by the effects of their revolution for the most part. Eventually, I made it to Europe, where it was safe, a product of your brother's work. I vowed never to forget about where I come from, and the state of my home country continually saddens me. A year ago, I started a mission to bring back democracy in the United States. It's long and convoluted, but I want, actually, I need, your help if I'm going to succeed." I sit quietly and stare at the ground, processing. So Nox knows how I feel. He comes from a similar background as Ivo and me, but that doesn't explain why he would need me. There has got to be more to this. He's coming off a bit too innocent for my liking.

"That's a moving story, and, yes, it's similar to my background, but it still doesn't explain why you want me and not my brother. What is your mission?" Nox gets up and starts pacing the length of the room, periodically stopping to warm his hands in the fire.

"I started my planning with identifying what exactly I'd like to achieve, what my goal was. I wanted to bring a sense of order, peace, and equality back to the United States, but I also want to be there to help guide it through its transformative years. Then I asked myself how I could get there. Realistically, I can't form a force on my own that can go up against the strongest military in the world. Not even the super team you and your brother made was good enough to go head-on against them. I needed to become in charge of a group of people that possessed the means to take down the United States hierarchy and military. After spending time here in Europe, I realized that it was only Europe that had those means. So, the first thing I need to do is take control of Europe, temporarily, of course. Then I can work my way up to invading the United States and seizing control of the country. That's my plan. I wanted your expertise to be head of the combat group and help lead with me. You're so young, but you've seen it all. You know what the migrant life is like, and you know what they will respond to. As soon as the East Coast sees your face, they will be on your side. You will become an icon, Zashil, a savior, not living under your brother's shadow. I didn't ask him because I wanted you. To be honest, I think you are a more capable fighter and have a more open-minded approach because of your age. Ivo is too far into his secret service work, and telling him about our plans would only mean abandoning our element of surprise." He sits back down, crossing his legs and looking at me. His breathing has quickened like he just finished an exam, and his green eyes are intent. What the hell did I just hear.

Nox basically wants to become a world leader, having no experience, and his entire plan is motivated pretty much by anger. Anyone logically thinking would think this man needs some mental assistance. But for some reason, his plan appeals to me. I don't know if it's the fact that he went out of the way to differentiate myself from my brother or the fact that his voice never wavered, fully committed to the words he was saying. In a lot of bizarre ways, he reminds me of Ivo. Nowadays, Ivo thinks too logically for this kind of thing. But, he used to be this radical and this open-minded. Nothing was impossible to him. I miss that.

"So what happens when you're done. Say, in a year. What happens to Europe, and who leads the United States? Or is it going to be you?" I skeptically ask.

"Oh god, no. It won't be me. I'm just going to get the United States stabilized and back on its feet using European resources. But then, I will step aside, find officials and people that are worthy leaders, and democratically have them elected. As for Europe, once my work is done, I will hand back the reigns, and everything should go back to how it all started. I wouldn't be so stupid as to think I would be able to lead the two biggest global powerhouses. As you can see, Zashil, I'm not a selfish person who wants glory, fame, or power. I want to do what's right for the Migrants who are suffering." He stands back up, brushing against the side of the couch as he goes to the snack table. He opens the fridge, grabs a plastic bottle of water, and starts to pour it into a glass.

"So, are you in? I can't do this without you." It's not a hard decision. I might as well go along with it. I'll be able to back out whenever if I want, and this is the opportunity I've been waiting for. This is what Ivo promised he would do but never did.

"Ok, Nox. I'm in." I stand up and face him from behind the couch. "But I have two conditions."

"Yes, anything." He takes sips of water.

"One, I get a say in everything we do, and you don't just order me around. You're not my boss. You're my partner."

"I wouldn't want it any other way. And two?"

"And two. I want a chance to convince Ivo. If I were to convince him, you can't argue he would be an irreplaceable asset."

"Fine. But remember, I don't need or want him. I want you. I'll only let him in because it means I get you for sure. But I can't let you leave just yet. I want to show you the crew and our humble abode. Then, if you still want to reach out to Ivo, we will find a way to do that discretely and secretly. But you only get one chance. If he says no, we need to make sure he doesn't tell the secret service, by any means necessary." I nod, my face stern but satisfied. I feel a bizarre sense of comfort when I'm around Nox. "Now, let me show you around." He walks back to the bookshelf and opens the door again.

"And Nox." I wait for him to turn around. "Call me Za." He nods to me and smiles before ushering me to follow. We walk into a metal hallway, the ceiling is dark glass and the floor a brushed matte stone. I lengthen my stride to catch up to him, and we walk down the hallway until we reach a sliding door the height of the entire floor. Sliding it open reveals a massive open space resembling an airplane hangar. Ironically, it's not unlike the first prison I stayed in years ago. The entire top is a glass dome, coming all the way down to the edge. Based on the lack of natural light, I assume we are underground.

"This is the home base of it all. Hopefully, this space will be filled with a lot more people soon. The people wandering around now are either guards that came in with Serge or some of the others that have been recruited." Above us, a second-floor circles around the edge of the dome, the floor of the balcony type thing is glass and the metal railing is the only interruption to the clean look. Nox sees me looking.

"Up there is where you will be staying. It has a suite and a training area for you. But of course, you're largely welcome to come and go. I expect it will be easier for you to stick around, but I understand that being underground might get suffocating. At least it does for me." We walk to the other side of the dome, where two pairs of large sliding doors on either side of the dome. "These two doors open up transport tunnels to the bases of our other team members." He points to the left. "That one on the left goes to Skylar's house. I heard you've already met her thanks to your ambitious and persistent brother. She's invaluable to our team. She's responsible for intel. She knows how to get everything we need and who might be a help or a nuisance." He rotates and points to the right.

"That one goes to the secret base of Tirique. He's the mind of this operation. If we need any hardware or software, he's the guy. Your brother has already caught on to one of our minor plans that involves Tirique. Usually, I would be a bit more unhappy that anyone has even got that close to finding anything but, in this case, it brought you." We walk to the right, and the massive door slides open automatically. It reveals what looks like a futuristic pod. We walk to the side, and I get to see it in its entirety. It's a white ball made of what looks like glossy painted glass. It's completely smooth except for an opening on each side for entry. The seats in the interior are a matching white leather, and two chairs face each other. I follow Nox into the pod, and we sit across from each other, he presses a metal button above his head, and we start moving, going at least fifty miles per hour.

"Serge rounds out our team. He may seem like an idiot, but he also controls the biggest and best private army service. For now, he's the firepower."

"So, how exactly do I fit into the team?" In the back of my mind, I'm thinking that if Nox could convince some of the most influential people to join him, I'm not alone in believing in his initiative.

"Think of yourself as my right-hand man. You can handle anything or everything. Please work with Serge to create an elite fighting team that you can lead into smaller incognito missions. These are some of the greatest minds, fighters, and politicians in the world. You should feel right at home here."

The pod stops at the end of the tunnel. A matching sliding door opens, and we step out into a more industrial space. Concrete, complimented by stained brown wood, surrounds us, only disrupted by a strip of glass wrapping around the whole bottom floor, looking into many tech labs. I can already see robots moving around. There is a concrete staircase in the middle of the circular space that leads to a similar upstairs setup as before, except now there are walkway bridges that lead to a center glass console that looks like it extends another floor above. It's an elaborate space. My thoughts are interrupted by Tirique gliding down the stairs towards us.

"Zashil. Welcome." Tirique's white lab coat covers a clean black suit that matches his round thin black glasses frames. Seeing a black man in tech always makes me happy. "I've heard so much about you, and I'm so excited that you decided to join us. This man can be very persuasive." He nods towards Nox and proceeds to shake his hand.

"Please, please. Let me show you around." We are about to start exploring the glass labs when an ear-wrenching beep starts to resonate through the entire building. It only takes one look from Nox to know that this is my problem, the first of many, I'm sure.

I V O

March 3, 2035

I decide to go back down to the underground HUB. I might as well start with the only actual place that I've found. I struggle to keep my eyes open as I make my way back towards the casino. I could try to find the other access points, but I figured it would not be a good use of my time, especially when I'm already familiar with the casino one. I weave towards the bathroom once I put on my glasses, trying to avoid being seen by the waiter and bartender earlier. I repeat the same actions and make my way down the long winding staircase to the underground again. I take off my glasses when I get myself down, slower than this morning.

I rub my eyes as I jog down the main street, now busy with well-dressed people. Some of them stare at me, which I usually avoid, but I'm too desperate and tired to care. It feels like I've been running forever by the time I get to the end. In front of me is a massive concrete wall, going from floor to ceiling of the underground, reinforced by military-grade steel, and simply daunting. The only way in that I can tell is a locked shut small door to the side. It's almost as if no one is supposed to enter from here. But if not from here, where? I run from side to side, scanning every inch of the concrete. My best bet is to knock down the door somehow. I

CYCLE

activate my suit and am about to generate a gun or sword to force my way through the door before I feel some dirt fall on my suit. I look up and see that some dirt is crumbling down, which focuses my attention on the very top of the wall. I can barely see it, but it looks as if there are some gaps between the wall and the dirty underground ceiling.

I step away from the door and look behind my shoulder. There is no one within a quarter-mile of me, so the likelihood of someone looking in my direction and then seeing me scale this massive wall is improbable. I can turn on the invisibility, too, just in case. I activate my suit, slide my right hand across my left forearm, turn on the grip, and make my way up the wall. It's a slow and arduous process, my hands and feet cramping and my arms weakening, but I make it up in fifteen minutes.

Grabbing the edge of the wall, I haul myself over and lay, stomach on the top. I glance to my right, it's a significant drop to the floor, but at least there aren't people crawling around. A massive glass dome valiantly stands in front of me. The best way to get on is probably to just jump and billet down the side of the wall, using my grip to grab onto the wall. I spin around on my stomach so that my head is facing where I came from. Dirt crumbles onto my head, and I'm careful not to bump into the top, which would subsequently cause me to fall. I'm very precariously balanced perpendicular to the wall when I jump backward without looking. I stop myself from spinning on my fall by moving towards the wall and gripping on before hitting the ground. One more bounce-off is all it takes for me to reach the ground. But then comes the first alarm beep, making me freeze, look down at the bottom of the wall, and see laser movement sensors. That explains the open space and lack of people. I'm an idiot. Of course, other vigilantes have tried this before. None of them have returned and told the tale because they get this far and then are ripped to pieces by Tirique's latest weaponry.

I stand up tall, generating a rifle in my left hand and a knife in my left. I guess this is how I die: caught underground and slaughtered by some madmen that I only need to ask a few questions. Ridiculous. A massive hangar door that serves as the entrance to the glass dome, which a metal strip along the bottom, opens and I brace myself for an army. But no army exits, weapons blazing ahead. No. Za stands a hundred feet in front of me, his matching suit gripping two knives and his facial expression blocked by a stone-cold emotionless helmet.

I retract my helmet and drop my weapons, the knife and gun clattering to the ground. Za does the same, his entire suit deactivating, revealing his tired face, but the intent of a new purpose is painted all over his expression. Those jerks better not have done anything to him. The weird part is that Za never changes pace. He strides up to me like nothing ever happened.

"Ivo. Where have you been?" He asks as he stands about four feet in front of me. A few men file out of the building and line up by the entrance. I recognize one of them as Tirique but have no idea who the other is. From a distance, he looks pretty young and is wearing a nice suit, so I'm assuming he holds some level of importance. I focus my attention back on Za.

"Where have I been? Where have you been? I wasn't the one kidnapped." He is about to speak, but I don't let him. "And what mind games are these guys playing? Why aren't you in constraints? They do realize that we can easily take all of them out when we are working together, right?" I start breathing heavily in anticipation. The information could not come faster. I need to know what's going on and quickly, before I randomly start assuming things. I anxiously look back at the men. They haven't moved and are simply staring ahead at our interaction.

CYCLE

"It's fine, Ivo." Za tries to reassure me as he tracks my eyes. "They aren't going to hurt you, but you have to listen to me." I nod, a bit discombobulated, partly from the strangeness of this whole situation and partly from straight-up exhaustion. I cross my legs and sit down as Za does and nervously start twiddling my thumbs." I'm going to tell you the whole story, Ivo, so you can't interrupt me. Some of the parts are going to freak you out but don't say anything until the end."

"Fine. I won't. But can you hurry up? I'm getting a bit stressed?" Za glares at me. "Fine, fine. I got it. I'll shut up."

"As you probably have deduced, I was captured in a pretty flawed and inelegant attempt. They knocked me out, and I woke up underground. That's where I met Nox." He points to the young guy with the suit. "Nox apologized for the rough nature and offered to let me go. But he wanted to explain himself first. I allowed it. Ivo, Nox was a migrant in the US just like us, except he was on the West Coast. He eventually escaped and made it here to Europe, and now he wants to go back and help the United States. He wants me to help him. And I said I would."

"You what! Are you insane, Zashil? You have to work on your trust issues. This man just kidnapped you. He claims he wants to save the world, I'm assuming by becoming a world leader, and you're just going to shrug your shoulders and go with it? Does none of that sound absurd to you?" I stand up and start walking in a small circle.

"Ivo. I can make my own decisions. They wanted me, and this is what I've been begging you to do. I want to save the people that we left behind."

"And we are going to do that, Za. But, inside the law. We are going to do it legally, with the consenting help of Europe and a willing nation. I always told you that we would help the Migrants. I needed to make my mark here before they would listen to me. And I'm so close. Really close, Za. You just have to hold on." Za shakes his head.

"I don't want to wait any longer. Nox is going to do it now, and I want to be with him. Now he's giving me a chance to convince you to join us. He doesn't want you, but I insisted. Please, Ivo. We can work together again. We can go back home and see our friends."

"I can't just leave the secret service, Za. They have done too much for us for me just to abandon them. And, Europe is safe. Who knows what would happen when we returned. Please, you have to trust me. Nox may seem like a good guy, but he's just like the rest of the monarchs. He's not going to let go of power when he has it, and the United States will end up in a worse position than they are in now."

"No. You're mistaken. Nox is different. You're the one that's doing this wrong." He turns around and walks away, leaving me helplessly standing still, unsure of what to say. Three soldiers suddenly drop down from the top around me. They handcuff me before I can do anything. I get dragged away to who knows where, the image of Za's back getting farther and farther away. This could be the beginning of the end.

ZA

March 3, 2035

I solemnly shake my head as soon as I turn around and make eye contact with Nox. He nods back with a saddened face and a grimace. He throws up his hands and gives the signal. I don't even look behind my shoulder to see three soldiers surround Ivo and take him away. Nox told me this would happen, but I always believed in myself to convince Ivo. He's so stubborn. Nox pats me on the back as he and Tirique follow behind me back into the building. I check my phone after I minimize my suit, which I can tell Tirique is coveting behind me. It's late in the evening, which I wouldn't know from the lack of natural light. I turn around.

"Imma head to my quarters, Nox. I'll see you in the morning."

"Get some rest, Za. We have a lot of work to do tomorrow." I've already turned around by the time he answers, but I nod my head anyway. I make my way back past the back end of the staircase and towards the pod transport tracks. The door slides open for me, and I get in the pod. As it zips back to Nox's headquarters, I start second-guessing my decision. Maybe Ivo was right. What if Nox isn't going to give power back, and he keeps it for himself? Would that be even worse than how it is now? For

Europe, of course. But, for the United States, I don't know. At least, with Nox, they would represent the Migrants, someone who would treat them equally. I ease my stress by reminding myself that I'm here by my own will. If I want to leave, I can just run away and find Ivo or, at the very least, warn the secret service.

Once the pod stops, I get out and re-enter into the vast expanse of the first floor. I look everywhere for the staircase and can't find it until I see a platform to my right. I step onto it and press the red 'up' button, crouching down to keep my balance. The platform rises almost too fast, but I safely make it onto the second floor. The glass walkway wraps around the whole perimeter, and I take a minute to admire its cleanliness. It really does look like I'm in a spaceship or something. I slowly make my way around to a glass door that already has my name embossed. I guess Nox was very confident that he could get me to say yes. I push open the door and walk into a vast open space. I'm already in the living room with high-end furniture left and right, a massive TV over a firing place the center point.

Meanwhile, a full-size kitchen surrounding a granite island is a step up to the right, and a bedroom is to the right with frosted sliding glass doors. I walk into the bedroom, collapsing onto the bed, already suited up with the most comfortable pillows. I turn over onto my back and look up into a massive circular window that sees the real world. I stare at the stars until my eyes can not stay open any longer.

IVO

March 4, 2035

I spend the night in a floating cage, literally. I wake up, my head resting against glass. I'm in a suspended glass box in god knows where. I think they knocked me out before I got here, but I vaguely remember getting in a truck, so I know I'm not in the underground HUB anymore. I look out of my cube, and it seems as if the steel wires holding me up are connected to the sides of a crater or something. All I know is that I'm in some mountainous landscape. With the global population nowadays, there aren't many of these left, so I would be in business if I could remember where they are. Too bad my memory is all a bit hazy right now. My neck is sore from the suit connector but, now that it's on permanently, the soreness should go away soon. I tap it to activate my suit and figure out a quick getaway, but I feel a ringing in my ear and a buzz. Damn. They must've put some electronics blocker somewhere. I check everywhere for guards, but they are nowhere to be seen. I guess their goal was to starve me to death in here. Too bad I won't be in here long enough for that to happen.

I punch the glass to see how reinforced it is, and to my shock, it cracks. Why the hell would they not use toughened glass on a prison cell. Bizarre.

I line it up and kick quickly through the side of the prison, and, after a few tries, I crack through the glass, making a hole big enough for me to squeeze through. It takes a couple of seconds for me to hear the glass shards shatter on the rocks below, so I'm very high up. I slowly lean my upper body through the hole, my back facing the ground and my feet facing towards the center of the cube. I reach up with my arms to grab the upper edge of the cube and lift myself. I manage to grab the slippery surface with my hands, and I put all my body weight on them as I pull my legs out through the hole. But as I'm about to lift my body over to the top of the cube, my hands slip, and I fall. I try to grab the cube with my hands, but it's too slippery. I start falling, the bottom of the cube becoming smaller and smaller. I close my eyes, bracing for the impact as I give up frantically flailing my arms.

***

My eyes open. I'm leaning up against a glass cube. My memory is hazy. It feels as though I've been in this exact position before. I stand up, seeing that I must be in a mountainous landscape. I rub my eyes, trying to shake off the weird feeling that I've been here before. I try to activate my suit, but I wince at the sharp pain in my neck and screech in my ears. I guess there must be an electronics blocker somewhere. I kick through the side of the glass, and it surprisingly cracks. With all their combined genius, these idiots didn't make the prison out of reinforced glass. Grinning at my luck, I put my fingers through some oxygen holes in the top of the cube. Lifting my body with my fingers, I continuously kick out through the side glass until it cracks. It eventually shatters and creates a gap wide enough for me to fit through. I jump down, but the floor cracks underneath my weight. I take one quick step to get through the gap and grab the side of the cube,

CYCLE

but it shatters beneath my feet. I fall, my body twisting and twirling in the air uncontrollably. I look at the fast-approaching ground with no way to cushion my fall. I close my eyes, bracing for impact.

***

I wake up leaning against some glass. My eyes flicker open, and I look around while I attempt to sit up. My whole body feels sore. It must have been from yesterday's long day. It felt as though that day would never end. I stand up and try to activate my suit, but a screech in my ear and a buzz against my neck tells me there must be an electronics blocker somewhere. Then suddenly, all of these memories flood in. One is of me falling through this very cube, and the other is me falling from the side of it. I look around, puzzled. How could my nightmares be of a situation I haven't lived yet?

I spin around multiple times, trying to shake the feeling that this has already happened. The memories are so vivid in my head. I bump against the glass and see a small hairline crack. The prison glass is not reinforced. Wait. I think I've said that before recently. But when recently would I have said that. I keep spinning around, staring at the hairline crack I made. And then I see it. Or rather, I don't see it. There is no reflection in the glass. That can't be possible. It's a glossy material. My fingerprints don't even show up on it—just the crack.

I sit down on the floor and think. How could glass not have a reflection, and why does it feel like I've been here before. Then it clicks. This can't be a real place, meaning I'm not actually here. I must be in a simulation loop. Every time I die, it just repositions me in the same spot. They didn't put me in a physical prison. They put me in a mental one. This has got to be something that Tirique is working on. Okay. How do I prove it? If I willingly jump to my death and then I come back, I'll know for sure. I kick a hole in the side of the cube and dive through it. I quickly fall to the bottom. I make my body into an arrow, so I fall faster and keep my eyes open. I look down and, before I hit the ground, everything goes black.

***

My eyes open, with me lying down in the same glass cube. Okay. My memory is still hazy, and it's hard to remember my first two falls, but now I know for sure that this is a simulation. How do I get out of this one? They want me to keep trying to get out, so I fail, and the simulation resets. They weren't scared of me realizing that this is a simulation because they must've thought I would try to escape successfully as my way out. But that doesn't work because they would just program a way to kill me, and the whole thing would repeat. There is always something someone can do inside mental traps that lets them out, just in case someone not supposed to be in here gets stuck, or they are doing testing to see how it looks.

The one thing they don't want me to do is not to do anything. So that's what I'm going to do. I crawl to the middle of the cube and sit cross-legged. Resting my hands on my knees like I'm meditating, I close my eyes, thinking about anything and everything that isn't how to escape this fake prison.

***

My eyes burst open. I'm strapped onto a metal table with a contraption connected to my temples. Two doctors are in front of me in

CYCLE

this glass lab, paying no attention to me. I don't try to move so that it stays that way. The straps around my ankles and wrists are leather and a bit loose. They are thin enough to generate my suit underneath the straps and squeeze between the head contraption and my hair. I just need to find a way to activate the suit. I see a sharp tool that's not entirely on the doctors' tray next to my head. Using all the force I can muster, I contract every muscle in my body to move the entire table, which happens to be on wheels, an inch closer to the sharp object. I'm successful, but I hear a screech beneath me. I quickly shut my eyes before the doctor can turn around and, once I listen to them continuing their conversation, I stretch my neck until it touches the suit activator on my neck. I miss it a few times and wince as the knife stabs a little into my skin, but I get it on the third try. I relax as I feel the suit develop around me.

"Welcome back, Ivo," the voice, Otto, says inside my suit.

"It's good to be back, Otto." By the time the doctors have heard my voice and spin around in their chairs, I've already snapped through the straps, the head thing clattering to the floor at the same time. Their faces spell straight fear, and I grin. I quickly run past them, generating a gun, and shooting the alarm before someone can press the button. I run into the main lobby and out of the door find myself in the countryside in the middle of nowhere. Signs everywhere inevitably have Tirique's name plastered all over. I generate the rod and activate the cycle. Checking the GPS, I'm in what used to be England. Instead of setting my course back towards the HUB, I put it to the docks. I speed away to find the only backup I know I can trust. I'm going home.

2 YEARS AGO

NOX

July 15, 2032

I drag my feet as I amble down the main city street. I stay close to the building, my shoulder brushing against the brick and glass. Even if it's only five in the morning, you can never be too careful. My sister told me we needed more food for the Migrants, but I can't be bothered to scavenge for anything. I've already lost hope for the US, no one is coming to save us, and there is nothing we can do about it. The only time I ever had any hope was when the conference building for the Board blew up. But, that was three years ago. I catch one of the last billboards that shows the news out of the corner of my eyes, and I glance up. I stand, my back against the one-way glass, my hood pulled halfway up my head, and stare up at the angled billboard. A massive portrait of Ivo Wolf is displayed with the title "The Savior of Europe," and the headline reads, "Hero Ivo Wolf honored for his work at last night's convention."

I take one more moment to examine everything there is to explore on the billboard and then keep walking. This street used to be littered with massive screens and billboards. Now, they are all replaced with blank surfaces. It's early adoption for new augmented reality tech that will 'change our reality' or something like that. The other day, I saw that there

CYCLE

is new construction of an entire city that's gonna basically run on this tech. Of course, migrants like me will never see or use any of this kind of stuff. I don't even know why they put this stuff in Los Angeles, there is practically no one here. Right now, LA is just a dumping ground for military resources. Now and again, a massive wave of soldiers and other companies will come by to collect resources, using LA as a camp of some kind. Otherwise, there are pretty much no civilians. They all fled once the US started to get into wars with pretty much everyone. The coasts stopped being an excellent place to live. We celebrated when people started leaving. It meant there was gonna be less trouble for us, the Migrants. But this is still no way to live. We have to find abandoned buildings to live in, and it's becoming hard to find new places with resources, food and what not.

 I walk for a few more blocks before taking a right and circling back. As of right now, my sister and I are camping out on the top floor of an abandoned conference building. There are about twenty floors, and the holes in the glass on the top floor make it easier to keep a lookout and maybe make a quick escape. Aria seldom leaves the building. She asks me to bring back food and other stuff, and she hands them out to other migrants that come and visit us. That's pretty much been our job since the Revolution. I want nothing more then to get out of this place and leave this wretched country. There are two problems, though. First, Aria doesn't want to go. She thinks it will be like abandoning the other migrants, even if I told her that we'd come back. Second, and probably more importantly, there is basically no way to leave even if I convinced Aria. We would either have to go by plane or boat and somehow make it past border control. That's impossible without a miracle.

  I hear cars in the distance, so I jog the rest of the way back, sprinting up the twenty flights of emergency concrete stairs and into the open office space. A few corner offices with broken glass and some chairs and monitors tossed around, but otherwise, there is nothing here. I emerge at the back left of the space. Our mattresses are to my far right. Aria is awake but just staring out the window, feeling the breeze of the draft against her face. I'm about to greet her when I remember that I have no food to give her. I pat myself down frantically, hoping I have something, anything.

"You didn't get any food, did you?" Aria calmly asks, her soft voice soothing. I hang my head before walking up and standing next to her. She doesn't even turn around to see if she's right.

"Sorry, sis. I got distracted and then started to hear some cars. Didn't feel like taking a risk today." She sighs.

"What distracted you this time, Nox?" Technically, we are twins. But to her, she's always been the oldest. It was great when our parents were around. They would always say she had to be the more responsible. But without them, it just gets annoying. There is a reason she doesn't go out. Her fighting and running skills aren't exactly ideal.

"They were broadcasting some news about Ivo on one of the last remaining billboards." Aria shakes her head.

"Jesus Nox. Why are you so obsessed with the Wolf brothers. They aren't any older than us."

"Because they took their chance, Aria. They wanted to make a change, so they did. Why don't you trust me when I say we can do that? They aren't any better than us. I guarantee you they aren't as smart." We walk towards our bags which lean against the wall next to our mattresses.

"We can't just get up and leave, Nox. Some people need our help here. It's better to make our difference with these few people than to try to save the whole world and die before we can help a single soul." She starts rummaging through her bag. Once she finds a granola bar, she unwraps it, breaking off half for me before slowly eating her half. I plop the entirety of my half in my mouth.

"I know we could help more people." I'm about to keep talking, but Aria gives me a look that says I'm not going to be able to change her mind, so I just sit down on my mattress, my back to her. After a few minutes of silence, I abruptly stand up and swivel to face her.

"I'm gonna head back out." I don't even ask what she needs. I stride back down the staircase and take a breath of fresh air once I push through the glass door at the bottom. Scanning the road for cars, I walk across the street and head towards the coast. Whenever I need a breath, I usually stare out at the ocean, now littered with plastic and all kinds of waste.

It takes thirty minutes for me to walk there. I couldn't find an abandoned bike. Once I get there, I hide behind some fences to make sure nobody is around the docks. I curse at myself as I see a few guards strolling back and forth along the edge of the pier. At first, I think it's just patrol, but when I see no other boat parked nearby, I wonder what they are guarding. I get down on my knees and put my hood back on, waiting to see what's going on.

I must have been sitting there for over an hour in the overcast weather before anything interesting happens. Until, out of nowhere, a massive plane appears, descending towards us. For a second, I think it's about to crash, and I scramble backward, but the plane starts to hover twenty feet above the water. A massive floating mechanism folds out from the bottom, and the plane simultaneously turns ninety degrees while also lowering to float on the water. I'm expecting a bunch of well-dressed governmental officials or something to come out of the massive black-painted plane. However, no one ever comes out. Instead, the four guards walk up to the side door, lower it, and start to drag out carts of food. I scurry around the fence and hide behind a bush twenty feet away from the guards.

"So when does this head back?" One guard asks in a deep voice.

"They said tonight. That's why they assigned four of us this time. We need to fill this guy up with some other resources by the late afternoon."

"These drone things still freak me out. I'm surprised they have us load it to the brim."

"Yeah, it's beyond me." The guards start loading all of the carts and boxes of food into their truck, leaving the door to the empty plane open. Once I see them drive away, I jump up from my hiding place and walk over to the plane. It's massive, at least as big as a regulation passenger plane. I peek inside, the glossy surface continuing onto the interior. It's cold but not uncomfortable, and there is a ton of space. 'This is it,' I think to myself. No guards, no pilot, a straight shot to wherever. It doesn't matter where it's going, just not here.

I jog all the way back home, smiling the entire time there. This is our chance. This is our only chance.

ARIA

July 15, 2032

I've just about finished packing my bag, and am I about to leave to help some migrants when I hear the familiar thumping of Nox sprinting up the stairs. I drop my cloth string bag on the mattress. What now? I turn to face the emergency stairwell exit just in time to see the door swing open and Nox stumble in. He puts up his finger as he leans over, catching his breath.

"Why are you running Nox?" I complain, annoyed. Sometimes I think that Nox doesn't care about helping our migrants. He is always thinking too big picture for him to be any help. That said, I can't really do anything without his athleticism and friendship with danger. Nox finally catches his breath and he stands up.

"I just came from the docks. I saw something I've never seen before." I roll my eyes.

"You can tell me when I get back. I have to help the new migrant family; they don't know what they are doing." I try to walk away, but he steps in front of me.

"You're going to want to hear this." He puts his hands on my shoulders. "This could change a lot."

"Fine." I instead walk towards the wall and slump to the ground, my spine feeling the roughness behind me.

"What is it?" He walks towards me and starts to sit down before he changes his mind and starts to anxiously pace back and forth between our mattresses and where I'm sitting.

"So I went to the docks to get some air. But there were guards there. I waited to a why the guards were there. Right?" He checks to make sure I'm still listening.

"They were probably just guarding a private boat or something."

"Yeah, that's what I thought. But there was no boat. I wait for like a long time before anything happens until a massive plane lands on the water right next to the dock." I sit up from my slump.

"Go on."

"When the guards opened the door, they didn't let anybody out. Instead, they just pulled out a bunch of carts of food." I get excited.

"That's great. Where are the carts? Did you bring back any food?"

"Well, no. And they loaded their truck with the food and drove somewhere. But that's not the point. I overheard them talking, and that plane is like a resource transport. It leaves tonight. The best part is, there is no pilot or anything. It's like a drone or something. Please, Aria. Listen to me. This is our chance. This is our one chance to get out of this trashy place and go out, make a difference. I promise we will come back and help these people, but we can't do it from here. There are millions of people around this country suffering. We can't help all of them if we are stuck here." I shake my head in disgust, walk over to the mattress, grab my bag, and walk towards the staircase.

"We won't be able to help all those people, Nox. But, we can help these people. With these few people, we are making a difference. I can't believe you didn't even get any of the food."

"Wait, Aria. Wait." Nox grabs my arm to pull me back. I shake it off. "We can't live like this forever, not when the whole world is moving on."

"I'm sorry, Nox. I'm not leaving. And if you're smart, you won't either. It's not what mom and dad would have wanted." I swing open the emergency staircase door, sliding down the railings until I get to the bottom. He's crazy. There is no way I'm getting into a random military drone and just leaving. Mom would want us to stay here, where we know we will be safe. We don't even know where the damn drone is going.

I keep shaking my head as I walk down the block. The family I'm going to doesn't speak English. I found them wandering down the street a few days ago. I have no idea where they came from, but they are acting like they have no idea what the Revolution even is. I hid them in a basement of an old grocery store; it's the go-to temporary place for any migrants we find. The store is only a few blocks away, and I don't run into any soldiers on my way there. The city is often pretty empty in the summer because no soldiers want to be in the heat on their off days. Similarly, no civilians come here because there really isn't a society to go to.

I cram my fingers in the small gap between the sliding doors and pull them open. They automatically open after a few inches, and I walk through, the sliding doors staying open behind me. I make my way through the bare aisles and push through the swinging doors that lead to the cold inventory room. My sneakers thud against the concrete, and I shiver from the quick temperature change. The staircase hides away to the right, and I check the freezers on my way there to make sure there isn't anything left over from the last time we looted. Sometimes soldiers will come by and put water and ice cream in the freezers here. Why the electrical is even still turned on in here is a mystery to me.

The staircase is a narrow wooden staircase. I honestly don't know why it exists. The stairs creak under my pressure. At one point, I'm sure one will fall through, so I quickly shift my pressure. I hear some bustling downstairs.

"It's me, Aria. It's okay. Don't be scared. I just came to check on you." I make it down and see the two kids huddled in the corner. The father smiles when he sees me, and I shake his hand. I swing around my bag and take out some fruit and a few granola bars. Technically, this food was for Nox and me, but he basically doesn't eat nowadays, and I don't mind giving up a meal for them. Handing the father the food, he immediately turns around and hands it to his wife, who distributes it to the kids. The family looks South Asian, but I can't be sure. I'm hoping my similar brown skin will make them feel that bit safer.

Nox and I's parents were born in Pakistan. Our dad was technically European. His family was just stationed in Pakistan to help a tech company establish themselves there. He grew up there, and when our parents got married, they came to America. It was the place to be back then. Everything changed when the Revolution happened. My dad tried to get us out of the country and instead got himself captured. Our mom had no idea what to do but eventually got herself caught too. The last time we saw her was when she dropped us off at the used clothes store where we hid in the backroom.

I look at the family, who are smiling at each other as they enjoy the food. They may have no idea of how wack this country is, but, for now, they at least have each other.

CYCLE

I keep the family company for the rest of the day. With the help of some drawing on my sketchbook and many hand signs, I think I'm able to tell them what's going on and vice versa. Apparently, they are from India, which is not doing well since the backing off of Europe. During the Revolution, India was re-colonized by Europe. After Ivo convinced Europe to stop, they gave India back their independence but took many resources. India is not in a good place according to this family. They found a way to be smuggled here, not knowing that it would be worse than India. More will come. They articulate with hand motions.

I tried to explain that this country is not in great shape. I told them it was getting better, which it's not. I so badly wish it was, but I don't think it ever will. Most of us migrants have just expected that survival is our life. We hoped Europe would have tried to help us, especially since one of us was the one that helped them, but nothing has happened so far. Even thinking about the Wolf brothers, after Nox can't shut up about them, annoys me.

I bid them farewell and walk back home. It's at least fifteen degrees cooler outside. The sun is setting in the distance. Slowly walking up the stairs, I eventually make it to the top. There is no sign of Nox when I get there, no surprise. He's probably off doing some night walk again. He's basically never around, always getting out and roaming around. He almost always comes back empty-handed, which frustrates me, but I've accepted he doesn't want to risk getting food every time. When he's not walking, he's hanging out on the roof, looking at the stars. I toss my bag down on my mattress and then head up to the top one more flight of stairs.

Peeping my head over the edge, I scan the roof—no sign of Nox. I'm about to head back down when I see a piece of paper being moved around by the breeze. I climb onto the roof, the ground rubbery. I pick up the piece of paper before it can blow off the edge. I already recognize the holes on the long edge as a sign that Nox ripped this out of his notebook. There is a short note written in black pen in the middle. It reads: "I'm sorry, Aria. One day, you will see. Love, Nox."

Oh, Jesus. I knew I made him angry. But I didn't think that he would actually go. He's never been that quick to make a decision like that. Damnit. I don't even bother to grab my bag. I slide down the staircase railing and scramble to find a trashed bike. I see an old rusty bike, the back tire almost flat. I hop on and peddle as fast as I can to the docks, my legs cramping as I go.

Once I get there, the docks are empty—nothing in sight except a few empty carts left behind. I drop the bike and walk to the edge of the dock. Kneeling at the edge, I break down. Small ripples grace the water as tears fall. I didn't think he would actually go. If I'd known that, I would've gone with him. Idiot. Of course, he was gonna go. He was waiting for an opportunity like this forever. There is no point finding him; I have no idea where the drone is even going.

I wipe my tears as I hear footsteps behind me.

"What do you want?!" I whimper.

"Your a hard woman to find, you know." I get up and turn around to see a military soldier cautiously walking towards me. He must've seen my disgusted and fight-ready face because he starts to back off. "Now, wait a minute. It's not what you think it is." I don't even care. I crouch low and glance towards where my bike is. He tracks my eyes, and we start sprinting towards the bike at the same time. I get there first and am about to swing myself onto the seat, but the soldier knocks me off and against a barbed-wire fence.

"I don't want to hurt you." I lunge at him, punching into his chest and knocking him off balance. As I get closer, he looks to be a few years older than me at most. His blonde hair peeks out from under his black cap. He falls next to the bike, which I jump towards. He manages to flick out a leg and kick the bicycle off the edge of the dock. I wince as I see it topple over, water splashing up onto my ankles. The guard catches me in my moment of hesitation, calmly swiveling his leg around and catching my legs. I fall to the ground, and he's on top of me, holding down my wrists before I can get up.

"Now listen to me, goddamnit. I'm not here to hurt you." I stop my frantic struggling and just stare at him with hatred. "I didn't come across the country, tasked with finding a mysterious girl, just to be knocked over and attacked by you. Now listen. Okay?" I don't change my facial expression, but I nod. Who wants to find me? I start struggling again when he reaches behind his back, I'm assuming for a gun.

"Goddamnit, man. I told you I'm not here to hurt you." The soldier gets up, letting me go, and puts out a hand to help me up. I reluctantly take it, and he pulls me to my feet. Once he's done rummaging in his back pocket, he pulls out a crumpled piece of paper. "They told me to give you this note. That's all, okay." I take the paper from his hands and look down. A migrant sign seals the black envelope. I look up to question the soldier, but he's already gone. I spin around in confusion, but he's nowhere to be found. I fall into a sitting position, crossing my legs.

Clumsily tearing open the envelope, I pull out a black piece of construction paper that has been folded three times. I unfold it, revealing neat cursive gold writing. The note is short. It says "Dear Aria. I think we can help each other. Please come find me in Boston. I hope to see you soon." Lower on the paper, the note is signed. "Aiko."

NOX

July 16, 2032

I try to sleep during the flight, struggling to find a comfortable position as I awkwardly lay across multiple food carts. I use my backpack as a pillow, but the most I get is a few minutes of shut-eye.

Not gonna lie, I hesitated for a second before I left. I wanted to tell Aria in person, but she took so long helping that migrant family that I needed to leave. Hopefully, she got my note. Otherwise, she would be worrying even more. I don't regret what I'm doing. At least, I don't regret it yet.

I spend my sleepless night thinking of my plan. However, I can't formulate that much of a plan since I still have no clue where this drone is going. I'm guessing that it's going to land somewhere in Asia, which is good. Much of Asia suffered less of a transformation after the Revolution. Their government was set up in a way where the Revolution didn't really alter it. Control of information already sort of existed. The only real thing that changed was who was in power and, even then, most of the public didn't care. None of this matters. In the end, I'm not planning on staying in Asia for very long. I just need to get food, find a phone, and then move on, getting to Europe as soon as possible. Once I'm there…I don't really know, but hopefully, something will happen that will make my brain click. Of course, I have to make it to Europe first.

I hide behind a cart closer to the door when I hear the drone starting to slow down and I feel the elevation drop. I'm not sure how many guards will be outside this plane, so I tense up in preparation for a possible fight. As we land, the door of the drone immediately swings open, but I hear no voices. Instead, a massive robotic arm swings over my head, lifts the cart from behind me, slowly backs out, and places it on an automated track. Realizing that this whole situation might not involve humans, I shuffle between the carts and carefully get out of the plane, weary of the swinging robotic arm above me.

My jaw drops as I see the extent of the operation. There are at least twenty drones docked here, locked into place by these connectors that extend from the metal dock floor. A massive rubber track goes the length of the dock and spirals into the middle, where another set of robots sort the food. I have never seen anything like it.

There are no signs or any indicators of where I am, so I stumble across the track, avoiding contact with the carts or the robots, and making my way to the center building. The building is fully plated in metal, with no windows and no doors. That's a problem. I walk around the building and see a road in the distance. Finally, some kind of civilization. I jog over to the road and take a moment to admire the landscape. Mountains dot the horizon, and beautiful green foliage surrounds me. I quickly shuffle behind a nearby tree when I hear a car coming. Peaking out from behind the tree, I see a pickup truck speeding down the windy road. I'm about to dip back down before I realize this could be my one chance to get out of this wacko robotic operation. The driver doesn't seem like he's paying attention and I slowly creep out from behind the tree as the truck approaches, ducking low enough to be slightly out of the driver's field of vision.

Once the truck passes, I leap up, grabbing the side of the truck bed with my hands. I lift my feet, so they don't drag against the asphalt. Using all of my strength, I flip myself over the side, landing on my back in the middle of the truck bed. I wince at the clang the impact makes, and I hurry to squeeze under the tarp which covers baskets of fruit. Gratefully, I grab an apple and bite into it. The juice drips down my chin as I proceed to shove strawberries into my mouth. Once I'm done indulging myself, I peek my head out of the tarp, lying down on my stomach, so that I can see the road. I scan the surroundings as we wind around the well-paved road. I breathe in the fresh air, reinvigorated with hope.

It's a very long drive before we even stop for gas, and I have to continue hiding in the fruit. I take a peek at the truck driver who has an outfit of a farmer, his brown overalls are stained brown, and his black boots are visibly falling apart. He struggles to unscrew the gas plug. After we stop for gas, we don't stop again for a few more hours until we get into the city. Once we are there, we turn into an alley, and that's where I get off. Grabbing my bag and rolling off, I land on the stone road, getting dirt all over me.

I only brought one set of clothes for the trip, couldn't be bothered to bring a whole bag of clothes. I wore my black jeans cuffed at the ankle, revealing my one pair of black Nike sneakers. I wore a gray long sleeve shirt underneath a maroon hoodie. I was freezing during the whole trip in the drone, but the sun now beats down on me, my black clothes not helping the cause. It's hot, humid, and I want nothing more than to take off my hoodie. But, I need it to keep my appearance a bit more low-key. My skin color still means I stick out here, even if race was way less of a driving force in their Revolution.

CYCLE

Walking out of the alley, my first order of business is to figure out where I am. The writing on all the signs is undoubtedly Asian, but I have no idea which language. The city is bustling, every single building looks brand new, and I can't remember the last time I was in a place this modern. Seeing people freely walking everywhere is almost off-putting. I wander around the city, keeping my head low when I walk by street vendors. Soon, I spot an abandoned tourists center, the only eyesore on the entire block. Tourism died during the Revolution, so it makes sense. I walk over to a square building stylized to look like a temple. Squinting at the worn-down paper signs in the windows, I'm able to find a small bit of English: "Welcome to South Korea" is all I get, but it's all I need.

Let's just say the situation could be better. The only country to really be affected by the Revolution in Asia was North Korea. It turns out, big tech companies don't like it when a country is that secluded. They launched multiple cyber attacks on the country and pretty much took it from the inside out. First, by taking over all of the cell phones, they ended up using multiple of North Korea's weapons on themselves. The country was practically decimated with bad air pollution, pushing many people out of the country. Instead of the tech companies trying to fix their idiotic mistake, they decided to put hundreds of servers down, basically making the entire country a server hub. Therefore, North Korea stayed the most secluded and secured area. Tech companies will do anything to protect their data. Anything.

In any other circumstance, I would just not go to North Korea. The only problem is the only way to travel by land out of South Korea is through North Korea. I can't take a boat to China because not only is that body of water extremely polluted and very highly secured but finding a boat is going to be very difficult. Anybody that wants to go to and from South Korea, which doesn't happen very often, has to go to Japan and then China or somehow get approved access to travel by boat. I can't do either of those. The information I read from many books about Asia after the Revolution is finally coming in handy. I never got to finish them because Aria threw all of them away when we started to move from place to place more often.

Well, this is not ideal. Forget a phone. I need weapons. There is no way I can get through North Korea without some weapons of my own. The problem is, I have no clue how to get those weapons.

I just mindlessly roam the city as the morning goes on and into the afternoon. I'm not really looking for anything particular, just anything that will help me with my mission. I wouldn't call myself an expert fighter, but I'm very good at navigating the streets. And, I'm always more intelligent than the guy I'm fighting. I also don't really know how to use weapons, but I just know they would help a lot. I start going into a few stores and checking out some vendors that sell knives of some sort, but as soon as I take a little bit too long checking out a more expensive knife, the vendors always give me a stare and scare me away. I think they can tell I don't have any money. I would just steal them, I'm very good at that. But, there are too many people, and this is not the time to start a chase.

Midway through the afternoon, as dusk begins, I finish the rest of the food in my bag. I leave the backpack stuffed in some street trash can, not wanting to deal with an empty bag on my shoulders. After a while, I feel myself getting tired and start thinking I'm going in circles. One of the smaller glass skyscrapers has defined ledges on each level. I walk up towards it, calculating the likelihood that I die or get seriously injured. I decide that it's worth it to get to the roof and have a nice risk-free sleep.

I'm about to make the first jump to the initial ledge when I spot a strangely empty trash bin. It's a massive bin pushed up against a brick and wooden building, across the alley from where I'm about to jump. I walk

CYCLE

over to the bin, which is made of sturdy metal and is painted green. I check the back. It appears that it's connected to the wall somehow. I try to push it, but it doesn't budge. Weird. I'm strong enough to make a trash bin like this at least move a little. That's what I'm going to tell myself at least. I decide to look inside it and I push myself to see over the ledge. There is almost no trash in it, and the interior walls are strangely clean, which makes me think there hasn't ever been much trash. In usual circumstances, I would say it's a new trash bin, but the exterior has collected the dirt for at least two years while the interior glistens. I jump into the trash bin, moving the trash to one side. The bottom looks normal at first glance. But, when I step on the cleared site, it flexes a little, and there is a noise that makes me think there is space underneath the bottom. I realize my foot is standing on one of two faint outlines in the shape of the soles of feet. I drag my right foot, so it is over the other outline. I stand there like that for five seconds, and nothing happens. But then the platform drops very fast. I start trying to grab the wall or something to slow down, but I'm already transported, at least thirty feet down, within half a second.

I look around, and I'm in a massive weapons storage unit, all of the guns and spy gear arranged very professionally. The name "Adam's Industry" is everywhere, but no one is in sight. It's just this room and a ton of weapons. God really wanted me to get these guns, I guess. I'm about to start picking up guns and gear myself up when it occurs to me that this is probably the best place to sleep for the night. I decide that's the way to go, and I grab some bulletproof vests, laying them down on the clear and empty floor in the middle of the small room. I lay on the ground, my head resting on the vests as pillows. Taking a deep breath, I shut my eyes. Tomorrow, I go to the border.

ARIA

July 16, 2032

The sun is just starting to rise as I begin my journey across the state. I started to walk last night but stopped after an hour. I thought I was going insane, so I decided to sleep on it. I woke up early this morning and decided to do it. I have no brother to keep in check now and, even though I have no idea who this Aiko person is, I have a gut feeling that this is the right thing to do. Based on her name, she's Asian, which means she's probably a migrant from the East Coast. If a migrant can send a white soldier in disguise across the entire country to give me a small note, they have power.

It makes sense. The East Coast Migrants have always been more established and have been a more considerable nuisance to the government. I hate to think about them because Nox idolized them so much, but the Wolf brothers are from the East Coast, and they've done quite a bit. I still have some disgust for them because they never came back to help their fellow migrants. I guess that's why Nox left. I scan the streets as I speed walk down block after block. Obviously, I can't just walk across the entire country but finding a vehicle will be difficult, mainly because there is security at every state border.

CYCLE

A couple of years ago, shortly after the Revolution was complete, I picked up a newspaper off of the ground and saw some futuristic plans for a cross-country speed train, one that traveled over and under the ground. This train could still be a pipe dream for the Board, but it's my last chance at a semi-safe passage to the other side of the country. The problem is I have no clue where it was built. If it was even built, that is. I keep walking along, ducking behind trash cans or into buildings when I see some soldiers or any cars.

It takes me a day before I get close enough to Arizona to start getting into the drylands. I only take small sips of my water to save it, but I'm dehydrated and find myself dragging my feet as evening approaches. I'm about to just to throw my bag down and sleep in the middle of nowhere, but I hear some bustle about two miles away in front of me, slightly to the left. I speed up, walking in that direction and using my remaining bit of energy. Once I get within a hundred yards, I see a few groups of very professional-looking people standing around a small brick building.

As I get closer, I struggle to hold in my excitement. Right in front of where the people are standing is a very wide train track, the metal glistening in all of its glory. I look left and right, and the track extends as far as I can see. I can't be sure that this is the train, but I don't know what else it would be.

I sit down behind a massive boulder, taking a breath. How do I get on the train? I look down at my ragged athletic tights and my forest green bomber coat covering my white t-shirt, the zippers of the coat pockets unable to zip up all of the way, and the main zipper completely missing. The white t-shirt is stained in multiple places from various adventures, while the fraying on my white leather sneakers just adds to their dustiness.

I don't look as homeless as I am, but I don't fit in with the men in expensive black suits and women in beautiful dresses waiting for the train.

I peek out from the side of the boulder. There is a long rectangular sign that has the impending time of arrival for the train. According to the sign, I have three minutes and twenty-seven seconds. Twenty-six now. Think, think. I would just jump onto the side of the train, but I feel a brand new high-tech train isn't going to have a place for me to do that. I'm imagining a smooth bullet train of some sort. I'm pretty sure that that's what the original newspaper article I saw had pictured.

I recheck the clock—just over two minutes. I decide to just pray that the train has some kind of storage car or something that I can get into. Otherwise, I'm kind of screwed. Unlike Nox, I can't just fight my way around things when in situations like this. All I got is my brain. I look to my left and see the train approaching in the distance. I look away for a few seconds and back to see it significantly closer. It sure is a high-speed train. Once the front of the train is past where I am, I stand up and quickly run-up to the train, making sure I don't make any noise as I get closer and closer to where the people are boarding. I'm guessing the storage part of the train would be at the back, so I make my way to the tail of the train.

I've almost made it to the back of the train when it starts to move, quickly speeding up. Oh god. I turn around and start sprinting as fast as I can, checking over my shoulder for the back of the train. To my relief, I spot a ladder on the side of the train connected to the side of the very last car. The train's glossy red surface turns into a blur as the train continues to speed up. In a split second, the ladder is right next to me. I brace myself, jumping off my right foot and grabbing the middle rung of the ladder with my left hand. I quickly force the rest of my flailing limbs towards the ladder and hug the side of the train as we speed away.

CYCLE

I frantically look up and down, left and right, looking for any way to get into the train. There is no entry on the side, that's for sure. I climb up, my feet on the very top rung, and my hands are aimlessly gripping the rounded corner of the train. I scan the top of the train, and there is an emergency door of sorts in the exact center of this car. I don't see a handle, I'm assuming because it's only for exiting the car, not entering. But, there is a large enough gap running around the door that I think I can cram my little fingers in there and force it open. I think it's my only option if I don't want to be dangerously against the side of the car the whole trip. If we were to go through a tunnel, that would very swiftly be the end of me.

I take a moment to center myself once I get back against the side of the car. I lean back to look at the track ahead. It looks like a straight shot for a while, so that's no problem. Letting out one last deep breath, I climb onto the top of the car. I basically look like a starfish, spreading out my limbs around the top of the car and using all of my strength to grip the smooth red surface. I slowly slide myself over to the center of the car. This is a significant risk. All of this hinges on this car being for storage or something. If this car has people in it or, worse, some security, then I pretty much helped myself to be captured. Once I slide myself over, I take my right hand and squeeze my finger into the left gap of the door. My knuckles hurt as I continue to shove my fingers into the gap. Once my fingers are deep enough, I feel around for the edge of the door. I grab it and pull with all my strength. The door is heavy and swings open with force, almost toppling my entire body over the train. I scramble to get back into the center and proceed to peak into the car. The interior has matte black on the walls; there are only two small circular windows that I can see and, to my relief, there are no chairs in sight, which means no people in sight.

With my stomach as the rotation point, I rotate one-hundred-and-eighty degrees. I move a little bit forward, so my feet are dangling over the gap. Slowly, I lower myself through the gap, holding onto the ledge with my hands at the end. I let go and fall to the floor, my legs crumpling beneath me from the fall. To my surprise, I don't end up with a sprained ankle or anything. Incredibly exhausted, I lay on the floor, my head resting on one of many metal crates. I take a deep breath before getting up to glance through the window leading to the rest of the cars.

I think I'm safe until we stop, which is hopefully not until we get to Boston. I crawl to the back of the train, resting my back against the opposite metal wall, the cold surface touching my back and making me shiver. I slump down, stretching my legs in the aisle. Looking through a larger round window, I don't see people for a few cars down. I zone out, staring at the door opposite from me which connects to the next car when it suddenly slides open. A guard with a helmet on stumbles in the door, catching his breath. He takes off his helmet, long blonde hair flowing out.

"Hey. It's you again. What are the chances?"

N O X

July 17, 2032

A few minutes after waking up, all of the doors and drawers of the weapons room are wide open, the ground is strewn with various guns, and I'm running around trying to narrow down my choices. It isn't easy. If I were realistic, I wouldn't take any big or heavy weapons because the chances of me winning in a shoot-off aren't so good. Even if using those automated weapons are incredibly entertaining. Not in a dark way, of course.

I kick all of the big guns to the back corner of the room, too lazy to put them back where they came from. I already scanned the entire room for security cameras, so I don't really care if whoever owns this place comes back to a mess. I pick up a couple of knives, their weight and balance perfect. I admire them for a second, imagining myself fighting through soldiers like the Wolf brothers. I guess my obsession is getting a bit too much. Plus, I don't really want to get that close to any soldier. I don't trust myself in close combat situations enough for that.

I put the knives down and wander over to the opposite counter. The spy gear stuff is here. I grab some compact bombs and shove them in my pockets. That makes me think about my outfit. The jeans and sweatshirt are probably not the best for this but, as I look around the room, I can't find any other clothing, not counting the bulletproof vests that I slept on. Those things are just uncomfortable to wear. Plus, their chunkiness will just annoy me to the point where I might not be as focused.

I decide to collect the stuff I want to bring and push them onto the corner of the counter. I take the bombs out of my pockets and put them there. Then I find a rectangular prism that, when activated, turns into a sniper gun. I've never tried aiming a gun like this, but the inherent long-distance use of the weapon is appealing. Next, I grab some pistols and decide to grab a blackout knife just in case. I find a drone that activates with a bracelet. To my surprise, the drone folds down and connects to the top of the bracelet so it almost looks like a watch. That will come in handy. Satisfied with my grouping of weapons, I shove them in my pockets in every way, deciding which ones I can carry by hand without being too uncomfortable. That is before I see a strange metal thing hidden away in the corner.

In the back left corner of the room, a chrome silver metal shield-looking thing is crammed in between two weapons cabinets. I pick it up and am immediately surprised by how light it feels. There is a strap on the backside to hold it like a shield. On the bottom right of the back, there is a sticker that says '1:1 Prototype.' That's weird. Why would a simple shield be a one-of-one prototype? There has got to be more to it. The shape is unique, a bit different from what I would expect from a traditional shield, the silhouette sharper and more streamlined. As I run my hand along the surface, it doesn't feel like conventional metal; it's not as smooth as I would expect. There are four rectangular outlines on the front, and I try to press them, but nothing happens. The edge of the shield on the back is painted black, but a section on the middle right side is red instead. This must be a touch-sensitive area. I slide my finger along that side, and then I hear a quick beep. Turning around the shield, the rectangles have retracting and, somehow, four wheels have generated. Basically, it became a skateboard.

Placing it down on the floor, I stand on the shield skateboard. I used to skateboard all around the city when I was younger, but I lost my skateboard when we made one of our many moves. As soon as I put any weight on the shield, I start moving forwards. When I lean backward, I go back. When I lean to one side, it turns slightly to that side. This is not just a normal skateboard. There is a motor of some kind, and, I can already tell, it can go pretty fast. I'm definitely bringing this thing. This means I won't have to walk all of the way to the border.

Picking up the shield, I scan it for any other tricks. When I remove the sticker, it reveals a very small and faint text print on the bottom. I squint and hold it very close to my face to read it. It says 'multi-functional suit.' The multi-functional part obviously makes sense to me. But what does it mean by 'suit.' I don't think I can wear this thing; I don't even know how I would try. I decide that the shield kind of resembles a chest plate. I don't really know how but that's all that I can come up with. Laughing at how stupid I must look, I bring the shield close to my chest. My laughing immediately disappears when I start to feel a weird force of attraction between me and shield. Now, this is just bizarre. When I get within an inch of my chest, the shield just snaps to my body like it's magnetic.

As soon as it connects, the metal starts to form around my body. It looks like nano-tech as it forms around my body. Finally, a helmet formulates around my head, and many screens appear over my field of vision. A voice in the helmet starts to speak, making me jump.

"Welcome. The suit has calibrated to your needs. You are now the sole owner and user of this suit. Would you like any help learning about the features of this suit?" A robotic female voice states.

"No, no, no." I frantically say.

"Ok, then. You may ask me anything at any time." There is a weird sound, and then the voice goes away. I start getting claustrophobic really fast and try to pull the helmet off. It doesn't budge. I start freaking out, shouting random words at the suit.

"Suit off! Off! No suit!" Finally, I get it. "Deactivate!" The suit quickly starts to detract, and I pull off the shield from my chest. Jesus. That thing is wack. But to be honest, it may be what I need to make this impossible mission work. I decide to give it a go. At the very least, for the skateboard.

I go back and collect my weapons, shoving the mini black bombs in my pockets. I put the detracting sniper in my back pocket and then take the pistol and precariously attach it to a carabiner which I then connect to a belt loop on the front right of my pants. Good thing my baggy sweatshirt covers most of the gun from sight. I decide to leave the knife. I walk over to the platform and line my feet up with the sole outlines. The platform quickly rises, and I find myself back, standing in a trash bin. I open the top a crack to peek out and climb out once I see that nobody is in the alley.

I toss down the shield after I slide my finger over the touch area. I hop on the board and ride away, pulling up my hood before I get into the congested area of the city. It's mid-afternoon, but I'm tired from the time change. I must've slept a lot last night. Rubbing my eyes, I try to remember the map I looked at this morning. If I follow this one bus path, I should get to the border within a few hours, especially on this thing. It would've taken me a day to walk to the border, so thank god.

After a couple of hours, I get so hungry I don't think I can stand any longer. Luckily, I drive by a gas station, where I rummage through the trash. I find some barely eaten chip bags and eat them as I continue riding. By the time I get near the border, the sun is already setting. Unsurprisingly, I don't pass another soul on my way here. At this moment, my plan doesn't really exist. I just need to get past the initial security, and then I should be good. Or at least I should be good enough to figure out what to do next.

A massive barbed wire fence signals the border. Guards line the outside as well as the inside. About a quarter-mile of the fence before the rest of the border is lined with a massive concrete wall with guards standing on top. No one said it would be easy. I deactivate the board and slowly scurry over to where the concrete wall starts. I'm guessing it would be easier if I gained the high ground. I pull the sniper out of my back pocket and activate it, fascinated as the entire sniper somehow folds out of the small case. I freak out for a second when I realize I didn't grab ammo but then realize that it came with some. That just means I can't mess up. I lay down behind some bushes and set up the sniper. I use the scope to scan the top of the wall. There is a guard about every fifty feet. If I want to take one out, I have to take all of them out. There are about eight that I should realistically shoot. The main problem is that I need to do all of them in quick succession so that none of them have time to react to someone else's death. Thank the lord this sniper is silent.

Once I have the height of the wall locked in, I aim for the person closest to the fence on the left. Here goes nothing. I shoot, missing just over the guard's right shoulder. Oops. The guard looks around like he's heard something, but I hit him the second time. He crumples to the ground, and I hit the second guard just as he sees the first guy. I keep going, hitting all of them the first time before I miss twice on the second to last guy. He's able to make it halfway through his cry for help before I finally hit him and then I hit the last one.

It could've been better, could've been worse, I tell myself. I throw the sniper to the side, realizing it only has one bullet left. I swing the shield around my neck, and I sprint towards the wall, hoping the darkness will cover me. Running up the wall, I'm able to use my momentum and grab the top ledge. I flip over the top and immediately crouch down. I take a breath before peeking over the edge and surveying the security scene. I took out a lot of guards, but the biggest problem is the automated weapons sitting on turrets down on the ground. If those weapons spot me, I'm dead.

My only realistic option is to take those out and just deal with having to fight the rest of the way. There is another fence fifty yards away that separates the security from the start of the servers. They can't use their weapons on me once I get in there because they can't damage the servers. Basically, getting over that fence means I'll be safe. I look back down at the ground. The foliage is definitely going to help my cause. There are four main automated turrets on the ground. I reach in my pockets and pull out three bombs. Well, that's unfortunate. I look to the farthest turret to my left and decide that I can probably throw the bomb that far. I activate the first bomb and line up the throw. Standing up, I wince as a guard on the ground beneath me spots me. I throw the bomb and duck back down. I wait for the explosion before I get ready to throw the second bomb. I hear the guard gathering his soldier buddies beneath me. I quickly stand up, line it up, and toss the bomb, taking out the second turret.

I activate the last bomb and stand up. I toss it as I jump from the top of the wall towards the last turret. I see the explosion of the third turret as I'm in the air. I swing the shield around my body and push it towards my chest while I take the pistol out. The suit generates just as I land over the last turret. I pull out the wires for automation as guards start sprinting towards me, some of their bullets denting my suit. I turn on the turret manually and start wildly spinning back and forth, taking out as many guards as possible. Once I take out most of them, I hop away from the turret and hide behind a tree. I hear multiple bullets graze the tree trunk, splinters flying everywhere and hitting my suit. I peek around the trunk, taking out a few more guards with my gun. Then I sprint. I sprint through bushes and grass, weaving around the trees. I hear more bullets whiz past my head.

I make it to the fence and closely climb over, hitting a server as I fall to the floor. Scrambling to get up, I roll behind a server for cover. I hear more guards run-up to the fence, yelling in Korean at their misfortune. I hear them walk away, so I deactivate the suit, letting out a sigh of relief. I rub the various bruises I have, leaning against the server.

All that keeps me from freedom now is a sea of black boxes. They line the horizon, going on for as far as I can see. At least I'm alive.

ARIA

July 17, 2032

I basically don't say anything to him until the morning. I don't even ask how he got in and where he came from or why the hell he is on the train in the first place. Instead, I say nothing, fall asleep for a bit, and then wake up the next day, still motivated to say absolutely zero as he sits across from me, leaning against the opposite door. I guess he gets a wave of confidence or is suddenly invigorated to speak because he attempts to make conversation.

"You know, I had a feeling that I might run into you." He waits for any reaction at all, and once he sees that I'm not staring with hatred at him, he continues.

"You seemed like a smart girl, and this train is the smartest way to go cross country." He waits again. Nothing. I give him nothing.

"Ok then...I guess I'll keep talking. I should probably introduce myself so it doesn't get weirder than it already is. Hi." He gives me a meek wave.

"My name is Tyler. I'm nineteen, and I'm from Boston. You're probably wondering what my deal is. Why, out of everybody, am I helping the Migrants? The answer is pretty simple. I'm an orphan." I sit up, his

CYCLE

sudden imperfection interesting me. I give him a slight nod for him to continue.

"My parents said that we would be safe during the Revolution. We were poor but not that poor, and our skin color was supposed to be enough for the Revolution to largely leave us alone. When some migrant boys asked for our help keeping care of some very young orphans of color, my parents couldn't refuse. See, they were very kind people. They weren't racist. They didn't have anything against the people of color, and they were largely disgusted by the Revolution. This was the case for lots of other families. But we had to go along with it to survive. When these boys dropped off the kids, we took care of them. We hid them when the soldiers came by looking and fed them. We did that for a few months. By then, the Revolution was largely dying down. My parents got too relaxed. The kids were running around the house when a mailman stopped by. He spotted the kids and called the police. They took the kids and my parents. I came home to an empty house. My neighbor told me the whole story. I never saw them again." I hesitate to speak, but I want to hear the rest of his story.

"What did you do?" He gives me a small smile when he hears my voice, but he continues to stare at the ground.

"Eventually, the government came to seize the house. I didn't want to join the labor camps or be forced into the military, so I escaped quickly. I was homeless for a long time, but a migrant found me in an alley once. His name was Idrissa. He told me to follow him, and I ended up in the migrant base. I told them my story, and they took care of me. Ever since I've basically been a migrant. I often go undercover for long periods. I've been deep undercover with the Board before. My skin color means that the Migrants can get the information they never could before."

"So you were sent on a mission to find me?" He looks up and nods. "But why me? How did they even know I existed?"

"I don't know why they wanted you. But the Migrants have been looking for help ever since the brothers left. Right now, Idrissa and Aiko lead the Migrants. I guess you're going to have to ask them yourself." I nod my head in agreement. We stay silent for a couple of minutes. I process what he's been saying. For so long, I just assumed that all white people were thriving—the untouchables. Never affected by the Revolution, I thought they just lived their lives. It didn't occur to me that they could suffer just as much as any of us.

"So what about you? What's your story?" I don't really want to tell him. I have never told anyone. But when I look at him, there is no malicious intent in his eyes—just curiosity.

"My brother and I were born here. Our parents immigrated long ago from Pakistan. When the Revolution happened, our father was captured pretty quickly, our mother soon after. We moved from place to place. Nothing was permanent. When the Revolution started to die down, we started to help others, creating the Migrants of the West, I suppose. We aren't really a group as much as we just share the name."

"And where's your brother now?"

"He left to find a new life. We didn't exactly see eye to eye on a lot of things." Tyler nods.

"My family used to cram into our old car every summer. We would drive and drive in a random direction, always exploring a new part of the country. That was my favorite time of the year. I was never good at school. See, I can't read very well. I suffer from dyslexia. I was bullied in school and, even with modern education, I still struggled to keep up. My parents never understood my struggle. They would always push me really hard. But, during the summer, the beautiful summer, they would forget all about it. Exploring the country made me love to travel, see new places, and meet new people. And, the food. Wow, the food. That was everything. Once, we went to New York City. We got the best pizza and sat in Central Square, all three of us, each eating an entire pizza. I kicked around the soccer ball, and we walked the whole park at night after we finished. I'll never forget those days. It's amazing how quickly everything has changed. I guess I'm old now." Tyler stares at the ground and wipes his eyes. He is hugging his legs, still wearing the military uniform.

"When I was younger, my parents would drive us to the national parks. We would see how many we could go to in a week, camping every night—staring at the stars at night and cooking food over the fire. My brother and I would always run around the forest. Once, we got lost and wandered around the national park for the whole day. Our parents were freaking out. We didn't care. We went swimming, playing hide and seek. Little did we know that our parents had called the park troops who were looking for us everywhere. When they finally found us, we had been missing for eight hours. We were ten miles away from our camp." I smile, remembering the story.

"When our parents found us. My brother walked up to my mom and said: "by any chance, do you have any extra trail mix." Everyone broke out laughing, even the troops. Sometimes I struggle to remember life before the Revolution. It's like we died, and we were born again in a whole new reality." I stand up and walk over to Tyler's side. He moves to the side, and I slide down against the door, sitting next to him.

"You don't happen to have any trail mix, do you?" Tyler asks. We both start laughing. The train comes to an abrupt halt, the screeching of the brakes snapping us out of it. Now it begins.

N O X

July 18, 2032

For a second, I don't think I can move. My limbs are so sore that they've lost all of their vigor, and the clumsy way I ended up collapsing to sleep against a server did not help the cause. I first straighten my torso, sitting up, so I'm leaning against the server like a normal human being. With all of the strength in my body, I lunge forward, fueling my legs enough to stand. I take a few steps, almost falling twice, but eventually, the pain dies down, and all I'm left with is a smooth and subtle throbbing of my entire body. Not great, but manageable. My stomach growls, reminding me that I haven't had nutrition in god knows how long. I shouldn't have been an idiot and just kept my stupid backpack and filled it with food.

I climb on top of the ten-foot server to get my bearings. In the distance, I see where I came from. I'm maybe a couple of miles away from the border security. I don't remember it, but I guess I walked quite a long way away from the border last night before I collapsed to sleep. Looking in the other direction, I see servers except for a larger than average gap between some. That gap continues further in the direction I want to go. I

CYCLE

decide that I'll go check that out before making any other decision since it's only about a mile away.

I activate the shield, praying that the multiple dents it picked up from yesterday aren't going to stop it from transforming. Clumsily, and after having to hear a few ear-wrenching screeches from metal against metal, the wheels come out and I hop on, riding in between servers.

It only takes me a few minutes to get over, and I smile at my good fortune once I get to the opening. There is a mini high-speed train that moves in between the servers. For what reason, I'm not sure. But the back cart is just big enough to me to sit in. Without hesitation, I hop in, hesitating for a moment when the train doesn't start moving. Eventually, the train gets going, and I lay back, shuffling around to find a comfortable position. As it starts to gather speed, I use my arms to tuck my legs into the cart so my flailing limbs don't get caught by a sharp edge of a server box.

I lose track of time staring at the sky, watching the sun slowly come up to the middle and around. The serenity of the train's hum against the tracks and feeling the breeze against my head is relaxation I haven't felt in a while. It reminds me of my time sitting at the docks, left alone while I thought of anything and everything, just letting my mind wander. The peace of it all makes me forget about my raging hunger, and I begin to brainstorm what my next steps are.

Assuming that this train goes to the opposite border, I would need to exit North Korea stealthily. While I will still have an element of surprise, going out without making a peep is significantly more complicated than going in and shooting everyone in sight. I feel my sore legs and empty guns will not be favorable in an all-out shoot-out.

If the border is set up the same way as the other one, my best bet will be going around the wall again, so I have the high ground. The problem is, I don't have a sniper to take anyone out, and I can't just run up the wall because only a bunch of idiots wouldn't see me. I decide that the only genuine and realistic way I can go about this is by observing the guards to see if there is a pattern in their shift changes or movement. Then, I could find the exact right moment to either climb the wall or slip out the fence.

Just as the night is starting to set in, I see the wall approaching in the distance. I jump off of the train, rolling off to the side and clambering into a server. I rub my shoulder as I activate my board and ride perpendicular to the track of the train to keep my distance and then turn again to head towards the wall. When I get within twenty yards, I remember that I have the drone bracelet on. I roll up my sleeve and check to make sure I didn't break it in yesterday's chaos.

When I see that it's okay, I hide behind a tree and turn my wrist over, pressing the activation button. The drone unfolds from the other side and rises into the air, its propellers rapidly spinning but completely silent. A screen suddenly projects from the inside of my wrist, displaying controls and showing what the drone sees. Carefully moving the directional controls, I navigate the drone away from me and towards the wall, avoiding bumping into all of the heavy foliage. I increase the elevation, so the drone isn't spotted against the night sky and quickly move above the wall. At first, I get excited to see the security setup is identical to the one I encountered on the other border. However, my excitement quickly fades when I fly the drone over the other side of the wall.

Sitting on the other side of the wall is a whole legion of soldiers with tanks, guns, and any other weapon you could imagine. I guess word moved fast that someone had broken into the server. They are just waiting for me. So much for a clean and quiet escape. Even if I were to get past the initial security, one of the many heavily armed soldiers on the other side would surely spot me. I fly the drone back, it docks itself back on the bracelet, and I pull my sweatshirt sleeve back over it. I slump down against the tree to think. I've already ruled out the sneaky approach, and I don't have the firepower to go all-out attack. So, what would be the happy medium? If I were to sneak over the wall and then somehow fight my way through the middle of the backup, then the soldiers I leave behind wouldn't be able to shoot at me as they would be scared to shoot their people.

Even then, though, I don't know what in god's name I'm going to use to fight through the soldiers. I put the shield to my chest and activate the suit.

"Lady?"

"Yes. What can I do for you today?"

"If I were to throw myself into combat against an ungodly amount of soldiers, what should I know about this suit?" The robotic voice proceeds to explain every feature the suit has, and I can feel my jaw beginning to drop as she keeps listing them off. For one, the suit can basically fly using wings that fold out from the back. I can also grab shards of metal off of my arms to use as knives or whatever. Not to mention that the suit is invincible to bombs. Others fly right over my head as I already start thinking about using this stuff when I attack.

After five minutes, the lady is still speaking, and I tell her to stop. I activate the custom sizing feature on the suit, and I feel the metal shrink and change to fit my body perfectly. Suddenly, it doesn't feel like I'm wearing anything, and I'm as mobile as I would be without the suit. Looking over my shoulder, I see a section of the wall partially covered by a massive tree.

When I'm sure that the closest guard isn't looking, I spin and sprint towards the twisty tree. I jump and grab the first limb, reveling at how well the suit is fitting me. Using my momentum from the initial swing, I reach for the next branch. I scurry up the tree and, within seconds, I am sliding myself along a long branch that reaches over the wall. The closest guard starts walking in my direction. As soon as he is directly below me, I jump onto his shoulders, the weight of me crumpling him to the ground. I hit him hard with my right fist, the metal of the suit heightening the effect. It only takes two punches to knock him out.

I crouch low to the ground, so no other guard on the wall notices me and activate the wings. They fold out in multiple long blades, spreading out from the suit's spine, mimicking the wings of a bird. I back up to the edge of the wall and get a running start. Sprinting towards the opposite edge, I jump at the very last moment. Instead of immediately plummeting to the ground, I stay at the same height. I hover, the wings slowly flapping, twenty feet above the soldiers who take a moment to stare at me. Finally, the one leading the lines starts screaming at them to fire, but their bullets just bounce off of me. I circle around them before folding in the wings and plunging into a tank with a fast spiraling motion. I cut right through it, taking out a guard on the way. The tank collapses around me, and I emerge from the wreckage unscathed. Five guards start running towards me, rifles swinging in their arms. I grasp five blades from my left arm and dart them forwards in one motion. They each hit a guard in the chest, their bulletproof vests no match for the razor-sharp pieces of metal. As the other guards increase their fire, I activate the wings again and bring them around me, creating a wall around my entire body. I take a breath, waiting for the guards to get closer and closer until they are basically knocking on the door. Then I thrust the wings open, blades flying in all directions, taking out at least thirty soldiers.

CYCLE

I grab two rifles from the ground and rise into the air. Rotating while I hover, I aim for every soldier in sight. Once I'm convinced I have adequately injured every person I see, I lower to the ground, deactivating the suit. I wince as my bruises flare up, but I am able to bundle myself into a nearby military car. I reverse it out into the road and spin the car around. I drive for who knows how long, leaving the horrors of North Korea. Adrenaline rushes through my veins, invigorated by my newfound power. I don't slow down until I see a massive metal sign on the side of the dirt road: "Welcome to China."

ARIA

July 17, 2032

"Let's go out the back," Tyler says as he gets up and puts on his helmet. "Here's what needs to happen. I've done this trip countless times. The security at this station is extremely thick. As in, no one has ever evaded their security. It's the best of the best." I stand up and walk over to my bag, swinging it over my shoulder.

"Than what are we going to do?" The helmet quickly covers Tyler's smile.

"Lucky for you, everyone thinks I'm a soldier. And you.." He points at me. "Are my very important prisoner." I nod and smile back.

"And what do I need to do to look like a dangerous criminal."

"Nothing, just follow my lead. But be quick about it, we have to exit the train before they find us here. Being in here wouldn't be a compelling look." Tyler kneels, putting his hands out to give me a boost. I step up on them and unlock the top door, swinging it open. Grabbing the ledge, I pull myself over and onto the top of the train, staying low the entire time. I peek down as Tyler jumps up and grabs the ledge, rolling onto the other side of the car. We use the ladder on the side to get down and then walk around to the landing platform. Passengers are filing out of the train while soldiers either let them pass after seeing their ticket or pat them down for weapons and escort them out of the station. I can't help myself from tilting my head and admiring the architecture of the place. The massive glass dome displays the blue sky, and the natural light makes it feel as though we aren't even indoors. The complimenting gold metal beams are shiny as if installed this morning, and the entire experience of the building is magical.

I'm snapped out of my trance by three soldiers walking towards us. The soldiers are all wearing black uniforms, similar to Tyler, but they have red caps and grey shoes instead of the complete blackout. Tyler copies their salute.

"And who might this be?" The most forward-standing soldier asks. His chubbier face and thick eyebrows aren't helping his cause at looking menacing or authoritative. I struggle to hold in a giggle.

"I captured her when posted on the West Coast. One of those disgusting rebels. They say she's one of their leaders. I was told to bring her here to be placed in a stronghold prison."

"Right then. Pass her over." The two men on the side step forward. One is holding handcuffs, and the other is holding a bag to put over my head. Tyler tugs my arm, so I move back.

"That won't be necessary. I was asked to transfer her myself. She's quite nifty."

"She doesn't look like any trouble."

"Well, looks can be deceiving."

"Very well then. Carry on." The soldiers salute Tyler again, who just nods this time before walking past us and allowing us to get through security. We walk out of the dome and onto the street. Tyler lets go of my arm and sidesteps away while I look to my right and left in amazement. There are so many people. All white, of course. But, still. This is what a city should look like, not the lame excuse of what Los Angeles has become. Tyler sees me scanning the roads.

"Boston has pretty much become the central hub of America in a lot of ways. Easier to protect against the impending Europeans and more stabilized than any other state. If you can believe it, real-estate is actually hard to come by."

"This is amazing," I respond.

"Come. Follow me." Tyler nudges my arm, and I follow him down the right side of the road. We walk briskly but not at an uncomfortable pace. My legs still ache from yesterday, but the presence of real society gives me a sudden push. My hood is still over my head, restricting my peripheral vision and hiding my face from view. I stare at Tyler's legs, his black boots dictating my pace.

"You can take off the hood now," Tyler says after slowing down for the first time in a couple of hours. I remove my hood hesitantly and look around to hear the ocean in the distance, the familiar smell of pollution still present even in a bustling place like this. There is barely a person in sight, and I look behind me to see the outskirts of the city. Finally, I spot some less than perfect buildings with plenty of blemishes. We keep walking until I can see the water to my left, the sidewalk is gone, and we are walking in practically the middle of the road, the pavement more worn and grey than the road I saw when we first arrived.

After we round the bend, Tyler walks to the right, towards a massive rock face. He rummages around in the side of the rock face before uncovering some kind of button that he presses.

"You might want to stand back," he says as he walks over and tugs me behind him. "There will be a lot of questions. Don't panic. I'll be here, and they are all good people, just curious." I nod as the entire middle of the road sinks below me, a ramp forming and dipping down to reveal an underground base.

"Welcome to the Migrants."

I follow Tyler down the ramp, looking behind me to see a worn metal hinge. This place must have existed for a while. Bounding down the ramp, Tyler interrupts many people who are running around doing tasks with purpose. Everyone drops what they are doing and looks towards Tyler.

"Sorry, everyone. Go back to what you were doing." Tyler apologizes as the ramp closes behind us. A few people come up to greet Tyler, and some more wave at him.

"Aria, come this way."

He leads me to the right and through a hallway. We walk past multiple bedrooms on the right before turning into a computer lab of sorts. There are computers everywhere, most of it old tech but some new stuff. Two people sit in the middle, talking to each other while they spin in their office chairs.

"Tyler!" The guy that is facing us gets up and does a handshake with Tyler. "I guess your trip was more than successful," he says, turning to me. "My name is Idrissa. Nice to meet you." I shake his hand. He is excited but collected. It's interesting. The girl sitting across from him spins around in her chair and gets up. She walks right past Tyler, who just smiles at the gesture.

"It didn't take you long to get over here, did it, Aria. I'm Aiko if it wasn't obvious. Come, let me show you to your room." She's Japanese, her outfit minimal but different than anything I've ever seen. I just nod and smile as I quickly follow her out of the room and back into the hallway.

We turn right into the hallway, passing a few more rooms on the way. We pass a room with posters on the wall, a desk, and more. There is dust collected on every surface and, despite the room looking very personalized, there is no sign that anyone has been in it for quite a while. Aiko sees me pause.

"We used to have a leader of sorts that wasn't me. He stayed in there. We decided to keep it open just in case he ever came back, but I'm not so sure that is ever going to happen anymore." She caresses the door, an emotional gaze captivated on the desk. Then she snaps out of it, and we continue walking down the hall to the back. At the very back, there is a large metal door.

"That's where all of the food is. It's cold in there, and you can easily get locked in by accident but take whatever you want. It's pretty much a free for all." She turns to her left to an empty room, there is a made bed and a small wooden desk with a desk lamp, but that's pretty much it.

"And this is you. Make yourself at home. I promise I won't harass you about your background and why you're here and all of that until you're all settled. I know what it feels like to be grilled by Tyler." She winks, and I smile before Aiko walks away and back down the hallway.

I throw my bag on the ground next to the desk and collapse onto the bed. Maybe, just maybe, this is the start of a new beginning.

CYCLE

PRESENT DAY

CYCLE

Z A

March 4, 2035

My eyes flutter open. I quickly sit up in my bed, disconcerted until I remember the previous day. I rub my eyes and look up, the light streaming down from the skylight. I swing my legs over the bed, taking a moment to contemplate before standing up. I pat myself down, realizing I've been in the same clothes forever. Disgusted, I don't even bother to check the closet to see if there are other clothes. I tear my crusty, dirty, worn clothes off my body and immediately scramble into the shower.

The hot water beats against my head. Where is Ivo? What was I thinking? Have I really just chosen the opposite side? I spend more time thinking about why I don't regret it then I do about why it went down as it did. 'He'll see,' I keep telling myself. When Ivo sees Nox and I succeed, bringing peace back home, he'll want to join us. I'm confident I can convince Nox to give me another chance at recruiting Ivo. When I get out of the shower, I've barely put on the expensive plain black clothes I found in the closet when Nox walks into the room.

"He's awoken." Nox calmly smiles as he strides into the living room. "I hope the sleep was all you hoped for. We have a long...." He glances at his watch. "Half a day ahead of us." I quickly glance at the oven clock. It's two in the afternoon. Unsurprisingly, my adolescent sleep schedule is wigged out.

"The sleep was good, Nox." I chuckle as I hurriedly get dressed, finally slipping on some designer black leather sneakers. I'm not sure how he managed it, but Nox has immediately made me look smart and more part of his clan just by giving me the right clothes. I meet him in the living room.

"So, what's first?" He smiles again before leading me out of my room after I grab a couple cereal bars.

"First, we need to get ready for tomorrow." We take the lift down and start walking towards the pod that leads to Skylar's house.

"Why, what's happening tomorrow?" I ask, following Nox through the automatic sliding doors and into the pod. Nox takes his time getting settled in his seat before answering my question.

"Well, tomorrow we start taking Europe, starting with London." He lets that sink in as the pod speeds towards Skylar's base. When it gets there, we climb out into a dark basement. The entire space is pretty much empty, like a subway station without the signs. Matte black paint covers everything, and the only way out is a glass staircase ahead. I struggle to keep up with Nox's fast strides and hurry to catch up.

"Nox. How exactly are we taking London tomorrow?" I feel dumb not knowing the plan.

"I think you know, Za." We climb the floating glass staircase, quickly moving into the first floor. "Think about how this all started in the first place." I start trying to remember as we turn the corner and walk up to another set of stairs. I glance to my left and recognize the large front windows. Then it hits me. I came to the HUB in the first place to help Ivo with a mission. The mission was to track down Tirique to see who he's working with because Ivo thought that Tirique's new bombs were strategically placed around London. I glimpse a subtle smile from Nox as he looks over his shoulder to see my realization. Once we get to the second floor, I snap out of it, and Skylar greets me.

"It's nice to meet you in a more civilized manner, Zashil," Skylar says, her menacing figure now seeming more relaxed. She reaches out to shake my hand. I meekly copy the gesture, and Nox immediately leads me to what seems like a control center in the far corner. Massive monitors line the entire wall, displaying all kinds of information. Two chairs are sitting behind an enormous control panel counter, and I sit down. Nox goes off to have a word with Skylar and then comes back. They stand on the other side of the counter, and both stare at me as I frantically make sense of my surroundings.

"Zashil." Skylar attempts to attract my attention, but I don't make eye contact with her until I've done a complete three-sixty in my chair and analyzed every part of the room. It's incredibly dull. The entire room is black, the doorways are all hidden, and there is absolutely no life to the space. It says a lot about Skylar that this is her house. Once she's convinced that I'm paying attention, Skylar starts talking again.

"Zashil. To be honest, we have no idea what we are doing here and could really use your help." That catches my attention, and I sit up in my chair.

"Yeah, what do you need. I guess that's why I'm here."

"So, as you know, we have placed bombs all over town, most of them being in or around major political buildings. We hope that we take out the politicians that are in our way and seize all of Europe in one swoop. It's a similar operation to what you and your brother pulled off those years ago, except on a larger scale."

"Well, first off. The civilians will be going absolutely crazy. Reassuring them is going to be the number one priority. You need to make it sound like you have everything under control even if you don't."

"How do we do that when bombs are going to be going off on virtually every other city block?" Nox asks as he paces back and forth. My confidence flows back as I realize I'm the expert right now.

"I think a live broadcast will do it. If you address everyone through the radio, billboards, and television, then you be able to reach virtually everyone in a single sweep."

"I guess you were right about the kid, Nox," Skylar says as Nox just nods back.

"I know. The only problem is that the controls needed for a mass broadcast like that are in the London center, which is heavily guarded." Nox finally sits down on the same side of the control board like me, burying his head in his hands.

"Send me with a small team, and I can take over the London center from the inside out. I already know the building pretty well from reporting to a mission there with Ivo for the secret service."

"That could work," Skylar says, already reaching for her phone. "They won't be the most elite fighters, but I know some guys that operate around the HUB and do clean up for some of the messier of workers." Nox is about to say something before his phone starts beeping. He takes a glance, grimaces, and starts to get up.

"Sorry. Excuse for me a minute," he says as he strides away and back downstairs—a smile of satisfaction forms on my face. I can't be sure, but if there is one thing I know about my brother, it's that you can't contain him for long.

IVO

March 5, 2035

I being to fall forward and am forced to put my hands up in front of me, grabbing the nearest stack of wooden crates, to stop my fall. I'm exhausted. My eyes are practically falling shut every ten seconds and not opening for another thirty. But, I still haven't been able to convince myself that this ship is safe in any way. I huddle behind many crates, but there are weapons across from me and some passengers through the door to my right. If I'm honest with myself, I could probably sleep, and nothing would happen to me, but it's the ease of mind part of that is keeping me awake.

I check my phone, thankful that I installed a super low power mode before this whole mission started. With the suit, though, I don't really need a phone. I've been on the boat for about a day now. The voyage is fast but not super fast like some other modern modes of transportation. We should be about halfway there by my calculation.

Once I got to the docks in Europe, I had to mentally sort through fifty different ships, all going to different places along the East Coast. Finding the Boston one didn't end up being that difficult, though, because it was

CYCLE

the only one that was heavily secured. Let's just say. I hope those two guards knew how to swim.

I wake up to beeping. My body is at a right angle. My upper body and head are collapsed on a wooden crate. Annoyed at myself, I grumble and stand up. I can't believe I fell asleep. I squeeze my way between the crates and immediately scurry behind the weapons boxes. I'm at the back of the boat, which means that getting off this thing without running into people will be pretty much impossible.

I decide to push through the ceiling. Most of the boat is made of sturdy materials, but the second level above me has the floor made of wood. I decide to punch through that. I open the closest weapons crate that doesn't have a special lock, pulling out a pretty basic rifle. I turn the gun around, making sure the safety is on before pointing the butt of the gun towards the ceiling. I climb on top of the weapons crate and start punching through the top with the gun and eventually creating a hole big enough to jump through. Before I grab the splintered edge of the hole, I hear commotion near the front of the boat with some people screaming and guns firing.

Pulling myself up and flipping through the hole, I activate my suit as I land. Looking towards the front of the boat, I see people running all around the bottom deck and a few people wearing all-black masks severely outnumbered by government soldiers through the window that wraps around this level. I spot a girl with a red tie around her forehead dart into the boat and towards the storage level where I just was.

I hear punches thrown beneath me and a body clatter into some weapons crates. I hop back down through the hole to see the same girl bombarded by five soldiers. She crouches low, swinging her left leg around and taking out two of the soldiers before being kicked back by a third. I decide to intervene, punching the first guard that turns to see me. I then generate a gun in my hand to shoot the next guard, firing at the one that kicked the girl next. The two on the ground barely get a chance to get up before I drop the gun, generate two knives, and toss them into their chests.

"Who are you?" The girl pushes off the wall and finds her footing again. I start to back away, realizing I may have meddled in business I shouldn't have. I look down at the guards I hit and get shivers when I realize they were part of the UN secret service, probably supplying someone in America.

I keep backing up, my arms in the air in innocence as the girl menacingly walks towards me. I see her looking me up and down, analyzing every inch of my suit. Her eyes lock on my chest. I look down to see the incredibly small emblem of the secret service. I silently curse at myself for not remembering to take that off. I see the girl quickly glance down, identifying the exact same secret service insignia.

"Your one of them?" Uh oh. She slowly starts to crouch down, shuffling her feet into a prowling position, reaching behind her back and pulling out a samurai sword. Wait. Only one person swears by a samurai sword as their primary weapon in the entire world.

"Aiko?" I stand up, lifting my arms higher in the air.

"How do you know my name?" She thrusts forward, her sword almost piercing my suit. I stumble back, falling against a crate. She holds me down with a hand on my shoulder, pulling back the sword, her hair falling out of its perfect position and glancing at my face.

"How. Do. You. Know. My. Name!" The breath from her angry exhalation fogs the glass of my suit helmet.

I quickly move my right arm before she can react. My finger just about hitting the spot behind my neck before she re-pins my arm back against the crate. My suit starts to deactivate. The nanotech consolidating around my neck before completely disappearing. I see her squint, staring into my eyes.

"Aiko. It's me. Ivo." Her eyes widen, her left hand touching my face. We must be there for two minutes, our breathing heavy. Then, she peels off her black mask, leaning in and kissing me in one motion. She hugs me tight. I wrap my arms around her.

"I can't believe you came back," she says. We both get up and stare at each other. She looks older but the same Aiko I left five years ago. Our eyes intently locked on each other, we both burst out laughing. Once we collect ourselves, we wander out of the boat.

"Why aren't you mad at me?" I'm almost scared to ask. She nudges my shoulder.

"Oh. Don't get me wrong. I'm furious. But it didn't seem appropriate to start with the anger." She smiles, and I just shake my head.

"I've been waiting five years to do that, Ivo. Five years." We walk out of the first level and onto the deck. I tip-toe over the various secret service bodies that litter the floor. The same few people wearing all black have taken off their masks and are leaning against the side of the boat. They snap out of the conversation as they see Aiko approaching. The girl in the middle steps forward.

"Where's the weapon?" She asks.

"Forget the weapon." They all throw up their hands in frustration and grunt. Aiko steps forward again, giving them a half glare. I try to hold back my smile.

IVO

"Do you know who this is?" They all shake their heads. I'm not surprised. I haven't been exactly present in the migrant life for quite some time.

"This is the greatest migrant weapon ever to grace the planet." They roll their eyes, and the same girl responds, looking me up and down.

"He doesn't look like much of a weapon to me, Aiko. Are you sure you got the right guy?" I find this the right time to introduce myself, and I pull Aiko behind me, shuffling in between the bodies. I reach out a hand to the girl, who reluctantly shakes it. I make uncomfortable eye contact with her.

"I didn't know I looked that harmless. My name is Ivo. I was with the Migrants at the very beginning." I see their jaws drop, and immediately the girl attempts to apologize.

"I'm so sorry, Mr. Wolf, I..I...I had no idea." She scrambles back against the side of the boat.

"No need to apologize. My absence probably deserves that. And please, it's Ivo. I'm not different than any of you."

"I tried to warn you," Aiko says as she starts to lead everyone off of the boat. I try to catch up to her as she shuffles everyone into a van that's parked right on the other side of the deck, in the middle of the empty road. I peek inside. No seat left untaken. "Sorry. It'll be tight, but you can sit on the ground in the van."

"It's all good. Same place?" I ask.

"Same place." She winks. I nod back to her, but she doesn't get in the van.

"What?"

"Oh. I wanna see this." She nods towards my arm, which is reaching behind my ear. "New one?"

"My best one yet."

CYCLE

"Every one is your best one yet, Ivo." Other than Za, she still knows me better than anyone else. I smile as I press the spot behind my ear. The suit quickly starts to form around me, the compliments of silver catching the sunlight. I give Aiko a two-finger wave as I notice the other migrants peaking out of the van in the corner of my eye. I turn to my left, the familiar Boston coming back in the form of my mental map. I run a few steps before jumping horizontally in the air. I activate the rod and the cycle fabricates beneath me just as I fall. I look behind me to see Aiko shake her head and get into the van.

I speed towards the base, passing by renovated buildings and spotting society in the city's center as I skirt around the city's outer edge. I suppose the government had to choose a city to be the epicenter of American society. I must admit, I didn't think it would be Boston, but I suppose it makes a lot of sense. Easy access to the coast, closest to Europe, and the best pre-existing infrastructure, other than New York City. I can't help but notice how far the city has come. It starts to remind me of the time before the Revolution, minus the absence of people of color. You can't win them all, I suppose.

Despite riding a much faster vehicle, I get to the base at pretty much the same time as the van. Aiko hops out right before the familiar crack. I bend down and run my finger along the perfectly straight crack in the pavement, just as I did all those years ago as a kid. I watch as Aiko walks over to the button that's hidden behind some rock.

"Still haven't automated that, I see." I tease her. The road starts to sink.

"And I lost the remote. Not everyone can tinker with everything and make it work, boy genius." She gets back in the van and drives it down the ramp. I follow, watching the ramp lift back up behind me.

There are so many more people. Everyone is running around doing tasks, some stopping to greet Aiko and the other migrants who are getting out of the van. Organized crates line the perimeter of the parking lot. No one is just sitting around. Even the kids are running around carrying things. Aiko walks up at me, laughing at my astonishment.

"It's like a well-oiled machine," I say. "How did you do this?"

"Five years, Ivo. You were gone for five years." I solemnly nod. I see Idrissa walk in from the hallway, see me, recognize me, glare at me with pure rage, and then turn around.

"Not all of us are happy you're here. You really hurt him when you left, Ivo. He didn't talk to anyone for weeks. Not even me." I curse at myself.

"Idri!" I scream after him, running into the hallway. I run up behind him and grab his arm before he can run into his room and close the door. "Please, Idri. Listen to me."

"No, Ivo. You listen to me." He turns around. "You think you can just leave and then come back, five years later, showing up out of nowhere, and everyone is going to celebrate you like the hero you think you are. You might've saved an entire continent. But, you left all of us here to dry. All of the Migrants suffered for months, Ivo. Without you, we had no savior, no person to get resources, to protect us. When you left, you took more than just yourself. You took what the essence of the Migrants was. We were a family. I waited, Ivo. I waited for weeks for you to come back. But then one year passed, two years, three, four, five. Life moved on. Aiko stepped up. More migrants showed up, and the Migrants continual suffering never stopped. So you listen. You left to save people, but you didn't save us. You're not my friend Ivo, at least not now. And, you're certainly not my brother anymore." He turns through the door and slams the door behind him. I hadn't even noticed, but Aiko had walked up behind me. She puts her hand on my arm.

"He will come around, Ivo. You're going to have to really try. But he will come around. You two were too close to be broken up indefinitely." I nod as she hugs me.

"Your room is still there, Ivo. I'll come back later; I have some errands to run." She starts to walk away but then quickly turns around, making it only about twenty feet.

"Ivo?"

"Yeah."

"Where's Zashil?" I break down, my emotions too high. A couple of tears run down my face. I walk towards the wall and slide down into a slump. Aiko walks over and sits next to me. "What happened? Tell me." I wipe my tears and collect myself.

"That's why I'm here. I didn't come just to visit. We are in massive trouble."

"Start from the beginning, Ivo." I nod.

"I took Za on a mission to investigate the origin of some bombings around Europe. But it all spiraled out of control. Someone named Nox kidnapped Za. He convinced Za to join him on his mission. I don't know what happened. I couldn't persuade him not to do it."

"What's the mission?"

"Nox wants to take control of Europe and then come save the Migrants in America by defeating the government. He's insane, Aiko. All of those people in Europe will be forgotten, and then he will become a dictator here. Yes, the Migrants will be free. But you will have no choice but to follow him blindly." I look to my side and see Aiko shaking her head.

"Oh god." The door next to me cracks open, Idri coming back out.

"What's the plan, boss?" he asks, no expression on his face. I confidently stand up. A common enemy is something Idri and I can team up for. I wipe my tears away.

"The plan is not to tell anyone until we have a plan. Aiko can go about her duties as normal, and I will get some rest before I acquaint myself with the current migrant situation. Idri, I'm gonna need you to fill me in later." He nods. Aiko nods as well before heading back down the hallway. Idri heads back into his room, and I walk towards my room. I'm about to head into my room, maintained just how I left it except for a layer of dust over everything, before I'm stopped outside by a couple of walking. There is a brown women about my age walking towards me. I'm taken aback by the guy whose arm is around her.

"Hi. Are you new? It's nice to meet you. My name is Aria."

"And I'm Tyler. Yes, I'm white. Yes, I'm still a migrant. Yes, it's a long story. And yes, I will tell it to you when you ask." Aria giggled. She peeks into my room.

"No one uses that room," she says, confused.

"That's because it's my room," I reply, exhausted. I see Aria contemplate for a second before something hits her.

"Wait a second. If that's your room." She looks me up and down. "And I've never seen you before. Then that means…Oh god. Ivo?"

"That's me," I reply, almost scared of the countless questions that will inevitably come.

"How? When? Why?"

"I really am quite tired." I start to shuffle back into my room, gently closing my door. "But it was very nice to meet you, Aria. And…" I hesitate for a second, thinking that I will definitely ask about his story. "Tyler." I close the door, walking back to my bed, and sitting down, my legs shooting with pain. It's been a while before I really got sleep. I wipe the dust off my pillow and lay down, staring at the all too familiar ceiling.

I'm back.

Z A

March 6, 2035

Today is the day. I walk out of my room door, and there is a metal box right outside. I drag it into the living room and open it, revealing all of the weapons and gear that I chose yesterday. I spent the day training with the team that they gave me. They are good. Not very good. But good. I was hoping they would be as qualified as the team assigned to me five years ago when I was in prison, but I suppose that that was just a pipe dream. Tirique and Skylar had picked out ten guys for me, but I only chose three of them, the ones I thought were the best and the most useful. It just so happened to be that they were the youngest, too, which didn't hurt. There is Michy, the sharpshooter, Kalvin, the combat fighter, and Pedro, the brains. I am quite satisfied with them.

I equip myself. I already have on some combat pants, a black compression long sleeve shirt, and a bulletproof vest with many pockets. The idea is that I only have to use the suit in an emergency. I grab the mini circular bombs and shove them in my pants pockets. I grab the two pistols, attaching them on either side of my hip. I put one knife near my right ankle and another over my heart. The only thing left is a small glass container. Inside are contacts, Tirique's newest invention. They do everything the glasses do, but they are contacts. I told the team that we will communicate through these instead of using transmitters. This is a relatively small mission, or at least it hopefully will be.

Once I'm geared up and put the contacts in, I head downstairs to find Nox, dressed in his usual suit, a team of bodyguards around him. I walk up to him. He said he would fight with me, but I told him he would need to look as professional as possible if he is going to address the whole population of Europe. He agreed.

"I will send you a message via the private messages with my contacts, so make sure to have your glasses on. Once we have cleared our London center, your people will need to get you upstairs to the top floor as fast as possible." I wait to see the bodyguards nod.

"It should just be a straight shot, but I'll have a sniper ready from across the street to take out anyone we didn't catch."

"Thank you, Za," Nox says. I nod back and head in the other direction, walking through the tunnel to the left and into the pod that runs towards Skylar's base. While I'm in the pod, I pat myself down, making sure I have everything.

When I get to Skylar's, I walk up the ground level and outside in front of her house. Waiting there are my three guys and four hover-bikes from Tirique. Skylar is there to greet me.

"Good luck, Zashil. Even if you may not need it." She smiles, and I smile back. I fist-bump the boys before mounting the closest hover-bike. I address the team before we leave.

"We fly in through the air and then drop to the ground. Michy, you land on the building across from us and start taking out anyone you see. We need to clear the path for Nox." He nods back. "Kalvin, you drop down to the ground and work your way up. Meanwhile, Pedro and I will crash through the roof and take control of the broadcasting system as quickly as possible. Everyone got it?" They all nod. I like that they are all quiet, silent killers, just like me. We lift off and start speeding towards London.

We reach London within a few hours, the high-speed hover-bikes helping the cause. As smoothly as possible, we hover over the London center. The building is about ten stories high and is all glass in the shape of a pyramid, coming to a very sharp point at the top. I gesture to the far less modern building across from it, and Michy veers off to land on the roof. We fly around in a circle before finding a good alley half a block away from the building for Kalvin to land. He heads down while Pedro and I get ready to drop down through the glass.

"This is gonna hurt." I send a text message through the contacts. His response hovers in front of my vision.

"I'm ready." We tilt forward, so our bodies are perpendicular to the ground before speeding towards the top of the building. We both crash through the glass. Shards are flying everywhere. We jump off the hover-bikes which keep crashing down the glass floors. Looking around as multiple guards run towards us, we are in the center console center, the broadcasting system accessed on the right. The tech people are already fleeing. I take out my pistols and shoot for injury towards all of them before turning my attention to the five onrushing guards.

"Pedro, go!" I quickly say, waiting for him to sprint towards the broadcasting section. I distract the guards by sprinting towards the opposite side. I flip over the middle console, shooting two guards in the process. I throw the gun at the third guard, hitting him in the forehead. I hear countless explosions in the distance as the various bombs start to go off. That's my cue to start hurrying it up. I take out my two knives, uppercutting the first guard that comes to me with my right fist before stabbing him with the knife in my second. I throw the knife in my right hand at the leg of the last guard before running up to him and knocking him out.

I look towards Pedro, who is furiously typing. I type a message to Kalvin.

"How's it going?" I ask.

"Look down." He responds. I proceed to look down through the glass floor. He waves right below me, a trail of bodies littering every single floor below him. He's good.

"Now." I message Nox. I peer down to the ground and see a black car pull up with Nox and his bodyguards getting out. Kalvin meets me as I walk towards Pedro.

"How close are you?"

"I…..Got it." He emphatically presses enter. All of the screens go black except for the one he is looking at. I scramble to turn on the camera which points at a plain background.

"Is everything working, Pedro?"

"Yeah, yeah. Everything is going good." Just in time, Nox bursts through the emergency staircase door, looking unfazed as ever. He nods to me before immediately standing in front of the camera.

"We are live in three…two…one." Pedro counts down.

"Hello, people of Europe. You are probably wondering why bombs are going off everywhere and who I am." I look across the street to see Nox on a massive billboard.

"My name is Nox. I am the one responsible for the bombs that have sufficiently taken out all of the highest-ranking governmental officials. I am here to take control of Europe. Please don't panic. Don't commit crimes. Trust me when I say that any opposing force would not be wise for your future. If you stay calm and move on with your lives, then, I promise you, everything will be completely fine." I take a deep breath of satisfaction as he finishes the speech he showed me with no flaws. But then he keeps going.

"This is the start of a new phase of history. A phase where all are equal and anybody that opposes this cause will pay the ultimate price. We are here to accomplish world peace and nothing less."

It's at that moment where I see Nox's eyes filled with control and rage. Maybe Ivo was right.

IVO

March 6, 2035

My head is buried in my hands. I can't believe it. I'm sitting in the computer room in front of the TV, a half-eaten bowl of cereal sitting in front of me. I had gotten up late in the morning and gathered breakfast together before sitting here. I was reveling in the fact that I'm back home. But, then I turned on the TV.

Shocking footage of multiple explosions around London are compiled on the screen. The red banner below says, "Europe taken by 'savior' Nox within hours." I am in a constant loop of staring at the scenes in astonishment and burying my head in my hands in disappointment. I even see a shot of Za dropping down through the top of London Center.

"How long until they're here?" Aiko comes up from behind me and puts her hands on my shoulders.

"I have no idea. I didn't think they were this far along." She comes around and sits across from me at the old wooden table. I run my fingers along the familiar cracks of the table.

"They have the full force of Europe Ivo. How are we...." She does a swoop of her hands, gesturing at the action on the TV. "Going to stop them."

"We have to stop them before they even get started. You're right. We can't take them by force, but we can by surprise."

"So, you're talking about a good old migrant ambush." She smiles.

"No. We have to come up with something new. Za will know everything we do if we don't." I clench my teeth at the thought that Za is the enemy.

"Well…While you think, you can help us out with a few things on our end." Aiko's not asking, so I just smile and get up, happy to have something to do. We walk out into the hallway and stop in front of my room.

"Get ready. We are taking a trip."

"Where are we going?" I ask as I stumble into my room and start getting clothes together.

"Just get ready, and you'll see." I nod and pull on new clean clothes. I put on a pair of clean black joggers, perfectly fitted, so I look put together. A black long-sleeved shirt goes on too, and a matte black waterproof zip-up jacket gets put over that. Finally, I put on some black athletic socks and a pair of black leather sneakers to look a little bit more professional. I go back into the hallway where Aiko is talking to the couple that I saw last night. I already forget their names. Walking up to them, I nod at Aiko and get close enough to hear her say.

"You guys are with us." And gesture at her and me. The lady, about the same age as me, has a beaming smile on her face like it's the first day of school, and the white guy next to her is not short of enthusiasm either.

I struggle to stride up next to Aiko, who is moving quickly towards the garage. As we enter the large open space, filled with organized rows of bins and crates and bustling with younger migrants, she turns to the wall on our left. A brick pops out after she presses it in, revealing a keypad. Once she puts in a passcode, an entire section of the wall, taller than me, pops out and moves to the side, revealing Aiko's sword in the center and other special weapons on either side. She grabs her sword and starts to sling it over her shoulder.

"And who made you this contraption?" I ask. I didn't know any of the Migrants could manage something like this.

"I'm not sure how, but I don't think you never met Marques right?" I shake my head, although the name rings a bell. "He's this inventor guy. Kinda prodigal as a kid. He's pretty amazing. I think he likes to think about himself as your competitor or something. I keep trying to tell him that nothing can surpass your expertise." I'm already skeptical about this guy, but that doesn't keep me from wanting to meet him.

"So when do I get to meet him?"

"Whenever we can find him." She turns around to see my furrowed brow. "He's been off the grid for a few months now. He went over to help set up a new migrant base on the West Coast." I turn around to see the couple waiting behind me—the lady chimes in.

"We planned to bring all of the West Coast Migrants here. It was difficult, but we managed to bring a lot of them. The problem is, immigrants keep showing up in America for some reason. Hence, the migrant group grew way faster there than we anticipated, and, as it turns out, this base does indeed have a limited capacity. I'm sure you've noticed that we've pretty much hit that number." I'm about to ask for her name again, but she anticipated it and put her hand out.

"I'm Aria, by the way. I know we met last night, but you looked pretty tired. It was probably a long journey from Europe." I shake her hand and nod. She seems sharp, which I like.

"That Nox guy must be giving you quite the headache." The blond guy next to Aria puts out his hand. I'm about to shake it and respond, but I see Adria have a guilty look out of the corner of my eye. When we make eye contact, she quickly turns away. Confused, I turn my attention back to the guy and shake his hand.

"I'm Tyler. They like to call me the resident white person of the group." He makes a similar joke as the one he did last night, and I'm too intrigued about how he became a migrant in the first place to enjoy it. I look over my shoulder to see Aiko smiling. She just gives me a look as if to say, 'I know he's weird, but he's useful.' Aiko wouldn't keep Tyler around unless she thought he was instrumental, and I trust her gut.

"Well, it's nice to meet both of you....again. One of these days, I want to hear both of your background stories." I say it to both of them but look at Aria. There has been something off about her ever since Tyler mentioned Nox.

"Okay. We should get going. We have a lot of work to do today, and security increases at night."

"You still haven't told me what we are doing." I say as Aiko moves towards the same van from yesterday.

"Depends. I'll tell you if you decide you're not too cool to drive in a van." I stop walking, tilt my head, and give her an annoyed look. She just laughs as I walk around the van and climb into the passenger seat. Meanwhile, Tyler and Adria open the side and load some empty crates into the van before climbing in and taking a seat.

"Oh, god damnit." Aiko was about to put her seat belt on before she pushes open the door, frustrated. She runs over the side trigger and opens the ramp. I just can't help myself from laughing as she climbs back in. She punches me in the shoulder as she just shakes her head.

"Maybe Marques can help with that." I hear Aria and Tyler struggling to hold back their laughter. I doubt they witness their boss bullied very often. Aiko can't hold her poker face for too long, and eventually, we all burst out laughing as we speed away from the base.

"Now, can you tell me where we are going?"

"We need weapons, now more than ever. Not only are we simply running out of weapons, but I'm assuming we are going to need some more firepower for the incoming invasion, no matter how much of a covert operation we end up doing. Usually, we try to pick up weapons when shipments come in, like the one you came on. Those tend to have lower security. But, there is a secret bunker full of all the higher-tech new weapons that I've always wanted to steal from. I had no idea it existed until Tyler over here told me about it from his time undercover as a soldier."

"That sounds perfect." I respond, excited to finally have an old fashion mission like the old days.

"There is just one problem...." I should have known better. There is always a catch.

"The bunker is hidden beneath the most secured conference building in the entire city. It's virtually impossible to sneak in without being spotted."

"I think you mean impossible until I got here." I wink at her, and she just shakes her head.

"But actually, what's the plan?" I look up, and we've made it into the outskirts of the city. Aiko pulls over, and we park next to an abandoned convenience store.

"I don't have the plan. Tyler does." I look behind at Tyler, who clears his throat at the sight of me turning around.

"I'm going to head into the building undercover as a soldier. There is a small door on the side of the building which only opens from the inside. When I make sure the coast is clear, I'll open the door and let you guys in. Then I can lead you to the bunker. We should be able to do it without causing too much of a scene. Once you and Aiko take out the guards on the way, I'll pose as a guard at the beginning of the hallway and guard it, while Aria will be the lookout. That's the plan." I look Tyler up and down and notice that he's wearing the same all-black military uniform as all of the guards and soldiers.

"Seems pretty legit," I say, impressed. Tyler grins, proud of himself.

"How far out are we from the building?"

"Only about a mile," Adria says, her demeanor back to normal. I nod.

"Let's get going then," Aiko says, jumping out of the van.

It takes us ten minutes to walk into the center of the city. We have to weave in and out of alleys and pull our hoods over our heads whenever we pass people. To our relief, since it's during the workday, most people are in their offices, and there isn't much street traffic. Once we are a block away from the building, Tyler peels off and joins a group of soldiers walking towards the conference building. I see it in the distance, the glass reflecting the sunlight. The building is a bizarre shape. It starts as a typical rectangular skyscraper, granted a little bit wider than average. But, after a few stories, it splits off into two narrow buildings with a substantial gap in the middle. About ten stories up, there is a glass skywalk that goes between the two towers. Not only does it look strange, but it looks very, very expensive. Never did I think I would see new and modern buildings like this built-in Boston again.

We all cross over a block and keep walking until we are across from the side of the building. Then we wait for Tyler. Aiko crouches, her hand ready to grab her sword at any moment while Aria kneels, a knife in each of her hands and a pistol hanging from her waist. We aren't waiting for long before the thick metal side door abruptly swings open. Tyler's face appears, ushering us in.

"The weapons bunker is down that way and some stairs. It's hard to miss." He points down to his right as we hear voices coming in the opposite directions.

"I'll take care of them," I say. Nodding at Aiko, who is heading towards the bunker. "Aria, you go with Aiko, Tyler, and I can take care of these guys." I run towards the voices, striding down the hallway and turning left at the corner. I see five soldiers running towards me, guns in their hands.

"Stay there," I say to Tyler, who needs to keep his cover if he's going to be helpful for the rest of this mission. Tyler looks confused before realizing what I was thinking. He notices I don't have any weapons on me and holds out his rifle.

"I'm good," I say as I shake my head.

I look to see the soldiers getting closer. I trigger my suit and start running towards the most forward soldier as the suit generates around me. I spring off the wall with my left foot and use my momentum to kick through the guard's chest. He stumbles to the ground, tripping up another guard who I throw a knife into before he can get back to his feet. Generating a gun in my hand, I put my hand on the next soldier, flipping over him and shooting him in the back. I then get low to the ground and swing my leg around and trip the next guard, who I shoot in the foot. The next guard lands a punch in my gut which makes me stumble back, but he gets too confident and tries to attack me with his fists again. I use his momentum to flip him onto the ground before kicking his head and knocking him out.

"What in god's name did I just witness." I spin around and see that Tyler has come out from around the corner. "I guess when they said you were the leader of the Migrants, they weren't kidding around."

"I'm going to check for any more guards that are nearby. You just make sure these guys don't wake up." He silently nods, his mouth still opens in awe. I hop over a couple of the bodies as I continue down the hallway. In the end, there is another perpendicular hallway. I decide to take a right. I'm wandering down the hall when I hear some faint voices. I look around to see where the voices could come from, but there is nothing. The wall on the right side is glossy black glass, and the ceiling and the opposite wall are made of just normal glass.

"Ivo?" I hear the voice clearer now. It sounds like someone is saying my name.

"Say it again," I say.

"Ivo?" This time it's said louder, and I hear it coming from the right wall. I lean against the wall, putting my ear to the glass.

"Again."

"Ivo. We are in here." The glass next to my head starts to pounding.

"How can you see me?"

"One-way glass."

"Okay. How do I get in?" I hear guards running my way, and there is a lot more of them which means there is no time to ask how whoever is on the other side of this wall knows my name.

"It's thin." Is all I get in reply. I generate two lasers, one in each of my hands.

"Step far away from the wall," I say. Hoping they heard me, I shoot the laser in my right hand through the glass. It slices through pretty easily. I drag it clumsily in an arc, cutting through the glass in the shape of a circle. I do the same for the other half of the circle with my other hand.

The glass falls forward and shatters on the ground in front of me, revealing two familiar faces. I just stare at them, tilting my head, trying to figure out how I know them. Then it hits me. I disable my helmet.

"Riz?"

"Yes," the one on the right says.

"Aziz?"

"Yes," the other says.

"Oh my god." I immediately help them out of the gap in the wall. At the same time, a ton of guards around the corner and start rushing towards us. I re-enable my helmet. "Hurry, hurry." My phone rings, and I pick it up through my suit.

"Ivo, where the hell is you. We are waiting for you outside the side door, but the commotion is beginning. Tyler said you went off somewhere. Get here right now!"

"I'm coming. I got sidetracked. You'll see, I found some friends." I hang up and generate a grenade in my hand, tossing it and waiting for it to explode with smoke. I then generate a pistol and start shooting towards the cloud as I run behind Riz and Ahmed. "Take a left!" I yell as a soldier gets close to me. I drop the gun and generate a knife, dodging a punch and stabbing the soldier in the knee. I pull the knife out and toss it at the next incoming soldier. Then I spin around and sprint around the turn.

"Right!" I yell again. They take a turn, and then I catch up to them, bursting through the metal door. Adria, Tyler, and Aiko are anxiously waiting against the opposite wall.

"You found the twins? How on earth did you find the twins?" Aiko asks.

"No time. There is a bunch of soldiers right behind us."

"Ivo. We don't have the van, and we can't outrun them."

"It's fine. I have an idea. Follow me." I sprint out of the opposite side of the alley and onto the main road. I generate the rod in my hands to enable the car mode, hoping to god it works. Pulling the rod apart, they each bend into a steering wheel shape as a high-speed car forms. Aiko hops in the passenger side, and the rest cram in the back. I speed away towards the base, seeing the soldiers throw their arms up in frustration as they turn the corner in my rearview window. Aiko lets out a sigh of relief and puts her hand on my shoulder. I notice her sword has crimson red blood splattered all over it.

"Looks like you didn't have an easy time of it either."

"No, but we got what we needed. She nods behind her." I glance behind my shoulder into the back seat and see Tyler and Aria with multiple weapons slung over their shoulders and each with a crate in their hands.

"Let's just say it could have been worse," Aria says. Aiko scans the car, taking a long moment to look at the twins.

"This is quite the gang."

"Just like old times," I reply.

"Yeah. Just like old times."

ZA

March 7, 2035

After Nox addressed Europe yesterday, I didn't talk to him or question him. We all just made our way back to the base, and I went into my room, laying in my bed for the rest of the day. Now I'm in the car with Nox, driving to the most extensive military base in Europe in Paris. I stare out the window, debris of buildings littering the ground and people still looking around in astonishment at the scenes. Nox said they should proceed as if life was normal. But how could they?

I catch reflections of Nox in the window. He looks calm and collected. Simply looking forward at the seat in front of him, not paying any attention to the chaos outside his door. I'm rubbing my hands together as I take note of all of the damage, which continues for so much longer than I imagined. I keep forgetting that explosions like this happened over all of Europe. At least Nox's crew will make some kind of an appearance in London. Other places will not be so fortunate. It will all be like the chaos just dropped from the sky.

"What is it, Za?" I spin my head around to see Nox staring into my eyes. I try to act like nothing is wrong, but he just glances at my legs which are both nervously shaking. He's too good. I hesitate to answer, frantically trying to come up with something to say in my head. Instead, he just continues.

"I know that my words yesterday were powerful, maybe even extreme. But, you know my plan. The last thing I want is to become the next dictator. I want to lead long enough and with enough power to establish a completely equal and sound society. That's it. Then I will let the real leaders take their place. But, I can't confirm the way people act without authority. They must respect me and, if they don't, they must fear me. There is simply no other way."

"What about all of the white people back home that are simply civilians like everyone here?" I gesture outside as we pass a large group of people, all of them staring at our car as we move smoothly down the road, a security detail vehicle in front and behind us. "Those people did nothing wrong. They were simply conformed as you want to do. You said that anyone that opposes would pay the ultimate price, but what about the people that are simply going along with the authoritative government because that's their only way to survive. You can't punish them. They are in a similar position as the Migrants." Nox grimaces at my last sentence.

"You are right. They may be innocent. But, their existence and their meekness are what fuels the revolution to live on. The Migrants have suffered but, for these people, they have been living good lives just because they were lucky enough to be born with the right color skin. Imagine if it was the other way around? Society had ten years of complete serenity. Discrimination simply didn't exist because the groups that discriminated were minimized, suppressed, and silenced. Za, we don't have that choice anymore. They are reminded too much of what kind of power they possess when they discriminate. Not to mention, these companies are affecting all civilians. They care not about the people and souls they sell to, but only about the financial gain they will get."

"I think that marching into the country with full military force sends off the wrong sign."

"Don't worry. That's not the plan anymore. I completely agree with you. So ,Tirique and I have been working on something."

"What is it?"

"You will see in due time."

"Fine. But that doesn't explain why we are headed to the military base. If we aren't going in with force, then why do we need to talk to the military?"

"Because, when we leave, they are going to be the ones responsible for keeping everything at bay here. Serge will be in charge of them, and then I will feel safe leaving Europe. I don't need a second revolution against me to start here in Europe."

We sit in silence for the rest of the trip. I continue to stare out of the window. I can't help but think about where Ivo must be right now. I'm sure he escaped whatever prison Nox put him in. They had no chance of trying to contain him. He's probably at the secret service headquarters, if it hasn't blown up, tracking this car right now.

When we reach the military base in Paris, I see the HUB in the distance. The military base is built at a point of elevation and is massive. Everything you could imagine is here, and generals are lined up waiting for us as we roll through the massive concrete construction and into an opening in the center of the building. I get out of the car, the generals of all different races and ages and all saluting us. Meanwhile, Serge peels off from the far right of the line and walks up to me.

"You know. I never really got to welcome you to the team. So welcome. I'm still sorry for the way your capture all went down, you know. It wasn't supposed to get messy, but all you Wolf brothers are wriggly."

"Yeah, calm down, Serge. All is forgiven." We shake hands, and he turns around, addressing the generals.

"Everyone, I would like you to meet your new leader, first in command, and current ruler of Europe! Nox!" He sweeps his arms around to present Nox, who salutes everyone. "I already prepped them. Just say a few words, and we should be on our way." Serge whispers to Nox as he walks past him and stands twenty feet away, facing us.

"It's a pleasure to meet all of you. I wouldn't call myself a ruler. But I do currently control Europe. My number one issue is the safety of the public here in Europe. Your job is to stop any threat before it has begun and keep the peace. It's very simple, but you must be smart about it. Don't scare the civilians. Instead, show them that you care. Serge is the best military leader I know, and you should be in good hands. That's all I got." Nox turns around and nods to me before getting back in the car. I can't believe that I drove all of this way just so that he could say that. I open the passenger door and lean in.

"I think I'm going to get back on my own. I'll see you later at the base."

"Don't be too late. We have a busy day tomorrow." I nod and shut the door. I quickly turn to Serge and give him a nod before getting a running start, activating my suit, and generating the cycle. I zoom down the paved hill and towards the HUB.

It only takes me about thirty minutes to get there. Once I get to the outskirts, I hop off the bike and deactivate my suit. I reach around in my pockets until I find my glasses. I put them on and turn them on. Virtual signs pop up everywhere, and I wander around, trying to get my bearings. When I finally stumble upon the restaurant that Ivo and I found Skylar in, I remember where I am, and it only takes a few more minutes for me to find the hotel we stayed in.

I walk in the front door but quickly slide off to the side and take the emergency stairwell up the floor we stayed on. Looking left and right before I walk into the hallway, I make my way to our room when I'm sure the coast is clear. I slowly open the door, which is unsurprisingly unlocked. Both Ivo and I must've left pretty spontaneously. Immediately, I walk to the living room space where Ivo's laptop is still open on the table. I glance towards my left. Pillows and sheets cover the floor.

I slide into the seat at the table and turn on the computer, hoping that it's still unlocked. It is. Thank the lord. I immediately navigate to the secret service database. I need to find the secret service location here at the HUB. I want to see if Nox was able to destroy the secret service. As long as they still exist, Nox doesn't really have control of Europe, which would make me feel a lot better. I scroll through many cryptic posts, all with a secret service name for the location and a small photograph of the entrance to the place. There are hundreds of these places everywhere, and the only way to narrow the search is by name. They make it purposefully difficult to find these places because they don't even like people within the secret service to know where all of them are. It makes sense to keep as much as possible on the down-low.

I scroll for about ten minutes before I think I find what I'm looking for. The code name is "PARhouseunderbars." I'm pretty sure the "PAR" is Paris, and "house under bars" is an acronym for HUB, so everything checks out to me. I find the location tag with coordinates in the description and then plug it into a virtual map of the HUB. I get my

CYCLE

bearings and then see that it's supposedly only a couple of blocks away from this hotel.

    I close the laptop this time and enable the auto-lock on the door on my out. I slide down the railing of the emergency staircase and make my back out of the hotel. I turn right in the direction of the secret base, which is weirdly further towards the center of the HUB. Once I find the building, I walk around until I find a piece of glass that's slightly out of place on the side of the building. I run my finger around the edge of the glass piece, which juts out a few millimeters from the rest of the wall. I feel a small hinge on the right side, so I drag my finger along the left side until I feel a tiny button. After pushing it, the door swings open, revealing a more secure metal door as an entrance. I notice black soot marks on the bottom of the door. That's not a good sign. I scan for any people before turning the handle that sits in a recessed semi-circle indent. The door opens in, and I climb into the space, standing up and closing the door behind me. My movement triggers automatic lights and reveals a horrific sight.

    Dead bodies are littering the floor. All of them are soldiers with secret service badges on their chests. The cement walls are splattered with blood, and all of the computers are bashed in. The room reeks of death. I wander to the back, where there is a security camera that isn't destroyed. I take it down and pull out the data card. Then I find a computer with the least cracked screen that is still somewhat functional and plug the data card in. I scrub the footage until I find the moment when the base was attacked. All of the soldiers are having a good time and laughing with each other. They were probably just posted here so that the secret service would have some people in the HUB. Suddenly, the door opens and takes all of them by surprise.

    The soldiers all scramble to get up and get their weapons ready. But it's too late. They are all shot on the spot as soldiers wearing all black file into the base and proceed to hit the computers. I see Nox walk into the base, slow-clapping at the cleanliness of the operation. A man in a suit is the last to step in. He has black hair and looks up at the camera after making sure all of the secret service soldiers are dead. I pause the footage and zoom in. The face is hard to not recognize. It's John Mane.

IVO

March 7, 2035

Aiko and I are sorting through the weapons that we stole yesterday. There are actually more weapons than I initially thought. It looks like the military finally caught up to the weapons I was inventing. There are a bunch of small black rectangular cartridges that become guns when triggered. They may have caught up, but they are five years too late. We are laying out the weapons into categories on the table in the tech lab. The unsorted weapons pile up in crates which Aiko and I put on the chairs we pulled out. On the far left, we have the really powerful and big guns that Adria and Tyler had swung around their soldiers, all of the collapsible guns are going in the middle, and the other miscellaneous stuff is on the far right, including grenades, knives, and other spy gear. We are almost done when the twins walk in. When we got back yesterday, they were so exhausted and hungry that they ate and then went straight to bed. Riz goes to the back corner and sits in an armchair while Aziz sits across from us at the table. Both of them have grown so much. Now they look like young adults. It's kind of making me feel a bit old.

"So, is now a good time to ask what the hell happened to you two?" Aiko asks, looking up to smile at Aziz.

"Depends," he replies.

"Depends on what?"

"Depends if you are going to tell us where you found this guy," Riz chimes in from the back and gestures towards me. Aziz puts his arms up in agreement.

"He will tell you once you tell us how you guys dropped off the face of the earth," Aiko replies.

"I don't think we can agree to those terms," Aziz says while Riz just cracks up in the back. Now they are just trying to get under Aiko's skin. I'm struggling to hold back a smile and, when Aiko notices, she just glares at me. I put up my arms in innocence.

"Alright boys, how about this. I will tell you how I came back, and then you tell us what happened to you."

"Yeah, that's acceptable," Riz says, who is now slumped back in the black leather chair, his right leg slung over the arm of the chair and his head propped up on a pillow against the opposite side.

"So let's hear it, God of Migrants," Aziz urges as he gets up, grabs a bag of chips, and then leans back in his chair. I shake my head before I begin.

"When am I starting? The beginning or the very beginning?"

"Well, we don't need to hear you brag about saving the free world, so let's just say the beginning?" Riz answers.

"Where is Za, by the way? I didn't see him around," Aziz asks.

"Oh boy. I guess I'm going to have to start from a couple of weeks ago." I look at Aiko, who is relaxing in her chair. "I'm going to summarize so that you guys don't fall asleep. Basically, I took Za on a mission to track down this sketchy but famous tech dude, Tirique."

"That's the guy that keeps coming up with those bombs and stuff, right?" Aziz asks in the middle of crunching his chips.

"Yeah. As I said, he's pretty famous. So, the mission started in the HUB, which is in what used to be Paris. It's an all-virtual city. Hard to explain. Anyways, after finishing one of our recon missions, Za goes to sleep in the hotel room, and I sneak out to do some extra exploring. When I got back, Za was gone."

"Wait. What the hell happened?" Riz perks up in the back. I hold up my finger to silence him.

"It took me a day to find him. But when I do, he's already committed to helping this guy Nox."

"Who's Nox?" Aziz asks. I smile to myself at the fact that the twins haven't lost their curiosity. It reminds me of the good old days.

"He is the psychopath that is trying to take over the world," Aiko responds.

"I thought that he was the guy that's trying to save the Migrants. That doesn't seem too bad to me," Riz adds.

"Well, he's not going about it the right way." Aiko shakes her head as she mostly says it to herself. She snaps out of it. "Anyways, will you guys shut up and let Ivo tell his story." I laugh at how motherly Aiko always is, especially around the twins.

"Somehow, Nox was able to convince Za to be on his side. When I finally found Za, he asked me to join them. Of course, I was like, 'hell no.' Then they took me, prisoner. I woke up in this glass cube. But the sketchiest part was that it was a mental prison or whatever." I glance at Riz, who is struggling to hold back a question, his left foot frantically tapping the ground. I just continue.

"Every time I tried to escape, I just snapped back to where I was from the beginning. Once I figured out how to break the loop, I was in some kind of wack lab owned by that Tirique guy. Once I escaped, I decided to find a way back home instead of trying to stop them here. I thought I was better off warning you guys." Riz is practically falling out of his chair when I look I his direction again.

"What, Riz?"

"I'm pretty sure that Aziz and I were put into one of those mental prison things."

"When?" I ask.

"It was when we were first captured," Aziz answers.

"Hold on. One story at a time. Let Ivo finish, and then you guys can tell us what happened."

"Fine." Riz grumpily sits back in his chair.

"I went to the docks and hitched a ride on some boat. When I arrived, there was some commotion on the boat, and that's when I ran into Aiko, who, it must be said, pretty much attacked me." Aiko gives me an annoyed look.

"To be fair, I thought that you were working for the bad guys." Aiko tries to defend herself.

"Those guards were from the secret service. Who are not the bad guys, I might add," I argue. Aiko just shrugs.

"Now it's your turn." I nod towards Aziz.

"Them two went on a special mission to find out about the new resources banks, and then we didn't see or hear from them," Aiko explains.

"How long were they gone?" I ask.

"Three months."

"Jeez." Aziz starts to tell the story, and I scoot my chair back to comfortably see him and Riz.

"Well, we did go on that mission. We made it to New York City because people were saying that the Board would stop building in Boston. Riz and I thought that New York City was the next obvious place for them to start building. It turns out we were right. When we got there, there was a ton of construction. Pretty much all of the civilians were locked in their homes because of how much construction was happening." Riz picks it up.

"We found a tiny group of migrants in New York City who helped us navigate the city. We planned to simply find and remember where we thought the resource bank was built to report that back. Then, in a few months, we could put together a more concerted and targeted mission to raid it when the building was finished. When we found the building, we overheard some discussion about some kind of attack. That's when Aziz was stupid." Aziz throws his arms up in frustration and growls at Riz.

"I admit that it wasn't my greatest decision. Out of the corner of my eye, I saw a guard that was slightly off to the side. I thought if I could somehow take him out without anyone seeing me, that we could grill him for some more information." I'm just shaking my head. First off, I don't remember you trying to abduct someone without cover. The likelihood that you take someone out and they can drag them away without anyone noticing is very low. Second, the twins were by themselves. It's going to take both of them just to pick the guy up. Aziz sees me shaking my head.

"I know, Ivo. I know. Anyways, I went for it. I was able to quietly knock him out, but when I ushered Riz to come to help me drag him away, he wasn't paying attention."

"Woah, woah, woah. I wasn't paying attention to you being an idiot because I was trying to fly the drone close to the group so I could get a picture or something and not try to get caught. It was your dumb idea to knock that guy out. Not my fault at all."

"Yeah, whatever, man. I tried to drag the guy away and around a corner on my own. He was a big dude, to say the least, and I didn't get very far before someone spotted me. Immediately I dropped the guy and threw a smoke grenade." Riz interrupts him.

"And that was a problem because my drone was still above them. We couldn't afford to get the drone because they could find a reverse hack to get our data. So while the soldiers were all sprinting towards Aziz, I ran to try to find the drone. It turns out it was crushed in the commotion."

"That's when they captured me. One guy shot and grazed my leg, which was very painful. Then they were able to get handcuffs on me. That was that. At this point, Riz should have vacated the scene so he could have had a chance to come back with more people to save me in some way."

"I've already been separated from you before, and I wasn't prepared for that to happen again," Riz says to Aziz. Then he turns to Aiko and me. "I was able to knock out a couple of guys and was about to get Aziz out of his mess, but then ten more guards just happened to walk out of the elevator at that exact moment. That's when we were really done. They handcuffed both of us and then knocked us out. Next thing we know, we have no idea where we are."

"That's the mental prison thingy. Except our's wasn't geared towards beating the system. It wasn't a loop or anything like that. It was more like a vacation type of scene to distract us and mess with our heads. When they turned it off, Riz and I had pretty much forgotten all our sense of direction, and we were super fatigued. Then they stuck us in some room with one-way glass. It was torture to continuously see people walking past our cell when no one even knew it existed. Also, they barely fed us."

"Wait. So when I broke you guys out, you had no idea that you were in Boston?" I inquire.

"Nope. Absolutely no clue," Riz says as he gets up from his chair and sits next to his brother, across from us at the table.

"That's crazy," I comment.

"Do you guys remember anything about the attack you overheard?" Aiko asks.

"Not really," Aziz answers, finishing his chips and tossing the empty bag into the trash can across the room. "But they kept saying this guy's name over and over again."

"Oh yeah. What was it? Serge something, I think," Riz adds.

"His last name was super dumb, I remember. One of those dumb American double first name situations."

"Adams. That's it. Serge Adams," Riz says definitively.

"That sounds familiar to me," Aiko says. "I'm pretty sure Adams is on a bunch of weapons and stuff that I've seen before."

"That's the guy that kidnapped Za. He's working with Nox. I think he's one of those private security-type people," I add.

"You know what this means, boys?" Aiko says to the twins.

"What?" They both say in unison. I answer it before Aiko has a chance.

"It means we are taking a field trip to New York City."

ZA

March 8, 2035

I wake up absolutely exhausted. Not only did I get up late last night, but I couldn't sleep because I was thinking of how the hell John Mane ended up working for Nox. Part of me just wants to ask Nox. I'm too valuable for him to cut me loose. However, I want to have Nox's trust, and if he knew that I went to a secret service base and then found footage of him, it would all sound a little suspicious. Well, it is questionable. Last time I saw Mr.Mane was before Ivo and I left. He found the Migrants and helped the whole gang with our attack. I can't see such a caring person changing sides like that. But, now that I think about it, Nox does paint the picture that he's on the side of the Migrants. That's basically his whole agenda: the Migrant savior.

I roll out of bed to a ferocious knocking on my door. I swing open the door to an anxious Nox, his left foot tapping the ground. He was knocking so hard that, when I open the door, he almost clocks my nose.

"What the hell Nox."

"What about 'we have a busy day tomorrow' do you not understand, Za." I rub my temples and shake my head.

"What time is it?"

"It's nine." I just stare at him, annoyed.

"Nine is late to you, Nox?"

"Yes. Yes, it is."

"Nox. You do realize that I'm a teenager, right?"

"So?"

"So we sleep like a lot. Nine is not late. You're insane." I keep my door open and walk to the kitchen to make some tea. I keep talking.

"Weren't you a teenager, like, not so long ago?"

"I never slept in. I always woke up early and went out. Wandering around the empty streets was a great time to let myself think." Maybe Nox is human, after all.

"Well. In that case, you're not normal." I put on the kettle and then slowly make my way to my closet. "I'll be down in five minutes." He shuffles backward out of the doorway with his hands up.

"Just please be ready."

"I'll be ready. But you don't want me to be too ready because then I'll make you look bad."

"Whatever makes you feel better." He shuts the door as he heads down the hallway. I smile while I pick out some clothes. I decide to grab some black jeans, white leather sneakers, and a dark grey sweatshirt. I'm not sure what work Nox has in mind, but I hope it doesn't require any running. I make myself some tea, stopping the kettle before the water is thoroughly heated up, and down it as fast as I can. I quickly eat a granola bar as I make my way downstairs and find Nox talking to Tirique in the middle of the floor. Nox ushers me into the conversation.

"Za, remember yesterday when you said that showing up with the whole military would look like too much of a force?"

"Yeah." I just think of the people I saw through the car window when he reminds me of that.

"Well, Tirique and I have been working very hard on a solution that we are very proud of." Tirique decides to hop in, pushing up his rectangular brown glasses.

"The problem is. We are missing a part of it. It's a scarce and costly piece to the equation."

"So you need me to get that piece?" I ask.

"You and your team." Nox corrects me.

"And what exactly is this amazing new solution you guys came up with?" I ask.

"We can't tell you quite yet. Think of it as a surprise." Nox replies. I become a bit skeptical. I have a feeling that, whatever this solution is, it's probably worse than just invading with military power. And, I didn't know you could get any worse than that.

"I don't like surprises." I blandly state.

"Well, you're going to like this one," Nox says as he nudges me away and waves to Tirique, who turns around and heads towards the tunnel that leads to his base. "The team is waiting at Skylar's base again. But if you wanna do this one alone, you can do that."

"Why would I want to go alone?"

"Well, I didn't know if you liked the team or not."

"Your crazy, Nox. I'm not that picky." He just shrugs, and I shake my head. "I'm gonna head to Skylar's. I'm assuming she has all of the details?"

"Yes, she does. I'll see you later." He walks towards his office. What in the world does he do all day? I walk towards Skylar's tunnel, hopping in the pod and arriving at her base within minutes. I step out into the ominous open space. It still feels so sterile. Making my way up the staircase, I look down and swear to myself as I realize that I'm still wearing my non-athletic clothes. Idiot. Once I get to the ground floor, Skylar is standing next to the next staircase.

"Hi, Zashil. I've been waiting for you." I glance out the big window. "The team is upstairs. I'm going to debrief you on the mission."

"Sounds good," I mutter as I follow her up the stairs. When we get into the control center, all of the guys are sitting in various spots. They all spin around in their office chairs to greet me.

"What's up, boys," I say. They all nod, and Pedro stands up to give me a fist bump. Skylar makes her way behind the control board that separates her and us. I take a seat in the last open chair, and Skylar starts the presentation.

"You guys are headed to Japan." We all kind of sit up, suddenly interested. If we are going to Japan, which no one ever does because you can get trapped there, it means that whatever we are getting is actually very rare. I know that Tirique said it was rare, but I didn't actually believe him.

"Yes, Pedro," Skylar calls on Pedro, who already has his hand up two seconds into the presentation. Michy giggles at Pedro, who gives him a death stare to shut him up.

"How are we going to get there?"

"Great question. We will have a helicopter for you guys. It should be landing outside in a few minutes. It's a very high-speed helicopter with all of the security and comfort needs you could ask for." Pedro immediately sits back in his chair, satisfied as if he just rose his hand to say something, not because he actually cared.

"You guys are going to be visiting this lab." She uses her clicker, and the massive screen displays a very new and modern glass building. It's massive.

"This is one of the leading labs for technology and is highly secured after being acquired by the Board, which is, of course, in turn, controlled by the tech companies. You can expect it to be very difficult to get in, and using brute force will not be an option." She clicks again. "You will be looking for this object." The screens show a small rectangular metal case labeled classified. "It should have a blue elixir in it. We have no idea where this is held, which is why you guys will need to be thorough. Whatever you end up doing better buys you a lot of time because searching for this is not going to be easy."

"Is there anything that would narrow our search? Like what department of the building it is held in or something." Pedro asks.

"Probably. I can't be sure, but most lab buildings are split up into different fields of study. This would most likely be under bio-tech. If you can find that part of the building, that would be your best bet. And remember, this is a very coveted material. It's extremely rare. Wherever they are keeping it will be very secure. So, don't waste your time rummaging through a bunch of chemicals stacked on shelves." She clicks to a screen that says 'good luck' in big black letters. "And that's all I got. It seems simple, but a lot could go wrong. I'm assuming that Za will be coming up with a plan as we speak." She looks at me, and I nod. I'm already trying to think about doing this; it's hard when you don't really know the building very well. Whatever we do has to be stealthy, which means everyone should stick together. But, at the same, splitting up would be most efficient for finding what we need. I hear a helicopter landing outside, and we all get up.

I shake Skylar's hand before bounding down the stairs and out the door. I climb into the helicopter, which has first-class chairs in two rows on either side of the helicopter—four seats for the four of us. Cases of weapons fill the rest of the space. All of the gear we could want hides behind the walls of the helicopter. After sitting down, I peer around to the back, where a massive case sits. It is highly secured with very thick glass and metal reinforcements around the edges. There is a keypad in front for a passcode. This must be for the elixir. I still don't understand what Tirique and Nox could need an elixir for. I don't think Nox would be dumb enough to drop bombs on the United States because of the risk of hitting some migrants.

When everyone has filed into the helicopter, we begin to rise into the air. I look over my shoulder and take a quick look at each of my team members. Pedro is already about to fall asleep. He's a pretty high-energy person, so when he's not bounding off the walls, he's passed out. He's wearing grey sweatpants with black sneakers and has a massive winter coat that goes to his knees over a black t-shirt. In front of him, and to my left, is Michy, sitting up in his chair, his headphones already on. I let out a sigh of relief seeing his outfit. He's wearing ripped black jeans with an expensive white t-shirt underneath a bomber jacket. Feel's good not to be the only one that looks like they are about to have a day out. Behind me is Kalvin, who has his blonde hair tucked underneath a black cap and has black joggers that cuff around the ankle with high-top Jordans and a blue hoodie on. He sees me looking and gives me a nod. Kalvin is the most zen out of all of us. Everything he does is with patience. He's probably going to just sit in a single position and contemplate the meaning of life or something for the entire trip.

I think about what the plan will be for the attack. They are probably going to drop us about a mile out from the lab. Hopefully, there will be enough cover around the lab for us to scout it out without being caught. I'll probably split us into two groups, with Michy and I going together. I'm going to want to find a place of elevation for Michy to be. Otherwise, we'd be wasting his best skill. I'm tapping my neck while I think when I accidentally press and hold on my suit trigger. Instead of the suit forming around me, a band of projected screens curves in front of my head. The screen goes from the bottom of my nose to the middle of my forehead. A voice in my ear says, "Smart View Unlocked." Being careful not to make too much noise, I whisper to prompt the voice in the suit.

"Hey, suit guy."

"Yes?" I cringe at how strange the voice is. I have no idea why Ivo would program it to be like this.

"What is this Smart View thing for?"

"Ivo designed this to be a way to use any of the digital functions of the suit without having to activate the entire suit. You can communicate, look things up, scroll through menus, and have GPS navigation without having to activate the entire suit."

"Ok. Can other people see what I'm seeing?"

"No. That is the best part. The Smart View is designed for only you to see. No one else can see what you see, so you can be using the Smart View in a very public area without any chance of blowing you're covered."

"Dang. That's pretty amazing."

"Do you have any other questions?"

"No. Not right now. Thanks." The voice disappears, and I flick through random menus. I can control everything with my eyes. After an hour of random swiping and scrolling, I begin to get a headache and disable the Smart View. I ask the pilot how much longer we have, and he says a couple of hours. I look around and see Pedro passed out, Michy calmly sleeping, and Kalvin still staring straight ahead. He nods at me again when he sees me looking. I nod back. I decide to shut my eyes for a few minutes after whispering to Kalvin to wake me up in an hour and a half.

I open my eyes to Kalvin repeatedly tapping my shoulder. When he sees my eyes open, he backs away as if he has awoken a beast.

"Wake them up," I say to him. He goes over to Pedro and gently brushes his neck. Pedro almost jumps out of his seat. Then Kalvin walks over to Michy and vigorously shakes his entire body until his headphones fly off.

"Rise and shine, boys," I say as I get up and stretch. "We land in thirty minutes, so get yourselves together." They all get up and start rummaging around in the closets for various clothes. We all get undressed and pull on black military cargo pants, black long sleeve compression shirts, bulletproof vests, and black sneakers. I grab two pistols and put them on either side of my vest while tucking four knives in various places. When we land, all of us are geared up and mentally prepared to brutally fight our way through the lab. Hopefully, it doesn't come to that.

The helicopter lands and a lush forest greets us in the middle of a mountainous landscape. It's beautiful. The pilot jumps out.

"I'll be waiting here. I'll let you guys know if I have to leave and find a new spot for any reason." He points to our right, through the forest. "The lab is that way. It's right next to a waterfall and pretty hard to miss. You guys will have plenty of covers. There is one thing you should know, though. When we were flying over, I spotted some turrets at the top of a mountain right above the lab. I think they are going to have somewhat of an aerial advantage so stay safe out there." He heads back into the helicopter. I turn to the team.

"First things first, we get close enough to the lab to find the turrets. That's when we find a place for Michy to set up and take them out. If we can be seen and shot from above, we have no chance sneaking into the lab discretely." Michy nods as I look at him for approval.

"After that's done, we can think about we want to get in. I think we are gonna have to fight some guards. It's just about what guards and where." The back of the helicopter opens, and four hover-bikes come out from the back. We hop on and speed away from the green meadow where we landed and into the forest. It only takes us a couple of minutes to get close enough to hear the rush of the water, and I signal to the boys to leave the hover-bikes and keep going on foot.

As we get closer to the water, the forest starts to thin out, the trees becoming more sparse and the foliage giving us less cover. Every thirty seconds, I look up to see if I can spot the turrets yet. After a few minutes, there are barely any trees to take cover behind, and I spot the edges of the building, which sits down the hill in a recessed area. I look at Michy.

"See if you can get a shot in from here. If we go any closer, I think the turrets will find us." Michy nods and swings his sniper from around his back. He unfolds the tripod and gets down on one knee as he adjusts the angle of the gun. For a few seconds, he scans the mountain top, and then he turns around to me and nods. He must see what he thinks are the turrets.

"Can you take them out?"

"Yes."

"Take the shots." Michy lines it up and then takes five shots in succession, moving horizontally as he takes out all of the turrets. Then he folds up his tripod and swings the sniper back around his back. This is why we have Michy. He does his job with no fuss and always get's it done. The only person with a sharper shot than Michy is Idrissa Mane. I can only imagine how much better it's gotten over the years. Of course, Aziz doesn't count. He is not even human.

We keep walking and start making our way down the hill with the added comfort that we can't be shot from above. As we descend, the lab building comes into view. It sits over the river with supports on either side. The entire building looks modern, and the waterfall next to it reflects on its glass sides. From our vantage point, we can see guards posted all around the perimeter, even some standing on floating platforms in the river but, crucially, there is no fence or barrier.

"Michy. Stay here and take out the guards on the side of the building that faces us when I give you the signal." He gets his sniper ready again as Kalvin, Pedro, and I continue our descent, keeping our cover behind the trees and bushes as much as possible. In about ninety seconds, we've bounded down to the building's level. I turn around, put up my thumb, and then look forward. I watch the ten guards on the side of the facility closest to us crumple to the ground. "Now. Now." I say to the group.

We sprint towards the building, crouching against it as soon as we get there. One guard manages to spot us on our way but, before any of us can get our weapons out, Michy shoots him down. There is a single side door on the back corner of the building, and we make our way there. Usually, shift changes happen every hour, so about ten minutes until the following shift change.

"We have ten minutes before the entire building is alerted, and we are screwed. Let's make them count," I say. Kalvin bursts through the door, and we find ourselves in a deserted hallway, the floor glossy and the wall wooden.

"Let's find this biotech section as fast as possible." We sprint down the hallway, taking a right and turning towards the middle of the building. The hallways are eerily empty, and we follow the signs to the biotech part of the building, which is on the opposite side. We find the lab, surrounded by thin glass walls. Scientists are nowhere to be seen. We stop running when we realize that there is not a single human in this building.

"Why is no one here?" Kalvin asks.

"This doesn't feel right. They couldn't have known we were coming. And, even if they did see it coming, they would bring in more guards, not vacate the area." Pedro comments as we wander into the lab.

"What if they decided to take the elixir and leave?" I ask.

"Nope," Kalvin says as he points to the back of the room where a metal case matching the one Skylar showed us sits in a glass box. Kalvin walks over, smashes the glass, and grabs the case. He opens it and shows me. Surrounded by black foam sits a small vial of bright blue elixir.

"Yeah, that's it," I say. "Well, let's go then." I look at Pedro, who has his head pointed up in curiosity. He's the group's brain, and when he's suspicious, we should all be suspicious. Everything does feel a bit off.

"Does anyone else hear that beeping?" I stand still and listen carefully. I hear a faint but constant beeping.

"It sounds like...." Kalvin starts.

"A bomb," I finish. "Run!" Kalvin passes me the case, and we all start sprinting back to the side of the building we came from. I check my watch, and we have thirty seconds before the following shift change. The beeping is getting louder and more frequent. Our feet pound silently against the glossy floor, and our rifles clang against our vests. Ten seconds. Nine. We are only halfway there. I toss the case back to Pedro trigger my suit, ripping off my layers so it can form around me. I generate a rod and then activate the cycle.

"Hop on!" I scream to Kalvin and Pedro, hoping their weight doesn't weigh down the cycle too much. As they get on, the cycle slumps down lower. Five. Four. I accelerate as much as possible, skidding across the floor and drifting around the corner. I almost lose control as the back tire clips the corner when I turn. Two. I drive straight through the door, and we all fall off the bike and go flying to the ground. We see guards walking around the corner towards us. One. The entire building blows up. I crouch and cover my head as the building goes up in flames. I hear a ringing in my ear as I see the guards get pushed into the river from the blow. My vision starts to get hazy as I see Michy sprinting towards us. He grabs my arm and pulls me up.

CYCLE

"Let's go, guys. Let's go." He helps us all up, and we stumble our way up the hill and back to our hover-bikes. I deactivate my suit to get a breather. Pedro and Kalvin have cuts and bruises all over them. Some burns are visible on their small sections of exposed skin. We make it back to the helicopter in a few minutes. We are battered and exhausted except for Michy. I collapse into my chair, too exhausted to take off my gear. I'm about to pass out when Pedro stumbles up to me and drops the case of elixir in my lap.

This new idea better be worth it because we all almost died for it.

IVO

March 8, 2035

We piled into the van. The twins squeezed between crates of food and piles of weapons. Aiko spent the rest of the day yesterday explain to Aria and Tyler how to keep the Migrants alive and what to do if they get attacked early. I told her to stay, but she insisted on coming. I'm not surprised, but nothing is gonna stop her from stressing out. It's funny how she still treats the Migrants like they are her children, especially since there are so many of them now. I look behind and see the twins slumped over each other, passed out. Aziz is curled in a ball, and Riz has his legs up on top of a pile of weapons with his head leaning on Aziz's shoulders. We are about halfway there, but they fell asleep fifteen minutes into the four-hour drive. I see Aiko roll her neck a couple of times in my peripheral vision.

"Pull over," I say to her, leaning back in my chair and cracking my knuckles.

"Why?"

"Let me drive us the rest of the way there." I smile at her, but she just gives me a mean glance.

"Don't worry. I got it." She meekly replies.

CYCLE

"Yeah, I know you do. But you're gonna let me do this one thing for you for once. Just because you're so kind." She playfully punches me in the arm.

"You are the worst, you know." I shrug and put my hands up.

"I know. But you like me anyways." She just shakes her head as she pulls off to the side of the road. I walk around to the driver's side of the van and climb in after Aiko gets out. Once I get going again, it only takes five minutes for Aiko to fall asleep. I reach in the back and grab Riz's pillow and blanket, which he doesn't need. I drape the blanket over her and slide the pillow behind her head. I pull my hood up as I notice more incoming traffic. If we are spotted, this mission will be over before it's even begun.

I stare at the road ahead and try to think of what Nox could be planning. I know that he probably took Europe to take all of its military resources and such. I have a gut feeling that if we are going to invade the country by force, we would have seen some news clips or something from Europe with the military preparing. For the entire continent's army to come over here would be quite the ordeal. It starts to seem more and more unlikely that Nox would come here and invade with military force. However, if he isn't coming with the military, how on Earth does he expect to defeat the resources of America? Trust me, if America were that easy to save, the secret service and I would've done it like three years ago. I shake my head in frustration as I run out of ideas. I glance up into the mirror and see the twins still passed out. Meanwhile, Aiko has grabbed the blanket tighter, and she is out, her head slowly sliding off the pillow.

We get into the edge of the city after a couple more hours. Aiko and the twins start to wake up as I circle, trying to find a discrete place to park the van. I find an alley with an old entrance to a parking garage. I park in the corner of the second floor of the garage. There are only a couple of cars on the first floor, so I'm not worried about being caught. The twins stumble out of the side of the van and immediately head to the edge of the building to look outside.

"Nice to see NYC again. Although I'm starting to get a little bit of PTSD," Riz says, leaning against the short sidewall with his back to the outside.

"You should talk. I was the one bombarded with heavily armed guards. I should be the one with more PTSD," Aziz says.

"I'll give you this one as long as you don't do anything stupid again while we are here. That'll be quite difficult for you." Riz replies. He glances at Aziz, who has a look of rage.

"I'll show you something worthy of PTSD." Riz sprints away and hides behind the van. Aziz smiles in satisfaction.

"Give it a break, you two," Aiko says, climbing out of the van. "Ivo, where are we going to stay? I don't think I can sleep in that van again. I'm already sore." She stretches her hips and bends down to touch her toes.

"I have absolutely no clue," I reply. Then I look at Aziz. "Any chance we could find a few migrants around here?"

"I mean, there is a chance. A very very very low chance. There are not that many of them, and the ones that do exist are very well hidden. Finding them before it gets really dark will be a challenge." I nod.

"Well. We aren't afraid of challenges," Aiko says. She has opened the back of the van and is tossing weapons to both Aziz and Riz. She looks at me and holds up a gun. "You want one, or is your fancy suit everything you need." I shake my head. The rough part is she's right.

"Nah. I'm good. I think if we get into a situation where we will need the guns, then we are kinda screwed anyways, so there is no point."

"Alright, negative, Nelly," she responds, smiling. She shuts the van door after winging her swords around her shoulder. A pistol is attached to her pants, but she's not carrying a big rifle like the twins.

"Ok. Let's go."

We walk to the emergency staircase in the opposite corner. When we get to the bottom, I push through the door and scan the empty streets. I have no idea where to start, and I look back at Aiko and the twins, who are just staring at me. I suppose I'm in charge of directions. If we turn right, we walk towards the middle of the city, and I doubt the very few migrants here will take a risk and be there. I defiantly turn left and pray that I made the correct decision. The sun is beginning to set, and the empty streets are becoming increasingly more sketchy. The abandoned skyscrapers line the streets, mixed with worn-down graffiti.

We mindlessly wander down the streets, walking away from the center of the city. We think we hear footsteps a few times, and we frantically spin around just to see a stray dog or a bird. We are on an unhealthy amount of high alert, and the farther we walk away from the city's safety, the less sure I am of finding the Migrants. When we pass old buildings that look habitable, we knock through the doors, but all of them are empty.

"I'm starting to think you guys made up the whole thing about finding migrants here," Aiko complains.

"I would like to remind everyone that I said the chances of us finding any migrants here were very, very slim. Just saying." Aziz responds.

"To be fair...the very few migrants that we did find before might just be captured by now. I mean, the security definitely looked like it was ramping up." Riz adds.

Disappointed, we turn back around to go back to the van. I'm walking behind everyone now, and I see a red dot on Aziz's back. I rub my eyes to

IVO

make sure it's not in my head. When I see the dot is still there, I run into the back of Aziz and tackle him to the ground.

"What the hell, Ivo!" Aziz whines.

"Sniper," I say. I scramble up into a crouching position. Enabling my suit, I track the trajectory to the roof of the building to our left. I zoom in with my suit's cameras. I see a guy and two women suited up with a lot of guns. They must notice me looking because they start to run towards the edge of the roof like they will jump.

"Run. Run now!" I yell as I turn around. Thankfully, the twins and Aiko have their rods handy. They pull them out and sprint towards the direction of the van, activating their cycles and rushing away. I take a split second to look back at the people who have jumped down the side of the building, and each has a very high-tech hover-bike. I don't like the look of this. I make a gun in my hand and shoot at them with no luck. Then I turn around, activate my bike, and catch up to the twins and Aiko. Aiko sees me pull up next to her.

"How do they have hover-bikes?" Aiko asks.

"I have no idea. But they don't look like they want peaceful talk. Why else would they have pointed a sniper at Aziz?" She shrugs. I see Riz take a look behind him.

"Wait a second. Those are hover-bikes?" He suddenly stops his cycle and stands in the middle of the road. Aziz looks behind and does the same, forcing Aiko and me to jump off and join them.

"Can someone explain why we are waiting for them to come and kill us?" Aiko frantically questions.

"Aiko. How do you think they got the hover-bikes? Ivo invented that kind of modification. This means that only the Boston Migrants have those kinds of hover-bikes," Riz says as the three people get closer. I prepare myself for a fight.

"I don't know. They could've just found them or something. Who knows?"

"Well, Aziz and I were staying with migrants. We were captured without our rods on us. Which means that the Migrants we were staying with still have the rods." The three people deactivate and hop off their bikes, each of them attaching the rods to their bulletproof vests. The woman on the left pushes her blond hair around her and then walks towards us. She looks about our age.

"Sup twins." She shrugs at them before smiling and hugging them.

"Told you," Riz explains, turning around and smirking at me.

"This is Tobin, this is Erling, and this is Ji." Aziz introduces us. "Guys, this is Aiko and…"

"Ivo. Yes. We know. It's great to meet you," Tobin says as she walks up to me and shakes my hand. Tobin backs away as I deactivate my suit. Erling, who is very tall, his lean muscular figure looks a little disproportionate, performs a handshake with each twin. Finally, Ji, who looks Korean, walks up to Aiko and hugs her.

"It's nice to have another East-Asian around." They laugh about it together.

"So you guys are the NYC Migrants," I say.

"We are indeed," Erling replies. "Us and all of our glory. I would give you guys a more warm welcome, but we have some bad news."

"What?" Aiko asks. Ji answers.

"They are here."

ZA

March 9, 2035

It's past midnight. I wake up to the sound of the helicopter's propellors slowing down, my arms clutching the all-valuable case, and the meek yellow lights from the helicopter's ceilings is the only illumination. I slide my back up the chair, rubbing my eyes and turning my head to check out the team. Everyone is awakening in a daze, our muscles sore and exhaustion sucking the life out of us. We all manage to stumble out of the helicopter, where there is an energized Skylar.

"Welcome back!" She starts. "How was it...." Her voice dies down as we all pass her without any greeting. The boys all collapse on the couch when they get inside. Nox is nervously waiting in the hallway, his sneaker tapping the ground and his hands moving around in the pockets of his suit pants. When he sees me, he stops leaning against the wall and strides towards me. He reaches out to shake his hand, but I frustratingly shove the elixir case into his chest, making him stumble back half a step. I just glare at him as he recollects himself in front of me.

"I'm way too tired to care about why my team and I almost just died for this tiny little vial of liquid. But tomorrow, you and I are sitting down, and you're going to tell me everything." He nervously swallows, and I

CYCLE

knock his shoulder as I walk past him. I briefly turn around to face him again.

"Partners, remember? You promised. Tell me everything tomorrow, or I'm gone." I turn towards the stairs, hobbling down them before clumsily placing myself in the transport in a heap. As I trigger the transport to start, I see Nox standing at the top of the stairs, staring in my direction. All we get is a split second of eye contact before the transport speeds away, and I lean back in my chair, licking the dried blood off my lip.

I slowly make my way to my room when the transport arrives. Opening the door, I shut it behind me with my heel and then throw off my shoes. I peel off my clothes, now plastered to my open cuts and burns. I get in a hot shower, watching the clear water be polluted with crimson red as it collects and then flows down the drain. I pretty much wince the whole time as the soap stings against my wounds. By the time I'm out of the shower, I can barely stand. I crumble onto my bed, and within minutes, I'm gone.

For the first time in a long time, I wake up when my body thinks it's ready. It's too bad that no amount of sleep was going to cure my physical ailments. I swing my legs over the bed, rearranging my pillows and taking a moment to collect myself. I put a little bit of weight on my legs to see how it feels and a sharp pain shoots up my leg greets me. Reluctantly, I stand up, feeling the blood flow down to my toes. I do some ankle rolls before pulling on a pair of socks, some sweatpants, and a t-shirt, all black. I fill up my kettle and rub my forehead as I sit at the kitchen table, waiting for the water to boil.

I grab some cereal and pour some into a black ceramic bowl. I'm about to get the milk when the kettle starts to whistle, continuing to whine as I ignore it, pouring in the milk, and then going to turn off the heat. I take my sweet time eating my breakfast and obnoxiously contemplating the purpose of life. I begin to think about where Ivo could possibly be if the secret service is practically gone. Before coming up with any concrete theories, I hear some quarreling downstairs, so I put on a pair of slides and make my way downstairs. In the smack-dab middle of the floor, Tirique and Nox are passionately arguing about something. Four guards are huddled in the corner, obviously unsure of what to do. I take the lift down, and as soon as Nox and Tirique hear my slides slap against the glossy floor, they lower their voices, stop talking, and turn to greet me. Tirique bounds up to me and puts his hand out.

"Great to see you again, Zashil." I smile and nod at Tirique, who vigorously shakes my hand. I glance at Nox, who is unwilling to give me a traditional greeting. I decide to turn back to Tirique.

"You guys seemed pretty passionate. What were you talking about?" Tirique seems to get uncomfortable and then backs away, trying to look innocent and prompting Nox forwards.

"We were discussing the next steps for our mission," Nox says, resting his hand on my shoulder.

"Ah, yes, yes." Tirique agrees before fully retreating and heading off to who knows where.

"Shall we?" Nox ushers me towards his office, which I haven't been in before. An out-of-place black wooden door separates us from him and his office. He puts his fingers in a scanner on the right side and slides the door open. Bizarre, to say the least. One of the most zen rooms I have ever set foot in welcomes me. Warm lighting splashes down on every surface, complimented by exclusively wood and gold. It's an incredibly luxurious, yet minimalist, setup and I find myself wandering around the room, exploring every nook and cranny. A bookshelf lined one wall, old elementary school awards sit in front of some of the books, all with the name: Nox Yavuz.

"Take a seat." Nox points at a streamlined black fabric couch that sits on four short wooden legs. I sit down, and he sits across from me in a smaller than average black armchair, metal gold buttons and accents adding to its royal flair. He leans back in his chair before changing his mind and deciding to alter his posture into a more professional one. His shoulders straighten, and he does a neck roll before sliding his, now unslumped, spine against the short back of the chair.

"I should've been more honest with you from the beginning." He looks at me, but I just nod. "To be honest, I was scared of how you might react to my new ideas. I guess we are partners, though, so if you disagree, that's kind of the point."

"It's fine. I was just angry last night because my team and I almost died yesterday for that elixir thing." He glances to a desk, and I follow his gaze to see the small bottle of elixir now displayed in a glass case.

"I don't even know what that thing is for. At the very least, I need something to tell my guys. You made me their leader. That was your idea. I can't expect them just to move on."

"Okay. Well. This is what Tirique and I have been working on, and I don't think you're going to like it." I don't think it could be that bad. I haven't known Nox for long, but I just have faith in what he's doing for some reason. It doesn't hurt that I think I'm right about what Nox is doing and Ivo isn't. It kinda makes me want to agree with Nox even more. I give Nox a look to tell him to continue, he obliges.

"Have you ever heard of bio-weapons?"

"Uhhhhh...can't say I have."

"Okay, well, I don't think knowing the definition of bio-weapons is necessary for you to understand our plan. So, I'll just explain what we've been working on. When you told me that attacking with force would be too violent, that made me think. What are our goals, and how do we get there? All we needed to do was temporarily take down the corrupt Board to free the Migrants and empower them, get them on our side, and then we will have enough power to figure out what we want to do from there." This is the vision that I believed in.

"Yeah, that checks out."

"Tirique had an idea for a way to release something discretely that takes care of all of our problems without having to invade anything."

"What was his idea?" Nox is stalling weirdly, almost like he's not completely sold on the plan. Tirique has some sketchy ideas. The military usually denies lots of his weapons because of safety reasons and such. That's why only private armies like Serge's have all of Tirique's newest and most expensive weapons. Nox hesitates some more until I give an annoyed stare.

"He created a virus. Well, he designed an airborne virus that would target the genetics of the white people who are the problem."

"Wait. You're kidding me, right. That's your brilliant idea? Nox. You can't do that. You can't put millions of innocent people at a health risk."

"It won't kill them. Or at least, it won't kill the healthy ones."

"This has to be a joke. So ,that thing.." I point to the elixir. "That thing that my team and I almost died for is the virus?"

"No. That's just one of the ingredients. That's the only ingredient that someone else had. That's why your mission was so important." I'm about to walk out of the room. I partially sit up, hovering above the soft surface of the couch and gripping the sidearm with my right hand.

"Wait. Wait. Just let me explain."

"You just explained. More explanation is not gonna make it any better. I agree with your goals, Nox. I want to save the Migrants as much, if not even more, than you do. But, this is not, and can not be the way to do it. You can't risk the health of and possibly kill thousands of innocent people. Just because they are white does not mean they are directly contributing to what the government is doing. They are simply complying, which, for them, is a means for survival." I stand up. I'm not sure what I'm going to do. I don't know if this is the end. I have no idea. I wish Ivo were beside me, working through the problem with me. I just shake my head. Am I supposed to warn them? Warn the same people that are directly responsible for my struggle? The struggle that killed my parents and killed so many others. Do I really have to go, surrender myself, just so that I can tell them there is a virus that will temporarily disable their entire population? But, that means it's over. No saving the Migrants. No chance that, without what Nox has done, there will ever be an opportunity again. If I warn them, am I saving those white lives just to take away the freedom and lives of countless migrants at the same time?

"Za." Nox stands up with me, wanders over to the entrance, and stands in the doorway, blocking my path. "Where are you going to go? Nothing has changed. Our purpose is still the same. My purpose is still the same. I made a promise to myself that I would save the Migrants. I made a promise to someone else too." He looks at the ground, obviously thinking about something emotional.

"This is our chance. It may be a bit of a weird chance. It may be a bit sketchy. But I just have to take it. I won't be able to do this again. Do you really want this life to confine the Migrants for generations?" I take another step closer towards the doorway.

"There will be other chances. Maybe not for you, Nox, but later on. Other people will have the chance to save the Migrants. It has to be done right. The whole point of saving the Migrants is to regain their freedom and bring back equality. We need to reset the clock and rebuild American society how it was five years ago when everything was working how it should be. That's the goal. And, that will happen. I can't stop you from doing this, Nox. Even if I were to try, you're too strong, and you have too many people that are already devoted to your cause. I think what you're doing is just going to shift the imbalance. The white people will be oppressed, and that's not the goal of your activism or your vision. If you continue with this plan, just know that you're doing it wrong, and while others could pursue what you're pursuing, later on, no one will ever be able to reverse what you're going to do to society now." He stands there, looking at me, squinting as he tries to get inside my head. I push past him and out the doorway. The glossy floors slap against my slides and the sterile look of the base flood my senses once again.

I look behind my shoulder to see Nox has not turned around yet. I'm not going to storm out of here. I'm not going to ditch him. At least, not yet. I just need to think. I hear Nox's door slam shut, and I pause to think if I should go back. I decide to keep walking, and I make it back up to my room. I toss my slides to the corner of the bedroom and sit at the kitchen table. My half-eaten cereal stares back at me, and the very last of the steam swirls up from my teacup. I rub my temples, trying to push the stress out of me. My body still aches. The mental duress just adds to my muscles constantly seizing up, culminating in inexplicable exhaustion.

There's just one thing I can't write figure out.

Is this the end or the beginning?

IVO

March 9, 2035

"Wait, wait, wait, wait, wait." It's already past midnight as we start walking, following Erling, Tobin, and Ji to wherever they call their base. Surprisingly, we are making our way towards the middle of the city. Riz is frantically trying to get some more information out of the crew; he's practical running around in circles trying to get something out of one of the three. Right now, he's more focused on Erling.

"What does that mean? Who's here? Why are they here? What is happening? Can someone get me some water?" Erling just chuckles at all his questions.

"Your still as bouncy as ever, Riz. All of your questions will be answered when we get back to the base. We can't talk about that kind of stuff in public. There are microphones and cameras everywhere. Even though we disabled most of them, you can never be too sure."

"How the hell are you not tired, man," Tobin adds. We were all going to use our cycles and hover-bikes, but apparently, I had landed some shots on theirs, so we have been suspended to the much slower and less safe walking for the time being. I wish the car that generates from my suit could fit more people. The buildings keep getting taller and taller as we keep moving. The lack of light means the glass-covered buildings all look very ominous, lurking in the shadows as if hundreds of government officials are waiting to pounce. Ji must see me looking around frantically because she shifts over to my side of the group and tries to console me.

"There aren't enough soldiers in the city for them to be out at night. It's as safe of a time to be wandering around as you can get." She pauses briefly as we walk a little longer. My soles start hitting the ground harder as my legs become increasingly tired. "We thought that putting the base in the middle of the city would make it harder to find. It worked so far, but it's not the safest bet. If we ever have to evacuate the city quickly, there is basically no way we make it out without at least a fight."

"So where are you guys from and, if you don't mind me asking, why are you guys the only migrants?"

"Well, there was a lot of us in the beginning. Tobin, Erling, and I all went to the same high school when the Revolution began. At first, the Board was focused much more on Boston, so all of the soon-to-be migrants were a bit lackadaisical. It was fine. First, everyone started messing around among all the authoritative chaos, but it was very short-lived. When the time came around where we needed to find organization, hiding places, and all that stuff, we weren't. The Migrants were basically gone before they even started. When a small group of us could come together, we didn't have a leader like you. We had no purpose or any idea of how to survive. This caught up to us in the end. A few times, teams would go out and almost get caught but luckily slip away. But then, the luck ended. In quick succession, teams were captured or killed and, before we knew it, it was just us three left. Thankfully, we were able to smarten up before they got us to. However, while you Boston Migrants have been saving people, we have only been trying to survive. Unfortunately, you didn't show up at a different time. We could've used your help to establish our group as more of a force."

"Damn. Well, at least we are here now." She nods, and we continue to walk in silence. Riz and Aziz are still bothering Erling, and I smile at their innocence. When we get to the very center of the city, we start proceeding with more caution, Tobin leading the way as we dodge into alleys and continuously scan the surroundings. After a few more minutes of walking in circles, I'm assuming to trick any cameras watching us, we approach a massive building covered in caution tape and blocked with wooden boards. It resembles something like a museum.

Erling walks up to what used to be the entrance, gripping each side of a six-foot board, the worn-down wood closer to brown and black than a natural brown. He moves the plank to the side, leaning it against the wall, and then motions for us to walk through. There is a gap just big enough for me to crouch through, trying to avoid the sharp edges of glass that remains from a revolving door. When we are all shuffled into a very dark hallway with smooth marble floors below us, Erling steps through and slides the wooden plank back into place. Tobin, Ji, and Erling all pull out flashlights from their pockets and shine them towards the middle of the building. There are glass tanks everywhere, and a cracked sign in front of us says, "Welcome to the Aquarium." Fascinated, I look up towards the high ceilings and spin around. I never thought I would be in an aquarium ever again. Of course, this isn't exactly the aquarium experience. Still, the curving paths and reflective glass remind me of times when Za and I would wander through the aquarium in Boston, mindlessly exploring as we walked farther and farther away from adult supervision.

Everything lights up when I reorient myself. Tobin walks back towards the group from what I now see as the power generator. The small dotted lights that guide you through the paths flicker awake, and lights of all different colors shine down from the ceiling. A massive tank, rising four stories, sits in the middle of the aquarium and defines the circular space. We slowly walk up to the top floor, going in circles around the tank. I notice a few hairline cracks as we continue to rise and see some platforms and office stuff. When we make it to the top, there is what resembles a diving board stretching over the center of the tank and then a ladder leading down. All of us make our way down onto the first platform. The ladder continues all of the way down, but we stand on a wooden platform attached to long horizontal metal beams. There are two beds on either side with a couple of desks and a couch.

"This is what we call home, I guess." Ji spreads her arms and gestures at the space as she spins around to face us. We are all huddled around the ladder. "The lowest level has all the food and such. Otherwise, there are a bunch of mattresses lying around on the second and third levels; there should be enough for you guys. Make yourself comfortable and get some sleep." The twins are the first to let out a sigh of relief and exhaustion, and they wave to us as they nervously make their way down the ladder. I peek down the hole in time to see them fall face first and collapse on two mattresses that are right next to each other.

"I think I'm gonna get some sleep too." Aiko hugs me before making her way down as well. Erling and Tobin take a seat in the office chairs while Ji sits on a mat on the ground. They look awake as ever, not at all prepared to sleep.

"How are you guys not tired?" I ask them.

"We don't really have a choice in terms of when we can leave this place. So, I guess we are just used to being up this late at night. It's a messed up schedule and is definitely not healthy, but it is what it is," Erling says as he leans farther back in his chair, rotating the chair around on its wheels.

"Once, we went a week without ever seeing daylight," Tobin adds.

CYCLE

"Oh yeah. That was wack, really messed with my head like there was some apocalypse where the sun disappeared or something," Ji comments. I walk over to a beanbag rested against the wall, slumping down, and resting the back of my head against the slick glass.

"So when you guys said 'they,' I'm pretty sure meant Nox and the bunch. Am I right?" I don't really feel like sleeping. Even if my exhausted body wanted a break, my focused brain wouldn't let it happen. Plus, I'd rather just hear the bad news and get it over with. At least, this way, I can think about how to solve the problem, which will calm me down.

"Well, yes and no." Erling sits up and begins to explain. "Basically, we found a bunch of empty shipping containers that had Tirique's name plastered all over them."

"Wait. How did you know that Tirique and Nox were working together?"

"I don't know. I guess Tobin just put two and two together at one point. New shipments of Tirique's stuff are starting to show up everywhere, which is pretty abnormal, seeing how the Board doesn't really buy his stuff. This all happened around the same time Nox started his whole takeover of Europe."

"Yeah, that's still pretty insane." Ji comments. She's now rotated herself and is lying down, staring up at the beams lining the top of the aquarium.

"Ok. I'm a little confused. I get that the shipping containers with Tirique's name on them are a sign of Nox coming. But I don't get why that's bad news. I mean, we knew he was going to be coming. Isn't it a good thing that he's not already here?" Tobin decides to answer after glancing awkwardly at Erling, who is already sitting back in his chair, uninterested in conversing for the foreseeable future.

"Yeah. I mean, no. That's what we thought when he saw that. But the weird thing is, there have been no people on any of the shipments, absolutely zero sign of anyone arriving here from Europe. We were assuming that weapons loaded up Tirique's containers, but there is literally no one here to use them."

"That is bizarre. Why would they ship a bunch of weapons and not bring anybody over? I mean, they took over all of Europe, which means they have the entire force of the European military."

"I mean, they can't seriously be considering not using that amount of force to take over America. That much power could crumple the Board's resources within a few days easily." Erling shakes his head as Ji says it.

"I guess the only way we can make any sense of this is if we find what's in those shipments. Even if we know what kind of weapons they are shipping here, that'll be enough to get us started on whatever preparation we may need." I say confidently.

"I guess our best chance of doing that is to get some sleep now so we can head out super early in the morning. That's usually when the shipments come in," Tobin says. I get up and position myself to climb down the ladder.

"I'll see you guys in the morning then. And don't bother waking the twins or Aiko up. It can just be us in the morning, and they need some rest." They all nod as I lower myself down the ladder and collapse onto the mattress next to Aiko. I take a deep breath before staring up at the bottom of the wooden platform, admiring the chrome metal beams, and then shut my eyes.

***

CYCLE

    I sit up in my bed, Aiko rolling over, annoyed, the platform above me starting to creak as I hear the team do their best to stay quiet. I go to get dressed, looking around for my bag, when I realize that we never went back to the van to get our stuff. Let's just hope some soldiers don't snoop around in that parking garage. I grab a torn piece of paper laying on the ground, a pen, and write Aiko and the twins a quick note: 'going out with the crew to get some more information. get the van when you wake up.' I slip it underneath Aiko's pillow and then head up the ladder. Already dressed in all black, Erling, Tobin, and Ji have flashlights strapped to their belts and guns slung over their shoulders.

    "You need one?" Ji asks, grabbing another gun from a crate in the corner.

    "Nah. I'm good, thanks," I reply.

    "He has that fancy suit thing, remember?" Tobin makes fun of Ji, smiling.

    "Don't forget. Ivo Wolf is in the building, people," Erling adds to the joke, standing up and walking to the ladder. "Ready?" He asks me. My stomach rumbles as I reluctantly nod. Erling barely waits for me to finish nodding before climbing up the ladder and descending the ramp. I let Ji and Tobin follow him before tiredly climbing the ladder myself. I have to make some strides in quick succession to catch up to the crew, who are practically jogging down the spiral ramp.

    When we get to the bottom, Erling carefully slides the massive piece of wood to the side again. We all crawl out, and I take a moment to revel at the glow of the sunrise, the golden light reflecting onto the countless glass facades of the towering skyscrapers. The sky fades into a darker blue the higher I look. I only get a split second of bliss before the trio activates their hover-bikes, which they apparently fixed last night, and look back at me, waiting. I get a running start, activating my suit and then activating my cycle. I slow down to let them get ahead of me, and then we proceed in a diamond formation, me taking up the rear and Tobin in front. We weave through the empty streets of New York City, the boarded up restaurant and shop fronts only interrupted by extravagant but fading graffiti. The city, once the epicenter of culture, is now abandoned and desolate, the lack of vibrancy signaled by silence.

When we get to the water, there are trucks lined up, all getting loaded with various crates. Deactivating our vehicles, we huddle behind a brick building, taking turns to peer around the corner. There is a massive ship by the dock, both Tirique's name and Serge's name painted onto the side in big block letters. They are obviously not scared of being noticed. About fifteen soldiers, all dressed in a bizarre orange uniform, are taking metal and wooden crates from the ship and loading them into various trucks. There doesn't seem to be any pattern that would clue us into which truck we should look into. Erling checks his watch and then whispers back to us.

"They should be done loading them up in about three minutes."

"Do we have a plan?" Ji asks, prompting all three of them to look at me.

"Oh. I guess that's my job then," I whisper back, deactivating my helmet. "Honestly, just take out any of the trucks you want. We just need to see what's in them, and the ten guards that I'm looking at right now don't seem like too much of a threat." They all nod as we hear the trucks start to leave the docks behind us. We wait another thirty seconds before we all trigger our vehicles and fan out onto the road, following the trucks that were are all lined up. Erling swings his gun over his shoulder and starts firing at the tires of the nearest trucks, the ones he hits start skidding out of control before crashing into buildings off of either side of the road. Ji and Tobin peel off to check what's in those trucks. I generate a knife in either hand, precisely throwing them into the back tires of two more trucks. I degenerate my cycle and pull open the back door of the truck.

Two guards start running towards me. One gets shot down before I can even attack him. I punch the other in the gut before stepping on his foot and generating a knife, stabbing it into his leg. He crumples into a heap on the ground, and I resume my search. Climbing into the back and opening two crates, regular guns, vests, and other pretty normal weapons greet me—nothing out of the ordinary, which is not very helpful knowledge. Tobin, Ji, and Erling run up from behind me.

"Anything special?" Ji asks.

"No. How about you guys?" I respond.

"Nothing. Just a bunch of guns and vests." We hear a truck with a flat tire skidding away. Erling looks at me like he wants to take it out.

"Let it go. We aren't going to get anything from it anyway."

"Just for fun?" Erling pleads. I deactivate my helmet, smiling.

"I suppose." He gets down on one knee, lining up the shot before firing the other back tire of the truck, which spins onto its side, a guard getting out and sprinting away. We walk up to it as crates topple out and smash onto the ground. Instead of weapons, many blue medical masks fly into the air, being blown around by the breeze. I catch one in my hand, the white string already dirtied and the nose bridge still straightened. I turn around to see the crew staring in confusion at the masks circling in the air.

I'm starting to think this is no normal war.

MEANWHILE

CYCLE

IDRI

March 9, 2035

To be fair, they did ask if I wanted to go. I think to myself as I sit up in my bed, my sore back not happy about me leaning against the wall. Both Aiko and Ivo came by to ask if I wanted to join the mission. Put simply, I just couldn't be bothered. But, I suppose that means it's a bit hypocritical for me to feel this way; angry, frustrated, annoyed. A part of me also didn't want everyone to abandon the base and, therefore, leave the base in the hands of Aria and Tyler, who are not the experienced leaders that can protect us. Not that they would even know I'm here to help them run the place. After all, I've spent the last two days buried in my room, furiously sorting through all of my emotions.

I've come to no serious or legitimate conclusion. I meant everything I said to Ivo, but as soon as I saw him, it was like I had just seen a long-lost family member for the first time. It angered me when he left. He said he would come back, come back to help the Migrants. Actually, he promised. They were just supposed to go warn Europe about the war and then come back. That was it. When Europe somehow, by the grace of God, believed everything Ivo said and, not only stopped the war, but also made a full one-eighty on their government, he called us to say that he was going to stay for a bit to make sure Europe stabilizes. He told us he would stay for a year. Of course, it wasn't just a year.

    Anyways, that's why I'm mad at him. Kinda dumb when I think about it because Ivo did so much for Europe, not just the stuff with the war. Whatever. I'm split. Plus, I never got a chance to talk about my uncle. I think he would've understood why I'd been so on edge. Now that I think about it, Aiko might have told him already. My uncle left a year ago for no reason. He just left. I've been scouring security footage and the internet to find any trace of him, but I had no chance from the beginning. If John Mane wants to disappear, he can disappear.

    My stomach gives me a frustrated grumble, so I get up and swing open my room door, glancing quickly at my clock. I haven't eaten all day, and it's practically dinner time. What did I do today? I helped unload some crates. Then, I watched some news while I did another sweep of the internet for my uncle. All of this searching stuff would be so much easier with Ivo's hacking skills. I take a step into the hallway before turning left, walking down the concrete hallway, and into the food pantry—all kinds of food line the shelf. The only thing they share in common is being sub-par. However, I can't really say that because the food that is average has obviously changed for the Migrants since the Revolution. I grab some microwavable mac and cheese and warm it up in the microwave that sits on a counter next to the empty space on the shelves. I'm woken up just that little bit more by the sudden beeping of the microwave, and I take my food out and bring it into the tech lab, sitting down at the worn-down wooden table.

    I'm only three bites into my meal when Tyler comes rushing into the room, panting as if he just ran a marathon.

"We have a massive problem." He barely gets out the sentence as he puts his hands on his knees in exhaustion. And this is why I didn't leave—this exact reason.

"What happened?" I say, taking another bite of my dinner. The chances that this is the most solvable problem known to mankind are very high.

"Aria," he coughs out. I stand up. If it's about Aria, it's serious. "She's gone. Well, they took her, but not really."

"Come and sit," I say, pulling out the chair next to mine. Tyler's feet barely leave the ground as he sits down, and they continue to nervously tap the ground. I rotate my chair ninety degrees so that I face him.

"Slowly, tell me what happened." Tyler takes a couple of deep breaths that, instead of being patient and meditative, just end up sounding like the beginning of hyperventilation.

"Well, Aria and I went out to get some food and other resources we could find. We do that every day." I nod. "Usually, there are parts of the city that are still under a lot of construction, so we can take cover there if we need a break. Not this time. The place is crawling with people. But, they aren't soldiers. They look like doctors. We couldn't get close enough to see what their jackets say, but there is no way it wasn't Nox and his gang. Anyways, Aria was adamant that she could get closer and check it out. I told her not to but she went anyways. And, I had to wait and protect all of the food we had gathered. She never came back. I waited for an hour. But eventually, someone spotted me, and I had to abandon my post and come back." I nestle my head in my hands, processing. Why the hell would there be doctors here?

"We have to get her back. We have to get her back. You have to help me." Now Tyler is really losing it

"Tyler. You have to calm down. We definitely won't be able to figure out how to get Aria back if you're just freaking out the whole time." This is what I mean by experience. I mean, we are technically the same age, maybe he's even a little older, but he has absolutely no clue how to compose himself. Most of the things I've taught him since finding him on the street have clearly gone over his head. I guide Tyler to sit down, who had stood up, and grabbed my shirt. I get him a glass of water and then head to my room.

There is only one thing going through my mind: thank God I didn't go with Ivo.

ARIA

March 9, 2035

"Let's go!" I scream back to Tyler, who is lazily pulling on clothes and just barely starting to wander out of our room.

"I'm coming!" He's said that three times now, never actually prompting him to go any faster. Just yesterday, Aiko gave us a whole lecture on how to run this place while she's gone, and we've already been dragging our feet on collecting more resources. First off, we slept in. Usually, Aiko comes knocking on the door in the morning to drag us off to bed so we can get out before Boston is crawling with people. Second off, we haven't eaten anything because I nagged Tyler to get up so much that he now just wants us to leave. My stomach grumbles as I jog towards the nearest van.

"We don't need to take the van if it's only the two of us," Tyler says, panting as he runs up from behind me.

"Fine," I say, pulling out the rod that Aiko gave me. Tyler does the same.

"Are you sure we shouldn't have Idrissa come with us? I mean, he is the most senior member of the Migrants at the base right now."

"What? No. It's fine. Plus, it's better if he's here while we are gone anyways in case something happens." Tyler shrugs, his shoulders in half-agreement, before walking over and triggering the door. We start running up the ramp, the sun splashing down on us as we activate our cycles and start heading towards the city, I check my shoulder to make sure the entrance closes, and then we are out on our adventure.

When we get into the city, I'm surprised. I knew it would be busy, but I didn't think it would be this busy. Doctors are crawling everywhere, their blue outfits creating an ocean in the center of the city. We skirt around them, hitting up any hidden storage containers that we know about, most of them scattered under or in buildings under construction. We duck and weave through scaffolding, occasionally taking a break to look back and try to figure out what the doctors are doing here. All of the doctors are just standing around in a group, as if they are waiting for something.

After about an hour, we had collected a healthy amount of resources and piled them up on the second floor of a skyscraper midway through construction, almost more than we could possibly carry on our way back. Tyler and I take another break, our backs against the pile, looking out at the crowd of doctors.

"I'm going to go check it out," I say as I spring to my feet.

"What? No. Why?" Tyler scrambles up to try to stop me.

"You just stay here and protect the resources." I pick up my bag and sling it around my back. I had packed some smoke grenades, a pistol or two, and some knives in here before we left. I usually don't bring any weapons because I always have Tyler to protect me if we ever get ourselves into a sticky situation. However, the number two point Aiko made to us before she left was to never leave without our own protection. Now, I'm starting to see why she would say that. I look back at Tyler, who has a facial expression mixed between confusion and worry. He knows he can't stop me.

"They don't look very dangerous. I just want to get close enough to either see what they are doing or see who they are working for." I need to know who these people are. Based on what I'm seeing, they don't look armed, and the soldier to doctor ratio favors me not getting swarmed by any armed bodies. Tyler is shaking his head.

"Seriously, Ty, it'll be fine."

I give him a quick kiss before sliding down the scaffolding and landing softly on the ground below. I look at the bright orange bars that cover this building to remember in case I get disoriented. I head straight into the crowd, none of the doctors giving me any suspect looks as I charge towards them. Once I'm near the edge of the group, I look at the emblem they all have sewn in over their heart. I can't tell what the letters are, or mean. But, based on information Aiko had given me, the design style of the logo reminds me both of Adams private army company and Tirique's weapons, which means these people are definitely with Nox. I see a young woman taking some syringes and other supplies out of a resource crate. I stride up to her, hoping I can start a friendly conversation.

Her blonde hair spirals far down her back, and her blue pants are stylishly cuffed, revealing a pair of sleek white sneakers. I gently tap her right shoulder, and she spins around quickly, her bright blue eyes staring into mine. I have a black snood pulled over my nose. Usually, people can't tell if my bronze skin is a dark tan or not until they see my whole face, and I'm trying to stay as calm as possible, hoping she doesn't get suspicious.

"Hi. Can I help you?" She asks. Thank the lord. I'm in.

"Hello. I was just going for my usual mid-morning walk, and I noticed all of this commotion. What's going on?"

"It's nothing you should be worried about. Everyone is safe, and you will see soon enough what's going on." She looks pretty unsure, but I don't think she knows any more than I do.

"Can I ask where you are from?" I shuffle a little closer to the crate and take a glance. Under all of the medical equipment, I see a massive rifle peeking out. I look back at the girl, making contact with her as I see she had followed my gaze. I bite my lip under my snood, but she just proceeds to answer my question.

"I grew up in Boston, so I've been here my whole life. I work in the public hospital around here as a nurse." I'm frantically trying to figure out how Nox could have gotten control of the local medical workers. Was she forced to be here? It's more likely that she volunteered because they offered some incentive, not knowing what she was getting herself into.

"Well. I'm going to continue my walk now, but it was great to meet you...."

"Sasha. Sasha Davis." I nod.

"I hope you have a wonderful rest of your day, and I'm looking forward to seeing what special surprise you all are whipping up." I wave to her, memorizing the name so I can look it up in the database when I get back. I find a bench and stand up on it, trying to get a better look. I notice that most of the soldiers seem to be guarding a single building. Interested, I walk along the outside of the crowd, making my way towards the building. When I get near it, I walk past it and onto the street parallel from the building. To my surprise, there is only one guard around the back. I reach around my back and grab a smoke grenade, remove the pin, and toss it as far away from the building as possible. The boom and then hiss of the released smoke distracts the one guard around the back who runs towards the explosion.

Once I'm confident he won't be able to hear me, I sprint towards the metal back door, swinging it open and locking it behind me. I squint through the tiny window in the door as the guard returns to his post and his original position, not noticing anything. I smile, satisfied with myself. I turn around to be greeted by an old hallway, the drywall only half there and the broken pipes hanging down from the ceiling. I carefully proceed down the hallway until it opens up into a massive room. The mix of tile and carpet on the ground tells me this used to be a lobby of some kind. However, instead of soft armchairs and reception desks, an electric babe-wired fence lines the entire perimeter of the space. Huddled around each other in a group, to my absolute shock, are Board soldiers and guards. One sees me approaching and limps over to the edge. They are all injured and in bad shape.

"You have to help us," the guard says, his leg obviously broken as he drags it behind him.

"Who did this? How did you get in here?" Another soldier, blood crusted over half his face, joins the other at the edge. He starts to answer in short sentences as he struggles to breathe properly.

"They all came so fast out of nowhere. They had all the new weapons. We never stood a chance. They beat us up and shoved all of us in here."

"Why are there doctors outside?" I ask. The first guard replies.

"We have no idea. We were all just minding our own business. One of our agents had received an anonymous message, so we were all called to the station ourselves in the middle of the city. It must have been some kind of trap." I know I'm a migrant, but I have to help these people. They need some kind of medical aid, but I can't do it on my own. I don't even know how to disengage this fence, so I can get in.

"I'm going to come back with more help. I promise," I say to them.

"Please. Be quick. Some of us are dying." I turn quickly and sprint in the opposite direction I came. Hopefully, this will spit me out in the front of the building. I walk out the side of the building, luckily there are no guards looking, and I walk through the crowd again.

"Hey. You there. Where do you think you're going?" A guard yells from behind me. I decide not to respond and keep walking.

"Hey!" I hear his boots stomp up from behind me, and he grabs my arm and spins me around. I make eye contact with him as his eyes get wider in shock. It doesn't take me long to realize that my snood has fallen down to my neck. I quickly kick out at the guard's crotch before spinning out and starting to run as fast as I can through the crowd. The guard gets up and yells from behind me.

"She's a migrant! Somebody get her!" I glance up at the familiar orange scaffolding, squinting to see the blonde hair of Tyler waving in the air.

As I'm looking up, I get tripped, tumbling to the ground. As my face lays against the hard concrete ground, my eyes set on a pair of stylish white sneakers. I slowly get to my knees, looking up into the bright blue eyes of Sasha. Now, instead of uncertainty, an expression of disappointment is painted over her face. I'm dragged to my feet by two more guards. I flail my arms to no success.

"Tyler!" I try to yell, but a shirt is shoved into my mouth before I can get out a peep. I get dragged away as I see the silhouette of Tyler getting smaller and smaller in the distance.

My heels bounce and click against the ground as they drag me back, their arms tightly gripped around my shoulders. I'm slumping in their grasp, and I stop flailing, realizing I probably shouldn't waste what's left of my energy on a pointless task. Doctors stare my way as I get pulled through the middle of the crowd, not long enough to show that they are surprised. They may seem clueless, but I'm sure most of them know exactly who they are working for and exactly what they are here to do. Sasha was probably just an exception. She seemed pretty young anyways.

My heart starts beating faster as I recognize the dismantled pipes and the musty smell. Please don't tell me they are putting me right back where I just came from. To my disappointment, I don't even get a chance to object before they quickly disable the electric fence, shove me in, and re-enable it. My instinct is to rush against the fence in rage, but a soldier pulls me back, preventing me from making contact with the fence.

"Woah there, miss." I turn around to be greeted by the same suffering, bruised, and worn-down face that greeted me before.

"I guess you didn't make it too far, huh?" His southern accent is deep, and there is a bit of a growl in his voice as he speaks. He's taller than I thought, his back permanently hunched over. Usually, I would be absolutely appalled to be in the vicinity, let alone be on the same side, as Board soldiers, but I guess we are fighting for our own survival at this point.

"It's okay. We all start off pretty energetic and hopeful until this place..." He motions to the lobby. "And that fence.." He points to the electric fence, "sucks all of the ambition you had left out of ya." I sit down, and he pats my back as I do it.

"What's your name?" I ask.

"Richard. Richard Ward."

"Nice to meet you, Richard. My name is Aria." I go to shake his hand, but he waves me off. I notice his battered hand. "So, how long have all of you been in here?"

"It's hard to keep track of the time in here." He nods towards the wooden boards that cover all of the windows. "But, if I had to guess, I'd say about two days."

CYCLE

"Jeez. If you don't mind me asking, what happened?" Richard chuckles.

"You tell me, kid. You have a better chance at figuring it out than us old farts." He shuffles his feet and hugs his knees to his chest. "We just minded our own business, doing our rounds. We were checking out some of the construction and, if we were lucky, catching some of you guys." He taps my head.

"Man, you migrants are a pain in our damn neck. You lot are sneaky. Ya know that? Anyways, we were doing our rounds, all of us in a group, and then it happened. Oh boy, it happened faster than any of us could keep up. They all dropped down from who knows where. They threw down ropes and slid down. Listen here, young one." He spins around on his butt so he can face me a little better.

"Most people that we've encountered make their move, and then there is a time of contemplation where they have to figure out their next move. Not these folks. They dropped down, and then they were…wooosh… straight into it. They took our legs out first, so we couldn't react. They disarmed all of us. And then…boom…we were all cuffed within seconds. And the funniest thing is, when we had time to get reorientated, they were gone, nowhere to be seen."

"Then what?" I anxiously ask, getting more intrigued, but simultaneously saddened, by the story.

"Then, after a few minutes, a bunch of guards, less lethal than the ones from before, pulled up in a few vans and knocked us out. Next thing we know, we are stuck in this contraption, all of us too wiped out to retaliate. They gave us some water and bread periodically, but that's it. Now that I think about it, the most interesting thing to happen since then is when you showed up."

"I'm sorry to keep asking questions, but do you have any memories of the attack that could be clues for who these people are?"

"I don't know, miss. Like most of these guys, I barely remember anything. All I remember seeing is a couple of guys that could've been your brothers related to you or something." Richard turns away, coughs a couple of times, and then collapses to the floor, immediately in a deep slumber. I sit for a while, not really thinking about anything, trying to make sense of what the hell could be happening. The fact that we went from thinking Nox would invade the United States with the power of all of Europe to a crowd of doctors is shocking. It's been hard the last few days, seeing Nox dismantling all of what was normal society and not being able to tell anyone. It's been hard not to tell Tyler. Of course, he has asked multiple times, but I just divert the conversation each time it happens. He's so much of a space cadet that he doesn't really notice. I would want to know if I were him, especially since he basically told me everything about his past and his family.

Ironically, I may be the key to convincing Nox to stop. I could be the only one left, actually. I've been trying to get in his head. I guess, at the very core, he is fulfilling a promise he made to me all those years before. But, we haven't talked in ages. He used to call me occasionally or text me after he had settled down in Europe. I never got to hear the details of his journey there; I'm sure it was much more dramatic than he made it seem. I never really had a chance to be an emotional mess after he left. I was kinda just thrown into a whole new life. It was probably good for me; it's what mom would've told me to do. She would always throw herself into her work. It's incredible to see how different the paths Nox and I took are. I guess someone could argue that we are fighting for the exact cause, but Nox's ways are too extreme for me, no matter the result they yield. I suppose my opinions are not too different than that of Ivo's. I can't imagine what he's going through.

I rub my eyes in exhaustion, a headache starting to emerge as my brain does extra work to supplement my body's weakness. I slowly lower myself to the ground, my head resting against the old carpet.

I wake up to flashlights beaming all around and over us. I sit up, as does everyone else except for the ones in really bad shape. A shadow of a man emerges on the balcony. I can't see any of his details, but as soon as he starts to speak, I recognize his voice as that of Tirique's, who I've heard speak in multiple tech conferences.

"Attention, guards. You should feel honored to be part of this momentous experiment. Finally, you can be part of something noble, unlike your joke of a government. In a matter of seconds, we will be releasing gas into the air. This gas is a virus. Don't worry, it's not lethal to most, but it will affect your respiratory systems and will most likely lead to unconsciousness. Again, we are eternally grateful for your participation." I squint towards the light as I see Tirique step back in preparation. Suddenly, a hiss starts, and a bluish gas starts to sneak out from the vents near the ceiling. It doesn't take long for it to fill up the space, and, as if on cue, all of the guards start coughing. I watch in horror as bodies crumple to the floor, struggling to breathe and eventually passing out. I grab Richard's arm as he finally curls over.

"See ya on the other side, kid." I don't have the words to respond. All I can think of is Nox. Oh, Nox. What the hell did you do now?

IDRI

March 10, 2035

I spent the entire night yesterday explaining to Tyler why we couldn't just run back out there and fight our way to finding Aria. He refused to believe me that the fight plan wouldn't work until I used the story of Za with him. When he heard that Za was missing for months, and that we got him back by waiting and figuring out how we could help Za without losing anyone else, he was convinced. I suppose it was an important lesson for him to learn and, if I'm honest, I was as reckless as he is back then. The 'sharpshooter,' as Ivo would call me, was never fazed and never scared. I still don't think I am.

It's five in the morning, and I roll out of bed, opening the left side of my closet, something I haven't done in three years. Behind the worn-down wooden door is a collection of all my old gear. An old black bulletproof vest is hanging next to a tight thermal long sleeve shirt. Below them, a shelf holds a pair of cargo pants and a bin with my old weapons. There used to be a point in time where I would be looking in this closet every day. Back when exploring the outside world was always a risk. No strategies and definitely no patterns were known back then.

CYCLE

I pull on the pants, the shirt, and the vest before dragging out a pair of sleek black boots from underneath the shelf and sliding my feet into them. I take out the bin with all my old weapons and find the two rectangular black boxes of collapsable rifles. Ivo made these for me five years ago, and they are still my favorite weapons of all time. I pick out a rusty knife, tucking it into the side of my pants, and then I push two pistols into my vest.

Swinging open the door, Tyler is already waiting for me, sitting curled up in a ball across from my door. He is wearing the clothes he wears when he impersonates a Board soldier. His face is forlorn, and his eyebrows furrowed as if he is in deep contemplation. He stands up in a smooth motion as he sees me open the door, his fear contradicts his readiness to fight. He looks me up and down.

"Why is all your gear from the old ages?" He jokingly asks. I just shake my head.

"Just because it's old doesn't mean it's not as good."

"I guess you and Aiko are together on that one. You know her, and that samurai sword are basically bonded for life." I chuckle, suddenly in the headspace to enjoy Tyler's humor.

"I think it's more superstition than anything else. We've had so much success with our trusty old gear in the past that we keep using it."

"Right, right, old man." Tyler hits back again. I roll my eyes as we make our way to the garage. I climb into the driver's seat of the van, but Tyler stops me.

"We aren't just going to take our hover-bikes?"

"Well, we could. But I doubt they didn't take all of Aria's stuff, and I'm not sure how well she could hang on during a quick getaway."

"That is true. I'm not sure that van is exactly the best vehicle for a quick getaway either." I nod in agreement and spin around in the garage, looking for another option. My eyes finally fall on a car covered in a protective hood. I walk over to it, throwing off the hood, and my eyes light up. I frantically wipe off the dust as memories of my dad's classic red Camry flow back into my mind.

"Man. You and the old stuff is for real, I guess. How old is this thing anyway?"

"Very old. But trust me, it has a little kick in it."

"You're not seriously considering actually taking this bad boy on our mission, right?"

"Oh no, no." Tyler lets out a sigh of relief

"Okay, good."

"I'm not considering anymore. I've decided. We are taking this guy on our mission."

"Oh my lord." Tyler starts to walk away. "That's it. I'm done. This is shocking. We will die in that thing. A quick getaway, forget it. There are even bullet holes in the damn back windshield." I'm already in the car and adjusting the seat. I look behind my shoulder and notice said bullet holes.

"It adds character." I know I'm annoying Tyler, but I figured this could be a good way to test his character. It's such a bad thing to do. I suppose it's why Aiko says I'm an old man in a young man's body.

"I suppose it does." Tyler walks around, tests the strength of the back windshield, opens the passenger door, and takes a seat, but not before he lets out a few huffs of frustration. He has officially passed the test. I start up the car, relieved to see it has a full tank of gas, and maneuver through the garage until we are right in front of the door. Instead of making Tyler do it, I step out and trigger the door, deciding it probably wouldn't be too good of an idea to annoy Tyler any more than he already is.

We speed up the ramp and out into the open road. Tyler points out where the commotion is as I maneuver around the edge of the city. We park in an alley around many buildings under construction, and Tyler guides me to a building covered in bright orange scaffolding. The metal bars surround the perimeter of the incomplete skyscraper in a grid. There is another level of scaffolding caving out the middle of the building, leaving the floors with a gaping hole. We climb up through the middle scaffolding, making our way from bar to bar and eventually landing on the highest partially complete level. A pile of resources lies there, and Tyler grabs a protein bar and starts to eat it from the top crate.

"I'm assuming those are the resources you gathered yesterday."

"Yes, indeed. I'm surprised they are still here, actually." I crouch down and look at what Tyler and Aria had gathered. It's a healthy mix of food and other stuff like old weapons, wires, batteries, and other necessities like that. I take a seat next to the pile, spinning around, so I'm facing out towards the city.

"So, where is this mob of doctors you were talking about?"

"Well, they were just over there." He points directly in front of us to a circular public opening sitting in between some of the tallest skyscrapers. A long stone bench wraps around the entire space, with some interruptions serving as entrances. Otherwise, there is nothing much else to it.

"Do you have the vaguest idea of where we can start looking?"

"I can't be positive, because I could be remembering this wrong, but I remember there was an abnormal amount of guards congregated around that building." He points again towards the middle of the city, this time at a tall, but aging, metal building on the far side of the circle.

"I guess we start there then. Unless you have any better ideas?"

"Nah. Sounds good to me." Tyler throws the empty wrapper to the side. We both get up, descending the scaffolding again, and we make our way to the building. We walk in a direct line, but something feels off to me. Why would there be hundreds of people working for Nox and then just none?

"Let's go around the long way just in case," I instruct Tyler.

"Oh c'mon, Idrissa." He whines.

"Nothing is ever wrong with being safe. Remember that." He reluctantly follows me as I turn right and walk a couple of blocks over from the circle. When we make it back around, the back of the building has a metal door entrance with a small glass window in it.

"I'll go in through here. You walk around from the front and walk in that way. We will cover more ground if we split up." Tyler nods, and I walk up to the door. He peels off to going around. I give the door handle a tug, but it's locked from the inside. I grab a pistol from my vest and shoot underneath the handle. A small bit of smoke comes out from the area and the door swings open, scorch marks lining the interior around the lock. I walk in, pistol up in case my entrance just woke up any more guards. I walk down a disgusting hallway, pipes falling to the ground and the once grey concrete covered in a layer of dust and dirt. The methodical drip of water compliments my steps on the sloppy wet ground.

I continue down the hallway until it opens up into some kind of lobby, the carpet soggy.

"Idrissa?" I look up and see Aria standing among a bunch of fallen bodies. All the guards look out cold, some of them lifting their heads and coughing before falling back to the floor. They are surrounded by an electric fence that goes around the perimeter of the lobby.

"Aria? What the hell is this?" As I get closer, Aria is shaking in fear, tears flowing down her face.

"They threw me in here yesterday. And, then…this morning….they said it was a test or something. And, this gas started coming out of the vents.." Her words are broken. "It's some kind of virus. The guards…

started coughing, and then the ones who weren't affected at first started coughing. I don't know why it didn't affect me. You have to help them, Idrissa. I promised I would help them."

"We will help them, Aria, but I need to get you out first." I take off my vest and my shirt. I wrap the shirt around my hands and start to climb up the chainlink fence, careful not to let any of my skin touch the metal. I jump up over the top, doing a flip before I land right next to Aria. I lean down and put my fingers behind the ear of the nearest guard.

"He's breathing," I say, relieved. I go to a few more guards, checking their pulses. All of them are alive, but they are obviously very, very sick. I stand up and walk back to Aria. I stand there thinking. Why would Aria not be sick right now? But, Aria beats me to it.

"Oh my god. They are all white. Idrissa, they are all white." Aria vigorously shakes my arm. I frantically spin around, scanning every face in the group. To my great disappointment, Aria is right.

"Idrissa. Please tell me you didn't bring Tyler."

"Oh. No." As if God was listening, Tyler bounds in through the opposite hallway and up to the fence.

"Aria. Thank god...." He starts furiously coughing, gasping for air. Crumpling to the floor, Aria just looks on in fright. I scan the ceiling, a balcony wraps around the top of the lobby space, and I spot a control box that must be powering the electric fence. I take out my collapsable gun, aiming at the control box and firing. Sparks fly out of the box. I take a deep breath, and then I touch the fence with my bare hand. Nothing happens. I hear Aria let out a sigh of relief. She starts to climb out, and I follow her. We rush to Tyler to who is lying on the floor.

"I'm okay, guys." He coughs again. "I'm okay." He starts to lose consciousness. I wrap my shirt around his forehead as a fever starts.

IDRI

"Help me carry him out of here," I say to Aria, who lifts his legs. I hold most of his weight as we move back the way I came. We are about to make our way across the street when a man in a black suit with gold accents drops down in front of us. I drop Tyler to the floor and pull out my knife, realizing I left my vest with all my weapons back in the building. The man strides right up to us before deactivating his helmet. I would recognize that frazzled black hair and those curious brown eyes anywhere.

"Idri?"

"Za?"

. . .

CYCLE

ZA

March 10, 2035

I couldn't sleep all night. I realized that I wouldn't be able to live with myself if I just kept my head down and served Nox like I didn't have a brain of my own. I plan to go along with Nox, maybe learn more about the specifics of his plan, and then escape somehow. I don't think it'll be too hard to escape, but I guess we will just have to wait and see. If all goes well, he has no idea I'm planning to dip, and he doesn't react quickly enough to stop me.

I'm already at the kitchen table, consuming some cereal and enjoying my tea. I keep waiting for a knock on the door from Nox, but one never comes. After eating, I head to my closet, careful to pick out some clothes that will last me through the imminent adventure. I'm sure Nox is going to be dressed in some luxurious suit, looking professional. I've usually been wearing clean cuffed black chinos with sneakers and a hoodie except for missions. I might have to wear something a bit more flexible and robust today. I pick out some thick water repellent joggers and wear my classic long sleeve black thermal with a black zip-up hoodie. Idri was the first one to introduce me to long sleeve thermals and, ever since, I haven't been able to find anything better. I decide not to gather too many weapons. I'll probably just use my suit when the time comes and, if I need any weapons, I can just take some from the nearest soldier.

I make my way downstairs, turning around and pausing in the doorway to take in my room for the last time. I wasn't really in here for long enough for it to hold any sentimental value to me, but it's what it represented. My first room attained myself, the first path I forged on my own. The fact that Ivo was right yet again is beside the point. I bound around the hallway and take the lift down. Nox is hanging out in the middle, instructing some guards to move some crates around. He sees me approaching and gives me a smile of relief.

"You look like you're ready for war. Why? This is a non-hostile takeover remember."

"Well. Your lead soldier is always ready for a fight." I give him a little wink, and he smiles in response. I can confidently say that Nox thinks that the tension just blew over harmlessly. It's going to be a challenge to keep it that way.

"Anyways, I've just been directing these guys to pack some food and other resources into the jet, and then we will be ready to go." He rubs his hands together in anticipation.

"Exciting stuff."

"Yes, indeed," I respond before walking to the metal circle that sits in the center of the tile floor. The shiny chrome reflects light and demands your attention, making the lavish tile floor around it seem bland and mundane. I slowly put both my feet in the center, the placement of my feet dictated by two very faint and thin black lines in the shape of feet. Once it feels my pressure, it starts to rise, a section of the honeycombed glass dome sliding away and revealing the open blue sky, today more of a gray, polluted with the occasional wispy cloud. The platform continues to rise as its metal legs don't stop extending. I spin around, admiring the horizon and the view. A massive glass loading dock, reinforced with more chrome metal, once again in the shape of a circle, floats over the ground halfway over the base and halfway over the ground. More metal beams extend downwards into the base and the ground. Sitting on top of the platform is a massive high-speed jet, matte black with massive turbines. It comes to a sharp tip and is slender all of the way through. When the lift is level with the loading dock, it stops, embedding perfectly with a path made of more overlapping chrome circles.

I walk towards the jet, a few guards and pilots already there, loading it with the resources I saw in the base. When they see me, they all stand up straight and salute me. I give them a meek salute back, still uncomfortable with that dynamic, and make my way into the jet, stepping up ridged metal steps. The middle of the plane looks like any other military transport, with mildly uncomfortable seats flanking either side with space in the middle, handles hanging down from the top ceiling, and weapons lining any open space on the wall. I walk to the back, where there is a whole kitchen and bathrooms, and then walk back through the middle and into the front. Brown leather seats, three rows of two seats split in the middle by a wider than average aisle, remind me of seats from an expensive movie theatre. I slump in the middle chair to the right, my left leg hanging over the side armrest. I stare through the top skylight and enjoy the sensation of the fluffy seat behind my head. This chair is the most comfortable thing I have ever sat in.

I must have been sitting in the plane, zoning out, for ten minutes when Nox finally joins me, followed by the guards and the pilots I saw before.

"I will let you get some more rest Za, but let me show something before you do." Nox leans over across the aisle, holding a tablet in his hands. He holds it out in front of me, showing me what looks like a drone shot.

"Where is this?" I ask as I continue to inspect it, Nox zooming in for me. There seem to be many people in blue uniforms congregated in some kind of opening within a city.

"This is in Boston. These are all of the medical practitioners we were able to collect and convince them of our cause." I have a slight feeling that 'convince' isn't exactly the right word to use, I'm not sure these people have any clue what or who they are working for, but I nod along to what Nox is saying anyways.

"Tirique had gone over early to do some preparatory work in New York City and Boston, where he is now." He must have left right after I saw him talking to Nox yesterday. "I took into account what you said about this being a health risk to innocent people, so I told Tirique to round up some doctors and nurses that could care for the innocent civilians." There may be some humanity left in Nox after all, although I'm quick to point out the flaw.

"But what about the cure?"

"Well, we can't work with that much haste. We have a vaccine ready, but we need this virus to spread how we intended before we can use it."

"I see." I want to argue back, but I don't have the energy, and I need to stay on Nox's good side for now. "Where are you releasing the virus first?"

"Tirique is going to release it on some Board soldiers in Boston who, after their immune systems fight the virus, will be released. We hope that with the amount of bustle in Boston, there are more than enough people from around the country to contract the virus and then bring it to wherever they are. Although, it's really just the East Coast we need to attack, that's where pretty much the entire Board is." He puts the tablet away, storing it in the compartment that's attached to the seat in front of him before turning back towards me.

"So, what do you think?"

"It sounds great, Nox." I try to sound as confident in my answer as possible, and he returns my remark with a satisfied nod.

"Ok. Good. I'll let you get some rest then." I give him a small smile before sitting back in my chair. I pull on my headphones and shut my eyes.

One more slice of peace before the chaos.

Instead of waking up to turbulence, which I expected, my eyes flutter open to realize we've just landed. Not only did the flight only take two hours, but the jet seemed to pierce the air perfectly and I didn't experience any disruptions. I tug my headphones off and glance to my right, where Nox is very awake and working on his computer. Looking over my shoulder, I spot the five soldiers already geared up. They are the ones that are replacing my team after I told them they didn't have to come back. Let's just say they didn't need a second invitation to bow out.

I step out of the plane and onto the concrete roof of a skyscraper. I pause for a moment to admire what Boston has become. Towering modern buildings have replaced the warm brick ones. The city is crawling with all kinds of people. Of course, the culture is gone, sterility has smothered it all out, but Boston now means something to the people that own this country, and I think that's special in a way, no matter how disappointed it makes me.

I let Nox walk by me and follow him down the emergency staircase of the building, walking over the massive painted 'H' that marks the roof as a landing zone. Once we go down the first flight of stairs, I'm expecting more, but we are instead graced by a glass elevator, big enough to fit all seven of us. The elevator takes us all the way down to what looks like a lobby of some kind. I can't be sure, but I think we are in a hotel. Tirique is waiting for us in one of the green lounge chairs, and he hurriedly gets up to greet us as we make our entrance.

"Nox. It's great to see you." He grabs Nox's hand and starts to shake it, and then turns to me, giving me a nod. "You as well, Mr. Wolf. Your room is just that way, Nox." Tirique points to his right down the hallway, and Nox begins to follow Tirique's directions. He turns around halfway there.

"Remember people. We do not leave this compound until we are absolutely ready. We don't need anyone to know that we are here." He is talking to everyone, but he takes careful attention to meet my gaze. Turning around, he heads down the hallway and into a room. The timing may not be ideal, but this could be my best window to get out of this place without causing a whole scene. I look at Tirique. I need to know what I'm dealing with first, which means seeing the soldiers that have already been given the virus.

"Tirique." He spins on one heel to look at me. "Can you tell me where the infected guards are being held?"

"Oh…well. I'm not sure anyone is supposed to leave for the time being." I give him a fake giggle.

"Don't be silly Tirique. I just want to find it on a map and get my bearings. After all, I haven't been in Boston for quite some time and, as the head security member, I think it would be appropriate for me to be acquainted with the surroundings." I talk formally, and Tirique, after a time of contemplation, obliges.

"Ok." He grabs a map out of his back pocket, unfolding it and pointing to a building not far from where I was a prisoner five years ago. I recognize the circular opening near it as the place where the doctors were gathered.

"Fantastic. Thank you. Now, would you mind showing me where my room is?"

"Of course. It's just down that way on your left." Tirique points to a hallway leading in the opposite direction as Nox. Perfect. I give Tirique one last nod of gratitude and then quickly walk down the hallway and into the room whose door was left ajar. I go straight to the window against the wall. I check for alarms and then slide it open, crawling through and landing on the cement sidewalk outside of the hotel.

"Where do you think you're going?" I look to my left and angrily exhale. Nox is standing to the side, casually leaning against the cement wall.

"I just needed some air," I calmly reply.

"You needed to crawl through your window to get air? This isn't a prison, and, last time I checked, the front door is working just fine." He seems casual and zen, but he is furiously glaring at me. He shuffles his feet a little, and I see his left hand is holding a taser. I hate those things. I take a step to my right, followed by Nox taking another step to his left.

"Nox. I thought we were good," I say, my heart starting to race.

"Are we good, Za? Tell me where you were really going, or I won't have a choice." He takes one more step towards me.

"I'm sorry, Nox." Before he can react, I launch off the wall with my left foot, spinning to the other side of Nox as I hang off a crevice in the wall from my left hand, my back touching the cement. As I lower myself to the ground, I grab the taser with my right hand, pressing the activation button as I push it into Nox's stomach. The only retaliation he can muster is an arm waving out at me, trying to grab my shirt or grapple me. In a matter of seconds, Nox is knocked out on the ground, his perfectly dry-cleaned suit now wrinkled. A dictator crumpled on the ground in front of a skyscraper. As I walk away, I can't shake the gut feeling that this was not our last violent encounter. It isn't over.

I activate my suit and trigger my bike, speeding away towards where the soldiers are held. I'm about to walk in when I get there, but I see the metal backdoor limply hanging open with scorch marks on it. It looks like someone has already broken in. I decide to hang out on the roof of the brick building across the street from it.

I wait for fifteen minutes before seeing a guy and a girl carrying a dude in their arms, his blonde hair waving in the air. The guy is shirtless and the girl is dressed like a migrant, their skin tones telling me that they are definitely migrants. Why the hell would they be helping him? Once they are right below me, I drop down ten feet in front of them. I notice the guy drop the white guy to the floor, but my eyes are locked on the black guy in front of me. I squint and step closer as he grabs a knife from his shoe. And then I see his pants. Two pockets on either side of the leg, the end of them tucked into black military boots. They are worn down, but only one person wears pants like that. I look back at his face, and then I see it. I deactivate my helmet, and we stare into each other's eyes.

"Idri?"

"Za?"

IVO

March 10, 2035

Bio-weapons. That's what we've come to. It's shocking. I'm zoning out as I drive back, a solid amount above the speed limit. It's interesting how I would be rushing back quicker if this was an out-and-out war with guns and soldiers. The truth is, we have no clue how to stop a virus. It's that simple. We could rush back all we want, but it won't come to anything. The team and I spent all day yesterday wandering the streets of New York City, trying to uncover any information. We would catch anybody affiliated with Nox and question them. Most of them didn't know what the hell was going on, but one spilled the beans on the virus. I was very tempted to ask them about Za, but I held myself back from going down that rabbit hole, didn't need to add emotions into the whole mix, and definitely didn't need to explain the entire situation to the team.

Unfortunately, the guy didn't have much more information for us, but I had a hunch that Nox wouldn't make the mistake of having too many people know his plans. The best are good at concealing their secrets. When we made it back, Aiko and the twins had found the van and parked it in front of the base. I explained everything to them, and we started brainstorming possible plans. Not before they had a mental breakdown, of course. The first thing we did was beg the team to come back with us. The more numbers we can get, the better. However, they were hesitant to leave their last and only post in the city, which was fair. We gave them detailed instructions on how to find us and how to get into our base if they want to come to help us later. We stayed over in New York last night, and now we are on the road. It's midday, and we are about halfway there. Aiko's face is smushed against the cloth passenger of the seat, and the twins are, once again, passed out in what seems like the most uncomfortable positions in the back, layered on top of each other.

Once again, I take the time to think on my own. If Nox, or Nox's team, I should say, is releasing a virus, then I suppose he doesn't actually have to come to the country. Although, based on his migrant background, I'm guessing he would want to be here to see his work in progress. Considering Boston is the country's epicenter at this point, it would be logical to release the virus in Boston. How he is going to release the virus, I have no idea, but it's probably extremely contagious. The only thing the soldier said was that the virus is "self-made" and "targeted towards white people." I didn't know you could attack a race of people like that. Technology has come a long way and, with Tirique leading your innovation, I suppose anything is possible.

To be honest, I can't shake the question stuck in the back of my head: where is Za? I smile to myself as I realize he's probably asking the exact same question wherever he is. As much as I want to berate him the next time I see him for not thinking things through and blindly joining an autocrat, I'm happy that he made a decision for himself and stayed strong in his choice. As an older brother, I know that I'm not very good at leaving the 'choose-your-own path' open.

When we get back, the first order of business is to have the Migrants start dropping off masks to all of the civilians we can. It seems like the humane thing to do, which it is, but convincing a group of oppressed people to help the survival of their oppressors is going to be a very difficult argument to make. If I get Aiko, Aria, Idri, and Tyler to argue with me, we will probably have more luck. Wait. Tyler. Oh, yikes. We have to protect Tyler too.

I continue to mull things over as more and more cars collect on the highway. Every time a car goes by on the lane next to us, I have to look in the opposite direction, so all they see is the back of my head. It gets annoying, but it's the only way we can guarantee not getting caught. I sit back in my seat, the fading plush cushion interrupted by the metal backbone of the seat digging into my back. My left hand rests on the top of the smooth black steering wheel, its cool temperature traveling up my arm. I have the heat on, blasting into my face, the heat hitting me in waves, as cool air from the cracked window keeps my temperature comfortable. The wind through the window creates a hiss that eventually just turns into white noise. This is me getting mentally prepared for a fight that could be harder than the one fives years ago.

I can't see much from the edge of the city, but as we get near to the base, the city looks as bustling as it always is, just as Nox would like it to be. I wind the last corner, and the base ramp door is already open. Idri is leaning against the rock on the right next to the trigger. Aiko's eyes slowly open, and the boys start arguing with each other about how they have cramps and dead arms because of how the other was sleeping on them. I park the van right before the ramp and get out, smiling as I see Idri.

"What are you doing out here?" I say, still unsure if I gave him enough time to process it. Instead of hugging him, I put out my fist, and we fist bump awkwardly.

"Let's just say you might wanna turn that van around. We have a lot of work to do." I nod, glad I don't have to break any news to the crew. I climb back into the driver's seat before getting out again and looking at Idri, confused.

"Wait. How do you guys know?"

"I could ask you the same question." He points down into the base garage. "Might wanna check down there before you ask any more questions." Even more, confused now, I wander down the ramp and into the garage.

Waiting there, sitting on a crate, and talking to Aria, is Za. He looks up at me like we just saw each other yesterday. At that moment, there is no malice in my mind.

"Whattup big bro," Za says, not feeling the need to formalize the situation and stand up.

"What's up."

ZA

March 10, 2035

Idri pauses for a minute before lowering into a fighting position. I can tell he's not sure what to do. The other lady is shuffling quickly behind Idri as the blonde dude lays on the floor. I deactivate my suit and then throw my hands up in the air.

"I'm not with them anymore," I defiantly state, it feels good to say actually.

"How do I know?" Idri says, not relaxing quite yet.

"C'mon, Idri. I never lie to you."

"The Za I knew would never disobey his brother and join a psychopath either, so I'm a bit confused." He brings up a fair point. I reach out my hands, squeezing my wrists together, and I drop down onto my knees.

"Just take me as a prisoner, and you can decide later if it's worth trusting me or not." Idri nods to that. The girl hands him handcuffs, and he tightens them on. We start walking back through the familiar circular gathering area.

"So who's that?" I ask, struggling to gesture towards the blonde kid who Idri is carrying over his right shoulder as he simultaneously tightens his grip on my left arm.

"I ask the questions, not you," Idri coldly replies.

"Fine, fine," I reply.

"First off. Why the hell are you working with Nox?" We continue to walk through the area. I recognize the stone benches that line the perimeter of the area. When we walk through, the girl nods towards a building under construction with orange scaffolding. Idri shakes his head in response, and she slowly nods back.

"First off. Worked. As in the past tense. And it's with, not for. Also, how do you know that I worked with him?" I don't think any of the news feeds showed me. There's no way a camera was ever near enough to me to get a good enough shot for Idri to identify me. Unless…

"Wait a second. Is Ivo here?"

"What do you not understand about I ask the questions?" Idri, as always, shows no emotion, giving me absolutely zero hints. We walk in silence for a couple more minutes, turning a corner and going down an alley.

"Are you going to answer the question or not?" Idri finally asks.

"Well, it's a very long story. Nox is a convincing guy. He used to be a migrant, you know." I catch an interesting expression from the girl out of the corner of my eye. "He came to me with an opportunity to help him save the Migrants. Of course, I said yes, not knowing what I was getting myself into. Fast forward to about one hour ago, one life or death situation, and one encounter with the psychopath version of Nox later, I escaped their compound here in Boston, and that's when I ran into you lot." Idri gives a slight nod, a sign that he mostly believes what I just told him.

"Why specifically did you run into us, though? It couldn't have just been by chance." Idri keeps it coming with the questions as we turn a corner into another alley. This time, Idri's classic red Camry is parked there. I smile at the sight go it.

"What?" Idri questions my smirk.

"It has been a while since I've seen that car. It brings back so many memories." I look back behind my shoulder to see a glimmer of realization in Idri's eyes; I know he is thinking about his memories with the car, tracing back to his days as a kid. Maybe he even remembers me as part of the original migrant group. I know that eventually, it will click that our history together is stronger than our past apart. I just have to wait until that happens. We approach the car, and the girl swings open the back left door.

"I haven't seen this car, well....ever." She comments. Idri starts to lower the blonde guy into the backseat, sliding him to the far right side of the car. He weakly readjusts himself in the seat and mutters a few words.

"Told you we shoulda taken the van." He giggles to himself before bursting out coughing and returning to his dazed state.

"Try to rest, Tyler. You're too sick for me to argue with you. I'll save that for later," Idri answers. At least I know one of their names then. I so badly want to ask why they are helping a white guy, but it looks like he is sick, pretty sure that's the virus. It makes me depressed to think that I was on the same side as the guy that made that virus come to life. Even worse, it wouldn't have been able to exist without my team finding that elixir stuff. Idri grabs my arm and gives me a light shove. I drop into the open space in the backseat. The girl walks around to the passenger seat as Idri gets in the driver's side and reverses. I decide to take the high road in this conversation.

"To answer your question, I was going to where they were testing the initial dose of the virus. I was going to see what the success of the virus was; I guess it was to see if I could help those people or not."

"What virus?" Idri asks. The blood is drained out of my face as I realize it's time for me to be the one to tell them that Nox is releasing a bioweapon on the United States government.

"You're telling me that that virus, the one I just saw take out twenty healthy Board soldiers within minutes, is the way Nox is attacking the country? Please, for the love of God, tell me that isn't true." The girl begs. I guess someone has seen it.

"How do you know about the virus?" I ask.

"Yeah, Aria, how do you know about that?" Idri then looks over his shoulder at me. "And what the hell are you talking about with this virus." I open my mouth to answer, but Aria, if that's her name, cuts me off. She's obviously passionate, so I decide I'll let her explain it.

"The gas that Tirique released when I was in that cage was a virus of some kind that affected everyone but me. That's why we saw it only affected white people, and that's why Tyler got sick. Tirique said we were the first initial experiment."

"So, what you're saying is...." Idri starts to collect his thoughts. I can tell his brain is rushing to process. "This virus is going to be released on a larger scale and spread through those soldiers which, essentially, is how Nox wants to take out the Board." Aria spins around and stares me down, awaiting my answer.

"I'm afraid that is indeed the case," I reply, trying to show as much guilt as I possibly can. Aria slumps back in her chair while Idri is quickly brainstorming possible solutions.

"So this is why you left." Idri addresses me. "You probably had no idea that Nox would go to extremes like this, and, as soon as you found out, you wanted to get out as soon as possible. It helped that it was in Boston. So, you were coming to warn us, not to spy on us." He leans back in his chair, and I can tell that something clicked in his brain, like he just solved a math problem when the solution was right in front of his face the whole time.

"Did you really think I was actually coming to spy on you guys, Idri?"

"Well, no. You aren't exactly stealth enough to do that, haven't yet accessed your inner ninja." There is the joke. Now, I know he fully trusts me now. It's good to have him back. He was practically another big brother for me. He notices my shoulders relax as we get more comfortable.

"Want me to take those cuffs off?" Idri asks.

"Yeah, no need. I got out of them ten minutes ago. I just kept them on so you guys wouldn't freak out." I slid my hands out of the cuffs. I had loosened them by taking a pin out of my pocket and unscrewing the middle screw.

"This is a lesson Aria. Next time you want to hold one of the Wolf brothers captives, you practically have to put them in an indestructible box, and sometimes that doesn't even work." Aria laughs before turning back to me.

"It was great to meet your brother, although we didn't get to talk for too long." I sit up in my chair at the confirmation that Ivo is here.

"When did he get here?" I ask. I had a feeling he was going to escape whatever prison they put him in, but how was he able to get all the way over here?

"A few days ago. As far as I know, he's in New York City right now, but I'm assuming he's going to be back in no time." I can't really pay attention to anything Idri says. All I'm thinking about is if Ivo is going to be mad at me or not. I snap out of it as Aria asks another question.

"I was going to ask your brother this but, since you're here, what was it like all those years ago at the beginning of the Revolution?"

"Weren't you here?" I ask. Very confused about the backstory of Aria and Tyler.

"No. I was on the West Coast. Oh. I guess I should introduce myself properly now that you aren't really our prisoner." She looks at Idri for approval, and he responds with a nod. "My name is Aria Yavuz. I'm from California on the West Coast; I had been there all my life, although my parents immigrated to the United States before the Revolution. I was kind of helping the Migrants on the West Coast, although there weren't too many of us. Two years ago, I made my way here to the East Coast and have been helping the Migrants ever since then. I have mostly helped with bringing migrants from the West Coast here, where we have more support and resources."

Her story is interesting, but something feels strangely familiar to me as I stare into her eyes. The piercing brown eyes, the flawless golden brown skin. She's obviously multi-racial because some of her features look European. And her name, Yavuz, so she's half Turkish. Why is that familiar to me? I don't waver in my eye contact with her, and she doesn't either. I sense some fear like she's hiding something. She pushes her hair behind her head and reveals a gold necklace around her neck. In the middle of that necklace is half a circle, almost like a crescent moon. Then it hits me. That's Nox's necklace. More like Nox has the other half. I look back into her eyes. She starts to realize I'm connecting the dots. Now her eyes look like Nox's eyes. They are siblings. Yavuz. I saw that somewhere in Nox's office. She sees I make the connection, and when I motion towards Idri, she shakes her head. She hasn't told anybody. I give her a minuscule nod.

"You guys got awfully quiet all of a sudden." Idri comments, his eyes never left the road.

"I was just thinking about how interesting it must have been to be on the West Coast; it's so different from over here." I start talking, which snaps Aria out of her trance.

"Ah yes. It was interesting." She looks at Tyler, putting her hand on his forehead and feeling his fever. "I guess I never introduced Tyler. You must be pretty confused. So was your brother. Too bad Tyler can't give his trademark 'I'm a white migrant' introduction. He's been with the Migrants for almost as long as you've been gone. Aiko and Idri brought him in when he was orphaned. He was the son of civilians that were helping the Migrants. Most of what he does is going undercover as a Board soldier. He was the one that found me on the West Coast and told me Aiko wanted me to come, it was a little bit more dramatic than that, but you get it."

I'm skeptical, but I'm sure that talking to him would make me feel better. I glance at Idri through his backseat mirror, and he gives me a nod of approval. I'm sure Idri put Tyler through the tests, and if he approves, I approve. Not that I have any authority anymore. He just reminds me of all the kids I would go to school with before the Revolution happened, the same kids that would later become the enemy and are now probably some kind of Board soldier or working for the big tech companies that own this country. Idri checks his phone.

"I just got an encrypted text from Ivo that says he's almost back." He looks at me. "You ready for a sibling reunion?"

"As ready as I will ever be, I suppose," I reply. Idri gets out of the van after we go around that last corner, the stone on the right still as rugged and raw as ever. The sounds of the ocean are pure, but the sight of the trash infecting the waves saddens me. Idri triggers the base door. Still, nothing has changed. After five years, it's still all the same. Aria jumps in the driver's seat and drives the van into the garage. People are walking everywhere. I never thought I would see this much bustle amongst the Migrants. The familiar red-brick foundation lines the outside of the garage, which is now full of vehicles of all kinds—organized crates with weapons and other resources off to the side. I get out of the van and sit on some crates in the middle. Admiring the evolution of the building, Aria comes and sits next to me, leaning against the crates.

"Is it different?" She asks.

"You don't even know. It's different, and it's the same. It's still the original home of the Migrants, but now it's filled with life. I never thought that we could make this into a real home, not just some temporary solution." She nods.

"Thanks for not saying anything."

"It would be kinda shitty for me to be here for an hour and wreck your whole life, wouldn't it?" She laughs.

"Well, when you say it like that...."

"But, why? Why haven't you told them? Nox has only been in the public eye for a few weeks at max. Why did you not tell them before when you got here two years ago?"

"At the time, I felt abandoned. I'm sure Nox didn't tell you about his rushed departure."

"No, he didn't."

"We don't have to get into that now, but let's just say it didn't leave me in a good state. Everything happened so fast and, before I knew it, I had a whole new life here. I wanted it to be just that—a new life. So I just never said anything, not even to Tyler. I just acted like I was a lone wolf."

"And, I thought I had it hard. Sheesh." I keep thinking how Nox never told me about his origin story. He probably wanted to keep it that way.

"The first time I saw that he was even still alive was a few days ago when we saw him on TV, wreaking havoc on Europe." I frown.

"Does he know you're here?"

"No." I'm not sure whether she realizes she could be the one to stop this whole war. Before I can ask, she brings it up. "I'm starting to think

I'm the secret weapon to this whole operation, secret even to my own team."

"Don't worry. You won't have to do this alone."

"How is he?" I take a moment to think about it. What does she wanna hear, brutal honesty? Do I tell her that her brother has become an absolute power monster bordering on psychopath, or should I tell her that he's doing pretty well. I mean, he is to a point. He's very successful at what he wants to do, and he's kinda doing whatever he wants with high efficiency and success.

"He's….pretty good. He's delighted with his work, and he is grounded in his mission, so I suppose you could say he is doing very well."

"Suppose?"

"I mean… you've seen the news. And the whole virus thing, I tried to talk him out of it, but he wouldn't listen." She solemnly nods.

"I can't believe he would do that. He was always proactive, but he was never that radical. I never pictured him as someone that thought hurting the enemy was the only way. I guess people change."

"People do change." At that moment, I notice a figure slowly walking down the ramp. First, I recognize the shoes, then the black pants, and then I see his face. Ivo stands thirty feet in front of me. I don't move. I just sit there. We hold eye contact before I open my mouth with a greeting.

"Whattup." I immediately cringe at my response to my own brother, who I haven't seen in a week because we chose opposing sides of a civil war. Idiot. I spot a glint of a smile start to form on his face. Aria is just looking on as if she was watching an intense movie scene, her brain telling her not to blink.

"What's up," Ivo replies. I hop down from my perch and stride up to him. I put out my hand, and he shakes it.

"We good?" I ask.

"You tell me?"

"I think we're good."

"That works for me." His shoulders relax. "Looks like someone finally came to their senses." He immediately resumes with his annoying big brother talk. Ivo notices I'm already getting annoyed.

"I'm playing with you, man. I'm glad you stuck with your decision. Nox must've been a pretty lucky dude to have a fighter like you on his side."

"Yeah, I'm sorry he put you in prison, by the way."

"Oh, I don't know if you can call that a prison. That was super wack. They had me in some kind of mind loop. I quickly learned I don't wanna be a prisoner of Tirique ever again." He looks to my right and sees Aria. "How are you doing, Aria? Any commotion while we were gone?" Idri walks past Ivo as he asks the question.

"Oh, you don't wanna know," he says. A wide grin appears on my face as the familiar face of Aiko pops up, walking down the ramp. She sees me and runs towards me, giving me a big hug.

"How are you doing, Za? Other than arguing with your brother again."

"I guess I'm good now."

"It's good to see you. Honestly, my hope for seeing the Wolf brothers together again was waning but, now that both of you are here, Nox has no idea what he just signed up for." She looks at Aria. "Idri just told me what happened. I'm so sorry you had to go through that. Where's Tyler?"

"He's resting in the car." More remorse flows through my veins as I notice migrants, probably former doctors, caring for Tyler. One looks back to give us a report.

"He's doing okay. It just looks like a bad cold, kind of like the flu. Tyler has a very strong immune system, but I'm sure this could hospitalize most healthy adults for at least a few days."

"That's all he needs," I say. Everyone looks at me as if they forgot I have all of the inside information. Idri is sitting off to the side, eating a bar, Aria is still beside me, Aiko and Ivo are next to each other in front of me, and I see the twins walking up to us.

"No way," Aziz says.

"Za is here!?" Riz exclaims. They stride up to me, Aziz punching the side of my arm in, what I hope, is affection and Riz messing up my hair.

"I see you two haven't matured at all." I tease them and they both hug me before they back up and sit with Idri. "Those first bunch of guards they infected is the original sample, but they are also hoping that those guards become the first super spreaders. The virus can hang in the air for up to an hour, so just walking in the same area as someone that was infected could cause possible infection."

"Is there a vaccine?" Aiko asks.

"Apparently, yes. But I don't know where or what it is, and Nox said he's not going to release that until he is confident that the targets of the attack have been successfully neutralized."

"So, what were all the doctors for yesterday?" Aria asks.

"I had a big argument with Nox about how it's not moral to cause any harm to civilians, which this virus obviously does. In an attempt to ease my worries, Nox somehow gathered and convinced a bunch of doctors to be on call to help civilians. Of course, not much care can be administered to those affected since it's mostly only a problem the vaccine can solve. It was basically just a massive ploy to convince me to stay on his side."

"So, how do we stop this thing?" We are all surprised as Tyler rises out of the car, slowly getting to his feet. He hobbles over to the group. Aria stands up to give him support and simultaneously hugs him.

"I'm fine, guys, don't worry. I had stomach bugs worse than this when I was a kid." Tyler is starting to grow on me.

"There is only one way we can stop this thing; we need to keep it from spreading," I say.

"I guess our first move is to check on the status of the first test group," Idri adds.

"Can we do that tomorrow? We are all super beat," Ivo says. This is how it used to be, Idri was always the one that wanted to get going and do the thing, not as reckless as me, of course, and Ivo was the one that kept him in check. They weren't too good at their respective roles, but it kinda worked.

"Yeah, but we better get up in the morning. Once they recover enough to walk around, Nox is going to let them out." I say defiantly. Everyone gives a slow nod and moves on to their rooms.

Tomorrow is when I really regret what I've done.

IVO

March 11, 2035

The whole team, which is now eight of us, is gathered in the garage. Everyone woke up early on their own except for Za, who, apparently, has had a rough go at it recently. We talked for a few minutes last night before going to bed. He apologized for not listening to me, I agreed, and then I apologized for never letting him pave his path. That was kind of it, and I think it was all we needed. In the grand scheme of things, it had only been about a week, so it was nothing compared to the six months apart that we had five years ago. It's interesting how that time can be seen as our origin story now.

"Ready?" Aiko asks the group. Everyone is decked out in stealthy black outfits, equipped with the best weapons. Tyler has pretty much fully recovered after a good night of sleep, his face once again filled with jubilance. He's wearing the clothes that fit in with the Board soldiers, which I'm not sure is a good or bad idea. It could make him more of a target, but it has the added benefit of meaning he can fit in with the other soldiers if we ever needed that. I guess we will have to wait and see.

Everyone starts to climb into the biggest van we have. It also happens to be the nicest. The matte back exterior contrasts with white leather seats on the inside. Shiny red accents line the bottom, the rims, and the sideview mirrors. There are four big seats in the van, not counting the drivers and passenger seat, which Aiko and I climb into. I take a look back and see Za right behind me, Aria next to him, Tyler in the back with Idri, and the twins hanging out on the ground, once again grappling with each other for the more comfortable position. They settle with Aziz laying down, parallel with the car and feet pointing to the front of the car, while Riz sits perpendicularly, his butt on one side of Aziz and his feet on the other. His back leans against the side of Tyler's seat. Weapons are piled up in the back.

"Let's get this show on the road," Aiko says, pulling out of the garage and riding up the ramp. "You ready for this?" She asks me.

"As ready as I'm ever going to be. I never thought my most formidable enemy would be a virus."

"Trust me. It's a surprise for all of us." We drive as fast as we can to the building where they infected the soldiers. Za had told me the building is close to the second prison he was held in, so I give Aiko instructions as we drive. We don't try to skirt around the city, time is of the essence, and we aren't really scared of people from the Board trying to stop a speeding van. I'm sure they have better things to worry about at the moment.

We pull into an alley across from the building, a metal door hanging open. It looks like the building is not in great shape from the outside, brick crumbling and debris littering the area around the building. The gray foundation is stained brown from repeated splatters of dirt. It must be one of the last taints on the perfect modern image that Boston embodies nowadays. We all climb out of the van, the twins electing to stay back with Tyler and keep a lookout. The rest of us head into the building. Aria leads the way, although a wave of PTSD is visibly washing over her. Our boots splash against the half an inch of water that covers the ground, and more drips onto our head from the low-hanging pipes. The darkness engulfs us as we roam down the hallway. A smell of rust radiates from the walls. The hallway quickly opens up into a tall open space, a balcony lining the edge. I immediately look at the electric fence lining the perimeter of the space, standing on what must be the grossest carpet I have ever seen, the combination of mustiness and scratchy material not doing it any favors.

"They are gone," Aria points out.

"That means they must have recovered enough to be let out," Za adds, coming up from behind me. I wander off and into the enclosure, which is accessible through a missing panel in the fence. I look up, sunlight peaking in through the cracks between the window and the boards trying to block it.

"What now?" Aiko asks. They all look at me. I guess my leadership position still holds, but I just direct everyone's attention to Za.

"Why don't we ask the inside man?" Za frowns at me but then crouches down, his furrowed brows deep in contemplation.

"The only way this virus spreads is if it can get out of the city. If the virus never leaves the city, the likelihood of it reaching all of the people Nox wants it to reach goes way down." Idri nods along.

"So, how do we do that?" Idri finally asks.

"There is only one way to do that. We need to…." Aiko starts.

"Block every exit point in the city," I finish.

"But that's nearly impossible. There are countless roads and highways where people can leave, not to mention the airport," Za comments.

"Not nearly as many as there used to be Za," Aria replies. "Since the rebuilding started, the government made it so there were only five or six main exit and entrance points for civilians, just in case they needed to regulate travel for any reason, they wanted it to be easier for them to control. As for the airport, there aren't going to be any flights anytime soon since all of the resource drops happened a couple of days ago."

"But there are still not enough of us to get to the exit and entrances in time. We just don't have the numbers," Za argues.

"You, young one, are forgetting that we have more than fifty migrants waiting to help out in any way they can," Aiko explains.

"Let's go corral the Migrants then," I defiantly say. Invigorated, we all jog out of the building and quickly hop back in the van.

"So, what's the word?" Tyler asks. Aiko starts driving as Aria turns around in her seat to explain to Tyler and the twins.

"Long story short, the soldiers aren't there anymore, so we need to stop all travel out of the city. We are going to get the Migrants for backup."

"Damn." The twins say in unison. Aiko drives back to the base as fast as she can. When we get there, I look back into the van.

"You guys stay here, I'll tell them what to do, and then we will figure out where we will go." I jump out and glide down the ramp. There is an alarm button next to the door trigger, which I hit, a blaring noise echoes through the whole base accompanied by a pulsating red light. The Migrants quickly begin to gather in front of me in the garage. The shock starts to sink in as the numbers keep on growing, people of all ethnicities and ages squeezing in between people to get a better view. The garage fills so much that people have to stand on crates or sit on the cars, the teenagers hanging off whatever they can.

"Hi, all. I know we've never used that alarm, but now is the time. You probably heard by now…." I'm pretty sure word travels in the base pretty fast, and Aria and Tyler are pretty in tune with almost everyone in here, so I'm sure they gave the information out to at least two people to spread. "…but the Nox attack is not a physical war, at least not yet. They have released an extremely contagious virus, and it's our goal not to let that virus spread outside of the city. That means that the five main exits out of the city need to be blocked. That's your job. Can someone tell me what the biggest exit and entrance to the city is?"

"The Zakim bridge," a woman sitting on top of one of the vans says.

"Thank you. Leave the Zakim bridge to us, and you guys split yourselves up and take the others." Aiko told me she has been training all of the Migrants to fight and use weapons, so hopefully, that training is about to pay off.

"Bring weapons and bring food. Anything that you would bring camping, bring that too. The idea is to block off these entrances for as long as we need to address this problem. I believe in you guys, stay safe, and thank you for your dedication. We will be in a better place after this is over, I promise." I wouldn't lie to the Migrants, and I truly believe that we can win this fight. I head back up the ramp and hop into the passenger seat again. Everyone sits up and lean towards me.

"So, how did it go?" Aiko asks.

"We are headed to the Zakim Bridge," I say with a smile. Aiko turns the van around and starts to speed towards the other side of the city, a satisfied grin plastered over her face.

ZA

March 11, 2035

"We are headed to the Zakim bridge," Ivo says, turned around to face us from the passenger seat. I look out the side window to see bunches of migrants flowing out of the base, driving various vehicles. I can't shake off this gut feeling that there will be more waiting for us at the Zakim bridge than we are expecting.

I continue to look out the window throughout the drive. I cringe at every person I see walking outside, knowing that they have every chance of being infected. Today, there is no sun to reflect against the endless rows of modern glass skyscrapers. Instead, the buildings are lavish mirrors for the clouds, creating a scene that transcends reality when driven past quickly. My hands sweat as they nervously grip my legs, and I rest my shiny forehead against the glass. While the twins crack jokes for the enjoyment of Aria and Tyler and the annoyance of Idri, I command my brain to tune them out. The last week has been chaotic, to say the least. I made countless mistakes, not including aiding Nox in his plan, which I now understand as being utterly diabolical. However, if I do my job today, if I am successful in my work today, then that's what I will remember from this week. I have only one thing on my mind; I want to bring Nox down as painfully as possible. The problem is, he's inevitably going to be two steps ahead of us. I stop looking out the window and shift my torso, so it's facing the front of the van. I look to my right, glancing at the flowing brown hair of Aria. She's the key. She's the play that Nox doesn't have in all one hundred of his playbooks. I don't know how, or when, but Aria is going to win us this thing. If she's as strong in her beliefs as I think she is, she will catch Nox off guard for a long enough time for us to strike.

I guess Aiko must have been harnessing the speed of god because we reach the Zakim bridge in only thirty minutes. I frown when I see no civilian cars as we pass through the tunnel leading up to the bridge. That's not normal. There should be plenty of people going back and forth, I'm pretty sure Nox and his team, our team, used everything in their power to make sure the city didn't know they were here. If that was the case, everyone should be proceeding at normal, which includes leaving the city.

"Oh no," Tyler says, who is leaning out of his seat, staring straight ahead through the windshield. Everyone in the back scrambles towards the front to get a better look. I don't move. I just need one glance to know that Nox is here. Not only is Nox here, but everyone is here; what was supposed to be my team, as well as a whole other flock of soldiers. And, just in case that wasn't enough, three massive tanks from Serge's army sit behind them. I'm not sure how long they've been there, but they are standing in perfect formation, all of them staring ahead at us. The gargantuan white arms of the bridge make them look comically small, but no one will be laughing. Aiko spins the van to the left, stopping the van perpendicular to the bridge. Everyone starts to get ready to file out of the van before Ivo stops us.

"Guys. Are we sure we want to do this? We can turn around, gather the proper weapons and strategize. I'm sure they aren't going anywhere. I don't want us to all die out there." Everyone takes a minute to think about it.

"I mean, have you seen those tanks? I don't know about you guys, but I'd rather not be blown to smithereens," Aziz says. Idri starts to shake his head.

"Well, at least that way, in a hundred years, someone can piece back together the legendary twins, like an ancient map," Riz adds, the twins cracking themselves up.

"Will you two shut up," Idri finally says. The twins immediately stop laughing. They both look down to the floor in shame.

"Yeah, we are in," Aziz mutters quietly.

"Anyone else opposed to risking our lives at this very moment?" Ivo asks one last time. "I'll take the silence as a no. Be smart, people. Nobody recklessly attack. Don't let him get in your head." Ivo looks at me as he said it. I return his stare with an affirmed nod. Tyler slides open the van door that's facing away from Nox. Everyone jumps out except for Aria. I look back at her.

"You will know when it's time," I say to her. She nods back before I turn around and catch up to the others who are peeling around the van. I join Ivo in the middle. To my right is Tyler and then Aziz. On Ivo's left is Aiko, Idri, and then Riz. It's quite a team. Nox comes forward to meet us.

"The famed East Coast migrant team. The team that defeated the Board. Temporarily, of course. And, the brothers that saved Europe. I'm getting goosebumps just seeing all of you together." He takes an extra-long second to look at Ivo. "

It's a shame we have to be this way. Why don't you join me?" Riz scoffs at the idea, and Idri punches him in the shoulder. "I don't see why that's ridiculous. We are all here for the same cause. I just want liberation for the

Migrants. That's what you want. Right? Are you really going to stand here and fight me? Because, essentially, that's you protecting and defending those oppressors."

"Your mind games aren't going to work on them, Nox," I say.

"Well, they worked on you, didn't they? We had a pretty good run. None of this would be possible without you." He gestures to the army behind him. I want to punch him so bad, just clock him in his pretty little jaw. He's trying to get in my head, he's always been trying to get in my head.

"The oppressors are the Board. We aren't defending the Board. We are here protecting the millions of civilians you could be affecting. It's not our fault that you can't get it through your thick skull that those are two different groups of people, not one and the same," I say. He shifts his gaze to Tyler.

"I see. That's a shame." He turns around, and slowly walks back, his perfectly tailored black suit lightly fluttering in the breeze. We are about a hundred feet away from the group. As Nox reaches them, he puts up his hand.

"Get down!" Ivo shouts. We all dive to the ground, covering our heads. "Take these!" Ivo tosses everyone these thin bracelets. He pulls him on his right wrist. "Like this!" He shouts as he double taps the side of the bracelet facing out. A shield appears that grows around him into a dome. At the same time, a piece of debris flies towards him, but it just bounces off the shield. He slides me one on the ground, which I put on and activate. We all hold them over our heads as the tanks continue to fire near us.

When I hear they are out of ammo, I deactivate the shield and run towards the onrushing soldiers. I feel the anger I get looking at Nox standing behind the battle scene, watching, turn into overwhelming rage. Two soldiers come towards me. I slide underneath one's legs as they swing with their right arm. I push into his back, and he topples forwards, accidentally tackling the other soldier. Tyler runs over, jumping on top of them and handcuffing their hands together. He winks at me before I spin around and run towards three more guards. Elbowing one in the gut, I twirl horizontally, pushing off both feet into another. The last guard tries to raise his gun, which I flick out of his hands with my foot before grabbing a knife from my vest and stabbing it into his leg. He cries in agony as the other two soldiers try to get up. I'm about to lean down and knock them out, but two shots quickly get fired into them. I spin around to see Idri behind me, lying on the ground with a sniper. I give him a quick nod which he returns. Debris is flying everywhere, and plumes of dust and dirt rise into the air, creating a thin fog. I spot the twins who have their backs together and are surrounded by five guards.

"Idri!" I yell back and point towards the twins. I grab and activate a collapsable rifle hanging from my waist and aim at two of them, taking both of them out with only two shots. By that time, Idri had already sufficiently injured the others. The twins look around in confusion before spotting us and smiling. They fist bump each other before moving on, their enthusiasm contagious.

I spin around to check on the others. Tyler is still ungracefully football tackling his opponents and then knocking them out. Idri is picking out anyone he can to shoot. Aiko is gracefully slicing through bodies with her swords as they continue to make the mistake of congregating together around her. It just makes it easier for her.

Meanwhile, Ivo has a pistol in each hand, blood dripping from his forehead as he takes out each soldier with more and more prowess. Blood leaks down my chin from my lip, and a guard runs towards me. He quickly punches me in the gut, pushing me to the ground and knocking the wind out of me. I try to flip back up onto my feet, but an elbow greets me in my cheek. Pain shoots up my jaw and into my forehead. This must be one of the guys that was supposed to replace my team. I wipe the blood off my chin with the back of my hand and kneel on the ground, one knee barely touching the rough asphalt. The soldier charges towards me again, and I use his momentum to place my hand on his hips, rise into a standing position, and flip him over my head. I quickly spin around and toss a knife into his foot.

"Za!" I hear from Ivo from across the bridge. I look at him, and he points as the three tanks are preparing to fire again. I nod back and start sprinting towards the tanks. They are massive, grey paint smoothly painted on, and three turrets extending out of the center bases. I bound up towards the nearest tank and glide up the side of it. I look at Ivo, who is on top of the tank on the other side. He tosses me a grenade that I pull the pin out of and drop down into the tank, but not before looking down and seeing nobody inside. Great. Now Tirique and Serge have invented robotic tanks. That's just great. I leap and grab onto the side of the other tank. It must feel that I am there before the turret turns down towards me to stop me. I reach to activate my shield, but I don't end up needing to as Ivo dives on top of it, forcing the turret to rotate and shoot towards the sky. A piece of the bridge starts to fall, and Ivo and I jump out of the way as it crushes the tank. The grenades go off, and a blaze of fire licks out at the sky from where the tanks used to be. Ivo nods at me and heads back towards the soldiers who are trying to trap the others.

That's when a soldier hits me to the ground, my back aching from the repeated contact—the soldier pins down my arms.

"Za." A deep methodical voice says. Why is this guy saying my name? I brush his arms off, pushing him away and scrambling backward in a crab walk before standing up and putting my fists up. "Za. Stop. It's me."

"I don't know who you are." I raise a pistol and point it at his chest.

"It's me. John. John Mane."

"I don't believe you." I rush towards him and push him to the ground. I sit on top of him, limiting his movement. "How do you know who John is? Tell me!"

"Because it's me. Please, just listen." His voice is much raspier than I remember John's being. I grab the side of his helmet and pull it off, lower his snood, and slide off his goggles. Staring back at me is the worn down, but unrecognizable, face of John Mane. Blood drips from a cut over his left eyebrow, and the crimson stand out against his dark skin. I back off of him, and he shakes the dirt off his vest before sitting up and leaning against a dismantled turret behind him. I take a seat next to him, in shock.

"I have something very important to tell you," he says, out of breath.

"Why are you here? How are you here?" I quickly ask.

"Please. We don't have much time. Nox will come to find me. Just let me tell you this." He sounds scared, and he is never scared.

"Fine."

"All of this." He gestures to the commotion continuing behind us. "All of this is a distraction."

"What do you mean?"

"Nox already sent assassins to kill every single Board official. He realized that you guys were too smart and too quick to let the virus leave the city, so he called in highly trained soldiers to go find them and kill them." This can't be happening.

"How do you know all this?"

"Six months, I left to go to Europe. To explore a new life. I met Serge and Nox there, and they seemed very suspicious to me. I told them I was a highly trained fighter. They said I could work for them. I've been undercover ever since."

"I...I don't understand."

"You're too late, Za. You may defeat Nox here, but he has accomplished what he wanted to. All of his targets have already been terminated. And, I think he has another secret project already started." He winces and grabs his gut. His hand is stained red with blood.

"What other project? We have to get you out of here and get you some help." I say to him, helping him to his feet as my mind scrambles for answers.

"I don't know what it is. But it cant' be good."

I guide him through the battle and drop him in twenty feet in front of Idri, who scrambles to his feet.

"Uncle!" He rushes towards us.

"I need to talk to Ivo, but take care of him." Idri nods back. I run as fast as I can to Ivo, who has just taken out another soldier.

"I found John."

"Who?"

"John Mane."

"What? Where?" He is just as out of breath as me.

"I dropped him over there with Idri." Ivo leans to the side to take a look.

"Oh my lord."

"Ivo."

"Yeah?"

"John said that Nox has already taken out the Board."

"But how? We haven't let the virus leave the city."

"He said that Nox knew we would try to stop him, so he sent assassins to kill them anyway." Ivo falls into a seated position on the ground.

"Damn."

"He also said Nox is working on another secret project."

CYCLE

"Your joking."

"Ivo. What do we do now?"

"Well, the virus is still out there. We may not be able to save those Board officials, but we can still take care of Nox, not let the virus spread, and find the vaccine." He lets out a sigh of frustration.

"Okay." I look at him for more instruction.

"Just keep fighting."

IVO

March 11, 2035

I get back up to my feet, pain shooting up through my whole body, culminating in a piercing headache. I don't have time to think about how Nox thought that much ahead or how John was here and knew what was going on. All I can do is finish this fight. I scan the battlefield for Nox. I spot him standing and observing the battle, hiding behind his last line of defense. That's it. I'm going straight for the heart of the beast.

"Cover me!" I shout back to everyone. I sprint past the debris of the tanks, peeling off my bulletproof vest and throwing away all of my guns, which are out of ammo anyway. Soldiers from behind me run towards me before crumpling to the ground. That's the cover. Now I just have to focus on the line of soldiers in front of me. Nox only takes a couple of steps back as he sees me coming, not wavering at all. He's not scared. Not one bit. And, that fills me with rage. As I approach the guards, I tap behind my ear, activating my suit. It grows around my body, and I wince as the tight fit squeezes all of my open gashes and bruises. Three soldiers rush towards me, and I generate a knife in either hand, slicing an 'X' into the chest of the first guard before tossing either knife into the torso of the other two. I punch the next soldier in the jaw, who spins off into the ground before trying to get up. I use the momentum of the next one to crash into the one on the floor, knocking each other out. I generate a gun in my right hand, shooting to my right and then to my left, taking out four more soldiers. Before I know it, it's just Nox and I.

Even after all that, Nox still stands, back straight, completely unfazed. I stride up to him, standing within ten feet of him. He just smirks at me.

"You know. I don't think I'm the helpless dictator that you think I am. If you think I was just cowering behind my strong army, then you're sadly mistaken. I simply wanted to enjoy the show, and, boy, your team disposed of my army. It was just the entertainment I was hoping for. I sincerely hope you aren't tired because this is just the beginning of the fight."

He takes off his suit jacket, dropping it on the ground. Underneath is a clean black t-shirt. Sitting on top of the shirt, in the middle of his chest, is a silver circle. He taps it, and a nano-tech suit forms around him. The suit is a shiny reflective silver, and it forms around his whole body, slightly more robust and thick than mine.

"Whatever you can do, I can do better," he says back. I rush towards him, but he just raises his hand at me, slices of his metal suit fly out, piercing my arm. I wince as I pull the shards of metal out of, revealing slits in my suit. I generate a gun in my hand and shoot out at him. He gracefully swivels around my shots before firing more slices of metal at me, which I dodge. I look at my suit, charged back up from all the hits I've taken, and I sprint towards him, punching his chest before he can do anything to stop me. All of the energy stored in my suit pushes him ten yards back, and he rolls onto the ground. He gets up to his feet and then puts his hands together like he's praying.

I look on in horror as massive metal wings fold out from his back. He rises effortlessly into the air. He generates a gun and starts to fire towards me. Time to try my new trick. I slide both of my forearms with the opposite hands. The suit starts to generate small thrusters everywhere on my body. Small flaps unfold, covering every inch of me. I quickly fly into the air and meet him, my body now floating effortlessly. I can't believe it worked. I wish I could see his face right now so I could tell him that whatever he can do, I can do too.

I generate more guns in my hands and start firing them towards him. One hits his shoulder, and he spins out of control for a split second before regaining his balance. He rises high above me and slaps his falcon wings in front of him. A massive charged gust hits me, and I helplessly get battered back into the ground, the rough concrete ripping my suit to shreds. My suit is now in pieces, only small parts of it left on my body. I have burn marks everywhere, and sparks fly from my feet where the turbine has disintegrated.

I glance up and see Nox descend towards me, unchanged in his stature and prowess. I wince as I try to get to my feet to no avail. He holds out his arms and I brace myself. I can see he's about to fire, and I see my life flash before my eyes before I see the back of Aria's head in front of me, her brown hair swirling in the breeze. She is shaking in fear, looking into the eyes of Nox, who still hasn't put down his arms.

"When I say go, go." She whispers over her shoulder to me, even her voice shaking.

"Aria?" He asks, lowering himself to the ground, his hands dropping by his sides. I have no idea what is happening. Nox deactivates his suit, his eyes looking at Aria in fascination.

"You have to stop, Nox." She replies, becoming more certain in her stance. I begin to get to my feet behind her.

"I told you I would do it, Aria. I promised you. Two years ago, I told you I would come back and save the Migrants. I'm doing it. This is me doing it." He takes a couple of steps towards Aria, whose shoulders tense up.

"This is not right, Nox. You can't hurt so many people; this is not how it's supposed to be. You have to stop. Please, stop."

"You can't be serious? Why aren't you happy? I'm doing what both of us always wanted. You told me that it wasn't possible. I'm showing you that it is. I did it. I have saved the Migrants. They just need a real leader, that can be me. It can be you too. We can lead together."

"Tell me where the vaccine is, Nox."

"You're seriously going to stand by them? By him?" He points at me. "You're really going to betray your own brother?" Tears are starting to flow down his face. I can't believe they are siblings. How did I not know this? Did anyone know this?

"You're the one that betrayed me, Nox. You shouldn't have left like that. You abandoned me."

"I said I would come back." He reiterates angrily. "I promised I would come back, and I did. I came back. I have so much power now. No longer are we some weak kids. We can control everything."

"I don't want to lead Nox. That's what you want. Not what I want." She takes a deep breath. "Tell me where the vaccine is, Nox. You have to tell me."

"Tell you or what? You can't do anything. I'm the one with the power. You have nothing." Aria looks behind her shoulder at me. I'm crouching, holding a gun behind my back.

"Go." I sprint around her, diving as I take a shot at the one gap in Nox's suit, the shoulder I hit before. He crumples backward, and I rush on top of him. His suit deactivated from underneath him, and I pin his wrists down to the asphalt.

"Tell me where the vaccine is. I swear to god, tell me, or you will never see daylight again. We are the Migrants. We believe in second chances. I'm sure your sister would love to give you another chance. You get to dictate your future, and that starts right now. Right at this moment. Now tell me where the vaccine is." His cheeks are damp and glossy with tears. His shirt is drenched in sweat, sticking to his body. A pool of blood forms underneath his shoulder. He opens his mouth before hesitating for a minute. I hear Aria's boots crunch against the ground behind me. He looks at her, staring into her eyes.

"It's in the hotel. Where we were staying, in my bedroom," he says weakly.

"How do we know you aren't lying?"

"What do I have to gain at this point?"

"Swear on Mom and Dad's life," Aria demands from behind me. He hesitates and then mutters.

"I swear." He responds.

"Say 'I swear on mom and dad's life.'" Aria repeats.

"I swear on mom and dad's life." He winces again, and I loosen my grip on him. I get up, and Aria goes up to him to care for his shoulder. I run back and find Za, who is looking on from a distance. He walks up to me.

"You are beaten up, man," he says to me, blood flowing down his chin.

"You don't look too good yourself. Nox claims the vaccine is in the hotel where he was staying. I'm assuming you know where that is."

"Yeah. I do." He starts to walk away, weaving around the countless bodies.

"Take Aiko with you." Aiko strides up and hugs me, kissing me on the cheek, before turning back to catch up with Za. They activate their cycles with their rods and start driving back into the city. I walk towards the van, collapsing to the ground, my back leaning against the van. Tyler walks towards me.

"We found this lady trying to make a run for it. She's tied down over there with the others." He points to my right to the side of the bridge.

"That's Skylar." I think if we are missing anyone, but my thoughts are scattered. I think Serge is still in Europe, or at least that's what I'm assuming. Hopefully, Za can confirm that for me later. But, where's Tirique?

"Where is Tirique?" I ask Tyler.

"Is that the tech guy?"

"Yeah."

"I'm not sure, but he isn't here, and we've pretty much rounded up everyone. Maybe he's back in Europe?"

"Can't be. He was the one running the tests on the first initial patients for the virus. Both Aria and Za told me he was here in the United States."

"Ivo. You might want to see this," Aziz comments as he and Riz walk towards me and lean down. Aziz shows me a video on his phone.

"Erling just sent this. Look who they found."

I take the phone and play the video. The video is of a dark room, a fluorescent light bulb hanging on a wire from the ceiling. In the middle is Tirique sitting in a chair. A headset, resembling the crazy mind prison thing they had on me before, sits on top of his face. He has a feeding tube connected to a mouthpiece, and he has locked himself to the feeding contraption. As we get closer, I'm horrified as I see that the headset is welded to his head somehow. The video pans to a table sitting next to him, zooming in on countless papers scattered everywhere. They look almost like blueprints, some kind of plan for something. Behind the table is a massive whiteboard with a huge web of ideas. There is only one thing connecting all of the papers and the whiteboard: they all say "A New World." This must be the secret project.

Aria is supporting a limping Nox, and they are coming towards us. I make myself get up and walk towards them.

"Nox. What the hell is this New World crap?" He just laughs. He's really out of it, his eyes closed. Aria has wrapped a white bandage around his shoulder, which is quickly turning bright red. I lightly slap his cheek.

"Hey. Nox. Wake up." He moves his head slightly like he's listening. "What is the New World?"

"So, they must have found Tirique. That's a real shame." He coughs. "I thought he was going to have longer than that."

"What is he building?"

"He's building what we all want, of course: A New World. We were tired of trying to save this one. It's pretty much unsalvageable. So we thought we would make a new one."

"How do we get in there?"

"Well. He's building it now. He has enough food in that tube for about a day, just enough time for him to finish. Then he will die. Glasses will suddenly appear on everyone's doorsteps."

"Why would he do that? Why would he sacrifice his life like that?"

"Oh. He's not actually dying. He will live forever in the new world, just as I will."

"But, you are alive."

"Not for long. I gave myself a poison that will kill me in a few seconds" He starts to furiously cough and slowly starts to lose consciousness. Aria is just looking on in horror, fresh tears pooling on the ground. Nox is only able to muster a few more words before he falls to the ground.

"Let the new society begin."

CYCLE

DIMENSION

FIND THE CHANGE

AUDEEP CARIENS

CYCLE

PROLOGUE

The Revolt left the United States torn apart. The Board had been completely decimated by the efforts of Nox and the Migrants were finally free. In the year following Nox's death, the Wolf brothers helped setup a new government, one that resembled life from ten years ago. With Nox gone, there was no one ruling Europe and the brothers returned to once again stabilize life in the opposite continent. Ivo and Za decided to step back, realizing that the world would hopefully need no more helping and they, for once, could live lives without crime fighting and a threat of global collapse. As Za and Ivo faded into the background, so did the rest of our migrant team. The twins found rich careers for themselves and Idri and Aiko disappeared. Only Tyler and Aria remained to lead.

But, the world wasn't done changing. Tirique did end up finishing his work, an alternate virtual world, AltD, before he died. AltD glasses, devices used to enter the virtual world, were dropped all over the planet. People everywhere, from the United States to Asia, became addicted and enveloped by their virtual lives. They were given a fresh start they didn't know they needed.

So, now, there is a new split. It's no longer Europe versus the United States, or the Board versus the Migrants. Now, it's AltD versus Reality.

KAI

November 1, 2040

My feet slam on the dirt with a methodical beat as I pant. The portal grows larger in the distance and shouts come from behind me as Bots chase me. Tall trees extend high into the air around me, a mirage of green and brown. The spring breeze runs through my legs and whips past my ears.

I run as hard as I can, my muscles seizing and my joints locking up. The portal and its black void are only two hundred meters away now. Glancing behind my shoulder, the Bots don't seem to be tiring at all, their white uniforms flitting through the foliage. Just a bit farther. I dive through the portal. A Bot's hand grabs onto my ankle but gets phased out when I fall through the portal. I crash against an uneven street, now only illuminated by moonlight and flickering street lamps.

That was close. I'm going to have to remember I'm on the watchlist before I go back in tomorrow, even if it's just for a day. I have no idea why I tried to steal four creator bricks at once but they were sitting right there. I get up, an old drunk guy staring at me from across the street. Brushing the dirt off my legs, I walk down the road. That's the problem with portals, quick getaways are challenging, and I dirty up all my Reality clothes. I should just start doing what everyone else does. They spend their days in AltD using their glasses and then go through the portals at night if they wanna sleep in AltD.

The buildings still have massive billboards angled down into the streets advertising for the Alternate Dimension. I think it's funny to think of a time when not everyone spent their days in AltD, when the streets weren't literally trash heaps. Litter now covers the streets, becoming a feature of the city. The street cleaners are too addicted to their new virtual lives to care about their job back in Reality. It wasn't too long ago when I was a kid roaming around the sparkling streets of Boston, the entire skyline filled with streamlined glass buildings. Now, just like the rest of the country, the city looks forgotten, depressing, and barren.

I rummage through the pockets of my sleek gray joggers, praying that my glasses aren't smashed to pieces as I keep walking down the street. I find them at the Bottom of my right pocket and anxiously slide them out, letting out a sigh of relief when I see no scratches. That's just straight luck. I love to see it. My glasses are a couple of years old now, not the fancy new ones that tons of companies have launched, but they still do the trick. I slide the sleek metal frames onto my face, and press the button on the right side. The right side triggers the older augmented Reality that started in the HUB. The left side sends you into AltD. Once the smart designer people could reverse engineer Tirique's original glasses, they started coming out with their own. I'm wearing a pair made by this guy called Riz.

As soon as I turn on the glasses, visuals pop up all around me. I swipe most of them away, especially the idiotic ads of businesses that don't even exist anymore. The only reason I turn my glasses on in the first place is for alerts and ghosts. When something really crazy or exciting happens in AltD, an alert pops up in that exact location in Reality. It's good to know for me because if an alert occurs around here in Boston, it means most people will head to Boston in AltD, so the city would be pretty empty. That's when I can go steal stuff.

I just have to watch out for ghosts. For the people that were super high up with Tirique, they can trigger their ghost. That basically means that when they go into AltD, they can see what's going on in Reality around them. It wasn't too bad until those people realized they could climb up to a roof and then enter AltD, meaning, when they checked up on Reality with their ghost, they could see a larger part of the city. My glasses start to pulse when I'm near a ghost, and I can look around and find them before I do something stupid while they could be looking.

Fortunately, I don't get any alerts or pulses as I weave through the dirty city streets. Because of all the visual ads, Boston starts to look like the HUB with identical glass buildings, so I turn directions back on. White arrows lay over the ground, dictating my turns towards home. It takes five minutes for me to get to the familiar pile of black trash bags stacked up in front of the heavy revolving doors of new a modern office building. I found it a few months ago and quickly realized that whoever worked here before wasn't exactly engaged with Reality anymore. I took it upon myself to slowly gather furniture and assemble a makeshift home on the fifth floor.

I stumble over the trash bags and push the spinning glass doors into the building in one smooth motion. Glossy black tiles cover the ground, still looking like it was only cleaned yesterday. A white reception desk in the shape of a semi-circle sits in the center of a big wooden backsplash wall. There are elevators to either side of the wall, but I take a sharp left, and I take off my glasses as I push through the silver emergency staircase door. I'm sure the elevators are working, but I never use them in case it notifies someone. I'm not really sure how any of that works, but I like to

DIMENSION

play it safe in Reality. It's kinda like I think being more careful and measured in Reality offsets how crazy and risky I am in AltD.

I climb up the five flights of stairs and walk into an empty office space. I have pushed all of the desks and chairs against the walls and into the corners. The space is warmly lit by a few mismatched lamps on the perimeter of a living area. A dark wooden kitchen table that was a pain to disassemble and assemble is next to a black couch. A few mattresses sit on the ground around the living room area. There are also a few beanbags scattered where two of my friends currently reside. They inevitably have their glasses on along with immersion headphones. Suddenly they start screaming at each other.

"God damnit, Azpi! Get out of the way," Kova yells from across the house, if you can call it a house.

"Will you just give me a minute!" Azpi yells back. They are obviously in it together, wherever they are.

"Shut up, you two!" I yell at Both of them, neither of them hearing me through their headphones. I'm about to pull off their glasses, but, realizing they might be in the middle of something important, I decide against it and instead sit at the kitchen table. A family-size bag of potato chips lies, half-finished, on the table, and I drag it over as I put my glasses back on. I wriggle around in the wooden chair, the worn-down slats digging uncomfortably into my back. I stand up and then sit back down again. It's crucial for me, as it is for most people, that I am comfortable before I enter AltD. Once I am adequately settled, I take one more deep breath and then press the button on the left side of my glasses.

The world around me starts to fade away, the table dematerializing first, followed by the other chairs near it. Before I know it, a new atmosphere is forming around me. For a split second, I can see the pixels magnetizing to each other, AltD looking like a two-dimensional facade before the three-dimensionality surrounds me once again. It took me a long time to get used to the 'Formulation' as they call it. The first time I did it, it made me feel like I was floating and not in a good way. Of course, I wasn't helping the process by not sitting down in the beginning. I quickly found out that Formulation should only be done sitting down, that's for going into AltD and coming out.

I wake up in AltD, where I had exited the last time I used my glasses. That's the only counter-intuitive part of entering and exiting it. You would think that you would appear in AltD in the parallel location that you entered from Reality, but that's not how it works. Instead, you enter back in AltD wherever you left off. In this case, I re-enter back into the same dark dungeon where I always leave from. I stand up, the hard metal chair only needing ten seconds to make me uncomfortable. Bricks surround me in the small lonely room. The glossy black paint is starting to chip away, revealing the rose-red brick underneath. The floor is hard concrete, gray and bare. A spiral gold staircase stands five feet in front of me, beckoning me up and into the much more lively AltD.

This has been my spot for the last year or so. It's located near the edge of ultra modern and exciting London, underneath an old castle estate. I'm not really sure if anybody in AltD has claimed this estate yet, but I only access this dungeon part from the secret outside entrance. I get up and begin my walk up the spiral staircase, sliding my hand on the round railing. The staircase is narrow, and a circular hatch separates me from the top of the staircase and the back of the castle estate. I unlock the hatch, swing it over and emerge into the open air. Skyscrapers surround me, skimming the clouds and making the archaic architecture of the castle look even more out of place. I walk around to the front of the building, where a row of old hedges and a medieval fence lines the perimeter of the estate. The grass is brown and rough. I stride over it and squeeze myself through the gaps in the fence. The road is busy. People are walking around, some in lavish clothing that they could never imagine owning in Reality and some in their normal garments, too lazy or too frugal to obtain new outfits.

Over the last few days, I've been on a mission to find some creator cubes. Creator cubes are the only ways to access and change how certain parts of AltD look. Some of the buildings in AltD are different than they are in Reality because someone got a creator cube and sat for hours and hours in AltD, re-coding and re-designing the buildings. It's extremely tedious, but even changing little things can give you an edge in the hierarchy. Tirique hid cubes around AltD and waited for people to find them. Those people that have them now are very special. A couple of years back, gangs started to appear with the sole purpose of destroying creator cubes because they didn't believe in the manipulation of AltD. I keep prowling around, trying to find the cubes and steal them somehow. It's my dream to one day build a luxurious first-class life for myself here.

I'm about to turn right and head down the road when a banner starts to circle around the skyscraper in front of me. It's a wanted list. There are Bots in AltD that Tirique programmed to be as much of a law enforcement force as possible. They look like humans, except they are all white and have no face. The wanted list is a way for the Bots to get some help tracking down people that they say are criminals in AltD. Some people are full-time bounty hunters, happy to spend their time tracking down criminals and receiving the small prizes that they get for turning them in. I take a quick look at the faces that are displayed on the banner just in case I happen to see one of them around. Then my heart drops into my stomach. The last face on the banner is mine. A question mark is displayed over the name and other information section below it, but it's me—my face. I immediately turn around, sliding back through the estate fence, and crouch down behind a hedge.

I knew that I had tried to steal creator cubes earlier today, but I didn't think they were even real, and I definitely didn't think they had seen my face or been around me long enough to ID me. Bots can only gather your identity and information if they are within ten feet of you for more than ninety seconds. Otherwise, there is no way they can find you in the database. Thank god the AltD database doesn't connect to any of your information in Reality. This is not good.

I carefully run back towards the secret dungeon door, covered in a layer of moss and grass. I swing it open and jump down onto the stairs, flipping the door back on my way down. I quickly reorient myself back in the chair and press the button on the left of my glasses. Taking off my glasses, I take a deep breath, resting my hands on the familiar wooden table. Kova and Azpi are still engaged in AltD. I quickly realize that I won't be able to go into AltD as an innocent man until I get this all sorted out.

I think my alternate life is suddenly becoming a true adventure.

T I M O

November 1, 2040

I pull my hood up after I feel a couple of raindrops touchdown on my dirty blonde hair. I only get to take a few more steps on the dry sidewalk before torrential rain starts to weigh down my brown leather backpack. I zip up my waterproof jacket, shivering as a drop of cold rain drips down my neck. As if that wasn't enough, high-speed winds lash at me, almost horizontal. The tall black skyscrapers, most now covered in billboards, do very little to dampen the effects of the weather.

It's early in the morning, the hazy sun barely visible through thick fog. I tighten my muscles to generate heat as I continue walking along the highway. I wave off a few taxis. I can't bring myself to take a taxi. They always make me feel awkward. I keep my head down so the wind and rain don't hit my face full force, staring at the perfectly clean sidewalk like it was made yesterday. The only reminders that Paris was once called the HUB are the countless identical black skyscrapers contributing to everyone's persistent sense that they are lost. They even rebuilt the Eiffel Tower, now a gorgeous and striking glass sculpture. The newer development here is all quite new. Europe only started developing this area a few months ago because they wanted a place for the government to be. I suppose you could call it the government hub now. They worked fast and more and more people came to live and work here. Or should I say work to live. Everyone that lives here in Paris works for some facet of the government.

I spot the government building for technology development a few hundred feet away and scurry to the revolving glass doors as quickly as possible. Two massive diagonal staircases start on either side and cross each other in the middle before leading to opposite sides of the second floor. The floor is a LED screen underneath glass, always displaying important information for the day. Because it's first thing in the morning, it just displays the date. I walk over to the "Y" on Tuesday as I make my way towards the staircase on the right. I climb up the stairs and then walk around the circular ledge. A massive metal and glass door with a tall vertical rod as a handle separates me from the "AltD department." I channel all my strength in my right arm, which pushes open the door before walking in. The familiar scene of frosted glass desks and tables greets me. Only a couple of people are in the office this early, and one of my co-workers walks over, pulls down my hood, and scruffs up my hair.

"How's our little intern doing?" She asks demeaningly.

"Scarred by the weather."

"Yes. I'm sure someone as young as you has never seen rain before," she replies.

"Leave him alone." The only other coworker in the office this morning comes over and shoves the lady away.

"How has your morning been so far, Timo, other than the weather?" Pernille kindly asks as Bethany scoffs and walks away.

"Bad weather days always make me a little more tired than normal," I reply. "How about you?"

DIMENSION

"Yeah, I'm the same way." She smiles at me. I think it's amusing how everyone in the office thinks I'm just this poor intern kid. In Reality, I know the loopholes and backdoors of AltD better than any of them. If I weren't under the age of eighteen, I would be their boss. They definitely don't know that I'm one of the notorious AltD Princes, or at least that's what they call us. The Princes are each very powerful individuals in AltD that no one knows the identity of. I'm essentially royalty in AltD, but I'm stuck as a government intern in Reality.

I mean, that's the real reason I am exhausted. Every day, I spend eight hours working here just to make minimum wage so my life, in Reality, doesn't degrade into shambles. After that, I get into AltD. I spend almost all night in AltD, resulting in an average amount of sleep of two to three hours. Weekends are the only times when I get a normal amount of shut-eye, but even then, I am only getting around nine hours, definitely not enough to compensate for the small amount I get during the week.

I smile back at Pernille before heading to my desk. Of course, they put my workstation in the back corner of the room, which is also the closest, out of all the desks, to the bathrooms. An ultra-wide curved monitor sits on an elegant metal base in the middle of the desk, with a keyboard and mouse sitting in the center. I sit down, swinging my bag around my shoulder and setting it down on the ground under the desk. I take off my dripping raincoat, hanging it on the back of my office chair before sitting down and turning on my computer.

My job is pretty simple, but it takes a whole team of experts in the government to get it done. Basically, we all identify loopholes into and out of AltD. We then take that information and report it back to other areas of the government so they can consider regulation. It's been a new trend starting within the last year. Nations quickly realize that having people too attached to their lives in AltD would result in a decrease in quality of life in Reality. Seeing how all of the European and Asian nations are currently thriving with extremely lively societies, it's hard to imagine anything changing quickly. The majority of people in Europe and Asia love their lives in Reality just as much, if not more than their lives in AltD, and the government would like to keep it that way. So, they have been thinking about ways to regulate the "borders"—the ways in and out of AltD. This way, they can keep track of how much their own people enter AltD, while they also have control over the foreigners entering their jurisdiction.

The funny part is that the government couldn't care less about what is happening in AltD itself. Most government officials are actually so out of touch that many of them barely go into AltD, if ever. I think it's a massive oversight. The way society changes inside of AltD is going to affect more people, including the nation's own citizens, than any border control in Reality is going to. Most of this work ends up being pretty straightforward because portals are usually well known and easy to find. However, people that have creator cubes and know what they are doing can reconfigure the surface function of the portals. In other words, criminals in AltD have been caught manipulating portals so that they lead straight out of another portal in Reality. In other words, they change the function of the portal so that people actually never enter AltD, but they think they have. They proceed with their AltD lives, creating enemies and committing crimes in Reality. It's pretty cruel, and it's not surprising that these criminal gangs almost exclusively do this in privileged areas.

The thing that makes everyone in this office so special is our knowledge of its history. Many of us have, at some point, vigorously studied Tirique Brown's and Nox Yavuz's journey, going all the way back since the original revolution. I have studied Tirique's entire career. Most of the information around the iconic Wolf brothers has been published, and Nox and Tirique certainly had a big part to play in their story. Tirique didn't just duplicate the world and call it AltD. He purposefully made some changes. The biggest thing he did was make sure that the money you have in Reality holds no value in AltD. Essentially, everyone entering AltD for the first time is completely equal, almost as if society started again. Based on Nox's initiatives from five years ago, it seemed like he wanted racial discrimination against migrants to be flipped on its head. Which basically would have meant that white people would have been the oppressed group. For that reason, it's somewhat surprising to see none of those dynamics exist within AltD; I guess Tirique had slightly different plans. Of course, that's all speculation seeing how both of them are dead. Following their death, cults and scholarly groups started to form to hash out the philosophy and stuff behind Nox's ideologies, initially starting forms of activism before being severely outnumbered. It's fair to say that Tirique has more of a lasting legacy than Nox.

As for the Wolf brothers, they are societal legends, akin to any other civil rights activist or famous athlete. They quickly walked away from the public eye a year after stopping Nox and helping to facilitate the vaccine to the virus Nox released. Now, no one knows where they are. There have been conspiracy theories that two of the AltD princes are actually them. I don't believe any of that. I think they are just enjoying peaceful lives away from society in some remote location where no one will ever find them. Either way, their mantles have been handed to the twins, Riz and Aziz. Riz has become a leader in tech, somewhat of a visionary, and Aziz is off-grid but shows up to stop crime around the world in Reality when no one else is doing it.

I roll my shoulders and am about to reopen my research on some sketchy portals in Japan when the door to our office shatters, the open metal frame clattering against the ground. Three very tall soldiers, wearing dark blue military gear, storm in.

"Hands up!" One yells. I immediately stand up, spinning around to face them, and raise my hands in the air—my entire body trembles in fear. Pernille and Bethany are doing the same from their respective sides of the office.

"Which one of you runs this place?"

"Take him! Take him!" Bethany yells. The soldier closest to her raises his rifle and shoots her in one smooth motion.

"I'm going to ask again. Which of you two is the smartest at this stuff?" I look at Pernille, who is staring back at me. Behind the extended wall of her desk is a phone for emergency calls. She is slowly sliding her hand along the glossy glass surface towards it. The soldiers can't see behind her desk from where they are standing. Subtly, I shake my head to tell her to stop. There is no way they don't see it soon. The soldier that just shot Bethany takes a couple of steps towards me.

"You're just a kid. You can't possibly know more than her." He tilts his head towards Pernille, who is to my left.

"Or maybe he's some kind of crazy prodigy." The third soldier adds. "He's scrawny like someone who sits at the computer all day."

"Prodigy....like the Wolf brothers?"

"Yeah. Like the wolf brothers."

"Will you guys shut up." The middle one, obviously the leader, growls. That's when Pernille's hand slips, holding the phone in her hand. She hits the ground, the phone clatters. She frantically tries to army-crawl towards it, but the same soldier who shot Bethany spins around and shoots her in the back before she can make any progress. I shudder, too scared to even process or react.

"I guess it's you then." The soldier who shot Bethany says. He clasps handcuffs around my wrists and guides me over the shattered glass. The

DIMENSION

other two soldiers follow behind us. I look around in fear as I see countless government bodies littering the open lobby floor.

Based on what they've done, I'm guessing they are pretty serious.

K A I

November 2, 2040

Tossing the covers off my sticky body, I roll out of bed. The orange light of the sunrise beams through the gaps in the skyline and floods the floor with ominous vibes. Azpi and Kova are still dead asleep on their respective mattresses. Their glasses, barely off their faces, bounce up and down as they snore. They spend their days in AltD messing around, playing sports or arcade games, doing everything fun that they can't do in Reality, which is a lot. Sometimes I join them, but I like to think I have higher aspirations within AltD.

I take a makeshift shower. The water flows somewhat uncontrollably from a pipe we attached to the water supply, which is surprisingly still running. Tossing on some clothes, grabbing my earbuds, and snagging a protein bar from the dining table, I start my morning with outside time. I put on my 90's rap and slide on my glasses as I step outside, the brisk November air slapping my face as a small amount of snow flurries down onto my face. I take this walk every morning, usually followed by my daily trip into AltD. But I don't think that's going to happen anytime soon, not unless I find a way to not be imprisoned within AltD for the rest of my life. That's what they do if your crime is really bad. Being imprisoned in

DIMENSION

AltD is significantly worse than just being taken in Reality because you are slowly dying in Reality and in AltD, you're literally dying twice.

As I walk a few blocks away from the office, I feel a couple of pulses from my glasses. I immediately duck behind the nearest trash heap and survey the roofs. I see one lady in a chair on her roof, surrounded by a glass enclosure locked from the inside. That's overkill. I keep scanning the buildings until I find the next ghost through the window of a fancy condo building. I slowly crawl away from the trash heap and back into the nearest alley. Then I spin around and quickly walk to the next block over, the pulses starting to fade in intensity. I let out a sigh of relief, my heartbeat starting to rest. Despite the fact I've encountered ghosts countless times, they always spook me out. That's mostly because I have no idea how that whole thing functions, only people that can activate a ghost know how it works.

I slow down and breathe in the dirty Boston air. A few remaining brick buildings line my left side as I venture farther out into the city. The old red brick peaks out from underneath tattered posters from a time AltD left behind. I love coming to this area and examining the old ads. Running my hand along the grooves of the wall, I squint at the fading text, trying to see what old gems I can uncover. I chuckle at the sight of car ads and athletic clinics. Five years ago, people would probably line up to get on the list for a shiny new car or get their kid into a soccer camp. Now they can have almost anything they want in AltD for free. Well, not for free. They are paying with their time. That's how AltD stays alive. If people don't go in there, it can't really exist. What makes AltD so captivating is that it had everybody flooding into the new world in a matter of months. Of course, Nox could never create the society he wanted from scratch, so it became somewhat of a people's world, owned and created by everyone.

KAI

I see a small picture of someone in combat positions hidden underneath a pile of other advertisements. I meticulously peel off the thin pieces of paper to uncover the post behind. It's a smaller than average poster, the only one on black paper with white text. It looks very stealthy, or at least it was in its prime. The top of the poster has modern blocky text that reads "Elite Combat Training," followed by a graphic I've never seen before. Below that, it says "open to everyone," and then there's a name "Flow Az." Strange name. At the very bottom, in abnormally small text, is an address. I don't really recognize the address format. I decide to go check it out. At the very least, I'm hoping I'll find an abandoned training gym where I can mess around and work out. At the very least.

I walk around the city until I find a skateboard on the ground, kind of beat up but usable. I skate around the city, scanning the numbers plastered above the doors. I must have made frantic rounds around the entire city a few times before sitting down on the curb in front of the original poster. Literally, none of the numbers match up with any that exist in this city. I stand back up and examine the poster one more time, carefully peeling it off the wall. Holding it up to the light, a series of faint grey lines appear in a shape that looks like some sort of map. On the other side of the empty street, a city map sits underneath glass on a post made for tourists. I walk over, wiping the dust off the glass and then placing down the poster. Moving it around the map, I finally get a match. The address now matches up with a building on the other side of the city, and I quickly realize that the numbers were coordinates and not addresses.

"Idiot," I mutter to myself. I grab the skateboard and make my way to the other side of the city. Despite the fact that it's mid-afternoon and as good of a day as you can ask for in November, the streets are still barren apart from the kid here and there, probably abandoned by a parent who went into AltD.

DIMENSION

It takes me an hour to get to the other side of the city, which has technically shrunk in size since the Revolt, if that's even what they still call it. I was always just call it the Zakim battle. I find the building the poster directed me to. It must be one of the last old skyscrapers standing because the quality of the glass is lower than usual, and it's only about ten stories high. I swing open the metal door, expecting to be greeted by the usual front-desk situation, or maybe a training gym of some kind, seeing how this is supposed to be an "elite combat training" clinic. Instead, I step into the most bizarre narrow hallway, glass on the sides and wood on the top and bottom. I walk down the hallway, the wood creaking underneath my every step as I walk for what seems like forever. At the end of the hallway, there is a small glass door, frosted over, so I can't see what's on the other side. The phrase "proceed at your own risk" is written on the door in the same font as the poster. At least I know I'm in the right place. Whether being here is a good idea or not is up for debate.

I crouch down on the floor to contemplate what could be on the other side of the door and if I even want to see what's on the other side of the door. I don't understand why a harmless clinic on combat training, probably made for kids and young adults, is so tucked away and hard to get to. Why on earth would the address actually be coordinates? No one used coordinates for navigation unless you were in the military or something, not even ten years ago. Also, the city map has changed so much in the last few years, yet the poster still lined up perfectly, like whoever made it knew that the streets were the only thing that weren't going to change.

I stand up. After all of this, I might just walk into a regular old training gym. I'm too curious not to check it out. Or, at least, that's what I'm going to tell myself. I turn the unconventional-looking handle and swing open the door. In front of me, a glass sphere hovers over a set of tracks. I walk up to it, and the closest quarter of the spherical pod slides around and lets me sit on a white leather armchair, like what I would imagine a first-class airplane seat to be like, but better. Before I can even really figure out what's going on, the sphere closes up again and starts moving very fast along the track. I sense the pod drop-down underground but, after that, I lose all my sense of direction.

I lose track of how long the pod is actually moving. It could be two minutes, could be thirty seconds. Eventually, the pod stops and opens up again, this time on the other side. I climb out, taking a moment to get my balance and recalibrate my body, and face a small frosted glass door, similar to before. Expecting to finally find this fabled training gym, I instead walk onto a bamboo floor and into what looks like someone's house. All three walls are glass. There is an opening on my right, which, I'm assuming, leads to the rest of the house. Everything else is wood, including the bookshelves floating on the glass walls.

At an enormous raw wood table in the middle of the room, with their back to me, sits a guy, his oversized grey hoodie showing through the back of his glass chair.

"It's been a while since someone has used that." His chuckle compliments his calm voice. "I actually forgot it existed. I suppose I should know the ways a complete stranger can enter my house." He still doesn't turn around, but I stay completely still, my legs shaking. Outside the windows, there is a sprawling forest with a view of the ocean in the background. He stands up and walks towards a shelf, putting away his book and pen he had been using to draw. His hoodie sags over his wide black pants—the Japanese style finished off with clean white leather sneakers. After carefully putting down his implements, he turns around. He has light brown skin, round thin black glasses, and messy straight black hair. He can't be older than mid-twenties. He looks familiar, but I can't really put my finger on why.

"Well. I'm not going to give you a grand introduction, and since you're the intruder, not in a bad way, of course, I think you should tell me who you are and how you found yourself into my private home." I meekly nod, try to swallow my anxiety, and open my mouth, readying myself to speak. Despite all of that, I decide against speaking and instead pull the crumpled poster that led me here in the first place out of my pocket. In the act of doing so, my earbuds fall to the floor, and I wince at the small ping of their impact. I quickly unfold the poster to the best of my ability and then hand it to him. He walks a few steps towards me and takes it from my hand, allowing me to squat to the ground and gather my earbuds quickly. I shove them deep into my pocket and stand back up.

"Still waiting." He says as he examines the poster.

"My name is Kai. I just followed that thing." I mutter as I point to the poster.

"Impressive that you could decipher this thing, Kai. It really isn't my best work in the slightest." He places the poster on the table.

"Are you Flow Az?" I ask. I am getting a bit more comfortable with his peaceful demeanor. Or uncomfortable, I can't quite tell. He chuckles again.

"I guess you can say that I am, yes." I do a quick scan of what's on his bookshelf. There are a lot of sketchbooks and then a couple of magazines framed. On the front of one magazine, there is a picture of the Wolf brothers when Time named them the most influential duo of the century. I immediately see the resemblance between Zashil Wolf in the picture and the man standing right in front of me. When I look back up, he's smiling, knowing I made the connection.

"Zashil Wolf?"

KAI

"Please, Za. I can't stand when people say my full name like I'm not just a twenty-three-year-old dude." Flow Az. Oh, my lord. I must have had a look of surprise, because he catches it.

"I know, right. Hence, it's not my best work. I can't believe I used my name backwards as some sort of alias. God, I was something else." He drags out another glass chair from the left side of the table. "Please, have a seat. Riding in that crazy pod can take something out of you. I had my brother reinvent the pods Nox used at his base. He didn't quite get the stability right." He looks at my face which is still displaying confusion.

"I doubt any of what I just said made sense." I walk over and sit in the glass chair, which is oddly comfortable, while Za stays standing, leaning against the table's edge.

"Anyways, what invigorated a young lad like you to do all that research and running around the city, and then to actually open that door that creepily says 'proceed at your own risk.'"

"Well, I didn't really have anything else to do. I'm kinda stuck out of AltD at the moment, and I found the poster and thought it looked interesting"

"Sorry to break it to you, but this is AltD. I am Tirique just in Za's body, and you are now in the custody of the government for all of your crimes." I stand up frantically. "Nah. I'm just kidding. It would've been pretty funny, though." I let out a massive sigh of relief, my heart beating so hard it feels like it'll break through my skin.

"I never really got into AltD stuff, couldn't really mentally prepare myself to enter into a world created by my enemy."

"So what's the deal with the poster? Was there actually a clinic you taught?" I ask once I recollect myself.

"I did actually start a clinic-type situation in that building you entered in Boston. We are in Canada now, by the way. But, it pretty quickly turned into a front for the Migrants. Basically, the Migrants would've known what that poster meant and would've come to me if they really needed anything. Of course, the Migrants were kinda dismantled by Nox and then this whole AltD thing. Wait, you're not a migrant, right?"

"No, no," I respond quietly as I try to contemplate how I got to Canada.

"Ok, good. That would've been awkward." He takes a moment to wait for me to respond, which I don't because I'm in complete shock.

"Well, since you appear to be temporarily out of service, it might be a good time to tell you that whatever your problem is in AltD, I can help you out with that."

TIMO

November 1, 2040

They shove me in a van and, even though the interior of the van has no windows, they tighten a bag around my head. I consider verbally retaliating somehow, but I am already scarred by seeing the piles of government bodies strewn across the floor. If they were able to do that, then they are legitimate enough just to kill me. It's not like I am more special than anyone else. At least, they don't know that I am.

It feels like we are driving for hours, the area of the bag by my mouth is now damp, constantly getting breathed in and touching my tongue. There are times when a wave of claustrophobia washes over me, the rough bag suddenly seeming like a means of transport to hell. Instead of screaming, I just calm myself down, imagining I'm in AltD, and the anxiety soon passes away. Sweat drips down my forehead and neck, my wrists sore from the handcuffs. When the car finally stops, everyone seems to get out and walk away, their voices fading in the distance. I'm not sure if I waited thirty seconds or thirty minutes, but eventually, someone removes the bag, and cool evening air brushes my cheeks.

My estimate of the trip being hours long was correct, and I notice dim moonlight squeezing in between wispy clouds. Two guards are around me,

DIMENSION

obviously not concerned by my ability to escape, loosely gripping my forearms. They guide me around the van and turn to face an ominous building. The building is the spitting image of what I would imagine a villain's lair to look like. Dark marble foundation rises halfway up the first story. Horizontal steel beams then finish off the wall. The doorway is a recessed opening followed by a vault door lock to complete the evil look. It's really something to behold. If I were reading a book about this building, I would probably be excited. However, this building doesn't do anything but instill a deep fear in my bones.

    I shake as two more guards appear out of nowhere just to open the door, each of them putting their two hands on the vault lock. I get dragged along into a dark hallway, the marble continuing onto the floor. I am dropped off into a very well-furnished room. An electric fireplace heats the space, and brown leather couches sit on top of what's now a waxed brown wood floor. The guards remove my handcuffs, usher me to sit, and then leave the room, locking it from the outside. I hesitantly sit on one of two of the couches. There are no windows, unsurprisingly. These people really have an issue with windows. Instead, bookshelves line every wall, covering a very strange red wallpaper. If I were to construct a stereotypical creepy library for some horror film, this would be it.

    I stay seated, tapping the slippery couch's surface with my fingers—now recovered from their shaking episode. I'm about to get up and start exploring when I feel myself begin to get lowered. I frantically look around, hugging my legs to my chest. I watch in astonishment as the entire floor, couches, bookshelves, and fireplace, all slowly lower, revealing the familiar steel and marble infrastructure. What is now a floating platform keeps lowering until it snaps into the floor of an open granite basement, almost like a parking garage.

In an almost identically furnished platform thing is a man in a red velvet suit. Wavy and bright blonde hair is tied in a bun behind his head. Hearing the sound of my platform click into place, he stands up and turns around, putting his arms out in delight.

"Ahhh...finally. I didn't know how much longer I was going to have to sit here. It's really not comfortable breathing in this musty air for more than ten minutes." He looks at me and smiles, obviously expecting me to laugh. I return his gaze with a meek grin.

"I mean, I'm kidding. I grew up breathing in much worse, highly polluted air. Not that you would understand..." He looks down at a piece of paper he has in his hand.

"...Timo. You have had a relatively easy go at it. Growing up in Europe is quite the privilege, not that you would recognize that or know what anything else could possibly feel like."

"Well. I'm not incompetent," I argue back. "Who are you anyway? How do you know who I am, and why did you take me? I'm just an office worker."

"Agree to disagree. My name is Tyler. I know who you are because you work for the government. I don't need to hack into any database to find your profile. It's all public." He strides over to me and hands me the partially crumpled piece of paper. I take a look and see pretty much all of my information laid out. I kinda recall signing a waiver for this. If I did, I regret it now.

"As for why you. It wasn't exactly like we had much of a choice. Trust me. We wanted one or two of the more experienced workers but, as things unfolded, we were stuck with you in the end."

"Ok. Tyler. Why would you want any of us in the first place?" I feel strange in the presence of this man. The fear I had before has started to fade but still exists under my skin. I'm starting to feel comfortable around him, which just makes me anxious because that's definitely what he wants.

"As you probably saw earlier today, I really don't like the government. You could say I've had a bad experience. Despite me being on the opposing side of Nox and Tirique during the war, I actually have grown to love AltD. The problem is, the government and people like you are dedicating time and effort to limit the freedom of AltD. In essence, I believe that AltD should stay as free as ever and be the haven where everyone starts in the same socio-economic class—no disparities of wealth or anything else. I did a little campaigning and found quite a few people that felt the same way. We are a movement."

I've heard of people trying to code in more and more loopholes as well as fight people that try to close them, like us. However, I didn't know that all of the attacks were tied together. If this quote-on-quote movement is as big as Tyler is saying, the government definitely isn't ready. I mean, these guys just walked in and got what they wanted in the middle of a government hub with barely a scratch.

"What do you want from me?" I hesitantly ask.

"You know how the government keeps patching the holes. So you're going to show us how that is done, and we will stop that work. Then we will see how useful you are after that. I don't want to hurt you, but you've inadvertently become part of the movement. Who knows, maybe by the end, I will have persuaded you to join us." I don't think I'll ever join Tyler. The people that don't abide by the government are criminals. The only reason we are regulating travel to AltD is that we don't want chaos to break out in Reality. We can't just have Europe cease to exist because everyone flees to AltD for the rest of their lives.

"That will never work. There are too many of us government workers doing this stuff around the world for you to stop them."

"Don't worry. You will help us out with that." He gives me one last grin before spinning around on his heel and walking away from me, his perfectly fitted suit barely wavering as he walks away. He takes a seat again, with his back to me, and his platform rises up, eventually disappearing like it was never there. I slide back in my chair, shutting my eyes to think. I'm going to have to be here for a while; I might as well make peace with that.

KAI

November 2, 2040

"What do you mean you can help me?" Za doesn't respond and starts quickly striding down the hallway I had noticed before.

"As you can imagine, I know some people." We walk into another space surrounded by windows and sunlight. This time, the light illuminates an office space, looking pretty similar to the last room. There are two wooden surfaces in an L shape as desks and more bookshelves, populated by various specimens. Za stands awkwardly next to a bookshelf and a few feet away from the desk. I go to stand next to him, but he puts an arm out to stop me.

"You're gonna wanna stay back a little for this." He tips back one of the specimen jars, which triggers a transformation. Chrome metal shutters slide over the windows, and ambient light turns on from the top. The two desks fold in and lower into the ground. In their place, a super long desk rises up from the ground, with steel bars as legs. On the desk is a super-wide monitor and all the tech you could ask for. The bookshelves all flip around, revealing every kind of weapon you could imagine mixed in with the odd musical instrument.

"Ok. Now you can come." We walk, and Za sits down at the black office chair. I realize that the wooden floor is now covered in clean black slate, split up into various rectangles with glossy stripes. "Stomp twice on that square," Za says, pointing at an outlined square a foot ahead of me. I stomp twice on the top of it and then back away. A stool, made up of all ninety-degree angles, rises out of the ground just as everything else did. I am speechless.

"Don't be so surprised by all of this. After all, my brother is the all-knowing inventor wonder kid."

"Makes sense, I guess."

"And speaking of Ivo, he's who I'm calling."

"I thought that the Wolf brothers didn't interact with AltD," Za smirks.

"Don't get me wrong. We don't, really. But, Ivo couldn't help but figure out how Tirique made AltD. It only took him a couple of weeks, but he figured out everything about AltD and how it works."

"I haven't even told you what my problem is."

"Yeah, well, there's no point in telling me. I'd barely understand it."

"So, who am I supposed to tell?"

"The one and only." Za starts typing on the sleek keyboard in front of him, looking up at the center monitor. He seems to open some kind of encrypted messaging system. He types 'you free?' Ivo almost immediately responds, 'of course' to which Za says, 'I have a friend." Ivo says, 'you don't have friends and then says, 'come.' Za looks back at me.

"You up for a field trip?" I excitedly nod.

Za walks back toward the original room and straight towards the bookshelf. He slides the entire wall of bookshelves seamlessly to the right, revealing an opening on the left just big enough for an entrance to a spiral staircase that winds down. Carefully and cautiously following Za down the stairs, we make it down to a garage. In the middle sits a clean Italian sports car, its minimalism appropriately matching Za's house and attire. It's matte silver with white leather seats inside. He opens up the passenger door for me and I sink into the seat, admiring the luxurious interior.

"Who makes this?" I ask.

"The Wolf brothers." He calmly responds. These brothers are something else. The engine rumbles as Za starts the car, and the seemingly unmovable concrete wall slides to the side. We speed out of the garage and down the spiraling road, making our way down the mountain.

We sit in silence for a while. I admire the fantastical landscape—no glass buildings or heaps of consumer trash. Hundred-year-old trees rise up from the uneven ground, bodies of water glisten in the sunlight, and the rawness of everything washes a calmness over me that I haven't felt in a long time. It feels like I'm protected.

"Why did you decide to go off-grid?" I finally ask.

"I think both of us wanted a break. It wasn't our plan to go completely off-grid in any way. But none of us expected AltD to shoot off as it did. After its launch, we tried to shut it down. We quickly realized that Tirique didn't finish and Nox wasn't around to make the final changes. Instead of becoming another segregated world, just with different people on top, AltD became something completely free, as you must know by now. We still didn't like it because it reminded us of Tirique, but we weren't mad it existed. Seeing how everyone at home started to abandon Reality, we took the opportunity to disappear."

"Well. I still remember you."

"You probably don't have too much company, kid."

"What happened to all the migrants?"

"Most of them went on to live their lives. The original crew, Aiko, Idri, Ivo, Tyler, Aria, we all disappeared together. I don't know where anyone else is. I guess Tyler and Aria are the most out there."

"So you guys have no friends, is what I'm hearing."

"I have friends. I see my boyfriend occasionally. But the quiet life suits us, especially Ivo, who was thrown into the spotlight very early. We've both had our fair share of war and fighting."

We sit in silence for another hour.

"How about you? What's your deal?"

"I live with my friends in an abandoned building in Boston." He chuckles.

"Kind of like I did. Parents?"

"I have no idea. My dad was half Japanese, so he always wanted to join the Migrants. My mom was white, and she knew she would never be accepted there. They split up for that reason when I was younger. My mom went to work somewhere and never came back after the Revolt. My dad went to help the migrants on the West Coast. Before I knew it, I was living by myself. My dad would usually come and check on me every couple of weeks. He hasn't shown up for four years now."

"So, you do know."

"Yeah. I guess so." Za smiles.

"I'm sorry you had to go through that. Unfortunately, many kids had to." Za leans back in his seat, his right hand resting on the bottom of the steering wheel and his left slowly tapping his thigh.

"How's Boston looking nowadays?"

"Trashed," I definitively state.

"Would you like to elaborate on that?"

"No, not really. It's just trashed."

"Ok then. Well, I expected it would be, honestly. I'm assuming people are pretty much living in AltD, so I don't see how the city would ever look normal. It's unfortunate because the Board had completely remodeled the city after the Revolution and then the government had done even more remodeling after the Revolt."

"I remember that. I was only like ten. Because I was white-passing, I could walk outside and see all of the construction surrounding me. I don't remember too much of the old Boston, but I think the Board and the government made it a bit too sterile."

"You can say that again." As we are having this conversation, the forest enveloped us and made our way through a valley, weaving between multiple massive mountains.

"You guys are certainly hellbent on not being found," I comment.

"Trust me. We don't need mountains and trees to disappear. But, it doesn't hurt." I look out of the window, the tree trunks blurring past us, creating a green and brown facade.

All of a sudden, Za takes a sharp left turn, heading right into the side of a mountain. Multiple sturdy trees stand valiantly in our way, but Za uses all of the agility of his car to swerve in between them. At first, I thought he was just cutting over to another parallel side road, but Za doesn't slow down as we get closer to the mountain.

"Hey. You good?" I frantically ask. Za doesn't react, so I start waving my hand in front of his face, trying to knock him out of whatever trance he's in.

"Will you stop the waving? I can't see anything."

"Well, that's not going to be an issue if you kill us." In response to that, Za starts to accelerate, even more, looking straight ahead at the dark grey stone of the mountain, the occasional patches of snow helping to define its sharp edges. I pull my hands away instead of moving them to cover myself, not that it would help me if we do end up barreling into the mountain, which looks increasingly more likely.

Za just keeps speeding up the mountain now, only yards away. Then, all of a sudden, and as soon as I think this is an abrupt end to my life, we completely phase through the mountain and into a tunnel. Pairs of glass tubes line the sides of the tunnel, one tube emitting a sterile blue light and the other a rich, warm orange. I sit up in my chair, squirming around to get a look at where we came from. I'm amazed as the entrance to the tunnel looks like a transparent opening, the trees and snow in the same place.

"The mountain you saw is a one-way hologram that Ivo designed. It can cover up any entrance, copying up the surroundings so you can't see in."

"Uh-huh," I reply in disbelief. We continue winding through the tunnel until we reach an abrupt drop. We start flying down the road at a sharp descent until leveling back out and slowing down as we slip into a garage. If I thought this car was impressive, these cars are mind-blowing. Cars of all different types line the garage, at least ten of them. They all only have one thing in common. They are all matte black. Saying that they are stealthy would be an understatement. Za parks the car in one of the last remaining gaps and gets out of the car. I follow suit, letting him guide me up the glass stairs, which are squeaky clean. We climb up into a massive open space, almost as large as the office building at home. I wonder if Azpi and Kova are wondering where I am. Probably not, since I'm usually gone during the day anyway, getting into AltD through a portal.

The ground is made up of massive black wooden planks, not painted and still raw. Light flashes down from the ceiling, which, after looking up, I realize is entirely glass. I see the roots of some trees and the bottom of

DIMENSION

their trunks above me. Patches of brown grass add to the natural feel, and I swiftly understand that we are directly underneath the ground, probably in some remote valley inaccessible by car. The furniture is completely different from Za's house. There is more glass than I thought was physically possible to have in a home. Glass chairs, glass tables, glass counters. What isn't glass is matte black and matches the aesthetic. It's sterile but, at the same time, so modern that I don't mind it. It's like my eyes are seeing something they've never seen before, so any words to describe the space feel unfitting. There is an elegant floating glass staircase going down from the middle of the room. I'm assuming that goes to bathrooms and bedrooms. I look at the walls. There are low bookshelves on most of the perimeter of the room, except for the kitchen. Above them are beautiful exposed lightbulbs. I hope I'm here long enough to see their glow.

"Za, it's great to see you." An Asian woman gets up from the black cloth couch in the far backside. She skips over to Za and gives him a big embrace.

"I see you brought a friend." She nods towards me before reaching out a hand. I shake it.

"This is Kai. His talking doesn't really work sometimes." I frown at Za, who just laughs at my annoyance.

"Hello, Kai. I'm Aiko. It's great to have someone in here that I don't know. We don't really get many guests, and I personally see it as a waste of the space." Aiko. I remember that name from some of the headlines. She's wearing a fitted black pantsuit with a flowing beige overcoat over it.

"Nice to meet you." I finally spurt out, Za still smiling at me, to my chagrin.

"I know you guys must be here for Ivo. I'll be right back." Aiko spins around on her heels and heads halfway down the staircase.

KAI

"They're here!" She yells down. She returns to stand in front of us and returns her attention to Za.

"How'd he find you?" She asks.

"Kids these days, almost as nifty as we were, I swear," he replies.

"Surprised you're not living your virtual life like every other teenager." She says to me.

"Not exactly by choice," I respond. "Although, if Boston hadn't become a trash bin, I would probably spend more time wandering about. Despite the fact that there isn't much stuff to do."

"I guess you're stuck hanging out with us then, aren't you?" She jokes.

"Oh boy. Here comes the menace," Za says, gesturing to Ivo, who is making his way up the stairs.

"Nice to see you too, bro," he replies with a smirk. Ivo is dressed in, unsurprisingly, all black. His perfectly slim black suit pants are fitted, and above them, he wears an oversized long sleeve sweater, the black hex pattern giving off a slight athletic vibe. A silver chain hangs around his neck and compliments a matching chrome ring on his left hand. His hair is long but not overgrown, curving messily around his head. He strides straight up to me, lightly punching Za on his way. He looks me up and down, studying my worn-down cuffed grey jeans and maroon sweatshirt.

"So, how did you figure out the map?" He asks me. In awe of his amazing deductive reasoning, I hesitate to speak again.

"He's a smart one," Za replies for me. "Or at least…I think he is. When he freezes up like this, I question it."

"Trust me, bro. We were worse." Za waves his hands in disagreement.

"I'm Ivo." He puts out his hand as Aiko did. It hits me like a brick wall that I'm in the presence of the Wolf brothers. I nervously shake his hand, cringing as I know my hand is furiously sweating.

"Kai," I say.

DIMENSION

"It's nice to meet you, Kai. So, why did my brother drag you all the way out here? Unless you're just here to hang out, which would be fine with me."

"I would love just to hang out. But, Za brought me here because I have an issue with AltD. He said you could help me fix it."

"Got it. Let me guess. Za said I spent a week studying everything about AltD, and now I'm a hidden master of how AltD works." I chuckle, looking at Za's annoyed grimace.

"Yeah, something like that."

"Za sometimes likes to over-advertise." Aiko jumps back in, who is now making tea in the kitchen.

"Well, am I wrong?" Za asks Ivo.

"Depends what the problem is," Ivo says to Za before turning back to me. "Let's head downstairs." Ivo turns around, and I follow him downstairs. Za starts to follow us.

"Not you," Ivo adds, not even turning around to confirm Za is following us. Za grumbles.

"Hang out with my wife. You haven't seen her in a minute."

"Fine," he reluctantly replies.

I step onto the floating glass staircase. The stairs are completely translucent, and I feel as if I'm floating or falling. We walk down into a dark space, partially lit by the right wall, which is another open space and is another window to the outside. This building must be on a slight hill. The other side has bedrooms and a bathroom. We walk towards the big window where a massive black desk somehow floats out of a triangular leg attached to the right side of the table. We both sit in black office chairs.

"So, what's up?" Ivo asks me.

"I tried to steal a few creator cubes. And now I'm a wanted criminal, even though the Bots took them away from me when I escaped."

"So, you're on the wanted board in AltD, and you don't have any creator cubes to change your appearance to disappear."

"Yes. Exactly."

"Let me see if this works." Ivo presses a button, and a massive computer rises from behind the table. These Wolf brothers just have to be stealthy about everything. He opens up some weird files and types in a long passcode. Once he's in, a bunch of code, that I definitely don't understand, pops up. I stare out the window as Ivo furiously types.

"I'm accessing the code of the Bots. Despite mostly being AI, there is basic code that will let me change who they actually go after. If you're not on their list anymore, then you will naturally be taken off the wanted list. That's how Tirique built it." He does a lot more typing and then two minutes later turns to me, hitting the table in satisfaction.

"Try that." I excitedly pull out my glasses and enter AltD. I appear in my familiar wooden chair and climb up the ladder. I roll myself onto the grass and walk to the fence. Just peeking around the corner, I check the wanted screen. To my disbelief, I'm no longer there. I wait for the list to cycle through a couple more times until I'm sure. Sprinting back to my chair and exiting AltD, I pull off the glasses.

"It worked," I say.

"Good, good." Ivo looks concerned.

"What's wrong?"

"This code is all messed up. This is not how it was five years ago, and it's definitely not how Tirique designed it."

"So, what's wrong with it?"

"I don't know. But from what I can tell, the Bots aren't being controlled by the AI code that Tirique and Nox built. Someone else is controlling the Bots. And if someone else is controlling the Bots."

"…someone else is governing and controlling AltD."

TIMO

November 2, 2040

I wake up on the same couch, very cushioned but almost uncomfortably so. My back is sweaty despite the cool temperature of the open basement, and, sitting up, I'm already bored of staring at the bookshelves. I'm sore from who knows what, probably being tossed around in a van for hours, and my head is in a daze. Out of all of the government AltD coders, it just had to be me, didn't it? My nice new pants are creasing, and my hair is probably all messed up because I didn't shower. I feel dead, both physically and mentally dead. I wait, unsure of what time of day it is, staring out into space, and fantasizing about a warm shower and my cozy Paris home.

Finally, the platform rises again, and the space I'm in returns to an innocent room. A door opens, and two bodyguards look at me.

"Come with us," they say curtly, and I obediently follow. We walk down the dark, ominous hallways and into a massive computer room. I'm greeted once again by the back of Tyler's head, his blonde hair now tumbling over his new attire. This time he wears a more casual black suit, still perfectly shaped to his body and still ten times more professional than I could ever envision myself wearing.

"Good morning, Timo," Tyler says, spinning around in his chair. "I think it's time to get started." Tyler pulls out a chair at the top of the computer room for me, looking down at all the other stations, already filled with people of all ages.

"Who are all these people?" I ask.

"This is your team. Let me explain." Tyler pulls up a chair and sits next to me. "You have two jobs. For now, at least. Let's just say this; until I give you more jobs, you have two jobs. The first is to track all of the hacks and secret entrances to AltD that the government is closing and keep them open. Basically, find a way to hide those from the government. I'm assuming you know how to do that. Yes?"

"I've never done it, but sure," I hesitantly reply. I don't want to seem like a complete expert because I want Tyler to let me go, but hiding these entrances shouldn't be that hard. I'm just going to need a lot of help.

"Great. So your second job is to track where the government is coming from and tell me the location of every government official closing AltD entrances. Got that?" I nod.

"Are you going to kill them?" I ask, immediately regretting it. Tyler winces.

"I don't kill. I just temporarily disable, and no, hopefully, we can round these folks up and get them working just like you are so kindly doing." Tyler stands up.

"Anyways. This entire team is at your disposal. Don't think about doing anything stupid because all twenty of these very capable soldiers aren't going anywhere. Play your cards right, do your jobs, and I might just let you go unfazed." He doesn't wait for me to agree or disagree and instead just walks out of the room and down a hallway. I turn to look at the rest of the room. It's like an auditorium, almost. There is one massive station where I'm sitting with countless computers. Stairs on either side of this platform go down to multiple descending levels, like a staircase, each lined with hundreds of desks. I notice that everyone, about thirty people, are all staring up at me. I almost feel like royalty, which I don't hate. I guess Tyler is trying to make it easy for me to forget that I'm still a prisoner.

"Hello." I address the group. Some of them meekly mutter a greeting, others just wave, and the rest just stare into space. "My name is Timo. Uhhhh...." I have no idea what to say. "I guess we have to get to work." I sit down, shaking my head at myself, and then abruptly stand up again, realizing I didn't actually explain what the work was.

"I'll get back to you on what that work is." I sit down again and get myself into the government AltD system from my station.

There are four bodyguards literally looking over my shoulder from a few feet behind me. I start creating anonymous, untraceable government accounts for the team while thinking about how I can escape or stall. It would be easy for me to program a way to slip into AltD, especially since they didn't take my glasses. However, seeing how they are not afraid of just killing me, leaving my physical body with them would probably not do me any good. I have to find a way to get through an AltD portal. The only way they would take me physically to a portal is if I convinced them I could only keep it open if I went there. That'll be hard to do since everyone knows that portals have been disappearing, meaning that all of them are closable from a remote location. I could just lock its code, meaning that no one can attempt to mess with it unless they can break through my security. That is definitely manageable for some people, but it would at least take them long enough to tell Tyler that something is wrong and we need to go check on it. Once I'm there, I can find a way to alert people about my presence. Not about my actual presence, but about my

AltD presence. If people catch wind of a Prince's public location, then they would flock like birds.

I press enter, sending login info for government accounts to the entire team and instructions on covering up secret portals from the government's radar. I see them all settle in their seats, satisfied that their work has finally arrived and, soon enough, the melodic punching of fingers on different kinds of keyboards fills the room. Meanwhile, I open a similar screen as everyone else's, trying to find the nearest secret portal to where I am. This building doesn't have a tag for a location, so I have no idea where we are. My bet is that we should be within a one hundred-mile radius of Paris. I search and search, going through government files and waiting for new alerts to pop up.

Two hours later, I'm starting to give up. Every area around Paris seems to be clean. It doesn't surprise me. No one would trust a secret portal this close to Paris, essentially the government center of the world. But, finally, something pops up. Deep in the middle of an overgrown forest, there seems to be a portal. The file pops up in my inbox as a security camera alert, meaning it was spotted by security cameras and automatically directed to our office instead of people reporting or something. I'm lightning quick to claim it as my job and then get to work. I first hide the file from the government by moving it onto a secure server I have set up back home. They'll catch onto its absence eventually, and I'll probably lose my job, but I don't think that matters at this point. I then code a lock over it, a twenty-digit alpha-numerical password. This is also easily hackable, but now there are two layers of protection between the portal's code and whoever wants to access it.

It's just dawning on me now that it's sketchy how the government has access to this code. Of course, messing with the entrances to AltD is barely

DIMENSION

scratching the surface. But, nonetheless, it seems odd to me that the government can manipulate things like this. I guess that's what Tyler is arguing. I'm just thinking how different AltD could become if the government could mess with something other than just the portals. I trigger a loud beeping warning from my laptop, which attracts the attention of the guards.

"What's happening?" One asks.

"I think there is something wrong with this portal. You might want to get Tyler." I plead that none of the guards know how this stuff works because that was a pretty lame excuse, and obviously, code from a portal wouldn't trigger a loud beeping noise. To my relief, the guard just nods and walks off to get Tyler. I wait for a couple of minutes before Tyler strides in.

"What's the problem?" I spin around my chair to face him.

"There is a portal right near us that I can't hide from the government like we are doing to the rest. I think it could be locked in some other way by the government. That would make sense because it's so close to the government center in Paris." I try hard not to smile at myself. I can't believe I came up with that on the spot.

"So, what do we do about that?"

"I think it would be a good idea to check it out in person. Often times the government has placed a physical tracker that bypasses the code and keeps it on the government's radar."

"But why wouldn't they just close it if they found it already?" Oh god.

"Uhhhh....they might just want to keep it open for their own use, which obviously means no one else can use it. Isn't that what you're trying to avoid."

"Yes. Exactly that regulation." Tyler frowns, contemplating his next decision. "Would you know what to look for?"

"Yes."

"Then you're coming with us. Go wait in your room. We will leave in five minutes."

I get up and walk as fast as possible to my room, closing the door behind me. I quickly slide my glasses out from beneath my pillow and enter AltD. I appear in my New York City high-rise apartment, a massive mansion looking out on the entire lively city. I'm sitting on one of my three white couches, which surround a gold coffee table. I walk up and through my modern living room, hints of gold everywhere, complimenting the white furniture and white walls. Expensive AltD fine art hangs in on my walls, along with various displays of objects. This is the life of a Prince.

I walk down the narrow hallway and into a completely black room covered in display cases. The most prominent of which houses three creator cubes. Each cube holds a different purpose, and there are only a few of each kind in all of AltD. They are all matte black and covered in intricate curves. The inside trim of the curves are different colors. The one on the left, which controls time, is laced in chrome red. The middle one, which controls objects, is complemented with gold. And the one on the right, with blue accents, controls the media. Of course, I can't change all of AltD. However, these let me change certain aspects of my own life in AltD and sometimes what others see. For instance, the time cube lets me go back up to thirty seconds of my life in AltD. I don't think that the Prince's know the full extent of what the cubes are capable of.

I pick up the right cube, gripping each corner with a finger. I then push in opposite directions, and the cube starts to open. A small projector is revealed, and I set the cube down on the big glass display case in the middle of the room. The cube projects a keyboard and screen floating in the air. I start typing, knowing I need to get back to Reality before Tyler shows up. I furiously type an anonymous announcement to show up on all the billboards and digital newspapers in AltD. It reads: 'Prince Odoi will be at the Paris entrance soon. Wearing a black suit with blonde hair." I send it and rush back to my couch, reaching to press the button and returning to Reality. I take off my glasses, shoving them in my pocket and turning around. To my horror, the door is already open, but no one is there. Tyler appears and looks at me.

"Ready to go?" I nod, confused. Whoever opened the door saw me with my glasses. But they also didn't care. This means someone that Tyler trusts isn't exactly on his side. I follow Tyler down the hallway and towards a van. I begin to climb into the front seat but Tyler stops me.

"You may be starting to prove your worth. But, that doesn't mean you're my partner. Get in the back and just be grateful I'm not cuffing you and putting a bag over your head." I solemnly head into the back and join four bodyguards sitting on the hard plastic seats.

My poor sense of direction means I have no idea where we are headed. It takes about thirty minutes to get there, though, which means I was right about our approximate location. We pull to a halt, and the bodyguards put cuffs over me, inevitably. I hobble out of the van, the bodyguards flanking me.

"What are we looking for?" Tyler asks, coming around the van and towards the portal. The van is parked narrowly between trees. Two massive trees sit about four feet ahead of us. The air seems to waver in between the trees indicating the portal, and Tyler walks up to the gap. He waves his hand in between them, his forearm disappearing. It's definitely here.

"We are looking for some kind of module somewhere along the perimeter of the portal," I say, at this point, making things up as I go along. Tyler looks at the bodyguards.

"What are you waiting for... let's get looking." The bodyguards look at me, then back at Tyler, then back at me. I shrug, and they walk over to the portal, searching the trees for whatever they think a module would like.

When I'm certain that no one is looking at me, I book it. I sprint as fast as I can towards the portal. Two guards try to step in front of me, but I just roll through them, dragging them with me into AltD. My appearance changes as I step through, changing from a government uniform to suit pants and a silk blue shirt. I hear Tyler shout from the other side.

"Follow him!" Getting up, I see a massive crowd of at least one hundred people eagerly waiting for a few paces away from the portal. Just as I had hoped, as Tyler walks through the portal, they sprint towards him, hoping to get a touch of him, an autograph, or a picture. In the midst of the chaos, I pull a cap off someone's head and pull it over my messy hair. Tyler is yelling, and I look behind my shoulder to see him retreat out of the portal.

I walk ahead, navigating through the forest until I see the familiar AltD Paris in the distance. My plan worked. Now, I just need to find a way to warn the government and make sure that Tyler's people don't continue to use the government accounts I gave them.

When I get into Paris, I rummage around in my pockets to find my glasses and feel a piece of paper. I pull it out and unfold it. The yellow edges are worn down. Written in oddly neat, all capitalized black letters in the middle of the paper is a message. No one signed it. All it says is, "Tyler isn't the real enemy. The real enemy is closer than you think but harder to find."

KAI

November 2, 2040

"What are we gonna do about this?" I ask Ivo as we walk back upstairs.

"We?"

"Yeah, we."

"Listen, Kai. Look around. AltD is your world, not mine."

"But you can't just let this happen. You have to have some endearment for the freedoms of AltD." We make it up the stairs and walk towards the couch where Za and Aiko are sitting.

"Of course I do. But I told myself I'd never get back into the thick of it. This would be the thick of it." Ivo plops himself next to Aiko while Za looks up at me.

"Did it work?"

"Yeah. I'm good now."

"That's great." He turns around and looks at Ivo. "Why do you look so serious?" I look at Ivo, who is staring at the ground, thinking.

"He does this often." Aiko tries to reassure me as she catches my gaze. Ivo doesn't respond, so I do.

"Ivo found something in the code of the AltD Bots that shows that someone could be controlling the Bots in AltD that's not just the algorithm written by Tirique."

"I literally only understood the last part you said," Aiko says. "In case you haven't noticed, I don't know much about AltD," she adds, looking at me.

"None of us do." Za chimes in.

"Care to enlighten us, Kai?" Aiko asks me. "A two minute crash course would be much appreciated."

"I'll try my best. How much do you know?" I ask.

"About what?" Aiko asks.

"About AltD."

"I know the origin story because I pretty much lived it with these fellas." She makes a sweeping gesture towards the brothers. "I know that AltD is so attractive to so many people because of its freedoms. That it's a reflection of what society could've been, and that's it's an ungoverned replica of our world, untouched in the way we've polluted it. In the eyes of Tirique and Nox, of course."

"Ungoverned except for the Bots."

"The what?"

"The Bots are basically the police of the AltD world. Tirique designed an AI algorithm that controls Bots all across AltD to help somewhat keep the peace. That is, no extreme violence, no stealing, no breaking basic rules. Any of these offenses would result in the Bots taking action. Of course, just like any police system, people run from the Bots, attacks the Bots, and so forth. But, if the Bots, and specifically their algorithm, identity a threat, they put it on the wanted board. The wanted board is public to everyone in AltD and rewards those who successfully neutralize a threat. That, essentially, is the law and the one function of governance that AltD has."

"Ok. So when you said that Ivo found something in the Bots' code, you were saying that someone was able to mess with the algorithm."

"Yes. Exactly."

"Isn't that supposed to be impossible?" Za asks.

"Theoretically, yes."

"So then?" Aiko asks.

"Well, we don't know who is doing it. The government in Europe has been getting more and more access to the code somehow. No one really knows how they are doing it."

"So you think the government is controlling the Bots?"

"I hope not." I slowly answer. As if on cue, all of us turn towards Ivo, who is still staring at the ground in concentration. Aiko puts her hand on Ivo's back.

"It always has to be the government, doesn't it." He mutters, not looking up. Za and Aiko both start zone out, probably remembering times that I will never know about.

"What do we do?" Za asks. I expect Ivo to have the same blunt answer when I asked the same question two minutes earlier, and I'm about to say just that, but Ivo responds differently.

"I don't think I'm going to be able to just sit here while the government messes up society again." I guess this is what happens in the mind of Ivo Wolf, a constant urge to do something right, to fight. Aiko nods along with what Ivo says and then looks up at me.

"Where do we start?" She asks me. I'm taken aback, and a look of confusion takes over my face, it's not the first time that has happened today.

"I don't think I'm the one to be asking."

"We go straight into the belly of the beast," Ivo says. He sits up, suddenly invigorated, like he was plotting a plan the entire time.

"This is how we are going to do this. Kai knows AltD better than all of us. At the very least, he's the only one that knows what it's like to be and live inside of AltD. So Za and Kai are our frontline guys. You both are going to find the fastest way to Europe and run some kind of stealth mission to gather information."

"What about you?" I ask Ivo.

"I need some time."

"You see, he's old now. He needs at least two days to find the right attire." Za jokes with me, trying to get a reaction out of Ivo.

"No. I need to find some friends."

TIMO

November 3, 2040

I spend the night in a hotel in AltD. Obviously, I didn't actually sleep. I'm almost too tired to sleep. I'm too scared I wouldn't wake up. I get off the soft white bed and look out the window. Paris in AltD is what I would imagine Paris to be before the HUB was built. Since Paris went through the most transformations over the last ten years out of all the major cities in the world, I'm not sure what time period Tirique tried to go for. Either way, the city is bustling. People with all different kinds of clothes and appearances are wandering around the streets. There are storefronts, bakeries, and everything in between lining pretty much every block. In the distance, the Eiffel tower basks in the sunlight, the tourist attraction acting as the perfect beacon for AltD Paris.

I turn around and walk out of the hotel doors. The hotels in AltD are pretty much self-sufficient. That is, there are Bots that clean everything up and make sure that the hotel doesn't become a mess. Otherwise, it's free and is basically everything free housing should be like. Of course, everyone and anyone can craft a better life for themselves in AltD than just living in a hotel. In AltD, most people have jobs. Every single job makes the same amount of money. You can either have a job or not have a job. I worked as an IT guy in AltD until I gathered my creator cubes. As a Prince, I pretty much have unlimited funds. The cube that makes objects literally lets me print money. I'm not sure this whole imbalance of power was intentional from Tirique. I'm guessing it wasn't. It doesn't make much of a difference anyway because only a few people in the entire world are Princes. Otherwise, everyone else enjoys a carefree and perfect life here.

I walk out of the hotel, squinting through the sunlight. I need to find a way to get back to the government centers, which means I need to exit back through a portal. But since the only portal around here is the one I came through, it's not going to be easy. Basically, I need to leave Paris, but the farther I go, the farther away from the government centers I will get. If I was in my AltD home, I could just find out where the other portals are, but I think I need to ask someone around here. I walk down the cobblestone street, the smell of fresh bread and coffee surrounding me. I see a kid walking across the street from me, and I approach him.

"Hey, man."

"Hey." He attempts to keep walking, clearly uninterested. I put out my arm to stop him, and he looks at me like I'm insane.

"I just want to know where the nearest portal is."

"It's over there." He points to the portal which I came through and tries to walk past me again. I don't move my arm, stopping him again. I can see he's getting frustrated.

"What's your deal?"

"The next closest."

"Don't you know anything about AltD, bro? There is no other portal near us unless you want to leave France. There are tons of portals in Spain and Germany."

"Why aren't there any near here?"

"Dude. No one, and I mean no one, wants to go anywhere near the government. They are sketchy, messing with AltD portals and everything. And, there was some chaos with some people that looked like the government over by that other portal yesterday. Crazy scenes."

"Oh really? Do you know if those government guys left?"

"There were tons of people there cuz a Prince said he would be around. So, everyone ran over there to see him. Then the government people were there, and then the Prince jumped out of the portal. I think there is still a massive crowd waiting outside the portal for the Prince. I don't know about the government. Some of my friends said that they left, but one guy told me that they are waiting on the other side for something."

"Huh."

"Can I go now? I'm hungry."

"Yeah, yeah. Sorry." I lower my arm, and he swiftly walks past me and straight into a bakery. I can't take the risk of walking out of the portal and straight back into the hands of Tyler, but I also don't want to end up all the way in Spain or Germany. I decide to go through the portal. But I'm going to need some help, like a car—a fast one.

I wander around until I find a car dealership. Lamborghini. Perfect. I walk in, and the car dealers look me up and down. I look at myself, realizing I don't fit the kind of customer they would be expecting. Even though everyone has the same opportunity for money, people still spend it in different ways. Of course, my account is full of money because I'm a Prince, not because I worked and saved up for a supercar.

"Hello, sir. What can I do for you today?" A cars salesman wearing a black pinstriped suit gracefully approaches me, buttoning his jacket.

"I need your fastest car," I reply.

"Do you now? You look a little young for a car like that." I'm about to respond by saying I worked really hard and saved my money or something, but I realize that's not what a snobby rich teenager would say.

"How dare you insult me and my money! If I can pay, I can pay."

"Right. Right. I'm sorry, sir." He starts to back off.

"Now. I'm going to try this again. I need your fastest car."

"Indeed. Right, this way." I follow him through the main garage, Lamborghini's of all different colors and configurations lined up in glorious rows. We walk straight through the general garage, the salesman types in a code of some kind to unlock the door, and we walk into an all-white garage. Just a single-car sits in the middle of the floor, chrome in color with red trim and clean black wheels. Every single angle, chamfer, and luxury detail stands out in the fluorescent light, which is beaming off the white walls.

"Is this the one?" I ask.

"This is the Veneno. The fastest they get. It has…" I cut his car explanation off.

"I'll take it."

"Right now?"

"Right now."

"Well, it will take a few minutes to set up the downpayment and everything. There is maintenance cost, warranty, and we are going to need proof that you'll be able to pay off the car eventually."

"No."

"Sir?"

"I'll pay in full."

"From the way you dress and the way you talk, I know you're of high status, sir. But there is just no chance you have that amount of money."

"Is that a challenge?" I lead him on.

DIMENSION

"No. It's a fact."

"Gimme a second." I reach into my pocket and pull out my glasses, the only object that can be carried through portals. I slide them on and access my virtual payment account. I then find my money, select the amount I think would be appropriate for the car, maybe a little more than that, and I find the account of this dealership. Then I wire the money. As if on cue, the salesman's work phone dings, and he pulls it out. He just looks at me, his jaw dropped, and the car keys dangling innocently in his hand. I snatch them without him giving me any resistance and take a seat in the car. I brush off the steering wheel, pushing the button on the car ceiling for the garage door, and accelerate, pulling out onto a shortened runway and then into the Paris streets.

Since my glasses are on, I also access the object cube. Because the cubes are programmed for me, I can access them remotely from my glasses. There isn't much I can do when I'm not physically around them, but one thing I can do is phase an object. This means that I can make an object exist in Reality through one portal pass. I enable that for this car which is now under my name, so that it doesn't disappear when I exist through the portal.

I drive towards the portal as fast as I can, first cutting perpendicularly across the street and then off-roading into the forest. I try my best to remember where the portal is before using my glasses as navigation. I spot Bots following me in police vehicles through my mirrors, probably for violating every traffic law that exists. But they aren't going to make it very far. They aren't equipped with weapons, and their cars aren't getting anywhere near mine. The plan is to drive through the portal as fast as possible, hopefully avoiding people, or making them jumping out of the way, and then use the car's speed to escape Tyler that waits on the other end. Maybe, if I get lucky, he won't be there at all.

I feel like I'm scraping the ground as I weave in between the trees, the ground in front of me rushing at me with pace. I notice the portal in the distance, marked by the massive crowd of people that stand in front of it, patiently waiting for me never to come. As I get closer and closer, they still don't move, and I start getting nervous. I know I need to keep gaining speed for this to work, but I don't plan on killing anybody's AltD lives. As I get yards away, they notice me not stopping and scramble away, scattering to the edges of the forest. With a grin on my face, I charge ahead and through the portal, popping out into the identical forest in Reality.

I frantically look left, right, and behind me, scanning every direction of the forest to make sure there are no signs of Tyler. And, luckily, there aren't. I make a U-turn and drive at full speed. The once again familiar signs of Paris, this time in Reality, getting closer and closer.

K A I

November 3, 2040

Sunlight brightens the guest room as my eyes slowly open, immediately squinting from the lights. For a second, I forget where I am until I remember that Za and I decided to stay the night at his house before we head out. I rub my eyes and roll out of bed, shedding the robes Za gave me and changing back into my clothes. I take a moment to admire the little touches of the room. Everything is, of course, wood. Sun shines in from three sides of the room, the last wall reserved for an opening to the bathroom. The bed has clean white sheets and pillows. Even the lamps are an elegant bamboo shape, clutching an exposed lightbulb. Everything is thought through. Every single element of the room matches the aesthetic of the house. No wonder Za never wants to leave this house.

I slide open the glass door with bamboo edges and into a complete glass hallway, not unlike the glass in Ivo's house. I walk forward, following the enticing smell of breakfast food. On my right, a massive kitchen is laid out in front of me. There are three island counters, all with glass and granite, and that's not including the wrap-around counter, massive sink, beautifully presented knives, and appliances. It's the kitchen of a professional chef. But instead of an arrogant private chef whipping up some extravagant meal, it's Za, still in his house clothes, which are still oddly stylish, making some omelettes. He smiles when he notices my arrival.

"I was about to wake you up." I look at the clock on the stove, telling me it's only five in the morning.

"But, it's early."

"Well. We have a lot to do, for one. And, for two, I wasn't going to let you eat breakfast cold." I walk over to him. "Don't get too close to the oven; I'm making banana bread."

"It smells really good."

"Us Wolf brothers aren't just robotic fighters. We have hobbies. Please, sit." I take a seat at the hexagonal wooden table. Two opposing sides of the hexagon are elongated to make this very edgy look, and the chairs have sharp and odd angles to compliment them. I admire Za's liveliness for a couple of minutes until he pulls out the banana bread, setting it on a cooling rack in front of me. Then he brings over two perfect omelets as well as a fruit bowl. "It's not anything fancy, but it'll do in a rush."

"Not fancy? This is the fanciest food I've had in who knows how long."

"In that case, I'm glad. It's nice to have someone around actually to eat with me. My boyfriend doesn't come here too often." We both start eating, reaching over each other's arms and sliding food onto our plates.

"What's he like?"

"Who?"

"Your boyfriend."

"Oh. Leon is great. He's an artist from Germany. He still paints and draws. He's a little bit famous, which is why I don't see him too often, especially since most of his shows are in Europe and I'm all the way over here."

"Where did you meet?"

"It was at a celebration for Ivo and I. For all of our quote on quote, 'countless achievements for world peace.' Whatever that means. He was there, as most of the well-known artists, writers, activists, and such were. I remember seeing his art a while ago, so meeting each other was probably fun for both of us."

"How long has it been?"

"I don't know. Maybe three years." We finish eating and clean up. Za goes to get dressed and he comes out in full stealth mode; slim black pants and an elegant, but functional, sweater. Even when gearing up for a fight, he still keeps the vibe.

"Now, let's get some help." He leads me back to the same room, tipping the specimen on the bookshelf to trigger the transformation. The weapons re-appear on the wall, and I stand there, admiring the assortment of artillery.

"Take your pick."

"I'm not sure that's a good idea," I reply.

"Why not?"

"I wouldn't trust me with any of those weapons, and I don't think we have time for you to teach me."

"Fair enough." He starts to equip himself with some guns, knives, and grenades, placing them in a big black duffel bag. "But, if we end up in AltD somehow, you're taking the lead."

"I can work with that," I say, satisfied.

He backs off the wall, the bag slung around his shoulder, and reverts the room back to its normal orientation. We head towards the garage. I start walking towards the car, but Za stops me.

"We aren't going to take my nice car on this." I look around, trying to spot another vehicle, and look back at Za in confusion. Out of his weapon's duffel bag, Za pulls out two small rods.

"We are going to take these." He hands me one. It's heavier than I expected and feels expensive. It's mostly smooth, but slight grooves start on either side of the rod, almost as if they are marking an area to grip.

"This is how you travel light and with some extra stealth." Za puts his duffel bag vertically on his back like a big backpack. He then widens his stance a little, takes a few steps back, and looks at me to make sure I'm watching. He holds the rod out in front of him, with each hand on the area I had noticed before with the grooves. Then he runs. After a few strides, he pulls the rod apart and then dives. Just as I think he's going to painfully belly flop onto the hard concrete of the garage, a clean electric cycle appears beneath him. It's long with big powerful wheels. All of its contents are inside a sleek silver body. Za starts to drive out of the garage before turning around to wait for me.

"I can do this," I mutter to myself, very unsure. I line myself up parallel to Za's approach and then back up a few steps. Then I start running.

"Trust it!" Za yells as I hesitate to make the jump. I position my hands and pull the rod apart, diving as high and quick as I can. I see the floor rushing towards me, and I flinch, getting ready for an impact. But, by the time I look back up, a matte black cycle has appeared beneath me, humming as it drives forward. Relieved, I pull up beside Za. I'm too shocked to really say anything, so Za just nods to me.

"Where are we headed?" I finally ask.

"To the coast."

"Isn't that a long drive?"

DIMENSION

"Not on these. Just follow me." Za speeds out of the garage. His cycle is completely silent as it smoothly drives off into the distance. I follow him, feeling the sheer power of the cycle beneath me. All I can think about is how this all came out of a small rod. We weave through streets, forests, and lakes. I can tell Za knows the quickest way to the coast, and he isn't holding back on the shortcuts. Not to mention we are driving very fast. It's too early in the morning for there to be anybody else on the roads, the early morning light that woke me up now intensifying.

It takes an hour for us to get to the coast. I don't know how far we were away from the coast initially, but it felt like we covered a lot of ground. We find ourselves stopped, the ocean almost at our feet, all of its glory and rampaging waves.

"What now?" I ask. Za hops off his cycle and slides the rod back together, the cycle disappearing in under a second. "And what the hell are these?"

"We just call it the Rod and it depends. Do you like the air or the water more?"

"Uh. Does it matter?"

"Yes. Because I just asked you."

"I guess the water. I haven't spent much time around it, but it seems cool."

"Damn."

"What?"

"I was really hoping you would choose the air."

"Why?"

"Water is too slow, so we were going to take the air regardless. It would've just been cooler."

"I'm so confused."

"I'll show you." Za steps back a few yards, just as he did with the cycle. As he runs towards the drop-off to the ocean, he opens up the Rod again, pushing it together first and then apart this time. He dives forward, and an entire flying vehicle appears, leaving Za hovering in the air. He is enclosed in a silver body, almost like the body of the cycle. Then there are two skinny wings on each side, forming an x of sorts. In each wing, there are many miniature turbines. At the moment, the two lower wings on either side of the pod are pointed parallel to the ground, so Za hovers. This just keeps getting better and better.

I hop off my cycle, backing up just as Za did. I run towards the drop-off to the ocean and do the same compression and pull motion with the Rod. I'm less afraid of dropping onto the earth below me this time, and I patiently wait for the hover thingy to form around me. Before I know it, I'm floating. Za gives me a nod, and I give him a grin. He chuckles before turning and speeding over the ocean. I follow excitedly behind him. We are well on our way to Europe.

TIMO

November 3, 2040

I park near the edge of the city. It wouldn't be surprising in the slightest if Tyler anticipated my move and was waiting in the government center. Or, he might've tried to go to my house, which I wasn't going to go back to anyways. I don't really have a plan. I thought I might as well come back to the government and warn whoever I can, assuming there are people left. Tyler said he doesn't like killing, so I'm hoping he didn't visit any other buildings.

I cautiously walk towards the center, constantly checking behind my back as well as around every corner. There aren't too many cars which freak me out initially until I realize it is the middle of the workday. The day is brisk but not freezing, and luckily, it's not raining. I turn corners quickly and walk at a fast pace, the government center buildings getting larger in the distance. If I did need to get away quickly for any reason, it wouldn't be easy. I parked too far away to get to my car, and I can't just enter AltD amid the anticipated chaos. I guess I'll play it by ear.

After twenty minutes of walking, the landscape around me slowly shifts from the city to the government center. Some people walk from building to building in their uniforms, and I'm thankful that mine is still on. I turn left to check out the tech building, and a swarm of people are against a police barrier. This must be the investigation, but I don't understand why it's just happening now. Tyler invaded two days ago, and there is no way nobody went into the building until then, especially since alarms and security cameras must have reacted to it. I walk up to the barrier and talk to the lady next to me.

"Hi. What happened?"

"You haven't heard?"

"Heard what?"

"The head of technology was killed." Uh oh. I guess Tyler knew exactly what he was doing. He must've come back and killed her because he gave up on me, as some sort of sign.

"Wow."

"I know. And just after the massacring two days ago, it's really horrible." I nod along. "And that's not even the craziest part."

"What?"

"Yeah. After she was brutally killed, they used her blood to write a message on her office wall."

"What did it say?"

"It said 'You can thank Timo for this.'" That's just great. Tyler is trying to frame me for something. Or, he is trying to stall me from telling people about his plan. Either way, he is implicating me to his benefit. I need to talk to someone high up in the government, like the head of another department or something. As I think about what to do, my colleague's gaze slowly dips from my face to the badge that sits so valiantly on top of my government jacket, which, I just noticed, is tattered and stained. It's almost like she doesn't know what to do. She takes a double-take, looking at my authentic government uniform and then at my equally authentic name tag. She starts to back up in fear and then mutters.

"It's him." And then louder.

"It's him." And then she screams.

"It's him! It's Timo!" She turns around and sprints away, and as people look towards me in unison, I cover up my badge with my hand, pulling it off and tossing it to the ground. I start to back up, reversing through all of the bodies, most of which are looking at me. Despite their brains realizing the connection between my name and the crime scene, they are just office workers, not interested in getting into some tussle. I convince myself that I will be able to back away successfully so I can hide and reevaluate, but, to my deep disappointment, a police officer hears the commotion and my name. I'm still confident that I can disappear amongst the bodies all wearing an identical uniform as he searches the crowd. However, the police must've looked me up in the database and found my picture because the policeman's eyes light up as they land on my blonde hair and shy stature.

"Hey! Stop!" He yells. I turn around, bodying my way through the rest of the crowd, and then start sprinting in the direction of my car. Within seconds, police cars are coming my way, their sirens blaring, and with additional reinforcements on foot closing in on me. Stretching every muscle in my body, I jump over fences and turn sharp corners, trying to lose as many of them as possible. I don't look back. The sirens fade, and the heavy slaps of boots against the ground disappear as well. I turn into an alley, a fence between me and the next block. I tiredly and clumsily jump the fence and run out into the street. A helicopter shines its light down on me as soon as I get there. Police cars surround me, each with two officers next to them, aiming their weapons. I drop down onto my knees in defeat, erecting my arms into the air. Four offices drag me to my feet, cuffing my hands and guiding me into a car. Like an ultimate law-making entourage, every car falls in line behind ours as we drive towards the government center yet again.

"You don't understand. I need to talk to a department head. I have some really important information about an enemy threat." I plead to the two officers in the front seat.

"We know you have information. That's why you're here."

"No. No. I'm not a criminal. I'm on your side. Look at my uniform. Please, just let me talk to a department head, and then you can do whatever you want with me."

"Kid. You just ran away from law enforcement. You have no authority to demand anything."

"Not to mention your name was written on a wall with the blood of the murdered head of tech." The policeman that's driving adds. I sit back, sighing deeply in frustration.

"You are wasting valuable time," I warn.

"I'm sure, bud."

The car pulls up in front of the tech building, where there is still a crowd of curious people. The door is opened for me and, as soon as I step out of the car, four police officers flank me, guiding me into the crime scene. People try to follow us into the building, but police officers block them off. I'm assuming they are going to question me here. We stride into the all-so-familiar tech building. Despite the floor and glass staircases being so recognizable, everything seems foreign. I don't think I had ever imagined myself being guided into this building, a place I've wanted to be for much of my life, as a criminal. I admire the architecture of the building, as I do every time I come here. We begin to pass underneath the second floor when I look up.

DIMENSION

Staring down at me is a kid my age and another slightly older man. The kid looks down at me, his black hair a mess on his head. The guy next to him stands a little farther back and, when he turns his face to look at me, there is something so strikingly recognizable about it, like I've seen it before. I look straight into the kid's piercing brown eyes. I get a weird gut feeling about them, and then they are gone as we pass underneath the second level.

I am turned into a conference room and pushed into a seat. In front of me is another police officer, one that seems to have more authority. He has short grey hair and a wrinkly but stern face. His eyes are unfriendly, and his resting face is one of someone who doesn't take any nonsense. I'm about to plead to him the same I did with the other officers, but he puts a finger up to stop me.

"So, you're Timo?"

"Yes. Sir."

"Ok, Timo. Here's how it's going to work. I'm going to ask some questions. You are going to answer the questions I ask. You will not talk when I don't ask you a question. If you give us the amount of information that we are looking for, then we will give you the benefit of the doubt. You are a worker for the government, after all. An intern, but still a worker. Do you understand?" I nod, upset that no one is listening to me.

"Great." He clicks open his pencil and slides over a notebook from the other side of the table, flipping through tons of interview notes until he gets to a blank page. "Let's start with where you've been for the past two days." This is good. Hopefully, I can thoroughly explain myself.

"Well, it's a long story."

"I'm sure."

"Do you want the abridged version?"

"Give me as much as you want, and I'll ask follow-up questions if I need to."

"Ok. I came into work on Monday, and everything was normal. I went to my desk and started my usual workflow. But then these guys came into the office and killed Bethany and Pernille, as you probably know. They took me hostage and brought me to this crazy secret evil base. I think it's somewhere outside of the city, but they put a bag over my head. This guy named Tyler was the boss or whatever, and, on Tuesday morning, he told me that I needed to help him. He wanted to hide portals from the government, so we, the government, can't hide them. Apparently, he's against government restrictions. Then, I managed to convince him to take me to the portal right outside Paris. I told him there was something wrong with it that could only be fixed in person. I lied of course. He took me there, and then I escaped through the portal. I then spent a night in AltD and then I came back out through the same portal and back to the government center to warn you guys about Tyler." I let out a deep breath and sit back in the hard office chair.

"Uh-huh. That's quite the story for a teenager to go through, don't you think?"

"I know. I thought so too. It's been a crazy couple of days."

"So why run away from the police?"

"Well, I thought that, after hearing about my name, that you were going to capture me mistakenly."

"But, you could have just said that instead of running away."

"It was an in-the-moment kind of thing." The officer leans forward in his chair, dropping the notebook and grasping his hands together.

"Here's what I think happened, Timo. I think you were not happy with your job, and you wanted some relief. I think you brought a weapon into work, killed Bethany and Pernille, and then ran. You then waited for the police to clean up the mess here and then came back to get your last kill. You then wrote the message, unsure if you would come back or stay away as a vigilante. You decided to come back and play the innocence card after realizing life wouldn't be too good to you in hiding. And here you are, coming up with a ridiculous story and hoping you will be released back into your old life." This can't be happening, and I stand up in frustration.

"I'm telling the truth. Tyler is out there, and you have to stop him! He wants to defeat the entire government, and he's relentless!" He waves towards the guards in the room.

"Please escort Timo to his cell." Before I can argue anymore, someone puts tape over my mouth and starts to drag me away, handcuffs hugging my wrists. There is no point in struggling. Tyler won.

KAI

November 3, 2040

We are almost going too fast. I have no time to admire the deep blue of the ocean and, as we speed over Ireland and the UK, I can't catch any of the details of the green hills or lush country. Before I know it, we are calmly cruising over the government center in Paris. I look at Za, who makes two extra loops to examine the buildings before looking back at me and nodding to a nearby concrete parking garage. It's one of the only buildings that has a flat roof big enough for us to land.

I carefully lower myself onto the grey roof and, as soon as I dismount, the jet disappears back into the Rod, which I hand back to Za. He's already crouched, scanning the government buildings, which all look identical from up here. I sit down next to him, my legs in that strange state where they feel tired from their lack of use.

"Devising a plan?" I ask.

"No." He replies. We sit in silence for a few seconds. "Last time I was here, it was completely different. It wasn't a government center. Actually, it was the opposite."

"The HUB, right?"

"Yeah." He looks at me, wondering how I knew about the HUB.

"I saw it on old advertisements in Boston."

"Right." He takes two more minutes to look at the buildings before pointing to one straight ahead.

"That's where we have to go."

"How do you know?" I squint.

"You see the police cars all around the front and the crowd of people?"

"Yeah."

"Who do you think caused that?"

"Someone that wanted some information."

"Yup. Let's go." He gets up and starts to walk down the ramp to the lower levels of the garage.

"Hold on. Don't we need to know what we are looking for or something? Do you have any idea where to start?"

"No clue. But that's why we are going to figure it out when we get there."

"That's a horrible plan. I thought you guys were the hyper-organized rebels that dismantle governments."

"That's Ivo. I'm not Ivo. I like to do things with a little more...a little more spice." I shake my head in disappointment. It would be ironic if this was when I died, accompanied by a Wolf brother.

We make our way down seven floors of ramps and walk out into the empty street. I blindly follow Za, who fast walks towards the building he pointed out. We stop behind the building next to the one we want to head into. Looking around the corner, Za grumbles in frustration as he sees the perimeter of the building guarded by the police force and barricaded by intrigued government officials. He points with his head to the back of the building, and I follow him around the corner and towards the back of the

KAI

government building. There are no doors that I can see, and I look at Za, who grumbles again.

With our backs against what I'm now assuming is the tech building, we slide slowly towards the front and wait on the corner, Za continually checking to look for an opening. Then, as if God wanted it to happen, a guy in a government uniform starts to sprint away, causing some chaos within the public and subsequently dragging all of the police away with him. Both Za and I immediately sneak into the building, right through the front door.

"Let's go up," Za says, and we climb the stairs on the side and up onto the second floor. We go from door to door, looking at the labels. Many of them just note different offices, all of them currently empty. I stumble upon a metal door that says 'Data Storage.'

"Za. Here." Za walks over to me, reads the label, and nods in satisfaction. I try to open the door, but it's locked. Za takes out another metal rod-type thing.

"Let me guess, that's going to pick the lock somehow." He proceeds to remove the tube's lid and fumble around with his fingers until he pulls out two bobby pins. He laughs at my face as I realize how stupid I must seem. Za proceeds to pick the lock, and the door swings open. We walk in, surrounding my data banks and rows of external storage. There is a small control center with an old laptop in the middle of it all. Za swings his bag off his back and reaches into it, pulling out a USB drive. He plugs it into the computer, and a program immediately starts to run.

"What's it doing?"

"It's automatically compressing and sorting through the data stored locally here. Then it will discern what information would be helpful and download it. Ivo made it." It's amazing how much stuff Ivo comes up with. The USB only takes about three minutes before it's done, flashing an indicator light. Za pulls it out, places it back into his bag, and swings his bag behind his back again. We head out the door and notice that the police are starting to come back. We walk over to the balcony. Below us, four police guards have surrounded a detained kid about my age. His blonde hair barely moves, and he looks at me, his piercing blue eyes meeting my gaze. It's only a second of eye contact, but it feels like an eternity before he passes beneath us.

"Let's get out of here while we still have a chance." Za comments. I follow him cautiously back down the stairs and around the building. We jog back to the parking garage and make our way back up to the roof.

"What now?"

"We have to get the USB to Ivo because I have no idea what to do with it."

We trace the exact path back, but it still looks like a whole new world to me. The ocean is calming and rough, and the wind against my face stings but adds to the exhilaration of it all. When we land back on the shore from where we left, Za calls Ivo to ensure we are still going to the right place.

"So?"

"Back to Ivo's place, I think."

"What has he been doing this whole time?"

"Gathering some help?"

"What does that mean?"

"How should I know? You act like I know what Ivo is always planning. I'm just as in the dark as you, and it's been like that for a while."

"Fine. Fine."

"C'mon. Let's get going." Za gets a running start before generating a cycle again, slowing down to let me catch up. I sprint forwards and jump, activating my cycle. This will never stop being exciting.

We drive through the varying Canadian landscape. I admire the tall trees and rugged mountains. We take a few stretch breaks before we finally get there, which doesn't do too much to help my pounding back ache. But, eventually, we get to Ivo's house. Driving straight through the mountain, this time without flinching, we emerge in the same garage, now with a few more new vehicles I don't recognize. One of them appears clearly out of place. It's an old red car, rusting around the edges and certainly not close to the luxurious aesthetic of Ivo's. The wheels look like they've been replaced, but the body of the car tells me it hasn't been through a car wash in about twenty years.

I turn around to see Za staring at the car in shock, his mouth open in awe.

"What?" I ask.

"There is no chance Ivo found him. No chance." I don't even have time to ask who he is talking about before Za bounds up the stairs. I quickly follow behind me and stand a few feet behind him at the top. Za is staring at a group of people sitting in the living room. The only people I recognize are Ivo and Aiko.

"Oh. My. God." Za is once again in shock. Ivo waves for me to come, so I skirt around Za's paralyzed body and towards the group of people.

"Give him some time," Ivo reassures. "It's been a while since he's seen these guys." On his left sits Aiko and then a black guy with a clean beard and scruffy hair. He has a yellow hoodie on above his black joggers and white sneakers. To Ivo's right, there are two brothers, or twins. They look almost identical, so they must be twins. One is wearing smart round glasses with a suit jacket over a t-shirt, finishing it off with some fitted black suit pants and black leather sneakers. The other one is wearing distressed jeans, white leather sneakers, a long-sleeved white shirt, and a white cap. Both of them have chains. One has a silver chain with a small cube on it, and the other one has a matching one except it's gold. Ivo looks left and right before taking a deep breath.

"I guess I should introduce you, Kai." He stands up and turns, so he's facing me and the group.

"Guys, this is Kai. How we found him is kinda a long story, so we will skip that. Kai, this is Idri." He points to the black guy, who gives me a confident little wave.

"This is Riz." He points to the one with glasses. That's how I know him. He invented my glasses.

"And this is Aziz." The last one puts out his hand for a fist bump. I oblige. All of a sudden, Za comes rushing from the back, giving each person a big hug.

"It's been too long," he whispers three times. Then he backs up to look at the twins. "Damn, you guys look good. Riz is like a super tech guru, and Aziz is…Aziz is…Aziz is crushing whatever Aziz is doing." Aziz rolls his eyes, and Riz playfully punches him in the shoulder.

"So, why everyone now?" Idri asks. "I mean, I love you people, and it's been a minute, but this was all kinda sudden." I pick up on a remnant of an African accent from Idri.

"Well. Kai here introduced us to a problem. And, I know we are retired or whatever, besides the twins, of course." They nod in agreement as Ivo continues. "But, I thought if we were gonna have one last hurrah as the Migrant squad, saving the world for the third time wouldn't be such a bad goodbye."

"Yeah, it does sound kinda cute when you put it like that," Riz comments.

"I mean...you say that now. But, what if I told you who the enemy was," Ivo explains with a grimace.

"Please, for all that is holy, please don't be the god damn government," Aziz pleads, dramatically dropping to the floor. Ivo just meekly smiles.

"Absolutely not, no." Idri gets up. "Not this again. Not a group of amateur fighters striving to take down entire nations and governments."

"Who you calling an amateur?" Za argues back, obviously offended.

"Everyone, calm down!" Aiko shuts everyone up as she yells. "This is ridiculous. We haven't seen each other for years, and this is what we are doing? We can't seriously be arguing right now. Ivo didn't say we have to save the world, he just said we could save the world."

"Oh, thanks, Aiko. When you put it like that, it makes me feel soooo much better," Aziz says sarcastically. Everyone sits in silence for another minute, and I finally decide it's my turn to say something.

"AltD is meant to be a free place. Of course, as you know, it wasn't built with the right intention. But, Nox never finished. He never completed the society he wanted, despite not knowing that. And, instead, Tirique left behind a completely free society. An entire free world. What this country wanted, actually. This world has pulled thousands of people out of their low-class lives and let them start anew. No bias, no history. Now, the government is trying to take that all away. They are actively trying to regulate our freedom, and they are choosing how they do it. Do you really want the last chance we have at total freedom just to disappear?" I sit down on the table emphatically and out of breath.

"Wow. I like this kid," Riz comments, to my delight.

"Me too," the brothers say in unison.

"So, is this settled?" Aiko asks.

DIMENSION

"War?" Za adds. Idri stands up and stretches his arms before collecting himself and fixing his hoodie.

"Let's get this over with."

TIMO

November 4, 2040

The prison isn't horrible. There is white furniture sitting inside of a completely blacked-out room. The paint on the walls is entirely smooth and, when I rub my hand over them, marks of moisture show up before slowly fading away. I didn't sleep very well last night, but I slept. I really don't know what to do from here. As soon as they put me in here, I jumbled around in my pockets for my glasses. But, I think they took them. That means I can't even get some help from AltD. I'm no fighter in the Reality, so busting my way out with brute force isn't really an option. I decide to just sit up in my bed and aimlessly think about how I got myself here. Three days ago, I was just an innocent intern working for the government, a simple job for a simple guy who wanted to get through his day so that he could satisfy his parents and then move on into AltD. Now, all of that got me here. I suppose one could say it was all just an unlucky chain of events.

I lean back against the wall and am about to shut my eyes again before food slides underneath the black door that fits perfectly with the walls, it looks like it's not even there. Seeing food makes my stomach loudly grumble. I have no idea when I last ate, and I scramble to pick up the tray.

DIMENSION

There is a milk carton on one side which I immediately chug before opening the cardboard box in the middle of the tray, excited just to have any food. And then there is nothing. No food, no drink, nothing. Just a small paper note about the size of a fortune cookie fortune sitting in the box. Great. That's just great.

I pick up the note and turn it around, revealing a small message in black print: 'Please, step away from the back wall.' Too tired and too hungry to ask questions or disobey any instruction, I slowly back away from the wall until I'm hugging the door and on the opposite wall of the cell. I wait ten seconds, but nothing happens. I'm about to walk back to the bed when a line starts to form from the ground, growing upwards in a straight line. It's like someone is laser cutting the wall from the other side. Before I know it, a rectangular opening starts to outline, and, eventually, a piece of the wall falls flat into my cell. It would've crushed me if I hadn't moved. Appearing in the doorway is a white guy, high twenties probably or maybe low thirties, in a blue tracksuit with white sneakers and a backwards white cap.

"C'mon, kid. We don't have much time." I just stare at him in confusion and fatigue. "Hey. Kid. Wanna stay in prison for the rest of your life? This is your chance." I nod and slowly step over the wall debris. Almost on cue, sirens start blaring from virtually every direction. We walk out onto the street behind the building, and a helicopter is hovering right above the street. I follow the man into the helicopter and take a seat, surprised that it's almost entirely silent inside.

"Let's go." The guy tells the pilot, who nods as we rise up and away from the helpless government soldiers waiting below.

"Why are you helping me?" I ask, prompting the man to look up from his phone and into my eyes. His eyes are bright green, and his hair is a ruffled brown.

"Well. You're a Prince, aren't you?" I'm in shock. No one is supposed to know my real-world identity. How does he know?

"Uh. Yeah."

"Right, then. Let's just say I have a history with AltD and the people that made it. I have made it my goal to find you Princes, because a man's dying wish to me was to give you all something very important when AltD set into place." I can barely muster a response.

"Who are you?"

"Serge. Serge Adams."

KAI

November 4, 2040

We all crashed in Ivo's living room except for Idri, who slept in the guest room. He called seniority or whatever, apparently. Somehow, I got a couch, Za got the other one, and the twins were kind of forced but also kind of volunteered to be on the floor. They seem very nice. To be honest, I'm still in shock that I'm around all of these famous people. I mean, the Wolf brothers were enough for me. But to also meet Riz, that's pretty insane.

I get up, pushing off the blanket, and walking over to the stove to check the time. It's only eight in the morning, but for Za, it's late. Stumbling over to his couch, I shake him awake.

"What?"

"It's late."

"How late?"

"Eight."

"Oh, for real?"

"Yeah." He grumbles, gracefully rolls out of bed, and immediately walks over to the open floor where the twins are sleeping.

"Wakey! Wakey!" He leans down and yells at them. They both quickly scurry out of their sleeping positions and up into a cautious stance. Za just laughs hysterically as they realize it was a prank. Riz shakes his head.

"Really, Za? We are supposed to be mature now."

"What? I can't have some fun?"

"I can't believe I actually missed you," Aziz adds. I look at the stairs to see Ivo emerge, Aiko, accompanying him, and Idri shortly behind. They are all dressed, making us look like children with our silk pajamas on.

"Ok. I think I'm ready," Ivo states.

"Ready for what?" Riz asks.

"This." Za fumbles around in his bag next to the couch he slept on and pulls out the USB, holding it in the air emphatically.

"Yeah. That." Ivo walks up to Za and snatches it out of his hand. "That seals our fate." He turns around and walks back down the stairs, not looking to demand my presence.

"Kai, you're with me." I excitedly follow behind him, and Za joins behind me.

"Not you, Za. Just Kai." Za throws up his arms in frustration as he peels off and joins the group on the couches. I don't even look at him as I walk down the stairs and sit next to Ivo in the same chair like last time. He plugs the USB into the back of the monitor and then rubs his hands in anticipation.

"Let's see what we got here." He opens the file that pops up, which takes a minute to load.

"How hard was it?"

"How hard was what?"

"Getting into the database."

"Oh, it wasn't too bad. There was an incident distracting the police, so we basically walked right in."

"Gotta love when it's easy." I nod in agreement as he turns backs towards the screen where the file has finished opening. He takes a few minutes to comb through the data and pictures, opening various folders, nodding, and then opening something else. I look at everything he looks at but still can't make heads or tails of any of it. Finally, he says something.

"Well. If we wanted all of the information that the European government has on every person in existence, we have that now, I guess."

"Nothing about the AltD thing?"

"There are some records of somebody messing with AltD portals. It doesn't say exactly what happened, and it's not like there is an investigation. It's kinda just the computer system logging events, and it noted people accessing the code of the portals."

"Well. That's odd. Why would they do that? That doesn't have anything to do with Bots."

"No, it doesn't. And you are the expert here, so I should be asking you that question." I nod, sinking into thought. If someone were to mess with portals, then they could be closing them. One of the best parts of AltD is the portals which mean people hypothetically don't have to own glasses to access AltD. I suppose that closing the portals would be a kind of regulation. That's the only guess I have.

"Closing the portals could be some kind of regulation for the European government, I suppose."

"How so? Do a lot of people use the portals?"

"I mean. I use them a lot, and I think other people do too."

"So, if the government were to close the portals, then what?"

"Then people can only get into AltD using their glasses."

"Is that bad?"

"Well, the glasses can be tracked, I think. I don't really know the specifics, but the glasses are kinda like people's individual key."

"So, if the government were to limit people to using their glasses, then they can force some kind of tracking on their entire population without them really knowing or realizing." He says it much better than I could. Plus, Ivo's questions helped me to get to these conclusions. I suppose this is why Ivo is Ivo.

"Yes. Exactly."

"Is it just me, or does that fit in the same category as controlling the Bots?"

"Sounds like it to me. Is this a lead?"

"Indeed it is. But we need to find a location. Any ideas as to where to start?" Back to thinking.

"If the government want to regulate the movements of its people, then they would probably want to close the portals on the borders of Europe. Specifically, the ones that are against other countries."

"Why?"

"Because someone could enter AltD using a portal in Europe and then easily exit using one that is in another country, it's like they traveled across borders without anyone knowing."

"Got it. It looks like we have ourselves a mission." He gets up, and I follow, satisfied with the part I played. He stops at the bottom of the stairs and turns around to face me.

"Nice job, kid." I can only respond with a grin, and I curse at myself for not saying thank you as we climb up the stairs. Everyone snaps out of their conversations and stands up to face us.

"So?" Za asks. I see Idri looking into Ivo's eyes, who responds with a nod.

DIMENSION

"I'll get the weapons and the cars ready." They must have some kind of telepathic connection.

"Mission?" Aiko asks.

"Mission," Ivo says with a nod.

"It's go time people," Za says, who holds Aziz's shoulder.

"Now this…this I actually missed."

TIMO

November 4, 2040

I just spend the rest of the helicopter trip trying to remember if I've heard the name Serge Adams before. And, once that doesn't produce anything of note, I move on to thinking how he knows the Princes. I mean, everyone knows that the Princes exist. Some have even met the Princes in AltD. But, never is anyone supposed to know their real-world identity. It's a privacy and safety thing for us. I guess it's not a rule, but we make it pretty hard to track down our real identity. I've found other Princes a couple of times and talked to them in AltD, but I have no idea who they really are in Reality.

I just lean back in my chair. It's black leather and overly comfortable. There is a mini-fridge of drinks in a middle console with two small displays for TVs. The helicopter is still completely silent, which I don't know how is possible, and the glass window that wrap around the entire body of the helicopter makes it feel like we are just floating in midair. To think that I was in prison with no foreseeable escape this morning is crazy. Serge is sitting across from me, and he notices me deep in thought.

"You probably want to hear a little more explanation about all of this." I sit up.

"Yeah, that'd be nice."

"It's not like I'm holding back any information or anything; it's just that I didn't want to shock you. I learned from my earlier recruits that jumping into things super fast and telling them a bunch of surprisingly, and borderline impossible, information kinda puts them in a state of self-contemplation." I take a deep breath.

"I think I'm ready."

"No self-contemplation?"

"I hope not."

"I suppose that's good enough." He shuffles around his feet and slides back in his chair, leaning forward to be a little closer to me.

"My name is Serge Adams, as I've already told you, and I'm sure it means even less the second time. When I was younger, I inherited the biggest private army and weapons company in the world from my father. That meant that, for a while, I was kinda in hot demand. A few years back, I joined a team of individuals you may recognize the names of; Nox, Tirique, and Skylar." Wow. That's quite the high-profile group. Now I at least know that this guy is semi-legit.

"I was Nox's firepower until he recruited Zashil Wolf. You know those Wolf brothers are something else." I had no idea that Zashil worked for Nox.

"I was assigned to keep Europe stable when everyone else went off and did whatever they were gonna do in the United States which, as we now know, did not pan out so well."

"So, what happened to you?"

"I'm getting there, kid. I had about six months of thinking nothing would happen to me like they just forgot about me or something. Of course, I was wrong. Soon enough, these two twins, I don't know their names, came for me. They single-handedly took down my entire army and then destroyed all of my weapons. They collected all of the remaining governmental officials and re-assembled the European government pretty quickly. The one thing they never did was find me, but I think when they got the government back on track and absolutely obliterated my army, they thought it didn't matter too much. What they didn't know was that Tirique had left me some secret missions and folders or whatever. This is where you come in. He told me about the Princes, telling me how AltD would have the cubes and that some individuals would find those objects. Of course, back then, he didn't call them Princes. The thing was, he didn't know much about how to find you guys, and I couldn't really even start looking until there were Princes to find. If there is something I am good at, it's tracking. So for the past few years, I've been tracking you all down."

That answers some of my questions, at least.

"But, why would Tirique want that?"

"Because there are a few small cool things you guys can do when working together with the cubes and one big thing."

"What's the big thing?"

"You know how Nox's famous last words were that himself and Tirique would live on forever in AltD." I'd seen it on occasional posters, new headlines, and stuff; it was used as more of a warning than anything else.

"Yeah."

"Well, Tirique couldn't make that happen right away because he needed to finish the world, and he knew he was dying, so he couldn't wait for AltD to be created and then add the programming for him and Nox. So he had to find a way to wait."

"So you're telling me that you've been gathering all of the Princes together so that we can finally carry on the prophecy and bring back Nox and Tirique?"

"Yeah. That's exactly right."

"And why would we want to do that?"

"What do you mean?"

"Why would we want to bring them back? They were objectively very dangerous people with an extremely dangerous mindset and a perspective that was radical in all of the wrong ways."

"But…but…"

"Yeah, I'm white, buddy. That's not how that works anymore. We aren't in 2035."

"But…"

"But what? I have no urge to bring Nox or Tirique back. There is literally nothing in it for me either; I can't believe I thought you were actually saving me." I'm sort of appalled, and my shyness is shedding away.

"Hey, kid. Be grateful for me busting you out of that prison. I don't think anyone else was going to that anytime soon."

"Plus. How do I know that Tirique and Nox aren't going to be some kind of crazy god-like figures in AltD that have control over everything?"

"How am I supposed to know that? I literally just told you everything I know. You know, you're way more annoying than the others."

"So, how many Princes have you found?"

"You're the last one." Wow. He's good. That could not have been easy.

After a few more minutes of silence and awkwardness, we land on the top of a massive mountain. I get out of the helicopter, and my jaw drops. It's like a massive glass castle surrounding the entire mountain. I can see through all of the glass and into lavish spaces. There is a massive training gym, an entire soccer field, and a huge dining hall. I don't even care that it's freezing and snow is wetting my hair.

"You know how you said there was nothing in it for you?"

"Uh-huh."

"Well. What's in it for you is to live like a Prince inside AltD and outside too. Now you tell me again that you don't want to do this, and I'll whisk you right back to that prison. For now, you might want to start a tour of your future home. It'll take a while."

Still in shock, I follow him through a grand door that leads straight into the mountain. We walk onto a transparent balcony that looks down on a massive living space, the exposed rock acting as walls. Many people are sitting in various chairs and couches, and they stare at me as I make it down the stairs.

"People. This is Timo or whatever his Prince name is. Timo, these are the other Princes." To my surprise, they are all relatively young, either a few years older or younger than me. Serge turns around and looks at a girl who is probably the closest to my age out of everyone. She's wearing black denim jeans with Jordan sneakers and a crop top with a classy white sweater. How is she not freezing? Her long brown hair does no work in distracting from her dark purple eyes.

"Cora, will you give Timo a tour and get him as far away from me as possible? He asks way too many questions." Cora springs up from her seat and walks over to me, looking at me before hugging me.

"Prince Odoi, right?"

"Yeah. But please, call me Timo."

"Ok, Timo, you ready for a crazy tour?"

"Always."

I follow her out of the room and into a suspended glass hallway. As the tour begins, all I'm thinking to myself is to stay strong. Don't let this entice you.

You can't let Nox back in.

KAI

November 4, 2040

Everyone immediately disperses to various places in the house. After getting dressed, I just stand by my bag, unsure of where to go as each team member moves with purpose. The twins go downstairs, following Idri to the weapons. Meanwhile, Ivo and Za go to the garage to figure out what vehicles to take. While all of this is happening, Aiko is rushing around packing sandwiches and various snacks, making me smile.

I decide to wander downstairs to check out the weapons situation. As I turn at the bottom, I see the familiar desk. Walking past it, I notice the twins and Idri at the back of the huge open floor. I stride past the open doors to various bedrooms and such, making my way to the back. The entire wall is lined with weapons, at least twice as many as Za's weapons wall at his house. There are guns of all kinds, grenades, vests, spy gear, and everything else you could imagine surrounding a suspended glass box in the middle. Idri sees me gawking at the array of artillery.

"You ever seen weapons like this before?"

"Never," I reply, almost embarrassed.

"Well, come here. I'll get you all geared up." The twins nod at me, now carrying a handful of weapons each, as they walk past me and back up the stairs. I step forward towards Idri, who starts pointing at weapons.

"Do you know how to shoot a gun?"

"Nope."

"I probably shouldn't give you these then." He jokes as he stops pointing at the side full of guns and moves towards the grenades and vests. He takes a couple of grenades down and hands them to me. I cautiously cradle them in my arms.

"I'm guessing you know how to use those. And, if you don't, it's not that hard to figure it out. It's pretty much the only thing the movies get right. Take the pin out and toss it and, unless you are god awful at throwing round objects, you should be fine. Just don't throw it at us."

"I'll try not to."

"Good man."

"Shouldn't I get one of those?" I point at the bulletproof vests.

"Yeah. That would probably be useful." He takes one down and hands it to me; it's much heavier than I imagined. How do people wear these all day? I very carefully lower the grenades to the ground, making sure they don't roll away, before starting to pull the vest on over my hoodie.

"You know what? Gimme that back," Idri says. I confusingly hand back the vest, which he places back on the wall. "And those." He points to the grenades on the ground, which I place in his arms, and he hands them back up.

"You won't need those."

"Won't I need something?"

"You won't need those because you will have this." Idri reaches into the suspended box and pulls out a small rectangular thing, almost like a sticker.

"Don't do anything with it now. Just save it for later." He hands it to me, and I put it into my pocket, perplexed as to how that little thing can solve our problems.

"Still not sure why I can't have some of that stuff too." I nod towards the vest and the grenades.

"Just trust me, kid. You'll see. You won't need that stuff."

"I don't want to die," I retaliate. Idri glares at me as if to say, 'shut up,' and I put my arms up in innocence as I walk away. I make my way back up the stairs, and Idri soon follows me. Just as we get to the top, Ivo approaches us from downstairs.

"Oh good, you guys got your stuff. We are just about ready to leave. Za helped me figure out the vehicle situation." I don't have a chance to tell him we don't need a vehicle situation before he turns around and rushes back down the garage, waving for us to follow. I shake my head and walk downstairs, where everyone else is gathered. All of the cars have been moved to the edges except for a massive blacked-out semi-truck. I have no idea where this thing came from because it definitely was not here before. Za walks up to us.

"So, of course, Ivo had me discuss which vehicles to take for like ten minutes before saying none of it mattered because he had this. Always the showman, I suppose." Ivo argues back from the other side of the garage.

"In my defense, I put a lot of work into this thing. It can literally transform into a boat and a plane. I mean, c'mon, I deserve a little credit for that." I'm almost so impressed with the fact that the semi-truck transforms into two other vehicles that I forget the entire thing is kind of redundant.

"Not to kill the vibe or anything, but I don't think we are gonna need all that." Ivo stops what he's doing, walks around the truck, and stands in front of me.

"What?"

"Well, there is a significantly more efficient and more realistic way to get to the border of Europe."

"How? I don't think you understand how fast this thing is."

"Yes, it's fast. But with that, we will have a massive vehicle and, therefore, a massive presence. It's a bit risky."

"The kid's right," Idri agrees from behind me.

"So, what do you propose?"

"There's only one other option."

"Which is?" Aiko asks.

"Through AltD."

"Oh god," Za complains yet again.

"I second that response," Aziz says, sitting in the passenger seat of the truck. I don't see what's wrong with my idea. It's the most plausible and would keep us the most low-key.

"What's so wrong with that?"

"In case you haven't noticed, we are kinda silently protesting AltD," Ivo explains.

"Not me," Riz comments.

"Everyone except for Riz."

"Just hear me out." I am confident in my ability to sell this. Ivo leans back on the hood of the truck.

"This has two massive advantages. For one, we can travel super lightly. So if anything goes south for any reason, or we need to pivot our plan of attack, it will be much easier to do that without leaving behind any traces. And, along the incognito line, we can look completely disguised in AltD. Not gonna lie, you Wolf brothers and Riz are pretty recognizable faces and names."

"He brings up good points, Ivo." Aiko joins Idri in supporting my argument. Ivo re-positions his legs, clearly considering my proposal.

"Ok."

"Ok?" I can't believe he agreed.

"But. You have to take the lead. You are bringing us into untravelled territory here. All of our know-how about how these missions usually go isn't going to be super useful. So, you're the leader now."

"Fair enough."

"You can't be serious, Ivo?" Aziz is angry.

"Did you hear Kai's plan? It's easily the smart option."

"I can't believe you people." He walks away annoyed, and Riz just laughs at him.

"So where now, boss?" Za asks as I try to get accustomed to my new leadership. It's not going to be very easy.

"To the nearest portal."

"And where's that?" Ivo asks.

"I have literally no clue."

"Well, you're not really doing such a great job leading, bud." Riz jokes, walking up next to me.

"It's not my fault that you guys plopped me into the middle of nowhere. If we were in Boston right now, I could recite the exact locations of all of the portals."

"Let me handle this," Riz says, resting his arm on my right shoulder. "I have access to all of the portal locations."

"How?" Za asks.

"He's kinda head of a big corporate company. Kinda like the ones we almost died trying to defeat a few years back," Aziz comments from the back with snark.

"More like the government understood I was creating a product to better the experience of AltD which all of their citizens we're using so, therefore, they gave me access to their data."

"So why didn't we just ask you for the data instead of Kai and I going to Paris to get it?" Za keeps the questions coming.

"Because he doesn't have unrestricted access, they would know what he was accessing, and some of the data we got is in-house stuff, like the profiles and whatnot," Ivo answers on behalf of Riz, flexing his knowledge yet again.

"Exactly," Riz agrees.

"So? What do we need to do this?" Idri finally chimes in.

"Gimme thirty seconds," Riz answers, reaching into his pocket and pulling out the cleanest pair of glasses I have ever seen. They look thinner than a standard pair of AltD glasses, the matte black finish with gold accents is delicious, and the slightly rounded glass perfect for Riz's face. Riz sees me coveting his glasses, and he smiles before putting them on. He leans against the garage, and we all look at him intently. After about a minute, he takes them off and looks at us in shock.

"What?" Ivo asks.

"There are multiple portals within a couple of miles of this house." That's shocking. Usually, portals aren't in super remote areas. Portals pop up in areas with high traffic. That's how Tirique designed them. So, it's very strange for there to be a bunch of portals in the middle of nowhere unless Ivo knows something that we don't. I guess it could just be a coincidence.

"That's great. Right?" Ivo replies.

"Yeah…" Riz looks at me, knowing that I realize what this means.

"Should we take the truck then?" Za asks.

"How about we take the Rods," I comment. Ivo smiles.

DIMENSION

"You've trained him well, Za. The kid knows what's up." Everyone proceeds to zip up their bags, taking out things they no longer need with the altered plan.

"What am I supposed to do with all of the food." I smile again at Aiko, who is scrambling to find a way to carry the sandwiches she made in the midst of everyone organizing their weaponry.

"We won't need the food," Za whines, briefly taking his attention off his collection of weapons.

"Screw it. I don't need any of this stuff," he finally says, tossing the bag to the side. What is it with these people and optionally choosing weapons? Ivo walks over and hugs Aiko.

"It's ok. We really don't need the food but thanks for making the sandwiches." She solemnly nods.

"Hold up. Ain't nobody throwing away any sandwiches. So, you don't want em? Fine. Speak for yourself." Idri bounds up to them from behind me and snatches a sandwich out of the bag, proceeding to gobble it down.

Everyone finally gets their stuff together, most people electing to travel even lighter, leaving their bigger weapons behind. We use ours Rods and ride our way towards the nearest portal, following Riz. After weaving through trees and over snow, we find ourselves well and truly in the middle of nowhere. I can't discern what direction we are in, every tree looks the same, and the landscape is continuous as far as I can see.

"This is it," Riz says, turning his torso towards a gap between two trees. I walk around him, curving my stride until I catch a glimmer and slight glare, like the space between the trees is really thin glass. It took a long time to train my eye to catch the portal's reflection, but now I can almost always find hidden portals with some time and lots of patience.

"Where?" Aiko asks. I hadn't noticed the swords on her back until right now. There are two of them, forming an 'x' on her back.

"You'll see. Just follow me," I tell her. Everyone folds in behind me, and I walk through the portal. My clothes slowly change as I make my way through the portal, my black combat clothes that Ivo lent me now replaced with baggy black sweatpants with an ankle cuff and a white sweatshirt. It's my low-key look. To my surprise, we walk onto a street covered in a dusting of snow. I look to my right, and we are on the outskirts of a city, crammed in between mountain tops. I step forward some more to let the rest follow and look behind as I see them emerge.

They all look exactly the same, although they are in grey outfits that look like prison uniforms. That's the default for people that haven't spent enough time in AltD to find other clothes. Ivo looks unsurprised, probably because he's been here. Same with Riz, who is decked out in a clean black suit. He still has glasses but now has silver tips in his wavy hair. Meanwhile, Aziz, Za, Aiko, and Idri are in shock. They keep looking at each other, examine themselves, and then looking out into the distance. AltD literally feels like a duplicate of the world which is obviously very real. It shocked me the first time I entered, and I kind of miss the novelty of experiencing it like a whole new world.

"Here. Take these." Riz pulls out outfit action tabs from his pocket. I've been trying to find those forever. They basically let you customize your outfit whenever and wherever you want to whatever you want. Of course, they are very rare and very expensive. Everyone takes one, and Riz demonstrates how to use it.

"Put it on the middle back of your right hand. Let it calibrate and attach to your skin. Then tap it and go crazy, selecting whatever you want. I would advise you to choose something low-key." Idri does it first, choosing practically the same thing he was wearing before. Aiko does the same, except she doesn't have the swords on her back anymore to finish off the outfit. Then Za and Ivo go. They are the ones that really matter. Ivo chooses a simple outfit with fitted suit pants, white sneakers, and a grey long-sleeved shirt. He adds a pair of glasses for good measure. Meanwhile, Za cycles through a bunch of stuff before choosing a designer hoodie with a picture of him and Ivo on it. The hoodie was a collaboration for when the brothers won the award for 'most influential' or something. He couples it with a pair of narrow black chinos and black sneakers.

"Really, bro?" Ivo makes fun of Za.

"What? I always wanted to get this. Let me have this one."

"Fine." Then everyone looks at Riz and I, signaling that they are ready so we begin to lead the group.

"Here." He hands me an outfit action tab. "I know you don't need it, but I also know you probably want it."

"I do. I really do." I eagerly take it and stick it into my pocket.

"So this is probably why there are so many portals, right?" He wonders. I join him in looking out at the city we are walking towards, following a path that descends the mountain.

"I guess so. I suppose the people found this place in AltD but haven't used the portals."

"Or they did and realized there is nothing in Reality there, so they didn't care."

"Yeah. Probably that." I nod in agreement. It's nice to have someone that knows everything about AltD like me. It's still kind of Earth-shattering to me that the team back there has never experienced AltD.

"So, where are we gonna find a vehicle?"

"No need."

"How come?"

"When I put my glasses on, I called for my jet."

"You have a jet?"

"Of course."

"Wait. Are you a Prince?"

"Oh, god no. I've just spent a lot of time in AltD, making some very high profile friends along the way and creating quite the life for myself here."

"I see." Almost on cue, a jet appears on the horizon, flying towards us before hovering five feet in front of me. A platform lowers off the side of the glossy chrome surface. This is going to make the trip quite a bit faster. We all pile in, sitting down in plush white seats. Ivo is impressed, distracting Za by pointing everything out about the jet.

Meanwhile, Aziz and Aiko are talking. Idri is already deep in contemplation. A pilot turns around from the front.

"Where to boss?" Riz perks his head up and replies.

"To the land border of Europe."

TIMO

November 4, 2040

The hallway leads into a massive dining hall. All of the furniture is wooden, and it looks like it's floating amongst all of the glass. I can see the building is attached and suspended to the declining side of the mountain, every metal beam jutting into the rock is noticeable. It's magical how the high ceilings and the glass combine to make it feel like we are suspended in the air.

"So this is the dining hall." I almost forget Cora is next to me, and she laughs at my face of awe. Embarrassed, I force myself to muster up a response.

"I was just admiring all of the glass." It isn't false, but it's also not like there is anything else I would be looking at.

"It's fine. I was the same way when Serge first brought me here." We start walking down the stairs and into the dining hall, passing the expensive tables and chairs, moving into another glass tunnel.

"When was that?"

"I'm not sure. Maybe six months ago."

"Oh wow. So, you've been here for a while."

"Yeah, I guess so. It really hasn't felt that way, though. There is so much to do here. We get to live such lavish lives. I don't know why any of us would ever want to leave." I can't tell if she truly believes what she's saying or Serge did a good job persuading her. I decide not to play into it and, instead, change the subject.

"So, where are you from?"

"My parents are American, but I grew up in Seoul."

"South Korea?"

"Yeah, I don't think there's another Seoul." She laughs, and I look stupid, yet again. When she recovers from my second embarrassment within the last two minutes, she asks me a question.

"How about you?"

"I grew up in Europe, around London. Then I moved closer to the government in Paris."

"Wow. So you work for the government?" She turns to face me, clearly intrigued. Her purples eyes are piercing. I'm barely taller than her, so her intense stare is kinda unavoidable. I scratch my head; I'm not great in social situations, especially with people my age.

"Yeah. As an intern in the tech department."

"Interesting." She turns, and we thankfully start walking again.

"So you must be super smart." Part of my social problems also leads to me not knowing how to respond to a compliment.

"I guess..." Idiot. "Soooo, did you work?"

"During the summer, I worked in a factory to make some money. It wasn't fun, but it was kinda necessary."

"Uh-huh." We exit the hallway, and this time we are in a massive glass sphere.

"This is the gym, as you can see. There is basketball and workout equipment here. And, if you drop through that hole in the middle, you

DIMENSION

will drop into the massive pool. Sometimes we heat it to be a hot tub of sorts."

"You guys really have everything, don't you?"

"Well. To be honest. Most of this is for you."

"What do you mean?"

"Has Serge told you his whole plan yet?"

"Yeah. Sounds a bit crazy to me."

"I suppose. Anyways. We all only have one cube. Except for me, I have two. But, you have three, which means you are inevitably the most important."

"Ok. That's a bit intimidating."

"Most crucially, you're the only one with a time cube."

"There's only one time cube?"

"We don't know that for sure. But, it's possible." I refuse to believe that there's only one time cube in all of AltD. Why would Tirique make it so there are over three of the others and only one time, and how did I get lucky enough to get that one time cube?

"Wow. That's kind of unbelievable."

"So, you see how this can't happen without you?"

"I mean, it can't happen with you either."

"We are like assistants. You're the main boss." Uncomfortable with how much my decision is going to impact things, I decide to change the subject again.

"So, what's this place?" As we walk out of the hallway, I pray that we don't end up at the soccer field or something which would make me look stupid yet again. To my relief, we walk onto a balcony that wraps around a big open space. The floors are an interesting hexagonal pattern made of what looks like concrete but painted a deep black. We walk down one of the four sets of stairs, and I notice big white glass panels are wrapping around the walls of the circular space, light still shining through the glass roof.

"This is the weapons room." That's a bit freaky. Why would there be a weapons room for a bunch of young people? It seems a bit dangerous if you ask me.

"Why?" I ask.

"Don't worry. It's mostly for Serge. He probably told you about how he used to have a private army and whatever. I think he misses those days. Sometimes he just comes here and hangs out." That's a bit creepy.

"I don't see any weapons."

"Well, he's not just gonna have them lying around." She excitedly jogs over to one of the panels. She slides her hand diagonally over the spotless glassy surface, and the panel gymnastically flips on a diagonal axis, revealing a whole host of weapons. I guess if someone were to ambush me here, I would know where to arm myself. Or have I already been ambushed? I walk up to Cora, who is so excited by the room's cool factor that she can barely stand still.

"Wow. It's quite an impressive array of artillery."

"I've never used a weapon, and I didn't have any urge to until I found this place. If you activate the panels on the other side of the room, some of them have targets in them and stuff. All of the glass in here is bulletproof. Have you ever used weapons?"

"I had to pass a government training test. They didn't have me do everything because I was too young, but I learned how to use some simple guns and stuff."

"Maybe you can teach me some of your skills some time."

"I wasn't very good."

"Doesn't matter." She replies. My social awkwardness results in us leaving the weapons room, walking through a much shorter hallway, and into a library. Now, this is my kind of place. I make loops around the books, fascinated by the collection while Cora struggles to keep up behind me.

"You must really like books."

"Yeah. I'm kinda a nerd."

"You don't seem like a nerd."

"Trust me. I'm a nerd."

"If you're a nerd, then I don't know what some other people I met here are." I so badly want to be alone in the library, enveloped in some knowledge, going through every book I possibly can, but Cora clearly doesn't share that sentiment. We are about to keep going when an alarm starts to beep. I get all frantic, looking around for threats and deciding which way would be the most advantageous. Meanwhile, Cora is bursting out laughing. My arms are up in a fighting position naturally, and she comes over and lowers them.

"That's the notice for dinner." She explains. I relax—the third embarrassing moment of the day. Three is the magic number, I guess.

"You had me for a second."

"I could tell. At least you looked valiant and ready for a fight."

"Did I? I think I looked like I was about to be knocked out by a single punch." She laughs.

"Don't worry. Nobody can find us here. If there is one place you were going to be safe, it's here."

"Good to know. That reminds me, I was gonna ask where we are."

"I have no idea."

"What do you mean? You said you have been here for six months."

"The single thing Serge refuses to tell us is where we are. He says it's a liability."

"Right." Serge is beginning to sound a lot more creepy than I originally thought.

"So. Ready for dinner?"

"Yeah, I'm starving. I haven't eaten today."

"How come?" We start retracing our steps back to the dining hall.

"This morning, I was in prison, if you can believe that."

"Oh my god. Are you ok?"

"I mean…yeah… I'm fine now."

"What happened?"

"It's kinda a long story."

"Give me the short version. Please."

"The short version is I was abducted by some serial killer people trying to take down the government. I escaped and then was framed for a murder and was thrown into prison." She stops walking, her jaw dropped.

"Your kidding."

"Nope."

"Later, I want the details."

"If you say so." We arrive in the dining hall, and everyone that I saw before is already at various tables eating. Cora and I sit down at our own table and, soon enough, a chef comes over and places a bountiful meal in front of both of us. We start eating.

"So, are you gonna teach me the names of everyone else?" I ask, eager to get to know other people.

"Are you kidding me? I don't know everybody's name. There's way too many of us, and none of us really like each other."

"Why don't you like each other."

"Well. We are all Princes. So, naturally, we are all pretty arrogant and full of ourselves. Which means every conversation just turns into an argument about who's better."

"But, that's in AltD."

"Yeah. It turns out you're the first person here I've met that has a real life outside of AltD and is actually a decent person to hold a conversation with. So, thanks for that."

"Anytime, I guess." I'm a little disappointed that I won't get to meet anybody else. I promise myself that I'll try to talk to someone else that isn't Cora tomorrow. That is, if Cora leaves me alone.

"You think a lot," she says, snapping me out of it.

"Uhhh. I guess it's just a habit."

"What do you think about?"

"I'm not sure. Sometimes, it's nothing that really matters. Sometimes, I just totally zone out."

"Got it." We finish eating in silence. The food is amazing. It's really good pasta with tomato sauce and chicken. Even when I wasn't a prisoner of the government, I didn't eat so well. My meals at home usually were either a pizza, a microwavable burrito, or a selection of snacks. Not too great.

"Let me show you where we sleep," Cora says. I nod and follow her back towards the start and into the mountain. We walk through the living room area I saw when I first got here and into a hallway area. Off of the hallway is a bunch of doors with name tags on them. Cora's is at the end of the hallway, where there is a single door against the dead-end with 'Odoi' on it.

"This is me. And, this is you." She opens the door to my room. "It's the biggest one. For reasons I explained before." I walk into what looks like a penthouse apartment. It's insane. There is inevitably glass everywhere, which is looking out the other side of the mountain, and the furniture is more lavish than I could ever imagine.

"Let me know if you need absolutely anything." She says before starting to close the door.

"Good night," I add.

"Night, Timo," she responds with a smile. I turn towards the glass table in the middle of the space and take a seat—a lavish life in trade for Nox and Tirique. As much as I didn't want Cora to convince me, I'm starting to feel a little convinced.

KAI

November 4, 2040

The flight feels much quicker than expected, but the innovation of high-speed planes probably happened at a higher rate in AltD. Either way, we get to the border in a fairly short amount of time, and the plane drops us off right near the edge. We all shuffle out of the plane and onto unkempt land. I've been around here before. Sometimes, I just hop through a portal and travel around to check out different places when I'm bored. I remember being quite uninterested by this area. It's not that there aren't any people. It's just that there isn't much excitement. When Tirique constructed AltD, he made the cities the place to be. Inevitably, people who went into AltD established themselves there first, which led to the general concentration of the AltD population in major cities.

"So, what now?" Aiko asks as everyone looks around to get their bearings. I wait for an answer, scanning the horizon before I turn back to see everyone waiting for my answer.

"You're the boss, remember?" Za reminds me.

"Right, right. Well, we have to find the portals."

"How do we do that?" Aziz asks. I guess this will be my first time trying to explain my portal locating technique.

"I've never tried to explain this to anyone, so stay with me. And if Riz has any other ideas, then he can help me out." I wait for everyone to nod before continuing.

"Some portals are pretty obvious within AltD; it doesn't look like there are any of those here, though. So, instead, you have to look for hiding portals that are pretty much invisible. However, they have a slight reflection, and they have a bit of a visual ripple." I squirm my arms around, making some desperate hand movements that I think look like ripples.

"Kinda like this?" Aziz asks. He's already standing about one hundred feet away. Riz and I look at each other and then jog over to Aziz. Surprisingly, he isn't wrong. The portal is in a very odd place, kinda hanging out in an open space.

"Yeah, that'll do it. Kind of exactly like that." I respond.

"Nice job, bro," Riz says before turning back towards the group and waving them over. Aiko and Ivo were already scouring the air like they were looking for a ghost or something. It's pretty funny. They all come over.

"Where is it?" Aiko asks, squinting and leaning down. Meanwhile, Ivo walks around, changing his perspective as I do.

"I see the ripples."

"Who's going through first?" Za asks.

"I vote the kid," Idri comments.

"And, just when I thought I had your confidence," I complain.

"No one said you didn't have my confidence. What if I want you to go through first because I trust you the most."

"Right, right. You just happen to trust me more than the rest of the team you've known for ten years. Yeah, that makes a lot of sense." Idri puts his hands up.

"Hey, man. No one said you have to listen to me."

"Fine. I'll do it. But, if I die, it's on you."

"Uh-huh." I notice Aiko smiling at the whole interaction before I head through the portal, my clothes from Reality re-appearing on my body as I move through it. Emerging from the portal, I look left and right. To my left, there is a massive gathering of soldiers in black uniforms. They look like government soldiers, and they have three tanks. These must be the people we are looking for. I hurriedly go back through the people before anyone can spot me.

"What?" Ivo asks.

"At least you didn't die." Idri continues to joke, but I think my scared face warns him because he immediately stops smiling.

"I think we've found who we were looking for."

"Well, that was fast," Za answers.

"How many?" Ivo asks.

"I don't know, but a lot. They look like government soldiers too, so this is proof that the government is messing with AltD stuff." I see everyone looking at each other and nodding over some unsaid agreement.

"What? What do we do?"

"Wanna have some fun?" Za asks me.

"Depends. Does it result in my death?"

"Not if you do it right."

"Then, why not?" In any other situation, I would not be going into a fight with a group of armed government soldiers, but I feel safe with the team around me.

"Good boy."

"Kai, when you step out, show what I gave you to put in your pocket to Ivo." Ivo looks at Idri when he hears his name, and Idri just taps an area behind his ear while nodding. Ivo smiles back in response and gives a short nod.

"Alright then, let's get moving, people." Aiko fearlessly leads the way through the portal, and everyone else follows behind. Immediately the crew starts to get their weapons ready, Aiko making sure her swords are still on her back. Then, before I know it, they are attracting the soldiers' attention by bounding towards them. The tanks even turn in their direction. I frantically try to find some kind of weapon.

"Calm down. I got you," Ivo says, walking up to me and putting his hand out for the little thing Idri gave me earlier. This better be helpful because Idri specifically didn't let me take anything else. I reach into my pocket and place the little thing in Ivo's hand. He walks around to the side of my head, and I feel a little zap and tug as he attaches the thing behind my right ear. Ivo steps back.

"Ok. Follow my instructions and gestures. Tap the surface of the device to calibrate." I nod and follow his instruction. I feel a couple more zaps and then a voice says calibrated. Ivo waits for my shock to wear off before continuing his instructions.

"Ok. Now, double-tap." I double-tap the device, and I feel a bizarre sensation of something growing over my body. I feel it cover my neck and slowly move down my body. I look down when I sense it gets to my chest and see a black suit with light chrome blue accents forming. It's very thin and looks almost like a living robot, the nanotech stuff fitting perfectly to my body. I lift up my feet so the suit can finish covering everywhere, and it finally goes over my head, digital elements appearing over my sight lines.

"Woah," I say.

"Now. If you want to generate a weapon, which can be a knife, a small gun, a big gun, or a grenade, then you make a fist in whichever hand, and then use your eyes to select the weapon you want quickly with your eyes. Then, after you select, immediately unclench your fist." He waits for me to practice. I make a fist in my right hand and see a virtual menu pop up over my field of vision with modern three-dimensional diagrams of each weapon. The knife is to the far left, and I move my eyes to the far left before unclenching my fist as Ivo said. I am left dumbfounded as I feel a knife appear in my hand. I guess this is what Idri meant. I look up, and Ivo nods, and then he peels off, running towards the battle. He starts running, then hops up into the air and a cycle, like the one I drove earlier, appears under him. I guess he'll teach me that later I think to myself as I jog towards the chaos.

I see a massive group of soldiers coming from around the back and generate a grenade in my hand. Pulling out the pin, I toss it into the group and watch as the explosion tosses the bodies to the side. There are already an unreal amount of bodies littering the ground. Some of them are bleeding badly. Those are probably from Aiko's swords. Meanwhile, others have been slightly more elegantly disabled, probably the work of the brothers. I use some knives and toss them at some people, clumsily punching out at soldiers that come near me before one of the others comes to help me out. The tanks are destroyed before I know it, and the soldiers are all writhing on the ground. I see the ripple of a portal along the same line as the one we saw but next to the far left tank.

"Well done, guys," Ivo says, praising us as we gather together.

"But what did that do?" I ask. "The government has limitless amounts of soldiers. We needed information."

"Most of them are still alive, so don't worry about that."

"Uh-huh." We are about to find the most alive person, but then someone walks through the portal. He has blonde hair in a bun behind his head and is wearing a smart-looking grey suit.

"What the hell happened here?" He says in frustration before looking at us. I generate a gun in my hand and begin to take aim before Za knocks the gun out of my hand.

"Not him."

"Why not?"

"Because." The man starts to walk up to us before stopping in front of Ivo, who met him halfway.

"Ivo?"

"Tyler?" They pull each other in for a hug before Tyler walks around, hugging everyone. Then he gets to me and gives me a fist bump.

"Thanks for not killing me, kid."

"Yeah, anytime," I respond, so confused. "Can someone please explain to me what the hell is happening?"

"I got this," Za says, reassuring the rest of the group. "This is Tyler. He was a migrant with us way back when. So, we know him and love him, which is why we didn't want you to kill him."

"Ok...so you aren't working for the government?" I ask Tyler.

"Oh, god no. Are you kidding me? Absolutely not. I'm trying to find the government, actually."

"And how exactly are you doing that?" I ask.

"Hold on, hold on. We can bombard him with questions later." Idri stops me.

"We will have plenty of time back home. You are coming back with us, right?" Idri looks at Tyler.

"I mean. You kinda took out all of my guys, so I don't exactly have anywhere else to be at the moment."

"Right. Sorry about that."

"It's fine. I'll call some ambulances and they'll end up somewhere." We walk back through the portal, and Riz calls for the jet again.

The entire flight back, I just have a bunch of questions in my head for Tyler. If he was the one messing with the portals, what was he doing? If he isn't with the government but rather against it, then what is the government doing? And, if Tyler was with the Migrants, then how did he end up on such a different path than everyone else? Why isn't he living underneath the radar?

I lean back in my plush seat, frustrated that I can't ask him any of this now. This whole thing just got so complicated. And, to think that, just a few days ago, I was roaming around trying to find a way to get back into AltD because I tried to steal some fake creator cubes, ridiculous.

TIMO

November 5, 2040

Somehow, the campus seems much less lavish in the morning. I'd say it feels barren almost. Last night, the dining hall felt lively, populated by plenty of people with voices to ring through the space. However, without the congregation of everyone, every space feels too big and too over the top. The ratio of people versus space feeling more and more stark. I think this to myself as I walk through the gym to continue exploring. I have no idea if Cora was up when I left my room. I didn't bother to check. I told myself I'd try to get to know some other people. I guess you know you're living with a bunch of other teenagers when you wake up at ten in the morning and still no one is out of bed. The dining hall was completely empty when I left.

    I make it to the weapons room, where I run into Serge. He is admiring some guns in his arms, surrounded by other big weapons scattered on the ground. Almost every panel is open, so I finally get a chance to see the variety of weapons in here. Unsurprisingly, there is everything I could possibly imagine and some more on top of that. I notice an entire section solely for knives. There must be fifty knives meticulously hung up to create a very menacing wall. Serge must catch me looking because he takes down the coolest looking knife off of the wall and walks towards me with it.

"Into knives, are we?" He asks, handing me the implement. It's heavy in my hands, the knife completely decked out in matte black, resulting in no glare or reflection.

"Not especially. I just haven't seen that many knives in one place."

"I see. It's quite the sight indeed. I'm sure Cora must've told you that I love this room."

"She did." I'm about to hand him the knife when he points to a touch indent in the circular handle. I touch it with my thumb, the blade facing away from me, and the small knife blade somehow extends into a sword, the handle adjusting accordingly.. The entire move was so graceful.

"So, what have you thought of your stay so far?" Serge asks as he takes the sword, changes it back into a knife, and returns it to the wall. He waits for me to answer by going around the room, putting the weapons on the walls, and closing the white panels. The space quickly goes from a scattered weapons room to an unidentifiable secret. He circles back around to me.

"I like it here. It's very...nice." I want to say unnecessary, but that's probably not the right word. Serge chuckles.

"Nice. Yes. It's very nice here."

"And, I haven't even seen the whole thing," I add to break the awkward silence, sounding overly enthusiastic.

"That's true. To be honest, this place can feel like it's going on forever. I got used to it. But, when I first came here, it was quite the shock."

"You mean you weren't here when it was built?"

"Oh, god no. With Nox and Tirique, they didn't tell me much. It didn't really bother me. I was able to lead my army and make my weapons which is really what I wanted to do."

"So, what happened?"

"Well. I told you this before, but when Tirique died, I suddenly found all of these hidden notes. One of them told me about this place, so I inevitably came to check it out. Ever since, this has been my home base. Can't really imagine any place better, to be honest."

"Yeah. If you're going to be stuck in hiding, this is definitely the place," I comment while looking around, admiring the landscape I can see through the glass.

"Indeed." We stand for a couple more minutes of awkward silence before Serge decides to say something.

"Have you thought about my proposal yet?" I hesitate. Have I? I haven't taken out some time to actually think about it, kind of just waiting for a gut feeling to show up, which hasn't appeared as of yet.

"I guess all of it is still ruminating."

"I think that after a couple of days, with the special group of people we have here and the special place that we are lucky enough to live in, you will come to make the right decision. At least, I hope so."

"To be clear, this can't happen without me, correct?"

"Yes. You are the most important piece. Actually, some of the Princes are just here because we might need them. I'm almost positive we only need one of each kind of cube." At least I have all of the leverage.

"So, technically, you only really needed me. Because, I have all three cubes."

"That's what I thought until…well, I'll tell you later. I want the entire group to hear about this. In terms of your decision, I think you're thinking too much about Nox and Tirique when you should be thinking about how good this would all be for your life." I'm positive I have one of each kind of cube that exists, so I'm not sure what Serge could've found.

"How could I not? They were some really influential people. Or, should I say dangerous."

"They weren't dangerous." Serge begins to get tense before calming himself down. "History painted the picture others wanted to paint. History says that Nox was too radical, that he was trying to attempt something that would have crumbled society. Of course, it didn't help that the Wolf brothers, the biggest public icons, agreed with that."

"And, that's wrong?"

"Of course, it's wrong. I will admit, Nox was swayed to go towards some pretty violent measures, but his psyche was pure. He was simply trying to eradicate the discrimination that plagued the United States for so long."

"By enforcing discrimination against the white people."

"See. That's the part that is misconstrued. Of course, we had to discriminate against the white people in the beginning, to stabilize the government how we wanted. But, that was never the end of our agenda."

"How am I supposed to believe that?"

"Because you can't believe what everyone says, even if almost everyone believes it and even if you have a personal connection with that belief."

"What do you mean?"

"Come with me. I'll show you." I hadn't even noticed that both of us had sat down across from each other, but now we stand up and walk into the next hallway, which leads to the gym. We keep walking through various rooms; I don't even have time to ask what they are. Then we stop in the middle of a hallway, a locked frosted glass door in between us and the next room with another small hallway extended at an angle away from us.

"You would say that you are completely immersed in AltD, wouldn't you?"

"Yeah."

"And, because you're a Prince, would you say that you are more accustomed, more familiar, and know more than an average person about AltD."

"I'd say I know everything there is to know about AltD."

"That's right." With a look of satisfaction on his face, he turns and walks up to the door, unlocking it with his fingerprint on the side of the door—the frosted glass slides into the sidewall, and we walk through. The room is circular and, inevitably, all transparent glass. I can see below us, above us, the mountain to the side of us. But, I only look through the glass for a split second because floating in midair is a portal in the middle of the room. It doesn't look like a typical AltD portal. It doesn't have that transparency with ripples. It actually is the opposite. It's the blackest black I have ever seen with no ripples, making it look almost two-dimensional.

"What is this?"

"This is the only portal to the third dimension."

"What do you mean, the third dimension?"

"It is what it sounds like. It's not an entire world like Tirique built for AltD, but it feels just as real."

"I don't believe you."

"Then try it yourself." He walks to the wall where there is a small console attached. He touches an unlock button, and a small ripple runs through the portal in response. He signals to me that I can go through it now. I didn't know you could actually lock a portal, but I suppose this isn't a normal portal.

I step through it, the sensation is almost the same as for AltD, except it feels thicker, like I'm temporarily walking through water. When I get on the other side, I'm wearing exactly what I was wearing when I entered, that's different from AltD, and I didn't know that was possible to do. I'm looking at a jungle of some kind. All of my senses are active, just like in AltD, and everything feels just as real. I am shocked as I notice wildlife jumping and flying amongst the vines. I step backward through the portal and to the room with Serge, who locks the portal again.

"But why? Why does that exist?"

"Because, that's where Nox and Tirique will show up when we bring them back."

"But that just means they would be stuck in there for their existence instead of in AltD."

"I don't know if you could notice, but that dimension doesn't exactly act like the rest."

"What's that supposed to mean?"

"If they walk out of that portal after being brought back, then they will appear at a checkpoint inside of AltD."

"So that portal is the only way?"

"Yeah."

"Isn't that a liability?"

"No. Because, no one can be in the third dimension right now."

"Are you sure?"

"Positive."

KAI

November 5, 2040

We got back very late, and everyone collapsed into slumber before the questioning of Tyler could resume. I, shockingly, wake up pretty early in the morning, probably because of my eagerness to ask Tyler some questions. I got a guest room this time, so I roll out of bed, get dressed, which makes me feel more awake, and slowly make my way up the stairs. I'm pleasantly surprised to see Tyler already up, struggling to locate things in the kitchen.

"What are you looking for?" I ask him, walking up to the counter.

"The teabags."

"Over there, I think." I point to a drawer on the far right of the counter, and he walks over, opens the drawer, and happily picks out a teabag.

"Thank the lord. I've been looking for like five minutes. It's been painful." I smile. He seems like such an easy-going guy. He makes his tea and then sits at the counter, facing me.

"I know you want to ask me questions, and that's totally fine, but you might as well start now because it's going to be so much more stressful when the whole group is up."

"I agree." I thought I had tons of questions, but I can't think of any at the moment.

"I think you just want to know who the hell I am, so I'll just give you an extended introduction if that works."

"Yeah, that's great." He must've read my mind. Everyone here is incredibly good at reading others. It's getting a bit creepy.

"Well, my name is Tyler. I joined the Migrants about eight years ago when Idri found me on the streets. I was orphaned because the Board captured my parents for helping some kids of color. I helped everyone fight back against Nox. I was especially helpful because of my race. I could fit in with the Board soldiers and stuff, so I could go undercover pretty easily. Any questions so far?"

"Why are you not hiding like everyone else?"

"Good question. I don't really know. I would ask them why they are hiding in the first place. When everyone started to disperse, I wanted to find something to do. That's when my girlfriend and I started to explore society in Reality and how AltD was affecting it. To be honest, it was pretty depressing. And then, we started noticing the government was doing weird stuff with portals and whatever, so we decided to try to stop them." He gets all sad all of a sudden.

"What?"

"That's when it happened. Something very rare occurred. Aria was out exploring the portals, and then something went wrong. A portal was shut down as she was passing through it."

"I'm so sorry."

"After it happened, she was nowhere to be found, and I felt scrambled. I looked everywhere for answers until I found old research papers from Nox and Tirique. They made a place called the third dimension, and I think that, somehow, she ended up there."

"How do we get to the third dimension?"

"I have no idea. I don't even know for sure that it's possible."

"So, what did you do?"

"I kept going with what Aria and I had started, investigating what the government was doing with portals. In truth, I just wanted to learn more about the third dimension, to see if somehow I could find my way there. I've started to spiral recently. A few days ago, I attacked the government center and kidnapped this intern. It was a little out of rage and a little bit of thinking he could give me hints or at least tell me more about the government. He ended up escaping, but it's not like he was super helpful anyway."

"What now?"

"I have no idea, kid. I haven't seen these people in ages, and they are gonna ask about Aria as soon as they get up. But, I can't shake this gut feeling that the third dimension and this stuff with the government are connected somehow. It's a stretch, but my gut isn't usually wrong."

"Good thing you have me around."

"What do you mean?"

"Well. I'm going to help you find out."

"You don't have to do that, kid."

"Trust me. I have nothing else better to do."

DIMENSION

1 YEAR AGO

TYLER

October 1, 2038

"Hey. Check this out." Aria puts her book down and gets up from the couch, ambling towards me. I point at the computer screen displaying a map of the world with orange dots."

"What are the dots?" She says, leaning over my shoulder.

"Each dot is a portal."

"Ok."

"But check this out." I press the play button on the map, and the orange dots start changing, some appearing and others disappearing.

"What am I looking at, Ty? You're gonna have to help me out here."

"This is a live map of the portals, showing a sped-up version of the last month. Obviously, dots appear because portals are constantly appearing in high concentration areas, which we already know."

"Uh-huh." She skeptically follows my argument.

"Some dots are disappearing, though. Do you see that?"

"Yeah, that's bizarre."

"I think someone is closing the portals."

"Is that even possible?"

"I have no idea. But according to this, yeah."

"So, what are we supposed to do about that?"

"I think we have to go check them out."

"Should I tell the team?"

"No. I got it. You go and get ready."

"Ok." Aria gets up and walks out of the office. It's not really an office. The table is cluttered, with empty glasses and books surrounding my laptop and monitor. It doesn't look messy. It just feels messy. The rest of the room is kind of the same. Aria is always reading while I'm investigating stuff, so a bunch of her books are stacked on the side of the coffee table and around in wooden bookshelves against the walls. There is an old and beat-up brown leather couch facing me from behind the table and a big matching armchair which no one ever occupies except for me. I slide back in my office chair and walk out of the door. The hallway is concrete and, excluding Aria and I's room, this is where the sterility is.

When the team split up, Aria and I wanted to have something to do, let the Migrant legacy live on somehow. Of course, the team didn't actually split up for any reason other than the fact that the brothers and Idri wanted to get some peace and quiet, and who could blame them for that. Aria and I found this abandoned warehouse in New York City and renovated it ourselves, recruiting some old migrants who wanted something to do. Then there are the soldiers who worked for Nox and felt bad, so they volunteered to be part of my army. I hate that word, but that's the best way to describe them. I don't really like any of them. They are kinda just terrible people, but it's not like I was going to put my beloved migrants in the way of harm, so I might as well use them if they volunteered.

The hallway quickly turns into a catwalk bridge, suspended above the open warehouse space. There are a few couches in various corners facing big TVs. Otherwise, the space is pretty open, with desk surfaces moving around on wheels and various office chairs. The work we do is pretty low-key, although we find it pretty important. Basically, we have just been traveling and doing online research, tracking how people interact with AltD and what different nations are going through. It's harmless work, and sometimes we can bring resources to people that need them. Over the past four years, we've noticed more and more people leaving Reality and spending their time in AltD. It's scary how different places are looking.

Most of the fighting team are conversing by the TVs. They are all wearing black, as I told them to do since the beginning. They always show up and hang out in the morning until I come down and tell them if I need them or not. Today, I think we will need everyone we have to cover as much ground as we possibly can. I bound down the wooden stairs descending from the catwalk and greet everyone.

"Hello, people." They all perk up and wander towards me. "We actually have something for you to do today." I wait for some kind of response, and they look at each other in shock before clapping.

"They never have anything to do," Aria jokes, walking up from behind me, her stylish jeans and white shirt traded for athletic tights and a long sleeve black shirt.

"Well, they do now. Here's the deal. There is some strange stuff going on with the portals, and we need to see what the hell is happening."

"What are we looking for?" One of them asks. I haven't learned their names yet.

"The portals are disappearing. So that, I guess." Everyone seems a bit confused, so I grab a handful of old printed maps on the table next to me.

"Here. Take these. They are old maps with marks of where all the portals are. If you go to that area and can't find the portal, it means it has disappeared."

"Ok. But what are we supposed to do with that information? You could just find that on your computer. Why do you need us to be in person there?" That's a great question. I actually hadn't thought this all of the way through, clearly. I look at Aria for help. She giggles at my lack of planning.

"For now, just ask people that live around the area if they noticed anything strange or if they know anything about the portals disappearing."

"And, if we see some sketchy government soldiers snooping around?" I can't help but smile to myself because that was very literally them not so long ago.

"If you see some sketchy soldiers…." This time Aria looks at me for help.

"Then take them out, keep them alive, of course, and we can ask them some questions." They all nod and start heading out. I'm assuming they will start in the city since we didn't tell them anywhere else to go. I look at Aria, who gives me an unconvincing shrug.

"What?" I ask.

"I've been walking around the city too many times; it's gotten a bit boring."

"Field trip?" She brightens up, hugging me. "Where to?"

"You decide."

"Have you ever wanted to check out Japan?" She hugs me even tighter in response before backing away.

"Wait. We can't afford to go to Japan."

"It's ok. I know a friend." She gives me a skeptical look.

"Really, Ty. Friend? You don't have any friends. I'm your only friend." Kind of true.

"Jeez. That's harsh. I have some friends."

"Who? Who are your friends?"

"Ivo, Za, Idri…"

"I'm going to stop you right there. They don't count."

"Why not?"

"Because you were introduced to them because it was for survival. You didn't just meet them as strangers and become best friends with them."

"That's what I did with you. Does that mean our friendship doesn't count?" She grumbles as she realizes I won the argument.

"How come you win the arguments now? I used to always win." She starts to turn around and write a note to leave for the team.

"And, for the record, we weren't friends when we first met."

"We weren't?"

"No. You tackled me remember?"

"What?"

"At the dock. Remember?"

"Oh yeah. I didn't tackle you. You were the one that hit me. I just had to make sure you got the note. I forgot all of that happened."

"Good thing you coincidently ended up on that train."

"Aria. I've tried to explain this to you so many times."

"What?"

"It was not a coincidence. I knew you were going to be there."

"So then why did you say 'what a coincidence.'" She uses air quotes.

"I was sarcastic clearly."

"I don't think so." We still frequently quarrel like this, but, generally, we have been pretty much inseparable since the moment we met, and we've been through it all together.

"How's this?" She holds up a note with black marker reading 'Out to check out international portals. Be back soon. Keep up the good work.' There are three smiley faces at the bottom, Aria's signature touch.

"Great. Now can we go, please?"

DIMENSION

"You're not even dressed." I look down and curse at myself, immediately running up the stairs as Aria laughs at me. I sprint into the room, shedding my house clothes and pulling on black chinos and a ribbed black shirt with a hood attached. Aria is going to be annoyed and claimed that I copied her outfit. I think it's funny when we match because it bothers her so much. I'm about to slip on some black leather sneakers when I catch a pair of Jordan 1s behind my dresser. Who we are going to see is going to appreciate these. I grab those instead and run back downstairs. Aria presses her phone.

"Forty-five seconds. Kinda slow if you ask me. Now, who's holding up the show?" I roll my eyes and walk through the front door. She follows me, and we start weaving through the once lively city.

There used to be all different kinds of people roaming the streets, always walking with purpose or lingering for entertainment. The aromas of ethnic cuisine would fill the air, complimenting the smell of drugs and cigarettes. As soon as you stepped outside, you felt invigorated, like you should do something or you wouldn't be doing the city itself justice. It took a couple of years, but eventually, the city lost its life. Now the buildings are just buildings, tall and sterile. The streets are barren and boring, and the few people that are still actually living in the city are tired and annoyed. That's what one of the most exciting cities in the world has come to. The problem is, it's not like Aria and I have anywhere else to go unless we wanted to go back to Boston, which is not too much better, I don't think.

We weave through the empty streets, using alleys as shortcuts until we find the nearest portal in Central Park. The park may be the only place that has resemblances of the old city life. It's much more unkept now, but I don't mind it, and the lush nature is a breath of fresh air, literally. The portal is right next to a bench, a bush literally sitting right in front of it.

TYLER

Aria found it not so long ago when we were hanging out here. We took a picture, and then she stepped back, tripped on the bush, and disappeared. She came back, shocked that she found a portal.

"Ready?" I ask.

"This never gets old," she replies, grabbing my hand as we step over the bush and the portal envelopes us.

.

ARIA

October 1, 2038

New York City in AltD is so different, so much better, to be honest. We walk out into Central Square. This time there is no bush in our way. There are people everywhere, and it's almost too crowded. Ty and I take a moment to admire it, the happiness on people's faces, the smell of food on the grill, it's all so livening. Our matching black outfits have been replaced with a suit on Tyler. He has a pair of sharp-looking black suit pants, a white t-shirt, a matching black blazer, and white leather sneakers. I'm now wearing a fancy summery top and tight jeans, basically what I was wearing earlier this morning before I got changed.

"What's the plan, boss?" I ask Tyler, who is deeply inhaling the AltD air. We don't like to spend an absurd amount of time here because we think it will take us too far away from Reality and the lives we have there. But, we definitely relish every excuse we have to enter AltD, and we try to make the most out of it every time. The last time we were here, Ty took me on a quote-on-quote 'date' to look at the stars. It was half dorky, half romantic. The pollution has gotten so bad in Reality that seeing the stars at night is very rare. Of course, climate change isn't really a thing in AltD. Tirique made sure of that when he made it.

"To be completely honest. I only had a small percentage of a plan."

"Of course you did," I complain. This always happens. Tyler is no Ivo Wolf, that's for sure. "Tell me what parts of the plan you have."

"You're going to make fun of me."

"I'm going to make fun of you either way Ty."

"Yeah, alright. Basically. I know where we are going, roughly. And I know that it would've been more enjoyable if we used AltD to get there."

"And…?"

"That's it. That's all I got."

"Really, Ty. You can't be serious." He has that look where he seems so disappointed in himself, but I know he's just doing it to make me feel bad for making fun of him.

"Well, if we are logical, then we should probably find a means of transportation. Right?" I slap my head.

"Yes, Ty. Yes. We can't just walk to Japan."

"Catch a flight?"

"And how are we going to pay for that flight?" He winks. "Oh god, no. No, Tyler. We are not sneaking illegally onto a flight."

"Cmon. It'll be fun."

"We could also get caught."

"Yeah, that's what makes it fun."

"Fine."

"Really?"

"Yeah. Let's go before I change my mind." He punches the air in celebration, and I shake my head as I follow him to the public bike area. We each hop on electric bikes, and Tyler starts furiously pedaling to get it started, which means I have to actually exercise my legs as we make our way to the airport.

We get to the area where everyone is being dropped off for their flights in around two hours. The circular sidewalk area filled with suitcases and goodbyes as the shade is illuminated by the glow of the various flight destinations. It's still so bizarre to me how real people's lives in AltD are. They have families with feelings, homes with jobs, travel with goodbyes. All of it is so immersive and real. It really has replaced Reality in a way I could have never imagined.

"What now?" I ask Tyler, who drops his bike on the ground.

"We have to find the right plane." I walk over the list of flights and their destinations.

"What's it lookin like?"

"Unsurprisingly, the only flight going to Japan is through Japan Airways." There aren't really any private airlines or anything because the flights are all run by robots and such. But, there are still different airlines just so that it feels more familiar to people. At least, that is what Tyler and I have always thought.

"That makes it pretty easy then. Let's go." He sneaks around to the side of the airport building. I see the lines of planes in the distance. Tyler takes out his glasses, puts them on, and uses them as binoculars, zooming in on the distance.

"I see it." He says, excited. "It's kinda far. When does the flight leave?"

"In fifteen minutes."

"Oh god. We better hurry." I follow him as he scurries around the side of the building. There aren't any human security guards, which doesn't really help us. Instead, there are Bots crawling around everywhere and security cameras that can alert them really quickly if they see any suspicious actions. He hugs the building very tight, barely staying in the blind spot of the cameras. It's a bit easier for me because I'm smaller.

There are small cars with carts driving around, the carts used for suitcases. The cars are all on tracks, as is pretty much everything else. Everything moves with no flaws and with extremely high efficiency. Tyler points to a car going in the direction we want to go in, and it helps it doesn't have too much luggage in the back. I nod at him, and he sprints towards it, heaving himself into the cart and turning around to help me up. We duck low in the cart so the cameras can't see us. The car doesn't move too fast, but it goes quickly enough for us to get to the plane with enough time to find a way in.

When we are directly underneath the aircraft that has 'Japan Airways' written in massive cursive pink on the side, we jump out, hiding behind the wheels of the plane. Tyler frantically scans the area, seeing how the hell we are going to get on the plane without anyone noticing us. I notice the latch to the luggage door unlocked and nudge Tyler, pointing at it. He smiles at me and kisses my forehead before running over, opening the door, and looking in. He shrugs his shoulders as if to say it's bearable and then ushers me over. We both dive through the door and onto a layer of suitcases, closing the door behind us.

The space is barely lit. Only small dim lights and sunlight peaking in through cracks serve as illumination of any kind. The suitcases below us are oddly comfortable, debatably better than our old couches at home, and the big open space means we aren't too cramped. It could be better, could be worse in my assessment.

"I can't believe we pulled that off," I exclaim.

"It wouldn't have happened without you pointing out the luggage door. That was smart. Nice job."

"Thanks. And it looks like your piece of a plan is working so far."

DIMENSION

"Don't jinx it."

"Fine. I won't." I lean against his shoulder, trying to get as comfortable as possible because this is a very long flight with a cloud of mystery over what's waiting for us on the other side.

TYLER

October 2, 2038

I could barely sleep on the plane, the constant jostling kept waking me up, and I needed to mentally go through all of the places my friend could be in Japan. I know he's in Tokyo, but there are a lot of people in Tokyo, and I have no idea where he is. Meanwhile, Aria pretty much slept the entire time, her head secured against my shoulder. When we finally land, I tap her awake.

"We are here." She rubs her eyes, and I laugh as she looks around like she's expecting to see a new place. Annoyed at me making fun of her, she slaps my chest and gets up. When the plane finally comes to a complete stop, I open the luggage latch to make sure the coast is clear.

"Let's go." I gesture to Aria when I see that the security Bots and luggage cars aren't here yet. She follows me out of the door and onto the concrete. The fresh air and breeze feel very refreshing against my skin, and the warm temperature is comforting. I notice passengers exiting the plane and walking into the airport, and I direct us towards them, seamlessly joining the line without anyone noticing. We walk into the airport and don't spend any time admiring the extremely modern architecture or the delicious-looking Japanese food before moving straight through the airport and out into the city. Lucky for us, we are already in Tokyo, and the city is even brighter and more lively than New York, accompanied by a completely different vibe.

"What now?" Aria asks.

"I honestly have no clue," I reply.

"Where do we start?"

"You hungry?" I ask, my stomach grumbling as I say it.

"Starving," she replies.

"Then, let's find some grub."

"Never say that again."

"What?"

"You said grub. That sounded god awful. It was so cringe I literally shuddered."

"Fine." I shake my head as we walk deeper into the city and spot a portal. When we step through it, there is literally good food everywhere we look, and neither Aria nor I is especially good at making decisions which means we are pretty much wandering around in circles for two hours. I'm shocked that the city is actually functioning and not like New York, and there's real stuff to do. For the first hour, we are looking at street vendors' menus, figuring out which breakfast food we would rather have. However, Aria mentioned that it was pretty much time for lunch once we thought we finally decided. That meant that we had to start all over again with an eye for different food. We finally end up finding some sushi, munching it down as we walk through a farmers market.

"We seriously have to start getting better at making decisions," Aria complains.

"Yeah, seriously. I mean, we were doing fine before you mentioned that it was lunchtime now."

"You're really going to blame this one me? I mean, I wasn't the one that said no to perfectly fine sushi because it didn't have the right kind of fish."

"What do you mean? The whole point of sushi is the fish. That's literally the one key ingredient."

"Whatever, Ty." We keep moving through the farmers market, stopping every two minutes so that Aria can examine some local fruit. We stop in front of the Japanese pears, Aria attempting to have a conversation with the vendor when I spot a pair of Jordans facing me from the opposite side of the stand. The shoes turn around and start walking away, and I step out into the open center of the market to see more of the person's body. The short but wavy jet black hair and high fashion street clothing look can only belong to one man. I run up to him and tap his shoulder, he spins around, and his backward black cap almost flies off his head in shock.

"Tyler?"

"Aziz."

"It's been a minute."

"It's been more than a minute."

"Couple years at least. Are you alone?"

"Nope. Aria is with me."

"What are you guys doing here?"

"I'll catch you up in a bit. For now, let's surprise Aria."

"Aight." I walk back to Aria, and Aziz stays close behind me but out of sight. I walk up from behind her, grabbing her hand.

"Where did you go?" She asks.

"Thought I saw someone I knew."

"And?"

"Well. It's like you said, I don't have any friends."

"Except for me." Aziz jumps out from behind me. Our unrehearsed surprise worked to perfection. Aria can't contain her excitement.

"Aziz!" She gives him a big hug and then looks at me in shock.

"This was who you were talking about?" She questions me.

"I can't believe you ever doubted me," I respond.

"Ok. Come on, you guys, I'll take you back to my place." We follow Aziz through the market and down the city's back streets until we get to a small storefront for what looks like a convenience store. He swings open the old wooden door and into a tiny space with snacks of all kinds lining the walls. An older man sits on a stool towards the back left corner, and Aziz waves.

"How are you, Cho?" Aziz asks in English. The man responds in Japanese, and Aziz continues in fluent Japanese. Aria looks at me in surprise at hearing Aziz speak another language. Aziz nods goodbye, and I wave to the man, who nods back before Aziz goes towards the drink fridge. He grabs the right side of the fridge with a slight lip and pulls, the entire thing swinging open to reveal a hallway. Now it's my turn to be surprised. The hallway has a battered wooden plank floor which is replaced by smooth black wooden planks once the space opens up. There is floor-to-ceiling glass on the back wall. A small but modern kitchen is in the far right corner, a living and dining area to its left, and a big desk in the middle. On the left wall, which is concrete, there is a bed that must fold down.

"I was about to talk about your modest livings, which I guess still counts, but it was definitely not what I was expecting," I comment.

"Yeah, it's not too shabby."

"Why did you settle here, Aziz?" Aria asks as Aziz gestures for us to sit, and we oblige.

"It wasn't really my initial plan. After the team kinda disbanded and my brother went off to do whatever tech thing he wanted to do, I wanted to travel the world. It was quite the time for a few months before I started helping my brother with Wolf brother-type missions. And then, I wanted to travel some more. But, by that time, every place was desolate. Except, for some crazy reason, Tokyo. This was always a dream place for me. I love the people, the language, and the culture. So, I guess I just stayed. I wanted as close to a normal life in Reality that I could get, and this was that."

"You and Riz really picked up the Wolf brother mantle." Aria comments.

"I never thought Riz and I could nearly do as much, but the brothers endorsed us kinda. They gave us these after all." He reaches for his neck and pulls out a necklace from under his shirt. It's gold with a cube on it.

"Oh-oh. This was before your time, I think. My bad." He tucks it under his shirt without any more explanation, leaving me wondering what the significance of that necklace is.

"So, what are you up to nowadays?" I ask.

"Not much, honestly. There's not too much to do. I help Cho out front-run the shop. He lives above me. Other than that, I've mostly been living a simple life, with tons of reading, eating, and sleeping. I was teaching combat courses for a while."

"If you've been reading all day, every day, for the past year, then I'm scared of how much you packed into your head," Aria mentions Aziz's photographic memory, which I completely forgot about. He chuckles at her comment.

"If you ever suddenly get seriously into mathematics, philosophy, or obscure nature facts, then I'm your guy." He gets up and grabs a small leather bag on one of the bookshelves before walking back over and sitting down on the ground next to my feet. He zips open the bag and pulls out a microfiber cloth and a spray thing.

"You think I didn't notice your shoes? They were the first thing I saw." He begins to rub out the skid marks and dirt, methodically spraying and then making circular motions with his hand.

"I wore them just for you, Aziz."

"I'm proud of you just for having them." I look at Aria with a look of immense satisfaction, and she just rolls her eyes at me.

"You guys ever going to tell me why you're here? I mean, I love having company, I've actually been in desperate need of it, but you did just surprise me."

"Before we get to that, you guys have to tell me how you stayed in touch," Aria demands.

"What do you mean?" Aziz asks.

"Yeah, we just never lost touch," I confidently reply.

"I mean, to be honest, Tyler and I were the best friend match within the team, and we made a deal to keep in touch. We've been texting ever since."

"Kinda fell off recently."

"It was your fault."

"Yeah, kinda was." In the beginning, when I didn't really have much to do, I was texting Aziz all of the time. I have no idea why I never told Aria about it; I just assumed she was still in touch with other people, like Aiko or Riz or something. Quickly life got a little bit more full, and I forgot to keep in contact. What was everyday communication quickly became chatting every month or so.

"So, can you please tell me why you're here?" He directs his question to Aria, but she looks at me and hands it off to me. I think I still know a little bit more about what's going on.

"Are you familiar with portals?"

"Yeah. There are a ton in Tokyo. It's for that AltD thing, right?"

"Exactly."

"Ok."

"So those portals pop up in places of high concentration, whether that's high population concentration in AltD or in Reality."

"That's why there are so many portals here in Tokyo," Aria adds.

"Got it."

"A few months ago, or maybe even farther back, we don't know, but, for a while, portals have started to disappear," I continue.

"And, that's bad?" Aziz asks.

"Well, not necessarily bad for the people because there are plenty of portals in most places."

"So then?"

"Well, it's just not supposed to be happening. That's not how AltD was designed."

"By Tirique?"

"Yeah. Tirique."

"So, what's happening?" Aria decides to take this one.

"We think that someone is regulating the portals. Like they found a way to turn them off or something. We aren't sure how, but it's got to be the government." I pick it up again.

"And the government shouldn't have control over anything in AltD. The whole point of AltD is that it's completely free, the only regulation being the coded AI and the Bots."

"So the government is messing with stuff yet again." We both nod.

"That's just fantastic," Aziz says sarcastically. "But why here?"

"Oh. Well, we were going to go investigate the portals anyways. We could've gone anywhere, but I thought we might as well make a trip out of it, and it was fun to surprise Aria with your presence."

"Understood. So, when are you guys starting this work? I would love to help. Give me something new to do."

"Thanks, Aziz. We are probably going to start tomorrow."

"No. Now. Let's start now."

"Now?"

"I'm already bored thinking of the nothingness I have to do between now and tomorrow morning."

"Ok, then. I guess we are starting now."

ARIA

October 2, 2038

"Great. So what's the plan." Aziz's excitement level has increased a lot from when we first started this conversation. I'm starting to have visions of him seven years ago when he was just a kid, bouncing at every opportunity he had to get into an adventure.

"Uhhhh. The plan…" Tyler struggles to think.

"Ty does not have a plan. It's kinda been a theme for this whole trip."

"Just lemme think. You people kinda just threw me into the deep end on this one." I decide to take over.

"I want to check out the portals, and we need someone monitoring the portals from back here. So, I will go check out the portal with a way to talk to you guys and Aziz and you will monitor stuff here. Plus, then you can catch Aziz up on AltD stuff, so he knows what's happening."

"Now that's a good plan. Was that so hard?" Aziz makes fun of Ty, and he punches Aziz's shoulder.

"I think I should be on plan duty from now on," I say.

"No. I still have a better track record with plans. Also, I don't like your plan," Ty replies.

"Why not?"

"Yeah, why? I like her plan." Aziz backs me up.

"Because, I don't like us splitting up. What if something happens?"

"Awwww. That's so romantic." Aziz continues to tease Tyler, and I laugh.

"C'mon, Ty. What's the worst that can happen?"

"Not sure if you remember this boss, but the last time we split up didn't go so well."

"Oh. Right." I forgot about that.

"And guess whose plan that was?" He got me there.

"Well. We are optimistically charging into the future."

"Uh-huh." I grab his hand.

"Seriously, it'll be fine. Plus, you and Aziz need your bro time or whatever."

"She has a point." Aziz backs me up again.

"Will you shut up," Tyler snaps back. Aziz and I both laugh. "Fine. Fine. I give up. We will use your plan." I get up and start walking out of the door.

"Use your glasses for communication. I have no idea where I'm going, so send me the nearest portal location as well." Tyler nods, and Aziz waves to me as I walk out of the door. I forget that the door is literally a drink fridge, and I clumsily stumble out of the doorway. Cho just looks at me, unchanged from the last position he was sitting in.

"Hi, Cho." I wave with a smile. He does the same nod back that he did the last time I waved. I put on my glasses, and I accept Tyler's invite for communication before walking out of the door and feeling the breeze against my skin again. I'm happy Ty accepted my plan, although somewhat reluctantly. I guess he posed a good argument and I suppose it was slightly romantic.

"Turn right and walk straight. There should be a portal in the middle of the city." Tyler says through the glasses.

"Can you send me the location?"

"Aria. It's literally just straight."

"Send it to me anyway."

"Why?"

"Cuz."

"Oh my lord. Fine." A file is sent, and I see it pop up in the top right of my vision. I open it and have the navigation system of the glasses overlay the directions onto my sightline, meaning arrows pop up over the street in front of me. Inevitably, it's just a straight arrow, like Tyler said. I enjoy the gradual modernization of the city as I walk closer and closer to the center. The buildings grow taller and taller, glass soon becomes the prominent material, and the number of people definitely becomes denser. I think Ty would've been just as surprised as me to see that Tokyo is still a city alive.

"Is Aziz there?"

"Yeah, I'm here," he responds.

"Aziz, why did the Tokyo population not revert to AltD? I don't get it. How, out of all of the major cities in the world, did Tokyo stay intact?"

"I honestly am not sure. Having a digital presence was a thing in Japan before any other country, so I guess people just weren't impressed. Japan is an island, so it was barely affected by the whole Revolution. They closed the borders and went on with life. I guess the stability they had meant that things like AltD were just so much less appealing. Could you not quote me on this, by the way? I'm just speculating."

"That makes sense, though." I keep walking until my glasses tell I'm within one hundred feet of my destination.

"Do you have any more details on the portal, Ty?"

"No, not really. Based on what I can see from here, I think it might be like right next to a building."

"That's just great. The portal that is very hard to find in the first place is right next to a complete glass building. Nice."

"Yeah, that's not ideal. Sorry about that."

"What do I do? Should I just walk into the side of the building, and hope I don't crash into glass?" I hear Aziz burst out laughing.

"Yes, do that. Please do that," he says.

"The depth will be slightly different with the portal so, if you look at it straight on, the reflection on the glass shouldn't be consistent. Try to look for that." Tyler comes in with honest advice.

"Ok. Thanks, Ty."

"Oh, cmon. The other thing would've been so much more entertaining," Aziz whines. I can hear Tyler slap his neck, and I smile at them joking around. I turn towards the glass buildings, which pretty much line every inch of each side of the street. I start on the right, carefully examine my reflection in the glass of each building as I walk by. The first two buildings look entirely normal, my reflection smooth throughout the entire glass sheet. But the third building does something weird. As I pass by the middle of the building, the top of my head gets kinda cut off and moved a bit lower. However, at the same point, it does this. There also happens to be the point where the new set of glass panels start.

"Guys. I have a bit of a situation over here."

"Yeah. What's up?" Aziz asks.

"Aziz. Even if she were to respond to you, would you have any idea how to help her?"

"Didn't you just explain to me how the portals work?"

"Yeah, for like thirty seconds. That doesn't make you an expert."

"Guys. Can you stop arguing and actually help me?" I demand.

"Yeah. Yeah. Sorry about him. What's up?"

"Well, I see what could be the portal. The problem is where the portal starts could also be the split between the two layers of glass panels, so I can't tell if it's actually the portal. Does that make sense?"

"Yes. It does."

"I think there is only one option here," Aziz comments again.

"Shut up, Aziz." Tyler retaliates.

"What? She obviously has to try the genius plan of trial and error and jump at it and see if it works."

"Your kidding," I argue.

"That actually might be the only way."

"And if it's not the portal?" I ask.

"It's gonna hurt. But, hopefully not too bad."

"I can't believe I'm actually going to do this."

"To be fair, I did say that we shouldn't split up if I remember correctly, and, in that case, I would've definitely jumped instead of you."

"Thanks for that backhanded reassurance, Ty."

"Yeah, no problem. Love you, and may God be with your soul."

I back up a few steps, visualizing where the rectangular portal is. I really hope I don't jump into glass which I will do if I can't figure out how to make this jump. I quickly realize that I'm no Zashil Wolf, not that I was even in the same stratosphere of athleticism in the first place, and I'm going to need some help with this. I frantically look left and right for anything I can step on, but all of the benches around are unstable and drilled into the ground. I'm about to throw in the towel and ask Tyler for help, but then I spot an old car idling with its windows down. I walk over, making sure the keys are still in the car, and when I see that they are, I unlock the door from the inside and climb into the car. Sorry to whoever's car this is, I guess. I drive it the two blocks over, so it's parked underneath the portal. I get out, climbing on the hood and then stumbling onto the top of the car. I really hope this works. Otherwise, I'm going to look really stupid.

"Make sure you mark this location, Ty. So you have a more specific location for later."

"Got it," he replies. Then I stand up and hop through the portal. However, instead of the usual feeling of my body phasing into a new Reality. I'm stuck in this void for an extra amount of time before finally exiting the portal. It felt like I was stuck in transit for a long time, although time can be really misconstrued when you're messing with dimensions. I get up in some kind of jungle. There is thick foliage everywhere I look. This doesn't really look like AltD Japan. I keep walking deeper into the jungle and then sit down, convinced that I'm not where I'm supposed to be. I walk back towards the portal, the exact spot I first entered, but the portal is gone. I slap at the empty air, waiting for something to happen.

"Tyler? Tyler? Aziz?" I frantically say, my glasses are still on my face, but no communication comes back. I sit down, my head in my hands. Where am I? How did I get here?

TYLER

October 2, 2038

"Aria? Are you ok? How's it looking on the other side." The communication still says it's online, but we sit in suspense for two minutes.

"Why isn't she responding?" Aziz asks.

"She probably just ran into some kind of situation on the other end. Just give her a minute." We wait for another minute, and then some static comes over the coms. "Do you know if those are words?" I ask Aziz. He leans in closer to the laptop speakers.

"I don't think those are words or, more likely, I just can't make any words out."

"Weird," I say as Aziz leans back.

"Maybe she just entered a dead zone or something and needs some time."

"There aren't really supposed to be any dead zones in AltD."

"Oh. Ok."

"I mean...I don't think so. I could be wrong. I suppose it's possible that the tether between our glasses could be disrupted when trying to communicate across dimensions."

"I only know what like half of that means, but it seems like you just agreed with me."

"Let's just give her some more time," I defiantly say. A little worry is starting to creep in, but I'm sure Aria is fine. She probably just forgot to change her communication settings. She might even be on her way home now, and we are questioning her for no reason.

"So you were telling me about the portals. Are they the only way to get into AltD?" I know Aziz is trying to distract me because he is sensing some kind of doubt in me, but I don't care because it's working. I was telling him about the portals for a bit while Aria was checking out the buildings, trying to get into the portal.

"No. You can use your glasses too, which is actually a more common mode."

"Glasses?"

"These." I take the glasses off my face and hand them to him.

"Weren't you just using these for communication?" I had wirelessly connected the communication from my glasses to my laptop so that Aziz could speak and listen.

"Yeah. They can do a lot of different things."

"Like what?"

"Well. They can do augmented Reality and display things over your field of vision. Most cities, in Reality, are still adjusted for this, and they can look really different when you see the overlays."

"I'm going to have to try that out."

"And then the glasses have basically replaced smartphones. So I can text people from it, call people, search the Internet and everything like that. The glasses can track my eyesight and is also connected to my neurons so it can basically respond to my thinking."

"Damn. And then, AltD?"

"Yeah. People can enter AltD using their glasses. They can do that from wherever they want, but people usually just do it from their homes."

"Do you do that a lot?"

"No, not really. I don't really like doing it."

"Why?"

"Well. If you use your glasses, then you appear in a set location in AltD. And then, when you want to return to Reality, you obviously return to where you are sitting."

"And?"

"It's just significantly less fun than moving through the portals and using AltD as a way to get to new places in Reality. For instance, we couldn't have done this trip had it not been for the portals."

"I see what you're saying. So, have you given me enough information for me to be proficient in AltD talk?"

"Let's not jump too far ahead, Aziz. I still haven't told you about ghosts, Bots, the cubes, Princes, or anything like that."

"That was a lot of words that a virtual dimension shouldn't have rebranded." I smile at that.

"That was a good one."

"What do you mean? All of my jokes are bangers. Anyways, are you gonna tell me about all that nonsense."

"Not right now. Right now, I wanna figure out where the hell my girlfriend is."

"Fair point." I stand up, taking my glasses back from Aziz and tucking them into my pocket.

"Let's go check it out."

"Aight." We walk out of the house, Aziz stopping to have a short conversation with Cho, who nods to me before walking away.

"How long did it take you to learn Japanese?"

"I don't know. Maybe a few months to get fluent."

"Wow. That's fast."

"Yeah, I guess so. Cho still helps me when I get something wrong but living in a place where everyone speaks Japanese helped a lot. I bought a few books to help me learn the language, but I barely used them. I think language learning is more about immersion than anything. I mean, my memory didn't hurt either, obviously."

"Interesting." I stop midway through the street. "Are we going the right way?"

"Yeah. It's straight this way and then a little turn at the fork." I'm about to ask him how he knows that, but then he tells me.

"Memory. Remember? I saw the map."

"What I would pay to get a photographic memory."

"Trust me. It's not always helpful. Sometimes it's just depressing."

"What do you mean?"

"Well, I don't get to choose everything I remember, do I?"

"Understood." It only takes us a few minutes to make it to the line of buildings that Aria was standing at. I immediately walk over to a car idling in front of a building. Aria probably used this to get a boost into the portal since it was so high up. There is a small dent in the hood where Aria must've put her weight, and I step up onto the same place. I then clamber onto the top of the car, but the portal is nowhere to be seen. I push my hand into where it should be, but I just feel the harsh cool glass, and I leave a guilty handprint smudge.

"It's not here," I say, a waver in my voice.

"How?"

"It disappeared."

"Ok. But how?"

"I don't know Aziz. No one knows. That's why the Aria and I were here in the first place, remember," I say, rushed and annoyed.

"Ok, ok. Are you, I mean we, sure that this is the right place?"

"Positive." I take a moment to think. If the portal disappeared, then it doesn't really explain anything. The communication line should still be working. And, Aria obviously got through the portal, so that means it disappeared after she went in. Hypothetically she should be in AltD in Japan, most likely trying to find another portal to get back here. If I could see footage of her going through, I could see exactly how it all happened. Then I remember that I have a way to track Aria's location, not in a creepy way. We tethered our glasses with locations to find each other in AltD if one of us was in AltD and the other in Reality. I pull out my glasses and slide them onto my face, accessing the feature. I check everywhere in Japan, there is no sign of her location, and there is no chance she could get out of Japan this fast. I mean, it's an island.

"Aziz, do you know where we can find security footage of this street."

"Yeah. Why?"

"You'll see. Can you take me there?"

"Sure. We aren't going to have to travel far; it's like a block away." I hop down from the car and start following Aziz through the city. I'm too anxious to admire the bustling life amongst the modern glass buildings, the absence of Aria starting to set in, and after that really comes the worry. I follow Aziz into a building and up the stairs. There is a security desk, but the guy just nods to Aziz and unlocks the door for us.

"Are you really on good terms like that with the security?"

"I have helped them with a few criminal missions here and there because Tokyo still has real crime because we have real society. So, they repay me with some access and sometimes some money. I really just do it because they told me they'd look out for Cho."

DIMENSION

"Why would they need to protect Cho?" I ask as we walk into the security camera room. Another guy at the desk nods to Aziz and then leaves.

"His son died in gang violence, and there is always a threat that somebody would come for him to get his money or something. I can't always be around to look out for him, so I made that deal with the police." Aziz is starting to seem like a much more mature person than he was acting like before, although I think he was just trying to annoy me on purpose. He pulls the chair out for me, and I sit down.

I swipe through the various cameras, each swipe getting me a certain distance farther away from the building we are in until I find the best camera angle looking at where we were. The camera is across the street, and I can zoom in, which helps a lot. I rewind the footage a couple of hours and then watch as Aria wanders around, finds the car, and parks it in front of the building.

"I guess you were right about that," Aziz comments as I continue to watch. She steps onto the hood of the car like I predicted and then jumps into the portal. She disappears through the building. So, she definitely made it through the portal. I know Aziz wants to comment on how cool that is, but I hear him swallow his words.

"I'm an idiot," I say.

"Why?"

"I came all this way to check out the timing of everything. Like when Aria went through the portal and then when the portal disappeared."

"Ok. And?"

"Well, portals are practically invisible, to begin with. And then, on top of that, this portal was in front of the glass. So there is absolutely no chance I would be able to discern anything from this footage."

"Oh."

"Are there alternate ways of viewing it by any chance?"

"Yeah. I think there is infrared."

"That might just work." Aziz nods and presses a button beside the keyboard. Suddenly all of the footage switches to infrared footage. All portals have very strong heat signatures because they appear in high concentration areas, or at least that's what I figured myself.

"The Japanese really like having all of the features, even if they are unnecessary."

"This is going to be helpful." I rewind and play back the footage again. This time I see Aria, now a moving red blob, enter the portal, an orange rectangle. Almost simultaneously, Aria's signature goes into the portal and disappears while the portal also goes away.

"Woah," Aziz says.

"You saw that, right?"

"Yeah. They were basically at the exact same time."

"Right."

"What does that mean?"

"I have no idea, but we have to find out." I get up and look at Aziz. I have no clue what I just witnessed, but I'm pretty sure Aria was just involved in some kind of AltD glitch or something, and I have no idea where that leaves her. She is either in AltD in some random place or something, in Reality somewhere else in the world, or gone. And, for the sake of her physical health and my mental state, I really hope it's one of the first two.

"You ready for an investigation?" I ask Aziz.

"Always."

ARIA

October 2, 3038

I use my sleeve to wipe the tears from my face. I've gone in five different directions, tried to find something that isn't an endless jungle, and then back again, so I remember my starting place. I decide to go around and grab some rocks, piling them where I'm standing so I have some kind of beacon, not that it will be helpful at all if I get lost in the endless jungle. I've already tried thinking to myself what could have gone wrong. I still can't figure out why the transit period felt so off. All I know is that I have no clue where the hell I am, and I would like to find that out before anything else. If I find where I am, I can slowly but surely make my way back to Japan, find another portal, and then give Ty a big hug back in Reality. That's my goal, and I'm hell-bent on reaching it.

After creating my meek pile of rocks, I turn around and walk in the opposite direction. The jungle starts to slowly thin out as I slap through vines and scurry away from various critters. A few times, I make eye contact with a monkey or two, and I swear that they have an intent to kill me, but then they look away, and I sink back into my paranoia. Occasionally, a small stream shows up, which I have to hop over not so gracefully. Other times, I'm stranded, contemplating if I'm about to step in quicksand or not. I must walk for a couple of miles before I see the landscape changing in the distance and start to run.

A rare smile emerges on my face as I see what looks to be the edge of the cliff. Some hope that my fate isn't sealed in this never-ending jungle suddenly floods me. However, the hope quickly fades when I scramble over the last fallen tree trunk and stand on the edge of the cliff. I look out into nothingness. Literally nothing, empty sky as far as I can see. I can't even tell if it's a light blue or a white. I look up and see that the clouds cease to exist beyond this point. I get down onto my stomach and look down to see that the ground beneath me must be some kind of floating island.

I spend the next three hours walking the perimeter of the floating thing that I'm on. I seem to be walking on a curve, so I'm assuming that this thing is a massive circle. There is still no sign of any other human life, and I get claustrophobic at the thought that I have only two options; either I learn how to survive on this floating island or I literally fall off a cliff.

Once I'm confident I'm walking around in a circle, I wander towards the center of the place. I am met with more and more jungle, the sounds of various insects no longer methodical and peaceful but instead driving me to insanity. A light rain starts to be filtered by the many trees, and the cool moisture feels good on my skin amidst all of the humidity. Soon enough, the jungle starts to thin out again, this time the ground underneath my feet completely changing. Very quickly, I walk onto sand, and then more sand, and then even more sand. I look left and right and see a circular desert in the middle of the jungle. That's not even the weirdest part. The sand is entirely black, the dunes barely discernible. The entire thing looks like a void.

DIMENSION

I back up, off of the sand, and sit down on a fallen tree trunk. I just stare out into the distance in shock. Nothing makes sense, and now I'm sitting in a jungle, looking at a black desert. I don't know how wack stuff like this keeps happening to me. I must sit for a couple of hours, and I'm about to get up and make my way back to my home base of sorts when the desert starts to cave in on itself like the island is living, and it's responding to its own hunger. I am left speechless for the third time in the last six hours as the desert disappears and a literal ocean, once again colorless, forms in its place. The entire thing happens in less than twenty minutes, and it was a sight to behold. I can't make sense of any of this in the slightest. All I know is this is definitely not AltD, this is definitely not Reality, and this is for sure not a dream.

I really am in a secret world.

TYLER

October 3, 2038

We waited the night to start our investigation, but both Aziz and I wake up early in the morning to get started. I roll off of the brown couch in the middle of the room and look up to see Aziz pushing his bed back against the wall. He must catch me looking at him because he asks a question.

"You want any tea?"

"Sure."

"Black tea good?"

"Do you have that good orange cinnamon black tea?"

"I actually do. That's my favorite."

"That works out well, doesn't it."

"Indeed it does." He excitedly fills the kettle and turns on the stove. He pulls out one of the drawers and grabs a couple of teabags. I catch a glimpse of the contents of the drawer, and it's pretty much just boxes upon boxes of orange cinnamon tea.

"Any ideas of where to start? Because, I've done a lot of thinking and still can't think of any."

"I'm new to all of this AltD stuff, but wouldn't it make some sense to start where it all began?"

"Like with Tirique and Nox?"

"Yeah. I don't know, but it seems like whatever happened to Aria, and that portal was quite the anomaly, and the creators of AltD would probably have been smart enough to find and research those."

"That's a very good point. But I have no idea what happened to Nox and Tirique's labs when they died."

"Nothing."

"What does nothing mean?"

"Literally nothing. I don't think anyone touched them. Everyone went to AltD so fast that no one cared enough. Maybe the government raided the buildings for files, but it's not like they were torn down or anything."

"How do you know that?"

"Because, I went and checked them out with Riz. Hold on. Let me see if I can find this thing." He walks up and strides towards his bookshelf. The tea kettle starts to whistle, so I go over and shut off the flame. I pour water into two mugs that Aziz had set up and gently drop the tea bags in.

"Honey?"

"Nah. I don't put anything in mine. But the honey is in the cupboard right above you."

"I don't put anything in either."

"Damn. We really are matching with the whole tea situation." I walk over with the tea in my hands and meet Aziz on the couch. He is holding a black notebook.

"What's that?" I ask as I hand him his tea.

"You're going to freak out when I tell you."

"Try me."

"When Riz and I were doing our missions, we would always check out any Nox bases and record any secret places we could find. Obviously, we didn't tell the government about what we found because we wouldn't want to give anyone that information. So, instead, to make sure we didn't forget, we wrote all of it down in here." He hands me the notebook. I can't believe something like this actually exists. I open it and am shocked. There are diagrams of the secret compartments, rooms, and floors accompanied by detailed instructions on how to get into the various spaces and a list of what's in them.

"This is amazing."

"Yeah. We are kinda proud of it. And, now, it will actually be useful." I continue to flip through it.

"Go to the end," Aziz tells me. I oblige. At the end is the final place, it's a secret underground research lab, and the contents says 'everything about AltD.' I look up at Aziz in immense happiness.

"I can't believe you found this. This is exactly what we need. Like exactly."

"Right? So you ready for a field trip?"

"Where is this?"

"We are headed to London."

"Say less." It only takes us a few minutes to gather everything because it isn't much, and then we are out the door.

"How are we getting there?" I ask Aziz, who just smiles at me and swings his backpack around to the ground.

"Ready for some nostalgia."

"Always." He pulls out two Rods.

"Wow. It's been a while since I've seen or used these. But, they are only for cycles, and we are kinda on an island Aziz."

"Don't worry. These are fresh off the Ivo assembly line." That's all he says before turning, waving to Cho again, who is somehow still unmoved in his position, and making his way down some back alleys. When we are in an area of fairly low population, Aziz ushers me to stand against the side of a building to give him space. I watch as he runs and then generates a mini plane contraption around him. A helmet forms around his head, and it's like he's on a cycle body but with four wings of sorts. I take my Rod and do the same, amazed as I seamlessly hover in the air.

"Cool, right?" Aziz yells so that I can hear him as we rise higher and higher into the sky, flying through some clouds which dissipate at my presence. I nod and follow him as he flies with purpose. This thing can go really fast. I hold down the accelerator, and it never levels out. It just keeps speeding up. I have no idea how we do it, but I recognize the London center building, no longer under repair from years ago, in only a few hours. I tilt forwards to descend, copying Aziz's movements, and we land on a dirt road near the city's outskirts.

"That was something. These things can speed man." I comment.

"To be honest, I had forgotten how fast they were. It's been a while since I've used it. Thanks for giving me an excuse to brush off the dust."

"No problem. So, where are we headed?"

"What do you mean? We are here."

"What?"

"We are here. This is it." He waves his arms, gesturing to the ground.

"It's underground?"

"Thanks, Sherlock, for that outstanding observation." I give him a look of annoyance, and he smiles.

"For someone with so much confidence, you should be showing me exactly where this base is," I argue.

"Ok. Give me the notebook."

"I thought you had it."

"I don't have it. I thought you grabbed it." I slap my head.

"You're kidding me, right?"

"No, you're kidding me."

"What do we do now?"

"Let's hope we aren't incompetent."

"What's that supposed to mean?"

"Well, I'm not about to go all the way back for a stupid notebook, so let's get looking. I'm sure we can find out how to get in here." I grumble in annoyance. I hate looking for secret bases. It's like the bane of my existence, an arduous task for no reason. I wouldn't consider Aria and I's quote on quote 'base' a secret one because I simply don't want to be put in that category. Aziz walks across the road and starts to examine various trees. I do the same on the other side.

"Found it."

"You're kidding. There is no chance you just found it in ten seconds." He steps out from behind the tree and just stands there, staring at me in disgust that I'm behind on something.

"What?"

"Am I seriously going to have to feed you this one myself?" I'm so confused, and I give him a thinking face. He just points at his head. I'm still confused.

"Nope. Nothing."

"I have a photographic memory, you dumbo. We were literally talking about this yesterday." Yeah, I thoroughly deserved the superlative. That was bad.

"So that whole thing about forgetting the notebook was a joke?"

"Yeah. I pranked you. And, got you pretty good." I walk over to the tree he emerged from and don't see anything.

"Nothing is here."

"Oh yeah. Nothing is there. It's over here." He walks over to the middle of the road. "Here. Stand next to me." I oblige as he pulls a gun out of his bag. Pointing at a tree in the distance, he uses his sharpshooting ability to hit something in the tree that triggers a circular platform from beneath us. The platform slowly pushes into the ground, and we are lowered into a base, dust covering almost everything in sight.

We stand in the middle of what looks like a lab and a data archive. Modern computers and screens are lining the entire back wall, with digital databases, as well as paper file boxes, filling every other available space. In the middle, there are long work tables with various engineering equipment and more computers. I'm sure this was quite the modern working environment when it was in its prime. Aziz walks over the paper files and pulls out the boxes, lifting them up and placing them on the table.

"Ok. Let's get going. You take the left side. I'll take the right." He directs me, and I pull out files, sitting on the opposite side of the table as him. I skim file after file, amazed at how much information is in these. Everything from the code of AltD to the more abstract vision of what the AltD society should look like is covered here, clearly outlined with signatures and checkmarks, mostly from Nox and Tirique. I wish I had Aziz's photographic memory right now because he must be catching all of this. Except, when I look up, he's not reading them.

"Why aren't you reading?"

"I don't really want to know about AltD. I am very content with my life, and I don't want any of this stuck in my head and coming back to haunt me in my dreams or something. You do your reading and, when you find what we are looking for, I'll memorize the important stuff."

"Fair enough. Your decision, I suppose. I guess this is what you mean by you don't always want to have the memory you have."

"Yes indeed." I nod and skim through the files faster.

I must be reading random things about AltD for hours before I find something that's even a little bit helpful. I thought that at least the other reading would teach me something interesting, but I knew most of the practical stuff, and everything else was completely over my head.

"This is it." I say as I flip the page and am greeted by the title 'Portal Defects.' I skim the page as Aziz walks over to my side of the table, flipping to the next section where it says 'the void between disappearing portals and the alternate dimension.' I keep reading, and I feel my heart drop to my stomach. The page says, 'if the rare occasion of someone passing through a portal when it disappears occurs, then said individual could be caught in the third dimension.'

"What the hell does that mean?" Aziz says.

"I don't know. But it doesn't sound good." The end of the section directs us to another page in the files, and I immediately flip there to the section titled 'The Third Dimension.' I skip over some nonsense about Nox and Tirique that doesn't sound relevant because they are dead, to the part where it describes the entrances and exits to the third dimension. For entrances, it says 'certain portal defects and the third dimension portal,' and for exits, it only says 'the third dimension portal.' Then it says 'location of the third dimension portal undetermined and completely classified.'

"I'm so sorry, Tyler." I slam the files close as a tear runs down my face. I have no idea how to find Aria because these files barely know how to find Aria. How was I supposed to know about a third dimension?

Wherever or whatever this third dimension is, I hope Aria stays alive because I'm not stopping until I find her.

ARIA

October 3, 2038

I fell asleep with the sound of waves as my lullaby, but I wake up to the silence of three black mountain peaks rising as high as I can see. As if they could not choose a more extreme landscape after the black desert and tumultuous ocean. I roll over and am about to find food when I notice that I'm not feeling any hunger. I guess something about being wherever I am means that I don't have to feed myself. That works for me, seeing how I was not prepared to actually go hunting or extract water from the jungle. Satisfied with that realization, I decided I might as well do some more wandering.

The jungle is, thankfully, unchanged as I walk through it in the morning light. I can't believe I'm actually saying that. The sun beams down through the vines, and the sound of insects is the only thing amongst the silence. I guess the animals around here sleep in or something. The ground is still a mix of dirt, mud, and rocks. I'm almost certain I'm going in circles before I run into a big stone pole that extends into the air. I can't believe I never noticed this, but I guess I was never at an appropriate elevation to see it. There are two stone plaques in front of the pole; each labeled with a floating virtual representation of the people.

I'm shocked as I read the plaque. One is labeled for Nox and the other for Tirique, each accompanied by a three-dimensional model of them. In the fine print, underneath a layer of vines which I push to the side, it says 'for the rebirth of our heroes.'

I got over my brother's death a while ago. I didn't think it would be as easy as it was. I know that's messed up to say, but we had barely had contact for years before his death, and I had grown to have some serious animosity towards his beliefs. I still grieved as I thought about everything our parents would think if they were still around. To be honest, having Ty around was a big lift for me. Having the Migrants, in general, acting as a functioning family was the reason why I was able to recover so quickly. It still crushes me to think how it all went down, and I wish my brother were still around. Throughout all of my recovery, I had never forgotten some of his final words: 'I will live on forever.' And, I can't help but think that this is what he meant.

I notice a path of some kind coming out from the pole, heavily covered in dirt and plants. I try to make out the grey concrete, and it leads me back to the center, stopping at the edge of the inner circle. There is no way in hell I'm continuing through the mountains, so I slump back down onto the ground.

Over the past day or so, I have found no way in, no way out, and no concept of where I am. The only thing I have found is a creepy foreboding of my dead brother's return and a scary possibility of his legacy continuing. I have to get out of here because the world, both in Reality and in AltD, is not going to like that one bit.

DIMENSION

ARIA

PRESENT DAY

DIMENSION

TIMO

November 5, 2040

Personally, I think Serge was a tad bit dramatic. It's not like everything I know has now become false just because I learned about a new dimension. Is it wild and almost concerning that no one knows that exists? Yes. But, does it really matter if it's a dimension no one can be in? No. So that's kind of the argument I'm telling myself. We are walking back towards the dining hall with some serious intent, and I'm thinking Serge is getting a little antsy about whatever this required piece of the puzzle is.

"I think it goes without saying that you don't tell anyone about this."

"The third dimension?"

"Yes. I only showed it to you because I wanted to make a point. But the others don't know, and I'd like to keep it that way."

"Fine." We walk the rest of the way to the dining hall in silence, Serge nervously playing with his fingers. I have a slight urge to reassure him somehow, like making him feel better by committing, but I can't bring myself to do it. I am still vacillating, and I don't want to promise to do anything that I'm just going to regret later on in life. When we make it to the dining hall, everyone is up and eating their breakfast. I spot Cora, and we make eye contact, resulting in her jumping out of her seat and jogging towards me.

"I was looking everywhere for you," she says.

"He was with me," Serge calmly states.

"I can see that. On some official Prince business are we?"

"Something like that," I respond.

"Cora. Will you please get everyone's attention? I have a couple of announcements to make," Serge demands, but in a way, that's not too intimidating.

"Of course," she happily replies before turning to the center of the dining hall.

"People!" She starts yelling. "Serge has a couple of announcements, so listen up!" Just by judging everyone's immediate response, I can tell that Cora holds some kind of authority already. That must be why Serge asked her to give me a tour.

"Yes. Hello everyone. I hope you guys are all enjoying your stay so far. As you know, I've been slowly ramping up our plan to bring Nox and Tirique back. Timo here was the last big piece of that. Or, so I thought. It turns out that Nox and Tirique required one last piece, what they called the 'Assembler.' It's a device that properly cradles the cubes so that the revival function can be performed. I have been trying to locate the owner of the Assembler, and I have successfully found his identity in Reality. His name is Tammy James, and he lives in Brazil currently. He's a young man about the age of all of you. I don't know how you young people are always the ones I am looking for. Anyways, I'm going to need some of you to volunteer to find him, convince him of our mission, and bring him back."

"Timo and I will do it." Cora volunteers us almost immediately.

"Great. I had predicted you two would be the ones," he replies. Everyone else goes back to eating like they knew that they never really had a chance at going on the mission in the first place. Cora looks at me excitedly, and I muster a smile and a nod. To be honest, I didn't really want to go; I wanted some time to think about what I was going to do about all of this, not get thrown into a search and rescue mission. Let's just hope that Cora is sufficient enough to convince Tammy to join the cause because I might be better at listing reasons why he shouldn't than anything else.

I sit down at an empty table, hoping to get some peace and quiet, but Cora takes it upon herself to move her food from where she was previously sitting to my table. Soon enough, a chef places some pizza in front of me, and my stomach demands that I shovel it down my mouth and, before Cora can make a peep, it's gone.

"Someone was hungry," she comments.

"Yeah. When I woke up, I thought I would just wander around and then get to eat early. Suffice to say, Serge had something else in mind."

"What did you guys talk about?" I filter the conversation Serge and I had in my brain, categorizing segments into 'can't tell Cora' and 'do tell Cora.' Before she can sense me thinking for too long, I just spit out some nonsense.

"He was just explaining the plan more to me."

"How come? Didn't he do that yesterday?"

"I mean, he did. But, I still have my doubts." This is a great time to test her persuasion skills. I'm a genius, and I struggle not to smile narcissistically at myself.

"You shouldn't have to be thinking about it. This is a once-in-a-lifetime opportunity to have an impact on everyone's life. Tirique and Nox literally created AltD from nothing. Imagine what else they could create if they have more time."

"But, how can you be so sure that the change will be a positive change?" So far, her persuasion skills are at a solid B-minus.

"I mean, you can never be sure. But, whatever they do, we will be on their good side for helping them." I hadn't thought about that, but that's a pretty selfish way of looking at it. "Trust me. If you don't do it, then you will create an enemy with Serge, and Serge is a powerful man."

"But Serge can't even come close to our power inside of AltD. And, isn't all of this for AltD?" I seem to find a loophole in her argument because she sits back and thinks about alternate routes. After a bit, she looks up at me and smiles.

"You're smart, Timo. No wonder you ended up with three cubes." I smile back. I'm about to open up and tell her about the third dimension, but Serge strides over to us.

"You guys better get going so you don't have to spend the night in Brazil." We both nod and get up.

"Hey boss...where are we going?" Cora asks as Serge walk away.

"Oh right. You guys don't know how to get out of this place. My bad. Walk up to the balcony but don't turn onto the landing platform, instead turn the other way." I follow Cora up the stairs, and she follows Serge's instructions, turning away from the landing platform and into a narrower than normal hallway. The hallway leads straight into yet another sphere, this time, the glass replaced with black carbon fiber of some kind. There is no natural light except for a small circular window at the top. Other than that, I can't see anything. Cora walks to a control pod in the middle of two semi-circular couches, and I follow her lead. There is a screen in the middle with a selection of missions to choose from. For now, there is only one listed, which is titled 'Tammy.' Cora presses it, and suddenly the navigation is set up, the sphere detaches from where we came from, a door forms in the entrance to the hallway, and we are off to Brazil.

"Do you have any idea how this thing is moving?" I ask Cora, who just shakes her head.

"I don't know how most of this stuff works, to be honest, but it feels like we are floating somehow."

"I wish we could see outside. I'm assuming Serge doesn't like us knowing anything about where we are."

"He says he will tell as soon as he knows all of us commit. I was going to say that you're the last one that needs to commit, but now we have Tammy." I can't help but ask her questions about how she's so certain that bringing someone who's objectively a psychopath back to life is a good idea.

"So. Can I ask you a kinda deep question?" She looks at me like some magical barrier has been broken between us and slides down against the wall, which I copy from the opposite side of the ship.

"Anything." She looks so eager for a question that's not about all of this, the cubes, or Serge, and I feel so bad that my social awkwardness means there is absolutely no chance I can think of any of the questions on the spot.

"Truly. Like, forgetting all of the lavish rooms, the cool tech, the general army guy directing, forgetting all of that. Truly, what do you think I should do?" I expect her to just make her whole spiel again, maybe with a slightly different argument this time, but a look of concern shows up on her usually bright face, like she's hit a crossroad.

"To be honest, Timo. I actually like you. I don't really like the other people. They are arrogant, they only care about their lives in AltD, and they are obsessed with the prospect of getting themselves some more power. You and me, we aren't like that. We have lives to care about, and brains that can function that can really think about the humane and moral thing to do. And, I really just don't know. I agreed to do it because I have always been paranoid about making the wrong decision when my parents always told me to make the safe one. Also, I knew I wasn't the decision that mattered. That's all you." I nod, shocked by Cora's change in character.

"I feel the same way. And my parents always wanted me to be calculated, never taking unnecessary risks. That's why I joined the government instead of some other cool startups or something." Cora gets up and walks over to my, sliding her back down the wall and sitting next to me, slightly leaning her head against my shoulder.

"It's fine. We will figure it out together. For now, we have to complete this mission."

"Ok," I mutter.

"Tell me a story."

"Like what?"

"I don't know. Any story. How about your cubes. Where did you find them?"

"It's kinda funny. I found my media cube first. I was playing street soccer by a construction zone. I accidentally kicked the ball into the contraction zone late at night and went to find it. I climbed the fence and everything, rummaging around in the dirt. Instead of my ball, I found the cube which I accidentally touched, so it automatically calibrated and became invisible."

"That's pretty funny."

"Yeah. I used the media cube to mess around a lot, pull pranks on my friends, and whatever. But then, I realized I could use it to help me find other cubes."

"How?"

"Well, I planted a fake media cube underground in a forest and used the media to show ads and stuff that someone thinks there is a cube there.

Naturally, everyone started to gravitate there. That means that I could walk around pretty public areas that were now empty. I don't know if you know this, but the cubes have a slight attraction to each other like they are magnets are something. So, for days, I wandered around discrete and natural landscapes with my media cube, trying to find some kind of force of attraction. Eventually, I found the object cube."

"Wow. What about the time cube."

"That's the weirdest part."

"What happened? You didn't use the same tactics again?"

"No. It just showed up on my doorstep."

"How did they know where you were?"

"I have no idea. I'm not even sure that whoever dropped it off had any clue who they were giving it to. It could've just been by accident. But it showed up in a cardboard box, unlocked and uncalibrated."

"That's a bit of a scary coincidence then."

"Yeah."

We sit, Cora drifting asleep against my shoulder, for the rest of the ride. I have no idea how long we are stuck in the sphere, but eventually, we land and the door opens.

"Hey. We are here." I shake Cora awake, who rubs her eyes and looks at me, and smiles, kissing my cheek before standing up and stretching.

"Ok. Let's go." We walk straight out into an abandoned parking lot of some village in Brazil. Cora hands me a picture of Tammy, and we start to scour the village for any signs of him.

After two hours, we are about to give up.

"I swear, I'm convinced this guy is some kind of ghost," Cora complains.

"A ghost that Serge is going to be really mad about if we don't bring back with us."

"Whatever, man. I'm starving, hot, and don't really care if Serge gets mad at us. It's not like he isn't going to find Tammy. He'll just do it himself or something."

"Wait, is this is a test?"

"A test for what?"

"Like a test for our competency to see if we are worthy of Nox's company. I don't know."

"Listen. Timo. I took a nap on the ride, as you know, and I am about to fall flat on my face and pass out again."

"Did you not sleep last night or something?" She shrugs. "Ok. At the very least, let's walk back to the ship and take a break." She nods, and we make our way back to the abandoned parking lot. When we get there, someone is leaning against the side of the ship."

"Sup guys," he says.

"Tammy?" I ask, and he nods.

"Are you kidding me, man? We've been looking everywhere for you." Cora continues to complain.

"Yeah, I know. I've been following you guys."

"Jesus. We really suck," I say.

"For real," Cora replies.

"Do you even know why we are looking for you?" I ask him.

"Yeah. I put two and two together. You're in a fancy whip, or whatever this thing is, you guys aren't dressed like you're from Brazil at all, and I have a thing that is of some pretty high value."

"Do you know what that thing is?" Cora asks.

"Hell yeah, I do. The damn thing came with digital instructions on how to use it. They were cryptic, don't get me wrong, but only an idiot wouldn't understand the pictures." Cora tosses her hands in the air.

"How is it that this guy already knows more than me?"

"So, where are we going?" He asks.

"Wait. Just like that?" I ask.

"Yeah, man. Look around. This place is boring and dead as hell. I don't really care what you all are tryna do. I'm tryna leave. Like now." I look at Cora, who just tiredly looks back at me.

"Who cares, Timo. Let's just bring him. I don't care if it's really suspicious."

"Fine." I walk back into the ship, Cora following, and then Tammy. I program the ship to go back to the base, and Cora and I slide back against the wall. I just stare at Tammy, his innocence and whole vibe seeming very, very suspicious.

KAI

November 5, 2040

When everyone else wakes up, Tyler explains what he told me to everyone else. My head hurts from trying to even think about the existence of a third dimension. Everyone else focuses on the loss of Aria, which makes sense. They are too busy consoling Tyler to think about the third dimension but, to be fair, it's not like a third dimension would mean much to anyone that experienced AltD for the first time yesterday. I must be completely zoning out because Aiko walks over and taps me on the shoulder. I jolt awake from whatever daze I'm in. Aiko looks surprised at my reaction.

"My bad," I say. "I was thinking."

"Yeah. There is a lot to think about, isn't there?"

"A lot," I emphasize.

"I just wanted to say it was great how you offered to help Tyler."

"Of course. Don't sweat it. I told Tyler that I have nothing else better to do, and whatever we find will be able to help a lot more people, I think."

"Well. You've only known us for three days, and you are already fully committed. You're pretty cool, man." She brushes my shoulder and walks back to the group, and I start thinking about how I would help Tyler in an actually useful way. Obviously, as he mentioned, he's been doing a lot of investigating at the portals. Still, we will have to find more information about the third dimension before knowing what we are looking for. When everyone finishes talking about Aria, I'm ushered over. Ivo, always the one with the level head, gets straight to the point.

"So, we aren't stopping until we find Aria. That's clear. Does anyone have any idea of where to start?" Everyone kinda sits in silence.

"Keep passing through portals until one of us gets sent to the third dimension?" Za proposes.

"Very funny, Za." Ivo comments, disappointed.

"No, I'm serious. The best way to help Aria is to get into the third dimension with more outside information and evaluate things with her. We could try to figure out how to get communication between dimensions to work. Maybe it's easier to talk if we are in AltD."

"Ok…"

"It won't work," Tyler says. "I mean…it could. But ,that's basically what I've been doing for the last year."

"And no luck?" Za asks again.

"Well, clearly not."

"Now that we know we can't do that, does anyone else have a better idea?" Ivo asks. I wait to see if anyone else wants to add before I speak up.

"What if there is more information on the third dimension, from Nox or Tirique?" I ask.

"Aziz?" Tyler asks.

"Why would Aziz know anything?" Riz asks.

"Because I was there when we lost Aria, and I was also there when Tyler found out about the third dimension," Aziz calmly states.

"Wait, what?" Ivo asks. I notice that Idri and Aiko have taken a seat on the couch and are just observing the conversation.

"Yeah, he was with me," Tyler says.

"So how bout it, boss?" Riz asks Aziz.

"Yeah, whip out that memory of yours," Za comments. Aziz grimaces.

"I didn't look at any of the documents because I didn't want any of that stuff stuck in my head. How was I supposed to know that we would be in this situation?"

"Jesus." Za throws his arms in the air.

"I mean, he's not completely useless. He did memorize the notebook that has all of the information on Nox's secret bases and whatnot." Tyler tries to calm Za down.

"This is true," Aziz says.

"Ok, I forgive you. That is very handy," Za apologies, and Idri chuckles from the back.

"So, where do we start?" Ivo asks. I wait for an answer before turning to see that he's looking at me.

"Oh. That's me again?"

"As long as you are the one coming up with the plans, you are the boss," he replies.

"Ok then. Uhhhh…" I really hadn't thought this far ahead. "The third dimension was probably one of the last things they made or thought of, right?"

"Yeah, probably," Ivo answers so I can continue my point.

"So we could probably find out the most recent base Nox, and Tirique went to before they died. And then we can go there and see if we can find anything about the third dimension that would be helpful. I'm guessing anything at all would be of some significance." Everyone kinda nods along as I go.

"God damn. Where has this kid been the last ten years," Aziz says.

"He was seven. That's where he was. Idiot," Riz bluntly states with his dry humor, and Aziz growls at him.

"Seven and a half, actually. If we are accurate."

"Really, kid?" Riz says to me. "You were doing so well until right there. Try not to ruin it anymore, will ya." I put my hands up and take a step back to let someone else take the lead.

"I like Kai's plan." Ivo gives me his second stamp of approval, and I think I feel confidence run through my veins.

"How are we supposed to find out where the last place they were in is?" Idri finally tunes in.

"That's a question for him." Ivo points across the room to Za, who is distracted, organizing the tea bags.

"Huh?" He looks up, completely lost.

"Did Nox's bases use security check-ins or something?" Idri asks.

"Oh yeah. Everything was digital, I warned him it was hackable too, but he said, 'I'm already too powerful.' Jokes on him, he clearly wasn't." Za uses air quotes and attempts to sound stoic when imitating Nox to emphasize his point. Almost on cue, everyone snaps their heads towards Ivo.

"Yeah, yeah. I can see if I can hack it."

"Can I come?" I ask, eager to see Ivo in his element.

"Of course, boss." He walks down the stairs, and I follow him as everyone resumes conversation behind us. We both sit down at the desk again.

"Imma be honest. I have no clue where even to start." He says. "I'm just gonna wing it." He rapidly types, windows beginning to pop up and disappear everywhere constantly.

"What are you doing?" I ask.

"So I had saved the program I used to hack into Nox's system from five years, and I'm using it to backchannel into his servers' data. Hopefully, there is some kind of file for security measures or something…speak of the devil." He opens a locked file, the program he's running automatically unlocks it, and a bunch of data I don't understand shows up.

"What about that?" I notice a file called eye scanner and point at it.

"Good eye." He waits for me to smile at his pun before pressing on it. "This is good. Assuming he put eye scanners that he himself used in most of his bases, we should be good." He scrolls through the folder. There is a list of locations with who went through the buildings.

"That looks promising," I comment.

"It does indeed. Let me try this…." He types something again, and suddenly all of the data is sorted by date access. He goes to the most recent, March 9th, 2035. Ivo highlights the coordinates next to the time, opens up a digital map, and plugs them in. A map marker shows up over somewhere in Germany.

"So?"

"That, my friend, is what you call another lead."

TIMO

November 5, 2040

Silence is the name of the game for the rest of the flight until Tammy decides to ask us some questions. It's shocking he can be at peace for that long, knowing absolutely nothing.

"So, where are we headed."

"We are..." Cora starts.

"We actually don't know because our boss hasn't told us, and he doesn't want us to know." I look at Cora, who is frowning up at me. I just shrug. I want to know if this guy can get spooked.

"Oh. Ok." He says before completely changing the subject. "I wish this thing had some speakers. I could really use some speakers." I roll my eyes.

"So, what do you do?" I ask.

"I'm an orphan. I have no clue where my parents are. But they left me a farm, so I ran that for a while before selling it. Now I kind of just roam around Brazil, sometimes finding work, sometimes stealing things." At least he's honest.

"Nice," I respond. I don't know if he can sense that I'm skeptical of him or my intense sarcasm.

"Is the place we are going nice?" He asks again.

"Actually, beautiful doesn't even start to...." Cora starts again before I cut her off.

"I think the aptest description would be that it's like an extremely lavish prison." This time Cora glares at me, incensed.

"Lavish. Dope." Tammy responds like he didn't hear the whole prison part.

"Do you really not care that you have no idea where you are going?" I finally ask out of frustration.

"Anywhere is better than my last living situation, which was kinda non-existent. Plus, the police may or may not have been looking for me, so the timing could not have been any better."

"That's great. That's just great. You're telling me we are now harboring a criminal."

"Woah. I'm not a criminal." Tammy attempts to defend himself.

"Didn't you just say that the police were looking for you?" I ask.

"I'm confused," Cora says, resting her chin on my shoulder.

"Ok. Fine. I'm a criminal, but it seems like kinda a harsh term."

"Well, it doesn't matter now anyway because you're with Serge and us now," Cora states.

"Right," I say with absolutely no confidence.

"Who's Serge?" Tammy asks.

"You'll see," I respond. The rest of the ride is silent, and I like it that way. I'm still very sketched out by Tammy. His whole vibe seems way too welcoming of all this. I would pay some serious money to see him be absolutely shocked by what Serge tells him about Nox and Tirique.

When we get back, I feel a secured click as we dock, and the door slides out of the way to unveil the hallway. I let Cora go first, Tammy behind her, then I go out last. We walk out onto the balcony, down the steps, and into the gathering area. Almost no one is there except Serge, who is calmly sipping coffee in an armchair. He's not doing anything else, just staring into space like he's a robot. By the size of the dent he leaves in the leather when he gets up, I can tell he's at least been sitting there for a couple of hours.

"Tammy. Nice to see you again." Serge puts out his hand, which Tammy shakes right away.

"This place is amazing, Mr.Adams. I wish you had brought me the first time we met." Gone is the muttering slang from Tammy, and incomes a thick British accent, I am left dumbfounded.

"What is going on?" Cora asks.

"Oh. Right. Well, this was a test. Surprise," Serge replies.

"You've got to be kidding me," I say. I can't believe I was right.

"Well. It kinda was, kinda wasn't. In truth, I met Tammy a long time ago. When I met him and didn't have any cubes, I was confused about why my search brought me to him. He told me about the Assembler, but I didn't know its significance. Anyways, I told him I might see him again eventually down the road. That was two years ago."

"So when you guys showed up, I knew it had to be Serge," Tammy adds.

"So the whole criminal and cops thing was made up?" I ask.

"Not entirely," Tammy replies. "I did kinda run into a problem with the cops because I stole some glasses. But, I was just tryna give them to some impoverished people."

"And. Let's be clear. I couldn't have just called him or something. Also, I knew his general location but not exactly where to find him. So your mission was actually kinda necessary." Serge reassures me as he sees me twitching in annoyance.

"Also, I have not been here, so those questions were legit. Sorry, my answers were kinda cringe, I was trying to play the clueless one."

"And you don't know anything about Serge's mission or why he's here?" Cora asks.

"Nope."

"Nice, this should be fun," she says, suddenly excited. As am I.

"Oh god, it's something highly unexpected and borderline hard to believe, isn't it," Tammy sighs and Serge manages a small smirk.

"Come. Sit over here." Serge guides all three of us to the couches, where Tammy slumps down into the couch.

"Ok, hit me," he says, sitting up on the couch. Meanwhile, Cora takes a seat next to me on the couch, tapping my leg in anticipation.

"Do either of you wanna take the lead on this?" Serge asks us.

"Nah. We are just gonna enjoy the show," Cora replies.

"Fair enough," Serge says with a chuckle. "Here's the deal, Tammy. For the last couple of years, I've been hunting down the Princes. I'm assuming you know what that means."

"Yep. The people with the cubes. Are these two Princes?" He nods towards us.

"I mean, I am, but he's the Prince of all Princes," Cora says, bumping me with her shoulder.

"Indeed. Timo here has three cubes," Serge adds.

"God damn. That's like all of them," Tammy comments before Serge continues.

"Anyways. I'm not just gathering all of the Princes because I think it's cool. In truth, Tirique left me a mission to fulfill after his planned demise. He gave me detailed instructions for how to bring Nox and Tirique back."

"What do you mean 'bring them back?'" Tammy says, continuing to scoot farther and farther forwards on the couch until I'm sure he's defying gravity by maintaining his sitting position.

"They made way for them to live on eternally in AltD," I state, as blandly and emotionless as possible.

"Wow. Now that, I was not expecting," Tammy says. "So why do you need me again?"

"You have the Assembler, which I didn't realize was part of this whole operation until a couple of days ago. Basically, the only way this can happen is if one of each cube is put into the assembler, which should trigger some kind of reaction," Serge answers.

"And then they will show up in AltD?"

"Not quite."

"So where?" Tammy asks.

"There may or may not be the third dimension," Cora responds, and I'm actually surprised she knew that. I guess Serge must've told everyone but didn't tell that there was a third dimension portal inside of this base.

"Ok...then," Tammy says, in shock just as I was. He takes a minute to stare at the ground, thinking.

"I'm in," he says.

"Just like that?" I ask. How can it be that he decided in two minutes when I still haven't been able to make a decision in the two days I've been thinking about it.

"Just like that."

"Your welcome to think about it," Serge says. I realize he doesn't actually mean that because he needs everyone, especially Tammy and me, to agree, but I think he just says it to seem like he's some kind of down-to-earth chill guy.

"I don't need to. Unlike you Princes, I don't have any kind of power or authority, in Reality, or in AltD. So if this puts me on the good side of some pretty powerful people, then I don't think I can say no." And, just like that, puzzle is now just waiting on me.

KAI

November 5, 2035

We have never run up the stairs faster. Ivo practically bulldozes the gathering in the living room.

"Everyone, get ready right now," he orders.

"Like right now," I say.

"You guys are gonna have to give us a little bit more than that before we are going anywhere. Or at least me because, as you can see, I am quite comfortable," Za says, leaning farther back into the couch.

"Yeah, I agree with that sentiment," Aziz adds, who's sitting across from Za, holding a cup of tea.

"Let's just say that Kai's plan worked," Ivo says.

"And?" Tyler asks.

"And we know the last place in Europe that Nox was," I answer. "It's somewhere in Germany."

"Oh, that place is insane," Aziz comments.

"You remember it?" Tyler asks.

"Clearly."

"Why is it insane?" Za asks.

"You'll see." Everyone seems to concur that this is the time to get up and start getting ready. Everyone goes to get dressed while I confidently take a seat at the counter, adrenaline running through my veins. When everyone is ready, we gather in the garage again.

"Can we please take the semi?" Ivo asks.

"Jesus, Ivo. Stop asking the kid to take your fancy truck." Za says, opening the back of the truck and tossing his stuff in before he jumps in. Ivo walks around to the driver's seat with a look of deep satisfaction as Aiko climbs into the passenger seat. I go around the back, admiring the truck's streamlined design, which has three pairs of massive wheels, almost as tall as me. Aziz helps me up into it, and my jaw drops. Not only are there leather cushions and entire computer setups at every station, but there are weapons against each wall as well as a shelf just full of Rods. If I were to imagine a vehicle for Ivo, this would be it. Ivo has to raise his voice to reach the back as I sit down at the farthest seat in the back.

"Everyone good?" He asks. We all put thumbs up. "Don't forget your seatbelts; you're really going to need them in about two minutes. I pull the seatbelt across my chest and click it into place as we exit the garage, go through the tunnel, and end up on the open road before stopping again.

"Brace yourselves," Ivo shouts from the front. I look out the window as the truck lifts into the air, and the wheels rotate to become thrusts. The truck's sides fold out and around to become wings, and, sooner than I know it, we are traveling through the air.

"Show off," Za comments from the seat next to me after he's done looking out his window.

"So tell me more about yourself, kid," Riz says to me, his head turned from the seat in front of me.

"Where are your parents from?"

"My dad immigrated to Germany from Turkey, and my mom was Japanese."

"Damn. And I was sitting here thinking that Ivo and I were unique." Za says, joining in on the conversation.

"And, you live in Boston now?" Tyler asks from the seat diagonal from me and next to Riz.

"Yeah. I live with two of my friends that are probably wondering where the hell I am right now."

"Very nice," Riz says. Everyone turns back and starts to zone out. I do the same.

It takes us a few hours to get to Germany, which is kinda incredible. We drive through the city, which has more people than I expected. Still nowhere near the concentration it used to have, but not even close to as bad as Boston. The truck, I guess it's a plane now, lands in a field and then transforms back, driving the rest of the way until I spot a 'Welcome to Berlin' sign. Ivo somehow squeezes the truck into an alley, and we all climb out.

"Ok. Where to?" Ivo asks Aziz as we all gather by the back of the truck.

"We have to find the subway."

"The subway?" I ask.

"Yeah."

"None of you German types happen to know your way around Berlin, do you?" Aziz asks us.

"I never visited here," I answer.

"We haven't been here since Ivo was like ten, so I don't think we are going to be any help either," Za says. I pull out my glasses and put them on, pulling up a three-dimensional map of the city. If this map is still accurate, there should be a subway access point a few blocks from where we are.

"Follow me," I say, not taking off my glasses or waiting for anyone to respond before I walk out of the alley and take a right onto the surprisingly clean road. We walk through rows of comforting old brick buildings. It's refreshing to see older buildings outnumber modern office skyscrapers, but I guess Europe never went through a massive remodeling like Boston did. The glasses keep asking me to turn on augmented reality, but I'm enjoying the scenery too much to bother with a bunch of floating objects and enticing signs. They are probably severely outdated anyways. Some people passing on the street stare at us. At first, I think it's because we are a big group but then I remember that the Wolf brothers are walking behind me. Hopefully, they are disguised enough not to attract too much-unneeded attention.

After ten minutes of walking, there is a staircase that goes down underground to the subway. Relieved that the map was accurate, I walk down the steps, checking over my shoulder to make sure everyone is still with me. Ivo gives me a reassuring nod and, when we get down to the middle of the station, I turn to stop to see what Aziz has to add to our directions.

"Nice job, Kai. It's all kinda coming back to me now," Aziz says, closing his eyes. He opens them with newfound purpose and leads us diagonally to the left, jumping over the payment stations. I follow directly behind as he maneuvers the station, stopping to check the subway maps a couple of times before leading us down a train tunnel. As we step off the path, I'm about to question him, but I see a stopped train hiding in the darkness further up. We all cautiously step over the train tracks, going slowly to give our eyes time to adjust to the darkness. Before we know it, we are standing in front of a permanently stopped train an out of service and caution warning playing on the led screen near the top.

"Any urge to enlighten us, Aziz?" Tyler asks.

"I remember this place," Riz answers instead, pushing his way to the front and swinging open the door to the train. For about twenty feet, the train looks completely normal, and then, all of a sudden, there is a steep ramp dipping in the ground. We all climb onto the train before following the twins down the ramp. We walk into a supremely lit glass room, modern computer setups everywhere and files all over the place.

"Let's get looking, people," Ivo says, not taking any time to admire the secrecy of this base. "We are looking for anything related to the third dimension."

I go to the nearest pile of files and start flipping through the various pages of reports, experiments, and concepts. Sometimes I find a handwritten report from Tirique or Nox, and I take extra time to skim them. I see some mentions of the third dimension and put them aside in the pile. I look up to see everyone doing the same as me, sorting the files by relevance. Ivo catches me noticing him taking pictures.

"As much as I hate to admit it, Tirique was a genius, and some of these ideas are just god-tier." I nod to him with a smile and go back to the files. When everyone is done, we stack all of the files with mentions of the third dimension onto the main middle desk. Idri is first to go to the pile and start flipping through them.

"None of these mentions are very detailed. There isn't much description in terms of the third dimension," he says.

"Let me see." Tyler walks over and looks over Idri's shoulder as they keep searching.

"We didn't happen to ever find Serge did we?" Idri asks.

"Nah. We tried looking for him, but he escaped after we took out his army. We didn't think he would really do much harm without his boss and his weaponry," Riz answers.

"Why do you ask?" Ivo asks.

"Because every single one of these reports or mentions to the third dimension are signed off to the one and only Serge Adams," Tyler says.

"Which means?" I ask.

"It means that we made a mistake," Aiko says. It's almost shocking to hear her voice. "And we once again need to find one man to get the answers we want."

TIMO

November 5, 2035

"Cora, can you show Tammy to his room."

"Of course." Cora gets up after squeezing my hand and leads Tammy off to the bedrooms.

"Timo, can I talk to you for a minute?" Serge asks, but really requesting. I nod, getting up to follow him to the weapons room again and I already know what he's going to ask me. Instead of walking to the weapons room, we stop in the library, and I am immediately comforted by the sight of books, covers, and spines. Of course, Serge probably knows this and is setting me up for some urgent ultimatum.

"What's up?" I ask. I can't be bothered to linger. I want him to get right to the point.

"I saw your face back there; I know you still haven't made a decision." I'm about to apologize, but he cuts me off. "I predicted this from you, though. From the start, you seemed very thoughtful and cautious. I knew you were skeptical of all of this, so I saved the biggest argument until the end."

"Argument?"

"Yes."

"Ok."

"Before I get started, I have a few questions."

"Ok..." This is all starting to feel very strange to me.

"Are you loyal to the government?"

"Yes." Despite the fact that my internship wasn't my first choice, I still chose the government because I think they are admirable.

"And, were you aware of the regulation the government was doing on the portals and other aspects of AltD?"

"Yes." For the most part, it was pretty obvious. I mean, I was literally tasked with closing portals. I thought the regulation was necessary because I hated seeing entire countries forgotten. After all, their population permanently fled to AltD.

"Even the Bots?"

"The Bots?"

"The government was strengthening its regulation by experimenting with controlling the Bots." I didn't know about this, and it seems contradictory to the whole objective of AltD.

"How were they able to do that?"

"I showed them." Now I'm very confused.

"And, why would you do that?"

"Because the government and I have an alliance of some kind. Actually, more than an alliance. We have a partnership. And, this is the point I wanted to make. For the last five years, the European government has been horrified by how it's losing its society in Reality because of AltD. They wanted order, regulation, and law."

"But AltD is supposed to be free. Isn't that the whole point?"

"No. And no, it wasn't. AltD is an unfinished product. For the past five years, people have been living in a prototype of sorts. Tirique and Nox were never able to finish, they wanted to organize society and government how they wanted, but they were killed and never resurrected in AltD." This is news to me.

"Ok."

"So, when I noticed the government struggling, I brokered a deal with them. I gave them ways to regulate AltD while they gave me resources and time to bring back Nox and Tirique. I made the promise that Nox would bring order to AltD in collaboration with the government. This power appealed to them."

"But, why talk to the government at all? You don't need them for any of this."

"That's true. But I couldn't set up the infrastructure that Nox and Tirique needed in AltD all by myself. I needed help, and that became the government. They have been laying the groundwork for what Nox needs, installing the proper software onto the Bots and regulating the portals how Nox wanted them to be regulated."

"So essentially, I've been working for you the whole time."

"Not quite. More like, you've been working for Nox the whole time, and now you need to play your part in bringing your boss back to help him finish his work."

"This is all very screwed up and convoluted."

"Yes. But, think about it. We are not against each other, me and you. We are actually the opposite. You have been working towards this for the last two years of your life. And, being a Prince in itself means fulfilling this prophecy." This is very quickly starting to become not just confusing, but mind-bending.

"Ok."

"So. Do you see it now?" For some reason, even though this just added so many more complications, the fact that this whole thing is backed by the government, which I trust because of how much good they have done for Europe, I feel more convinced.

"This can't happen without you, Timo. I know you want to do the right thing, and you didn't know what that was before. But now you know, and now you can make the right decision with a clear mind and complete confidence."

"Fine. I'll do it." I'm still not totally convinced. Not because I disagree with the mission, I think I do now, but because I don't know how much I like the idea of bringing Nox back to life. I've read the books and, no matter how many times Serge says history was written harshly, it doesn't change what he did and was trying to do.

"That's great to hear, and I was really hoping you'd make that decision because the entire team is waiting for you in the weapons room."

"Why?"

"I'll tell you as we walk."

"Do they already know?"

"Yeah, I told them." I guess Serge was very confident that I would agree with the plan. I suppose he was right in the end. We both stand up and walk towards the room. I saw a farewell to the library, still perturbed that I haven't had a chance to spend more time in here.

"So, what's the deal?"

"There is a secret structure in AltD that only you can open."

"Why me?"

"Because you have the time cube."

"Ok. And what's the building for?"

"The building is for charging the cubes."

"Charging the cubes?"

"The cubes need to be charged with this special energy for a day before they are placed in the Assembler."

"Ok. So why do you need the whole team for that?"

"Technically, I only need you and maybe Tammy. But the rest are there so that they don't feel completely left behind and because having extras of the cubes is never a bad thing."

"Makes sense." We walk into the weapons room and everyone, even Cora and Tammy, are in conversation, pausing to look at us.

"It's go time, people," Serge says. "Everyone needs to use their glasses, get into AltD, and bring their cubes to the designated location I will send to you. Do this fast and secretly, no lingering and definitely no media messages for all you media cube owners." Everyone nods, and Cora walks over to me as she puts on her glasses.

"See you on the other side, boss."

"Don't judge my AltD outfits," I reply with a wink. She smiles, and I put on my glasses, pressing the button for AltD. I wake up in my apartment again and go straight to the cubes. I hold the object cube, using its power to create a backpack that fits each softball-sized cube comfortably. The bag appears floating in front of me, and I grab it and carefully place each cube in it. As I'm doing that, a message appears in my sightline from Serge, coordinates and directions to whatever building he was talking about. I open the link and start the directions as I walk up to the roof of my building, where a high-speed helicopter is waiting for me. It's always here for my beckoning, and it's wholly auto-piloted, so, after I climb in and take a seat, I give it the directions. I'm swiftly on my way, probably far ahead of everyone else, which is fine seeing they technically only need Tammy and I.

When I get to the coordinates, Serge is already there, calmly leaning against a tree. The helicopter lands in a gap in the forest, and I realize I didn't actually pay attention to where I am.

DIMENSION

"That was quite the entrance," Serge comments as I walk up to him, cubes in my backpack slung around my shoulders.

"What can I say? I'm a Prince."

"So am I, and I don't have a private helicopter." I hear Cora's voice behind me, and I turn around to see her, looking almost the same apart from her clothes, with a tote bag housing her cubes.

"Exactly my point," Serge says. "Timo likes the lavish life, I suppose. However, I am not surprised you two are the first ones here."

"Hey, I want some credit." I hadn't even seen Tammy sitting against a tree ten yards behind Serge.

"You don't count because you're not a Prince." Cora makes a joke, and Tammy frowns.

"Serge, c'mon," Tammy pleads for some support.

"She's kinda right, though," Serge says, prompting Tammy to punch the air in frustration.

"Ok. Are we doing this thing?" I ask Serge. He nods and turns towards a tree, sliding his finger along the bark in a certain way that triggers the entire top portion of the tree trunk to disconnect and slide back, somehow staying balanced so it doesn't fall over. In the platform created, there is a small indent for me to place the cube. I swing my bag around and pull out the time cube, which immediately attracts the attention of both Cora and Tammy, who flock over to examine it. I ignore their interest and their curious eyes and walk over to the tree and place the cube in its designated place. To my disappointment, nothing happens.

"What did I do wrong?" I ask Serge.

"Take it off," Serge instructs me. I remove the cube and place it meticulously back into the bag while I step away. As a horizontal crack reveals itself about a hundred feet long along the ground, everyone backs away. I watch in amazement as an entire semi-circular section of the land raises on a hinge like an accordion, glass appearing in the space it creates. Simultaneously, holes appear in the ground where the folded land appears to be headed so that the trees fit in perfectly. In a matter of minutes, the forest landscape has been replaced by an accordion dome of glass and has left all four of us, now joined by a couple of other Princes, in utter shock.

We enter the dome through a sliding door and pedestals are surrounding the perimeter. Tammy clicks the assembler into place in the middle as I place each of my cubes on a pedestal, the charging mechanism responding with a glow. We are hours away from the return of Nox and Tirique.

KAI

November 6, 2040

"And you are sure that there isn't anything on Serge or something that we can track?" Aziz asks the group. We got back last night and collectively collapsed into sleep for the third time. Now, we are semi-rested and gathered in the living room again, trying to brainstorm exactly how to find Serge. At least we've got it down to knowing that we are looking for Serge. But that also means that Aziz and Riz were complaining the entire ride back about how they should have hunted down and killed Serge instead of letting him get away. To which Ivo agreed and added the fact that he should've finished the job himself. It made the whole drive back a little tenser for everyone except Tyler and I. Tyler was thinking about how much closer we have gotten to finding Aria within the last 24 hours than he had within a year. Meanwhile, I was just excited to be on this mission with everyone.

"No, Aziz. I'm not sure," Ivo replies. "But, we keep asking that question, we keep realizing there is no way to track him, then we figure out other solution which also don't work, and then we end up back at that question. We've been doing this for two hours."

"It's fine. We can figure this out." Aiko reassures everyone, but mostly Ivo.

"What if we make some kind of decoy of something he would find desirable inside of AltD and draw him out that way?" Aziz asks.

"I could get that done easily for pretty much whatever," Riz adds.

"Guys. Serge is a smart man. He has stayed completely under the radar for the better part of five years now. He's not going to fall for some trick like that," Za argues back.

Meanwhile, I'm furiously sorting through my brain for anything that could be helpful. The main problem is that we don't know much about Serge. We don't know where he's been hiding out, we don't know why everything about the third dimension connects to him, and we certainly don't know anything about him personally that would lead to finding him. Za is the only one to have personally talked to him, and he couldn't really add anything other than the fact that he likes his weapons. Oh my god, that could be it.

"Guys." I get everyone's attention, and they all look at me like they forgot I was here. "I might have an idea."

"Kid, you're acting all vague," Za comments.

"For real," Aziz responds.

"Ok, ok. I remember Za saying that Serge likes weapons." I look at Za for confirmation

"It's practically an addiction," he confirms.

"So, wouldn't he have some kind of supplier or something?" Idri sits up, clearly intrigued. "And, in turn, wouldn't said supplier have an idea of when Serge would stop by?"

"The kid's done it again. I can not believe this teenager is making us look bad," Za half complains and half compliments.

"I approve of this idea," Idri says, which, for some reason, means more to me than anyone else's opinion.

"Now we have to find which supplier," Aiko states.

"Well, he's not going to risk his undercover status for some dinky pistols, so whoever it has to be pretty legitimate," Za says. I slide on my glasses, deciding not to wait for Ivo to go down to his laptop because this is a maneuver I can actually manage myself. I go to map search, a feature added to the glasses a year before AltD really rose to fame. It kind of went under the radar, but someone literally invented a complete database of every single business in the entire world and even marked it with the status of people that go that. The last part of that is going to be especially useful in this instance. I first sort it so only places that sell or make weapons are showing. Then I remove places that just sell knives, pistols, or swords; I doubt Serge will bounce around to four different places to find what he wants. Surprisingly, that doesn't leave too many places on the map, and they are all in Europe, three locations exact. I flip through them, one doesn't actually sell the weapons, or it claims. The other two look very commercial like they aren't hiding anything. Both of them literally have tags that read 'high premium weapons for sale' and, for the same reason Serge is not going to fall for a trick like Aziz proposed, he's not going to be dumb enough to go to that place.

"Russia?" I completely forgot that people were still brainstorming, and I hear Riz propose Russia.

"Actually, you're not far off." Just as they did, everyone looks at me as if they forgot I was there as I take my glasses off.

"Let me guess. You already know where we have to go because you're just that much better at making plans than us," Aziz comments.

"Well, no to the second part, but yes to the first part. It's a place in Finland, kinda a low-key profile with very high profile weapons, so it's a good bet that Serge is there."

"And you know this because...." Za starts.

"Because I used the company map on my glasses, it let me sort through all of the places Serge could go by category, and I just narrowed it down from there."

"I actually remember when that feature came out. I was too busy to try it out properly, but I remember it seemed very, very impressive. Did Tirique make sure it was in all glasses?" Ivo asks.

"No, but this guy does." I point to Riz, who nods in response.

"Yeah, I make sure they are in all of our glasses, although I kinda forgot that that feature even existed until right now."

"Not that it really matters because we are going to listen to him anyway, but who votes to follow the kid to Finland?" Ivo asks, and pretty much everyone raises their hands. It still feels bizarre to be the one with the answers around this group of people, but it continues to fuel my confidence.

"To the truck." Everyone is already ready because, as we've been brainstorming, everybody kinda expected we would end up out on a mission and periodically left to get dressed. We all file out of the room, Aiko stopping me before we enter the garage.

"You've been a huge help, Kai," she says. "I really cared about Aria, so thanks for helping." I nod, unsure of what to say. She looks deflated, almost discouraged. She gives me a small hug before getting back into the passenger seat, and I again jump into the back seat.

"Kai, toss me the coordinates, will you?" Ivo shouts from the front.

"Yeah." I put my glasses back on and message them to him.

"Thanks, boss," he says, and then we are out of the garage and into the air just as seamlessly as yesterday, the transformation never going to get old.

We are probably about halfway through the flight when Tyler decides to start a conversation again, Za on the verge of sleep.

"So, you live with your friends, huh?"

"Yeah, Azpi and Kova."

"Interesting names. European?"

"Spanish and Croatian."

"Very cool. Living with your friends is always a fun experience. It's how all of us were living in our teen years and a little beyond that. How'd you guys meet?"

"We were all on the same soccer team for a while."

"Not anymore?"

"The team was migrated to AltD, and I can't really be bothered to do that. It's just not the same."

"I feel that."

"What are they like?" Za asks, not evening opening his eyes.

"They are both kinda crazy. Kova gets irritated quickly when people are loud, and Azpi is always loud, so they just end up yelling at each other all the time. Suffice to say, I don't spend much time in the house."

"Remind me of those two back in the day." Za points to the twins, who just happen to be bickering about something or other. I smile as everyone goes back to sleep. I just think about what Azpi and Kova could be doing right now. Who knows if they have even noticed my absence. They spend so much time in AltD that I wouldn't be surprised if they thought they just keep missing me. I would usually leave for most of the day anyway because I prefer using the portals.

KAI

It takes about the same time to get to Finland as it did to get to Berlin. This time, we land pretty much smack dab where we want to be, Ivo finding a spot to land in the middle of Helsinki. Everyone files out of the truck, leaning against the vehicle while they stretch.

"Where the hell is everyone?" Za asks.

"I mean, I was going to land on the outskirts of the city, but Aiko was actually looking out of the window, and she told me she didn't see any people," Ivo says.

"I'm not gonna walk all of the way into the city to be subtle when no one is in the city," Aiko adds.

"I agree with that assessment," Idri confirms.

"None of that answers my question," Za says. I'm just as confused as Za. Finland has always been the pinnacle of living conditions. Literally, everyone wanted to live in Finland. I will be shocked if the entire population of Finland has decided to go into AltD and abandon their lives here.

"This is creepy," I comment.

"Whatever, let's go to the place we came here for." Ivo tries to re-focus us as everyone else spins around in confusion. We follow Ivo, who has moved the navigation to his phone, weaving through the beautiful streets of the city, the bricks buildings all have glass additions to make them look more modern, and it makes the city quite the collector's item. There are houses with the lights turned off and no one inside, there are grocery stores completely stocked, but with no shoppers, and there are even scents from fresh pastries and steam from recently made coffee still floating out of cafes. This is bizarre.

"Guys, I think I found all of the people," Aiko says, pointing into a window of a massive mill building. We all peak inside and see hundreds of

Finnish people with their glasses on and in AltD. We walk around to the front of the building, Ivo not following us and visibly anxious to finish the mission and find what we came here for. The front of the building is like a chapel, two oversized oak doors separating the AltD congregation and us. There is a plaque next to the door that reads 'The AltD Finland Initiative."

"Wow. That's something," I say, examining the plaque for any other details which there aren't.

"What's going on here, kid? You're the expert." Riz asks.

"I'm not an expert on this, but it looks like the entire country has, or at least this entire city, has decided to all enter AltD together to form a similar society to their own in Reality in AltD. I knew that was possible, but I didn't think people would actually do that."

"So they are basically trying to make Reality Finland in AltD Finland," Aziz says.

"Exactly," I respond. "And, that explains the lack of people."

"That lack of people is making this place a much more enticing offer for Serge, and I'd love it if we can get back to that as quickly as possible," Ivo says from behind us, trying to get us back on task again. We all nod and follow Ivo the rest of the way to the location. It's not exactly a subtle building. The entire wooden cube is painted entirely black. It's kind pf the exact opposite of a secret location. But, I guess Serge wouldn't care since pretty much everyone in this place is gone during the day.

We walk around the back, which is completely open, resembling an airplane hangar. And, almost as if on cue and sent from the gods, a man is examining and packing weapons into a duffel bag. He turns around and I can see, from how the blood drains from his face, that it's Serge, and he was not expecting this. Ivo already has a gun in his hand pointed at Serge while Za takes the lead on the intimidation.

"Guns down, Serge. Hands above your head and get down on your knees." He silently obliges with no fuss, aware of the fact that a group of elite fighters is surrounding the Wolf brothers, not me, of course.

"Hey, Za. Long time no see. What seems to be going on...." He gets up and starts to sprint away, but Idri has pulled out a gun and cleanly shot Serge in the foot before I can blink. He screams out in agony as he writhes around on the ground.

"I was just going to get my business card." He hysterically jokes as Aziz pulls over a chair from the weapons room and heaves Serge onto it, Riz going around the back to wrap him up with metal wire and rope. Aiko walks around the back, kneels, and sprays Serge's wound so he can focus on us and not the pain.

"You were doing so so well, Serge. Too bad I know your guilty pleasure."

"I'm a different person than I was back then." Serge tries to reassure him.

"Are you? It seems like you're still subservient to whatever Nox and Tirique say, even though they are both dead. Care to explain that?" He looks up at Za, almost in shock, but I sense a little bit of satisfaction. We all stand in silence for about twenty minutes, no one caring to expedite the process.

"How do you know that?"

"It doesn't really matter, does it?" I'm realizing now that Za is a very good interrogator. "But, I'll tell you anyway because you're an old friend. Here's how it's going to work. I'm going to tell you some stories. Then I'm going to ask you some questions. You're going to answer my question, or we will do something very, very bad."

"You already took away my army, or at least they did, and my boss. I don't think there is anything else you can take away." Five more minutes of nothing.

"If there is one thing that I know about you, Serge, is that you're arrogant and you're arrogant because you love yourself and you love yourself because no one, definitely not your rich dad, has told you any reason not to." Serge spits at Za's feet in retaliation.

"I'll take that as meaning that you're ready for the story. This is Tyler." Za points behind to Tyler. "Tyler lost someone a year ago as she was going through a portal. Tyler did his research and figured that the only place she could be is in the third dimension." Serge's eyes grow big. "By that reaction, I'm assuming this is news to you. Now, we did our due diligence with our additional research, and it seems that everything about the third dimension has been relayed to you. Hence, your imprisonment here. So, you are going to tell us everything about the third dimension. That means where the portal is and why the hell this dimension even exists in the first place. Clear?" Another seven minutes of quiet, everyone seems to be thinking, but Serge seems to be stalling.

"I'm not answering any of your questions." Serge is smart. "You aren't going to kill me because I'm the only way left in this world that you can get your answers. So, I'm perfectly fine sitting here for the rest of my life, knowing that I have secrets that you all want but will never get."

"What if you didn't sit here forever, but you were able to roam free somewhere else?" Riz says, walking over to Serge, holding a small device in his hand.

"What?"

"This little thing I'm holding is a recent invention of mine for scenarios like this. When attached to your glasses and your head, this device will trap you in AltD for eternity. I'm sure you have a lot of your life left to live and certain things you want to happen. I don't think you want to be stuck in AltD for the rest of your life, although it would be quite the dedication to your dead bosses." I can see that this threatens Serge, but he just stares intently back. Riz walks up to him, pulling Serge's glasses out of his pocket and sliding them onto his face after attaching them to the small black device. He inches the contraption closer and closer to Serge's head until it's millimeters away from making contact.

"Fine, fine. I'll tell you. I guess it doesn't matter because we are too far along for you to stop us." Riz backs away, letting Za retake center stage.

"Stop what?" Za asks.

"The return of Nox and Tirique."

"They are dead, Serge."

"But Nox's last words were…."

"I will live on forever." Ivo finishes.

"Exactly."

"How is that possible?" Za asks. More silence until Za moves forwards, getting impatient.

"The third dimension is a landing place for them. When the Princes, that I have gathered, activate their cubes together, Tirique and Nox will return there, then I will open the single portal that exists to the third dimension, and they will use it to walk into AltD. Voila, the continuation of a perfect legacy." That's not good. I see Idri and Ivo both clenching their fists at the thought of Nox coming back. Remarkably, Za seems to be keeping his calm despite his background with both Nox and Tirique.

"So what? They are going to rule AltD?"

"They are going to finish creating the society that they always wanted to see. The one, in Reality, you didn't let them make."

"Wouldn't that require some preparation?"

"Of course. Tons of it. That's why my government friends have been helping me out."

"So those regulations, the Bots, and the portals, that's all been in partnership with you?" Ivo asks.

"Of course."

"But why would they want to help you?" Za continues questioning.

"Because, they want order. They want to rule more than anything. They want some authority in the virtual world and want to re-establish their dominance over their people. All governments are corrupt. No matter how many times you Wolf brother stripped them down and rebuilt them from scratch, it will never change. The flaw is never the system. The flaw is always the people."

And that's the last thing he's able to say before ten people holding some serious firepower drop down from the roof in front of Serge and all hell breaks loose.

TIMO

November 6, 2040

Ear-piercing would be how I'd describe it. I have finally gotten a chance to relax and take a seat in the library, a stack of rare and unfamiliar books in front of me. I'm not even three sentences into the first book when the most horrifying alarm goes off, vibrating the glass walls and scratching my soul. I get up, pushing my chair back in frustration and emphatically closing the dated raw book cover. I swear the binding almost breaks with the impact. I run to the dining hall, where I see Cora trying to clean up a spilled glass of water. I pick up the glass, careful not to touch any of the deep cracks, and then I pick up some paper towels and help her, crouching to the ground.

"What is happening?" I ask.

"How should I know?"

"Where's Serge?" I ask.

"I saw him this morning. He told me he was going out to look at some weapons or something, you know him." The alarm just keeps getting louder.

"God damnit. I need to turn this thing off." I sprint to the lobby space and search the ground. Last time, I noticed a series of panels that seemed to not fit in with the rest of the floor. I find a small hole in the ground, stick my finger in, and remove the panel. There are tons of electrical switches and exposed wires, and I frantically search for anything that mentions a security alarm. I find a switch for security, and I switch it off, praying that the only security in this place is the alarm. I put the panel back and collapse against the couch, relieved by the silence. Cora walks through the hallway towards me, a group of Princes behind her, and Tammy emerges from the opposite end that leads to the bedrooms.

"What in god's name was that?" Tammy asked, walking over and offering his hand to lift me. I take it and bring myself back to my feet.

"Did anyone actually go through the whole orientation booklet?" Cora asks the group.

"That's a thing?" I ask.

"Yeah. I was way too lazy to read it, and then I lost mine. I'm sure Serge just didn't bother to give either you or Tammy a copy."

"I think I remember something that was in there." A guy from the back says. We all turn towards him, and he takes it as a cue to continue.

"I'm almost positive that the alarm has to be triggered by Serge himself."

"Ok. So, Serge is in danger," I say.

"And we know he's at some kind of weapons supplier or something," Cora adds.

"If he pinged the alarm wirelessly, then we should be able to trace that signal," I say.

"We?" Cora says. "That's all you tech guy. Go for it."

"Fine. Gimme like two minutes." I slump onto the couch and slide on my glasses. I have no idea where to start since I still don't know where in the world this base is. I decide to just use the company map to find possible places where Serge could have gone, and then I check to see if any place has a strong signal pulse which is kinda rare to see these days. Wherever that would be is probably where Serge is and, since he seems to be a pretty capable man, being in trouble is perhaps an extremely urgent matter. I let the filters I set run, mindlessly watching the loading bar until the results come through. Thankfully, there is only one spot, and it's a place in Finland.

"Well, that's going to be a problem," I complain.

"What?" Tammy asks.

"I found the place."

"That's great," Cora says.

"But, it's in Finland."

"Oof." Tammy exhales. "That's tough."

"Indeed. Does anyone have any clue at all how the hell we are going to get to Finland?" I ask.

"Garage?" Tammy asks.

"That's a thing?" Cora responds with another question which seems to be a recurring theme so far today.

"Oh, I have no idea. It was more of a question type thing."

"Ok...then," Cora remarks before turning to the guy that had the information about the alarm.

"Yeah, I don't know about any garage, but if you walk to like the end of the base, through all of those rooms, there is supposed to be a couple of top-secret rooms. The map shows them but they were redacted and with no labels." He must be talking about the third dimension portal room, but I vaguely remember another hallway leading off of that. Whatever is at the end of that hallway is probably still locked.

"Ok. You guys stay there. Cora and I will check it out." I was going to invite Tammy, but I don't trust him enough yet and, just in case the whole third dimension portal thing comes up, I feel more confident in explaining things to Cora.

"Cool," Cora replies, and she follows me as I speed walk. We have a lot of ground to cover between here and where we are going.

"Wow. You are a fast walker."

"I mean, I've already committed to all of this. I can't be bothered to let the organizer of it all just die now."

"That's a fair point." She agrees as we walk through the library, and I grab a roll of cello tape as we walk by. "What's that for?"

"You'll see." My mind is bouncing everywhere in a craze, theorizing about possible plans of approach. If there is a plane here, who's gonna pilot it? If there is nothing, what are we gonna do? If we end up getting all of the ways there and then have to fight some criminals, how are we going to that? Do any of us even know how to wield weapons, because I certainly do not? This leads me to the realization that all of us are basically useless unless we are in AltD, which is kind of a depressing thought.

"For the love of all god, will you please slow down." I don't even realize that Cora has been trying to get my attention this whole time as we pass through the gym.

"What?" I say, turning around to face her. She pulls me closer, lands a kiss, and then spins me back around.

"Just that. Now you can go."

"Ok…" I am mentally slapping my forehead. How am I supposed to respond to that? That kiss just compounded the complications in my brain, and I have a hard time separated the things in my head for long enough to process them individually. When we finally make it to the split in the hallway, I walk to the third dimension portal lock and then turn around.

"I'm sorry, I'm like kinda all over the place. And, like, awkward in general." She smiles.

"Your funny." She responds. "Now, are you going to tell me what the tape is for?"

"Right. The tape." I turn back around to face the fingerprint lock and then turn back to Cora, lean in, kiss her on the cheek, and then back away. She can't help but laugh.

"Focus, Timo." I turn to the lock, break off a piece of the tape and let it grip the fingerprint scanner. I hold the tape up to the light to see if it picked up the fingerprint grooves, which I see clearly. Satisfied, I turn and walk down the tangent hallway, Cora following behind me. We make it to another frosted glass door with a fingerprint lock, as I suspected. I use the tape to unlock the door.

"Damn. That was clean. No wonder you worked for the government," Cora comments as the door swings open, revealing exactly what we needed. There are four mini jets, each able to hold two people. I walk closer to them to admire their figure. They are very compact, chrome in color, and clearly high in tech. I open the cockpit to one and lean in, letting out a sigh of relief as I see an automated piloting system.

"These will work, right?" I ask her.

"Yeah, these will definitely work." We leave the door open behind us as we jog back to the lobby where the Princes are.

"So?" Tammy asks.

"Go to the end of the base and then turn onto the side hallway. I left the door open. There are four mini jets. Each one can fit two people."

"Great," he responds.

"How many of you want to go?" Cora asks the group. Seven of them raise their hands.

"Good stuff, people. Come with me." Tammy starts to jog towards the jets, the seven volunteers following behind him. I take out my glasses and quickly send Tammy the coordinates.

"I sent you the location," I shout at Tammy, who puts his thumb up in the air as he jogs away.

"Thanks!"

"Ok. What are we going to do?" I ask Cora as the people that didn't volunteer, only a few of them, dissipate.

"There might be something we can use. Follow me." This time she's the one to walk swiftly, and I follow her as she leads me to the weapons room. She goes straight to the perimeter and counts out the panels, pressing in the seventh one, revealing two black shield-looking things.

"What are these?" I ask.

"I don't really know, but they aren't labeled like the rest." I take one down and turn it around. It kind of starts to resemble a chest plate, and I read the fine print at the bottom, which says 'multi-functional suit.'

"I don't think they are just shields. That's for sure." I decide to press it into my chest, and then all of a sudden, at if it's magnetically connecting to my body, it snaps into place. Nanotech starts to grow over my body, black metal covering every inch and finally growing over my head.

"Woah. Yeah. Definitely, not just a shield," she says as she puts hers on. It's even more incredible to watch it grow over someone else's body; it's like it's alive.

"Still not positive how this helps us," I remark.

"This is true," she replies. "Wait a second, what does this do?" She seems to trigger something in the suit because I back away as metal wings fold out from her back.

"Angelic," I say, which she laughs at. "It's a button on the top corner of your sightline." I see it and press it. The sensation is bizarre like someone is extracting something from my back, but wings unfurl within seconds.

"Angelic." She copies me.

"Ok. Let's go. No time to waste." I retract the wings and jog towards the jet hangar again, amazed at how light and fitted the suit feels. It literally has molded to my body. Cora runs from behind me, and we make it to the hangar.

"Woah. Where did you find that?" Tammy asks as he climbs into his jet, which everyone else has already done.

"In the weapons room," Cora answers.

"Did you guys grab weapons?" I ask.

"Nah, but these things have a ton of weapons stashed in the back compartments."

"Nice."

"See you on the other side." He closes the cockpit and presses a button. An entire wall of the hangar slides up and over the roof, revealing the cold air of wherever we are. As soon as the jets leave, I reactivate the wings and take flight, gliding through the air. I immediately recognize the unforgettable landscape. We are in Norway, that's convenient.

"Timo?" I hear Cora's voice through my suit.

"Yeah?"

"You can hear me?"

"Yeah."

"Ok, cool. There seems to be a speed mode in the top left. Imma try it out."

"I'll do the same." I see the button and trigger it. I feel the wings lock in, and I see a set of mini thrusters appear on Cora's feet and back. Suddenly we are going very, very fast, almost flying by the jets. We follow the jets for the quick flight, less than ten minutes, until we are in Finland. The city is empty, which is bizarre. We land and take cover a couple of blocks from the exact building we need to be at, and I retract the wings while everyone else grabs weapons from the compartments in the jet.

"Let's hope this thing has some weapons in it," Cora says as we cautiously walk towards the building, staying close to the building and back alleys. When we make it to the location, Tammy leads us up the emergency staircase on the side of the big black building and onto the roof. I get on my stomach and slide myself towards the edge and back of the building. I see Serge tied to a chair, eight heavily armed people around him. It looks like they are interrogating him. I wait for everyone to match my position near the edge of the roof and put my hand up in a countdown. Three. Two. One.

I jump, landing confidently in between the people and Serge in the chair. Everyone else joins me, and we form a wall of bodies in front of the chair. I scan the crowd. I am left in shock at seeing the Wolf brothers in their element. I also see Tyler, I wonder what the connection is there, and the same kid I saw from before in that government building, he's about my age. They all raise their weapons, and I nod to Cora, who goes behind us and starts to untie Serge. After the Wolf brothers and that kid activate suits of their own. We start rushing towards them, none of us really knowing how to fire our weapons. They all cleanly dodge our shots, getting close enough to land a few punches on our people.

"I got him!" Cora yells from behind me.

"Everyone back!" I yell to the team, who fall back, continuing to fire their weapons to maintain their threat. When we have backed at least a hundred feet away, we turn around and sprint towards our jet. I hear the sound of muted engines from behind us and look behind my shoulder to see three of the guys in suits now on motorcycles of some kind, seriously gaining on us. We manage to make it to the jets a couple of seconds before they do.

"The jets have an off-grid invisible switch." Serge manages to mutter as Tammy hauls him into the jet.

"So do the suits," he says, looking at us. We nod back, and the jets rise into the air just as the three guys around the corner. I start throwing slices of metal towards them, waving my arms and letting the suit do the rest, surprised that I'm actually being effective. I activate the wings, and Cora does the same, rising into the air and activating invisibility. Then I spiral around and fly back towards the base.

The so-called icons are left behind.

KAI

November 7, 2040

Back to brainstorming is the name of the game. There is a combination of defeated minds in the room from yesterday's encounter and active ones, making sense of the information that Serge dumped onto us. Ivo and Za are in shock, both being the most scarred from Nox's whole initiative. I don't have all the details, but I know that Za initially worked with Nox. So that means that we are left with the saddened Aiko, the silent Idri, and the energetic twins. The only ones actively trying to find the next step in this saga are Tyler and me, Tyler with his mind completely set on finding Aria at whatever cost and me, still with nothing else better to do. Suffice to say. It's not the elite group of fighters and thinkers that we started yesterday with, at least not until they get some motivation.

While everyone is deflated in the living room, Tyler and I are leaned over the kitchen counter, trying to work things out between the two of us. We are trying to figure out where Serge's base is because we have deduced that the third dimension portal must be highly secured somewhere he would most likely be camped out.

"We definitely don't have any clue of where to start, right?"

"Well, we know it's in Reality. We also know that it can't be in a place where people would see it, so it has to be in some kind of remote location. And, we know that it's probably big if he's found all the Princes."

"So we have narrowed it down to half the world."

"Yeah. I guess when you put it like that, we don't really know where to start."

"Well, he's not going to be in central Europe, I don't think."

"Why not?"

"The government."

"But he's working with the government."

"I doubt they would have been friends in the beginning.

"Ok. I buy that. And we can rule out the US because it's the US."

"Yep."

"So, what are we left with?"

"Everything that's not central Europe and the US."

"Right. I don't think this is going to work."

"What about construction contracts or records?"

"I don't think Nox or Serge would use a public service like that. They would probably just do it themselves."

"That's valid."

"If we are thinking about Serge's possible destinations based on his history, then we could probably do some cross-referencing with the twins since they spent a while tracking him and his team down." Tyler obviously agrees with my plan because he tries to get Aziz's attention.

"Hey. Aziz." Aziz looks up. "Where did you look when you were trying to track down Serge?"

"Oh, pretty much everywhere, that guy was probably the most evasive person I have ever tried to catch."

"Aisa?'

"Yep."

"All of Asia?"

"Yep"

"Europe?"

"Yep."

"Africa?"

"Yep."

"Ok. Where didn't you look?"

"I'm not sure. I don't think we checked the islands. They were too difficult to get to. And, we didn't check the edges of Europe."

"So you didn't check all of Asia. Or, all of Europe."

"I mean…I guess not."

"What does that leave us with?" Tyler turns back to me, more and more of the group deciding to tune in. I start listing off places that haven't been named yet.

"Jamaica?"

"Not remote enough."

"Hawaii?"

"Mostly underwater."

"Alaska?"

"No. I think it has to be close to Finland because otherwise how would all those people show up to protect Serge that fast, we were only with him for an hour."

"You're right. So we should probably focus on the edge of Europe close to Finland."

"Agreed."

"Norway?"

"That sounds interesting. Do we have anything else that could possibly prove that?"

"Nox was apparently a big admirer of Norway. He went to visit there a couple of times. It was all before I joined up with him, which wasn't long, but I definitely heard about it," Za comments.

"So, do we just guess and commit?" Tyler asks. I look at Ivo for an answer.

"I don't really like guessing. I'm not tryna go all of the way to Norway just for Serge not to be there."

"What about cloaking?" Aziz asks.

"What about it?" Tyler follows up.

"Is cloaking technology trackable? Like the kind that Serge could have on his base?" The question is obviously directed to Ivo.

"Yeah, but only if the security system is off, and I have no idea why Serge would ever do that."

"Shall we give it a try?" Za asks, some pleading in his voice. I think everyone wants to be done with the brainstorming and take their emotions out on Nox in a more physical way than just out-thinking him.

"We've already been sat here for two hours, so why not." Ivo heads downstairs, and I instinctively follow him. Sitting down at the computer with a sigh, he logs on.

"Is cloaking technology hard to track?" I ask.

"No, not at all. But, again, the security system it's connected to has to be turned off or has been switched off recently. Otherwise, there is no way to track its signal and then no way to find its location." He opens up a terminal and starts to type. I try to keep up, but, as always, I'm lost within the first thirty seconds. All of a sudden, a map pops up with red and green markers.

"Red means?"

"Red means it's detecting a similar technology, but not cloaking. Green means it's confident that there is cloaking."

"And?"

"Well, I'll be damned. Will you look at that." He presses a toggle to see only green markers, and the map zooms in the only green marker on the entire work. And it's in Norway.

"I'll admit, I was skeptical of your guys' theorizing, but I was wrong. I guess we have to basically go to back to where we came from. He gets up, and I follow, running up the stairs to catch up to him.

"So?" Tyler asks.

"To Norway, we go," I defiantly say. The twins break out into furious clapping while Idri just nods his head, appreciating the result. This time, people were too tired and lazy to get dressed after waking up, so everyone slowly shuffles to their bag or to their room, wherever their clothes are— everyone except Tyler and me, who both need to get dressed as part of our morning routine. The nice thing about the suit is that I don't really have to put too much care into what I wear because the suit will cover it anyway.

"Looks like our lucky guess wasn't too far off," Tyler proudly remarks.

"Not far off at all, actually." He smiles.

"True." It kinda hits me like a brick wall that I have spent the last six days with the original migrants. The people that saved the entire continent of Europe from world war. The same people that saved all of society from the rule of Nox. And, the same people that are about to save the world from Nox for the second time. Crazy stuff.

I'm jolted out of my daze when Za bounds up the stairs, followed by everyone else, fist-bumping me before heading straight for the garage. For the third time, we shuffle into the Ivo truck, as we've come to call it.

KAI

The flight is dead silent. No one speaks. Everyone takes deep breath after deep breath, coming to familiar terms with their emotions so that they can shove them as far down as they can go and open up laser focus. It's a feeling I'm not used to, and I don't even have much baggage to hide. My trip to Norway is quite beautiful, the serenity of the blurring mountains, snowy forests, and deep blue ocean, a welcome addition to our collective mediation. I notice Tyler tapping his foot, either anxious, stressed, nervous, or a combination of all of that. It wouldn't be an understatement to say that this mission, or should I say the success of this mission, is probably weighing the heaviest on him.

"We will get her." I defiantly whisper, just loud enough for him to hear me. He doesn't turn and nod or give me any response, but I know he heard me and his foot slowly approaches a pitter-patter instead of a thump. I don't know if I just made a promise I can't keep. Nobody here seemed to have the same question as me; can Aria even come out of AltD? I guess there is only one way to find out.

The whole trip ends up being predictably long, but locating the base proves to be a bit of an issue. We know that the cloaking of the base shouldn't be on because that's how we found it, but Ivo's location from the search was not very specific. It couldn't be that exact because it didn't know where the base could be in the mountains, which means Ivo spends a solid twenty minutes circling in the air, having all of us stare out the windows until something catches our eye.

"There!" Aziz says, and everyone looks across, and through the window he's sitting at. I unbuckle myself and walk over, standing over this shoulder and following his point to a part of the mountain that seems to look like some kind of reflection or something as our angle of sight changes. Ivo continues to turn, Aziz giving him directions.

"A little right. Too much, right. Ok, there, stop. It's right in front of us." Ivo inches closer and closer, and suddenly I see it. The base is massive, which I was not expecting. What I had mistaken as a reflection of some kind is actually just the result of the entire base being glass, every single inch of it. We can start to see into the rooms as Ivo directs us down towards it, the expansiveness and luxury of the base prominent. There is a gym with a pool beneath it, the depth of the water visible because of the glass. A library, housing thousands of books, floats in the air as well as a full-fledged sparring area, or at least that's what it looks like. Ivo must spot the landing platform at the top the same time I do because he starts to speed towards it, slowing us down to land on the platform. We all climb out, breathing in the high-altitude air.

"Everyone ready?" Ivo begins to prep us. "I have no idea what is going to be waiting for us when we get in. But, by the glimpse I got of it through the glass as we landed, it's a lot of bodies, a lot of guns, and a lot of glass. Everyone looks out for each other, especially if there is any structural damage done this place because then it could all collapse and fall down the mountain at any time." Everyone nods, attaching weapons to various areas of their bodies. The twins have replaced their usual guns and such with just their necklaces. I still don't know what the cubes do, but I guess I'll find out. Meanwhile, Aiko has swung swords around her back, and Idri has attached a gun, knife, or grenade to pretty much every inch of his body. Tyler, who's clearly more comfortable with hand-to-hand combat, has a circular contraption on each of his hands and knives tucked away in his pants.

"Alright, team. The objective is to find the portal, get in, get Aria, get out. Other than that, we just have to wing it. Let's hope that Aria has a bit more information for us about the whole Nox and Tirique situation." We all nod in agreement again, and we, as confidently as we possibly can, charge our way into the big entrance to the base. We emerge on some kind of balcony, looking down at a lobby area with couches, armchairs, and coffee tables. But, that's not the first thing I see. The first thing I see is many people around my age, holding their glasses and surrounded by a healthy number of soldiers. Damnit. We forgot about the whole AltD thing. Whatever the Princes are going to do, we can't let it happen. I look at Ivo, who makes the same realization I do.

"I need to go in," I say to him. He nods.

"Take Za and Aziz."

"Ok," I reply. Riz hears us and hands a pair of glasses to both Za and Aziz. He hands another pair to me, and I have no time to revel in the fact that it's the new model I coveted so much.

"I modded the glasses so that you all show up where they show up." I don't even know how that's possible but thank the lord Riz remembered to do that. I look down at the group of people just in time to see them putting their glasses on. The last one to do it was the same kid I saw earlier in the government center, his blonde hair flourishing over his forehead. I sit down and slide my glasses on after Aziz and Za. It's time for a confrontation. The final confrontation.

TIMO

November 7, 2040

We show up at the same place as before, now the dome fully exposed after being unlocked. The last time we were here, we all programmed our glasses so that we showed up here. Serge barely talked to us yesterday before he went to bed early. He seemed shaken like he found out something that he wasn't expecting or that could really compromise us. He didn't seem prepared to share, so he didn't, and I didn't press him. An hour ago, the last thing he said was, "some people are probably going to find us." And he was suddenly accompanied by a bunch of soldiers. They looked like they were from the government. Of course, Serge was right. The same group from yesterday showed up just as we were entering AltD. It turns out it's possibly the most threatening group of people I am ever going to encounter. Maybe Serge was hit with some instantaneous wave of PTSD.

"Ok, people! You know what we have to do!" Cora shouts to everyone.

"Cover Tammy and me at all costs and, if one of the cubes breaks, someone needs to put in theirs. I'm going to do the time cube last and, as you know, there is only one of them, so that's the most important moment." Then, somehow, the kid I saw, Za, and one of the twins show up. I have no clue how they spawned in this exact spot, but it means that our time is much less. I don't think our people can fend them off, even though we severely outnumber them.

"Ok. Go, go!" Cora orders, but it's kind of confusing. Half of the people flock into the base, and the other half turn to face a threat. I slap my head and look at Cora, who just shrugs.

"Really?" I complain.

"C'mon. Cut me some slack. Does it look like I've commanded a team before?"

"I mean, no. But, that was about as vague as it possibly could've been."

"Yeah, yeah. Just do your job, Timo." I shake my head as I stride into the base, laying my eyes on the cubes in the back. Tammy is already waiting in the center, trying to understand the instructions on the Assembler.

"This is a god damn maze."

"Are the instructions not helping?" I ask, leaning down to check it out.

"I've been following the instructions. I think I'm doing it right, and then all of a sudden, I end up exactly where I started, and I have no idea which step I messed up on. It's like a cycle of unexpected failure."

"Uh-huh." He's kind of right. The instructions themselves would take some time to understand. The Assembler is basically just a black skeleton. It starts with a cross of metal bars that have clicked into the ground. Then it becomes a web of thinner bars that create this pole, or pedestal of some kind, that provides the height. At the top, there are three crosses again with tangent bars to place a cube in and then lock it in. Those are suspended at different heights and have special little sensors. Right now, Tammy is trying to extend the height with the web of bars and make sure everything is facing the right way, which requires a bunch of fiddling until they all click. Tammy continues to swear at himself, and I take a look out of the base. The Princes that entered before thankfully circled back to join the fight, but it's kind of in vein. The twin and Za won't let a single hit get even close to them, dodging them with ease and then landing a firm hit somewhere else. The weak point is clearly the kid my age who is looking valiant but not doing too much. I guess when you have the other two also on your side, it doesn't really matter. I walk over to my object cube, feeling the energy force as my hand gets closer to it.

"What are you doing? I'm don't think I'm even close to being ready."

"This is not for that," I say. I pick up the cube, activating it, so I see the screen. I stand there, placing my legs shoulder-width apart, cube in my hand, and I get to work. I generate some weapons around Tammy and me, just in case. And then, slowly but surely, I build a brick wall around the base. Bricks fly down from the sky and build upon themselves.

"That's going to use a lot of energy, Timo," Tammy says.

"It's fine. We have more of these."

"Ok, but you can't touch the others."

"Cora has one."

"And?"

"Cora will get here in time." Tammy looks skeptical. "Listen. If we both die or they get close enough to the cubes to destroy them, then all of this was for nothing."

"Fine." I continue generating a wall, starting another layer three feet behind it. The Princes realize what's happening, and they step behind the walls, letting it generate between them and the others.

"Everyone grab a gun," Cora says, pointing to the weapons I generated on the floor. "Aim it at the top of the wall."

"I got it. I think I got it," Tammy says, collapsing to the ground in relief. I continue to construct the wall, using all of the brainpower I have to properly align the bricks, focusing on the next spot I want the brick to go, waiting for it to get there, and then moving on. Slowly but surely, a two-layer wall starts to form around the entrance of the base. I nod to Cora, who nods back. She puts down her weapon and carefully picks up her object cube, the lines glowing with energy. Placing it in the highest capsule, the frame automatically connects to the cube, which gets locked in. The Assembler responds with a golden glow rippling through each beam.

"Do Both," I tell Cora.

"Both?"

"Yeah, Both."

"Ok." She goes back to the next pedestal and grabs her media cube, walking it over and placing it in the lowest capsule, the Assembler responding with the same glow, now blue.

"One to go," Tammy says, looking at me. I walk over to my pedestals, place the object cube back on the charger, and grab the time cube next to it, the red lines pulsating. I'm about to turn around when I hear a gunshot, a scream, and the crash of glass behind me.

ARIA

November 7, 2040

A thick fog prevents me from seeing more than twenty feet ahead of me, and a warm mist falls from the sky. I'm over the jungle weather. I'm mindlessly doing my daily walk around the perimeter of the island. That's what I've been calling it. I stare out into the open, the emptiness, the never-ending reminder that I'm stuck. I haven't drunk water, I haven't eaten, in what I counted to be a year. I've been sleeping deeper into the jungle, and there is a rare mango tree there where've I've been marking the days as they pass by me. There's physically no way for me to look at myself, so I don't know if my appearance literally hasn't changed or if I look like I'm doubly homeless, without a physical home, and without a dimension to call home.

    I haven't been able to theorize much. However, by the realism of this place and the clear designation towards Nox and Tirique, I have determined that this must be another dimension, probably with only one way out, meant for the sole purpose of a landing spot for Nox and Tirique for their great prophetic return. How that's going to happen is beyond me, and where the portal resides is equally as confusing. The thing is, I know that Tirique and Nox are going to appear where their three-dimensional holograms are. It only makes sense. And, the path that leads out from that is probably the path towards the portal. The problem is, I knew just as much within my first twenty-four hours here, so it's not like I've made any breakthroughs. Despite that, my theory was at least confirmed three days ago when a beam of light shot up from where the portal probably is. I was going to make a run for it, but two things were stopping me. For one, it's in the middle of the Darkness as I've come to know it, and, at the time of the portal's activation, the Darkness was an ocean, and I wasn't swimming a quarter-mile. Plus, the beam only appeared for about two minutes before rescinding, so I wouldn't have been able to make it anyways. I have still not stepped into the Darkness. The mere possibility, no matter how slim it is, of me, just being swallowed up by the void is scary enough. I might not have made any progress over the last year, but at least I'm alive.

Towards the end of my loop, I see the tree I marked, and I cut off into the jungle again. The vines slap my face with a little more zip today as I can't see them swinging before I'm already whacked. My stumble from the jungle is a repetition of staring at the ground, so I don't trip and die, then looking up to be greeted by a swinging vine, then almost tripping and dying, then looking back at the ground again, so that doesn't happen again, which it obviously does. All of that just about sums up how the last year has gone for me. Finally, after some subpar bushwhacking and an extra spoonful of patience, I make it to the plaques and what I see is not a great sign.

The holograms have stopped rotating, and each figure's arms are outstretched like they are either Jesus on the cross or Lionel Messi after scoring a goal. Meanwhile, the letters on each plaque have a holy glow and pulse, like they are living. I stand up, and the path to the portal is subtly illuminated, spots of light peeking out from the dirt and vines. I follow the path back to the Darkness and, as if God just has his way today, a beam extends from the middle of the landscape, which is a desert this time. Is a desert better than an ocean? Yes. But, both still have an intent to kill that is hard to ignore. That is until I hear a voice. I try to block out all of the jungle bustle so I can listen to it better, inching as close to the Darkness as I can possibly get. Then I hear it.

"Aria!" It's Tyler. It doesn't matter that I haven't heard a single human voice that isn't mine in a year. It doesn't matter that it's a quarter of a mile away. It doesn't matter that I don't know how to get to him. It's Tyler, and nothing is going to stop. I almost can't look as I take a step onto the sand. I step down with my left foot, but I don't feel sand beneath it. I make myself look, and my eyes grow wide as I see my foot landing straight on a solid platform of glass. I take my foot off, and the platform disintegrates back into the sand. I place my foot down again, the glass forming immediately. Ok. Left foot. Right foot. Left foot again. And then I'm running, sprinting, actually. The occasional stumble means my hands press down against the desert, but, they too, just feel solid glass. I can not believe I could've done this the entire time. The desert that once was never-ending seems to become a story of the past quicker than I could ever imagine. I leave everything in my wake, the jungle, my stupid calendar makings, the nothingness off of the edge, everything. And then I see him. I see the bright blonde hair waving within the frame of the transparent portal, which also gives me a look into a glass room and hallway. The sight of natural light is refreshing, and the mountains in the background of the scene are almost like looking at a foreign world to me because it's been so long.

But I also see the flailing arms, the knife held to his neck, and the silhouette of a man behind him. Nothing is ever, can ever, be this easy.

TYLER

November 7, 2040

Kai, Aziz, and Za all sit down in meditative positions and slide on their glasses. I'm assuming it's to stop the gathering of, who I'm assuming to be the Princes, below. Ivo, who's always prepared to make us look bad, backs up a few steps before flinging himself off the side of the balcony, kicking through a soldier as he lands, standing up, taking a gun from the next soldier, and shooting him in the leg. Then he turns around, activates his suit, which never gets old, generates a knife in each of his hands, and throws it at the two incoming soldiers. They all look to be from the government, so it gives me great pleasure to watch. By the time Aiko, Idri, Riz, and I have walked down the balcony steps, the wall of soldiers is pretty much already gone, Idri nonchalantly crouching down and shooting the last two.

"What about these fellas?" Riz asks, obnoxiously leaning down and staring at the Princes, who obviously can't see him back. Riz waves his hand in front of their faces for good measure before walking to a kid with blonde hair. I get closer and immediately recognize the kid as Timo. I guess our paths crossing again was really meant to be, although it would've been kinda helpful to know he was a Prince before letting him even remotely close to an AltD portal.

"Oh, that's cute. This kid is sweating." Riz says, staring at Timo.

"Jesus, Riz. Out of all the times to have an attention span and curiosity of a five-year-old, you had to choose now?" Idri complains. Aiko chuckles behind him.

"Make fun of the kids later, Riz," she adds.

"Preferably after we save the world for the third time," Ivo says.

"Where to?" I ask Ivo. Idri walks back from the hallway that goes deeper into the mountain. I didn't even notice him leave; he's always been stealthy like that, I suppose.

"Not that way. It's just bedrooms."

"This way it is," Ivo says, starting to stride the other way down the hallway. Soldiers are periodically placed in each hallway. We each decide to take a turn with the lead. We pass through the dining hall, and I pull out a knife, generating a shield with my special gloves Ivo made me earlier. I deflect all of their gunshots and then stab one in the leg, spinning around his crumpling figure and pulling out a pistol before shooting it at the next incoming guard.

"When did you get so good at fighting?" Ivo asks.

"What do you mean? I've always been this good." I jokingly reply.

"Since I trained him," Idri bluntly says from the back.

"Ah. That makes a lot more sense." Aiko takes the lead on the next one as we move swiftly through a gym and a sparring room with white panels. She unsheathes her swords from around her back, taking out the first guy in one fluid motion. The next makes the mistake of charging at her, which she dodges and then sticks out the handle of the sword, which knocks the guy down. She puts her swords back as we walk past her.

"It's so gruesome to watch but so impressive at the same time," I say, walking by Idri.

"I could've done that with one shot. Why she has to look like some super ninja is beyond me," he remarks. I smile, and we keep moving through the rooms, taking out soldiers like it's nobody's business. To be honest, there are not as many soldiers as I would've thought. I don't mind because it gives me plenty of time to admire the sheer architecture of this place. The amount of glass is overwhelming, the transparency meaning the rooms feel like they are floating against the mountain. It all seems wildly unnecessary, but I could see how this place would be enticing to live in, and I'm sure Serge had to do his fair share of convincing to gather all of the Princes here. I just don't know how all of those kids are so sure they want to do this. Of course, the events of Nox were five years ago when they were a lot younger, but they couldn't have not learned or heard about it. I just hope that Kai, Aziz, and Za can take them out before we have to worry about any Nox and Tirique reincarnation. We keep walking, our shoes slapping against the thick glass until we get to a fork in the hallway. There is a frosted glass door straight ahead and then a narrower hallway leading off the side.

"I can take this one; you guys go check that one out."

"You sure?" Ivo asks.

"Yeah, yeah. It doesn't seem too far. I can just holler if I need any help."

"Ok." The three of them cut off, and I walk up closer to the door. I push on the handle, but it's pretty well locked. A fingerprint scanner is sitting on a console to my right. Damn. I probably need Serge's fingerprint. Then I feel a knee in my back, and I'm thrust forwards into the door, my face smashing against the glass and pain shooting from my cheekbone and into my jaw. I turn around just in time to dodge a boot coming towards my face. Serge is standing right above me. A gun pointed at me. I punch him in the shin, which I think hurts my hand more than it does his shin, but it throws him off long enough for me to push off of the door behind my head and slide myself in between his legs. Now I'm able to get to my feet and put my fists up, ready for the next blow. Serge turns around, immediately points his gun, and pulls the trigger. I crouch into the ground, activating both shields from my hands which stop the bullets. I slide a knife out of my pants, propelling myself backward as I toss it at Serge. He doesn't just dodge, he catches it and throws it back. I roll over quickly before it hits me, the knife clattering to the ground.

"Tyler!" I hear Riz's voice, and I look to my right, seeing the three of them in the distance, occupied by a healthy amount of government soldiers. He slides his silver necklace across the glass floor and into my outstretched hand. I slide it over my neck, double-tapping the cube as I hop to my feet. I feel nanotech surround my body in a matter of milliseconds, the helmet finally stretching over my head. The suit immediately calibrates to my body and is fully operational just in time to see Serge charging towards me. I generate a gun in my hand, but I cannot fire it before Serge punches the gun away and lands another hit in my stomach. I dodge the next punch, ducking underneath his arm, and then I generate a knife and stab it into his leg before swinging my head back around and hitting him in the face. He gets tossed against the glass but uses his momentum to kick back off and pin me against the opposite wall.

"Don't try to mess with things you don't understand. This is inevitable, and nothing was ever, or will ever, stop it from happening." His raspy, short of breath voice, threatens. I frantically try to generate another knife in my hand, but he pins my arm behind my body, head butting my chest and then kneeing my leg. Excruciating pain shoots up every inch of me, culminating in a raging burn.

"Whatever you tell yourself to sleep at night," I reply and look down at my suit, where each miniature line of the nanotech is glowing. Oh, he isn't ready for this one. I wait for Serge to come back at me with his own momentum, and then I explode, activating every muscle in my body to break free and use the energy charge to slam Serge against the fall. He crumples to the ground and, as he tries to stumble to his feet, I hit him one last time in the head, and he hits the deck for the last time. I drag his half-conscious body over to the fingerprint scanner, a streak of blood from his leg crimson against the glass floor. I attempt to prop his body against the glass wall, using my body weight to keep it in place. I pick up his hand with my one free arm, wipe it clean of any blood or sweat, and place his pointer finger on the scanner. I hear a click as the door unlocks, and I let Serge's body drop to the floor as the door swings open, and I walk in. The portal is like nothing I've ever seen before. Its color is so black that it looks like a void, like it's beyond the power of light and color. There is another locking system to the side, and I walk over, pressing the unlock button just as I'm tackled to the floor again. Serge pins me to the ground this time.

"Not so fast." I flip him around, so I'm pinning him against the ground. He kicks me out with his legs and sends me flying to the other side of the room. Before I have time to get up, he jumps on top of me, rolls me over, and pins my stomach down, grabbing my chin and pulling my head up. He reaches for the cube around my neck, and he deactivates the suit, pulling the chain off my neck and throwing the necklace down the hallway. I manage to free an elbow, which I flail towards his gut. He winces and rolls back in pain while I tiredly get to my feet and walk towards the portal, which now has slight ripples. I'm about to walk through when Serge comes from behind me and puts me in a headlock, sinking a knife into the back of my leg. I feel light-headed from the pain, retaining all the strength I have so I can stay standing and close to the portal.

"Aria!" I yell, hoping Aria is somewhere on the other side of this darkness.

"She's too far. Maybe she'll make it in time to see your dead body against the ground." Serge hisses behind my ear, clasping his hand over my mouth as it holds another knife.

"You're a deranged asshole. You know that?" I manage to mutter before he tightens his grip over my mouth.

"Whatever you tell yourself to help you sleep at night." He uses my comeback against me, and then, just as quickly, he crumbles to the ground. I look back, and Ivo has punched his head, and Serge now lays on the blood-stained floor, actually unconscious this time.

"Go." He says to me. I nod and walk through the portal and straight into a body. I feel arms tightly hold onto me as I stare out into a black desert.

"Tyler." I hear Aria's voice, backing away from the embrace so I can see her. She looks just as healthy as when she left through the portal a year ago. I hug her even tighter, lifting her feet off of the ground.

"Tyler. We don't have time. Something is happening."

"We know. You have to show and tell me everything you know so that we can get this over with and we can move on with our lives, with you never ever leaving my side." She manages a smile and then turns around, holding my hand as we stride over the desert, glass platforms forming underneath our feet. I already think this place is bizarre, but that's even before we get to the jungle.

"Welcome to the island," Aria exclaims with a wave of her hands.

"You mean the third dimension?"

"That's what this is?"

"Yeah."

"Oh, god."

"Why did you call it the island?"

"Because it's literally a floating piece of land, about a mile and a half in diameter. The entire thing is a jungle except for a little bit around the edge and this middle bit called the Darkness, which is where we are now."

"Yeah, what's up with this?"

"It constantly changes between different landscapes, but it's always black. Trust me, Ty, you haven't seen it all until now."

"I don't know, Aria. I saw a lot of stuff trying to look for you."

"How did you find me?"

"I'll tell you later. Right now, Ivo, Aiko, Riz, and Idri are frantically trying to fight off an abundance of government soldiers."

"I already have so many questions."

"I'm sure." She guides me off of the sand and straight into the jungle, her grip on my hand not wavering.

"Where are we headed?"

"You'll see. I notice that your patience hasn't changed."

"Listen. I had to wait one year to see the love of my life again. I'd say I've been doing enough waiting."

"You have a point," she admits. I keep stepping over roots while ducking underneath low-hanging vines. A faint glow beneath all of the dirt and roots tell me that this is leading somewhere. Then she shows me two plaques. "See. The glow has been gradually getting brighter in response to something." That must be because of whatever is happening in AltD. One of them is for Nox, the other for Tirique. Above the plaques, there are two floating holograms of their respective people, the arms of the holograms outstretched in some holy position.

"What am I looking at?"

"You are looking at the resurrection point for Nox and Tirique, and I'm hoping you know the other side of the story."

"Unfortunately, I do."

"And?"

"Well. At this very moment, Kai, Za, and Aziz are in AltD trying to stop the Princes that Serge Adams gathered from putting their cubes together, which would somehow bring back Tirique and your lovely brother."

"Woah. Who's Kai?"

"A kid that Za found that's been helping us. You would like him, actually. But, that's not important right now."

"Ok. So what are we supposed to do about that?"

"At the moment, we are hoping that the three in AltD can do their thing. But, if they can't, then we were kind of praying that you would know what to do."

"This is all beyond me."

"But, you've been here for a year."

"In case you haven't noticed Ty, there really isn't much to do here and certainly not any library flowing with information."

"Yes. Yes. I see that now. I just want this to be over. It's been quite the saga." Aria leans over for a kiss.

"That is clear. But, at least the team is back together. That's pretty cool." I'm about to tell her how it all went down, but the holograms float into the air and grow in size until they are the size of us. The plaque suddenly disintegrates, the ash floating in the sky, and two circular portals, the same black from the one I used to get in here, appear in their place.

Something is happening. Something not good.

KAI

November 7, 2040

It takes us an extra minute to show up in AltD. I think it's because whatever software or feature Riz added needed to determine where the Princes were going, but eventually, we end up in AltD, standing a hundred feet in front of a glass dome where I can see every single cube sitting on pedestals. I swear it takes some serious self-control not to return to my old urges and steal some cubes. Like they are right there. All of them. Literally a hundred feet away. However, I re-focus myself with some self reminders that I have now been given a greater purpose. I see the blonde kid running into the building along with a few of the other Princes. They all look a bit scattered, the girl in front who seems to have some authority over the others clearly lost with her instructions. I look at Aziz, who just shrugs at me, both of us thinking this might be easier than we initially thought.

"Let's get this done as quick as possible," Za says. "I really just need to see my boyfriend and one long night of stressless sleep."

"I agree with this," I respond. "Obviously not the boyfriend part because I don't have one of those, but the stressless sleep definitely."

"Jesus, you two. Will, you shut up and pay attention," Aziz complains.

"What?" Za asks.

"We don't even have a plan. Like, are we destroying the cubes? Are we taking out the Princes? Are we just kinda stalling until something happens on the other end of things? How is literally no one else concerned with the fact that we have no plan of attack?" Aziz argues.

"I guess we are just gonna have to wing it," I say, gesturing towards the onrushing Princes, all wielding weapons.

"You guys are the worst," Aziz complains again, putting his fists up. I look forwards and brace myself as a big kid about my age runs towards me with a sword in his hand. He definitely does not know how to use that. I say to myself as he completely miscues his first swing. I kick the sword out of his hand and then perform my best karate kick, pushing him back. He gets up and runs back towards me when I pick up the sword and hit him as hard as I can with the handle, knocking him out. Another girl is already prepared to fight behind her fallen colleague, and she pulls out a rifle. I scurry behind a tree until I hear her run out of ammo. I quickly spring around the tree and sprint towards her, using her own momentum to trip her. I grab the belt from the other guy and tie the girl's hands together, leaving her face down on the ground.

I look to the side to see Aziz and Za just toying with the others, dodging all of their hits gracefully and then landing a few light hits to annoy them. They are clearly enjoying themselves way too much. I'm distracted by them so much that I don't even notice bricks flying through the air and creating a brick wall between us and the base. As the Princes that Za and Aziz are fighting flee behind the wall, we gather together, admiring the bricks being rapidly placed with perfection.

"Well. Not even our non-existent plan accounted for that. So I guess our lack of organization didn't actually matter in the end," Za says, and Aziz slaps his forehead. I'm enjoying how they've switched roles, Aziz taking the lead and getting made fun of by Za instead of the other way around.

"We could've still made a plan, idiot. Just because we didn't account for one of them creating a brick wall out of thin air doesn't mean our plan would've been useless."

"Yeah, yeah."

"Too bad our suits don't work in here," I comment.

"They do," Za states.

"What? Why did I have to be in Reality when I first used it then?"

"That was just for calibration. Ivo is too smart to have it not work in AltD," Za replies.

"Did you know this?" I ask Aziz.

"Yeah, of course. Riz told me all about him using his suit in AltD."

"Jeez. So then why were you guys not using your suits just now."

"Because that's less fun," Za says.

"Yeah. What he said," Aziz agrees. At these moments, I realize that both Za and Aziz are still kids at heart that just want to mess around and have some fun.

"So." I start to devise a real plan that we can orchestrate. "I think we use our suits to drop in from above. We can climb the wall and then jump down into the dome."

"I like this so far," Aziz says.

"Oh. That's all I got," I say as Aziz frowns. Za decides to pick it up.

"They may not be great fighters, but they aren't stupid. They are definitely going to be waiting in there with guns pointed at us. Our suits are semi-bullet proof but not from a hundred bullets."

"So, what do we do?" I ask.

"Shock them," Aziz says.

"What?" Za questions.

"Quite literally shock them. As you said, they aren't experienced fighters. So, we jump, one of us lands a hit, and they should hesitate long enough for us to take out their weapons at the very least."

"So who takes the shot?" I ask, knowing that it's not going to be me.

"I got it," Za says confidently.

"The knifeman has turned into Idri real quick," Aziz jokes. I don't really get it because Za has used guns primarily over the last few days but whatever.

"Ok. Let's not waste any more time. Let the plan commence," I say, reaching behind my ear and activating my suit, the same sensation of the tech growing over my body causing an extra dose of adrenaline to flow through my body. I look at Aziz double-tap the cube on his neck which automatically snaps to his chest, a suit similar to mine growing out of it. I guess I know what the necklaces are for now. When all three of us have our suits activated, we scale the first brick wall, crouching when we get to the top so no one can see us.

"On five," Aziz says, the communication automatically switching to the suits. I look at Za, who is stretching his arm, preparing himself to generate a gun and take the shot. Meanwhile, I readjust my feet to launch myself off the thirty-foot walls.

"Five. Four." I shake out my hands.

"Three. Two." I do a neck roll and stand up.

"One." I fully leap, the power and agility of the suit helping my athleticism. I push my feet together as I crash through the glass head first. Looking to the side, I see a gun generate in Za's hand, and a shot hit the right thigh of the tall kid in the middle. I land solidly on the ground with a summersault and then generate a couple of knives in each hand. Swinging around, I toss each knife into the leg of the two closest people. Then I stand up, rushing towards the next person and knocking them out.

KAI

When the attacks are over, I relax and take a moment to get my bearings. There is a black contraption in the middle of the room, connected to the ground. The contraption is like a web that rises and cradles two creator cubes, one media cube and one object cube. I look ahead and straight into the eyes of the blonde kid who's tightly holding the time cube—the girl that was leading before stands in front, guarding him. I look at Za and Aziz, who are both bracing themselves for something.

"Kid. You're gonna have one shot." I hear Aziz's voice as a whisper through my helmet.

"Me?"

"Yeah. Hit the cube."

"What if it doesn't do anything?"

"It'll do something."

"Shouldn't one of you take the shot?"

"We can't."

"Why not?"

"Za is hit, and I'm standing in front of him, so they don't know our weak point. I'm going to dive towards the girl and draw her out. You will have to take the shot cuz that kid is gonna sprint towards the thing in the middle. Got it?"

"Got it."

"Ok. Go." I see Aziz dive forwards and grab the legs of the girl and drag her down. I generate a gun in my hand and dive to get a better angle. The kid is already running with the cube in his hands. I take aim, my eyes tracking the movement of the cube, my fingers hovering over the trigger. I take the shot and watch as the bullet flies perfectly in the direction of the cube. And then it hits a body. My body slams against the ground as I see the kid place the cube in the thing.

It's done.

TIMO

November 7, 2040

The twin makes a flailing dive towards Cora and grabs her legs, dragging her down. I sprint towards the Assembler, then I hear a shot and look to see a bullet coming right at me. And then I see Tammy's long body jump in front of me. He gets hit, but I don't have time. I place the cube in the Assembler, and it locks in place. The three cubes all open up in a way I didn't know was possible, and they combine in front of our eyes, creating a very dark glow. I close my eyes to the light, and when I open them, the cubes are literally disintegrating into ash—all of my power, all our power, everything is gone in a matter of seconds. The twin, Za, and the kid all disappear, returning to Reality. I hear the groaning of Tammy and rush towards him. In addition to the shot he took in the leg, he took one in the gut too. Blood is spilling everywhere. Cora crawls over from where she was tackled.

"It's ok, Tammy. We did it. We got it done." She reassures him, squeezing his hand. He solemnly nods, and then his eyes close, and then he's gone too.

"This better not have been in vain," I say.

"Is everyone else ok?" Cora asks the rest, a couple of tears running down her face. After three days with Cora, I can confidently say that she gets attached very, very quickly. I look around, and most people are nodding, some nodding on behalf of unconscious people who are injured. It seems that most of us came out of this alive. Of course, Serge couldn't care less if we survived this. As long as we completed the mission, that's all he's concerned about, which we did.

We successfully put the cubes together, triggered whatever was going to bring Nox and Tirique back, and then agonizingly watched our only stamp of authority literally crumble in front of our eyes. All because we've been promised another path to glory, to more tremendous success. To be part of a legacy or to build a legacy. And, if it doesn't work out, we have a life of normality to live out, in Reality, and in AltD. It came at a cost, but, hey, at least we are alive right?

ARIA

November 7, 2035

We scurry backwards as the holograms continue to grow and grow, the plaques simultaneously getting magically wiped away. And then, in scary fashion, the holograms drop through the holes.

"Get ready," Tyler warns.

"Ready for what?"

"I don't know. The worst." Then it happens. Levitating out of the two-dimensional-looking black portal holes are two bodies, Nox and Tirique, their eyes fluttering open like they are emerging from a long slumber. They both look impeccable, not a scratch on their skin like they have been rejuvenated by mother nature or something. Ageless. Nox's eyes burst open before his body lands effortlessly on the ground. He looks at Tyler, who's in a combat-ready position.

"That's cute." Tyler pulls out a knife, runs towards him with a battle scream, and stabs him right in the heart. Meanwhile, Tirique is just standing on the ground next to him with no expression on his face. No shock. No surprise. Nothing.

"Just give it a minute." Is all he says. Nox's body turns to ash and floats away in the air, just as the plaques and holograms did. We wait about fifteen seconds, and then Nox, again looking as young as ever, emerges from the portal. Tyler, who has, at this point, gone insane, decides to turn to Tirique to stab him instead. I grab his arm before he can go any further.

"Ty. Stop."

"But…"

"They can't die. You just saw that they couldn't die."

"It's nice to see you, sis," Nox says, walking towards me.

"Right, right asshole. Calm down. Just because you made yourself into some kind of psychotic demigod does not mean that you are truly back," I reply.

"You're right. You're right. It's even better than that. I am immortal, and I have all of the power. I quite literally have been reborn with a world in my hand."

"Not until you get to the portal," Tyler exclaims defiantly.

"Right. That…that shouldn't be a problem," he says. I don't know how to react right now. Part of me is so triggered to see Nox come back with his arrogant dictator self; it's almost like his ego grew when he died.

On the other hand, something in me yearns for a brother again, to be reunited in that way with someone that was part of me for so long. I see that Tyler knows I'm feeling caught in between two minds because he decides to buy us some time. He unexpectedly grabs two new knives from his pants, throwing one into the heart of Nox, who immediately crumples to the floor. Tirique hesitates for a little out of shock, and Tyler takes the opportunity to sprint up to him and stab him in the gut. He then immediately turns to me.

"That gives us a couple of minutes. Are you good? I mean, I know what's going on through your head, but you know what we have to do, right?" I nod along. "We just have to do the right thing this one last time, and you will finally be free of him and his insane methods. I know a part of you wants him back, but your greater judgment knows what the right thing to do is. You have to do it for yourself, and you have to do it for everyone on the other side of that portal. You have to do it for the world. Wow, this is sounding awfully dramatic, but you know what I mean." He talks in an extremely hurried manner, out of breath and out of time.

"Let's go," I say. Tyler, inevitably, helps me clear my head with his rushed but inspired speech, and I have learned to trust my gut feeling on things. My gut is telling me that we need to get rid of Nox, and we are doing that without any hesitation.

"Let's go?"

"Well, we obviously have no idea how to be rid of them and stop this whole thing. That is unless you were planning on staying here for the rest of your life and stabbing them over and over again."

"I definitely was not planning on that."

"So, then we have to get out of the third dimension and talk it through with the others. It's the only way we will have a chance at stopping them."

"Your right. Let's go." He turns around, jogging through the jungle and onto the Darkness. For a second, I think that the glass platforms might have gone away since Nox and Tirique are here now, but they thankfully reappear beneath Tyler's feet.

"Don't run." I hear the insane voice of Nox behind me, and I block it out. We quite literally ignore him by starting to run as fast as we can to the portal. How the glass platforms can keep up is beyond me, but they do, and I rely on their solid surface not to lose my momentum. I see the portal ahead of me. The translucent shape that will take me to Reality is the only thing I want right now. I see the back of who I think is Ivo. Tyler and I dive through the portal as soon as we get there, the steps of Nox and

Tirique no more than twenty feet behind us. I bundle into Ivo's body and slam my hip against the ground.

"Close it! Close it!" Tyler screams at Za, who's standing by the lock, and he frantically presses the button, the portal safely locking behind us. For now, we are good. But, a stall isn't going to save the world.

TYLER

November 7, 2040

"What happened? What happened?" Ivo and Za both question me simultaneously as I'm able to lift myself to my feet. I look to the other side of the room, where Aria is strongly embracing Aiko.

"Hey. Tyler. We are gonna need some words here, buddy." Idri comes over and snaps me out of it, which seems to be his special ability with me.

"Yeah, yeah, sorry. What was the question?"

"Oh, Jesus help us," Ivo starts. "We need to know what in tarnation is happening in the third dimension. I can see you're kind of dazed, so if you need some easier question, you can start with why the hell your girlfriend has practically just football tackled me, and hopefully, things will naturally roll on from there."

"Uh-huh. Ok. Uhhhh. Well, Serge wasn't bluffing." I can barely speak.

"I can explain, Ty, cuz you are clearly struggling." Aria begins to help me out. "Hi, by the way." Everyone takes a collective deep breath at the sight of her, and each takes a turn to hug her.

"Hi, I'm Kai," Kai says, putting out his hand, but Aria brings him into an embrace in typical Aria fashion.

"Ok. Tyler was trying to say that Tirique and Nox are indeed back in the worst way we could have possibly imagined. Funny enough, Tyler killed Nox already."

"Two times, actually." I correct her.

"Yes. Two times."

"I'm so lost," Za says.

"They won't bloody die," I complain in agony.

"I'm still so lost," Za says.

"I concur," Ivo says. Aria picks it up again.

"Basically, every time we kill them, they disintegrate, and the debris flies into the air, and then they just come back."

"Seriously?" Za asks with a look of shock, deep concern all over his face.

"Tell me about it, bro." I continue my complaints. "As if the fact his ego hasn't been inflated from dying wasn't enough. I don't regret getting to kill him two times in three minutes, though." Idri chuckles. We got closer when he spent some time training me, which means he occasionally responds to my humor.

"So, we have to figure out how the hell we are going to end this." Aiko thinks out loud.

"We have to destroy the portal," Kai says.

"Explain," I demand.

"Well, since Nox and Tirique can't die, then we have to destroy the portal, which is their only way for them to actually succeed. If there is no portal, they have no purpose. And if they have no purpose, then, who knows, they might just disappear."

"Kid has a point. Yet again," Za says.

DIMENSION

"I don't care what happens or if this is how it works but dibs on keeping the kid," Aziz says as seriously as he possibly can before cracking a smile. This time Idri is silent, deep in contemplation.

"But, that would mean someone needs to know if it actually gets destroyed from the other end and to hold Nox and Tirique off," Riz says.

"I'll do it," Ivo says, everyone a little confused.

"We'll do it." Za joins. Then it sets in what they mean.

IVO

November 7, 2040

Everyone just stares at Za and I, their faces either in the initial phase of realization or they've already realized, and now they are either in disbelief or are slowly pushing into sadness. In truth, I want it to just be me, but I know I won't be able to persuade Za to leave me behind, so there's really no point spending what's left of my energy. As if they are robots turned off by their annoyed owners, everyone starts to slump down in their place. I look at the twins. They are just staring ahead. They know there is no stopping us. We already left them the first time when Za and I retreated into a more peaceful life, handing them our necklaces like they were taking up the mantle and continuing the legacy. Although, it would be a stretch to describe Za and I's up and down adventure and dogged pursuit of dictators as a legacy. It was more a condition of life in response to our need for something to do. We did a lot of good, but we also wore ourselves down.

"No. Absolutely not. There has to be another way. There is another way," Idri argues, he is the only one not standing, and now he paces back and forth.

"There isn't," Za states, as bluntly as possible. He looks at me, knowing that we've both done the mental calculation, the pros, and the cons. It's painful, but there is absolutely no chance either of us will let any of them go instead of us. Idri looks at me, and I just nod at him. He deflates likes he's lost a battle. I suppose it's not the most fairytale ending to our rocky and tumultuous relationship, but I know that he understands that I think this is my responsibility. It hasn't changed from the early days when I would complain when he would accompany me on trips to get resources because I was only comfortable risking myself. "You always have to be the hero," he would say. And, to a point, he's right. I still think I failed my parents, that they shouldn't be dead right now. Maybe it's arrogance or a constant need for a confidence boost like Idri alluded to ten years ago. But, it could also be an overcompensation to make up for a series of events I had no power over. I look up to see Aiko walking towards me, cuts in her clothes from slight miss-hits with her swords, blood dripping from her back where the swords have been returned, and tears flowing down her face. She walks up to me. Talking just loud enough for me to hear through her tired exhales.

"Are you sure?" I nod. "Why?"

"I have to."

"No, you don't."

"You know there isn't any other way."

"I know. But why? Why do you always have to be the savior? Why do you always have to leave me?" The one promise I made before the Nox fight was to leave together and make up for lost time. Of course, the lost time was all my fault, my ignorant idiot self leaving a void between us by cowardly fleeing to Europe and, even more disappointingly, staying there for five years. She still resents the fact that the only thing that brought me back was a global threat and an astray brother.

"I'm sorry. I will always love you." I whisper into her ear before hugging her as tight as I can, her tears pooling and dripping down my shoulder and mine dropping innocently onto her straight black hair.

"Will you come back this time?" I take a minute to let the moment sink in, to think.

"I don't know." She backs away, and Idri immediately brings me in for an unexpected hug. I can tell that he's still tense and a little mad at me, but he's not going to leave me with those emotions. Aria and Tyler both give me hugs. Aria backing off and opening her mouth to say something, probably thank you for doing this or thank you for saving me, but nothing comes out, and Tyler just grabs her hand and leads her away. I get a collective embrace from the twins before Kai walks up to me. He's unsure what to do, so I pull him in for a hug, and then he stands there.

"Tell me what I need to do." I smile. Something about this kid reminds me of me. His shyness at the beginning that morphed into a master planning attitude. And, he knows at this moment, he just knows.

"This is the end of the base. You need to blow up this room and that hallway. Let this entire section collapse into the mountain. If that doesn't destroy the portal, I don't know what will." He solemnly nods back and then walks down the hallway, probably to get some bombs or something.

"Not to rush us or anything, Ivo, but this lock thing here says that it can only hold for another two minutes before it's forced open. It must be some fail safe that Tirique programmed in," Za says, standing by the lock.

"Ok." It only takes thirty seconds for Kai to come back with a variation of different sticker bombs and a grenade. He hands me some sticker bombs, and the grande and I start placing them in the hallway in a coherent line the goes up the walls, travels on the ceiling, and comes back to the ground in a loop. It's funny that these little rectangles will blow this entire glass hallway and some more to smithereens. Once Kai has done the

DIMENSION

same to the other end of the hallway, closer to the room before the portal, he walks over to me, and I hand him the big grenade.

"As soon as we are through the portal, trigger the sticker bombs and then, before the room starts to fall, throw this as close to the portal as you can get." He nods again.

"So this time, I should aim for you guys." He says with a little grin.

"This time. Yes." I smile back. I walk back into the room with Za. "You ready, bro?"

"Always. There's no one else I'd rather mindlessly walk into the third dimension with."

"Wolf brothers?"

"Wolf brothers." He gives me a handshake, and he walks over to the locking system. I look at Idri, who starts to herd everyone out of the room and as far down the hallway they can get while still seeing us. I nod at Za, who unlocks the portal, and I nod at Kai, who triggers the bombs. I watch the glass explode, shards being sent everywhere, and the hallway slowly starting to lose its existence, the gazes of my family blurring in the distance. Za and I turn towards the portal.

This may be the end. But we are migrants for life.

LATER

ZA

August 1, 2041

I close one eye and squint as if it's going to help me aim any better. The makeshift bow feels fragile in my hand, and I swear I hear a couple of crackles when I pull back the string. The rough wood of the arrow is definitely gifting the inside of my fingers with plenty of splinters; they will be a pain in the neck to take out later, especially with no tweezers. The target on Ivo's back swerves in between trees, the vines really not helping me, and the discomfort of using this makeshift bow also throws me off. Of course, these are all valid reasons for why I might miss. But, Ivo is going to say that I'm making up excuses, tell me that he can prove it, and then proceed to hit a bullseye from two hundred feet away with ease. I wait for Ivo to run into a little opening in the jungle ahead, and then I release, dropping the bow and looking ahead in anticipation. I see it miss Ivo's head by a few inches, and I immediately crouch behind the nearest tree.

"Jesus Christ. I almost died, you scoundrel!" Ivo screams, running back towards me. I peek around the tree, Ivo is already there, and he knocks my head with the target which he has taken off his back.

"I told you this game was a bad idea," I argue.

"It's only a bad game for incompetent shooters. How was I supposed to know you're horrible at bow and arrow."

"Let me guess. You want to show me how it's done."

"To be honest, I don't think I have to because your shot was so god awful that I think I can just say that there is no chance I can possibly hit a worse shot."

"Fine. I concede."

"No, you can't because you already lost like five minutes ago."

"Uh-huh." He smiles.

"Anyways, I think it's changing to the ocean soon. Wanna go watch it?"

"Of course." We make our way back through the jungle. When we tossed ourselves through the portal, Tirique and Nox were waiting for us. We fought with them for a bit. Both Ivo and I had forgotten how good of a fighter Nox was, and it didn't help that he was as fit as superman. We held them off long enough for the beam above the portal to disappear, and then the portal just drifted away. Nox couldn't believe it. He couldn't believe that we had sacrificed ourselves so that he could die. He actually made fun of us for it. God, I hate that guy so much. Just thinking about him makes me pulsate with anger. It took a few minutes, but eventually, Tirique and Nox started to levitate. Some force brought them back to their two portals, they were sent back in, and the portals closed. That was the last we saw of those dictators.

"Here?" Ivo asks, pointing to a fallen trunk.

"Works for me." We sit down on the trunk and look at the desert in front of us.

"It still feels so weird that we just don't eat," I say.

"Kind of works for me."

"Yeah, well, you didn't like to eat. But me, my taste buds, and my stomach loved food like it was my child, so it's tough."

"I see." We stare ahead as the desert starts to fall through, funneling down some kind of black hole in the middle.

"So, what are we rating that game?" Ivo asks.

"I don't know. Like a three."

"And how bout if you were good at it."

"Like a three and a half."

"Bull crap."

"Well, if I had hit you in the head, maybe it would be a four."

"You're the worst." He punches me in the shoulder. As the sand disappears, water spurts up from the same point and, before I can blink five times, there is an ocean in front of us, waves and all. The landscape transformations never get old, and Ivo loves that they are all black. I like the ocean the most because I love the peace of it. The whole vibe suits the fact that we are bound to this life for the rest of eternity. We don't even know if we can die. It doesn't seem like we are aging but, then again, we haven't been in here for too long.

"Do you miss them?" Ivo asks this every time we sit and watch the transformation.

"Every day," I reply. He nods. I'm about to ask him the same question when a strange light appears coming from the middle of the ocean. It keeps growing until it looks like the same beam that was there when the original third dimension portal was open. I look at Ivo, who sees the same thing. He looks at me. And we smile at each other.

"About time," he exclaims.

"About time," I repeat.

Our life is always a maze. The fight of the Migrants will always be a cycle. But, no dimension is going to keep us down for long.

DIMENSION

BIO

Audeep Cariens, born in 2004, attends high school in greater Boston, Massachusetts. He has always had a dystopian world growing in his brain, but never quite knew what to do about it. Since starting high school, Audeep has found a passion in social justice advocacy and raising awareness about systemic issues of inequity. The Change Trilogy serves as the marriage between these two interests. When not staring at math homework or frolicking on the soccer field, Audeep writes digestible, page-turning adventures about oppression, for younger audiences.

Made in the USA
Middletown, DE
27 November 2022